ALEXANDER McCALL SMITH

THE NO. 1 LADIES' DETECTIVE AGENCY

In addition to the huge international phenome-non The No. 1 Ladies' Detective Agency series, Alexander McCall Smith is the author of The Sunday Philosophy Club series, the Portuguese Irregular Verbs series, *The Girl Who Married a Lion*, and *44 Scotland Street*. He was born in what is now Zimbabwe and taught law at the University of Botswana and Edinburgh Univer-sity. He lives in Scotland and returns regularly to Botswana.

THE NO. 1

LADIES'

DETECTIVE AGENCY

THE NO. 1

LADIES'

DETECTIVE AGENCY

Alexander McCall Smith

Anchor Books

A Division of Random House, Inc.

New York

First Anchor Books Edition, August 2002

Copyright © 1998 by Alexander McCall Smith

All rights reserved under International and Pan-American
Copyright Conventions. Published in the United States by
Anchor Books, a division of Random House, Inc., New York,
and simultaneously in Canada by Random House of Canada
Limited, Toronto. Originally published in softcover
in Scotland by Polygon, Edinburgh, in 1998.

Anchor Books and colophon are registered trademarks
of Random House, Inc.

Library of Congress Cataloging-in-Publication Data
McCall Smith, R. A.
The No. 1 Ladies' Detective Agency / Alexander McCall Smith.
p. cm.
1. Women private investigators—Botswana—Fiction. 2. Botswana—Fiction.
I. Title: Number One Ladies' Detective Agency. II. Title.
PR6063.C326 N6 2002
821'.914—dc21
2002018694

Vintage ISBN 10: 1-4000-3477-9
Vintage ISBN 13: 978-1-4000-3477-2

www.anchorbooks.com

Printed in the United States of America
40   39   38   37   36   35   34   33   32

This book is for
Anne Gordon-Gillies
in Scotland

and for
Joe and Mimi McKnight
in Dallas, Texas

THE NO. 1

LADIES'

DETECTIVE AGENCY

CHAPTER ONE

THE DADDY

MMA RAMOTSWE had a detective agency in Africa, at the foot of Kgale Hill. These were its assets: a tiny white van, two desks, two chairs, a telephone, and an old typewriter. Then there was a teapot, in which Mma Ramotswe—the only lady private detective in Botswana—brewed redbush tea. And three mugs—one for herself, one for her secretary, and one for the client. What else does a detective agency really need? Detective agencies rely on human intuition and intelligence, both of which Mma Ramotswe had in abundance. No inventory would ever include those, of course.

But there was also the view, which again could appear on no inventory. How could any such list describe what one saw when one looked out from Mma Ramotswe's door? To the front, an acacia tree, the thorn tree which dots the wide edges of the Kalahari; the great white thorns, a warning; the olive-grey leaves, by contrast, so delicate. In its branches, in the late afternoon, or in the cool of the early morning, one might see a Go-Away Bird, or hear it, rather. And beyond the acacia, over the dusty road, the roofs of the town under a cover of trees and scrub bush; on the horizon, in a blue shimmer of heat, the hills, like improbable, overgrown termite mounds.

Everybody called her Mma Ramotswe, although if people had wanted to be formal, they would have addressed her as Mme Mma Ramotswe. This is the right thing for a person of stature, but which she had never used of herself. So it was always Mma Ramotswe, rather than Precious Ramotswe, a name which very few people employed.

She was a good detective, and a good woman. A good woman in a good country, one might say. She loved her country, Botswana, which is a place of peace, and she loved Africa, for all its trials. I am not ashamed to be called an African patriot, said Mma Ramotswe. I love all the people whom God made, but I especially know how to love the people who live in this place. They are my people, my brothers and sisters. It is my duty to help them to solve the mysteries in their lives. That is what I am called to do.

In idle moments, when there were no pressing matters to be dealt with, and when everybody seemed to be sleepy from the heat, she would sit under her acacia tree. It was a dusty place to sit, and the chickens would occasionally come and peck about her feet, but it was a place which seemed to encourage thought. It was here that Mma Ramotswe would contemplate some of the issues which, in everyday life, may so easily be pushed to one side.

Everything, thought Mma Ramotswe, has been something before. Here I am, the only lady private detective in the whole of Botswana, sitting in front of my detective agency. But only a few years ago there was no detective agency, and before that, before there were even any buildings here, there were just the acacia trees, and the riverbed in the distance, and the Kalahari over there, so close.

In those days there was no Botswana even, just the Bechuanaland Protectorate, and before that again there was Khama's Country, and lions with the dry wind in their manes. But look at it now: a detective agency, right here in Gaborone, with me, the fat lady detective, sitting outside and thinking these thoughts about how what is one thing today becomes quite another thing tomorrow.

Mma Ramotswe set up the No. 1 Ladies' Detective Agency with the proceeds of the sale of her father's cattle. He had owned a big herd, and had no other children; so every single beast, all one hundred and eighty of them, including the white Brahmin bulls whose grandparents he had bred himself, went to her. The cattle were moved from the cattle post, back to Mochudi where they waited, in the dust, under the eyes of the chattering herd boys, until the livestock agent came.

They fetched a good price, as there had been heavy rains that year, and the grass had been lush. Had it been the year before, when most of that southern part of Africa had been wracked by drought, it would have been a different matter. People had dithered then, wanting to hold on to their cattle, as without your cattle you were naked; others, feeling more desperate, sold, because the rains had failed year after year and they had seen the animals become thinner and thinner. Mma Ramotswe was pleased that her father's illness had prevented his making any decision, as now the price had gone up and those who had held on were well rewarded.

"I want you to have your own business," he said to her on his death bed. "You'll get a good price for the cattle now. Sell them and buy a business. A butchery maybe. A bottle store. Whatever you like."

She held her father's hand and looked into the eyes of the man she loved beyond all others, her Daddy, her wise Daddy, whose lungs had been filled with dust in those mines and who had scrimped and saved to make life good for her.

It was difficult to talk through her tears, but she managed to say: "I'm going to set up a detective agency. Down in Gaborone. It will be the best one in Botswana. The No. 1 Agency."

For a moment her father's eyes opened wide and it seemed as if he was struggling to speak.

"But . . . but . . ."

But he died before he could say anything more, and Mma Ramotswe fell on his chest and wept for all the dignity, love and suffering that died with him.

SHE HAD a sign painted in bright colours, which was then set up just off the Lobatse Road, on the edge of town, pointing to the small building she had purchased: THE NO. 1 LADIES' DETECTIVE AGENCY. FOR ALL CONFIDENTIAL MATTERS AND ENQUIRIES. SATISFACTION GUARANTEED FOR ALL PARTIES. UNDER PERSONAL MANAGEMENT.

There was considerable public interest in the setting up of her agency. There was an interview on Radio Botswana, in which she thought she was rather rudely pressed to reveal her qualifications, and a rather more satisfactory article in *The Botswana News,* which drew attention to the fact that she was the only lady private detective in the country. This article was cut out, copied, and placed prominently on a small board beside the front door of the agency.

After a slow start, she was rather surprised to find that her services were in considerable demand. She was consulted about missing husbands, about the creditworthiness of potential business partners, and about suspected fraud by employees. In almost every case, she was able to come up with at least some information for the client; when she could not, she waived her fee, which meant that virtually nobody who consulted her was dissatisfied. People in Botswana liked to talk, she discovered, and the mere mention of the fact that she was a private detective would let loose a positive outpouring of information on all sorts of subjects. It flattered people, she concluded, to be approached by a private detective, and this effectively loosened their tongues. This happened with Happy Bapetsi, one of her earlier clients. Poor Happy! To have lost your daddy and then found him, and then lost him again . . .

"I USED to have a happy life," said Happy Bapetsi. "A very happy life. Then this thing happened, and I can't say that anymore."

Mma Ramotswe watched her client as she sipped her bush tea. Everything you wanted to know about a person was written in the face, she believed. It's not that she believed that the shape of the head was what counted—even if there were many who still clung to that belief; it was more a question of taking care to scrutinise the lines and the general look. And the eyes, of course; they were very important. The eyes allowed you to see right into a person, to penetrate their very essence, and that was why people with something to hide wore sunglasses indoors. They were the ones you had to watch very carefully.

Now this Happy Bapetsi was intelligent; that was immediately apparent. She also had few worries—this was shown by the fact that there were no lines on her face, other than smile lines of course. So it was man trouble, thought Mma Ramotswe. Some man has turned up and spoilt everything, destroying her happiness with his bad behaviour.

"Let me tell you a little about myself first," said Happy Bapetsi. "I come from Maun, you see, right up on the Okavango. My mother had a small shop and I lived with her in the house at the back. We had lots of chickens and we were very happy.

"My mother told me that my Daddy had left a long time ago, when I was still a little baby. He had gone off to work in Bulawayo and he had never come back. Somebody had written to us—another Motswana living there—to say that he thought that my Daddy was dead, but he wasn't sure. He said that he had gone to see somebody at Mpilo Hospital one day and as he was walking along a corridor he saw them wheeling somebody out on a stretcher and that the dead person on the stretcher looked remarkably like my Daddy. But he couldn't be certain.

"So we decided that he was probably dead, but my mother did not mind a great deal because she had never really liked him very much. And of course I couldn't even remember him, so it did not make much difference to me.

"I went to school in Maun at a place run by some Catholic missionaries. One of them discovered that I could do arithmetic rather well and he spent a lot of time helping me. He said that he had never met a girl who could count so well.

"I suppose it was very odd. I could see a group of figures and

I would just remember it. Then I would find that I had added the figures in my head, even without thinking about it. It just came very easily—I didn't have to work at it at all.

"I did very well in my exams and at the end of the day I went off to Gaborone and learned how to be a bookkeeper. Again it was very simple for me; I could look at a whole sheet of figures and understand it immediately. Then, the next day, I could remember every figure exactly and write them all down if I needed to.

"I got a job in the bank and I was given promotion after promotion. Now I am the No. 1 subaccountant and I don't think I can go any further because all the men are worried that I'll make them look stupid. But I don't mind. I get very good pay and I can finish all my work by three in the afternoon, sometimes earlier. I go shopping after that. I have a nice house with four rooms and I am very happy. To have all that by the time you are thirty-eight is good enough, I think."

Mma Ramotswe smiled. "That is all very interesting. You're right. You've done well."

"I'm very lucky," said Happy Bapetsi. "But then this thing happened. My Daddy arrived at the house."

Mma Ramotswe drew in her breath. She had not expected this; she had thought it would be a boyfriend problem. Fathers were a different matter altogether.

"He just knocked on the door," said Happy Bapetsi. "It was a Saturday afternoon and I was taking a rest on my bed when I heard his knocking. I got up, went to the door, and there was this man, about sixty or so, standing there with his hat in his hands. He told me that he was my Daddy, and that he had been living in Bulawayo for a long time but was now back in Botswana and had come to see me.

"You can understand how shocked I was. I had to sit down, or I think I would have fainted. In the meantime, he spoke. He told me my mother's name, which was correct, and he said that he was sorry that he hadn't been in touch before. Then he asked if he could stay in one of the spare rooms, as he had nowhere else to go.

"I said that of course he could. In a way I was very excited to see my Daddy and I thought that it would be good to be able to make up for all those lost years and to have him staying with me, particularly since my poor mother died. So I made a bed for him in one of the rooms and cooked him a large meal of steak and potatoes, which he ate very quickly. Then he asked for more.

"That was about three months ago. Since then, he has been living in that room and I have been doing all the work for him. I make his breakfast, cook him some lunch, which I leave in the kitchen, and then make his supper at night. I buy him one bottle of beer a day and have also bought him some new clothes and a pair of good shoes. All he does is sit in his chair outside the front door and tell me what to do for him next."

"Many men are like that," interrupted Mma Ramotswe.

Happy Bapetsi nodded. "This one is especially like that. He has not washed a single cooking pot since he arrived and I have been getting very tired running after him. He also spends a lot of my money on vitamin pills and biltong.

"I would not resent this, you know, except for one thing. I do not think that he is my real Daddy. I have no way of proving this, but I think that this man is an impostor and that he heard about our family from my real Daddy before he died and is now just pretending. I think he is a man who has been looking for a retirement home and who is very pleased because he has found a good one."

Mma Ramotswe found herself staring in frank wonderment at Happy Bapetsi. There was no doubt but that she was telling the truth; what astonished her was the effrontery, the sheer, naked effrontery of men. How dare this person come and impose on this helpful, happy person! What a piece of chicanery, of fraud! What a piece of outright theft in fact!

"Can you help me?" asked Happy Bapetsi. "Can you find out whether this man is really my Daddy? If he is, then I will be a dutiful daughter and put up with him. If he is not, then I should prefer for him to go somewhere else."

Mma Ramotswe did not hesitate. "I'll find out," she said. "It may take me a day or two, but I'll find out!"

Of course it was easier said than done. There were blood tests these days, but she doubted very much whether this person would agree to that. No, she would have to try something more subtle, something that would show beyond any argument whether he was the Daddy or not. She stopped in her line of thought. Yes! There was something biblical about this story. What, she thought, would Solomon have done?

MMA RAMOTSWE picked up the nurse's uniform from her friend Sister Gogwe. It was a bit tight, especially round the arms, as Sister Gogwe, although generously proportioned, was slightly more slender than Mma Ramotswe. But once she was in it, and had pinned the nurse's watch to her front, she was a perfect picture of a staff sister at the Princess Marina Hospital. It was a good disguise, she thought, and she made a mental note to use it at some time in the future.

As she drove to Happy Bapetsi's house in her tiny white van, she reflected on how the African tradition of support for relatives could cripple people. She knew of one man, a sergeant of police, who was supporting an uncle, two aunts, and a second cousin. If you believed in the old Setswana morality, you couldn't turn a relative away, and there was a lot to be said for that. But it did mean that charlatans and parasites had a very much easier time of it than they did elsewhere. They were the people who ruined the system, she thought. They're the ones who are giving the old ways a bad name.

As she neared the house, she increased her speed. This was an errand of mercy, after all, and if the Daddy were sitting in his chair outside the front door he would have to see her arrive in a cloud of dust. The Daddy was there, of course, enjoying the morning sun, and he sat up straight in his chair as he saw the tiny white van sweep up to the gate. Mma Ramotswe turned off the engine and ran out of the car up to the house.

"Dumela Rra," she greeted him rapidly. "Are you Happy Bapetsi's Daddy?"

The Daddy rose to his feet. "Yes," he said proudly. "I am the Daddy."

Mma Ramotswe panted, as if trying to get her breath back.

"I'm sorry to say that there has been an accident. Happy was run over and is very sick at the hospital. Even now they are performing a big operation on her."

The Daddy let out a wail. "Aiee! My daughter! My little baby Happy!"

A good actor, thought Mma Ramotswe, unless . . . No, she preferred to trust Happy Bapetsi's instinct. A girl should know her own Daddy even if she had not seen him since she was a baby.

"Yes," she went on. "It is very sad. She is very sick, very sick.

And they need lots of blood to make up for all the blood she's lost."

The Daddy frowned. "They must give her that blood. Lots of blood. I can pay."

"It's not the money," said Mma Ramotswe. "Blood is free. We don't have the right sort. We will have to get some from her family, and you are the only one she has. We must ask you for some blood."

The Daddy sat down heavily.

"I am an old man," he said.

Mma Ramotswe sensed that it would work. Yes, this man was an impostor.

"That is why we are asking you," she said. "Because she needs so much blood, they will have to take about half your blood. And that is very dangerous for you. In fact, you might die."

The Daddy's mouth fell open.

"Die?"

"Yes," said Mma Ramotswe. "But then you are her father and we know that you would do this thing for your daughter. Now could you come quickly, or it will be too late. Doctor Moghile is waiting."

The Daddy opened his mouth, and then closed it.

"Come on," said Mma Ramotswe, reaching down and taking his wrist. "I'll help you to the van."

The Daddy rose to his feet, and then tried to sit down again. Mma Ramotswe gave him a tug,

"No," he said. "I don't want to."

"You must," said Mma Ramotswe. "Now come on."

The Daddy shook his head. "No," he said faintly. "I won't. You see, I'm not really her Daddy. There has been a mistake."

Mma Ramotswe let go of his wrist. Then, her arms folded, she stood before him and addressed him directly.

"So you are not the Daddy! I see! I see! Then what are you doing sitting in that chair and eating her food? Have you heard of the Botswana Penal Code and what it says about people like you? Have you?"

The Daddy looked down at the ground and shook his head.

"Well," said Mma Ramotswe. "You go inside that house and get your things. You have five minutes. Then I am going to take you to the bus station and you are going to get on a bus. Where do you really live?"

"Lobatse," said the Daddy. "But I don't like it down there."

"Well," said Mma Ramotswe. "Maybe if you started doing something instead of just sitting in a chair you might like it a bit more. There are lots of melons to grow down there. How about that, for a start?"

The Daddy looked miserable.

"Inside!" she ordered. "Four minutes left now!"

WHEN HAPPY Bapetsi returned home she found the Daddy gone and his room cleared out. There was a note from Mma Ramotswe on the kitchen table, which she read, and as she did so, her smile returned.

THAT WAS not your Daddy after all. I found out the best way. I got him to tell me himself. Maybe you will find the real Daddy one day. Maybe not. But in the meantime, you can be happy again.

CHAPTER TWO

ALL THOSE YEARS AGO

WE DON'T forget, thought Mma Ramotswe. Our heads may be small, but they are as full of memories as the sky may sometimes be full of swarming bees, thousands and thousands of memories, of smells, of places, of little things that happened to us and which come back, unexpectedly, to remind us who we are. And who am I? I am Precious Ramotswe, citizen of Botswana, daughter of Obed Ramotswe who died because he had been a miner and could no longer breathe. His life was unrecorded; who is there to write down the lives of ordinary people?

I AM Obed Ramotswe, and I was born near Mahalapye in 1930. Mahalapye is halfway between Gaborone and Francistown, on that road that seems to go on and on forever. It was a dirt road in those days, of course, and the railway line was much more important. The track came down from Bulawayo, crossed into Botswana at Plumtree, and then headed south down the side of the country all the way to Mafikeng, on the other side.

As a boy I used to watch the trains as they drew up at the siding. They let out great clouds of steam, and we would dare one another to run as close as we could to it. The stokers would shout at us, and the station master would blow his whistle, but they never managed to get rid of us. We hid behind plants and boxes and dashed out to ask for coins from the closed windows of the trains. We saw the white people look out of their windows, like ghosts, and sometimes they would toss us one of their Rhodesian pennies—large copper coins with a hole in the middle—or, if we were lucky, a tiny silver coin we called a tickey, which could buy us a small tin of syrup.

Mahalapye was a straggling village of huts made of brown, sun-baked mud bricks and a few tin-roofed buildings. These belonged to the Government or the Railways, and they seemed to us to represent distant, unattainable luxury. There was a school run by an old Anglican priest and a white woman whose face had been half-destroyed by the sun. They both spoke Setswana, which was unusual, but they taught us in English, insisting, on the pain of a thrashing, that we left our own language outside in the playground.

On the other side of the road was the beginning of the plain that stretched out into the Kalahari. It was featureless land, cluttered with low thorn trees, on the branches of which there perched the hornbills and the fluttering molopes, with their long, trailing tail feathers. It was a world that seemed to have no end, and that, I think, is what made Africa in those days so different. There was no end to it. A man could walk, or ride, forever, and he would never get anywhere.

I am sixty now, and I do not think God wants me to live much longer. Perhaps there will be a few years more, but I doubt it; I saw Dr Moffat at the Dutch Reformed Hospital in Mochudi who listened to my chest. He could tell that I had been a miner, just by listening, and he shook his head and said that the mines have many different ways of hurting a man. As he spoke, I remembered a song which the Sotho miners used to sing. They sang: "The mines eat men. Even when you have left them, the mines may still be eating you." We all knew this was true. You could be killed by falling rock or you could be killed years later, when going underground was just a memory, or even a bad dream that visited you at night. The mines would come back for their payment, just as they were coming back for me now. So I was not surprised by what Dr Moffat said.

Some people cannot bear news like that. They think they must live forever, and they cry and wail when they realise that their time is coming. I do not feel that, and I did not weep at that news which the doctor gave me. The only thing that makes me sad is that I shall be leaving Africa when I die. I love Africa, which is my mother and my father. When I am dead, I shall miss the smell of Africa, because they say that where you go, wherever that may be, there is no smell and no taste.

I'm not saying that I'm a brave man—I'm not—but I really don't seem to mind this news I have been given. I can look back over my sixty years and think of everything that I have seen and of how I started with nothing and ended up with almost two hundred cattle. And I have a good daughter, a loyal daughter, who looks after me well and makes me tea while I sit here in the sun and look out to the hills in the distance. When you see these hills from a distance, they are blue; as all the distances in this country are. We are far from the sea here, with Angola and Namibia between us and the coast, and yet we have this great empty ocean of blue above us and around us. No sailor could be lonelier than a man standing in the middle of our land, with the miles and miles of blue about him.

I have never seen the sea, although a man I worked with in the mines once invited me to his place down in Zululand. He told me that it had green hills that reached down to the Indian Ocean and that he could look out of his doorway and see ships in the distance. He said that the women in his village brewed the best beer in the country and that a man could sit in the sun there for many years and never do anything except make children and drink maize beer. He said that if I went with him, he might be able to get me a wife and that they might overlook the fact that I was not a Zulu—if I was prepared to pay the father enough money for the girl.

But why should I want to go to Zululand? Why should I ever want anything but to live in Botswana, and to marry a Tswana girl? I said to him that Zululand sounded fine, but that every man has a map in his heart of his own country and that the heart will never allow you to forget this map. I told him that in Botswana we did not have the green hills that he had in his place, nor the sea, but we had the Kalahari and land that stretched farther than one could imagine. I told him that if a man is born in a dry place, then although he may dream of rain, he does not want too much, and that he will not mind the sun that beats down and down. So I never went with him to Zululand and I never saw the sea, ever. But that has not made me unhappy, not once.

So I sit here now, quite near the end, and think of everything that has happened to me. Not a day passes, though, that my mind does not go to God and to thoughts of what it will be like to die. I am not frightened of this, because I do not mind pain, and the pain that I feel is really quite bearable. They gave me pills—large white ones—and they told me to take these if the pain in my chest became too great. But these pills make me sleepy, and I prefer to be awake. So I think of God and wonder what he will say to me when I stand before him.

Some people think of God as a white man, which is an idea which the missionaries brought with them all those years ago and which seems to have stuck in people's mind. I do not think this is so, because there is no difference between white men and black men; we are all the same; we are just people. And God was here anyway, before the missionaries came. We called him by a different name, then, and he did not live over at the Jews' place; he lived here in Africa, in the rocks, in the sky, in places where we knew he liked to be. When you died, you went somewhere else, and God would have been there too, but you would not be able to get specially close to him. Why should he want that?

We have a story in Botswana about two children, a brother and sister, who are taken up to heaven by a whirlwind and find that heaven is full of beautiful white cattle. That is how I like to think of it, and I hope that it is true. I hope that when I die I find myself in a place where there are cattle like that, who have sweet breath, and who are all about me. If that is what awaits me, then I am happy to go tomorrow, or even now, right at this moment. I should like to say goodbye to Precious, though, and to hold my daughter's hand as I went. That would be a happy way to go.

*   *   *

I LOVE our country, and I am proud to be a Motswana. There's no other country in Africa that can hold its head up as we can. We have no political prisoners, and never have had any. We have democracy. We have been careful. The Bank of Botswana is full of money, from our diamonds. We owe nothing.

But things were bad in the past. Before we built our country we had to go off to South Africa to work. We went to the mines, just as people did from Lesotho and Mozambique and Malawi and all those countries. The mines sucked our men in and left the old men and the children at home. We dug for gold and diamonds and made those white men rich. They built their big houses, with their walls and their cars. And we dug down below them and brought out the rock on which they built it all.

I went to the mines when I was eighteen. We were the Bechuanaland Protectorate then, and the British ran our country, to protect us from the Boers (or that is what they said). There was a Commissioner down in Mafikeng, over the border into South Africa, and he would come up the road and speak to the chiefs. He would say: "You do this thing; you do that thing." And the chiefs all obeyed him because they knew that if they did not he would have them deposed. But some of them were clever, and while the British said "You do this," they would say "Yes, yes, sir, I will do that" and all the time, behind their backs, they did the other thing or they just pretended to do something. So for many years, nothing at all happened. It was a good system of government, because most people want nothing to happen. That is the problem with governments these days. They want to do things all the time; they are always very busy thinking of what things they can do next. That is not what people want. People want to be left alone to look after their cattle.

We had left Mahalapye by then, and gone to live in Mochudi, where my mother's people lived. I liked Mochudi, and would have been happy to stay there, but my father said I should go to the mines, as his lands were not good enough to support me and a wife. We did not have many cattle, and we grew just enough crops to keep us through the year. So when the recruiting truck came from over the border I went to them and they put me on a scale and listened to my chest and made me run up and down a ladder for ten minutes. Then a man said that I would be a good miner and they made me write my name on a piece of paper. They asked me the name of my chief and asked me whether I had ever been in any trouble with the police. That was all.

I went off on the truck the next day. I had one trunk, which my father had bought for me at the Indian Store. I only had one pair of shoes, but I had a spare shirt and some spare trousers. These were all the things I had, apart from some biltong which my mother had made for me. I loaded my trunk on top of the truck and then all the families who had come to say goodbye started to sing. The women cried and we waved goodbye. Young men always try not to cry or look sad, but I knew that within us all our hearts were cold.

It took twelve hours to reach Johannesburg, as the roads were rough in those days and if the truck went too fast it could break an axle. We travelled through the Western Transvaal, through the heat, cooped up in the truck like cattle. Every hour, the driver would stop and come round to the back and pass out canteens of water which they filled at each town we went through. You were allowed the canteen for a few seconds only, and in that time you had to take as much water as you could. Men who were on their second or third contract knew all about this, and they had bottles of water which they would share if you were desperate. We were all Batswana together, and a man would not see a fellow Motswana suffer.

The older men were about the younger ones. They told them that now that they had signed on for the mines, they were no longer boys. They told us that we would see things in Johannesburg which we could never have imagined existing, and that if we were weak, or stupid, or if we did not work hard enough, our life from now on would be nothing but suffering. They told us that we would see cruelty and wickedness, but that if we stuck with other Batswana and did what we were told by the older men, we would survive. I thought that perhaps they were exaggerating. I remembered the older boys telling us about the initiation school that we all had to go to and warning us of what lay ahead of us. They said all this to frighten us, and the reality was quite different. But these men spoke the absolute truth. What lay ahead of us was exactly what they had predicted, and even worse.

In Johannesburg they spent two weeks training us. We were all quite fit and strong, but nobody could be sent down the mines until he had been made even stronger. So they took us to a building which they had heated with steam and they made us jump up and down onto benches for four hours each day. This was too much for some men, who collapsed, and had to be hauled back to their feet, but somehow I survived it and passed on to the next part of our training. They told us how we would be taken down into the mines and about the work we would be expected to do. They talked to us about safety, and how the rock could fall and crush us if we were careless. They carried in a man with no legs and put him down on a table and made us listen to him as he told us what had happened to him.

They taught us Funagalo, which is the language used for giving orders underground. It is a strange language. The Zulus laugh when they hear it, because there are so many Zulu words in it but it is not Zulu. It is a language which is good for telling people what to do. There are many words for push, take, shove, carry, load, and no words for love, or happiness, or the sounds which birds make in the morning.

Then we went down to the shafts and were shown what to do. They put us in cages, beneath great wheels, and these cages shot down as fast as hawks falling upon their prey. They had trains down there—small trains—and they put us on these and took us to the end of long, dark tunnels, which were filled with green rock and dust. My job was to load rock after it had been blasted, and I did this for seven hours a day. I grew strong, but all the time there was dust, dust, dust.

Some of the mines were more dangerous than others, and we all knew which these were. In a safe mine you hardly ever see the stretchers underground. In a dangerous one, though, the stretchers are often out, and you see men being carried up in the cages, crying with pain, or, worse still, silent under the heavy red blankets. We all knew that the only way to survive was to get into a crew where the men had what everybody called rock sense. This was something which every good miner had. He had to be able to see what the rock was doing—what it was feeling—and to know when new supports were needed. If one or two men in a crew did not know this, then it did not matter how good the others were. The rock would come down and it fell on good miners and bad.

There was another thing which affected your chances of

survival, and this was the sort of white miner you had. The white miners were put in charge of the teams, but many of them had very little to do. If a team was good, then the boss boy knew exactly what to do and how to do it. The white miner would pretend to give the orders, but he knew that it would be the boss boy who really got the work done. But a stupid white miner—and there were plenty of those—would drive his team too hard. He would shout and hit the men if he thought they were not working quickly enough and this could be very dangerous. Yet when the rock came down, the white miner would never be there; he would be back down the tunnel with the other white miners, waiting for us to report that the work had been finished.

It was not unusual for a white miner to beat his men if he got into a temper. They were not meant to, but the shift bosses always turned a blind eye and let them get on with it. Yet we were never allowed to hit back, no matter how undeserved the blows. If you hit a white miner, you were finished. The mine police would be waiting for you at the top of the shaft and you could spend a year or two in prison.

They kept us apart, because that is how they worked, these white men. The Swazis were all in one gang, and the Zulus in another, and the Malawians in another. And so on. Everybody was with his people, and had to obey the boss boy. If you didn't, and the boss boy said that a man was making trouble, they would send him home or arrange for the police to beat him until he started to be reasonable again.

We were all afraid of the Zulus, although I had that friend who was a kind Zulu. The Zulus thought they were better than any of us and sometimes they called us women. If there was a fight, it was almost always the Zulus or the Basotho, but never the Batswana. We did not like fighting. Once a drunk Motswana wandered into a Zulu hostel by mistake on a Saturday night. They beat him with sjamboks and left him lying on the road to be run over. Fortunately a police van saw him and rescued him, or he would have been killed. All for wandering into the wrong hostel.

I worked for years in those mines, and I saved all my money. Other men spent it on town women, and drink, and on fancy clothes. I bought nothing, not even a gramophone. I sent the money home to the Standard Bank and then I bought cattle with it. Each year I bought a few cows, and gave them to my cousin to look after. They had calves, and slowly my herd got bigger.

I would have stayed in the mines, I suppose, had I not witnessed a terrible thing. It happened after I had been there for fifteen years. I had then been given a much better job, as an assistant to a blaster. They would not give us blasting tickets, as that was a job that the white men kept for themselves, but I was given the job of carrying explosives for a blaster and helping him with the fuses. This was a good job, and I liked the man I worked for.

He had left something in a tunnel once—his tin can in which he carried his sandwiches—and he had asked me to fetch it. So I went off down the tunnel where he had been working and looked for this can. The tunnel was lit by bulbs which were attached to the roof all the way along, so it was quite safe to walk along it. But you still had to be careful, because here and there were great galleries which had been blasted out of the rock. These could be two hundred feet deep, and they opened out from the sides of the tunnel to drop down to another working level, like underground quarries. Men fell into these galleries from time to time, and it was always their fault. They were not looking where they were walking, or were walking along an unlit tunnel when the batteries in their helmet lights were weak. Sometimes a man just walked over the edge for no reason at all, or because he was unhappy and did not want to live anymore. You could never tell; there are many sadnesses in the hearts of men who are far away from their countries.

I turned a corner in this tunnel and found myself in a round chamber. There was a gallery at the end of this, and there was a warning sign. Four men were standing at the edge of this, and they were holding another man by his arms and legs. As I came round the corner, they lifted him and threw him forwards, over the edge and into the dark. The man screamed, in Xhosa, and I heard what he said. He said something about a child, but I did not catch it all as I am not very good at Xhosa. Then he was gone.

I stood where I was. The men had not seen me yet, but one turned round and shouted out in Zulu. Then they began to run towards me. I turned round and ran back along the tunnel. I knew that if they caught me I would follow their victim into the gallery. It was not a race I could let myself lose.

Although I got away, I knew that those men had seen me and that I would be killed. I had seen their murder and could be a witness, and so I knew that I could not stay in the mines.

I spoke to the blaster. He was a good man and he listened to me carefully when I told him that I would have to go. There was no other white man I could have spoken to like that, but he understood.

Still, he tried to persuade me to go to the police.

"Tell them what you saw," he said in Afrikaans. "Tell them. They can catch these Zulus and hang them."

"I don't know who these men are. They'll catch me first. I am going home to my place."

He looked at me and nodded. Then he took my hand and shook it, which is the first time a white man had done that to me. So I called him my brother, which is the first time I had done that to a white man.

"You go back home to your wife," he said. "If a man leaves his wife too long, she starts to make trouble for him. Believe me. Go back and give her more children."

So I left the mines, secretly, like a thief, and came back to Botswana in 1960. I cannot tell you how full my heart was when I crossed the border back into Botswana and left South Africa behind me forever. In that place I had felt every day that I might die. Danger and sorrow hung over Johannesburg like a cloud, and I could never be happy there. In Botswana it was different. There were no policemen with dogs; there were no *totsis* with knives, waiting to rob you; you did not wake up every morning to a wailing siren calling you down into the hot earth. There were not the same great crowds of men, all from some distant place, all sickening for home, all wanting to be somewhere else. I had left a prison—a great, groaning prison, under the sunlight.

When I came home that time, and got off the bus at Mochudi, and saw the *kopje* and the chief's place and the goats, I just stood and cried. A man came up to me—a man I did not know—and he put his hand on my shoulder and asked me whether I was just back from the mines. I told him that I was, and he just nodded and left his hand there until I had stopped weeping.

Then he smiled and walked away. He had seen my wife coming for me, and he did not want to interfere with the home-coming of a husband.

I had taken this wife three years earlier, although we had seen very little of one another since the marriage. I came back from Johannesburg once a year, for one month, and this was all the life we had had together. After my last trip she had become pregnant, and my little girl had been born while I was still away. Now I was to see her, and my wife had brought her to meet me off the bus. She stood there, with the child in her arms, the child who was more valuable to me than all the gold taken out of those mines in Johannesburg. This was my first-born, and my only child, my girl, my Precious Ramotswe.

Precious was like her mother, who was a good fat woman. She played in the yard outside the house and laughed when I picked her up. I had a cow that gave good milk, and I kept this nearby for Precious. We gave her plenty of syrup too, and eggs every day. My wife put Vaseline on her skin, and polished it, so that she shone. They said she was the most beautiful child in Bechuanaland and women would come from miles away to look at her and hold her.

Then my wife, the mother of Precious, died. We were living just outside Mochudi then, and she used to go from our place to visit an aunt of hers who lived over the railway line near the Francistown Road. She carried food there, as that aunt was too old to look after herself and she only had one son there, who was sick with sufuba and could not walk very far.

I don't know how it happened. Some people said that it was because there was a storm brewing up and there was lightning that she may have run without looking where she was going.

But she was on the railway line when the train from Bulawayo came down and hit her. The engine driver was very sorry, but he had not seen her at all, which was probably true.

My cousin came to look after Precious. She made her clothes, took her to school and cooked our meals. I was a sad man, and I thought: Now there is nothing left for you in this life but Precious and your cattle. In my sorrow, I went out to the cattle post to see how my cattle were, and to pay the herd boys. I had more cattle now, and I had even thought of buying a store. But I decided to wait, and to let Precious buy a store once I was dead. Besides, the dust from the mines had ruined my chest, and I could not walk fast or lift things.

One day I was on my way back from the cattle post and I had reached the main road that led from Francistown to Gaborone. It was a hot day, and I was sitting under a tree by the roadside, waiting for the bus that would go that way later on. I fell asleep from the heat, and was woken by the sound of a car drawing up.

It was a large car, an American car, I think, and there was a man sitting in the back. The driver came up to me and spoke to me in Setswana, although the number plate of the car was from South Africa. The driver said that there was a leak in the radiator and did I know where they might find some water. As it happened, there was a cattle-watering tank along the track to my cattle post, and so I went with the driver and we filled a can with water.

When we came back to put the water in the radiator, the man who had been sitting in the back had got out and was standing looking at me. He smiled, to show that he was grateful for my help, and I smiled back. Then I realised that I knew who this man was, and that it was the man who managed all those mines in Johannesburg—one of Mr Oppenheimer's men.

I went over to this man and told him who I was. I told him that I was Ramotswe, who had worked in his mines, and I was sorry that I had had to leave early, but that it had been because of circumstances beyond my control.

He laughed, and said that it was good of me to have worked in the mines for so many years. He said I could ride back in his car and that he would take me to Mochudi.

So I arrived back in Mochudi in that car and this important man came into my house. He saw Precious and told me that she was a very fine child. Then, after he had drunk some tea, he looked at his watch.

"I must go back now," he said. "I have to get back to Johannesburg."

I said that his wife would be angry if he was not back in time for the food she had cooked him. He said this would probably be so.

We walked outside. Mr Oppenheimer's man reached into his pocket and took out a wallet. I turned away while he opened it; I did not want money from him, but he insisted. He said I had been one of Mr Oppenheimer's people and Mr Oppenheimer liked to look after his people. He then gave me two hundred rands, and I said that I would use it to buy a bull, since I had just lost one.

He was pleased with this. I told him to go in peace and he said that I should stay in peace. So we left one another and I never saw my friend again, although he is always there, in my heart.

CHAPTER THREE

LESSONS ABOUT BOYS AND GOATS

O BED RAMOTSWE installed his cousin in a room at the back of the small house he had built for himself at the edge of the village when he had returned from the mines. He had originally planned this as a storeroom, in which to keep his tin trunks and spare blankets and the supplies of paraffin he used for cooking, but there was room for these elsewhere. With the addition of a bed and a small cupboard, and with a coat of whitewash applied to the walls, the room was soon fit for occupation. From the point of view of the cousin, it was luxury almost beyond imagination; after the departure of her husband, six years previously, she had returned to live with her mother and her grandmother and had been required to sleep in a room which had only three walls, one of which did not quite reach the roof. They had treated her with quiet contempt, being old-fashioned people, who believed that a woman who was left by her husband would almost always have deserved her fate. They had to take her in, of course, but it was duty, rather than affection, which opened their door to her.

Her husband had left her because she was barren, a fate which was almost inevitable for the childless woman. She had spent what little money she had on consultations with traditional healers, one of whom had promised her that she would conceive within months of his attentions. He had administered a variety of herbs and powdered barks and, when these did not work, he had turned to charms. Several of the potions had made her ill, and one had almost killed her, which was not surprising, given its contents, but the barrenness remained and she knew that her husband was losing patience. Shortly after he left, he wrote to her from Lobatse and told her— proudly—that his new wife was pregnant. Then, a year and a half later, there came a short letter with a photograph of his child. No money was sent, and that was the last time she heard from him.

Now, holding Precious in her arms, standing in her own room with its four stout, whitewashed walls, her happiness was complete. She allowed Precious, now four, to sleep with her in her bed, lying awake at night for long hours to listen to the child's breathing. She stroked her skin, held the tiny hand between her fingers, and marvelled at the completeness of the child's body. When Precious slept during the afternoon, in the heat, she would sit beside her, knitting and sewing tiny jackets and socks in bright reds and blues, and brush flies away from the sleeping child.

Obed, too, was content. He gave his cousin money each week to buy food for the household and a little extra each month for herself. She husbanded resources well, and there was always money left over, which she spent on something for Precious. He never had occasion to reprove her, or to find fault in her upbringing of his daughter. Everything was perfect.

The cousin wanted Precious to be clever. She had had little education herself, but had struggled at reading, and persisted, and now she sensed the possibilities for change. There was a political party, now, which women could join, although some men grumbled about this and said it was asking for trouble. Women were beginning to speak amongst themselves about their lot. Nobody challenged men openly, of course, but when women spoke now amongst themselves, there were whispers, and looks exchanged. She thought of her own life; of the early marriage to a man she had barely met, and of the shame of her inability to bear children. She remembered the years of living in the room with three walls, and the tasks which had been imposed upon her, unpaid. One day, women would be able to sound their own voice, perhaps, and would point out what was wrong. But they would need to be able to read to do that.

She started by teaching Precious to count. They counted goats and cattle. They counted boys playing in the dust. They counted trees, giving each tree a name: crooked one; one with no leaves; one where mopani worms like to hide; one where no bird will go. Then she said: "If we chop down the tree which looks like an old man, then how many trees are there left?" She made Precious remember lists of things—the names of members of the family, the names of cattle her grandfather had owned, the names of the chiefs. Sometimes they sat outside the store nearby, the Small Upright General Dealer, and waited for a car or a truck to bump its way past on the pothole-pitted road. The cousin would call out the number on the registration plate and Precious would have to remember it the next day when she was asked, and perhaps even the day after that. They also played a variety of Kim's Game, in which the cousin would load a basket-work tray with familiar objects and a blanket would then be draped over it and one object removed.

"What has been taken from the tray?"

"An old marula pip, all gnarled and chewed up."

"And what else?"

"Nothing."

She was never wrong, this child who watched everybody and everything with her wide, solemn eyes. And slowly, without anybody ever having intended this, the qualities of curiosity and awareness were nurtured in the child's mind.

By the time Precious went to school at the age of six, she knew her alphabet, her numbers up to two hundred, and she could recite the entire first chapter of the Book of Genesis in the Setswana translation. She had also learnt a few words of English, and could declaim all four verses of an English poem about ships and the sea. The teacher was impressed and complimented the cousin on what she had done. This was virtually the first praise that she had ever received for any task she had performed; Obed had thanked her, and done so often, and generously, but it had not occurred to him to praise her, because in his view she was just doing her duty as a woman and there was nothing special about that.

"We are the ones who first ploughed the earth when Modise (God) made it," ran an old Setswana poem. "We were the ones who made the food. We are the ones who look after the men when they are little boys, when they are young men, and when they are old and about to die. We are always there. But we are just women, and nobody sees us."

Lessons About Boys

Mma Ramotswe thought: God put us on this earth. We were all Africans then, in the beginning, because man started in Kenya, as Dr Leakey and his Daddy have proved. So, if one thinks carefully about it, we are all brothers and sisters, and yet everywhere you look, what do you see? Fighting, fighting, fighting. Rich people killing poor people; poor people killing rich people. Everywhere, except Botswana. That's thanks to Sir Seretse Khama, who was a good man, who invented Botswana and made it a good place. She still cried for him sometimes, when she thought of him in his last illness and all those clever doctors in London saying to the Government: "We're sorry but we cannot cure your President."

The problem, of course, was that people did not seem to understand the difference between right and wrong. They needed to be reminded about this, because if you left it to them to work out for themselves, they would never bother. They would just find out what was best for them, and then they would call that the right thing. That's how most people thought.

Precious Ramotswe had learned about good and evil at Sunday School. The cousin had taken her there when she was six, and she had gone there every Sunday without fail until she was eleven. That was enough time for her to learn all about right and wrong, although she had been puzzled—and remained so—when it came to certain other aspects of religion. She could not believe that the Lord had walked on water—you just couldn't do that—nor had she believed the story about the feeding of the five thousand, which was equally impossible. These were lies, she was sure of it, and the biggest lie of all was that the Lord had no Daddy on this earth. That was untrue because even children knew that you needed a father to make a child, and that rule applied to cattle and chickens and people, all the same. But right and wrong—that was another matter, and she had experienced no difficulty in understanding that it was wrong to lie, and steal, and kill other people.

If people needed clear guidelines, there was nobody better to do this than Mma Mothibi, who had run the Sunday School at Mochudi for over twelve years. She was a short lady, almost entirely round, who spoke with an exceptionally deep voice. She taught the children hymns, in both Setswana and English, and because they learned their singing from her the children's choir all sang an octave below everybody else, as if they were frogs.

The children, dressed in their best clothes, sat in rows at the back of the church when the service had finished and were taught by Mma Mothibi. She read the Bible to them, and made them recite the Ten Commandments over and over again, and told them religious stories from a small blue book which she said came from London and was not available anywhere else in the country.

"These are the rules for being good," she intoned. "A boy must always rise early and say his prayers. Then he must clean his shoes and help his mother to prepare the family's breakfast, if they have breakfast. Some people have no breakfast because they are poor. Then he must go to school and do everything that his teacher tells him. In that way he will learn to be a clever Christian boy who will go to Heaven later on, when the Lord calls him home. For girls, the rules are the same, but they must also be careful about boys and must be ready to tell boys that they are Christians. Some boys will not understand this . . ."

Yes, thought Precious Ramotswe. Some boys do not understand this, and even there, in that Sunday School there was such a boy, that Josiah, who was a wicked boy, although he was only nine. He insisted on sitting next to Precious in Sunday School, even when she tried to avoid him. He was always looking at her and smiling encouragingly, although she was two years older than he was. He tried also to make sure that his leg touched hers, which angered her, and made her shift in her seat, away from him.

But worst of all, he would undo the buttons of his trousers and point to that thing that boys have, and expect her to look. She did not like this, as it was not something that should happen in a Sunday School. What was so special about that, anyway? All boys had that thing.

At last she told Mma Mothibi about it, and the teacher listened gravely.

"Boys, men," she said. "They're all the same. They think that this thing is something special and they're all so proud of it. They do not know how ridiculous it is."

She told Precious to tell her next time it happened. She just had to raise her hand a little, and Mma Mothibi would see her. That would be the signal.

It happened the next week. While Mma Mothibi was at the back of the class, looking at the Sunday School books which the children had laid out before them, Josiah undid a button and whispered to Precious that she should look down. She kept her eyes on her book and raised her left hand slightly. He could not see this, of course, but Mma Mothibi did. She crept up behind the boy and raised her Bible into the air. Then she brought it down on his head, with a resounding thud that made the children start.

Josiah buckled under the blow. Mma Mothibi now came round to his front and pointed at his open fly. Then she raised the Bible and struck him on the top of the head again, even harder than before.

That was the last time that Josiah bothered Precious Ramotswe, or any other girl for that matter. For her part, Precious learned an important lesson about how to deal with men, and this lesson stayed with her for many years, and was to prove very useful later on, as were all the lessons of Sunday School.

The Cousin's Departure

The cousin looked after Precious for the first eight years of her life. She might have stayed indefinitely—which would have suited Obed—as the cousin kept house for him and never complained or asked him for money. But he recognised, when the time came, that there might be issues of pride and that the cousin might wish to marry again, in spite of what had happened last time. So he readily gave his blessing when the cousin announced that she had been seeing a man, that he had proposed, and that she had accepted.

"I could take Precious with me," she said. "I feel that she is my daughter now. But then, there is you . . ."

"Yes," said Obed. "There is me. Would you take me too?"

The cousin laughed. "My new husband is a rich man, but I think that he wants to marry only one person."

Obed made arrangements for the wedding, as he was the cousin's nearest relative and it fell to him to do this. He did it readily, though, because of all she had done for him. He arranged for the slaughter of two cattle and for the brewing of enough beer for two hundred people. Then, with the cousin on his arm, he entered the church and saw the new husband and his people, and other distant cousins, and their friends, and people from the village, invited and uninvited, waiting and watching.

After the wedding ceremony, they went back to the house, where canvas tarpaulins had been hooked up between thorn trees and borrowed chairs set out. The old people sat down while the young moved about and talked to one another, and sniffed the air at the great quantities of meat that were sizzling on the open fires. Then they ate, and Obed made a speech of thanks to the cousin and the new husband, and the new husband replied that he was grateful to Obed for looking after this woman so well.

The new husband owned two buses, which made him wealthy. One of these, the Molepolole Special Express, had been pressed into service for the wedding, and was decked for the occasion with bright blue cloth. In the other, they drove off after the party, with the husband at the wheel and the new bride sitting in the seat immediately behind him. There were cries of excitement, and ululation from the women, and the bus drove off into happiness.

They set up home ten miles south of Gaborone, in an adobe-plastered house which the new husband's brother had built for him. It had a red roof and white walls, and a compound, in the traditional style, with a walled yard to the front.

At the back, there was a small shack for a servant to live in, and a lean-to latrine made out of galvanised tin. The cousin had a kitchen with a shining new set of pans and two cookers. She had a large new South African paraffin-powered fridge, which purred quietly all day, and kept everything icy cold within. Every evening, her husband came home with the day's takings from his buses, and she helped him to count the money. She proved to be an excellent bookkeeper, and was soon running that part of the business with conspicuous success.

She made her new husband happy in other ways. As a boy he had been bitten by a jackal, and had scars across his face where a junior doctor at the Scottish Missionary Hospital at Molepolole had ineptly sewn the wounds. No woman had told him that he was handsome before, and he had never dreamed that any would, being more used to the wince of sympathy. The cousin, though, said that he was the most good-looking man she had ever met, and the most virile too. This was not mere flattery—she was telling the truth, as she saw it, and his heart was filled with the warmth that flows from the well-directed compliment.

"I know you are missing me," the cousin wrote to Precious. "But I know that you want me to be happy. I am very happy now. I have a very kind husband who has bought me wonderful clothes and makes me very happy every day. One day, you will come and stay with us, and we can count the trees again and sing hymns together, as we always used to. Now you must look after your father, as you are old enough to do that, and he is a good man too. I want you to be happy, and that is what I pray for, every night. God look after Precious Ramotswe. God watch her tonight and forever. Amen."

Goats

As a girl, Precious Ramotswe liked to draw, an activity which the cousin had encouraged from an early age. She had been given a sketching pad and a set of coloured pencils for her tenth birthday, and her talent had soon become apparent. Obed Ramotswe was proud of her ability to fill the virgin pages of her sketchbook with scenes of everyday Mochudi life. Here was a sketch which showed the pond in front of the hospital— it was all quite recognisable—and here was a picture of the hospital matron looking at a donkey. And on this page was a picture of the shop, of the Small Upright General Dealer, with things in front of it which could be sacks of mealies or perhaps people sitting down—one could not tell—but they were excellent sketches and he had already pinned several up on the walls of the living room of their house, high up, near the ceiling, where the flies sat.

Her teachers knew of this ability, and told her that she might one day be a great artist, with her pictures on the cover of the Botswana Calendar. This encouraged her, and sketch followed sketch. Goats, cattle, hills, pumpkins, houses; there was so much for the artist's eye around Mochudi that there was no danger that she would run out of subjects.

The school got to hear of an art competition for children. The Museum in Gaborone had asked every school in the country to submit a picture by one of its pupils, on the theme "Life in Botswana of Today." Of course there was no doubt about whose work would be submitted. Precious was asked to draw a special picture—to take her time doing it—and then this would be sent down to Gaborone as the entry from Mochudi.

She drew her picture on a Saturday, going out early with her sketchbook and returning some hours later to fill in the details inside the house. It was a very good drawing, she thought, and her teacher was enthusiastic when she showed it to her the following Monday.

"This will win the prize for Mochudi," she said. "Everybody will be proud."

The drawing was placed carefully between two sheets of corrugated cardboard and sent off, registered post, to the Museum. Then there was a silence for five weeks, during which time everybody forgot about the competition. Only when the letter came to the Principal, and he, beaming, read it out to Precious, were they reminded.

"You have won first prize," he said. "You are to go to Gaborone, with your teacher and myself, and your father, to get the prize from the Minister of Education at a special ceremony."

It was too much for her, and she wept, but soon stopped, and was allowed to leave school early to run back to give the news to her Daddy.

They travelled down with the Principal in his truck, arriving far too early for the ceremony, and spent several hours sitting in the Museum yard, waiting for the doors to open. But at last they did, and others came, teachers, people from the newspapers, members of the Legislature. Then the Minister arrived in a black car and people put down their glasses of orange juice and swallowed the last of their sandwiches.

She saw her painting hanging in a special place, on a room divider, and there was a small card pinned underneath it. She went with her teacher to look at it, and she saw, with leaping heart, her name neatly typed out underneath the picture: PRE-

CIOUS RAMOTSWE (10) (MOCHUDI GOVERNMENT JUNIOR SCHOOL). And underneath that, also typed, the title which the Museum itself had provided: Cattle Beside Dam.

She stood rigid, suddenly appalled. This was not true. The picture was of goats, but they had thought it was cattle! She was getting a prize for a cattle picture, by false pretences.

"What is wrong?" asked her father. "You must be very pleased. Why are you looking so sad?"

She could not say anything. She was about to become a criminal, a perpetrator of fraud. She could not possibly take a prize for a cattle picture when she simply did not deserve that.

But now the Minister was standing beside her, and he was preparing to make a speech. She looked up at him, and he smiled warmly.

"You are a very good artist," he said. "Mochudi must be proud of you."

She looked at the toes of her shoes. She would have to confess.

"It is not a picture of cattle," she said. "It is a picture of goats. You cannot give me a prize for a mistake."

The Minister frowned, and looked at the label. Then he turned back to her and said: "They are the ones who have made a mistake. I also think those are goats. I do not think they are cattle."

He cleared his throat and the Director of the Museum asked for silence.

"This excellent picture of goats," said the Minister, "shows how talented are our young people in this country. This young lady will grow up to be a fine citizen and maybe a famous artist. She deserves her prize, and I am now giving it to her."

She took the wrapped parcel which he gave her, and felt his

hand upon her shoulder, and heard him whisper: "You are the most truthful child I have met. Well done."

Then the ceremony was over, and a little later they returned to Mochudi in the Principal's bumpy truck, a heroine returning, a bearer of prizes.

CHAPTER FOUR

LIVING WITH THE COUSIN AND
THE COUSIN'S HUSBAND

AT THE age of sixteen, Mma Ramotswe left school ("The best girl in this school," pronounced the Principal. "One of the best girls in Botswana.") Her father had wanted her to stay on, to do her Cambridge School Certificate, and to go even beyond that, but Mma Ramotswe was bored with Mochudi. She was bored, too, with working in the Upright Small General Dealer, where every Saturday she did the stocktaking and spent hours ticking off items on dog-eared stock lists. She wanted to go somewhere. She wanted her life to start.

"You can go to my cousin," her father said. "That is a very different place. I think that you will find lots of things happening in that house."

It cost him a great deal of pain to say this. He wanted her to stay, to look after him, but he knew that it would be selfish to expect her life to revolve around his. She wanted freedom; she wanted to feel that she was doing something with her life. And of course, at the back of his mind, was the thought of marriage. In a very short time, he knew, there would be men wanting to marry her.

He would never deny her that, of course. But what if the man who wanted to marry her was a bully, or a drunkard, or a womaniser? All of this was possible; there was any number of men like that, waiting for an attractive girl that they could latch on to and whose life they could slowly destroy. These men were like leeches; they sucked away at the goodness of a woman's heart until it was dry and all her love had been used up. That took a long time, he knew, because women seemed to have vast reservoirs of goodness in them.

If one of these men claimed Precious, then what could he, a father, do? He could warn her of the risk, but whoever listened to warnings about somebody they loved? He had seen it so often before; love was a form of blindness that closed the eyes to the most glaring faults. You could love a murderer, and simply not believe that your lover would do so much as crush a tick, let alone kill somebody. There would be no point trying to dissuade her.

The cousin's house would be as safe as anywhere, even if it could not protect her from men. At least the cousin could keep an eye on her niece, and her husband might be able to chase the most unsuitable men away. He was a rich man now, with more than five buses, and he would have that authority that rich men had. He might be able to send some of the young men packing.

THE COUSIN was pleased to have Precious in the house. She decorated a room for her, hanging new curtains of a thick yellow material which she had bought from the OK Bazaars on a shopping trip to Johannesburg. Then she filled a chest of drawers with clothes and put on top of it a framed picture of the Pope. The floor was covered with a simply patterned reed mat. It was a bright, comfortable room.

Precious settled quickly into a new routine. She was given a job in the office of the bus company, where she added invoices and checked the figures in the drivers' records. She was quick at this, and the cousin's husband noticed that she was doing as much work as the two older clerks put together. They sat at their tables and gossiped away the day, occasionally moving invoices about the desk, occasionally getting up to put on the kettle.

It was easy for Precious, with her memory, to remember how to do new things and to apply the knowledge faultlessly. She was also willing to make suggestions, and scarcely a week went past in which she failed to make some suggestion as to how the office could be more efficient.

"You're working too hard," one of the clerks said to her. "You're trying to take our jobs."

Precious looked at them blankly. She had always worked as hard as she could, at everything she did, and she simply did not understand how anybody could do otherwise. How could they sit there, as they did, and stare into the space in front of their desks when they could be adding up figures or checking the drivers' returns?

She did her own checking, often unasked, and although everything usually added up, now and then she found a small discrepancy. These came from the giving of incorrect change, the cousin explained. It was easy enough to do on a crowded bus, and as long as it was not too significant, they just ignored it. But Precious found more than this. She found a discrepancy of slightly over two thousand pula in the fuel bills invoices and she drew this to the attention of her cousin's husband.

"Are you sure?" he asked. "How could two thousand pula go missing?"

"Stolen?" said Precious.

The cousin's husband shook his head. He regarded himself as a model employer—a paternalist, yes, but that is what the men wanted, was it not? He could not believe that any of his employees would cheat him. How could they, when he was so good to them and did so much for them?

Precious showed him how the money had been taken, and they jointly pieced together how it had been moved out of the right account into another one, and had then eventually vanished altogether. Only one of the clerks had access to these funds, so it must have been him; there could be no other explanation. She did not see the confrontation, but heard it from the other room. The clerk was indignant, shouting his denial at the top of his voice. Then there was silence for a moment, and the slamming of a door.

This was her first case. This was the beginning of the career of Mma Ramotswe.

The Arrival of Note Mokoti

There were four years of working in the bus office. The cousin and her husband became accustomed to her presence and began to call her their daughter. She did not mind this; they were her people, and she loved them. She loved the cousin, even if she still treated her as a child and scolded her publicly. She loved the cousin's husband, with his sad, scarred face and his large, mechanic's hands. She loved the house, and her room with its yellow curtains. It was a good life that she had made for herself.

Every weekend she travelled up to Mochudi on one of the cousin's husband's buses and visited her father. He would be waiting outside the house, sitting on his stool, and she would curtsey before him, in the old way, and clap her hands.

Then they would eat together, sitting in the shade of the lean-to verandah which he had erected to the side of the house. She would tell him about the week's activity in the bus office and he would take in every detail, asking for names, which he would link into elaborate genealogies. Everybody was related in some way; there was nobody who could not be fitted into the far-flung corners of family.

It was the same with cattle. Cattle had their families, and after she had finished speaking, he would tell her the cattle news. Although he rarely went out to the cattle post, he had reports every week and he could run the lives of the cattle through the herd-boys. He had an eye for cattle, an uncanny ability to detect traits in calves that would blossom in maturity. He could tell, at a glance, whether a calf which seemed puny, and which was therefore cheap, could be brought on and fattened. And he backed this judgement, and bought such animals, and made them into fine, butterfat cattle (if the rains were good).

He said that people were like their cattle. Thin, wretched cattle had thin, wretched owners. Listless cattle—cattle which wandered aimlessly—had owners whose lives lacked focus. And dishonest people, he maintained, had dishonest cattle—cattle which would cheat other cattle of food or which would try to insinuate themselves into the herds of others.

Obed Ramotswe was a severe judge—of men and cattle—
and she found herself thinking: what will he say when he finds
out about Note Mokoti?

SHE HAD met Note Mokoti on a bus on the way back from
Mochudi. He was travelling down from Francistown and was
sitting in the front, his trumpet case on the seat beside him.
She could not help but notice him in his red shirt and seer-
sucker trousers; nor fail to see the high cheekbones and the
arched eyebrows. It was a proud face, the face of a man used
to being looked at and appreciated, and she dropped her eyes
immediately. She would not want him to think she was looking
at him, even if she continued to glance at him from her seat.
Who was this man? A musician, with that case beside him; a
clever person from the University perhaps?

The bus stopped in Gaborone before going south on the
road to Lobatse. She stayed in her seat, and saw him get up.
He stood up, straightened the crease of his trousers, and then
turned and looked down the bus. She felt her heart jump; he
had looked at her; no, he had not, he was looking out of the
window.

Suddenly, without thinking, she got to her feet and took her
bag down from the rack. She would get off, not because she
had anything to do in Gaborone, but because she wanted to
see what he did. He had left the bus now and she hurried,
muttering a quick explanation to the driver, one of her cousin's
husband's men. Out in the crowd, out in the late afternoon
sunlight, redolent of dust and hot travellers, she looked about
her and saw him, standing not far away. He had bought a roast
mealie from a hawker, and was eating it now, making lines

down the cob. She felt that unsettling sensation again and she stopped where she stood, as if she were a stranger who was uncertain where to go.

He was looking at her, and she turned away flustered. Had he seen her watching him? Perhaps. She looked up again, quickly glancing in his direction, and he smiled at her this time and raised his eyebrows. Then, tossing the mealie cob away, he picked up the trumpet case and walked over towards her. She was frozen, unable to walk away, mesmerised like prey before a snake.

"I saw you on that bus," he said. "I thought I had seen you before. But I haven't."

She looked down at the ground.

"I have never seen you," she said. "Ever."

He smiled. He was not frightening, she thought, and some of her awkwardness left her.

"You see most people in this country once or twice," he said. "There are no strangers."

She nodded. "That is true."

There was a silence. Then he pointed to the case at his feet.

"This is a trumpet, you know. I am a musician."

She looked at the case. It had a sticker on it; a picture of a man playing a guitar.

"Do you like music?" he asked. "Jazz? Quella?"

She looked up, and saw that he was still smiling at her.

"Yes. I like music."

"I play in a band," he said. "We play in the bar at the President Hotel. You could come and listen. I am going there now."

They walked to the bar, which was only ten minutes or so from the bus stop. He bought her a drink and sat her at a table at the back, a table with one seat at it to discourage others.

Then he played, and she listened, overcome by the sliding, slippery music, and proud that she knew this man, that she was his guest. The drink was strange and bitter; she did not like the taste of alcohol, but drinking was what you did in bars and she was concerned that she would seem out of place or too young and people would notice her.

Afterwards, when the band had its break, he came to join her, and she saw that his brow was glistening with the effort of playing.

"I'm not playing well today," he said. "There are some days when you can and some days when you can't."

"I thought you were very good. You played well."

"I don't think so. I can play better. There are days when the trumpet just talks to me. I don't have to do anything then."

She saw that people were looking at them, and that one or two women were staring at her critically. They wanted to be where she was, she could tell. They wanted to be with Note.

He put her on the late bus after they had left the bar, and stood and waved to her as the bus drew away. She waved back and closed her eyes. She had a boyfriend now, a jazz musician, and she would be seeing him again, at his request, the following Friday night, when they were playing at a braaivleis at the Gaborone Club. Members of the band, he said, always took their girlfriends, and she would meet some interesting people there, good-quality people, people she would not normally meet.

And that is where Note Mokoti proposed to Precious Ramotswe and where she accepted him, in a curious sort of way, without saying anything. It was after the band had finished and they were sitting in the darkness, away from the noise of the drinkers in the bar. He said: "I want to get married soon and I want to get married to you. You are a nice girl who will do very well for a wife."

Precious said nothing, because she was uncertain, and her silence was taken as assent.

"I will speak to your father about this," said Note. "I hope that he is not an old-fashioned man who will want a lot of cattle for you."

He was, but she did not say so. She had not agreed yet, she thought, but perhaps it was now too late.

Then Note said: "Now that you are going to be my wife, I must teach you what wives are for."

She said nothing. This is what happened, she supposed. This is how men were, just as her friends at school had told her, those who were easy, of course.

He put his arm around her and moved her back against the soft grass. They were in the shadows, and there was nobody nearby, just the noise of the drinkers shouting and laughing. He took her hand and placed it upon his stomach, where he left it, not knowing what to do. Then he started to kiss her, on her neck, her cheek, her lips, and all she heard was the thudding of her heart and her shortened breath.

He said: "Girls must learn this thing. Has anybody taught you?"

She shook her head. She had not learned and now, she felt, it was too late. She would not know what to do.

"I am glad," he said. "I knew straightaway that you were a virgin, which is a very good thing for a man. But now things will change. Right now. Tonight."

He hurt her. She asked him to stop, but he put her head back and hit her once across the cheek. But he immediately kissed her where the blow had struck, and said that he had not meant to do it. All the time he was pushing against her, and scratching at her, sometimes across her back, with his finger-nails. Then he moved her over, and he hurt her again, and struck her across her back with his belt.

She sat up, and gathered her crumpled clothes together. She was concerned, even if he was not, that somebody might come out into the night and see them.

She dressed, and as she put on her blouse, she started to weep, quietly, because she was thinking of her father, whom she would see tomorrow on his verandah, who would tell her the cattle news, and who would never imagine what had happened to her that night.

Note Mokoti visited her father three weeks later, by himself, and asked him for Precious. Obed said he would speak to his daughter, which he did when she came to see him next. He sat on his stool and looked up at her and said to her that she would never have to marry anybody she did not want to marry. Those days were over, long ago. Nor should she feel that she had to marry at all; a woman could be by herself these days—there were more and more women like that.

She could have said no at this point, which is what her father wanted her to say. But she did not want to say that. She lived for her meetings with Note Mokoti. She wanted to marry him. He was not a good man, she could tell that, but she might change him. And, when all was said and done, there remained those dark moments of contact, those pleasures he snatched from her, which were addictive. She liked that. She felt ashamed even to think of it, but she liked what he did to her, the humiliation, the urgency. She wanted to be with him, wanted him to possess her. It was like a bitter drink which bids you back. And of course she sensed that she was pregnant. It was too early to tell, but she felt that Note Mokoti's child was within her, a tiny, fluttering bird, deep within her.

THEY MARRIED on a Saturday afternoon, at three o'clock, in the church at Mochudi, with the cattle outside under the trees, for it was late October and the heat was at its worst. The countryside was dry that year, as the previous season's rains had not been good. Everything was parched and wilting; there was little grass left, and the cattle were skin and bones. It was a listless time.

The Reformed Church Minister married them, gasping in his clerical black, mopping at his brow with a large red handkerchief.

He said: "You are being married here in God's sight. God places upon you certain duties. God looks after us and keeps us in this cruel world. God loves His children, but we must remember those duties He asks of us. Do you young people understand what I am saying?"

Note smiled. "I understand."

And, turning to Precious: "And do you understand?"

She looked up into the Minister's face—the face of her father's friend. She knew that her father had spoken to him about this marriage and about how unhappy he was about it, but the Minister had said that he was unable to intervene. Now his tone was gentle, and he pressed her hand lightly as he took it to place in Note's. As he did so, the child moved within her, and she winced because the movement was so sudden and so firm.

*   *   *

AFTER TWO days in Mochudi, where they stayed in the house of a cousin of Note's, they packed their possessions into the back of a truck and went down to Gaborone. Note had found somewhere to stay—two rooms and a kitchen in somebody's house near Tlokweng. It was a luxury to have two rooms; one was their bedroom, furnished with a double mattress and an old wardrobe; the other was a living room and dining room, with a table, two chairs, and a sideboard. The yellow curtains from her room at the cousin's house were hung up in this room, and they made it bright and cheerful.

Note kept his trumpet there and his collection of tapes. He would practise for twenty minutes at a time, and then, while his lip was resting, he would listen to a tape and pick out the rhythms on a guitar. He knew everything about township music—where it came from, who sang what, who played which part with whom. He had heard the greats, too; Hugh Masekela on the trumpet, Dollar Brand on the piano, Spokes Machobane singing; he had heard them in person in Johannesburg, and knew every recording they had ever made.

She watched him take the trumpet from its case and fit the mouthpiece. She watched as he raised it to his lips and then, so suddenly, from that tiny cup of metal against his flesh, the sound would burst out like a glorious, brilliant knife dividing the air. And the little room would reverberate and the flies, jolted out of their torpor, would buzz round and round as if riding the swirling notes.

She went with him to the bars, and he was kind to her there, but he seemed to get caught up in his own circle and she felt that he did not really want her there. There were people there who thought of nothing but music; they talked endlessly about music, music, music; how much could one say about music?

They didn't want her there either, she thought, and so she stopped going to the bars and stayed at home.

He came home late and he smelled of beer when he returned. It was a sour smell, like rancid milk, and she turned her head away as he pushed her down on the bed and pulled at her clothing.

"You have had a lot of beer. You have had a good evening."

He looked at her, his eyes slightly out of focus.

"I can drink if I want to. You're one of these women who stays at home and complains? Is that what you are?"

"I am not. I only meant to say that you had a good evening."

But his indignation would not be assuaged, and he said: "You are making me punish you, woman. You are making me do this thing to you."

She cried out, and tried to struggle, to push him away, but he was too strong for her.

"Don't hurt the baby."

"Baby! Why do you talk about this baby? It is not mine. I am not the father of any baby."

MALE HANDS again, but this time in thin rubber gloves, which made the hands pale and unfinished, like a white man's hands.

"Do you feel any pain here? No? And here?"

She shook her head.

"I think that the baby is all right. And up here, where these marks are. Is there pain just on the outside, or is it deeper in?"

"It is just the outside."

"I see. I am going to have to put in stitches here. All the way across here, because the skin has parted so badly. I'll spray something on to take the pain away but maybe it's better for you not to watch me while I'm sewing! Some people say men can't sew, but we doctors aren't too bad at it!"

She closed her eyes and heard a hissing sound. There was cold spray against her skin and then a numbness as the doctor worked on the wound.

"This was your husband's doing? Am I right?"

She opened her eyes. The doctor had finished the suture and had handed something to the nurse. He was looking at her now as he peeled off the gloves.

"How many times has this happened before? Is there anybody to look after you?"

"I don't know. I don't know."

"I suppose you're going to go back to him?"

She opened her mouth to speak, but he interrupted her.

"Of course you are. It's always the same. The woman goes back for more."

He sighed. "I'll probably see you again, you know. But I hope I don't. Just be careful."

SHE WENT back the next day, a scarf tied around her face to hide the bruises and the cuts. She ached in her arms and in her stomach, and the sutured wound stung sharply. They had given her pills at the hospital, and she had taken one just before she left on the bus. This seemed to help the pain, and she took another on the journey.

The door was open. She went in, her heart thumping within her chest, and saw what had happened. The room was empty, apart from the furniture. He had taken his tapes, and their new metal trunk, and the yellow curtains too. And in the bedroom, he had slashed the mattress with a knife, and there was kapok lying about, making it look like a shearing room.

She sat down on the bed and was still sitting there, staring at the floor, when the neighbour came in and said that she would get somebody to take her in a truck back to Mochudi, to Obed, to her father.

There she stayed, looking after her father, for the next fourteen years. He died shortly after her thirty-fourth birthday, and that was the point at which Precious Ramotswe, now parentless, veteran of a nightmare marriage, and mother, for a brief and lovely five days, became the first lady private detective in Botswana.

CHAPTER FIVE

WHAT YOU NEED TO OPEN
A DETECTIVE AGENCY

MMA RAMOTSWE had thought that it would not be easy to open a detective agency. People always made the mistake of thinking that starting a business was simple and then found that there were all sorts of hidden problems and unforeseen demands. She had heard of people opening businesses that lasted four or five weeks before they ran out of money or stock, or both. It was always more difficult than you thought it would be.

She went to the lawyer at Pilane, who had arranged for her to get her father's money. He had organised the sale of the cattle, and had got a good price for them.

"I have got a lot of money for you," he said. "Your father's herd had grown and grown."

She took the cheque and the sheet of paper that he handed her. It was more than she had imagined possible. But there it was—all that money, made payable to Precious Ramotswe, on presentation to Barclays Bank of Botswana.

"You can buy a house with that," said the lawyer. "And a business."

"I am going to buy both of those."

The lawyer looked interested. "What sort of business? A store? I can give you advice, you know."

"A detective agency."

The lawyer looked blank.

"There are none for sale. There are none of those."

Mma Ramotswe nodded. "I know that. I am going to have to start from scratch."

The lawyer winced as she spoke. "It's easy to lose money in business," he said. "Especially when you don't know anything about what you're doing." He stared at her hard. "Especially then. And anyway, can women be detectives? Do you think they can?"

"Why not?" said Mma Ramotswe. She had heard that people did not like lawyers, and now she thought she could see why. This man was so certain of himself, so utterly convinced. What had it to do with him what she did? It was her money, her future. And how dare he say that about women, when he didn't even know that his zip was half undone! Should she tell him?

"Women are the ones who know what's going on," she said quietly. "They are the ones with eyes. Have you not heard of Agatha Christie?"

The lawyer looked taken aback. "Agatha Christie? Of course I know her. Yes, that is true. A woman sees more than a man sees. That is well-known."

"So," said Mma Ramotswe, "when people see a sign saying

No. 1 Ladies' Detective Agency, what will they think? They'll think those ladies will know what's going on. They're the ones."

The lawyer stroked his chin. "Maybe."

"Yes," said Mma Ramotswe. "Maybe." Adding, "Your zip, Rra. I think you may not have noticed . . ."

SHE FOUND the house first, on a corner plot in Zebra Drive. It was expensive, and she decided to take out a bond on part of it, so that she could afford to buy somewhere for the business too. That was more difficult, but at last she found a small place near Kgale Hill, on the edge of town, where she could set up. It was a good place, because a lot of people walked down that road every day and would see the sign. It would be almost as effective as having an advertisement in the *Daily News* or the *Botswana Guardian*. Everybody would soon know about her.

The building she bought had originally been a general dealer's shop, but had been converted into a dry cleaners and finally a bottle store. For a year or so it had lain empty, and had been lived in by squatters. They had made fires inside, and in each of the rooms there was a part of the wall where the plaster had been charred and burned. The owner had eventually returned from Francistown and had driven out the squatters and placed the dejected-looking building on the market. There had been one or two prospective purchasers, but they had been repelled by its condition and the price had dropped. When Mma Ramotswe had offered cash, the seller had leapt at her offer and she received the deeds within days.

There was a lot to do. A builder was called in to replace the damaged plaster and to repair the tin roof and, again with the offer of cash, this was accomplished within a week. Then

Mma Ramotswe set to the task of painting, and she had soon completed the outside in ochre and the inside in white. She bought fresh yellow curtains for the windows and, in an unusual moment of extravagance, splashed out on a brand new office set of two desks and two chairs. Her friend, Mr J.L.B. Matekoni, proprietor of Tlokweng Road Speedy Motors, brought her an old typewriter which was surplus to his own requirements and which worked quite well, and with that the office was ready to open—once she had a secretary.

This was the easiest part of all. A telephone call to the Botswana College of Secretarial and Office Skills brought an immediate response. They had just the woman, they said. Mma Makutsi was the widow of a teacher and had just passed their general typing and secretarial examinations with an average grade of 97 percent; she would be ideal—they were certain of it.

Mma Ramotswe liked her immediately. She was a thin woman with a rather long face and braided hair in which she had rubbed copious quantities of henna. She wore oval glasses with wide plastic frames, and she had a fixed, but apparently quite sincere smile.

They opened the office on a Monday. Mma Ramotswe sat at her desk and Mma Makutsi sat at hers, behind the typewriter. She looked at Mma Ramotswe and smiled even more broadly.

"I am ready for work," she said. "I am ready to start."

"Mmm," said Mma Ramotswe. "It's early days yet. We've only just opened. We will have to wait for a client to come."

In her heart of hearts, she knew there would be no clients. The whole idea was a ghastly mistake. Nobody wanted a private detective, and certainly nobody would want her. Who was she, after all? She was just Precious Ramotswe from Mochudi.

She had never been to London or wherever detectives went to find out how to be private detectives. She had never even been to Johannesburg. What if somebody came in and said "You know Johannesburg of course," she would have to lie, or just say nothing.

Mma Makutsi looked at her, and then looked down at the typewriter keyboard. She opened a drawer, peered inside, and then closed it. At that moment a hen came into the room from the yard outside and pecked at something on the floor.

"Get out," shouted Mma Makutsi. "No chickens in here!"

At ten o'clock Mma Makutsi got up from her desk and went into the back room to make the tea. She had been asked to make bush tea, which was Mma Ramotswe's favourite, and she soon brought two cups back. She had a tin of condensed milk in her handbag, and she took this out and poured a small amount into each cup. Then they drank their tea, watching a small boy at the edge of the road throwing stones at a skeletal dog.

At eleven o'clock they had another cup of tea, and at twelve Mma Ramotswe rose to her feet and announced that she was going to walk down the road to the shops to buy herself some perfume. Mma Makutsi was to stay behind and answer the telephone and welcome any clients who might come. Mma Ramotswe smiled as she said this. There would be no clients, of course, and she would be closed at the end of the month. Did Mma Makutsi understand what a parlous job she had obtained for herself? A woman with an average of 97 percent deserved better than this.

Mma Ramotswe was standing at the counter of the shop looking at a bottle of perfume when Mma Makutsi hurtled through the door.

"Mma Ramotswe," she panted. "A client. There is a client in the office. It is a big case. A missing man. Come quickly. There is no time to lose."

THE WIVES of missing men are all the same, thought Mma Ramotswe. At first they feel anxiety, and are convinced that something dreadful has happened. Then doubt begins to creep in, and they wonder whether he's gone off with another woman (which he usually has), and then finally they become angry. At the anger stage, most of them don't want him back anymore, even if he's found. They just want to have a good chance to shout at him.

Mma Malatsi was in the second stage, she thought. She has begun to suspect that he is off somewhere having a good time, while she's left at home, and of course it's beginning to rankle. Perhaps there are debts to be paid, even if she looks as if she's got a fair bit of money.

"Maybe you should tell me a little bit more about your husband," she said, as Mma Malatsi began to drink the cup of strong bush tea which Mma Makutsi had brewed for her.

"His name is Peter Malatsi," Mma Malatsi said. "He's forty and he has—had—has a business selling furniture. It's a good business and he did well. So he hasn't run away from any creditors."

Mma Ramotswe nodded. "There must be another reason," she began, and then, cautiously: "You know what men are like, Mma. What about another woman? Do you think . . ."

Mma Malatsi shook her head vigorously.

"I don't think so," she said. "Maybe a year ago that would have been possible, but then he became a Christian and took up with some Church that was always singing and marching around the place in white uniforms."

Mma Ramotswe noted this down. Church. Singing. Got religion badly? Lady preacher lured him away?

"Who were these people?" she said. "Maybe they know something about him?"

Mma Malatsi shrugged. "I'm not sure," she said, slightly irritably. "In fact, I don't know. He asked me to come with him once or twice, but I refused. So he just used to go off by himself on Sundays. In fact, he disappeared on a Sunday. I thought he'd gone off to his Church."

Mma Ramotswe looked at the ceiling. This was not going to be as hard as some of these cases. Peter Malatsi had gone off with one of the Christians; that was pretty clear. All she had to do now was find which group it was and she would be on his trail. It was the old predictable story; it would be a younger Christian, she was sure of that.

BY THE end of the following day, Mma Ramotswe had compiled a list of five Christian groups which could fit the description. Over the next two days she tracked down the leaders of three of them, and was satisfied that nothing was known of Peter Malatsi. Two of the three tried to convert her; the third merely asked her for money and received a five-pula note.

When she located the leader of the fourth group, the Reverend Shadreck Mapeli, she knew that the search was over. When she mentioned the Malatsi name, the Reverend gave a shudder and glanced over his shoulder surreptitiously.

"Are you from the police?" he asked. "Are you a policeman?"

"Policewoman," she said.

"Ah!" he said mournfully. "Aee!"

"I mean, I'm not a policewoman," she said quickly. "I'm a private detective."

The Reverend appeared to calm down slightly.

"Who sent you?"

"Mma Malatsi."

"Ooh," said the Reverend. "He told us that he had no wife."

"Well, he did," said Mma Ramotswe. "And she's been wondering where he is."

"He's dead," said the Reverend. "He's gone to the Lord."

Mma Ramotswe sensed that he was telling the truth, and that the enquiry was effectively at an end. Now all that remained to be done was to find out how he had died.

"You must tell me," she said. "I won't reveal your name to anybody if you don't want me to. Just tell me how it happened."

They drove to the river in Mma Ramotswe's small white van. It was the rainy season, and there had been several storms, which made the track almost impassable. But at last they reached the river's edge and parked the van under a tree.

"This is where we have our baptisms," said the Reverend, pointing to a pool in the swollen waters of the river. "This is where I stood, here, and this is where the sinners entered the water."

"How many sinners did you have?" asked Mma Ramotswe.

"Six sinners altogether, including Peter. They all went in together, while I prepared to follow them with my staff."

"Yes?" said Mma Ramotswe. "Then what happened?"

"The sinners were standing in the water up to about here." The Reverend indicated his upper chest. "I turned round to tell the flock to start singing, and then when I turned back I noticed that there was something wrong. There were only five sinners in the water."

"One had disappeared?"

"Yes," said the Reverend, shaking slightly as he spoke. "God had taken one of them to His bosom."

Mma Ramotswe looked at the water. It was not a big river, and for much of the year it was reduced to a few stagnant pools. But in a good rainy season, such as that year's, it could be quite a torrent. A nonswimmer could easily be swept away, she reflected, and yet, if somebody were to be swept away the body would surely be found downstream. There were plenty of people who went down to the river for one purpose or another and who would be bound to notice a body. The police would have been called. There would have been something in the newspaper about an unidentified body being found in the Notwane River; the paper was always looking for stories like that. They wouldn't have let the opportunity go by.

She thought for a moment. There was another explanation, and it made her shiver. But before she went into that, she had to find out why the Reverend had kept so quiet about it all.

"You didn't tell the police," she said, trying not to sound too accusing. "Why not?"

The Reverend looked down at the ground, which, in her experience, was where people usually looked if they felt truly sorry. The shamelessly unrepentant, she found, always looked up at the sky.

"I know I should have told them. God will punish me for it. But I was worried that I would be blamed for poor Peter's accident and I thought they would take me to court. They might make me pay damages for it, and that would drive the Church into bankruptcy and put a stop to God's work." He paused. "Do you understand why I kept quiet, and told all the flock not to say anything?"

Mma Ramotswe nodded, and reached out to touch the Reverend gently on the arm.

"I do not think that what you did was bad," she said. "I'm sure that God wanted you to continue and He will not be angry. It was not your fault."

The Reverend raised his eyes and smiled.

"Those are kind words, my sister. Thank you."

THAT AFTERNOON, Mma Ramotswe asked her neighbour if she could borrow one of his dogs. He had a pack of five, and she hated every one of them for their incessant barking. These dogs barked in the morning, as if they were roosters, and at night, when the moon rose in the sky. They barked at crows, and at hammerkops; they barked at passersby; and they sometimes barked just because they had got too hot.

"I need a dog to help me on one of my cases," she explained. "I'll bring him back safe and sound."

The neighbour was flattered to have been asked.

"I'll give you this dog here," he said. "It's the senior dog, and he has a very good nose. He will make a good detective dog."

Mma Ramotswe took the dog warily. It was a large yellow creature, with a curious, offensive smell. That night, just after sunset, she put it in the back of her van, tying its neck to a handle with a piece of string. Then she set off down the track that led to the river, her headlights picking out the shapes of the thorn trees and the anthills in the darkness. In a strange way, she felt glad of the company of the dog, unpleasant though it was.

Now, beside the pool in the river, she took a thick stake from the van and drove it into the soft ground near the water's edge. Then she fetched the dog, led it down to the pool, and tied its string firmly to the stake. From a bag she had with her, she took out a large bone and put it in front of the yellow dog's nose. The animal gave a grunt of pleasure and immediately settled down to gnaw the bone.

Mma Ramotswe waited just a few yards away, a blanket tucked round her legs to keep off the mosquitoes and her old rifle over her knees. She knew it could be a long wait, and she hoped that she would not go to sleep. If she did, though, she was sure that the dog would wake her up when the time came.

Two hours passed. The mosquitoes were bad, and her skin itched, but this was work, and she never complained when she was working. Then, suddenly, there came a growling noise from the dog. Mma Ramotswe strained her eyes in the darkness. She could just make out the shape of the dog, and she could see that it was standing now, looking towards the water. The dog growled again, and gave a bark; then it was silent once more. Mma Ramotswe tossed the blanket off her knees and picked up the powerful torch at her side. Just a little bit longer, she thought.

There was a noise from the water's edge, and Mma Ramotswe knew now that it was time to switch on her torch. As the beam came on, she saw, just at the edge of the water, its head turned towards the cowering dog, a large crocodile.

The crocodile was totally unconcerned by the light, which it probably took for the moon. Its eyes were fixed on the dog, and it was edging slowly towards its quarry. Mma Ramotswe raised the rifle to her shoulder and saw the side of the crocodile's head framed perfectly in her sights. She pulled the trigger.

When the bullet struck the crocodile, it gave a great leap, a somersault in fact, and landed on its back, half in the water, half out. For a moment or two it twitched and then was still. It had been a perfectly placed shot.

Mma Ramotswe noticed that she was trembling as she put the rifle down. Her Daddy had taught her to shoot, and he had done it well, but she did not like to shoot animals, especially crocodiles. They were bad luck, these creatures, but duty had to be done. And what was it doing there anyway? These creatures were not meant to be in the Notwane River; it must have wandered for miles overland, or swum up in the flood waters from the Limpopo itself. Poor crocodile—this was the end of its adventure.

She took a knife and slit through the creature's belly. The leather was soft, and the stomach was soon exposed and its contents revealed. Inside there were pebbles, which the crocodile used for digesting its food, and several pieces of foul-smelling fish. But it was not this that interested her; she was more interested in the undigested bangles and rings and wristwatch she found. These were corroded, and one or two of them were encrusted, but they stood out amongst the stomach contents, each of them the evidence of the crocodile's sinister appetites.

"IS THIS your husband's property?" she asked Mma Malatsi, handing her the wristwatch she had claimed from the crocodile's stomach.

Mma Malatsi took the watch and looked at it. Mma Ramotswe grimaced; she hated moments like this, when she had no choice but to be the bearer of bad news.

But Mma Malatsi was extraordinarily calm. "Well at least I know that he's with the Lord," she said. "And that's much better than knowing that he's in the arms of some other woman, isn't it?"

Mma Ramotswe nodded. "I think it is," she said.

"Were you married, Mma?" asked Mma Malatsi. "Do you know what it is like to be married to a man?"

Mma Ramotswe looked out of the window. There was a thorn tree outside her window, but beyond that she could see the boulder-strewn hill.

"I had a husband," she said. "Once I had a husband. He played the trumpet. He made me unhappy and now I am glad that I no longer have a husband." She paused. "I'm sorry. I did not mean to be rude. You've lost your husband and you must be very sorry."

"A bit," said Mma Malatsi. "But I have lots to do."

CHAPTER SIX

BOY

THE BOY was eleven, and was small for his age. They had tried everything to get him to grow, but he was taking his time, and now, when you saw him, you would say that he was only eight or nine, rather than eleven. Not that it bothered him in the slightest; his father had said to him: I was a short boy too. Now I am a tall man. Look at me. That will happen to you. You just wait.

But secretly the parents feared that there was something wrong; that his spine was twisted, perhaps, and that this was preventing him from growing. When he was barely four, he had fallen out of a tree—he had been after birds' eggs—and had lain still for several minutes, the breath knocked out of him; until his grandmother had run wailing across the melon field and had lifted him up and carried him home, a shattered egg still clasped in his hand. He had recovered—or so they thought at the time—but his walk was different, they thought.

They had taken him to the clinic, where a nurse had looked at his eyes and into his mouth and had pronounced him healthy.

"Boys fall all the time. They hardly ever break anything."

The nurse placed her hands on the child's shoulders and twisted his torso.

"See. There is nothing wrong with him. Nothing. If he had broken anything, he would have cried out."

But years later, when he remained small, the mother thought of the fall and blamed herself for believing that nurse who was only good for doing bilharzia tests and checking for worms.

THE BOY was more curious than other children. He loved to look for stones in the red earth and polish them with his spittle. He found some beautiful ones too—deep-blue ones and ones which had a copper-red hue, like the sky at dusk. He kept his stones at the foot of his sleeping mat in his hut and learned to count with them. The other boys learned to count by counting cattle, but this boy did not seem to like cattle—which was another thing that made him odd.

Because of his curiosity, which sent him scuttling about the bush on mysterious errands of his own, his parents were used to his being out of their sight for hours on end. No harm could come to him, unless he was unlucky enough to step on a puff adder or a cobra. But this never happened, and suddenly he would turn up again at the cattle enclosure, or behind the goats, clutching some strange thing he had found—a vulture's feather, a dried tshongololo millipede, the bleached skull of a snake.

Now the boy was out again, walking along one of the paths that led this way and that through the dusty bush. He had found something which interested him very much—the fresh dung of a snake—and he followed the path so he might see the creature itself. He knew what it was because it had balls of fur in it, and that would only come from a snake. It was rock rabbit fur, he was sure, because of its colour and because he knew that rock rabbits were a delicacy to a big snake. If he found the snake, he might kill it with a rock, and skin it, and that would make a handsome skin for a belt for him and his father.

But it was getting dark, and he would have to give up. He would never see the snake on a night with no moon; he would leave the path and cut back across the bush towards the dirt road that wound its way back, over the dry riverbed, to the village.

He found the road easily and sat for a moment on the verge, digging his toes into soft white sand. He was hungry, and he knew that there would be some meat with their porridge that night because he had seen his grandmother preparing the stew. She always gave him more than his fair share—almost more than his father—and that angered his two sisters.

"We like meat too. We girls like meat."

But that did not persuade the grandmother.

He stood up and began to walk along the road. It was quite dark now, and the trees and bushes were black, formless shapes, merging into one another. A bird was calling somewhere—a night-hunting bird—and there were night insects screeching. He felt a small stinging pain on his right arm, and slapped at it. A mosquito.

Suddenly, on the foliage of a tree ahead, there was a band of yellow light. The light shone and dipped, and the boy turned round. There was a truck on the road behind him. It could not be a car, because the sand was far too deep and soft for a car.

He stood on the side of the road and waited. The lights were almost upon him now; a small truck, a pickup, with two bounding headlights going up and down with the bumps in the road. Now it was upon him, and he held up his hand to shade his eyes.

"Good evening, young one." The traditional greeting, called out from within the cab of the truck.

He smiled and returned the greeting. He could make out two men in the cab—a young man at the wheel and an older man next to him. He knew they were strangers, although he could not see their faces. There was something odd about the way the man spoke Setswana. It was not the way a local would speak it. An odd voice that became higher at the end of a word.

"Are you hunting for wild animals? You want to catch a leopard in this darkness?"

He shook his head. "No. I am just walking home."

"Because a leopard could catch you before you caught it!"

He laughed. "You are right, Rra! I would not like to see a leopard tonight."

"Then we will take you to your place. Is it far?"

"No. It is not far. It is just over there. That way."

THE DRIVER opened the door and got out, leaving the engine running, to allow the boy to slide in over the bench seat. Then he got back in, closed the door and engaged the gears. The boy drew his feet up—there was some animal on the floor and he had touched a soft wet nose—a dog perhaps, or a goat.

He glanced at the man to his left, the older man. It would be rude to stare and it was difficult to see much in the darkness. But he did notice the thing that was wrong with the man's lip and he saw his eyes too. He turned away. A boy should never stare at an old man like this. But why were these people here? What were they doing?

"There it is. There is my father's place. You see—over there. Those lights."

"We can see it."

"I can walk from here if you like. If you stop, I can walk. There is a path."

"We are not stopping. You have something to do for us. You can help us with something."

"They are expecting me back. They will be waiting."

"There is always somebody waiting for somebody. Always."

He suddenly felt frightened, and he turned to look at the driver. The younger man smiled at him.

"Don't worry. Just sit still. You are going somewhere else tonight."

"Where are you taking me, Rra? Why are you taking me away?"

The older man reached out and touched the boy on the shoulder.

"You will not be harmed. You can go home some other time. They will know that you are not being harmed. We are kind men, you see. We are kind men. Listen, I'm going to tell you a little story while we travel. That will make you happy and keep you quiet.

"There were some herd boys who looked after the cattle of their rich uncle. He was a rich man that one! He had more cattle than anybody else in that part of Botswana and his cattle were big, big, like this, only bigger.

"Now these boys found that one day a calf had appeared on

the edge of the herd. It was a strange calf, with many colours on it, unlike any other calf they had ever seen. And, ow! they were pleased that this calf had come.

"This calf was very unusual in another way. This calf could sing a cattle song that the boys heard whenever they went near it. They could not hear the words which this calf was using, but they were something about cattle matters.

"The boys loved this calf, and because they loved it so much they did not notice that some of the other cattle were straying away. By the time that they did notice, it was only after two of the cattle had gone for good that they saw what had happened.

"Their uncle came out. Here he comes, a tall, tall man with a stick. He shouts at the boys and he hits their calf with his stick, saying that strange calves never brought any luck.

"So the calf died, but before it died it whispered something to the boys and they were able to hear it this time. It was very special, and when the boys told their uncle what the calf had said he fell to his knees and wailed.

"The calf was his brother, you see, who had been eaten by a lion a long time before and had come back. Now this man had killed his brother and he was never happy again. He was sad. Very sad."

The boy watched the man's face as he told the story. If he had been unaware of what was happening until that moment, now he knew. He knew what was going to happen.

"Hold that boy! Take his arms! He's going to make me go off the road if you don't hold him."

"I'm trying. He is struggling like a devil."

"Just hold him. I'll stop the truck."

CHAPTER SEVEN

MMA MAKUTSI DEALS WITH THE MAIL

THE SUCCESS of the first case heartened Mma Ramotswe. She had now sent off for, and received, a manual on private detection and was going through it chapter by chapter, taking copious notes. She had made no mistakes in that first case, she thought. She had found out what information there was to be had by a simple process of listing the likely sources and seeking them out. That did not take a great deal of doing. Provided that one was methodical, there was hardly any way in which one could go wrong.

Then she had had a hunch about the crocodile and had followed it up. Again, the manual endorsed this as perfectly acceptable practice. "Don't disregard a hunch," it advised. "Hunches are another form of knowledge." Mma Ramotswe had liked that phrase and had mentioned it to Mma Makutsi. Her secretary had listened carefully, and then typed the sentence out on her typewriter and handed it to Mma Ramotswe.

Mma Makutsi was pleasant company and could type quite
well. She had typed out a report which Mma Ramotswe had
dictated on the Malatsi case and had typed out the bill for
sending to Mma Malatsi. But apart from that she had not
really been called on to do anything else and Mma Ramotswe
wondered whether the business could really justify employing
a secretary.

And yet one had to. What sort of private detective agency
had no secretary? She would be a laughingstock without one,
and clients—if there were really going to be any more, which
was doubtful—could well be frightened away.

Mma Makutsi had the mail to open, of course. There was
no mail for the first three days. On the fourth day, a catalogue
was received, and a property tax demand, and on the fifth day
a letter which was intended for the previous owner.

Then, at the beginning of the second week, she opened a
white envelope dirty with finger marks and read the letter out
to Mma Ramotswe.

Dear Mma Ramotswe,

I read about you in the newspaper and about how you
have opened this big new agency down there in town. I
am very proud for Botswana that we now have a person
like you in this country.

   I am the teacher at the small school at Katsana Village,
thirty miles from Gaborone, which is near the place where
I was born. I went to Teachers' College many years ago and
I passed with a double distinction. My wife and I have two
daughters and we have a son of eleven. This boy to which

I am referring has recently vanished and has not been seen for two months.

We went to the police. They made a big search and asked questions everywhere. Nobody knew anything about our son. I took time off from the school and searched the land around our village. We have some *kopjes* not too far away and there are boulders and caves over there. I went into each one of those caves and looked into every crevice. But there was no sign of my son.

He was a boy who liked to wander, because he had a strong interest in nature. He was always collecting rocks and things like that. He knew a lot about the bush and he would never get into danger from stupidity. There are no leopards in these parts anymore and we are too far away from the Kalahari for lions to come.

I went everywhere, calling, calling, but my son never answered me. I looked in every well of every farmer and village nearby and asked them to check the water. But there was no sign of him.

How can a boy vanish off the face of the Earth like this? If I were not a Christian, I would say that some evil spirit had lifted him up and carried him off. But I know that things like that do not really happen.

I am not a wealthy man. I cannot afford the services of a private detective, but I ask you, Mma, in the name of Jesus Christ, to help me in one small way. Please, when you are making your enquiries about other things, and talking to people who might know what goes on, please ask them if they have heard anything about a boy called Thobiso, aged eleven years and four months, who is the son of the teacher at Katsana Village. Please just ask them, and if you hear anything at all, please address a note to the undersigned, myself, the teacher.

In God's name, Ernest Molai Pakotati, Dip.Ed.

Mma Makutsi stopped reading and looked across the room at Mma Ramotswe. For a moment, neither spoke. Then Mma Ramotswe broke the silence.

"Do you know anything about this?" she asked. "Have you heard anything about a boy going missing?"

Mma Makutsi frowned. "I think so. I think there was something in the newspaper about a search for a boy. I think they thought he might have run away from home for some reason."

Mma Ramotswe rose to her feet and took the letter from her secretary. She held it as one might hold an exhibit in court— gingerly, so as not to disturb the evidence. It felt to her as if the letter—a mere scrap of paper, so light in itself—was weighted with pain.

"I don't suppose there's much I can do," she said quietly. "Of course I can keep my ears open. I can tell the poor daddy that, but what else can I do? He will know the bush around Katsana. He will know the people. I can't really do very much for him."

Mma Makutsi seemed relieved. "No," she said. "We can't help that poor man."

A letter was dictated by Mma Ramotswe, and Mma Makutsi typed it carefully into the typewriter. Then it was sealed in an envelope, a stamp stuck on the outside, and it was placed in the new red out-tray Mma Ramotswe had bought from the Botswana Book Centre. It was the second letter to leave the No. 1 Ladies' Detective Agency, the first being Mma Malatsi's bill for two hundred and fifty pula—the bill on the top of which Mma Makutsi had typed: "Your late husband—the solving of the mystery of his death."

THAT EVENING, in the house in Zebra Drive, Mma Ramotswe prepared herself a meal of stew and pumpkin. She loved standing in the kitchen, stirring the pot, thinking over the events of the day, sipping at a large mug of bush tea which she balanced on the edge of the stove. Several things had happened that day, apart from the arrival of the letter. A man had come in with a query about a bad debt and she had reluctantly agreed to help him recover it. She was not sure whether this was the sort of thing which a private detective should do—there was nothing in the manual about it—but he was persistent and she found it difficult to refuse. Then there had been a visit from a woman who was concerned about her husband.

"He comes home smelling of perfume," she said, "And smiling too. Why would a man come home smelling of perfume and smiling?"

"Perhaps he is seeing another woman," ventured Mma Ramotswe.

The woman had looked at her aghast.

"Do you think he would do that? My husband?"

They had discussed the situation and it was agreed that the woman would tackle her husband on the subject.

"It's possible that there is another explanation," said Mma Ramotswe reassuringly.

"Such as?"

"Well . . ."

"Many men wear perfume these days," offered Mma Makutsi. "They think it makes them smell good. You know how men smell."

The client had turned in her chair and stared at Mma Makutsi.

"My husband does not smell," she said. "He is a very clean man."

Mma Ramotswe had thrown Mma Makutsi a warning look. She would have to have a word with her about keeping out of the way when clients were there.

But whatever else had happened that day, her thoughts kept returning to the teacher's letter and the story of the missing boy. How the poor man must have fretted—and the mother, too. He did not say anything about a mother, but there must have been one, or a grandmother of course. What thoughts would have been in their minds as each hour went past with no sign of the boy, and all the time he could be in danger, stuck in an old mine shaft, perhaps, too hoarse to cry out anymore while rescuers beat about above him. Or stolen perhaps—whisked away by somebody in the night. What cruel heart could do such a thing to an innocent child? How could anybody resist the boy's cries as he begged to be taken home? That such things could happen right there, in Botswana of all places, made her shiver with dread.

She began to wonder whether this was the right job for her after all. It was all very well thinking that one might help people to sort out their difficulties, but then these difficulties could be heartrending. The Malatsi case had been an odd one. She had expected Mma Malatsi to be distraught when she showed her the evidence that her husband had been eaten by a crocodile, but she had not seemed at all put out. What had she said? But then I have lots to do. What an extraordinary, unfeeling thing for somebody to say when she had just lost her husband. Did she not value him more than that?

Mma Ramotswe paused, her spoon dipped half below the surface of the simmering stew. When people were unmoved in that way, Mma Christie expected the reader to be suspicious. What would Mma Christie have thought if she had seen Mma Malatsi's cool reaction, her virtual indifference? She would have thought: This woman killed her husband! That's why she's unmoved by the news of his death. She knew all along that he was dead!

But what about the crocodile and the baptism, and the other sinners? No, she must be innocent. Perhaps she wanted him dead, and then her prayer was answered by the crocodile. Would that make you a murderer in God's eyes if something then happened? God would know, you see, that you had wanted somebody dead because there are no secrets that you can keep from God. Everybody knew that.

She stopped. It was time to take the pumpkin out of the pot and eat it. In the final analysis, that was what solved these big problems of life. You could think and think and get nowhere, but you still had to eat your pumpkin. That brought you down to earth. That gave you a reason for going on. Pumpkin.

CHAPTER EIGHT

A CONVERSATION WITH
MR J.L.B. MATEKONI

THE BOOKS did not look good. At the end of the first month of its existence, the No. 1 Ladies' Detective Agency was making a convincing loss. There had been three paying clients, and two who came for advice, received it, and declined to pay. Mma Malatsi had paid her bill for two hundred and fifty pula; Happy Bapetsi had paid two hundred pula for the exposure of her false father; and a local trader had paid one hundred pula to find out who was using his telephone to make unauthorised long-distance calls to Francistown. If one added this up it came to five hundred and fifty pula; but then Mma Makutsi's wages were five hundred and eighty pula a month. This meant that there was a loss of thirty pula, without even taking into account other overheads, such as the cost of petrol for the tiny white van and the cost of electricity for the office.

Of course, businesses took some time to get established—Mma Ramotswe understood this—but how long could one go on at a loss? She had a certain amount of money left over from her father's estate, but she could not live on that forever. She should have listened to her father; he had wanted her to buy a butchery, and that would have been so much safer. What was the expression they used? A blue-chip investment, that was it. But where was the excitement in that?

She thought of Mr J.L.B. Matekoni, proprietor of Tlokweng Road Speedy Motors. Now that was a business which would be making a profit. There was no shortage of customers, as everybody knew what a fine mechanic he was. That was the difference between them, she thought; he knew what he was doing, whereas she did not.

Mma Ramotswe had known Mr J.L.B. Matekoni for years. He came from Mochudi, and his uncle had been a close friend of her father. Mr J.L.B. Matekoni was forty-five—ten years older than Mma Ramotswe, but he regarded himself as being a contemporary and often said, when making an observation about the world: "For people of our age . . ."

He was a comfortable man, and she wondered why he had never married. He was not handsome, but he had an easy, reassuring face. He would have been the sort of husband that any woman would have liked to have about the house. He would fix things and stay in at night and perhaps even help with some of the domestic chores—something that so few men would ever dream of doing.

But he had remained single, and lived alone in a large house near the old airfield. She sometimes saw him sitting on his verandah when she drove past—Mr J.L.B. Matekoni by himself, sitting on a chair, staring out at the trees that grew in his garden. What did a man like that think about? Did he sit there and reflect on how nice it would be to have a wife, with children running around the garden, or did he sit there and think about the garage and the cars he had fixed? It was impossible to tell.

She liked to call on him at the garage and talk to him in his greasy office with its piles of receipts and orders for spare parts. She liked to look at the calendars on the wall, with their simple pictures of the sort that men liked. She liked to drink tea from one of his mugs with the greasy fingerprints on the outside while his two assistants raised cars on jacks and cluttered and banged about underneath.

Mr J.L.B. Matekoni enjoyed these sessions. They would talk about Mochudi, or politics, or just exchange the news of the day. He would tell her who was having trouble with his car, and what was wrong with it, and who had bought petrol that day, and where they said they were going.

But that day they talked about finances, and about the problems of running a paying business.

"Staff costs are the biggest item," said Mr J.L.B. Matekoni. "You see those two young boys out there under that car? You've no idea what they cost me. Their wages, their taxes, the insurance to cover them if that car were to fall on their heads. It all adds up. And at the end of the day there are just one or two pula left for me. Never much more."

"But at least you aren't making a loss," said Mma Ramotswe. "I'm thirty pula down on my first month's trading. And I'm sure it'll get worse."

Mr J.L.B. Matekoni sighed. "Staff costs," he said. "That secretary of yours—the one with those big glasses. That's where the money will be going."

Mma Ramotswe nodded. "I know," she said. "But you need a secretary if you have an office. If I didn't have a secretary, then I'd be stuck there all day. I couldn't come over here and talk to you. I couldn't go shopping."

Mr J.L.B. Matekoni reached for his mug. "Then you need to get better clients," he said. "You need a couple of big cases. You need somebody rich to give you a case."

"Somebody rich?"

"Yes. Somebody like . . . like Mr Patel, for example."

"Why would he need a private detective?"

"Rich men have their problems," said Mr J.L.B. Matekoni. "You never know."

They lapsed into silence, watching the two young mechanics remove a wheel from the car on which they were working.

"Stupid boys," said Mr J.L.B. Matekoni. "They don't need to do that."

"I've been thinking," said Mma Ramotswe. "I had a letter the other day. It made me very sad, and I wondered whether I should be a detective after all."

She told him of the letter about the missing boy, and she explained how she had felt unable to help the father.

"I couldn't do anything for him," she said. "I'm not a miracle worker. But I felt so sorry for him. He thought that his son had fallen in the bush or been taken by some animal. How could a father bear that?"

Mr J.L.B. Matekoni snorted. "I saw that in the paper," he said. "I read about that search. And I knew it was hopeless from the beginning."

"Why?" asked Mma Ramotswe.

For a moment, Mr J.L.B. Matekoni was silent. Mma Ramotswe looked at him, and past him, through the window to the thorn tree outside. The tiny grey-green leaves, like blades of grass, were folded in upon themselves, against the heat; and beyond them the empty sky, so pale as to be white; and the smell of dust.

"Because that boy's dead," said Mr J.L.B. Matekoni, tracing an imaginary pattern in the air with his finger. "No animal took him, or at least no ordinary animal. A santawana maybe, a thokolosi. Oh yes."

Mma Ramotswe was silent. She imagined the father—the father of the dead boy, and for a brief moment she remembered that awful afternoon in Mochudi, at the hospital, when the nurse had come up to her, straightening her uniform, and she saw that the nurse was crying. To lose a child, like that, was something that could end one's world. One could never get back to how it was before. The stars went out. The moon disappeared. The birds became silent.

"Why do you say he's dead?" she asked. "He could have got lost and then . . ."

Mr J.L.B. Matekoni shook his head. "No," he said. "That boy would have been taken for witchcraft. He's dead now."

She put her empty mug down on the table. Outside, in the workshop, a wheel brace was dropped with a loud, clanging sound.

She glanced at her friend. This was a subject that one did not talk about. This was the one subject which would bring fear to the most resolute heart. This was the great taboo.

"How can you be sure?"

Mr J.L.B. Matekoni smiled. "Come on, now, Mma Ramotswe. You know as well as I do what goes on. We don't like to talk about it do we? It's the thing we Africans are most ashamed of. We know it happens but we pretend it doesn't. We know all right what happens to children who go missing. We know."

She looked up at him. Of course he was telling the truth,

because he was a truthful, good man. And he was probably right—no matter how much everybody would like to think of other, innocent explanations as to what had happened to a missing boy, the most likely thing was exactly what Mr J.L.B. Matekoni said. The boy had been taken by a witch doctor and killed for medicine. Right there, in Botswana, in the late twentieth century, under that proud flag, in the midst of all that made Botswana a modern country, this thing had happened, this heart of darkness had thumped out like a drum. The little boy had been killed because some powerful person somewhere had commissioned the witch doctor to make strengthening medicine for him.

She cast her eyes down.

"You may be right," she said. "That poor boy . . ."

"Of course I'm right," said Mr J.L.B. Matekoni. "And why do you think that poor man had to write that letter to you? It's because the police will be doing nothing to find out how and where it happened. Because they're scared. Every one of them. They're just as scared as I am and those two boys out there under that car are. Scared, Mma Ramotswe. Frightened for our lives. Every one of us—maybe even you."

MMA RAMOTSWE went to bed at ten that night, half an hour later than usual. She liked to lie in bed sometimes, with her reading lamp on, and read a magazine. Now she was tired, and the magazine kept slipping from her hands, defeating her struggles to keep awake.

She turned out the light and said her prayers, whispering the words although there was nobody in the house to hear her. It was always the same prayer, for the soul of her father, Obed, for Botswana and for rain that would make the crops grow and the cattle fat, and for her little baby, now safe in the arms of Jesus.

In the early hours of the morning she awoke in terror, her heartbeat irregular, her mouth dry. She sat up and reached for the light switch, but when she turned it on nothing happened. She pushed her sheet aside—there was no need for a blanket in the hot weather—and slipped off the bed.

The light in the corridor did not work either, nor that in the kitchen, where the moon made shadows and shapes on the floor. She looked out of the window, into the night. There were no lights anywhere; a power cut.

She opened the back door and stepped out into the yard in her bare feet. The town was in darkness, the trees obscure, indeterminate shapes, clumps of black.

"Mma Ramotswe!"

She stood where she was, frozen in terror. There was somebody in the yard, watching her. Somebody had whispered her name.

She opened her mouth to speak, but no sound came. And it would be dangerous to speak, anyway. So she backed away, slowly, inch by inch, towards the kitchen door. Once inside, she slammed the door shut behind her and reached for the lock. As she turned the key the electricity came on and the kitchen was flooded with light. The fridge started to purr; a light from the cooker winked on and off at her: 3:04; 3:04

THE BOYFRIEND

THERE WERE three quite exceptional houses in the country, and Mma Ramotswe felt some satisfaction that she had been invited to two of them. The best-known of these was Mokolodi, a rambling chateau-like building placed in the middle of the bush to the south of Gaborone. This house, which had a gate-house with gates on which hornbills had been worked in iron, was probably the grandest establishment in the country, and was certainly rather more impressive than Phakadi House, to the north, which was rather too close to the sewage ponds for Mma Ramotswe's taste. This had its compensations, though, as the sewage ponds attracted a great variety of bird life, and from the verandah of Phakadi one could watch flights of flamingos landing on the murky green water. But you could not do this if the wind was in the wrong direction, which it often was.

The third house could only be suspected of being a house of distinction, as very few people were invited to enter it, and

Gaborone as a whole had to rely on what could be seen of the house from the outside—which was not much, as it was surrounded by a high white wall—or on reports from those who were summoned into the house for some special purpose. These reports were unanimous in their praise for the sheer opulence of the interior.

"Like Buckingham Palace," said one woman who had been called to arrange flowers for some family occasion. "Only rather better. I think that the Queen lives a bit more simply than those people in there."

The people in question were the family of Mr Paliwalar Sundigar Patel, the owner of eight stores—five in Gaborone and three in Francistown—a hotel in Orapa, and a large outfitters in Lobatse. He was undoubtedly one of the wealthiest men in the country, if not the wealthiest, but amongst the Batswana this counted for little, as none of the money had gone into cattle, and money which was not invested in cattle, as everybody knew, was but dust in the mouth.

Mr Paliwalar Patel had come to Botswana in 1967, at the age of twenty-five. He had not had a great deal in his pocket then, but his father, a trader in a remote part of Zululand, had advanced him the money to buy his first shop in the African Mall. This had been a great success; Mr Patel bought goods for virtually nothing from traders in distress and then sold them on at minimal profit. Trade blossomed and shop was added to shop, all of them run on the same commercial philosophy. By his fiftieth birthday, he stopped expanding his empire, and concentrated on the improvement and education of his family.

There were four children—a son, Wallace, twin daughters, Sandri and Pali, and the youngest, a daughter called Nandira. Wallace had been sent to an expensive boarding school in Zimbabwe, in order to satisfy Mr Patel's ambition that he become a gentleman. There he had learned to play cricket, and to be cruel. He had been admitted to dental school, after a large donation by Mr Patel, and had then returned to Durban, where he set up a practice in cosmetic dentistry. At some point he had shortened his name—"for convenience's sake"—and had become Mr Wallace Pate BDS (Natal).

Mr Patel had protested at the change. "Why are you now this Mr Wallace Pate BDS (Natal) may I ask? Why? You ashamed, or something? You think I'm just a Mr Paliwalar Patel BA (Failed) or something?"

The son had tried to placate his father.

"Short names are easier, father. Pate, Patel—it's the same thing. So why have an extra letter at the end? The modern idea is to be brief. We must be modern these days. Everything is modern, even names."

There had been no such pretensions from the twins. They had both been sent back to the Natal to meet husbands, which they had done in the manner expected by their father. Both sons-in-law had now been taken into the business and were proving to have good heads for figures and a sound understanding of the importance of tight profit margins.

Then there was Nandira, who was sixteen at the time and a pupil at Maru-a-Pula School in Gaborone, the best and most expensive school in the country. She was bright academically, was consistently given glowing reports from the school, and was expected to make a good marriage in the fullness of time—probably on her twentieth birthday, which Mr Patel had felt was precisely the right time for a girl to marry.

The entire family, including the sons-in-law, the grandparents, and several distant cousins, lived in the Patel mansion near the old Botswana Defence Force Club. There had been several houses on the plot, old colonial-style houses with wide verandahs and fly screens, but Mr Patel had knocked them down and built his new house from scratch. In fact, it was several houses linked together, all forming the family compound.

"We Indians like to live in a compound," Mr Patel had explained to the architect. "We like to be able to see what's going on in the family, you know."

The architect, who was given a free rein, designed a house in which he indulged every architectural whimsy which more demanding and less well-funded clients had suppressed over the years. To his astonishment, Mr Patel accepted everything, and the resulting building proved to be much to his taste. It was furnished in what could only be called Delhi Rococo, with a great deal of gilt in furniture and curtains, and on the walls expensive pictures of Hindu saints and mountain deer with eyes that followed one about the room.

When the twins married, at an expensive ceremony in Durban to which over fifteen hundred guests were invited, they were each given their own quarters, the house having been considerably expanded for the purpose. The sons-in-law were also each given a red Mercedes-Benz, with their initials on the driver's door. This required the Patel garage to be expanded as well, as there were now four Mercedes-Benz cars to be housed there; Mr Patel's, Mrs Patel's car (driven by a driver), and the two belonging to the sons-in law.

An elderly cousin had said to him at the wedding in Durban: "Look, man, we Indians have got to be careful. You shouldn't go flashing your money around the place. The Africans don't like that, you know, and when they get the chance they'll take it all away from us. Look at what happened in Uganda. Listen to what some of the hotheads are saying in Zimbabwe. Imagine what the Zulus would do to us if they had half a chance. We've got to be discreet."

Mr Patel had shaken his head. "None of that applies in Botswana. There's no danger there, I'm telling you. They're stable people. You should see them; with all their diamonds. Diamonds bring stability to a place, believe me."

The cousin appeared to ignore him. "Africa's like that, you see," he continued. "Everything's going fine one day, just fine, and then the next morning you wake up and discover your throat's been cut. Just watch out."

Mr Patel had taken the warning to heart, to an extent, and had added to the height of the wall surrounding his house so that people could not look in the windows and see the luxury. And if they continued to drive around in their big cars, well, there were plenty of those in town and there was no reason why they should be singled out for special attention.

MMA RAMOTSWE was delighted when she received the telephone call from Mr Patel asking her whether she could possibly call on him, in his house, some evening in the near future. They agreed upon that very evening, and she went home to change into a more formal dress before presenting herself at the gates of the Patel mansion. Before she went out, she telephoned Mr J.L.B. Matekoni.

"You said I should get a rich client," she said. "And now I have. Mr Patel."

Mr J.L.B. Matekoni drew in his breath. "He is a very rich man," he said. "He has four Mercedes-Benzes. Four. Three of them are all right, but one has had bad problems with its transmission. There was a coupling problem, one of the worst I've seen, and I had to spend days trying to get a new casing . . ."

YOU COULD not just push open the gate at the Patel house; nor could you park outside and hoot your horn, as everybody did with other houses. At the Patel house you pressed a bell in the wall, and a high-pitched voice issued from a small speaker above your head.

"Yes. Patel place here. What do you want?"

"Mma Ramotswe," she said. "Private . . ."

A crackling noise came from the speaker.

"Private? Private what?"

She was about to answer, when there was another crackling sound and the gate began to swing open. Mma Ramotswe had left her tiny white van round the corner, to keep up appearances, and so she entered the compound by foot. Inside, she found herself in a courtyard which had been transformed by shade netting into a grove of lush vegetation. At the far end of the courtyard was the entrance to the house itself, a large doorway flanked by tall white pillars and tubs of plants. Mr Patel appeared before the open door and waved to her with his walking stick.

She had seen Mr Patel before, of course, and knew that he had an artificial leg, but she had never seen him at really close quarters and had not expected him to be so small. Mma Ramotswe was not tall—being blessed with generous girth, rather than height—but Mr Patel still found himself looking up at her when he shook her hand and gestured for her to come inside.

"Have you been in my house before?" he asked, knowing, of

course, that she had not. "Have you been at one of my parties?"

This was a lie as well, she knew. Mr Patel never gave parties, and she wondered why he should pretend to do so.

"No," she said simply. "You have never asked me."

"Oh dear," he said, chuckling as he spoke. "I have made a big mistake."

He led her through an entrance hall, a long room with a shiny black and white marble floor. There was a lot of brass in this room—expensive, polished brass—and the overall effect was one of glitter.

"We shall go through to my study," he said. "That is my private room in which none of the family are ever allowed. They know not to disturb me there, even if the house is burning down."

The study was another large room, dominated by a large desk on which there were three telephones and an elaborate pen and ink stand. Mma Ramotswe looked at the stand, which consisted of several glass shelves for the pens, the shelves being supported by miniature elephant tusks, carved in ivory.

"Sit down, please," said Mr Patel, pointing to a white leather armchair. "It takes me a little time to sit because I am missing one leg. There, you see. I am always on the lookout for a better leg. This one is Italian and cost me a lot of money, but I think there are better legs to be had. Maybe in America."

Mma Ramotswe sank into the chair and looked at her host.

"I'll get straight to the point," said Mr Patel. "There's no point in beating about the bush and chasing all sorts of rabbits, is there? No, there isn't."

He paused, waiting for Mma Ramotswe's confirmation. She nodded her head slightly.

"I am a family man, Mma Ramotswe," he said. "I have a happy family who all live in this house, except for my son, who is a gentleman dentist in Durban. You may have heard of him. People call him Pate these days."

"I know of him," said Mma Ramotswe. "People speak highly of him, even here."

Mr Patel beamed. "Well, my goodness, that's a very pleasing thing to be told. But my other children are also very important to me. I make no distinction between my children. They are all the same. Equal-equal."

"That's the best way to do it," said Mma Ramotswe. "If you favour one, then that leads to a great deal of bitterness."

"You can say that again, oh yes," said Mr Patel. "Children notice when their parents give two sweets to one and one to another. They can count same as us."

Mma Ramotswe nodded again, wondering where the conversation was leading.

"Now," said Mr Patel. "My big girls, the twins, are well married to good boys and are living here under this roof. That is all very excellent. And that leaves just one child, my little Nandira. She is sixteen and she is at Maru-a-Pula. She is doing well at school, but . . ."

He paused, looking at Mma Ramotswe through narrowed eyes. "You know about teenagers, don't you? You know how things are with teenagers in these modern days?"

Mma Ramotswe shrugged. "They are often bad trouble for their parents. I have seen parents crying their eyes out over their teenagers."

Mr Patel suddenly lifted his walking stick and hit his artificial leg for emphasis. The sound was surprisingly hollow and tinny.

"That's what is worrying me," he said vehemently. "That's what is happening. And I will not have that. Not in my family."

"What?" asked Mma Ramotswe. "Teenagers?"

"Boys," said Mr Patel bitterly. "My Nandira is seeing some boy in secret. She denies it, but I know that there is a boy. And this cannot be allowed, whatever these modern people are saying about the town. It cannot be allowed in this family—in this house."

AS MR Patel spoke, the door to his study, which had been closed behind them when they had entered, opened and a woman came into the room. She was a local woman and she greeted Mma Ramotswe politely in Setswana before offering her a tray on which various glasses of fruit juice were set. Mma Ramotswe chose a glass of guava juice and thanked the servant. Mr Patel helped himself to orange juice and then impatiently waved the servant out of the room with his stick, waiting until she had gone before he continued to speak.

"I have spoken to her about this," he said. "I have made it very clear to her. I told her that I don't care what other children are doing—that is their parents' business, not mine. But I have made it very clear that she is not to go about the town with boys or see boys after school. That is final."

He tapped his artificial leg lightly with his walking stick and then looked at Mma Ramotswe expectantly.

Mma Ramotswe cleared her throat. "You want me to do something about this?" she said quietly. "Is this why you have asked me here this evening?"

Mr Patel nodded. "That is precisely why. I want you to find out who this boy is, and then I will speak to him."

Mma Ramotswe stared at Mr Patel. Had he the remotest idea, she wondered, how young people behaved these days, especially at a school like Maru-a-Pula, where there were all those foreign children, even children from the American Embassy and such places? She had heard about Indian fathers trying to arrange marriages, but she had never actually encountered such behaviour. And here was Mr Patel assuming that she would agree with him; that she would take exactly the same view.

"Wouldn't it be better to speak to her?" she asked gently. "If you asked her who the young man was, then she might tell you."

Mr Patel reached for his stick and tapped his tin leg.

"Not at all," he said sharply, his voice becoming shrill. "Not at all. I have already been asking her for three weeks, maybe four weeks. And she gives no answer. She is dumb insolent."

Mma Ramotswe sat and looked down at her feet, aware of Mr Patel's expectant gaze upon her. She had decided to make it a principle of her professional life never to turn anybody away, unless they asked her to do something criminal. This rule appeared to be working; she had already found that her ideas about a request for help, about its moral rights and wrongs, had changed when she had become more aware of all the factors involved. It might be the same with Mr Patel; but even if it were not, were there good enough reasons for turning him down? Who was she to condemn an anxious Indian father when she really knew very little about how these people ran their lives? She felt a natural sympathy for the girl, of course; what a terrible fate to have a father like this one, intent on keeping one in some sort of gilded cage. Her own Daddy had never stood in her way over anything; he had trusted her and she, in turn, had never kept anything from him—apart from the truth about Note perhaps.

She looked up. Mr Patel was watching her with his dark eyes, the tip of his walking stick tapping almost imperceptibly on the floor.

"I'll find out for you," she said. "Although I must say I don't really like doing this. I don't like the idea of watching a child."

"But children must be watched!" expostulated Mr Patel. "If parents don't watch their children, then what happens? You answer that!"

"There comes a time when they must have their own lives," said Mma Ramotswe. "We have to let go."

"Nonsense!" shouted Mr Patel. "Modern nonsense. My father beat me when I was twenty-two! Yes, he beat me for making a mistake in the shop. And I deserved it. None of this modern nonsense."

Mma Ramotswe rose to her feet.

"I am a modern lady," she said. "So perhaps we have different ideas. But that has nothing to do with it. I have agreed to do as you have asked me. Now all that you need to do is to let me see a photograph of this girl, so that I can know who it is I am going to be watching."

Mr Patel struggled to his feet, straightening the tin leg with his hands as he did so.

"No need for a photograph," he said. "I can produce the girl herself. You can look at her."

Mma Ramotswe raised her hands in protest. "But then she will know me," she said. "I must be able to be unobserved."

"Ah!" said Mr Patel. "A very good idea. You detectives are very clever men."

"Women," said Mma Ramotswe.

Mr Patel looked at her sideways, but said nothing. He had no time for modern ideas.

As she left the house, Mma Ramotswe thought: He has four children; I have none. He is not a good father this man, because he loves his children too much—he wants to own them. You have to let go. You have to let go.

And she thought of that moment when, not even supported by Note, who had made some excuse, she had laid the tiny body of their premature baby, so fragile, so light, into the earth and had looked up at the sky and wanted to say something to God, but couldn't because her throat was blocked with sobs and no words, nothing, would come.

IT SEEMED to Mma Ramotswe that it would be a rather easy case. Watching somebody could always be difficult, as you had to be aware of what they were doing all the time. This could mean long periods of waiting outside houses and offices, doing nothing but watching for somebody to appear. Nandira would be at school for most of the day, of course, and that meant that Mma Ramotswe could get on with other things until three o'clock came round and the school day drew to an end. That was the point at which she would have to follow her and see where she went.

Then the thought occurred to Mma Ramotswe that following a child could be problematic. It was one thing to follow somebody driving a car—all you had to do was tail them in the little white van. But if the person you were watching was riding a bicycle—as many children did on their way home from school—then it would look rather odd if the little white van were to be seen crawling along the road. If she walked home, of course, then Mma Ramotswe could herself walk, keeping a reasonable distance behind her. She could even borrow one of her neighbour's dreadful yellow dogs and pretend to be taking that for a walk.

On the day following her interview with Mr Patel, Mma Ramotswe parked the tiny white van in the school car park shortly before the final bell of the day sounded. The children came out in dribs and drabs, and it was not until shortly after twenty past three that Nandira walked out of the school entrance, carrying her schoolbag in one hand and a book in the other. She was by herself, and Mma Ramotswe was able to get a good look at her from the cab of her van. She was an attractive child, a young woman really; one of those sixteen-year-olds who could pass for nineteen, or even twenty.

She walked down the path and stopped briefly to talk to another girl, who was waiting under a tree for her parents to collect her. They chatted for a few minutes, and then Nandira walked off towards the school gates.

Mma Ramotswe waited a few moments, and then got out of the van. Once Nandira was out on the road, Mma Ramotswe followed her slowly. There were several people about, and there was no reason why she should be conspicuous. On a late winter afternoon it was quite pleasant to walk down the road; a month or so later it would be too hot, and then she could well appear out of place.

She followed the girl down the road and round the corner. It had become clear to her that Nandira was not going directly home, as the Patel house was in the opposite direction to the route she had chosen. Nor was she going into town, which meant that she must be going to meet somebody at a house somewhere. Mma Ramotswe felt a glow of satisfaction. All she would probably have to do was to find the house and then it would be child's play to get the name of the owner, and the boy. Perhaps she could even go to Mr Patel this evening and reveal the boy's identity. That would impress him, and it would be a very easily earned fee.

Nandira turned another corner. Mma Ramotswe held back a little before following her. It would be easy to become over-confident following an innocent child, and she had to remind herself of the rules of pursuit. The manual on which she relied, *The Principles of Private Investigation* by Clovis Ander-sen, stressed that one should never crowd one's subject. "Keep a long rein," wrote Mr Andersen, "even if it means losing the subject from time to time. You can always pick up the trail later. And a few minutes of non-eye contact is better than an angry confrontation."

Mma Ramotswe judged that it was now time to go round the corner. She did so, expecting to see Nandira several hundred yards down the road, but when she looked down it, the road was empty—non-eye contact, as Clovis Andersen called it, had set in. She turned round, and looked in the other direc-tion. There was a car in the distance, coming out of the drive-way of a house, and nothing else.

Mma Ramotswe was puzzled. It was a quiet road, and there were not more than three houses on either side of it—at least in the direction in which Nandira had been going. But these houses all had gates and driveways, and bearing in mind that she had only been out of view for a minute or so, Nandira would not have had time to disappear into one of these houses. Mma Ramotswe would have seen her in a driveway or going in through a front door.

If she has gone into one of the houses, thought Mma

Ramotswe, then it must be one of the first two, as she would certainly not have been able to reach the houses farther along the road. So perhaps the situation was not as bad as she had thought it might be; all she would have to do would be to check up on the first house on the right-hand side of the road and the first house on the left.

She stood still for a moment, and then she made up her mind. Walking as quickly as she could, she made her way back to the tiny white van and drove back along the route on which she had so recently followed Nandira. Then, parking the van in front of the house on the right, she walked up the driveway towards the front door.

When she knocked on the door, a dog started to bark loudly inside the house. Mma Ramotswe knocked again, and there came the sound of somebody silencing the dog. "Quiet, Bison; quiet, I know, I know!" Then the door opened and a woman looked out at her. Mma Ramotswe could tell that she was not a Motswana. She was a West African, probably a Ghanaian, judging by the complexion and the dress. Ghanaians were Mma Ramotswe's favourite people; they had a wonderful sense of humor and were almost inevitably in a good mood.

"Hallo Mma," said Mma Ramotswe. "I'm sorry to disturb you, but I'm looking for Sipho."

The woman frowned.

"Sipho? There's no Sipho here."

Mma Ramotswe shook her head.

"I'm sure it was this house. I'm one of the teachers from the secondary school, you see, and I need to get a message to one of the form four boys. I thought that this was his house."

The woman smiled. "I've got two daughters," she said. "But no son. Could you find me a son, do you think?"

"Oh dear," said Mma Ramotswe, sounding harassed. "Is it the house over the road then?"

The woman shook her head. "That's that Ugandan family," she said. "They've got a boy, but he's only six or seven, I think."

Mma Ramotswe made her apologies and walked back down the drive. She had lost Nandira on the very first afternoon, and she wondered whether the girl had deliberately shrugged her off. Could she possibly have known that she was being followed? This seemed most unlikely, which meant that it was no more than bad luck that she had lost her. Tomorrow she would be more careful. She would ignore Clovis Andersen for once and crowd her subject a little more.

At eight o'clock that night she received a telephone call from Mr Patel.

"You have anything to report to me yet?" he asked. "Any information?"

Mma Ramotswe told him that she unfortunately had not been able to find out where Nandira went after school, but that she hoped that she might be more successful the following day.

"Not very good," said Mr Patel. "Not very good. Well, I at least have something to report to you. She came home three hours after school finished—three hours—and told me that she had just been at a friend's house. I said: what friend? and she just answered that I did not know her. Her. Then my wife found a note on the table, a note which our Nandira must have dropped. It said: "See you tomorrow, Jack." Now who is this Jack, then? Who is this person? Is that a girl's name, I ask you?"

"No," said Mma Ramotswe. "It sounds like a boy."

"There!" said Mr Patel, with the air of one producing the

elusive answer to a problem. "That is the boy, I think. That is the one we must find. Jack who? Where does he live? That sort of thing—you must tell me it all."

Mma Ramotswe prepared herself a cup of bush tea and went to bed early. It had been an unsatisfactory day in more than one respect, and Mr Patel's crowing telephone call merely set the seal on it. So she lay in bed, the bush tea on her bedside table, and read the newspaper before her eyelids began to droop and she drifted off to sleep.

THE NEXT afternoon she was late in reaching the school car park. She was beginning to wonder whether she had lost Nandira again when she saw the girl come out of the school, accompanied by another girl. Mma Ramotswe watched as the two of them walked down the path and stood at the school gate. They seemed deep in conversation with one another, in that exclusive way which teenagers have of talking to their friends, and Mma Ramotswe was sure that if only she could hear what was being said, then she would know the answers to more than one question. Girls talked about their boyfriends in an easy, conspiratorial way, and she was certain that this was the subject of conversation between Nandira and her friend.

Suddenly a blue car drew up opposite the two girls. Mma Ramotswe stiffened and watched as the driver leant over the passenger seat and opened the front door. Nandira got in, and her friend got into the back. Mma Ramotswe started the engine of the little white van and pulled out of the school car park, just as the blue car drew away from the school. She followed at a safe distance, but ready to close the gap between them if there was any chance of losing them. She would not repeat yesterday's mistake and see Nandira vanish into thin air.

The blue car was taking its time, and Mma Ramotswe did not have to strain to keep up. They drove past the Sun Hotel and made their way towards the Stadium roundabout. There they turned in towards town and drove past the hospital and the Anglican Cathedral towards the Mall. Shops, thought Mma Ramotswe. They're just going shopping; or are they? She had seen teenagers meeting one another after school in places like the Botswana Book Centre. They called it "hanging around," she believed. They stood about and chatted and cracked jokes and did everything except buy something. Perhaps Nandira was going off to hang around with this Jack.

The blue car nosed into a parking place near the President Hotel. Mma Ramotswe parked several cars away and watched as the two girls got out of the car, accompanied by an older woman, presumably the mother of the other girl. She said something to her daughter, who nodded, and then detached herself from the girls and walked off in the direction of the hardware stores.

Nandira and her friend walked past the steps of the President Hotel and then slowly made their way up to the Post Office. Mma Ramotswe followed them casually, stopping to look at a rack of African print blouses which a woman was displaying in the square.

"Buy one of these Mma," said the woman. "Very good blouses. They never run. Look, this one I'm wearing has been washed ten, twenty times, and hasn't run. Look."

Mma Ramotswe looked at the woman's blouse—the colours had certainly not run. She glanced out of the corner of her eye at the two girls. They were looking in the shoe shop window, taking their time about wherever they were going.

"You wouldn't have my size," said Mma Ramotswe. "I need a very big blouse."

The trader checked her rack and then looked at Mma Ramotswe again.

"You're right," she said. "You are too big for these blouses. Far too big."

Mma Ramotswe smiled. "But they are nice blouses, Mma, and I hope you sell them to some nice small person."

She moved on. The girls had finished with the shoe shop and were strolling up towards the Book Centre. Mma Ramotswe had been right; they were planning to hang about.

THERE WERE very few people in the Botswana Book Centre. Three or four men were paging through magazines in the periodical section, and one or two people were looking at books. The assistants were leaning over the counters, gossiping idly, and even the flies seemed lethargic.

Mma Ramotswe noticed that the two girls were at the far end of the shop, looking at a shelf of books in the Setswana section. What were they doing there? Nandira could be learning Setswana at school, but she would hardly be likely to be buying any of the schoolbooks or biblical commentaries that dominated that section. No, they must be waiting for somebody.

Mma Ramotswe walked purposefully to the African section and reached for a book. It was *The Snakes of Southern Africa,* and it was well illustrated. She gazed at a picture of a short brown snake and asked herself whether she had seen one of these. Her cousin had been bitten by a snake like that years ago, when they were children, and had come to no harm. Was that the snake? She looked at the text below the picture and read. It could well have been the same snake, because it was described as nonvenomous and not at all aggressive. But it had attacked her cousin; or had her cousin attacked it? Boys attacked snakes. They threw stones at them and seemed unable to leave them alone. But she was not sure whether Putoke had done that; it was so long ago, and she could not really remember.

She looked over at the girls. They were standing there, talking to one another again, and one of them was laughing. Some story about boys, thought Mma Ramotswe. Well, let them laugh; they'll realise soon enough that the whole subject of men was not very funny. In a few years' time it would be tears, not laughter, thought Mma Ramotswe grimly.

She returned to her perusal of *The Snakes of Southern Africa*. Now this was a bad snake, this one. There it was. Look at the head! Ow! And those evil eyes! Mma Ramotswe shuddered, and read: "The above picture is of an adult male black mamba, measuring 1.87 metres. As is shown in the distribution map, this snake is to be found throughout the region, although it has a certain preference for open veld. It differs from the green mamba, both in distribution, habitat, and toxicity of venom. The snake is one of the most dangerous snakes to be found in Africa, being outranked in this respect only by the Gaboon Viper, a rare, forest-dwelling snake found in certain parts of the eastern districts of Zimbabwe.

"Accounts of attacks by black mambas are often exaggerated,

and stories of the snake's attacking men on galloping horses, and overtaking them, are almost certainly apocryphal. The mamba can manage a considerable speed over a very short distance, but could not compete with a horse. Nor are the stories of virtually instantaneous death necessarily true, although the action of the venom can be speeded if the victim of the bite should panic, which of course he often does on realising that he has been bitten by a mamba.

"In one reliably recorded case, a twenty-six-year-old man in good physical condition sustained a mamba bite on his right ankle after he had inadvertently stepped on the snake in the bush. There was no serum immediately available, but the victim possibly succeeded in draining off some of the venom when he inflicted deep cuts on the site of the bite (not a course of action which is today regarded as helpful). He then walked some four miles through the bush to seek help and was admitted to hospital within two hours. Antivenom was administered and the victim survived unscathed; had it been a puff-adder bite, of course, there would have been considerable necrotic damage within that time and he may even have lost the leg . . ."

Mma Ramotswe paused. One leg. He would need to have an artificial leg. Mr Patel. Nandira. She looked up sharply. The snake book had so absorbed her that she had not been paying attention to the girls and now—where were they?—gone. They were gone.

She pushed *The Snakes of Southern Africa* back onto the shelf and rushed out into the square. There were more people about now, as many people did their shopping in the latter part of the afternoon, to escape the heat. She looked about her. There were some teenagers a little way away, but they were boys. No, there was a girl. But was it Nandira? No. She looked in the other direction. There was a man parking his bicycle under a tree and she noticed that the bicycle had a car aerial on it. Why?

She set off in the direction of the President Hotel. Perhaps the girls had merely gone back to the car to rejoin the mother, in which case, everything would be all right. But when she got to the car park, she saw the blue car going out at the other end, with just the mother in it. So the girls were still around, somewhere in the square.

Mma Ramotswe went back to the steps of the President Hotel and looked out over the square. She moved her gaze systematically—as Clovis Andersen recommended—looking at each group of people, scrutinising each knot of shoppers outside each shop window. There was no sign of the girls. She noticed the woman with the rack of blouses. She had a packet of some sort in her hand and was extracting what looked like a Mopani worm from within it.

"Mopani worms?" asked Mma Ramotswe.

The woman turned round and looked at her.

"Yes." She offered the bag to Mma Ramotswe, who helped herself to one of the dried tree worms and popped it into her mouth. It was a delicacy she simply could not resist.

"You must see everything that goes on, Mma," she said, as she swallowed the worm. "Standing here like this."

The woman laughed. "I see everybody. Everybody."

"Did you see two girls come out of the Book Centre?" asked Mma Ramotswe. "One Indian girl and one African girl. The Indian one about so high?"

The trader picked out another worm from her bag and popped it into her mouth.

"I saw them," she said. "They went over to the cinema. Then they went off somewhere else. I didn't notice where they were going."

Mma Ramotswe smiled. "You should be a detective," she said.

"Like you," said the woman simply.

This surprised Mma Ramotswe. She was quite well-known, but she had not necessarily expected a street trader to know who she was. She reached into her handbag and extracted a ten-pula note, which she pressed into the woman's hand.

"Thank you," she said. "That's a fee from me. And I hope you will be able to help me again some time."

The woman seemed delighted.

"I can tell you everything," she said. "I am the eyes of this place. This morning, for example, do you want to know who was talking to whom just over there? Do you know? You'd be surprised if I told you."

"Some other time," said Mma Ramotswe. "I'll be in touch."

There was no point in trying to find where Nandira had got to now, but there was every point in following up the information that she already had. So Mma Ramotswe went to the cinema and enquired as to the time of that evening's performance, which is what she concluded the two girls had been doing. Then she returned to the little white van and drove home, to prepare herself for an early supper and an outing to the cinema. She had seen the name of the film; it was not something that she wanted to sit through, but it had been at least a year since she had been to the cinema and she found that she was looking forward to the prospect.

Mr Patel telephoned before she left.

"My daughter has said that she is going out to see a friend about some homework," he said peevishly. "She is lying to me again."

"Yes," said Mma Ramotswe. "I'm afraid that she is. But I know where she's going and I shall be there, don't you worry."

"She is going to see this Jack?" shouted Mr Patel. "She is meeting this boy?"

"Probably," said Mma Ramotswe. "But there is no point in your upsetting yourself. I will give you a report tomorrow."

"Early-early, please," said Mr Patel. "I am always up at six, sharp-sharp."

THERE WERE very few people in the cinema when Mma Ramotswe arrived. She chose a seat in the penultimate row, at the back. This gave her a good view of the door through which anybody entering the auditorium would have to pass, and even if Nandira and Jack came in after the lights had gone down, it would still be possible for Mma Ramotswe to pick them out.

Mma Ramotswe recognised several of the customers. Her butcher arrived shortly after she did, and he and his wife gave her a friendly wave. Then there was one of the teachers from the school and the woman who ran the aerobics class at the President Hotel. Finally there was the Catholic bishop, who arrived by himself and ate popcorn loudly in the front row.

Nandira arrived five minutes before the first part of the pro-gramme was about to start. She was by herself, and she stood for a moment in the door, looking around her. Mma Ramotswe felt her eyes rest on her, and she looked down quickly, as if inspecting the floor for something. After a moment or two she looked up again, and saw that the girl was still looking at her.

Mma Ramotswe looked down at the floor again, and saw a discarded ticket, which she reached down to pick up.

Nandira walked purposefully across the auditorium to Mma Ramotswe's row and sat down in the seat next to her.

"Evening, Mma," she said politely. "Is this seat taken?"

Mma Ramotswe looked up, as if surprised.

"There is nobody there," she said. "It is quite free."

Nandira sat down.

"I am looking forward to this film," she said pleasantly. "I have wanted to see it for a long time."

"Good," said Mma Ramotswe. "It is nice to see a film that you've always wanted to see."

There was a silence. The girl was looking at her, and Mma Ramotswe felt quite uncomfortable. What would Clovis Andersen have done in such circumstances? She was sure that he said something about this sort of thing, but she could not quite remember what it was. This was where the subject crowded you, rather than the other way round.

"I saw you this afternoon," said Nandira. "I saw you at Maru-a-Pula."

"Ah, yes," said Mma Ramotswe. "I was waiting for somebody."

"Then I saw you in the Book Centre," Nandira continued. "You were looking at a book."

"That's right," said Mma Ramotswe. "I was thinking of buying a book."

"Then you asked Mma Bapitse about me," Nandira said quietly. "She's that trader. She told me that you were asking about me."

Mma Ramotswe made a mental note to be careful of Mma Bapitse in the future.

"So, why are you following me?" asked Nandira, turning in her seat to stare at Mma Ramotswe.

Mma Ramotswe thought quickly. There was no point in denying it, and she may as well try to make the most of a difficult situation. So she told Nandira about her father's anxieties and how he had approached her.

"He wants to find out whether you're seeing boys," she said. "He's worried about it."

Nandira looked pleased.

"Well, if he's worried, he's only got himself to blame if I keep going out with boys."

"And are you?" asked Mma Ramotswe. "Are you going out with lots of boys?"

Nandira hesitated. Then, quietly: "No. Not really."

"But what about this Jack?" asked Mma Ramotswe. "Who's he?"

For a moment it seemed as if Nandira was not going to reply. Here was another adult trying to pry into her private life, and yet there was something about Mma Ramotswe that she trusted. Perhaps she could be useful; perhaps . . .

"Jack doesn't exist," she said quietly. "I made him up."

"Why?"

Nandira shrugged. "I want them—my family—to think I've got a boyfriend," she said. "I want them to think there's somebody I chose, not somebody they thought right for me." She paused. "Do you understand that?"

Mma Ramotswe thought for a moment. She felt sorry for this poor, overprotected girl, and imagined just how in such circumstances one might want to pretend to have a boyfriend.

"Yes," she said, laying a hand on Nandira's arm. "I understand."

Nandira fidgeted with her watchstrap.

"Are you going to tell him?" she asked.

"Well, do I have much choice?" asked Mma Ramotswe. "I can hardly say that I've seen you with a boy called Jack when he doesn't really exist."

Nandira sighed. "Well, I suppose I've asked for it. It's been a silly game." She paused. "But once he realises that there's nothing in it, do you think that he might let me have a bit more freedom? Do you think that he might let me live my life for a little without having to tell him how I spend every single minute?"

"I could try to persuade him," said Mma Ramotswe. "I don't know whether he'll listen to me. But I could try."

"Please do," said Nandira. "Please try."

They watched the film together, and both enjoyed it. Then Mma Ramotswe drove Nandira back in her tiny white van, in a companionable silence, and dropped her at the gate in the high white wall. The girl stood and watched as the van drove off, and then she turned and pressed the bell.

"Patel place here. What do you want?"

"Freedom," she muttered under her breath, and then, more loudly: "It's me, Papa. I'm home now."

MMA RAMOTSWE telephoned Mr Patel early the next morning, as she had promised to do. She explained to him that it would be better for her to speak to him at home, rather than to explain matters over the telephone.

"You've got bad news for me," he said, his voice rising. "You are going to be telling me something bad-bad. Oh my God! What is it?"

Mma Ramotswe reassured him that the news was not bad,

but she still found him looking anxious when she was shown into his study half an hour later.

"I am very worried," he said. "You will not understand a father's worries. It is different for a mother. A father feels a special sort of worry."

Mma Ramotswe smiled reassuringly.

"The news is good," she said. "There is no boyfriend."

"And what about this note?" he said. "What about this Jack person? Is that all imagination?"

"Yes," said Mma Ramotswe simply. "Yes, it is."

Mr Patel looked puzzled. He lifted his walking stick and tapped his artificial leg several times. Then he opened his mouth to speak, but said nothing.

"You see," said Mma Ramotswe, "Nandira has been inventing a social life for herself. She made up a boyfriend for herself just to bring a bit of . . . of freedom into her life. The best thing you can do is just to ignore it. Give her a bit more time to lead her own life. Don't keep asking her to account for her time. There's no boyfriend and there may not even be one for some time."

Mr Patel put his walking stick down on the floor. Then he closed his eyes and appeared deep in thought.

"Why should I do this?" he said after a while. "Why should I give in to these modern ideas?"

Mma Ramotswe was ready with her answer. "Because if you don't, then the imaginary boyfriend may turn into a real one. That's why."

Mma Ramotswe watched him as he wrestled with her advice. Then, without warning he stood up, tottered for a while before he got his balance, and then turned to face her.

"You are a very clever woman," he said. "And I'm going to

take your advice. I will leave her to get on with her life, and then I am sure that in two or three years she will agree with us and allow me to arra . . . to help her to find a suitable man to marry."

"That could easily happen," said Mma Ramotswe, breathing a sigh of relief.

"Yes," said Mr Patel warmly. "And I shall have you to thank for it all!"

MMA RAMOTSWE often thought about Nandira when she drove past the Patel compound, with its high white wall. She expected to see her from time to time, now that she knew what she looked like, but she never did, at least not until a year later, when, while taking her Saturday morning coffee on the verandah of the President Hotel, she felt somebody tap her shoulder. She turned round in her seat, and there was Nandira, with a young man. The young man was about eighteen, she thought, and he had a pleasant, open expression.

"Mma Ramotswe," said Nandira in a friendly way. "I thought it was you."

Mma Ramotswe shook Nandira's hand. The young man smiled at her.

"This is my friend," said Nandira. "I don't think you've met him."

The young man stepped forward and held out his hand.

"Jack," he said.

MMA RAMOTSWE THINKS ABOUT THE LAND WHILE DRIVING HER TINY WHITE VAN TO FRANCISTOWN

MMA RAMOTSWE drove her tiny white van before dawn along the sleeping roads of Gaborone, past the Kalahari Breweries, past the Dry Lands Research Station, and out onto the road that led north. A man leaped out from bushes at the side of the road and tried to flag her down; but she was unwilling to stop in the dark, for you never knew who might be wanting a lift at such an hour. He disappeared into the shadows again, and in her mirror she saw him deflate with disappointment. Then, just past the Mochudi turnoff, the sun came up, rising over the wide plains that stretched away towards the course of the Limpopo. Suddenly it was there, smiling on Africa, a slither of golden red ball, inching up, floating effortlessly free of the horizon to dispel the last wisps of morning mist.

The thorn trees stood clear in the sharp light of morning, and there were birds upon them, and in flight—hoopoes, louries, and tiny birds which she could not name. Here and there cattle stood at the fence which followed the road for mile upon mile. They raised their heads and stared, or ambled slowly on, tugging at the tufts of dry grass that clung tenaciously to the hardened earth.

This was a dry land. Just a short distance to the west lay the Kalahari, a hinterland of ochre that stretched off, for unimaginable miles, to the singing emptinesses of the Namib. If she turned her tiny white van off on one of the tracks that struck off from the main road, she could drive for perhaps thirty or forty miles before her wheels would begin to sink into the sand and spin hopelessly. The vegetation would slowly become sparser, more desert-like. The thorn trees would thin out and there would be ridges of thin earth, through which the omnipresent sand would surface and crenellate. There would be patches of bareness, and scattered grey rocks, and there would be no sign of human activity. To live with this great dry interior, brown and hard, was the lot of the Batswana, and it was this that made them cautious, and careful in their husbandry.

If you went there, out into the Kalahari, you might hear lions by night. For the lions were there still, on these wide landscapes, and they made their presence known in the darkness, in coughing grunts and growls. She had been there once as a young woman, when she had gone with her friend to visit a remote cattle post. It was as far into the Kalahari as cattle could go, and she had felt the utter loneliness of a place without people. This was Botswana distilled; the essence of her country.

It was the rainy season, and the land was covered with green. Rain could transform it so quickly, and had done so;

now the ground was covered with shoots of sweet new grass, Namaqualand daisies, the vines of Tsama melons, and aloes with stalk flowers of red and yellow.

They had made a fire at night, just outside the crude huts which served as shelter at the cattle post, but the light from the fire seemed so tiny under the great empty night sky with its dipping constellations. She had huddled close to her friend, who had told her that she should not be frightened, because lions would keep away from fires, as would supernatural beings, *tokoloshes* and the like.

She awoke in the small hours of the morning, and the fire was low. She could make out its embers through the spaces between the branches that made up the wall of the hut. Somewhere, far away, there was a grunting sound, but she was not afraid, and she walked out of the hut to stand underneath the sky and draw the dry, clear air into her lungs. And she thought: I am just a tiny person in Africa, but there is a place for me, and for everybody, to sit down on this earth and touch it and call it their own. She waited for another thought to come, but none did, and so she crept back into the hut and the warmth of the blankets on her sleeping mat.

Now, driving the tiny white van along those rolling miles, she thought that one day she might go back into the Kalahari, into those empty spaces, those wide grasslands that broke and broke the heart.

CHAPTER ELEVEN

BIG CAR GUILT

T WAS three days after the satisfactory resolution of the Patel case. Mma Ramotswe had put in her bill for two thousand pula, plus expenses, and had been paid by return of post. This astonished her. She could not believe that she would be paid such a sum without protest, and the readiness, and apparent cheerfulness with which Mr Patel had settled the bill induced pangs of guilt over the sheer size of the fee.

It was curious how some people had a highly developed sense of guilt, she thought, while others had none. Some people would agonise over minor slips or mistakes on their part, while others would feel quite unmoved by their own gross acts of betrayal or dishonesty. Mma Pekwane fell into the former category, thought Mma Ramotswe. Note Mokoti fell into the latter.

Mma Pekwane had seemed anxious when she had come into the office of the No. 1 Ladies' Detective Agency. Mma Ramotswe had given her a strong cup of bush tea, as she always did with nervous clients, and had waited for her to be ready to speak. She was anxious about a man, she thought; there were all the signs. What would it be? Some piece of masculine bad behaviour, of course, but what?

"I'm worried that my husband has done a dreadful thing," said Mma Pekwane eventually. "I feel very ashamed for him."

Mma Ramotswe nodded her head gently. Masculine bad behaviour.

"Men do terrible things," she said. "All wives are worried about their husbands. You are not alone."

Mma Pekwane sighed. "But my husband has done a terrible thing," she said. "A very terrible thing."

Mma Ramotswe stiffened. If Rra Pekwane had killed somebody she would have to make it quite clear that the police should be called in. She would never dream of helping anybody conceal a murderer.

"What is this terrible thing?" she asked.

Mma Pekwane lowered her voice. "He has a stolen car."

Mma Ramotswe was relieved. Car theft was rife, almost unremarkable, and there must be many women driving around the town in their husbands' stolen cars. Mma Ramotswe could never imagine herself doing that, of course, and nor, it seemed, could Mma Pekwane.

"Did he tell you it's stolen?" she asked. "Are you sure of it?"

Mma Pekwane shook her head. "He said a man gave it to him. He said that this man had two Mercedes-Benzes and only needed one."

Mma Ramotswe laughed. "Do men really think they can fool us that easily?" she said. "Do they think we're fools?"

"I think they do," said Mma Pekwane.

Mma Ramotswe picked up her pencil and drew several lines

on her blotter. Looking at the scribbles, she saw that she had drawn a car.

She looked at Mma Pekwane. "Do you want me to tell you what to do?" she asked. "Is that what you want?"

Mma Pekwane looked thoughtful. "No," she replied. "I don't want that. I've decided what I want to do."

"And that is?"

"I want to give the car back. I want to give it back to its owner."

Mma Ramotswe sat up straight. "You want to go to the police then? You want to inform on your husband?"

"No. I don't want to do that. I just want the car to get back to its owner without the police knowing. I want the Lord to know that the car's back where it belongs."

Mma Ramotswe stared at her client. It was, she had to admit, a perfectly reasonable thing to want. If the car were to be returned to the owner, then Mma Pekwane's conscience would be clear, and she would still have her husband. On mature reflection, it seemed to Mma Ramotswe to be a very good way of dealing with a difficult situation.

"But why come to me about this?" asked Mma Ramotswe. "How can I help?"

Mma Pekwane gave her answer without hesitation.

"I want you to find out who owns that car," she said. "Then I want you to steal it from my husband and give it back to the rightful owner. That's all I want you to do."

LATER THAT evening, as she drove home in her little white van, Mma Ramotswe thought that she should never have agreed to help Mma Pekwane; but she had, and now she was committed. Yet it was not going to be a simple matter—unless, of course, one went to the police, which she clearly could not do. It may be that Rra Pekwane deserved to be handed over, but her client had asked that this should not happen, and her first loyalty was to the client. So some other way would have to be found.

That evening, after her supper of chicken and pumpkin, Mma Ramotswe telephoned Mr J.L.B. Matekoni.

"Where do stolen Mercedes-Benzes come from?" asked Mma Ramotswe.

"From over the border," said Mr J.L.B. Matekoni. "They steal them in South Africa, bring them over here, respray them, file off the original engine number, and then sell them cheaply or send them up to Zambia. I know who does all this, by the way. We all know."

"I don't need to know that," said Mma Ramotswe. "What I need to know is how you identify them after all this has happened."

Mr J.L.B. Matekoni paused. "You have to know where to look," he said. "There's usually another serial number some-where—on the chassis—or under the bonnet. You can usually find it if you know what you're doing."

"You know what you're doing," said Mma Ramotswe. "Can you help me?"

Mr J.L.B. Matekoni sighed. He did not like stolen cars. He preferred to have nothing to do with them, but this was a request from Mma Ramotswe, and so there was only one answer to give.

"Tell me where and when," he said.

*   *   *

THEY ENTERED the Pekwane garden the following evening, by arrangement with Mma Pekwane, who had promised that at the agreed time she would make sure that the dogs were inside and her husband would be busy eating a special meal she would prepare for him. So there was nothing to stop Mr J.L.B. Matekoni from wriggling under the Mercedes-Benz parked in the yard and flashing his torch up into the bodywork. Mma Ramotswe offered to go under the car as well, but Mr J.L.B. Matekoni doubted whether she would fit and declined her offer. Ten minutes later, he had a serial number written on a piece of paper and the two of them slipped out of the Pekwane yard and made their way to the small white van parked down the road.

"Are you sure that's all I'll need?" asked Mma Ramotswe. "Will they know from that?"

"Yes," said Mr J.L.B. Matekoni. "They'll know."

She dropped him off outside his gate and he waved goodbye in the darkness. She would be able to repay him soon, she knew.

THAT WEEKEND, Mma Ramotswe drove her tiny white van over the border to Mafikeng and went straight to the Railway Café. She bought a copy of the *Johannesburg Star* and sat at a table near the window reading the news. It was all bad, she decided, and so she laid the paper to one side and passed the time by looking at her fellow customers.

"Mma Ramotswe!"

She looked up. There he was, the same old Billy Pilani, older now, of course, but otherwise the same. She could just

see him at the Mochudi Government School, sitting at his
desk, dreaming.

She bought him a cup of coffee and a large doughnut and
explained to him what she needed.

"I want you to find out who owns this car," she said, passing
the slip of paper with the serial number written on it in the
handwriting of Mr J.L.B. Matekoni. "Then, when you've found
out, I want you to tell the owner, or the insurance company, or
whoever, that they can come up to Gaborone and they will find
their car ready for them in an agreed place. All they have to do
is to bring South African number plates with the original number on them. Then they can drive the car home."

Billy Pilani looked surprised.

"All for nothing?" he asked. "Nothing to be paid?"

"Nothing," said Mma Ramotswe. "It's just a question of
returning property to its rightful owner. That's all. You believe
in that, don't you Billy?"

"Of course," said Billy Pilani quickly. "Of course."

"And Billy I want you to forget you're a policeman while all
this is going on. There's not going to be any arrest for you."

"Not even a small one?" asked Billy in a disappointed tone.

"Not even that."

BILLY PILANI telephoned the following day.

"I've got the details from our list of stolen vehicles," he said.
"I've spoken to the insurance company, who've already paid
out. So they'd be very happy to get the car back. They can send
one of their men over the border to pick it up."

"Good," said Mma Ramotswe. "They are to be in the African

Mall in Gaborone at seven o'clock in the morning next Tuesday, with the number plates."

Everything was agreed, and at five o'clock on the Tuesday morning, Mma Ramotswe crept into the yard of the Pekwane house and found, as she had been expecting, the keys of the Mercedes-Benz lying on the ground outside the bedroom window, where Mma Pekwane had tossed them the previous night. She had been assured by Mma Pekwane that her husband was a sound sleeper and that he never woke up until Radio Botswana broadcast the sound of cowbells at six.

He did not hear her start the car and drive out onto the road, and indeed it was not until almost eight o'clock that he noticed that his Mercedes-Benz was stolen.

"Call the police," shouted Mma Pekwane. "Quick, call the police!"

She noticed that her husband was hesitating.

"Maybe later," he said. "In the meantime, I think I shall look for it myself."

She looked him directly in the eye, and for a moment she saw him flinch. He's guilty, she thought. I was right all along. Of course he can't go to the police and tell them that his stolen car has been stolen.

She saw Mma Ramotswe later that day and thanked her.

"You've made me feel much better," she said. "I shall now be able to sleep at night without feeling guilty for my husband."

"I'm very pleased," said Mma Ramotswe. "And maybe he's learned a lesson too. A very interesting lesson."

"What would that be?" asked Mma Pekwane.

"That lightning always strikes in the same place twice," said Mma Ramotswe. "Whatever people say to the contrary."

CHAPTER TWELVE

MMA RAMOTSWE'S HOUSE IN
ZEBRA DRIVE

THE HOUSE had been built in 1968, when the town inched out from the shops and the Government Buildings. It was on a corner site, which was not always a good thing, as people would sometimes stand on that corner, under the thorn trees that grew there, and spit into her garden, or throw their rubbish over her fence. At first, when she saw them doing that, she would shout from the window, or bang a dustbin lid at them, but they seemed to have no shame, these people, and they just laughed. So she gave up, and the young man who did her garden for her every third day would just pick up the rubbish and put it away. That was the only problem with that house. For the rest, Mma Ramotswe was fiercely proud of it, and daily reflected on her good fortune in being able to buy it when she did, just before house prices went so high that honest people could no longer pay them.

The yard was a large one, almost two-thirds of an acre, and

it was well endowed with trees and shrubs. The trees were nothing special—thorn trees for the most part—but they gave good shade, and they never died if the rains were bad. Then there were the purple bougainvillaeas which had been enthusiastically planted by the previous owners, and which had almost taken over by the time Mma Ramotswe came. She had to cut these back, to give space for her pawpaws and her pumpkins.

At the front of the house there was a verandah, which was her favourite place, and which was where she liked to sit in the mornings, when the sun rose, or in the evenings, before the mosquitoes came out. She had extended it by placing an awning of shade netting supported by rough-hewn poles. This filtered out many of the rays of the sun and allowed plants to grow in the green light it created. There she had elephant-ear and ferns, which she watered daily, and which made a lush patch of green against the brown earth.

Behind the verandah was the living room, the largest room in the house, with its big window that gave out onto what had once been a lawn. There was a fireplace here, too large for the room, but a matter of pride for Mma Ramotswe. On the mantelpiece she had placed her special china, her Queen Elizabeth II teacup and her commemoration plate with the picture of Sir Seretse Khama, President, *Kgosi* of the Bangwato people, Statesman. He smiled at her from the plate, and it was as if he gave a blessing, as if he knew. As did the Queen, for she loved Botswana too, and understood.

But in pride of place was the photograph of her Daddy, taken just before his sixtieth birthday. He was wearing the suit which he had bought in Bulawayo on his visit to his cousin there, and he was smiling, although she knew that by then he was in pain. Mma Ramotswe was a realist, who inhabited the present, but one nostalgic thought she allowed herself, one indulgence, was to imagine her Daddy walking through the door and greeting her again, and smiling at her, and saying: "My Precious! You have done well! I am proud of you!" And she imagined driving him round Gaborone in her tiny white van and showing him the progress that had been made, and she smiled at the pride he would have felt. But she could not allow herself to think like this too often, for it ended in tears, for all that was passed, and for all the love that she had within her.

The kitchen was cheerful. The cement floor, sealed and polished with red floor paint, was kept shining by Mma Ramotswe's maid, Rose, who had been with her for five years. Rose had four children, by different fathers, who lived with her mother at Tlokweng. She worked for Mma Ramotswe, and did knitting for a knitting cooperative, and brought her children up with the little money that there was. The oldest boy was a carpenter now, and was giving his mother money, which helped, but the little ones were always needing shoes and new trousers, and one of them could not breathe well and needed an inhaler. But Rose still sang, and this was how Mma Ramotswe knew she had arrived in the morning, as the snatches of song came drifting in from the kitchen.

CHAPTER THIRTEEN

WHY DON'T YOU MARRY ME?

APPINESS? MMA Ramotswe was happy enough. With her detective agency and her house in Zebra Drive, she had more than most, and was aware of it. She was also aware of how things had changed. When she had been married to Note Mokoti she had been conscious of a deep, overwhelming unhappiness that followed her around like a black dog. That had gone now.

If she had listened to her father, if she had listened to the cousin's husband, she would never have married Note and the years of unhappiness would never have occurred. But they did, because she was headstrong, as everybody is at the age of twenty, and when we simply cannot see, however much we may think we can. The world is full of twenty-year-olds, she thought, all of them blind.

Obed Ramotswe had never taken to Note, and had told her that, directly. But she had responded by crying and by saying that he was the only man she would ever find and that he would make her happy.

"He will not," said Obed. "That man will hit you. He will use you in all sorts of ways. He thinks only of himself and what he wants. I can tell, because I have been in the mines and you see all sorts of men there. I have seen men like that before."

She had shaken her head and rushed out of the room, and he had called out after her, a thin, pained, cry. She could hear it now, and it cut and cut at her. She had hurt the man who loved her more than any other, a good, trusting man who only wanted to protect her. If only one could undo the past; if one could go back and avoid the mistakes, make different choices . . .

"If we could go back," said Mr J.L.B. Matekoni, pouring tea into Mma Ramotswe's mug. "I have often thought that. If we could go back and know then what we know now . . ." He shook his head in wonderment. "My goodness! I would live my life differently!"

Mma Ramotswe sipped at her tea. She was sitting in the office of Tlokweng Road Speedy Motors, underneath Mr J.L.B. Matekoni's spares suppliers' calendar, passing the time of day with her friend, as she sometimes did when her own office was quiet. This was inevitable; sometimes people simply did not want to find things out. Nobody was missing, nobody was cheating on their wives, nobody was embezzling. At such times, a private detective may as well hang a closed sign on the office door and go off to plant melons. Not that she intended to plant melons; a quiet cup of tea followed by a shopping trip to the African Mall was as good a way of spending the afternoon as any. Then she might go to the Book Centre and see if any interesting magazines had arrived. She loved magazines. She loved their smell and their bright pictures. She loved interior design magazines which showed how people lived in faraway countries. They had so much in their houses, and such beautiful things too. Paintings, rich curtains, piles of velvet cushions which would have been wonderful for a fat person to sit upon, strange lights at odd angles . . .

Mr J.L.B. Matekoni warmed to his theme.

"I have made hundreds of mistakes in my lifetime," he said, frowning at the recollection. "Hundreds and hundreds."

She looked at him. She had thought that everything had gone rather well in his life. He had served his apprenticeship as a mechanic, saved up his money, and then bought his own garage. He had built a house, married a wife (who had unfortunately died), and become the local chairman of the Botswana Democratic Party. He knew several ministers (very slightly) and was invited to one of the annual garden parties at State House. Everything seemed rosy.

"I can't see what mistakes you've made," she said. "Unlike me."

Mr J.L.B. Matekoni looked surprised.

"I can't imagine you making any mistakes," she said. "You're too clever for that. You would look at all the possibilities and then choose the right one. Every time."

Mma Ramotswe snorted.

"I married Note," she said simply.

Mr J.L.B. Matekoni looked thoughtful.

"Yes," he said. "That was a bad mistake."

They were silent for a moment. Then he rose to his feet. He was a tall man, and he had to be careful not to bump his head when he stood erect. Now, with the calendar behind him and the fly paper dangling down from the ceiling above, he cleared his throat and spoke.

"I would like you to marry me," he said. "That would not be a mistake."

Mma Ramotswe hid her surprise. She did not give a start, nor drop her mug of tea, nor open her mouth and make no sound. She smiled instead, and stared at her friend.

"You are a good kind man," she said. "You are like my Daddy . . . a bit. But I cannot get married again. Ever. I am happy as I am. I have got the agency, and the house. My life is full."

Mr J.L.B. Matekoni sat down. He looked crestfallen, and Mma Ramotswe reached out to touch him. He moved it away instinctively, as a burned man will move away from fire.

"I am very sorry," she said. "I should like you to know that if I were ever to marry anybody, which I shall not do, I would choose a man like you. I would even choose you. I am sure of this."

Mr J.L.B. Matekoni took her mug and poured her more tea. He was silent now—not out of anger, or resentment—but because it had cost him all his energy to make his declaration of love and he had no more words for the time being.

CHAPTER FOURTEEN

HANDSOME MAN

ALICE BUSANG was nervous about consulting Mma Ramotswe, but was soon put at ease by the comfortable, overweight figure sitting behind the desk. It was rather like speaking to a doctor or a priest, she thought; in such consultations nothing that one could possibly say would shock.

"I am suspicious of my husband," she said. "I think that he is carrying on with ladies."

Mma Ramotswe nodded. All men carried on with ladies, in her experience. The only men who did not were ministers of religion and headmasters.

"Have you seen him doing this?" she asked.

Alice Busang shook her head. "I keep watching out but I never see him with other women. I think he is too cunning."

Mma Ramotswe wrote this down on a piece of paper.

"He goes to bars, does he?"

"Yes."

"That's where they meet them. They meet these women who hang about in bars waiting for other women's husbands. This city is full of women like that."

She looked at Alice, and there flowed between them a brief current of understanding. All women in Botswana were the victims of the fecklessness of men. There were virtually no men these days who would marry a woman and settle down to look after her children; men like that seemed to be a thing of the past.

"Do you want me to follow him?" she said. "Do you want me to find out whether he picks up other women?"

Alice Busang nodded. "Yes," she said. "I want proof. Just for myself. I want proof so that I can know what sort of man I married."

MMA RAMOTSWE was too busy to take on the Busang case until the following week. That Wednesday, she stationed herself in her small white van outside the office in the Diamond Sorting Building where Kremlin Busang worked. She had been given a photograph of him by Alice Busang and she glanced at this on her knee; this was a handsome man, with broad shoulders and a wide smile. He was a ladies' man by the look of him, and she wondered why Alice Busang had married him if she wanted a faithful husband. Hopefulness, of course; a naïve hope that he would be unlike other men. Well, you only had to look at him to realise that this would not be so.

She followed him, her white van trailing his old blue car through the traffic to the Go Go Handsome Man's Bar down by the bus station. Then, while he strolled into the bar, she sat for a moment in her van and put a little more lipstick on her lips and a dab of cream on her cheeks. In a few minutes she would go in and begin work in earnest.

IT WAS not crowded inside the Go Go Handsome Man's Bar and there were only one or two other women there. Both of them she recognised as bad women. They stared at her, but she ignored them and took a seat at the bar, just two stools from Kremlin Busang.

She bought a beer and looked about her, as if taking in the surroundings of the bar for the first time.

"You've not been here before, my sister," said Kremlin Busang. "It's a good bar, this one."

She met his gaze. "I only come to bars on big occasions," she said. "Such as today."

Kremlin Busang smiled. "Your birthday?"

"Yes," she said. "Let me buy you a drink to celebrate."

She bought him a beer, and he moved over to the stool beside her. She saw that he was a good-looking man, exactly as his photograph had revealed him, and his clothes were well chosen. They drank their beers together, and then she ordered him another one. He began to tell her about his job.

"I sort diamonds," he said. "It's a difficult job, you know. You need good eyesight."

"I like diamonds," she said. "I like diamonds a lot."

"We are very lucky to have so many diamonds in this country," he said. "My word! Those diamonds!"

She moved her left leg slightly, and it touched his. He noticed this, as she saw him glance down, but he did not move his leg away.

"Are you married?" she asked him quietly.

He did not hesitate. "No. I've never been married. It's better to be single these days. Freedom, you know."

She nodded. "I like to be free too," she said. "Then you can decide how to spend your own time."

"Exactly," he said. "Dead right."

She drained her glass.

"I must go," she said, and then, after a short pause: "Maybe you'd like to come back for a drink at my place. I've got some beer there."

He smiled. "Yes. That's a good idea. I had nothing to do either."

He followed her home in his car and together they went into her house and turned on some music. She poured him a beer, and he drank half of it in one gulp. Then he put his arm around her waist, and told her that he liked good, fat women. All this business about being thin was nonsense and was quite wrong for Africa.

"Fat women like you are what men really want," he said.

She giggled. He was charming, she had to admit it, but this was work and she must be quite professional. She must remember that she needed evidence, and that might be more difficult to get.

"Come and sit by me," she said. "You must be tired after standing up all day, sorting diamonds."

SHE HAD her excuses ready, and he accepted them without protest. She had to be at work early the next morning and he could not stay. But it would be a pity to end such a good evening and have no memento of it.

"I want to take a photograph of us, just for me to keep. So that I can look at it and remember tonight."

He smiled at her and pinched her gently.

"Good idea."

So she set up her camera, with its delayed switch, and leapt back on the sofa to join him. He pinched her again and put his arm around her and kissed her passionately as the flash went off.

"We can publish that in the newspapers if you like," he said. "Mr Handsome with his friend Miss Fatty."

She laughed. "You're a ladies' man all right, Kremlin. You're a real ladies' man. I knew it first time I saw you."

"Well somebody has to look after the ladies," he said.

ALICE BUSANG returned to the office that Friday and found Mma Ramotswe waiting for her.

"I'm afraid that I can tell you that your husband is unfaithful," she said. "I've got proof."

Alice closed her eyes. She had expected this, but she had not wanted it. She would kill him, she thought; but no, I still love him. I hate him. No, I love him.

Mma Ramotswe handed her the photograph. "There's your proof," she said.

Alice Busang stared at the picture. Surely not! Yes, it was her! It was the detective lady.

"You . . ." she stuttered. "You were with my husband?"

"He was with me," said Mma Ramotswe. "You wanted proof, didn't you? I got the best proof you could hope for."

Alice Busang dropped the photograph.

"But you . . . you went with my husband. You . . ."

Mma Ramotswe frowned. "You asked me to trap him, didn't you?"

Alice Busang's eyes narrowed. "You bitch!" she screamed. "You fat bitch! You took my Kremlin! You husband-stealer! Thief!"

Mma Ramotswe looked at her client with dismay. This would be a case, she thought, where she might have to waive the fee.

CHAPTER FIFTEEN

MR J.L.B. MATEKONI'S DISCOVERY

ALICE BUSANG was ushered out of the agency still shouting her insults at Mma Ramotswe.

"You fat tart! You think you're a detective! You're just man hungry, like all those bar girls! Don't be taken in everyone! This woman isn't a detective. No. 1 Husband Stealing Agency, that's what this is!"

When the row had died away, Mma Ramotswe and Mma Makutsi looked at one another. What could one do but laugh? That woman had known all along what her husband was up to, but had insisted on proof. And when she got the proof, she blamed the messenger.

"Look after the office while I go off to the garage," said Mma Ramotswe. "I just have to tell Mr J.L.B. Matekoni about this."

He was in his glass-fronted office cubicle, tinkering with a distributor cap.

"Sand gets everywhere these days," he said. "Look at this."

He extracted a fragment of silica from a metal duct and showed it triumphantly to his visitor.

"This little thing stopped a large truck in its tracks," he said. "This tiny piece of sand."

"For want of a nail, the shoe was lost," said Mma Ramotswe, remembering a distant afternoon in the Mochudi Government School when the teacher had quoted this to them. "For want of a shoe, the . . ." She stopped. It refused to come back.

"The horse fell down," volunteered Mr J.L.B. Matekoni. "I was taught that too."

He put the distributor cap down on his table and went off to fill the kettle. It was a hot afternoon, and a cup of tea would make them both feel better.

She told him about Alice Busang and her reaction to the proof of Kremlin's activities.

"You should have seen him," she said. "A real ladies' man. Stuff in his hair. Dark glasses. Fancy shoes. He had no idea how funny he looked. I much prefer men with ordinary shoes and honest trousers."

Mr J.L.B. Matekoni cast an anxious glance down at his shoes—scruffy old suede boots covered with grease—and at his trousers. Were they honest?

"I couldn't even charge her a fee," Mma Ramotswe went on. "Not after that."

Mr J.L.B. Matekoni nodded. He seemed preoccupied by something. He had not picked up the distributor cap again and was staring out of the window.

"You're worried about something?" She wondered whether her refusal of his proposal had upset him more than she imagined. He was not the sort to bear grudges, but did he resent her? She did not want to lose his friendship—he was her best friend in town, in a way, and life without his comforting presence would be distinctly the poorer. Why did love—and sex—complicate life so much? It would be far simpler for us not to have to worry about them. Sex played no part in her life now and she found that a great relief. She did not have to worry how she looked; what people thought of her. How terrible to be a man, and to have sex on one's mind all the time, as men are supposed to do. She had read in one of her magazines that the average man thought about sex over sixty times a day! She could not believe that figure, but studies had apparently revealed it. The average man, going about his daily business, had all those thoughts in his mind; thoughts of pushing and shoving, as men do, while he was actually doing something else! Did doctors think about it as they took your pulse? Did lawyers think about it as they sat at their desks and plotted? Did pilots think about it as they flew their aeroplanes? It simply beggared belief.

And Mr J.L.B. Matekoni, with his innocent expression and his plain face, was he thinking about it while he looked into distributor caps or heaved batteries out of engines? She looked at him; how could one tell? Did a man thinking about sex start to leer, or open his mouth and show his pink tongue, or . . . No. That was impossible.

"What are you thinking about, Mr J.L.B. Matekoni?" The question slipped out, and she immediately regretted it. It was as if she had challenged him to confess that he was thinking about sex.

He stood up and closed the door, which had been slightly ajar. There was nobody to overhear them. The two mechanics were at the other end of the garage, drinking their afternoon tea, thinking about sex, thought Mma Ramotswe.

"If you hadn't come to see me, I would have come to see you," said Mr J.L.B. Matekoni. "I have found something, you see."

She felt relieved; so he was not upset about her turning him down. She looked at him expectantly.

"There was an accident," said Mr J.L.B. Matekoni. "It was not a bad one. Nobody was hurt. Shaken a bit, but not hurt. It was at the old four-way stop. A truck coming along from the roundabout didn't stop. It hit a car coming from the Village. The car was pushed into the storm ditch and was quite badly dented. The truck had a smashed headlight and a little bit of damage to the radiator. That's all."

"And?"

Mr J.L.B. Matekoni sat down and stared at his hands.

"I was called to pull the car out of the ditch. I took my rescue truck and we winched it up. Then we towed it back here and left it round the back. I'll show it to you later."

He paused for a moment before continuing. The story seemed simple enough, but it appeared to be costing him a considerable effort to tell it.

"I looked it over. It was a panel-beating job and I could easily get my panel-beater to take it off to his workshop and sort it out. But there were one or two things I would have to do first. I had to check the electrics, for a start. These new expensive cars have so much wiring that a little knock here or there can make everything go wrong. You won't be able to lock your doors if the wires are nicked. Or your antitheft devices will freeze everything solid. It's very complicated, as those two boys out there drinking their tea on my time are only just finding out."

"Anyway, I had to get at a fuse box under the dashboard, and while I was doing this, I inadvertently opened the glove compartment. I looked inside—I don't know why—but something made me do it. And I found something. A little bag."

Mma Ramotswe's mind was racing ahead. He had stumbled upon illicit diamonds—she was sure of it.

"Diamonds?"

"No," said Mr J.L.B. Matekoni. "Worse than that."

SHE LOOKED at the small bag which he had taken out of his safe and placed on the table. It was made of animal skin—a pouch really—and was similar to the bags which the Basarwa ornamented with fragments of ostrich shell and used to store herbs and pastes for their arrows.

"I'll open it," he said. "I don't want to make you touch it."

She watched as he untied the strings that closed the mouth of the bag. His expression was one of distaste, as if he were handling something with an offensive smell.

And there was a smell, a dry, musty odour, as he extracted the three small objects from the bag. Now she understood. He need say nothing further. Now she understood why he had seemed so distracted and uncomfortable. Mr J.L.B. Matekoni had found muti. He had found medicine.

She said nothing as the objects were laid out on the table. What could one say about these pitiful remnants, about the bone, about the piece of skin, about the little wooden bottle, stoppered, and its awful contents?

Mr J.L.B. Matekoni, reluctant to touch the objects, poked at the bone with a pencil.

"See," he said simply. "That's what I found."

Mma Ramotswe got up from her chair and walked towards the door. She felt her stomach heave, as one does when confronted with a nauseous odour, a dead donkey in a ditch, the overpowering smell of carrion.

The feeling passed and she turned round.

"I'm going to take that bone and check," she said. "We could be wrong. It could be an animal. A duiker. A hare."

Mr J.L.B. Matekoni shook his head. "It won't be," he said. "I know what they'll say."

"Even so," said Mma Ramotswe. "Put it in an envelope and I'll take it."

Mr J.L.B. Matekoni opened his mouth to speak, but thought better of it. He was going to warn her, to tell her that it was dangerous to play around with these things, but that would imply that one believed in their power, and he did not. Did he?

She put the envelope in her pocket and smiled.

"Nothing can happen to me now," she said. "I'm protected."

Mr J.L.B. Matekoni tried to laugh at her joke, but found that he could not. It was tempting Providence to use those words and he hoped that she would not have cause to regret them.

"There's one thing I'd like to know," said Mma Ramotswe, as she left the office. "That car—who owned it?"

Mr J.L.B. Matekoni glanced at the two mechanics. They were both out of earshot, but he lowered his voice nonetheless while he told her.

"Charlie Gotso," he said. "Him. That one."

Mma Ramotswe's eyes widened.

"Gotso? The important one?"

Mr J.L.B. Matekoni nodded. Everyone knew Charlie Gotso. He was one of the most influential men in the country. He had the ear of . . . well, he had the ear of just about everyone who counted. There was no door in the country closed to him, nobody who would turn down a request for a favour. If Charlie Gotso asked you to do something for him, you did it. If you did not, then you might find that life became more difficult later on. It was always very subtly done—your application for a licence for your business may encounter unexpected delays; or you may find that there always seemed to be speed traps on your particular route to work; or your staff grew restless and went to work for somebody else. There was never anything you could put your finger on—that was not the way in Botswana, but the effect would be very real.

"Oh dear," said Mma Ramotswe.

"Exactly," said Mr J.L.B. Matekoni. "Oh dear."

CHAPTER SIXTEEN

THE CUTTING OF FINGERS
AND SNAKES

IN THE beginning, which in Gaborone really means thirty years ago, there were very few factories. In fact, when Princess Marina watched as the Union Jack was hauled down in the stadium on that windy night in 1966 and the Bechuanaland Protectorate ceased to exist, there were none. Mma Ramotswe had been an eight-year-old girl then, a pupil at the Government School at Mochudi, and only vaguely aware that anything special was happening and that something which people called freedom had arrived. But she had not felt any different the next day, and she wondered what this freedom meant. Now she knew of course, and her heart filled with pride when she thought of all they had achieved in thirty short years. The great swathe of territory which the British really had not known what to do with had prospered to become the best-run state in Africa, by far. Well could people shout Pula! Pula! Rain! Rain! with pride.

Gaborone had grown, changing out of all recognition. When she first went there as a little girl there had been little more than several rings of houses about the Mall and the few government offices—much bigger than Mochudi, of course, and so much more impressive, with the government buildings and Seretse Khama's house. But it was still quite small, really, if you had seen photographs of Johannesburg, or even Bulawayo. And no factories. None at all.

Then, little by little, things had changed. Somebody built a furniture workshop which produced sturdy living-room chairs. Then somebody else decided to set up a small factory to make breeze-blocks for building houses. Others followed, and soon there was a block of land on the Lobatse Road which people began to call the Industrial Sites. This caused a great stir of pride; so this is what freedom brought, people thought. There was the Legislative Assembly and the House of Chiefs, of course, where people could say what they liked—and did—but there were also these little factories and the jobs that went with them. Now there was even a truck factory on the Francistown Road, assembling ten trucks a month to send up as far as the Congo; and all of this started from nothing!

Mma Ramotswe knew one or two factory managers, and one factory owner. The factory owner, a Motswana who had come into the country from South Africa to enjoy the freedom denied him on the other side, had set up his bolt works with a tiny amount of capital, a few scraps of secondhand machinery bought from a bankruptcy sale in Bulawayo, and a workforce consisting of his brother-in-law, himself, and a mentally handicapped boy whom he had found sitting under a tree and who had proved to be quite capable of sorting bolts. The business had prospered, largely because the idea behind it was so sim-

ple. All that the factory made was a single sort of bolt, of the
sort which was needed for fixing galvanised tin roof sheeting
onto roof beams. This was a simple process, which required
only one sort of machine—a machine of a sort that never
seemed to break down and rarely needed servicing.

Hector Lepodise's factory grew rapidly, and by the time
Mma Ramotswe got to know him, he was employing thirty
people and producing bolts that held roofs onto their beams
as far north as Malawi. At first all his employees had been
his relatives, with the exception of the mentally handicapped
boy, who had subsequently been promoted to tea-boy. As the
business grew, however, the supply of relatives dwindled, and
Hector began to employ strangers. He maintained his earlier
paternalistic employment habits, though—there was always
plenty of time off for funerals as well as full pay for those who
were genuinely sick—and his workers, as a result, were usually
fiercely loyal to him. Yet with a staff of thirty, of whom only
twelve were relatives, it was inevitable that there would be
some who would attempt to exploit his kindness, and this is
where Mma Ramotswe came in.

"I can't put my finger on it," said Hector, as he drank coffee
with Mma Ramotswe on the verandah of the President Hotel,
"but I've never trusted that man. He only came to me about six
months ago, and now this."

"Where had he been working before?" asked Mma
Ramotswe. "What did they say about him?"

Hector shrugged. "He had a reference from a factory over
the border. I wrote to them but they didn't bother to reply.
Some of them don't take us seriously, you know. They treat us
as one of their wretched Bantustans. You know what they're
like."

Mma Ramotswe nodded. She did. They were not all bad, of course. But many of them were awful, which somehow eclipsed the better qualities of some of the nice ones. It was very sad.

"So he came to me just six months ago," Hector continued. "He was quite good at working the machinery, and so I put him on the new machine I bought from that Dutchman. He worked it well, and I upped his pay by fifty pula a month. Then suddenly he left me, and that was that."

"Any reason?" asked Mma Ramotswe.

Hector frowned. "None that I could make out. He collected his pay on a Friday and just did not come back. That was about two months ago. Then the next I heard from him was through an attorney in Mahalapye. He wrote me a letter saying that his client, Mr Solomon Moretsi, was starting a legal action against me for four thousand pula for the loss of a finger owing to an industrial accident in my factory."

Mma Ramotswe poured another cup of coffee for them both while she digested this development. "And was there an accident?"

"We have an incident book in the works," said Hector. "If anybody gets hurt, they have to enter the details in the book. I looked at the date which the attorney mentioned and I saw that there had been something. Moretsi had entered that he had hurt a finger on his right hand. He wrote that he had put a bandage on it and it seemed all right. I asked around, and somebody said that he had mentioned to them that he was leaving his machine for a while to fix his finger which he had cut. They thought it had not been a big cut, and nobody had bothered any more about it."

"Then he left?"

"Yes," said Hector. "That was a few days before he left."

Mma Ramotswe looked at her friend. He was an honest man, she knew, and a good employer. If anybody had been hurt she was sure that he would have done his best for them.

Hector took a sip of his coffee. "I don't trust that man," he said. "I don't think I ever did. I simply don't believe that he lost a finger in my factory. He may have lost a finger somewhere else, but that has nothing to do with me."

Mma Ramotswe smiled. "You want me to find this finger for you? Is that why you asked me to the President Hotel?"

Hector laughed. "Yes. And I also asked you because I enjoy sitting here with you and I would like to ask you to marry me. But I know that the answer will always be the same."

Mma Ramotswe reached out and patted her friend on the arm.

"Marriage is all very well," she said. "But being the No. 1 lady detective in the country is not an easy life. I couldn't sit at home and cook—you know that."

Hector shook his head. "I've always promised you a cook. Two cooks, if you like. You could still be a detective."

Mma Ramotswe shook her head. "No," she said. "You can carry on asking me, Hector Lepodise, but I'm afraid that the answer is still no. I like you as a friend, but I do not want a husband. I am finished with husbands for good."

MMA RAMOTSWE examined the papers in the office of Hector's factory. It was a hot and uncomfortable room, unprotected from the noise of the factory, and with barely enough space for the two filing cabinets and two desks which furnished it. Papers lay scattered on the surface of each desk; receipts, bills, technical catalogues.

"If only I had a wife," said Hector. "Then this office would not be such a mess. There would be places to sit down and flowers in a vase on my desk. A woman would make all the difference."

Mma Ramotswe smiled at his remark, but said nothing. She picked up the grubby exercise book which he had placed in front of her and paged through it. This was the incident book, and there, sure enough, was the entry detailing Moretsi's injury, the words spelled out in capitals in a barely literate hand:

MORETSI CUT HIS FINGER. NO. 2 FINGER COUNTING FROM THUMB. MACHINE DID IT. RIGHT HAND. BANDAGE PUT ON BY SAME. SIGNED: SOLOMON MORETSI. WITNESS: JESUS CHRIST.

She reread the entry and then looked at the attorney's letter. The dates tallied: "My client says that the accident occurred on 10th May last. He attended at the Princess Marina Hospital the following day. The wound was dressed, but osteomyelitis set in. The following week surgery was performed and the damaged finger was amputated at the proximal phalangeal joint (see attached hospital report). My client claims that this accident was due entirely to your negligence in failing adequately to fence working parts of machinery operated in your factory and has instructed me to raise an action for damages on his behalf. It would clearly be in the interests of all concerned if this action were to be settled promptly and my client has accordingly been advised that the sum of four thousand pula will be acceptable to him in lieu of court-awarded damages."

Mma Ramotswe read the remainder of the letter, which as far as she could make out was meaningless jargon which the attorney had been taught at law school. They were impossible, these people; they had a few years of lectures at the University

of Botswana and they set themselves up as experts on everything. What did they know of life? All they knew was how to
parrot the stock phrases of their profession and to continue to
be obstinate until somebody, somewhere, paid up. They won
by attrition in most cases, but they themselves concluded it
was skill. Few of them would survive in her profession, which
required tact and perspicacity.

She looked at the copy of the medical report. It was brief
and said exactly what the attorney had paraphrased. The date
was right; the headed note paper looked authentic; and there
was the doctor's signature at the bottom. It was a name she
knew.

Mma Ramotswe looked up from the papers to see Hector
staring at her expectantly.

"It seems straightforward," she said. "He cut his finger and
it became infected. What do your insurance people say?"

Hector sighed. "They say I should pay up. They say that
they'll cover me for it and it would be cheaper in the long run.
Once one starts paying lawyers to defend it, then the costs can
very quickly overtake the damages. Apparently they'll settle up
to ten thousand pula without fighting, although they asked me
not to tell anybody about that. They would not like people to
think they're an easy touch."

"Shouldn't you do what they say?" asked Mma Ramotswe. It
seemed to her that there was no real point in denying that the
accident had happened. Obviously this man had lost a finger
and deserved some compensation; why should Hector make
such a fuss about this when he did not even have to pay?

Hector guessed what she was thinking. "I won't," he said. "I
just refuse. Refuse. Why should I pay money to somebody who

I think is trying to cheat me? If I pay him this time, then he'll go on to somebody else. I'd rather give that four thousand pula to somebody who deserved it."

He pointed to the door that linked the office to the factory floor.

"I've got a woman in there," he said, "with ten children. Yes, ten. She's a good worker too. Think what she could do with four thousand pula."

"But she hasn't lost a finger," interrupted Mma Ramotswe. "He might need that money if he can't work so well anymore."

"Bah! Bah! He's a crook, that man. I couldn't sack him because I had nothing on him. But I knew he was no good. And some of the others didn't like him either. The boy who makes the tea, the one with a hole in his brain, he can always tell. He wouldn't take tea to him. He said that the man was a dog and couldn't drink tea. You see, he knew. These people sense these things."

"But there's a big difference between entertaining suspicions and being able to prove something," said Mma Ramotswe. "You couldn't stand up in the High Court in Lobatse and say that there was something about this man which was not quite right. The judge would just laugh at you. That's what judges do when people say that sort of thing. They just laugh."

Hector was silent.

"Just settle," said Mma Ramotswe quietly. "Do what the insurance people tell you to do. Otherwise you'll end up with a bill for far more than four thousand pula."

Hector shook his head. "I won't pay for something I didn't do," he said through clenched teeth. "I want you to find out what this man is up to. But if you come back to me in a week's time and say that I am wrong, then I will pay without a murmur. Will that do?"

Mma Ramotswe nodded. She could understand his reluctance to pay damages he thought he didn't owe, and her fee for a week's work would not be high. He was a wealthy man, and he was entitled to spend his own money in pursuit of a principle; and, if Moretsi was lying, then a fraudster would have been confounded in the process. So she agreed to act, and she drove away in her little white van wondering how she could prove that the missing finger had nothing to do with Hector's factory. As she parked the van outside her office and walked into the cool of her waiting room, she realised that she had absolutely no idea how to proceed. It had all the appearances of a hopeless case.

THAT NIGHT, as she lay in the bedroom of her house in Zebra Drive, Mma Ramotswe found that sleep eluded her. She got up, put on the pink slippers which she always wore since she had been stung by a scorpion while walking through the house at night, and went through to the kitchen to make a pot of bush tea.

The house seemed so different at night. Everything was in its correct place, of course, but somehow the furniture seemed more angular and the pictures on the wall more one-dimensional. She remembered somebody saying that at night we are all strangers, even to ourselves, and this struck her as being true. All the familiar objects of her daily life looked as if they belonged to somebody else, somebody called Mma Ramotswe, who was not quite the person walking about in pink slippers.

Even the photograph of her Daddy in his shiny blue suit seemed different. This was a person called Daddy Ramotswe, of course, but not the Daddy she had known, the Daddy who had sacrificed everything for her, and whose last wish had been to see her happily settled in a business. How proud he would have been to have seen her now, the owner of the No. 1 Ladies' Detective Agency, known to everybody of note in town, even to permanent secretaries and Government ministers. And how important he would have felt had he seen her that very morning almost bumping into the Malawian High Commissioner as she left the President Hotel and the High Commissioner saying: "Good morning, Mma Ramotswe, you almost knocked me down there, but there's nobody I would rather be knocked down by than you, my goodness!" To be known to a High Commissioner! To be greeted by name by people like that! Not that she was impressed by them, of course, even high commissioners; but her Daddy would have been, and she regretted that he had not lived to see his plans for her come to fruition.

She made her tea and settled down to drink it on her most comfortable chair. It was a hot night and the dogs were howling throughout the town, egging one another on in the darkness. It was not a sound you really noticed anymore, she thought. They were always there, these howling dogs, defending their yards against all sorts of shadows and winds. Stupid creatures!

She thought of Hector. He was a stubborn man—famously so—but she rather respected him for it. Why should he pay? What was it he had said: If I pay him this time then he'll go on to somebody else. She thought for a moment, and then put the mug of bush tea down on the table. The idea had come to her suddenly, as all her good ideas seemed to come. Perhaps Hector was the somebody else. Perhaps he had already made claims elsewhere. Perhaps Hector was not the first!

Sleep proved easier after that, and she awoke the next morning confident that a few enquiries, and perhaps a trip up to Mahalapye, would be all that was required to dispose of Moretsi's spurious claim. She breakfasted quickly and then drove directly to the office. It was getting towards the end of winter, which meant that the temperature of the air was just right, and the sky was bright, pale blue, and cloudless. There was a slight smell of wood-smoke in the air, a smell that tugged at her heart because it reminded her of mornings around the fire in Mochudi. She would go back there, she thought, when she had worked long enough to retire. She would buy a house, or build one perhaps, and ask some of her cousins to live with her. They would grow melons on the lands and might even buy a small shop in the village; and every morning she could sit in front of her house and sniff at the wood-smoke and look forward to spending the day talking with her friends. How sorry she felt for white people, who couldn't do any of this, and who were always dashing around and worrying themselves over things that were going to happen anyway. What use was it having all that money if you could never sit still or just watch your cattle eating grass? None, in her view; none at all, and yet they did not know it. Every so often you met a white person who understood, who realised how things really were; but these people were few and far between and the other white people often treated them with suspicion.

The woman who swept her office was already there when she arrived. She asked after her family, and the woman told her of their latest doings. She had one son who was a warder at the prison and another who was a trainee chef at the Sun Hotel. They were both doing well, in their ways, and Mma Ramotswe was always interested to hear of their achievements. But that morning she cut the cleaner short—as politely as she could—and got down to work.

The trade directory gave her the information she needed. There were ten insurance companies doing business in Gaborone; four of these were small, and probably rather specialised; the other six she had heard of and had done work for four of them. She listed them, noted down their telephone numbers, and made a start.

The Botswana Eagle Company was the first she telephoned. They were willing to help, but could not come up with any information. Nor could the Mutual Life Company of Southern Africa, or the Southern Star Insurance Company. But at the fourth, Kalahari Accident and Indemnity, which asked for an hour or so to search the records, she found out what she needed to know.

"We've found one claim under that name," said the woman on the other end of the line. "Two years ago we had a claim from a garage in town. One of their petrol attendants claimed to have injured his finger while replacing the petrol pump dispenser in its holder. He lost a finger and they claimed under their employer's policy."

Mma Ramotswe's heart gave a leap. "Four thousand pula?" she asked.

"Close enough," said the clerk. "We settled for three thousand eight hundred."

"Right hand?" pressed Mma Ramotswe. "Second finger counting from the thumb?"

The clerk shuffled through some papers.

"Yes," she said. "There's a medical report. It says something about . . . I'm not sure how to pronounce it . . . osteomy . . ."

"Elitis," prompted Mma Ramotswe. "Requiring amputation of the finger at the proximal phalangeal joint?"

"Yes," said the clerk. "Exactly."

There were one or two details to be obtained, and Mma Ramotswe did that before thanking the clerk and ringing off. For a few moments she sat quite still, savouring the satisfaction of having revealed the fraud so quickly. But there were still several loose ends to be sorted out, and for these she would have to go up to Mahalapye. She would like to meet Moretsi, if she could, and she was also looking forward to an interview with his attorney. That, she thought, would be a pleasure that would more or less justify the two-hour drive up that awful Francistown Road.

The attorney proved to be quite willing to see her that afternoon. He assumed that she had been engaged by Hector to settle, and he imagined that it would be quite easy to browbeat her into settling on his terms. They might try for a little bit more than four thousand, in fact; he could say that there were new factors in the assessment of damages which made it necessary to ask for more. He would use the word quantum, which was Latin, he believed, and he might even refer to a recent decision of the Court of Appeal or even the Appellate Division in Bloemfontein. That would intimidate anyone, particularly a woman! And yes, he was sure that Mr Moretsi would be able to be there. He was a busy man, of course; no, he wasn't in fact, he couldn't work, poor man, as a result of his injury, but he would make sure that he was there.

Mma Ramotswe chuckled as she put down the telephone.

The attorney would be going to fetch his client out of some bar, she imagined, where he was probably already celebrating prematurely the award of four thousand pula. Well, he was due for an unpleasant surprise, and she, Mma Ramotswe, would be the agent of Nemesis.

She left her office in the charge of her secretary and set off to Mahalapye in the tiny white van. The day had heated up, and now, at noon, it was really quite hot. In a few months' time it would be impossible at midday and she would hate to have to drive any distance through the heat. She travelled with her window open and the rushing air cooled the van. She drove past the Dry Lands Research Station and the road that led off to Mochudi. She drove past the hills to the east of Mochudi and down into the broad valley that lay beyond. All around her there was nothing—just endless bush that stretched away to the bounds of the Kalahari on the one side and the plains of the Limpopo on the other. Empty bush, with nothing in it, but some cattle here and there and the occasional creaking wind-mill bringing up a tiny trickle of water for the thirsty beasts; nothing, nothing, that was what her country was so rich in—emptiness.

She was half an hour from Mahalapye when the snake shot across the road. The first she saw of it was when its body was about halfway out onto the road—a dart of green against the black tar; and then she was upon it, and the snake was beneath the van. She drew in her breath and slowed the car, looking behind her in the mirror as she did so. Where was the snake? Had it succeeded in crossing the road in time? No, it had not; she had seen it go under the van and she was sure that she had heard something, a dull thump.

She drew to a halt at the edge of the road, and looked in the mirror again. There was no sign of the snake. She looked at the steering wheel and drummed her fingers lightly against it. Perhaps it had been too quick to be seen; these snakes could move with astonishing speed. But she had looked almost immediately, and it was far too big a snake to disappear just like that. No, the snake was in the van somewhere, in the works or under her seat perhaps. She had heard of this happening time and time again. People picked up snakes as passengers and the first thing they knew about it was when the snake bit them. She had heard of people dying at the wheel, as they drove, bitten by snakes that had been caught up in the pipes and rods that ran this way and that under a car.

Mma Ramotswe felt a sudden urge to leave the van. She opened her door, hesitantly at first, but then threw it back and leaped out, to stand, panting, beside the vehicle. There was a snake under the tiny white van, she was now sure of that; but how could she possibly get it out? And what sort of snake was it? It had been green, as far as she remembered, which meant at least it wasn't a mamba. It was all very well people talking about green mambas, which certainly existed, but Mma Ramotswe knew that they were very restricted in their distribution and they were certainly not to be found in any part of Botswana. They were tree-dwelling snakes, for the most part, and they did not like sparse thorn bush. It was more likely to be a cobra, she thought, because it was large enough and she could think of no other green snake that long.

Mma Ramotswe stood quite still. The snake could have been watching her at that very moment, ready to strike if she approached any closer; or it could have insinuated itself into the cab of the van and was even now settling in under her seat. She bent forward and tried to look under the van, but she could not get low enough without going onto her hands and knees. If she did that, and if the snake should choose to move, she was worried that she would be unable to get away quickly enough. She stood up again and thought of Hector. This was what husbands were for. If she had accepted him long ago, then she would not be driving alone up to Mahalapye. She would have a man with her, and he would be getting under the van to poke the snake out of its place.

The road was very quiet, but there was a car or a truck every so often, and now she was aware of a car coming from the Mahalapye direction. The car slowed down as it approached her and then stopped. There was a man in the driver's seat and a young boy beside him.

"Are you in trouble, Mma?" he called out politely. "Have you broken down?"

Mma Ramotswe crossed the road and spoke to him through his open window. She explained about the snake, and he turned off his engine and got out, instructing the boy to stay where he was.

"They get underneath," he said. "It can be dangerous. You were right to stop."

The man approached the van gingerly. Then, leaning through the open door of the cab, he reached for the lever which released the bonnet and he gave it a sharp tug. Satisfied that it had worked, he walked slowly round to the front of the van and very carefully began to open the bonnet. Mma Ramotswe joined him, peering over his shoulder, ready to flee at the first sight of the snake.

The man suddenly froze.

"Don't make any sudden movement," he said very softly. "There it is. Look."

Mma Ramotswe peered into the engine space. For a few moments she could make out nothing unusual, but then the snake moved slightly and she saw it. She was right; it was a cobra, twined about the engine, its head moving slowly to right and left, as if seeking out something.

The man was quite still. Then he touched Mma Ramotswe on the forearm.

"Walk very carefully back to the door," he said. "Get into the cab, and start the engine. Understand?"

Mma Ramotswe nodded. Then, moving as slowly as she could, she eased herself into the driving seat and reached forward to turn the key.

The engine came into life immediately, as it always did. The tiny white van had never failed to start first time.

"Press the accelerator," yelled the man. "Race the engine!"

Mma Ramotswe did as she was told, and the engine roared throatily. There was a noise from the front, another thump, and then the man signalled to her to switch off. Mma Ramotswe did so, and waited to be told whether it was safe to get out.

"You can come out," he called. "That's the end of the cobra."

Mma Ramotswe got out of the cab and walked round to the front. Looking into the engine, she saw the cobra in two pieces, quite still.

"It had twined itself through the blades of the fan," said the man, making a face of disgust. "Nasty way to go, even for a snake. But it could have crept into the cab and bitten you, you know. So there we are. You are still alive."

Mma Ramotswe thanked him and drove off, leaving the cobra on the side of the road. It would prove to be an eventful journey, even if nothing further were to happen during the final half hour. It did not.

"NOW," SAID Mr Jameson Mopotswane, the Mahalapye attorney, sitting back in his unprepossessing office next to the butchery. "My poor client is going to be a little late, as the message only got to him a short time ago. But you and I can discuss details of the settlement before he arrives."

Mma Ramotswe savoured the moment. She leaned back in her chair and looked about his poorly furnished room.

"So business is not so good these days," she said, adding: "Up here."

Jameson Mopotswane bristled.

"It's not bad," he said. "In fact, I'm very busy. I get in here at seven o'clock, you know, and I'm on the go until six."

"Every day?" asked Mma Ramotswe innocently.

Jameson Mopotswane glared at her.

"Yes," he said. "Every day, including Saturdays. Sometimes Sundays."

"You must have a lot to do," said Mma Ramotswe.

The attorney took this in a reconciliatory way and smiled, but Mma Ramotswe continued: "Yes, a lot to do, sorting out the lies your clients tell you from the occasional—occasional—truth."

Jameson Mopotswane put his pen down on his desk and glared at her. Who was this pushy woman, and what right did she have to talk about his clients like that? If this is the way

she wanted to play it, then he would be quite happy not to settle. He could do with fees, even if taking the matter to court
would delay his client's damages.

"My clients do not lie," he said slowly. "Not more than anybody else, anyway. And you have no business, if I may say so,
to suggest that they are liars."

Mma Ramotswe raised an eyebrow.

"Oh no?" she challenged. "Well, let's just take your Mr
Moretsi, for example. How many fingers has he got?"

Jameson Mopotswane looked at her disdainfully.

"It's cheap to make fun of the afflicted," he sneered. "You
know very well that he's got nine, or nine and a half if you want
to split hairs."

"Very interesting," said Mma Ramotswe. "And if that's the
case, then how can he possibly have made a successful claim
to Kalahari Accident and Indemnity, about three years ago, for
the loss of a finger in an accident in a petrol station? Could you
explain that?"

The attorney sat quite still.

"Three years ago?" he said faintly. "A finger?"

"Yes," said Mma Ramotswe. "He asked for four thousand—
a bit of a coincidence—and settled for three thousand eight
hundred. The company have given me the claim number, if
you want to check up. They're always very helpful, I find, when
there's any question of insurance fraud being uncovered.
Remarkably helpful."

Jameson Mopotswane said nothing, and suddenly Mma
Ramotswe felt sorry for him. She did not like lawyers, but he
was trying to earn a living, like everybody else, and perhaps she
was being too hard on him. He might well have been supporting elderly parents, for all she knew.

"Show me the medical report," she said, almost kindly. "I'd be interested to see it."

The attorney reached for a file on his desk and took out a report.

"Here," he said. "It all seemed quite genuine."

Mma Ramotswe looked at the piece of headed paper and then nodded.

"There we are," she said. "It's just as I thought. Look at the date there. It's been whited out and a new date typed in. Our friend did have a finger removed once, and it may even have been as a result of an accident. But then all that he's done is to get a bottle of correction fluid, change the date, and create a new accident, just like that."

The attorney took the sheet of paper and held it up to the light. He need not even have done that; the correction fluid could be seen clearly enough at first glance.

"I'm surprised that you did not notice that," said Mma Ramotswe. "It doesn't exactly need a forensic laboratory to see what he's done."

It was at this point in the shaming of the attorney that Moretsi arrived. He walked into the office and reached out to shake hands with Mma Ramotswe. She looked at the hand and saw the stub of the finger. She rejected the proffered hand.

"Sit down," said Jameson Mopotswane coldly.

Moretsi looked surprised, but did as he was told.

"So you're the lady who's come to pay . . ."

The attorney cut him short.

"She has not come to pay anything," he said. "This lady has come all the way from Gaborone to ask you why you keep claiming for lost fingers."

Mma Ramotswe watched Moretsi's expression as the attorney spoke. Even if there had not been the evidence of the changed date on the hospital report, his crestfallen look would have convinced her. People always collapsed when confronted with the truth; very, very few could brave it out.

"Keep claiming . . . ?" he said limply.

"Yes," said Mma Ramotswe. "You claim, I believe, to have lost three fingers. And yet if I look at your hand today I see that two have miraculously grown back! This is wonderful! Perhaps you have discovered some new drug that enables fingers to grow back once they have been chopped off?"

"Three?" said the attorney, puzzled.

Mma Ramotswe looked at Moretsi.

"Well," she said. "There was Kalahari Accident. Then there was . . . Could you refresh my memory? I've got it written down somewhere."

Moretsi looked to his attorney for support, but saw only anger.

"Star Insurance," he said quietly.

"Ah!" said Mma Ramotswe. "Thank you for that."

The attorney picked up the medical report and waved it at his client.

"And you expected to be able to fool me with this . . . crude alteration? You expected to get away with that?"

Moretsi said nothing, as did Mma Ramotswe. She was not surprised, of course; these people were utterly slippery, even if they had a law degree to write after their names.

"Anyway," said Jameson Mopotswane, "that's the end of your tricks. You'll be facing fraud charges, you know, and you'll have to get somebody else to defend you. You won't get me, my friend."

Moretsi looked at Mma Ramotswe, who met his gaze directly.

"Why did you do it?" she asked. "Just tell me why you thought you could get away with it?"

Moretsi took a handkerchief out of his pocket and blew his nose.

"I am looking after my parents," he said. "And I have a sister who is sick with a disease that is killing everybody these days. You know what I'm talking about. She has children. I have to support them."

Mma Ramotswe looked into his eyes. She had always been able to rely on her ability to tell whether a person was telling the truth or not, and she knew that Moretsi was not lying. She thought quickly. There was no point in sending this man to prison. What would it achieve? It would merely add to the suffering of others—of the parents and of the poor sister. She knew what he was talking about and she understood what it meant.

"Very well," she said. "I will not tell the police about any of this. And my client will not either. But in return, you will promise that there will be no more lost fingers. Do you understand?"

Moretsi nodded rapidly.

"You are a good Christian lady," he said. "God is going to make it very easy for you in heaven."

"I hope so," said Mma Ramotswe. "But I am also a very nasty lady sometimes. And if you try any more of this nonsense with insurance people, then you will find that I will become very unpleasant."

"I understand," said Moretsi. "I understand."

"You see," said Mma Ramotswe, casting a glance at the

attentive attorney, "there are some people in this country, some men, who think that women are soft and can be twisted this way and that. Well I'm not. I can tell you, if you are interested, that I killed a cobra, a big one, on my way here this afternoon."

"Oh?" said Jameson Mopotswane. "What did you do?"

"I cut it in two," said Mma Ramotswe. "Two pieces."

CHAPTER SEVENTEEN

THE THIRD METACARPAL

ALL THAT was a distraction. It was gratifying to deal with a case like that so quickly, and to the clear satisfaction of the client, but one could not put out of one's mind the fact that there was a small brown envelope in the drawer with contents that could not be ignored.

She took it out discreetly, not wanting Mma Makutsi to see it. She thought that she could trust her, but this was a matter which was very much more confidential than any other matter they had encountered so far. This was dangerous.

She left the office, telling Mma Makutsi that she was going to the bank. Several cheques had come in, and needed to be deposited. But she did not go to the bank, or at least not immediately. She drove instead to the Princess Marina Hospital and followed the signs that said PATHOLOGY.

A nurse stopped her.

"Are you here to identify a body, Mma?"

Mma Ramotswe shook her head. "I have come to see Dr Gulubane. He is not expecting me, but he will see me. I am his neighbour."

The nurse looked at her suspiciously, but told her to wait while she went to fetch the doctor. A few minutes after she returned and said that the doctor would be with her shortly.

"You should not disturb these doctors at the hospital," she said disapprovingly. "They are busy people."

Mma Ramotswe looked at the nurse. What age was she? Nineteen, twenty? In her father's day, a girl of nineteen would not have spoken to a woman of thirty-five like that—spoken to her as if she was a child making an irritating request. But things were different now. Upstarts showed no respect for people who were older, and bigger too, than they were. Should she tell her that she was a private detective? No, there was no point in engaging with a person like this. She was best ignored.

Dr Gulubane arrived. He was wearing a green apron—heaven knows what awful task he had been performing—and he seemed quite pleased to have been disturbed.

"Come with me to my office," he said. "We can talk there."

Mma Ramotswe followed him down a corridor to a small office furnished with a completely bare table, a telephone, and a battered grey filing cabinet. It was like the office of a minor civil servant, and it was only the medical books on a shelf which gave away its real purpose.

"As you know," she began, "I'm a private detective these days."

Dr Gulubane beamed a broad smile. He was remarkably cheerful, she thought, given the nature of his job.

"You won't get me to talk about my patients," he said. "Even if they're all dead."

She shared the joke. "That's not what I want," she said. "All I would like you to do is to identify something for me. I have it with me." She took out the envelope and spilled its contents on the desk.

Dr Gulubane immediately stopped smiling and picked up the bone. He adjusted his spectacles.

"Third metacarpal," he muttered. "Child. Eight. Nine. Something like that."

Mma Ramotswe could hear her own breathing.

"Human?"

"Of course," said Dr Gulubane. "As I said, it's from a child. An adult's bone would be bigger. You can tell at a glance. A child of about eight or nine. Possibly a bit older."

The doctor put the bone down on the table and looked up at Mma Ramotswe.

"Where did you get it?"

Mma Ramotswe shrugged. "Somebody showed it to me. And you won't get me to talk about my clients either."

Dr Gulubane made an expression of distaste.

"These things shouldn't be handed round like that," he said. "People show no respect."

Mma Ramotswe nodded her agreement. "But can you tell me anything more? Can you tell me when the . . . when the child died?"

Dr Gulubane opened a drawer and took out a magnifying glass, with which he examined the bone further, turning it round in the palm of his hand.

"Not all that long ago," he said. "There's a small amount of tissue here at the top. It doesn't look entirely dessicated. Maybe a few months, maybe less. You can't be sure."

Mma Ramotswe shuddered. It was one thing to handle bone, but to handle human tissue was quite a different matter.

"And another thing," said Dr Gulubane. "How do you know that the child whose bone this is is dead? I thought you were the detective—surely you would have thought: this is an extremity—people can lose extremities and still live! Did you think that, Mrs Detective? I bet you didn't!"

SHE CONVEYED the information to Mr J.L.B. Matekoni over dinner in her house. He had readily accepted her invitation and she had prepared a large pot of stew and a combination of rice and melons. Halfway through the meal she told him of her visit to Dr Gulubane. Mr J.L.B. Matekoni stopped eating.

"A child?" There was dismay in his voice.

"That's what Dr Gulubane said. He couldn't be certain about the age. But he said it was about eight or nine."

Mr J.L.B. Matekoni winced. It would have been far better never to have found the bag. These things happened—they all knew that—but one did not want to get mixed up in them. They could only mean trouble—particularly if Charlie Gotso was involved in them.

"What do we do?" asked Mma Ramotswe.

Mr J.L.B. Matekoni closed his eyes and swallowed hard.

"We can go to the police," he said. "And if we do that, Charlie Gotso will get to hear about my finding the bag. And that will be me done for, or just about."

Mma Ramotswe agreed. The police had a limited interest in pursuing crime, and certain sorts of crime interested them not at all. The involvement of the country's most powerful figures in witchcraft would certainly be in the latter category.

"I don't think we should go to the police," said Mma Ramotswe.

"So we just forget about it?" Mr J.L.B. Matekoni fixed Mma Ramotswe with a look of appeal.

"No. We can't do that," she said. "People have been forgetting about this sort of thing for long enough, haven't they? We can't do that."

Mr J.L.B. Matekoni lowered his eyes. His appetite seemed to have deserted him now, and the stew was congealing on his plate.

"The first thing we do," she said, "is to arrange for Charlie Gotso's windscreen to be broken. Then you telephone him and tell him that thieves have broken into his car while it was in the garage. You tell him that there does not appear to have been anything stolen, but that you will willingly pay for a new windscreen yourself. Then you wait and see."

"To see what?"

"To see if he comes back and tells you something's missing. If he does, you tell him that you will personally undertake to recover this thing, whatever it is. You tell him that you have a contact, a lady private detective, who is very good at recovering stolen property. That's me, of course."

Mr J.L.B. Matekoni's jaw had dropped. One did not simply go up to Charlie Gotso just like that. You had to pull strings to see him.

"And then?"

"Then I take the bag back to him and you leave it up to me. I'll get the name of the witch doctor from him and then, well, we'll think about what to do then."

She made it sound so simple that he found himself convinced that it would work. That was the wonderful thing about confidence—it was infectious.

Mr J.L.B. Matekoni's appetite returned. He finished the stew, had a second helping, and then drank a large cup of tea before Mma Ramotswe walked with him to his car and said good-night.

She stood in the drive and watched the lights of his car disappear. Through the darkness, she could see the lights of Dr Gulubane's house. The curtains of his living room were open, and the doctor was standing at the open window, looking out into the night. He could not see her, as she was in darkness and he was in the light, but it was almost as if he was watching her.

CHAPTER EIGHTEEN

A LOT OF LIES

ONE OF the young mechanics tapped him on the shoulder, leaving a greasy fingerprint. He was always doing this, that young man, and it annoyed Mr J.L.B. Matekoni intensely.

"If you want to attract my attention," he had said on more than one occasion, "you can always speak to me. I have a name. I am Mr J.L.B. Matekoni, and I answer to that. You don't have to come and put your dirty fingers on me."

The young man had apologised, but had tapped him on the shoulder the next day, and Mr J.L.B. Matekoni had realised that he was fighting a losing battle.

"There's a man to see you, Rra," said the mechanic. "He's waiting in the office."

Mr J.L.B. Matekoni put down his spanner and wiped his hands on a cloth. He had been involved in a particularly delicate operation—fine-tuning the engine of Mrs Grace Mapondwe, who was well-known for her sporty style of driving. It was a matter of pride to Mr J.L.B. Matekoni that people knew that Mrs Mapondwe's roaring engine note could be put down to his efforts; it was a free advertisement in a way. Unfortunately, she had ruined her car and it was becoming more and more difficult for him to coax life out of the increasingly sluggish engine.

The visitor was sitting in the office, in Mr J.L.B. Matekoni's chair. He had picked up a tyre brochure and was flipping through it when Mr J.L.B. Matekoni entered the room. Now he tossed it down casually and stood up.

Mr J.L.B. Matekoni rapidly took in the other man's appearance. He was dressed in khaki, as a soldier might be, and he had an expensive, snakeskin belt. There was also a fancy watch, with multiple dials and a prominent second hand. It was the sort of watch worn by those who feel that seconds are important, thought Mr J.L.B. Matekoni.

"Mr Gotso sent me," he said. "You telephoned him this morning."

Mr J.L.B. Matekoni nodded. It had been easy to break the windscreen and scatter the fragments of glass about the car. It had been easy to telephone Mr Gotso's house and report that the car had been broken into; but this part was more difficult—this was lying to somebody's face. It's Mma Ramotswe's fault, he thought. I am a simple mechanic. I didn't ask to get involved in these ridiculous detective games. I am just too weak.

And he was—when it came to Mma Ramotswe. She could ask anything of him, and he would comply. Mr J.L.B. Matekoni even had a fantasy, unconfessed, guiltily enjoyed in which he helped Mma Ramotswe. They were in the Kalahari together and Mma Ramotswe was threatened by a lion. He called out, drawing the lion's attention to him, and the animal turned and snarled. This gave her the chance to escape, while he dispatched the lion with a hunting knife; an innocent enough fantasy, one might have thought, except for one thing: Mma Ramotswe was wearing no clothes.

He would have loved to save her, naked or otherwise, from a lion, but this was different. He had even had to make a false report to the police, which had really frightened him, even if they had not even bothered to come round to investigate. He was a criminal now, he supposed, and it was all because he was weak. He should have said no. He should have told Mma Ramotswe that it was not her job to be a crusader.

"Mr Gotso is very angry," said the visitor. "You have had that car for ten days. Now you telephone us and tell us that it is broken into. Where's your security? That's what Mr Gotso says: where's your security?"

Mr J.L.B. Matekoni felt a trickle of sweat run down his back. This was terrible.

"I'm very sorry, Rra. The panel-beaters took a long time. Then I had to get a new part. These expensive cars, you can't put anything in them . . ."

Mr Gotso's man looked at his watch.

"All right, all right. I know how slow these people are. Just show me the car."

Mr J.L.B. Matekoni led the way out of the office. The man seemed less threatening now; was it really that easy to turn away wrath?

They stood before the car. He had already replaced the windscreen, but had propped what remained of the shattered one against a nearby wall. He had also taken the precaution of leaving a few pieces of broken glass on the driver's seat.

The visitor opened the front door and peered inside.

"I have replaced the windscreen free of charge," said Mr J.L.B. Matekoni. "I will also make a big reduction in the bill."

The other man said nothing. He was leaning across now and had opened the glove compartment. Mr J.L.B. Matekoni watched quietly.

The man got out of the car and brushed his hand against his trousers; he had cut himself on one of the small pieces of glass.

"There is something missing from the glove compartment. Do you know anything about that?"

Mr J.L.B. Matekoni shook his head—three times.

The man put his hand to his mouth and sucked at the cut.

"Mr Gotso forgot that he had something there. He only remembered when you told him about the car being broken into. He is not going to be pleased to hear that this item has gone."

Mr J.L.B. Matekoni passed the man a piece of rag.

"I'm sorry you've cut yourself. Glass gets everywhere when a windscreen goes. Everywhere."

The man snorted. "It doesn't matter about me. What matters is that somebody has stolen something belonging to Mr Gotso."

Mr J.L.B. Matekoni scratched his head.

"The police are useless. They didn't even come. But I know somebody who can look into this."

"Oh yes? Who can do that?"

"There's a lady detective these days. She has an office over that way, near Kgale Hill. Have you seen it?"

"Maybe. Maybe not."

Mr J.L.B. Matekoni smiled. "She's an amazing lady! She

knows everything that's going on. If I ask her, she'll be able to find out who did this thing. She might even be able to get the property back. What was it, by the way?"

"Property. A small thing belonging to Mr Charlie Gotso."

"I see."

The man took the rag off his wound and flung it on the floor.

"Can you ask that lady then," he said grudgingly. "Ask her to get this thing back to Mr Gotso."

"I will," said Mr J.L.B. Matekoni. "I will speak to her this evening, and I am sure she will get results. In the meantime, that car is ready and Mr Gotso can collect it anytime. I will clear up the last bits of glass."

"You'd better," said the visitor. "Mr Gotso doesn't like to cut his hand."

Mr Gotso doesn't like to cut his hand! You're a little boy, thought Mr J.L.B. Matekoni. You're just like a truculent little boy. I know your type well enough! I remember you—or somebody very like you—in the playground at Mochudi Government School—bullying other boys, breaking things, pretending to be tough. Even when the teacher whipped you, you made much about being too brave to cry.

And this Mr Charlie Gotso, with his expensive car and sinister ways—he's a boy too. Just a little boy.

HE WAS determined that Mma Ramotswe should not get away with it. She seemed to assume that he would do whatever she told him to do and very rarely asked him whether he wanted to take part in her schemes. And of course he had been far too meek in agreeing with her; that was the problem, really—she thought that she could get away with it because he never stood up to her. Well, he would show her this time. He would put an end to all this detective nonsense.

He left the garage, still smarting, busy rehearsing in his mind what he would say to her when he reached the office.

"Mma Ramotswe, you've made me lie. You've drawn me into a ridiculous and dangerous affair which is quite simply none of our business. I am a mechanic. I fix cars—I cannot fix lives."

The last phrase struck him for its forcefulness. Yes—that was the difference between them. She was a fixer of lives—as so many women are—whereas he was a fixer of machines. He would tell her this, and she would have to accept its truth. He did not want to destroy their friendship, but he could not continue with this posturing and deception. He had never lied—never—even in the face of the greatest of temptations, and now here he was enmeshed in a whole web of deceit involving the police and one of Botswana's most powerful men!

She met him at the door of the No. 1 Ladies' Detective Agency. She was throwing the dregs from a teapot into the yard as he drew up in his garage van.

"Well?" she said. "Did everything go as planned?"

"Mma Ramotswe, I really think . . ."

"Did he come round himself, or did he send one of his men?"

"One of his men. But, listen, you are a fixer of lives, I am just . . ."

"And did you tell him that I could get the thing back? Did he seem interested?"

"I fix machines. I cannot . . . You see, I have never lied. I have never lied before, even when I was a small boy. My tongue would go stiff if I tried to lie, and I couldn't."

Mma Ramotswe upended the teapot for a final time.

"You've done very well this time. Lies are quite all right if you are lying for a good cause. Is it not a good cause to find out who killed an innocent child? Are lies worse than murder, Mr J.L.B. Matekoni? Do you think that?"

"Murder is worse. But . . ."

"Well there you are. You didn't think it through, did you? Now you know."

She looked at him and smiled, and he thought: I am lucky. She is smiling at me. There is nobody to love me in this world. Here is somebody who likes me and smiles at me. And she's right about murder. It's far worse than lies.

"Come in for tea," said Mma Ramotswe. "Mma Makutsi has boiled the kettle and we can drink tea while we decide what to do next."

CHAPTER NINETEEN

MR CHARLIE GOTSO, BA

MR CHARLIE Gotso looked at Mma Ramotswe. He respected fat women, and indeed had married one five years previously. She had proved to be a niggling, troublesome woman and eventually he had sent her down to live on a farm near Lobatse, with no telephone and a road that became impassable in wet weather. She had complained about his other women, insistently, shrilly, but what did she expect? Did she seriously think that he, Mr Charlie Gotso, would restrict himself to one woman, like a clerk from a Government department? When he had all that money and influence? And a BA as well? That was the trouble with marrying an uneducated woman who knew nothing of the circles in which he moved. He had been to Nairobi and Lusaka. He knew what people were thinking in places like that. An intelligent woman, a woman with a BA, would have known better; but then, he reminded himself, this fat woman down in Lobatse had borne him five children already and one had to acknowledge that fact. If only she would not carp on about other women.

"You are the woman from Matekoni?"

She did not like his voice. It was sandpaper-rough, and he slurred the ends of the words lazily, as if he could not be bothered to make himself clear. This came from contempt, she felt; if you were as powerful as he was, then why bother to communicate properly with your inferiors? As long as they understood what you wanted—that was the essential thing.

"Mr J.L.B. Matekoni asked me to help him, Rra. I am a private detective."

Mr Gotso stared at her, a slight smile playing on his lips.

"I have seen this place of yours. I saw a sign when I was driving past. A private detective agency for ladies, or something like that."

"Not just for ladies, Rra," said Mma Ramotswe. "We are lady detectives but we work for men too. Mr Patel, for example. He consulted us."

The smile became broader. "You think you can tell men things?"

Mma Ramotswe answered calmly. "Sometimes. It depends. Sometimes men are too proud to listen. We can't tell that sort of man anything."

He narrowed his eyes. The remark was ambiguous. She could have been suggesting he was proud, or she could be talking about other men. There were others, of course . . .

"So anyway," said Mr Gotso. "You know that I lost some property from my car. Matekoni says that you might know who took it and get it back for me?"

Mma Ramotswe inclined her head in agreement. "I have done that," she said. "I found out who broke into your car. They were just boys. A couple of boys."

Mr Gotso raised an eyebrow. "Their names? Tell me who they are."

"I cannot do that," said Mma Ramotswe.

"I want to smack them. You will tell me who they are."

Mma Ramotswe looked up at Mr Gotso and met his gaze. For a moment neither said anything. Then she spoke: "I gave them my word I would not give their names to anybody if they gave me back what they had stolen. It was a bargain." As she spoke, she looked around Mr Gotso's office. It was just behind the Mall, in an unprepossessing side street, marked on the outside with a large blue sign, GOTSO HOLDING ENTER-PRISES. Inside, the room was simply furnished, and if it were not for the photographs on the wall, you would hardly know that this was the room of a powerful man. But the photographs gave it away: Mr Gotso with Moeshoeshoe, King of the Basotho; Mr Gotso with Hastings Banda; Mr Gotso with Sobhuza II. This was a man whose influence extended beyond their borders.

"You made a promise on my behalf?"

"Yes, I did. It was the only way I could get the item back."

Mr Gotso appeared to think for a moment; Mma Ramotswe looked at one of the pictures more closely. Mr Gotso was giv-ing a cheque to some good cause and everybody was smiling; "Big cheque handed over for charity" ran the cut-out newspa-per headline below.

"Very well," he said. "I suppose that was all you could do. Now, where is this item of property?"

Mma Ramotswe reached into her handbag and took out the small leather pouch.

"This is what they gave me."

She put it on the table and he reached across and took it in his hand.

"This is not mine, of course. This is something which one of my men had. I was looking after it for him. I have no idea what it is."

"Muti, Rra. Medicine from a witch doctor."

Mr Gotso's look was steely.

"Oh yes? Some little charm for the superstitious?"

Mma Ramotswe shook her head.

"No, I don't think so. I think that is powerful stuff. I think that was probably rather expensive."

"Powerful?" His head stayed absolutely still as he spoke, she noticed. Only the lips moved as the unfinished words slid out.

"Yes. That is good. I would like to be able to get something like that myself. But I do not know where I can find it."

Mr Gotso moved slightly now, and the eyes slid down Mma Ramotswe's figure.

"Maybe I could help you, Mma."

She thought quickly, and then gave her answer. "I would like you to help me. Then maybe I could help you in some way."

He had reached for a cigarette from a small box on his table and was now lighting it. Again the head did not move.

"In what way could you help me, Mma? Do you think I'm a lonely man?"

"You are not lonely. I have heard that you are a man with many women friends. You don't need another."

"Surely I'm the best judge of that."

"No, I think you are a man who likes information. You need that to keep powerful. You need muti too, don't you?"

He took the cigarette out of his mouth and laid it on a large glass ashtray.

"You should be careful about saying things like that," he said. The words were well articulated now; he could speak clearly when he wanted to. "People who accuse others of witchcraft can regret it. Really regret it."

"But I am not accusing you of anything. I told you myself that I used it, didn't I? No, what I was saying was that you are a man who needs to know what's going on in this town. You can easily miss things if your ears are blocked with wax."

He picked up the cigarette again and drew on it.

"You can tell me things?"

Mma Ramotswe nodded. "I hear some very interesting things in my business. For example, I can tell you about that man who is trying to build a shop next to your shop in the Mall. You know him? Would you like to hear about what he did before he came to Gaborone? He wouldn't like people to know that, I think."

Mr Gotso opened his mouth and picked a fragment of tobacco from his teeth.

"You are a very interesting woman, Mma Ramotswe. I think I understand you very well. I will give you the name of the witch doctor if you give me this useful information. Would that suit you?"

Mma Ramotswe clicked her tongue in agreement. "That is very good. I shall be able to get something from this man which will help me get even better information. And if I hear anything else, well I shall be happy to let you know."

"You are a very good woman," said Mr Gotso, picking up a

small pad of paper. "I'm going to draw you a sketch-map. This man lives out in the bush not far from Molepolole. It is difficult to find his place, but this will show you just where to go. I warn you, by the way—he's not cheap. But if you say that you are a friend of Mr Charlie Gotso, then you will find that he takes off twenty percent. Which isn't at all bad, is it?"

CHAPTER TWENTY

MEDICAL MATTERS

SHE HAD the information now. She had a map to find a murderer, and she would find him. But there was still the detective agency to run, and cases which needed to be dealt with—including a case which involved a very different sort of doctor, and a hospital.

Mma Ramotswe had no stomach for hospitals; she disliked the smell of them; she shuddered at the sight of the patients sitting on benches in the sun, silenced by their suffering; she was frankly depressed by the pink day-pyjamas they gave to those who had come with TB. Hospitals were to her a *memento mori* in bricks and mortar; an awful reminder of the inevitable end that was coming to all of us but which she felt was best ignored while one got on with the business of life.

Doctors were another matter altogether, and Mma Ramotswe had always been impressed by them. She admired, in particular, their sense of the confidential and she took comfort in the fact that you could tell a doctor something and, like a priest, he would carry your secret to the grave. You never found this amongst lawyers, who were boastful people, on the whole, always prepared to tell a story at the expense of a client, and, when one came to think of it, some accountants were just as indiscreet in discussing who earned what. As far as doctors were concerned, though, you might try as hard as you might to get information out of them, but they were inevitably tight-lipped.

Which was as it should be, thought Mma Ramotswe. I should not like anybody else to know about my . . . What had she to be embarrassed about? She thought hard. Her weight was hardly a confidential matter, and anyway, she was proud of being a traditionally built African lady, unlike these terrible, stick-like creatures one saw in the advertisements. Then there were her corns—well, those were more or less on public display when she wore her sandals. Really, there was nothing that she felt she had to hide.

Now constipation was quite a different matter. It would be dreadful for the whole world to know about troubles of that nature. She felt terribly sorry for people who suffered from constipation, and she knew that there were many who did. There were probably enough of them to form a political party—with a chance of government perhaps—but what would such a party do if it was in power? Nothing, she imagined. It would try to pass legislation, but would fail.

She stopped her reverie, and turned to the business in hand. Her old friend, Dr Maketsi, had telephoned her from the hospital and asked if he could call in at her office on his way home that evening. She readily agreed; she and Dr Maketsi were both from Mochudi, and although he was ten years her senior she felt extremely close to him. So she cancelled her hair-braiding appointment in town and stayed at her desk, catching up on some tedious paperwork until Dr Maketsi's familiar voice called out: Ko! Ko! and he came into the office.

They exchanged family gossip for a while, drinking bush tea and reflecting on how Mochudi had changed since their day. She asked after Dr Maketsi's aunt, a retired teacher to whom half the village still turned for advice. She had not run out of steam, he said, and was now being pressed to stand for Parliament, which she might yet do.

"We need more women in public life," said Dr Maketsi. "They are very practical people, women. Unlike us men."

Mma Ramotswe was quick to agree. "If more women were in power, they wouldn't let wars break out," she said. "Women can't be bothered with all this fighting. We see war for what it is—a matter of broken bodies and crying mothers."

Dr Maketsi thought for a moment. He was thinking of Mrs Gandhi, who had a war, and Mrs Golda Meir, who also had a war, and then there was . . .

"Most of the time," he conceded. "Women are gentle most of the time, but they can be tough when they need to be."

Dr Maketsi was eager to change the subject now, as he feared that Mma Ramotswe might go on to ask him whether he could cook, and he did not want a repetition of the conversation he had had with a young woman who had returned from a year in the United States. She had said to him, challengingly, as if the difference in their ages were of no consequence: "If you eat, you should cook. It's as simple as that." These ideas came from America and may be all very well in theory, but had they made the Americans any happier? Surely there had to be some limits to all this progress, all this unsettling change. He had heard recently of men who were obliged by their wives to change the nappies of their babies. He shuddered at the thought; Africa was not ready for that, he reflected. There were some aspects of the old arrangements in Africa which were very appropriate and comfortable—if you were a man, which of course Dr Maketsi was.

"But these are big issues," he said jovially. "Talking about pumpkins doesn't make them grow." His mother-in-law said this frequently, and although he disagreed with almost everything she said, he found himself echoing her words only too often.

Mma Ramotswe laughed. "Why have you come to see me?" she said. "Do you want me to find you a new wife, maybe?"

Dr Maketsi clicked his tongue in mock disapproval. "I have come about a real problem," he said. "Not just about a little question of wives."

Mma Ramotswe listened as the doctor explained just how delicate his problem was and she assured him that she, like him, believed in confidentiality.

"Not even my secretary will get to hear what you tell me," she said.

"Good," said Dr Maketsi. "Because if I am wrong about this, and if anybody hears about it, I shall be very seriously embarrassed—as will the whole hospital. I don't want the Minister coming looking for me."

"I understand," said Mma Ramotswe. Her curiosity was thoroughly aroused now, and she was anxious to hear what juicy matter was troubling her friend. She had been burdened with several rather mundane cases recently, including a very demeaning one which involved tracing a rich man's dog. A dog! The only lady detective in the country should not have to stoop to such depths and indeed Mma Ramotswe would not have done so, had it not been for the fact that she needed the fee. The little white van had developed an ominous rattle in the engine and Mr J.L.B. Matekoni, called upon to consider the problem, had gently broken the news to her that it needed expensive repairs. And what a terrible, malodorous dog it had turned out to be; when she eventually found the animal being dragged along on a string by the group of urchins which had stolen it, the dog had rewarded its liberator with a bite on the ankle.

"I am worried about one of our young doctors," said Dr Maketsi. "He is called Dr Komoti. He's Nigerian."

"I see."

"I know that some people are suspicious of Nigerians," said Dr Maketsi.

"I believe that there are some people like that," said Mma Ramotswe, catching the doctor's eye and then looking away again quickly, almost guiltily.

Dr Maketsi drank the last of his bush tea and replaced his mug on the table.

"Let me tell you about our Dr Komoti," he said. "Starting from the time he first turned up for interview. It was my job to interview him, in fact, although I must admit that it was rather a formality. We were desperately short of people at the time and needed somebody who would be able to lend a hand in casualty. We can't really be too choosy, you know. Anyway, he seemed to have a reasonable C.V. and he had brought several references with him. He had been working in Nairobi for a few years, and so I telephoned the hospital he was at and they confirmed that he was perfectly all right. So I took him on.

"He started about six months ago. He was pretty busy in

casualty. You probably know what it's like in there. Road accidents, fights, the usual Friday evening business. Of course a lot of the work is just cleaning up, stopping the bleeding, the occasional resuscitation—that sort of thing.

"Everything seemed to be going well, but after Dr Komoti had been there about three weeks the consultant in charge had a word with me. He said that he thought that the new doctor was a bit rusty and that some of the things he did seemed a bit surprising. For example, he had sewed several wounds up quite badly and the stitching had to be redone.

"But sometimes he was really quite good. For example, a couple of weeks ago we had a woman coming in with a tension pneumothorax. That's a pretty serious matter. Air gets into the space round the lungs and makes the lung collapse, like a popped balloon. If this happens, you have to drain the air out as quickly as you can so that the lung can expand again.

"This is quite a tricky job for an inexperienced doctor. You've got to know where to put in the drain. If you get it wrong you could even puncture the heart or do all sorts of other damage. If you don't do it quickly, the patient can die. I almost lost somebody myself with one of these a few years ago. I got quite a fright over it.

"Dr Komoti turned out to be pretty good at this, and he undoubtedly saved this woman's life. The consultant turned up towards the end of the procedure and he let him finish it. He was impressed, and mentioned it to me. But at the same time, this is the same doctor who had failed to spot an obvious case of enlarged spleen the day before."

"He's inconsistent?" said Mma Ramotswe.

"Exactly," said Dr Maketsi. "One day he'll be fine, but the next day he'll come close to killing some unfortunate patient."

Mma Ramotswe thought for a moment, remembering a news item in *The Star*. "I was reading the other day about a bogus surgeon in Johannesburg," she said. "He practised for almost ten years and nobody knew that he had no qualifications. Then somebody spotted something by chance and they exposed him."

"It's extraordinary," said Dr Maketsi. "These cases crop up from time to time. And these people often get away with it for a long time—for years sometimes."

"Did you check up on his qualifications?" asked Mma Ramotswe. "It's easy enough to forge documents these days with photocopiers and laser printers—anybody can do it. Maybe he's not a doctor at all. He could have been a hospital porter or something like that."

Dr Maketsi shook his head. "We went through all that," he said. "We checked with his Medical School in Nigeria—that was a battle, I can tell you—and we also checked with the General Medical Council in Britain, where he did a registrar's job for two years. We even obtained a photograph from Nairobi, and it's the same man. So I'm pretty sure that he's exactly who he says he is."

"Couldn't you just test him?" asked Mma Ramotswe. "Couldn't you try to find out how much he knows about medicine by just asking him some tricky questions?"

Dr Maketsi smiled. "I've done that already. I've taken the opportunity to speak to him about one or two difficult cases. On the first occasion he coped quite well, and he gave a fairly good answer. He clearly knew what he was talking about. But on the second occasion, he seemed evasive. He said that he wanted to think about it. This annoyed me, and so I mentioned something about the case we had discussed before.

This took him off his guard, and he just mumbled something inconsequential. It was as if he had forgotten what he'd said to me three days before."

Mma Ramotswe looked up at the ceiling. She knew about forgetfulness. Her poor Daddy had become forgetful at the end and had sometimes barely remembered her. That was understandable in the old, but not in a young doctor. Unless he was ill, of course, and in that case something could have gone wrong with his memory.

"There's nothing wrong with him mentally," said Dr Maketsi, as if predicting her question. "As far as I can tell, that is. This isn't a case of pre-senile dementia or anything like that. What I'm afraid of is drugs. I think that he's possibly abusing drugs and that half the time he's treating patients he's not exactly there."

Dr Maketsi paused. He had delivered his bombshell, and he sat back, as if silenced by the implications of what he had said. This was almost as bad as if they had been allowing an unqualified doctor to practise. If the Minister heard that a doctor was treating patients in the hospital while high on drugs, he might begin to question the closeness of supervision in the hospital.

He imagined the interview. "Now Dr Maketsi, could you not see from the way this man was behaving that he was drugged? Surely you people should be able to spot things like that. If it's obvious enough to me when I walk down the street that somebody has been smoking *dagga,* then surely it should be obvious enough to somebody like you. Or am I fondly imagining that you people are more perceptive than you really are . . ."

"I can see why you're worried," said Mma Ramotswe. "But I'm not sure whether I can help. I don't really know my way around the drug scene. That's really a police matter."

Dr Maketsi was dismissive. "Don't talk to me about the police," he said. "They never keep their mouths shut. If I went to them to get this looked into, they'd treat it as a straightforward drugs enquiry. They'd barge in and search his house and then somebody would talk about it. In no time at all word would be all about town that he was a drug addict." He paused, concerned that Mma Ramotswe should understand the subtleties of his dilemma. "And what if he isn't? What if I'm wrong? Then I would have as good as killed his reputation for no reason. He may be incompetent from time to time, but that's no reason for destroying him."

"But if we did find out that he was using drugs," said Mma Ramotswe. "And I'm not sure how we could do this, what then? Would you dismiss him?"

Dr Maketsi shook his head vigorously. "We don't think about drugs in those terms. It isn't a question of good behaviour and bad behaviour. I'd look on it as a medical problem and I'd try to help him. I'd try to sort out the problem."

"But you can't 'sort out' with those people," said Mma Ramotswe. "Smoking *dagga* is one thing, but using pills and all the rest is another. Show me one reformed drug addict. Just one. Maybe they exist; I've just never seen them."

Dr Maketsi shrugged. "I know they can be very manipulative people," he said. "But some of them get off it. I can show you some figures."

"Well, maybe, maybe not," said Mma Ramotswe. "The point is: what do you want me to do?"

"Find out about him," said Dr Maketsi. "Follow him for a few days. Find out whether he's involved in the drug scene. If he is, find out whether he's supplying others with drugs while you are about it. Because that will be another problem for us.

We keep a tight rein on drugs in the hospital, but things can go missing, and the last thing we want is a doctor who's passing hospital drug supplies to addicts. We can't have that."

"You'd sack him then?" goaded Mma Ramotswe. "You wouldn't try to help him?"

Dr Maketsi laughed. "We'd sack him good and proper."

"Good," said Mma Ramotswe. "And proper too. Now I have to tell you about my fee."

Dr Maketsi's face fell. "I was worried about that. This is such a delicate enquiry, I could hardly get the hospital to pay for it."

Mma Ramotswe nodded knowingly. "You thought that as an old friend . . ."

"Yes," said Dr Maketsi quietly. "I thought that as an old friend you might remember how when your Daddy was so ill at the end . . ."

Mma Ramotswe did remember. Dr Maketsi had come unfailingly to the house every evening for three weeks and eventually had arranged for her Daddy to be put in a private room at the hospital, all for nothing.

"I remember very well," she said. "I only mentioned the fee to tell you that there would be none."

SHE HAD all the information she needed to start her investigation of Dr Komoti. She had his address in Kaunda Way; she had a photograph, supplied by Dr Maketsi; and she had a note of the number of the green station wagon which he drove. She had also been given his telephone number, and the number of his postal box at the Post Office, although she could not imagine the circumstances in which she might need these. Now all she had to do was to start to watch Dr Komoti and to learn as much as she could about him in the shortest possible time.

Dr Maketsi had thoughtfully provided her with a copy of the duty rota in the casualty department for the following four months. This meant that Mma Ramotswe would know exactly when he might be expected to leave the hospital to return home and also when he might be on night duty. This would save a great deal of time and effort in sitting waiting in the street in the tiny white van.

She started two days later. She was there when Dr Komoti drove out of the staff car park at the hospital that afternoon and she followed him discreetly into town, parking a few cars away from him and waiting until he was well away from the car park before she got out of the van. He visited one or two shops and picked up a newspaper from the Book Centre. Then he returned to his car, drove straight home, and stayed there—blamelessly, she assumed—until the lights went out in the house just before ten that evening. It was a dull business sitting in the tiny white van, but Mma Ramotswe was used to it and never complained once she had agreed to take on a matter. She would sit in her van for a whole month, even more, if asked to do so by Dr Maketsi; it was the least she could do after what he had done for her Daddy.

Nothing happened that evening, nor the next evening. Mma Ramotswe was beginning to wonder whether there was ever any variety to the routine of Dr Komoti's life when suddenly things changed. It was a Friday afternoon, and Mma Ramotswe was ready to follow Dr Komoti back from work. The doctor was slightly late in leaving the hospital, but eventually he came out of the casualty entrance, a stethoscope tucked into the pocket of his white coat, and climbed into his car.

Mma Ramotswe followed him out of the hospital grounds, satisfied that he was not aware of her presence. She suspected that he might go to the Book Centre for his newspaper, but this time instead of turning into town, he turned the other way. Mma Ramotswe was pleased that something at last might be happening, and she concentrated carefully on not losing him as they made their way through the traffic. The roads were busier than usual, as it was a Friday afternoon at the end of the month, and this meant payday. That evening there would be more road accidents than normal, and whoever was taking Dr Komoti's place in casualty would be kept more than occupied stitching up the drunks and picking the shattered windscreen glass out of the road accident cases.

Mma Ramotswe was surprised to find that Dr Komoti was heading for the Lobatse Road. This was interesting. If he was dealing in drugs, then to use Lobatse as a base would be a good idea. It was close enough to the border, and he might be passing things into South Africa, or picking things up there. Whatever it was, it made him a much more interesting man to follow.

They drove down, the tiny white van straining to keep Dr Komoti's more powerful car in sight. Mma Ramotswe was not worried about being spotted; the road was busy and there was no reason why Dr Komoti should single out the tiny white van. Once they got to Lobatse of course, she would have to be more circumspect, as he could notice her in the thinner traffic there.

When they did not stop in Lobatse, Mma Ramotswe began to worry. If he was going to drive straight through Lobatse it was possible that he was visiting some village on the other side of the town. But this was rather unlikely, as there was not much on the other side of Lobatse—or not much to interest somebody like Dr Komoti. The only other thing, then, was the border, some miles down the road. Yes! Dr Komoti was going over the border, she was sure of it. He was going to Mafikeng.

As the realisation dawned that Dr Komoti's destination was out of the country, Mma Ramotswe felt an intense irritation with her own stupidity. She did not have her passport with her; Dr Komoti would go through, and she would have to remain in Botswana. And once he was on the other side, then he could do whatever he liked—and no doubt would—and she would know nothing about it.

She watched him stop at the border post, and then she turned back, like a hunter who has chased his prey to the end of his preserve and must now give up. He would be away for the weekend now, and she knew as little about what he did with his time as she did about the future. Next week, she would have to get back to the tedious task of watching his house by night, in the frustrating knowledge that the real mischief had taken place over the weekend. And while she was doing all this, she would have to postpone other cases—cases which carried fees and paid garage bills.

When she arrived back in Gaborone, Mma Ramotswe was in a thoroughly bad mood. She had an early night, but the bad mood was still with her the following morning when she went into the Mall. As she often did on a Saturday morning, she had a cup of coffee on the verandah of the President Hotel and enjoyed a chat with her friend Grace Gakatsla. Grace, who had a dress shop in Broadhurst, always cheered her up with her stories of the vagaries of her customers. One, a Government Minister's wife, had recently bought a dress on a Friday and brought it back the following Monday, saying that it did not really fit. Yet Grace had been at the wedding on Saturday where the dress had been worn, and it had looked perfect.

"Of course I couldn't tell her to her face she was a liar and that I wasn't a dress-hire shop," said Grace. "So I asked her if she had enjoyed the wedding. She smiled and said that she had. So I said I enjoyed it too. She obviously hadn't seen me there. She stopped smiling and she said that maybe she'd give the dress another chance."

"She's just a porcupine, that woman," said Mma Ramotswe. "A hyena," said Grace. "An anteater, with her long nose."

The laughter had died away, and Grace had gone off, allowing Mma Ramotswe's bad mood to settle back in place. It seemed to her that she might continue to feel like this for the rest of the weekend; in fact, she was worried that it could last until the Komoti case was finished—if she ever finished it.

Mma Ramotswe paid her bill and left, and it was then, as she was walking down the front steps of the hotel, that she saw Dr Komoti in the Mall.

FOR A moment Mma Ramotswe stood quite still. Dr Komoti had crossed the border last night just before seven in the evening. The border closed at eight, which meant that he could not possibly have had time to get down to Mafikeng, which was a further forty minutes' drive, and back in time to cross again before the border closed. So he had only spent one evening there and had come back first thing that morning.

She recovered from her surprise at seeing him and realised that she should make good use of the opportunity to follow him and see what he did. He was now in the hardware store, and Mma Ramotswe lingered outside, looking idly at the contents of the window until he came out again. Then he walked purposefully back to the car park and she watched him getting into his car.

Dr Komoti stayed in for the rest of the day. At six in the evening he went off to the Sun Hotel where he had a drink with two other men, whom Mma Ramotswe recognised as fellow Nigerians. She knew that one of them worked for a firm of accountants, and the other, she believed, was a primary schoolteacher somewhere. There was nothing about their meeting which seemed suspicious; there would be many such groups of people meeting right at this moment throughout the town— people thrown together in the artificial closeness of the expatriate life, talking about home.

He stayed an hour and then left, and that was the extent of Dr Komoti's social life for the weekend. By Sunday evening, Mma Ramotswe had decided that she would report to Dr Maketsi the following week and tell him that there was unfortunately no evidence of his moving in drug-abusing circles and that he seemed, by contrast, to be the model of sobriety and respectability. There was not even a sign of women, unless they were hiding in the house and never came out. Nobody had arrived at the house while she was watching, and nobody had left, apart from Dr Komoti himself. He was, quite simply, rather a boring man to watch.

But there was still the question of Mafikeng and the Friday evening dash there and back. If he had been going shopping down there in the OK Bazaars—as many people did—then he would surely have stayed for at least part of Saturday morning, which he clearly did not. He must have done, then, whatever it was he wanted to do on Friday evening. Was there a woman down there—one of those flashy South African women whom

men, so unaccountably, seemed to like? That would be the simple explanation, and the most likely one too. But why the hurry
back on Saturday morning? Why not stay for Saturday and take
her to lunch at the Mmbabatho Hotel? There was something
which did not seem quite right, and Mma Ramotswe thought
that she might follow him down to Mafikeng next weekend, if
he went, and see what happened. If there was nothing to be
seen, then she could do some shopping and return on Saturday afternoon. She had been meaning to make the trip anyway,
and she might as well kill two birds with one stone.

DR KOMOTI proved obliging. The following Friday he left the
hospital on time and drove off in the direction of Lobatse, followed at a distance by Mma Ramotswe in her van. Crossing
the border proved tricky, as Mma Ramotswe had to make sure
that she did not get too close to him at the border post, and
that at the same time she did not lose him on the other side.
For a few moments it looked as if she would be delayed, as a
ponderous official paged closely through her passport, looking
at the stamps which reflected her coming and going to Johannesburg and Mafikeng.

"It says here, under occupation, that you are a detective," he
said in a surly tone. "How can a woman be a detective?"

Mma Ramotswe glared at him. If she prolonged the encounter, she could lose Dr Komoti, whose passport was now
being stamped. In a few minutes he would be through the border controls, and the tiny white van would have no chance of
catching up with him.

"Many women are detectives," said Mma Ramotswe, with
dignity. "Have you not read Agatha Christie?"

The clerk looked up at her and bristled.

"Are you saying I am not an educated man?" he growled. "Is that what you are saying? That I have not read this Mr Christie?"

"I am not," said Mma Ramotswe. "You people are well educated, and efficient. Only yesterday, when I was in your Minister's house, I said to him that I thought his immigration people were very polite and efficient. We had a good talk about it over supper."

The official froze. For a moment he looked uncertain, but then he reached for his rubber stamp and stamped the passport.

"Thank you, Mma," he said. "You may go now."

Mma Ramotswe did not like lying, but sometimes it was necessary, particularly when faced with people who were promoted beyond their talents. An embroidering of the truth like that—she knew the Minister, even if only very distantly—sometimes gingered people up a bit, and it was often for their own good. Perhaps that particular official would think twice before he again decided to bully a woman for no good reason.

She climbed back into the van and was waved past the barrier. There was now no sight of Dr Komoti and she had to push the van to its utmost before she caught up with him. He was not going particularly fast, and so she dropped back slightly and followed him past the remnants of Mangope's capital and its fantouche Republic of Bophuthatswana. There was the stadium in which the president had been held by his own troops when they revolted; there were the government offices that administered the absurdly fragmented state on behalf of its masters in Pretoria. It was all such a waste, she thought, such an utter folly, and when the time had come it had just faded away like the illusion that it had always been. It was all part of the farce of apartheid and the monstrous dream of Verwoerd; such pain, such long-drawn-out suffering—to be added by history to all the pain of Africa.

Dr Komoti suddenly turned right. They had reached the outskirts of Mafikeng, in a suburb of neat, well-laid-out streets and houses with large, well-fenced gardens. It was into the driveway of one of these houses that he turned, requiring Mma Ramotswe to drive past to avoid causing suspicion. She counted the number of houses she passed, though—seven—and then parked the van under a tree.

There was what used to be called a sanitary lane which ran down the back of the houses. Mma Ramotswe left the van and walked to the end of the sanitary lane. The house that Dr Komoti entered would be eight houses up—seven, and the one she had had to walk past to get to the entrance to the lane.

She stood in the sanitary lane at the back of the eighth house and peered through the garden. Somebody had once cared for it, but that must have been years ago. Now it was a tangle of vegetation—mulberry trees, uncontrolled bougainvillaea bushes that had grown to giant proportions and sent great sprigs of purple flowers skywards, paw-paw trees with rotting fruit on the stems. It would be a paradise for snakes, she thought; there could be mambas lurking in the uncut grass and boomslangs draped over the branches of the trees, all of them lying in wait for somebody like her to be foolish enough to enter.

She pushed the gate open gingerly. It had clearly not been used for a long time, and the hinge squeaked badly. But this did not really matter, as little sound would penetrate the vegetation that shielded the back fence from the house, about a hundred yards away. In fact, it was virtually impossible to see the house through the greenery, which made Mma Ramotswe feel safe, from the eyes of those within the house at least, if not from snakes.

Mma Ramotswe moved forward gingerly, placing each foot carefully and expecting at any moment to hear a hiss from a protesting snake. But nothing moved, and she was soon crouching under a mulberry tree as close as she dared to get to the house. From the shade of the tree she had a good view of the back door and the open kitchen window; yet she could not see into the house itself, as it was of the old colonial style, with wide eaves, which made the interior cool and dark. It was far easier to spy on people who live in modern houses, because architects today had forgotten about the sun and put people in goldfish bowls where the whole world could peer in through large unprotected windows, should they so desire.

Now what should she do? She could stay where she was in the hope that somebody came out of the back door, but why should they bother to do that? And if they did, then what would she do?

Suddenly a window at the back of the house opened and a man leaned out. It was Dr Komoti.

"You! You over there! Yes, you, fat lady! What are you doing sitting under our mulberry tree?"

Mma Ramotswe experienced a sudden, absurd urge to look over her shoulder, as if to imply that there was somebody else under the tree. She felt like a schoolgirl caught stealing fruit, or doing some other forbidden act. There was nothing one could say; one just had to own up.

She stood up and stepped out from the shade.

"It is hot," she called out. "Can you give me a drink of water?"

The window closed and a moment or two later the kitchen door opened. Dr Komoti stood on the step wearing, she noticed, quite different clothes from those he had on when he left Gaborone. He had a mug of water in his hand, which he gave to her. Mma Ramotswe reached out and drank the water gratefully. She was, in fact, thirsty, and the water was welcome, although she noticed that the mug was dirty.

"What are you doing in our garden?" said Dr Komoti, not unkindly. "Are you a thief?"

Mma Ramotswe looked pained. "I am not," she said.

Dr Komoti looked at her coolly. "Well, then, if you are not a thief, then what do you want? Are you looking for work? If so, we already have a woman who comes to cook in this house. We do not need anybody."

Mma Ramotswe was about to utter her reply when somebody appeared behind Dr Komoti and looked out over his shoulder. It was Dr Komoti.

"What's going on?" said the second Dr Komoti. "What does this woman want?"

"I saw her in the garden," said the first Dr Komoti. "She tells me she isn't a thief."

"And I certainly am not," she said indignantly. "I was looking at this house."

The two men looked puzzled.

"Why?" one of them asked. "Why would you want to look at this house? There's nothing special about it, and it's not for sale anyway."

Mma Ramotswe tossed her head back and laughed. "Oh,

I'm not here to buy it," she said. "It's just that I used to live here when I was a little girl. There were Boers living in it then, a Mr van der Heever and his wife. My mother was their cook, you see, and we lived in the servants' quarters back there at the end of the garden. My father kept the garden tidy . . ."

She broke off, and looked at the two men in reproach.

"It was better in those days," she said. "The garden was well looked after."

"Oh, I'm sure it was," said one of the two. "We'd like to get it under control one day. It's just that we're busy men. We're both doctors, you see, and we have to spend all our time in the hospital."

"Ah!" said Mma Ramotswe, trying to sound reverential. "You are doctors here at the hospital?"

"No," said the first Dr Komoti. "I have a surgery down near the railway station. My brother . . ."

"I work up that way," said the other Dr Komoti, pointing vaguely to the north. "Anyway, you can look at the garden as much as you like, mother. You just go ahead. We can make you a mug of tea."

"Ow!" said Mma Ramotswe. "You are very kind. Thank you."

IT WAS a relief to get away from that garden, with its sinister undergrowth and its air of neglect. For a few minutes, Mma Ramotswe pretended to inspect the trees and the shrubs—or what could be seen of them—and then, thanking her hosts for the tea, she walked off down the road. Her mind busily turned over the curious information she had obtained. There were two Dr Komotis, which was nothing terribly unusual in itself; yet somehow she felt that this was the essence of the whole matter. There was no reason, of course, why there should not be twins who both went to medical school—twins often led mirrored lives, and sometimes even went so far as to marry the sister of the other's wife. But there was something particularly significant here, and Mma Ramotswe was sure that it was staring her in the face, if only she could begin to see it.

She got into the tiny white van and drove back down the road towards the centre of town. One Dr Komoti had said that he had a surgery in town, near the railway station, and she decided to take a look at this—not that a brass plate, if he had one, would reveal a great deal.

She knew the railway station slightly. It was a place that she enjoyed visiting, as it reminded her of the old Africa, the days of uncomfortable companionship on crowded trains, of slow journeys across great plains, of the sugarcane you used to eat to while away the time, and of the pith of the cane you used to spit out of the wide windows. Here you could still see it—or a part of it—here, where the trains that came up from the Cape pulled slowly past the platform on their journey up through Botswana to Bulawayo; here, where the Indian stores beside the railway buildings still sold cheap blankets and men's hats with a garish feather tucked into the band.

Mma Ramotswe did not want Africa to change. She did not want her people to become like everybody else, soulless, selfish, forgetful of what it means to be an African, or, worse still, ashamed of Africa. She would not be anything but an African, never, even if somebody came up to her and said "Here is a pill, the very latest thing. Take it and it will make you into an American." She would say no. Never. No thank you.

She stopped the white van outside the railway station and got out. There were a lot of people about; women selling roasted maize cobs and sweet drinks; men talking loudly to their friends; a family, travelling, with cardboard suitcases and possessions bundled up in a blanket. A child pushing a home-made toy car of twisted wire bumped into Mma Ramotswe and scurried off without an apology, frightened of rebuke.

She approached one of the woman traders and spoke to her in Setswana.

"Are you well today, Mma?" she said politely.

"I am well, and you are well too, Mma?"

"I am well, and I have slept very well."

"Good."

The greeting over, she said: "People tell me that there is a doctor here who is very good. They call him Dr Komoti. Do you know where his place is?"

The woman nodded. "There are many people who go to that doctor. His place is over there, do you see, where that white man has just parked his truck. That's where he is."

Mma Ramotswe thanked her informant and bought a cob of roasted maize. Then, tackling the cob as she walked, she walked across the dusty square to the rather dilapidated tin-roofed building where Dr Komoti's surgery was to be found.

Rather to her surprise, the door was not locked, and when she pushed it open she found a woman standing directly in front of her.

"I am sorry, the doctor isn't here, Mma," said the woman, slightly testily. "I am the nurse. You can see the doctor on Monday afternoon."

"Ah!" said Mma Ramotswe. "It is a sad thing to have to tidy up on a Friday evening, when everybody else is thinking of going out."

The nurse shrugged her shoulders. "My boyfriend is taking

me out later on. But I like to get everything ready for Monday before the weekend starts. It is better that way."

"Far better," Mma Ramotswe answered, thinking quickly. "I didn't actually want to see the doctor, or not as a patient. I used to work for him, you see, when he was up in Nairobi. I was a nurse on his ward. I wanted just to say hallo."

The nurse's manner became markedly more friendly.

"I'll make you some tea, Mma," she offered. "It is still quite hot outside."

Mma Ramotswe sat down and waited for the nurse to return with the pot of tea.

"Do you know the other Dr Komoti?" she said. "The brother?"

"Oh yes," said the nurse. "We see a lot of him. He comes in here to help, you see. Two or three times a week."

Mma Ramotswe lowered her cup, very slowly. Her heart thumped within her; she realised that she was at the heart of the matter now, the elusive solution within her grasp. But she would have to sound casual.

"Oh, they did that up in Nairobi too," she said, waving her hand airily, as if these things were of little consequence. "One helped the other. And usually the patients didn't know that they were seeing a different doctor."

The nurse laughed. "They do it here too," she said. "I'm not sure if it's quite fair on the patients, but nobody has realised that there are two of them. So everybody seems quite satisfied."

Mma Ramotswe picked up her cup again and passed it for refilling. "And what about you?" she said. "Can you tell them apart?"

The nurse handed the teacup back to Mma Ramotswe. "I

can tell by one thing," she said. "One of them is quite good—the other's hopeless. The hopeless one knows hardly anything about medicine. If you ask me, it's a miracle that he got through medical school."

Mma Ramotswe thought, but did not say: He didn't.

SHE STAYED in Mafikeng that night, at the Station Hotel, which was noisy and uncomfortable, but she slept well nonetheless, as she always did when she had just finished an enquiry. The next morning she shopped at the OK Bazaars and found, to her delight, that there was a rail of size 22 dresses on special offer. She bought three—two more than she really needed—but if you were the owner of the No. 1 Ladies' Detective Agency you had to keep up a certain style.

She was home by three o'clock that afternoon and she telephoned Dr Maketsi at his house and invited him to come immediately to her office to be informed of the results of her enquiry. He arrived within ten minutes and sat opposite her in the office, fiddling anxiously with the cuffs of his shirt.

"First of all," announced Mma Ramotswe, "no drugs."

Dr Maketsi breathed a sigh of relief. "Thank goodness for that," he said. "That's one thing I was really worried about."

"Well," said Mma Ramotswe doubtfully. "I'm not sure if you're going to like what I'm going to tell you."

"He's not qualified," gasped Dr Maketsi. "Is that it?"

"One of them is qualified," said Mma Ramotswe.

Dr Maketsi looked blank. "One of them?"

Mma Ramotswe settled back in her chair with the air of one about to reveal a mystery.

"There were once two twins," she began. "One went to medical school and became a doctor. The other did not. The one with the qualification got a job as a doctor, but was greedy and thought that two jobs as a doctor would pay better than one. So he took two jobs, and did both of them part-time. When he wasn't there, his brother, who was his identical twin, you'll recall, did the job for him. He used such medical knowledge as he had picked up from his qualified brother and no doubt also got advice from the brother as to what to do. And that's it. That's the story of Dr Komoti, and his twin brother in Mafikeng."

Dr Maketsi sat absolutely silent. As Mma Ramotswe spoke he had sunk his head in his hands and for a moment she thought that he was going to cry.

"So we've had both of them in the hospital," he said at last. "Sometimes we've had the qualified one, and sometimes we've had the twin brother."

"Yes," said Mma Ramotswe simply. "For three days a week, say, you've had the qualified twin while the unqualified twin practised as a general practitioner in a surgery near Mafikeng Railway Station. Then they'd change about, and I assume that the qualified one would pick up any pieces which the unqualified one had left lying around, so to speak."

"Two jobs for the price of one medical degree," mused Dr Maketsi. "It's the most cunning scheme I've come across for a long, long time."

"I have to admit I was amazed by it," said Mma Ramotswe. "I thought that I'd seen all the varieties of human dishonesty, but obviously one can still be surprised from time to time."

Dr Maketsi rubbed his chin.

"I'll have to go to the police about this," he said. "There's going to have to be a prosecution. We have to protect the public from people like this."

"Unless . . ." started Mma Ramotswe.

Dr Maketsi grabbed at the straw he suspected she might be offering him.

"Can you think of an alternative?" he asked. "Once this gets out, people will take fright. We'll have people encouraging others not to go to hospital. Our public health programmes rely on trust—you know how it is."

"Precisely," said Mma Ramotswe. "I suggest that we transfer the heat elsewhere. I agree with you: the public has to be protected and Dr Komoti is going to have to be struck off, or whatever you people do. But why not get this done in somebody else's patch?"

"Do you mean in Mafikeng?"

"Yes," said Mma Ramotswe. "After all, an offence is being committed down there and we can let the South Africans deal with it. The papers up here in Gaborone probably won't even pick up on it. All that people here will know is that Dr Komoti resigned suddenly, which people often do—for all sorts of reasons."

"Well," said Dr Maketsi. "I would rather like to keep the Minister's nose out of all this. I don't think it would help if he became . . . how shall we put it, upset?"

"Of course it wouldn't help," said Mma Ramotswe. "With your permission I shall telephone my friend Billy Pilani, who's a police captain down there. He'd love to be seen to expose a bogus doctor. Billy likes a good, sensational arrest."

"You do that," said Dr Maketsi, smiling. This was a tidy solution to a most extraordinary matter, and he was most impressed with the way in which Mma Ramotswe had handled it.

"You know," he said, "I don't think that even my aunt in Mochudi could have dealt with this any better than you have."

Mma Ramotswe smiled at her old friend. You can go through life and make new friends every year—every month practically—but there was never any substitute for those friendships of childhood that survive into adult years. Those are the ones in which we are bound to one another with hoops of steel.

She reached out and touched Dr Maketsi on the arm, gently, as old friends will sometimes do when they have nothing more to say.

THE WITCH DOCTOR'S WIFE

A DUSTY track, hardly in use, enough to break the springs; a hill, a tumble of boulders, just as the sketch map drawn by Mr Charlie Gotso had predicted; and above, stretching from horizon to horizon, the empty sky, singing in the heat of noon.

Mma Ramotswe steered the tiny white van cautiously, avoiding the rocks that could tear the sump from the car, wondering why nobody came this way. This was dead country; no cattle, no goats; only the bush and the stunted thorn trees. That anybody should want to live here, away from a village, away from human contact, seemed inexplicable. Dead country.

Suddenly she saw the house, tucked away behind the trees, almost in the shadow of the hill. It was a bare earth house in the traditional style; brown mud walls, a few glassless windows, with a knee-height wall around the yard. A previous owner, a long time ago, had painted designs on the wall, but neglect and the years had scaled them off and only their ghosts remained.

She parked the van and drew in her breath. She had faced down fraudsters; she had coped with jealous wives; she had even stood up to Mr Gotso; but this meeting would be different. This was evil incarnate, the heart of darkness, the root of shame. This man, for all his mumbo-jumbo and his spells, was a murderer.

She opened the door and eased herself out of the van. The sun was riding high and its light prickled at her skin. They were too far west here, too close to the Kalahari, and her unease increased. This was not the comforting land she had grown up with; this was the merciless Africa, the waterless land.

She made her way towards the house, and as she did so she felt that she was being watched. There was no movement, but eyes were upon her, eyes from within the house. At the wall, in accordance with custom, she stopped and called out, announcing herself.

"I am very hot," she said. "I need water."

There was no reply from within the house, but a rustle to her left, amongst the bushes. She turned round, almost guiltily, and stared. It was a large black beetle, a setotojane, with its horny neck, pushing at a minute trophy, some insect that had died of thirst perhaps. Little disasters, little victories; like ours, she thought; when viewed from above we are no more than setotojane.

"Mma?"

She turned round sharply. A woman was standing in the doorway, wiping her hands on a cloth.

Mma Ramotswe stepped through the gateless break in the wall.

"Dumela Mma," she said. "I am Mma Ramotswe."

The woman nodded. "Eee. I am Mma Notshi."

Mma Ramotswe studied her. She was a woman in her late fifties, or thereabouts, wearing a long skirt of the sort which the Herero women wore; but she was not Herero—she could tell.

"I have come to see your husband," she said. "I have to ask him for something."

The woman came out from the shadows and stood before Mma Ramotswe, peering at her face in a disconcerting way.

"You have come for something? You want to buy something from him?"

Mma Ramotswe nodded. "I have heard that he is a very good doctor. I have trouble with another woman. She is taking my husband from me and I want something that will stop her."

The older woman smiled. "He can help you. Maybe he has something. But he is away. He is in Lobatse until Saturday. You will have to come back some time after that."

Mma Ramotswe sighed. "This has been a long trip, and I am thirsty. Do you have water, my sister?"

"Yes, I have water. You can come and sit in the house while you drink it."

IT WAS a small room, furnished with a rickety table and two chairs. There was a grain bin in the corner, of the traditional sort, and a battered tin trunk. Mma Ramotswe sat on one of the chairs while the woman fetched a white enamel mug of water, which she gave to her visitor. The water was slightly rancid, but Mma Ramotswe drank it gratefully.

Then she put the mug down and looked at the woman.

"I have come for something, as you know. But I have also come to warn you of something."

The woman lowered herself onto the other chair.

"To warn me?"

"Yes," said Mma Ramotswe. "I am a typist. Do you know what that is?"

The woman nodded.

"I work for the police," went on Mma Ramotswe. "And I have typed out something about your husband. They know that he killed that boy, the one from Katsana. They know that he is the man who took him and killed him for muti. They are going to arrest your husband soon and then they will hang him. I came to warn you that they will hang you also, because they say that you are involved in it too. They say that you did it too. I do not think they should hang women. So I came to tell you that you could stop all this quickly if you came with me to the police and told them what happened. They will believe you and you will be saved. Otherwise, you will die very soon. Next month, I think."

She stopped. The other woman had dropped the cloth she had been carrying and was staring at her, wide-eyed. Mma Ramotswe knew the odour of fear—that sharp, acrid smell that people emit through the pores of their skin when they are frightened; now the torpid air was heavy with that smell.

"Do you understand what I have said to you?" she asked.

The witch doctor's wife closed her eyes. "I did not kill that boy."

"I know," said Mma Ramotswe. "It is never the women who do it. But that doesn't make any difference to the police. They have evidence against you and the Government wants to hang you too. Your husband first; you later. They do not like witchcraft, you know. They are ashamed. They think it's not modern."

"But the boy is not dead," blurted out the woman. "He is at the cattle post where my husband took him. He is working there. He is still alive."

MMA RAMOTSWE opened the door for the woman and slammed it shut behind her. Then she went round to the driver's door, opened it, and eased herself into the seat. The sun had made it burning hot—hot enough to scorch through the cloth of her dress—but pain did not matter now. All that mattered was to make the journey, which the woman said would take four hours. It was now one o'clock. They would be there just before sunset and they could start the journey back immediately. If they had to stop overnight because the track was too bad, well, they could sleep in the back of the van. The important thing was to get to the boy.

The journey was made in silence. The other woman tried to talk, but Mma Ramotswe ignored her. There was nothing she could say to this woman; nothing she wanted to say to her.

"You are not a kind woman," said the witch doctor's wife finally. "You are not talking to me. I am trying to talk to you, but you ignore me. You think that you are better than me, don't you."

Mma Ramotswe half-turned to her. "The only reason why you are showing me where this boy is is because you are afraid.

You are not doing it because you want him to go back to his parents. You don't care about that, do you? You are a wicked woman and I am warning you that if the police hear that you and your husband practise any more witchcraft, they will come and take you to prison. And if they don't, I have friends in Gaborone who will come and do it for them. Do you understand what I am saying?"

The hours passed. It was a difficult journey, out across open veld, on the barest of tracks, until there, in the distance, they saw cattle stockades and the cluster of trees around a couple of huts.

"This is the cattle post," said the woman. "There are two Basarwa there—a man and a woman—and the boy who has been working for them."

"How did you keep him?" asked Mma Ramotswe. "How did you know that he would not run away?"

"Look around you," said the woman. "You see how lonely this place is. The Basarwa would catch him before he could get far."

Something else occurred to Mma Ramotswe. The bone—if the boy was still alive, then where did the bone come from?

"There is a man in Gaborone who bought a bone from your husband," she said. "Where did you get that?"

The woman looked at her scornfully "You can buy bones in Johannesburg. Did you not know that? They are not expensive."

THE BASARWA were eating a rough porridge, seated on two stones outside one of the huts. They were tiny, wizened people, with the wide eyes of the hunter, and they stared at the intruders. Then the man rose to his feet and saluted the witch doctor's wife.

"Are the cattle all right?" she asked sharply.

The man made a strange, clicking noise with his tongue. "All right. They are not dead. That cow there is making much milk."

The words were Setswana words, but one had to strain to understand them. This was a man who spoke in the clicks and whistles of the Kalahari.

"Where is the boy?" snapped the woman.

"That side," replied the man. "Look."

And then they saw the boy, standing beside a bush, watching them uncertainly. A dusty little boy, in torn pants, with a stick in his hand.

"Come here," called the witch doctor's wife. "Come here."

The boy walked over to them, his eyes fixed on the ground in front of him. He had a scar on his forearm, a thick weal, and Mma Ramotswe knew immediately what had caused it. That was the cut of a whip, a sjambok.

She reached forward and laid a hand on his shoulder.

"What is your name?" she asked gently. "Are you the teacher's son from Katsana Village?"

The boy shivered, but he saw the concern in her eyes and he spoke.

"I am that boy. I am working here now. These people are making me look after the cattle."

"And did this man strike you?" whispered Mma Ramotswe. "Did he?"

"All the time," said the boy. "He said that if I ran away he would find me in the bush and put a sharpened stick through me."

"You are safe now," said Mma Ramotswe. "You are coming with me. Right now. Just walk in front of me. I will look after you."

The boy glanced at the Basarwa and began to move towards the van.

"Go on," said Mma Ramotswe. "I am coming too."

She put him in the passenger seat and closed the door. The witch doctor's wife called out.

"Wait a few minutes. I want to talk to these people about the cattle. Then we can go."

Mma Ramotswe moved round to the driver's door and let herself in.

"Wait," called the woman. "I am not going to be long."

Mma Ramotswe leaned forward and started the engine. Then, slipping the van into gear, she spun the wheel and pressed her foot on the accelerator. The woman shouted out and began to run after the van, but the dust cloud soon obscured her and she tripped and fell.

Mma Ramotswe turned to the boy, who was looking frightened and confused beside her.

"I am taking you home now," she said. "It will be a long journey and I think we shall have to stop for the night quite soon. But we will set off again in the morning and then it should not be too long."

She stopped the van an hour later, beside a dry riverbed. They were completely alone, with not even a fire from a remote cattle post to break the darkness of the night. Only the starlight fell on them, an attenuated, silver light, falling on the sleeping figure of the boy, wrapped in a sack which she had in the back of the van, his head upon her arm, his breathing regular, his hand resting gently in hers, and Mma Ramotswe herself, whose eyes were open, looking up into the night sky until the sheer immensity of it tipped her gently into sleep.

AT KATSANA Village the next day, the schoolmaster looked out of the window of his house and saw a small white van draw up outside. He saw the woman get out and look at his door, and the child—what about the child—was she a parent who was bringing her child to him for some reason?

He went outside and found her at the low wall of his yard.

"You are the teacher, Rra?"

"I am the teacher, Mma. Can I do anything for you?"

She turned to the van and signalled to the child within. The door opened and his son came out. And the teacher cried out, and ran forward, and stopped and looked at Mma Ramotswe as if for confirmation. She nodded, and he ran forward again, almost stumbling, an unlaced shoe coming off, to seize his son, and hold him, while he shouted wildly, incoherently, for the village and the world to hear his joy.

Mma Ramotswe walked back towards her van, not wanting to intrude upon the intimate moments of reunion. She was crying; for her own child, too—remembering the minute hand that had grasped her own, so briefly, while it tried to hold on to a strange world that was slipping away so quickly. There was so much suffering in Africa that it was tempting just to shrug your shoulders and walk away. But you can't do that, she thought. You just can't.

MR J.L.B. MATEKONI

EVEN A vehicle as reliable as the little white van, which did mile after mile without complaint, could find the dust too much. The tiny white van had been uncomplaining on the trip out to the cattle post, but now, back in town, it was beginning to stutter. It was the dust, she was sure of it.

She telephoned Tlokweng Road Speedy Motors, not intending to bother Mr J.L.B. Matekoni, but the receptionist was out to lunch and he answered. She need not worry, he said. He would come round to look at the little white van the following day, a Saturday, and he might be able to fix it there on the spot, in Zebra Drive.

"I doubt it," said Mma Ramotswe. "It is an old van. It is like an old cow, and I will have to sell it, I suppose."

"You won't," said Mr J.L.B. Matekoni. "Anything can be fixed. Anything."

Even a heart that is broken in two pieces? he thought. Can

they fix that? Could Professor Barnard down in Cape Town cure a man whose heart was bleeding, bleeding from loneliness?

MMA RAMOTSWE went shopping that morning. Her Saturday mornings had always been important to her; she went to the supermarket in the Mall and bought her groceries and her vegetables from the women on the pavement outside the chemist's. After that, she went to the President Hotel and drank coffee with her friends; then home, and half a glass of Lion Beer, taken sitting out on the verandah and reading the newspaper. As a private detective, it was important to scour the newspaper and to put the facts away in one's mind. All of it was useful, down to the last line of the politicians' predictable speeches and the church notices. You never knew when some snippet of local knowledge would be useful.

If you asked Mma Ramotswe to give, for instance, the names of convicted diamond smugglers, she could give them to you: Archie Mofobe, Piks Ngube, Molso Mobole, and George Excellence Tambe. She had read the reports of the trials of them all, and knew their sentences. Six years, six years, ten years, and eight months. It had all been reported and filed away.

And who owned the Wait No More Butchery in Old Naledi? Why, Godfrey Potowani, of course. She remembered the photograph in the newspaper of Godfrey standing in front of his new butchery with the Minister of Agriculture. And why was the Minister there? Because his wife, Modela, was the cousin of one of the Potowani women who had made that dreadful fuss at the wedding of Stokes Lofinale. That's why. Mma

Ramotswe could not understand people who took no interest in all this. How could one live in a town like this and not want to know everybody's business, even if one had no professional reason for doing so?

HE ARRIVED shortly after four, driving up in his blue garage bakkie with TLOKWENG ROAD SPEEDY MOTORS painted on the side. He was wearing his mechanic's overalls, which were spotlessly clean, and ironed neatly down the creases. She showed him the tiny white van, parked beside the house, and he wheeled out a large jack from the back of his truck.

"I'll make you a cup of tea," she said. "You can drink it while you look at the van."

From the window she watched him. She saw him open the engine compartment and tap at bits and pieces. She saw him climb into the driver's cab and start the motor, which coughed and spluttered and eventually died out. She watched as he removed something from the engine—a large part, from which wires and hoses protruded. That was the heart of the van perhaps; its loyal heart which had beaten so regularly and reliably, but which, ripped out, now looked so vulnerable.

Mr J.L.B. Matekoni moved backwards and forwards between his truck and the van. Two cups of tea were taken out, and then a third, as it was a hot afternoon. Then Mma Ramotswe went into her kitchen and put vegetables into a pot and watered the plants that stood on the back windowsill. Dusk was approaching, and the sky was streaked with gold. This was her favourite time of the day, when the birds went dipping and swooping through the air and the insects of the night started to shriek. In this gentle light, the cattle would be walking home and the fires outside the huts would be crackling and glowing for the evening's cooking.

She went out to see whether Mr J.L.B. Matekoni needed more light. He was standing beside the little white van, wiping his hands on lint.

"That should be fine now," he said. "I've tuned it up and the engine runs sweetly. Like a bee."

She clapped her hands in pleasure.

"I thought that you would have to scrap it," she said.

He laughed. "I told you anything could be fixed. Even an old van."

He followed her inside. She poured him a beer and they went together to her favourite place to sit, on the verandah, near the bougainvillaea. Not far away, in a neighbouring house, music was being played, the insistent traditional rhythms of township music.

The sun went, and it was dark. He sat beside her in the comfortable darkness and they listened, contentedly, to the sounds of Africa settling down for the night. A dog barked somewhere; a car engine raced and then died away; there was a touch of wind, warm dusty wind, redolent of thorn trees.

He looked at her in the darkness, at this woman who was everything to him—mother, Africa, wisdom, understanding, good things to eat, pumpkins, chicken, the smell of sweet cattle breath, the white sky across the endless, endless bush, and the giraffe that cried, giving its tears for women to daub on their baskets; O Botswana, my country, my place.

Those were his thoughts. But how could he say any of that to her? Any time he tried to tell her what was in his heart, the words which came to him seemed so inadequate. A mechanic cannot be a poet, he thought, that is not how things are. So he simply said:

"I am very happy that I fixed your van for you. I would have been sorry if somebody else had lied to you and said it was not worth fixing. There are people like that in the motor trade."

"I know," said Mma Ramotswe. "But you are not like that."

He said nothing. There were times when you simply had to speak, or you would have your lifetime ahead to regret not speaking. But every time he had tried to speak to her of what was in his heart, he had failed. He had already asked her to marry him and that had not been a great success. He did not have a great deal of confidence, at least with people; cars were different, of course.

"I am very happy sitting here with you . . ."

She turned to him. "What did you say?"

"I said, please marry me, Mma Ramotswe. I am just Mr J.L.B. Matekoni, that's all, but please marry me and make me happy."

"Of course I will," said Mma Ramotswe.

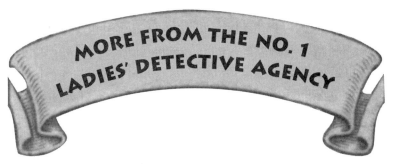

MORE FROM THE NO. 1 LADIES' DETECTIVE AGENCY

THE NO. 1 LADIES' DETECTIVE AGENCY

Millions of readers have fallen in love with the witty, wise Mma Ramotswe and her Botswana adventures. Share the magic of Alexander McCall Smith's No. 1 Ladies' Detective Agency series in two alternate editions:

1-4000-3477-9 (pbk)
0-375-42387-7 (hc)

TEARS OF THE GIRAFFE

The No. 1 Ladies' Detective Agency is growing, and in the midst of solving her usual cases—from an unscrupulous maid to a missing American—eminently sensible and cunning detective Mma Ramotswe ponders her impending marriage, promotes her talented secretary, and finds her family suddenly and unexpectedly increased by two.

Volume 2
1-4000-3135-4 (pbk)

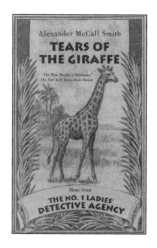

MORALITY FOR BEAUTIFUL GIRLS

While trying to resolve some financial problems for her business, Mma Ramotswe finds herself investigating the alleged poisoning of a government official as well as the moral character of the four finalists of the Miss Beauty and Integrity contest. Other difficulties arise at her fiancé's Tlokweng Road Speedy Motors, as Mma Ramotswe discovers he is more complicated than he seems.

Volume 3
1-4000-3136-2 (pbk)

The mysteries are "smart and sassy . . . [with] the power to amuse or shock or touch the heart, sometimes all at once."
—*Los Angeles Times*

THE KALAHARI TYPING SCHOOL FOR MEN

Mma Precious Ramotswe is content. But, as always, there are troubles. Mr J.L.B. Matekoni has not set the date for their wedding, her assistant Mma Makutsi wants a husband, and worst of all, a rival detective agency has opened up in town. Of course, Precious will manage these things, as she always does, with her uncanny insight and good heart.

Volume 4
1-4000-3180-X (pbk)
0-375-42217-X (hc)

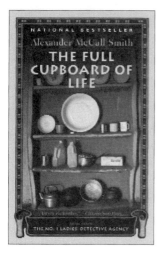

THE FULL CUPBOARD OF LIFE

Mma Ramotswe has weighty matters on her mind. She has been approached by a wealthy lady to check up on several suitors. Are these men interested in her or just her money? This may be difficult to find out, but it's just the kind of case Mma Ramotswe likes.

Volume 5
1-4000-3181-8 (pbk)
0-375-42218-8 (hc)

IN THE COMPANY OF CHEERFUL LADIES

Precious Ramotswe is busier than usual at the No. 1 Ladies' Detective Agency when the appearance of a strange intruder in her house and a mysterious pumpkin in her yard add to her concerns. But what finally rattles Mma Ramotswe's normally unshakable composure is the visitor who forces her to confront a painful secret from her past.

Volume 6
0-375-42271-4 (hc)
Paperback available Spring 2006

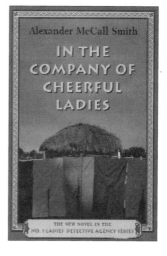

A New Series Begins

THE SUNDAY PHILOSOPHY CLUB

**THE SUNDAY
PHILOSOPHY CLUB**
Isabel Dalhousie is fond of problems,
and sometimes she becomes
interested in problems that are,
quite frankly, none of her business—
including some that are best left to
the police. Filled with endearingly
thorny characters and a Scottish
atmosphere as thick as a highland
mist, *The Sunday Philosophy Club* is
an irresistible pleasure.

Volume 1
1-4000-7709-5 (pbk)
0-375-42298-6 (hc)

"The literary equivalent of herbal tea and a cozy fire. . . .
McCall Smith's Scotland [is] well worth future visits."
—*The New York Times*

THE SUNDAY PHILOSOPHY CLUB

FRIENDS, LOVERS, CHOCOLATE

While taking care of her niece Cat's delicatessen, Isabel meets a heart transplant patient who has had some strange experiences in the wake of surgery. Against the advice of her housekeeper, Isabel is intent on investigating. Matters are further complicated when Cat returns from vacation with a new boyfriend, and Isabel's fondness for him lands her in another muddle.

Volume 2
0-375-42299-4 (hc)
Paperback available Fall 2006

ANCHOR BOOKS
ORIGINAL TRADE PAPERBACKS

44 SCOTLAND STREET
All of Alexander McCall Smith's trademark warmth and wit come into play in this novel chronicling the lives of the residents of an Edinburgh boardinghouse. Complete with colorful characters, love triangles, and even a mysterious art caper, this is an unforgettable portrait of Edinburgh society.
1-4000-7944-6

THREE NEW NOVELLAS
INTRODUCING THE ECCENTRIC AND EVER-LIKABLE
PROFESSOR DR VON IGELFELD

Welcome to the insane and rarified world of Professor Dr Moritz-Maria von Igelfeld of the Institute of Romance Philology. Von Igelfeld is engaged in a never-ending quest to win the respect he feels certain is due him—a quest which has a way of going hilariously astray.

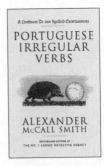

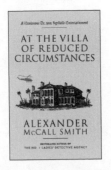

1-4000-7708-7   1-4000-9508-5   1-4000-9509-3

JOIN THE FAN CLUB TODAY!

ALEXANDER McCALL SMITH

Photo © Chris Watt

WWW.ALEXANDERMCCALLSMITH.COM

Membership to the Alexander McCall Smith Fan Club is absolutely FREE! You can register online at **www.alexandermccallsmith.com** or simply complete the form below and mail it to: **Alexander McCall Smith Fan Club, c/o Anchor Books, 1745 Broadway, New York, NY 10019**. As a member, you will receive a quarterly newsletter covering all of Alexander McCall Smith's beloved series, his latest work and travels, and details about where you can see him on tour. Additionally, members will have exclusive opportunities to hear from the author, participate in contests, and receive excerpts of McCall Smith's titles before the books are available in stores. Don't miss this chance to have a greater connection to one of your favorite authors!

NAME: _____

ADDRESS: _____

CITY: _____ STATE: _____ ZIP: _____

E-MAIL: _____

WHERE DO YOU BUY BOOKS? _____

ALEXANDER McCALL SMITH

TEARS OF THE GIRAFFE

In addition to the huge international phenomenon The No. 1 Ladies' Detective Agency series, Alexander McCall Smith is the author of The Sunday Philosophy Club series, the Portuguese Irregular Verbs series, *The Girl Who Married a Lion*, and *44 Scotland Street*. He was born in what is now Zimbabwe and taught law at the University of Botswana and Edinburgh University. He lives in Scotland and returns regularly to Botswana.

TEARS OF THE GIRAFFE

TEARS OF THE

GIRAFFE

Alexander McCall Smith

Anchor Books

A Division of Random House, Inc.

New York

First Anchor Books Edition, August 2002

Copyright © 2000 by Alexander McCall Smith

Library of Congress Cataloging-in-Publication Data
McCall Smith, R. A.
Tears of the giraffe / Alexander McCall Smith.
p. cm.
1. Ramotswe, Precious (Fictitious character)—Fiction.   2. Women private
investigators—Botswana—Fiction.   3. Botswana—Fiction.   I. Title.
PR6063.C326 T4 2002
823'.914—dc21
2002018695

Anchor ISBN 10: 1-4000-3135-4
Anchor ISBN 13: 978-1-4000-3135-1

www.anchorbooks.com

Printed in the United States of America
23   25   27   29   30   28   26   24

This book is for
Richard Latcham

TEARS OF THE GIRAFFE

MR J.L.B. MATEKONI'S HOUSE

MR J.L.B. Matekoni, proprietor of Tlokweng Road Speedy Motors, found it difficult to believe that Mma Ramotswe, the accomplished founder of the No. 1 Ladies' Detective Agency, had agreed to marry him. It was at the second time of asking; the first posing of the question, which had required immense courage on his part, had brought forth a refusal—gentle, and regretful—but a refusal nonetheless. After that, he had assumed that Mma Ramotswe would never remarry; that her brief and disastrous marriage to Note Mokoti, trumpeter and jazz aficionado, had persuaded her that marriage was nothing but a recipe for sorrow and suffering. After all, she was an independent-minded woman, with a business to run, and a comfortable house of her own in Zebra Drive. Why, he wondered, should a woman like that take on a man, when a man could prove to be difficult to manage once vows were exchanged and he had settled himself in her house? No, if he were in Mma Ramotswe's shoes, then he might well decline an offer of marriage, even from somebody as eminently reasonable and respectable as himself.

But then, on that noumenal evening, sitting with him on her verandah after he had spent the afternoon fixing her tiny white van, she had said yes. And she had given this answer in such a simple, unambiguously *kind* way, that he had been confirmed in his belief that she was one of the very best women in Botswana. That evening, when he returned home to his house near the old Defence Force Club, he had reflected on the enormity of his good fortune. Here he was, in his mid-forties, a man who had until that point been unable to find a suitable wife, now blessed with the hand of the one woman whom he admired more than any other. Such remarkable good fortune was almost inconceivable, and he wondered whether he would suddenly wake up from the delicious dream into which he seemed to have wandered.

Yet it was true. The next morning, when he turned on his bedside radio to hear the familiar sound of cattle bells with which Radio Botswana prefaced its morning broadcast, he realised that it had indeed happened and that unless she had changed her mind overnight, he was a man engaged to be married.

He looked at his watch. It was six o'clock, and the first light of the day was on the thorn tree outside his bedroom window. Smoke from morning fires, the fine wood smoke that sharpened the appetite, would soon be in the air, and he would hear the sound of people on the paths that criss-crossed the bush near his house; shouts of children on their way to school; men going sleepy-eyed to their work in the town; women calling out to one another; Africa waking up and starting the day. People

arose early, but it would be best to wait an hour or so before he
telephoned Mma Ramotswe, which would give her time to get
up and make her morning cup of bush tea. Once she had done
that, he knew that she liked to sit outside for half an hour or
so and watch the birds on her patch of grass. There were
hoopoes, with their black and white stripes, pecking at insects
like little mechanical toys, and the strutting ring-neck doves,
engaged in their constant wooing. Mma Ramotswe liked birds,
and perhaps, if she were interested, he could build her an aviary.
They could breed doves, maybe, or even, as some people did,
something bigger, such as buzzards, though what they would
do with buzzards once they had bred them was not clear. They
ate snakes, of course, and that would be useful, but a dog was
just as good a means of keeping snakes out of the yard.

When he was a boy out at Molepolole, Mr J.L.B. Matekoni
had owned a dog which had established itself as a legendary
snake-catcher. It was a thin brown animal, with one or two
white patches, and a broken tail. He had found it, abandoned
and half-starved, at the edge of the village, and had taken it
home to live with him at his grandmother's house. She had
been unwilling to waste food on an animal that had no apparent function, but he had won her round and the dog had
stayed. Within a few weeks it had proved its usefulness, killing
three snakes in the yard and one in a neighbour's melon patch.
From then on, its reputation was assured, and if anybody was
having trouble with snakes they would ask Mr J.L.B. Matekoni
to bring his dog round to deal with the problem.

The dog was preternaturally quick. Snakes, when they saw
it coming, seemed to know that they were in mortal danger.
The dog, hair bristling and eyes bright with excitement, would
move towards the snake with a curious gait, as if it were stand-

ing on the tips of its claws. Then, when it was within a few feet of its quarry, it would utter a low growl, which the snake would sense as a vibration in the ground. Momentarily confused, the snake would usually begin to slide away, and it was at this point that the dog would launch itself forward and nip the snake neatly behind the head. This broke its back, and the struggle was over.

Mr J.L.B. Matekoni knew that such dogs never reached old age. If they survived to the age of seven or eight, their reactions began to slow and the odds shifted slowly in favour of the snake. Mr J.L.B. Matekoni's dog eventually fell victim to a banded cobra, and died within minutes of the bite. There was no dog who could replace him, but now . . . Well, this was just another possibility that opened up. They could buy a dog and choose its name together. Indeed, he would suggest that she choose both the dog and the name, as he was keen that Mma Ramotswe should not feel that he was trying to take all the decisions. In fact, he would be happy to take as few decisions as possible. She was a very competent woman, and he had complete confidence in her ability to run their life together, as long as she did not try to involve him in her detective business. That was simply not what he had in mind. She was the detective; he was the mechanic. That was how matters should remain.

HE TELEPHONED shortly before seven. Mma Ramotswe seemed pleased to hear from him and asked him, as was polite in the Setswana language, whether he had slept well.

"I slept very well," said Mr J.L.B. Matekoni. "I dreamed all the night about that clever and beautiful woman who has agreed to marry me."

He paused. If she was going to announce a change of mind, then this was the time that she might be expected to do it.

Mma Ramotswe laughed. "I never remember what I dream," she said. "But if I did, then I am sure that I would remember dreaming about that first-class mechanic who is going to be my husband one day."

Mr J.L.B. Matekoni smiled with relief. She had not thought better of it, and they were still engaged.

"Today we must go to the President Hotel for lunch," he said. "We shall have to celebrate this important matter."

Mma Ramotswe agreed. She would be ready at twelve o'clock and afterwards, if it was convenient, perhaps he would allow her to visit his house to see what it was like. There would be two houses now, and they would have to choose one. Her house on Zebra Drive had many good qualities, but it was rather close to the centre of town and there was a case for being farther away. His house, near the old airfield, had a larger yard and was undoubtedly quieter, but was not far from the prison and was there not an overgrown graveyard nearby? That was a major factor; if she were alone in the house at night for any reason, it would not do to be too close to a graveyard. Not that Mma Ramotswe was superstitious; her theology was conventional and had little room for unquiet spirits and the like, and yet, and yet . . .

In Mma Ramotswe's view there was God, *Modimo,* who lived in the sky, more or less directly above Africa. God was extremely understanding, particularly of people like herself, but to break his rules, as so many people did with complete disregard, was to invite retribution. When they died, good people, such as Mma Ramotswe's father, Obed Ramotswe, were undoubtedly welcomed by God. The fate of the others was unclear, but they were sent to some terrible place—perhaps a bit like Nigeria, she thought—and when they acknowledged their wrongdoing they would be forgiven.

God had been kind to her, thought Mma Ramotswe. He had given her a happy childhood, even if her mother had been taken from her when she was a baby. She had been looked after by her father and her kind cousin and they had taught her what it was to give love—love which she had in turn given, over those few precious days, to her tiny baby. When the child's battle for life had ended, she had briefly wondered why God had done this to her, but in time she had understood. Now his kindness to her was manifest again, this time in the appearance of Mr J.L.B. Matekoni, a good kind, man. God had sent her a husband.

AFTER THEIR celebration lunch in the President Hotel—a lunch at which Mr J.L.B. Matekoni ate two large steaks and Mma Ramotswe, who had a sweet tooth, dipped into rather more ice cream than she had originally intended—they drove off in Mr J.L.B. Matekoni's pickup truck to inspect his house.

"It is not a very tidy house," said Mr J.L.B. Matekoni, anxiously. "I try to keep it tidy, but that is a difficult thing for a man. There is a maid who comes in, but she makes it worse, I think. She is a very untidy woman."

"We can keep the woman who works for me," said Mma Ramotswe. "She is very good at everything. Ironing. Cleaning.

Polishing. She is one of the best people in Botswana for all these tasks. We can find some other work for your person."

"And there are some rooms in this house that have got motor parts in them," added Mr J.L.B. Matekoni hurriedly. "Sometimes I have not had enough room at the garage and have had to store them in the house—interesting engines that I might need some day."

Mma Ramotswe said nothing. She now knew why Mr J.L.B. Matekoni had never invited her to the house before. His office at Tlokweng Road Speedy Motors was bad enough, with all that grease and those calendars that the parts suppliers sent him. They were ridiculous calendars, in her view, with all those far-too-thin ladies sitting on tyres and leaning against cars. Those ladies were useless for everything. They would not be good for having children, and not one of them looked as if she had her school certificate, or even her standard six. They were useless, good-time girls, who only made men all hot and bothered, and that was no good to anybody. If only men knew what fools of them these bad girls made; but they did not know it and it was hopeless trying to point it out to them.

They arrived at the entrance to his driveway and Mma Ramotswe sat in the car while Mr J.L.B. Matekoni pushed open the silver-painted gate. She noted that the dustbin had been pushed open by dogs and that scraps of paper and other rubbish were lying about. If she were to move here—*if*—that would soon be stopped. In traditional Botswana society, keeping the yard in good order was a woman's responsibility, and she would certainly not wish to be associated with a yard like this.

They parked in front of the stoop, under a rough car shelter that Mr J.L.B. Matekoni had fashioned out of shade-netting. It was a large house by modern standards, built in a day when builders had no reason to worry about space. There was the whole of Africa in those days, most of it unused, and nobody bothered to save space. Now it was different, and people had begun to worry about cities and how they gobbled up the bush surrounding them. This house, a low, rather gloomy bungalow under a corrugated-tin roof, had been built for a colonial offi-cial in Protectorate days. The outer walls were plastered and whitewashed, and the floors were polished red cement, laid out in large squares. Such floors always seemed cool on the feet in the hot months, although for real comfort it was hard to better the beaten mud or cattle dung of traditional floors.

Mma Ramotswe looked about her. They were in the living room, into which the front door gave immediate entrance. There was a heavy suite of furniture—expensive in its day—but now looking distinctly down-at-heel. The chairs, which had wide wooden arms, were upholstered in red, and there was a table of black hardwood on which an empty glass and an ashtray stood. On the walls there was picture of a mountain, painted on dark velvet, a wooden kudu-head, and a small pic-ture of Nelson Mandela. The whole effect was perfectly pleas-ing, thought Mma Ramotswe, although it certainly had that forlorn look so characteristic of an unmarried man's room.

"This is a very fine room," observed Mma Ramotswe.

Mr J.L.B. Matekoni beamed with pleasure. "I try to keep this room tidy," he said. "It is important to have a special room for important visitors."

"Do you have any important visitors?" asked Mma Ramotswe.

Mr J.L.B. Matekoni frowned. "There have been none so far," he said. "But it is always possible."

"Yes," agreed Mma Ramotswe. "One never knows."

She looked over her shoulder, towards a door that led into the rest of the house.

"The other rooms are that way?" she asked politely.

Mr J.L.B. Matekoni nodded. "That is the not-so-tidy part of the house," he said. "Perhaps we should look at it some other time."

Mma Ramotswe shook her head and Mr J.L.B. Matekoni realised that there was no escape. This was part and parcel of marriage, he assumed; there could be no secrets—everything had to be laid bare.

"This way," he said tentatively, opening the door. "Really, I must get a better maid. She is not doing her job at all well."

Mma Ramotswe followed him down the corridor. The first door that they reached was half open, and she stopped at the doorway and peered in. The room, which had obviously once been a bedroom, had its floors covered with newspapers, laid out as if they were a carpet. In the middle of the floor sat an engine, its cylinders exposed, while around it on the floor there were littered the parts that had been taken from the engine.

"That is a very special engine," said Mr J.L.B. Matekoni, looking at her anxiously. "There is no other engine like it in Botswana. One day I shall finish fixing it."

They moved on. The next room was a bathroom, which was clean enough, thought Mma Ramotswe, even if rather stark and neglected. On the edge of the bath, balanced on an old white face-cloth, was a large bar of carbolic soap. Apart from that, there was nothing.

"Carbolic soap is very healthy soap," said Mr J.L.B. Matekoni. "I have always used it."

Mma Ramotswe nodded. She favoured palm-oil soap,

which was good for the complexion, but she understood that men liked something more bracing. It was a bleak bathroom, she thought, but at least it was clean.

Of the remaining rooms, only one was habitable, the dining room, which had a table in the middle and a solitary chair. Its floor, however, was dirty, with piles of dust under the furniture and in each corner. Whoever was meant to be cleaning this room had clearly not swept it for months. What did she do, this maid? Did she stand at the gate and talk to her friends, as they tended to do if not watched closely? It was clear to Mma Ramotswe that the maid was taking gross advantage of Mr J.L.B. Matekoni and relying on his good nature to keep her job.

The other rooms, although they contained beds, were cluttered with boxes stuffed with spark plugs, windscreen-wiper blades, and other curious mechanical pieces. And as for the kitchen, this, although clean, was again virtually bare, containing only two pots, several white enamelled plates, and a small cutlery tray.

"This maid is meant to cook for me," said Mr J.L.B. Matekoni. "She makes a meal each day, but it is always the same. All that I have to eat is maizemeal and stew. Sometimes she cooks me pumpkin, but not very often. And yet she always seems to need lots of money for kitchen supplies."

"She is a very lazy woman," said Mma Ramotswe. "She should be ashamed of herself. If all women in Botswana were like that, our men would have died out a long time ago."

Mr J.L.B. Matekoni smiled. His maid had held him in thrall for years, and he had never had the courage to stand up to her. But now perhaps she had met her match in Mma Ramotswe, and she would soon be looking for somebody else to neglect.

"Where is this woman?" asked Mma Ramotswe. "I would like to talk to her."

Mr J.L.B. Matekoni looked at his watch. "She should be here soon," he said. "She comes here every afternoon at about this time."

THEY WERE sitting in the living room when the maid arrived, announcing her presence with the slamming of the kitchen door.

"That is her," said Mr J.L.B. Matekoni. "She always slams doors. She has never closed a door quietly in all the years she has worked here. It's always slam, slam."

"Let's go through and see her," said Mma Ramotswe. "I'm interested to meet this lady who has been looking after you so well."

Mr J.L.B. Matekoni led the way into the kitchen. In front of the sink, where she was filling a kettle with water, stood a large woman in her mid-thirties. She was markedly taller than both Mr J.L.B. Matekoni and Mma Ramotswe, and, although rather thinner than Mma Ramotswe, she looked considerably stronger, with bulging biceps and well-set legs. She was wearing a large, battered red hat on her head and a blue housecoat over her dress. Her shoes were made of a curious, shiny leather, rather like the patent leather used to make dancing pumps.

Mr J.LB. Matekoni cleared his throat, to reveal their presence, and the maid turned round slowly.

"I am busy . . ." she started to say, but stopped, seeing Mma Ramotswe.

Mr J.L.B. Matekoni greeted her politely, in the traditional

way. Then he introduced his guest. "This is Mma Ramotswe," he said.

The maid looked at Mma Ramotswe and nodded curtly.

"I am glad that I have had the chance to meet you, Mma," said Mma Ramotswe. "I have heard about you from Mr J.L.B. Matekoni."

The maid glanced at her employer. "Oh, you have heard of me," she said. "I am glad that he speaks of me. I would not like to think that nobody speaks of me."

"No," said Mma Ramotswe. "It is better to be spoken of than not to be spoken of. Except sometimes, that is."

The maid frowned. The kettle was now full and she took it from under the tap.

"I am very busy," she said dismissively. "There is much to do in this house."

"Yes," said Mma Ramotswe. "There is certainly a great deal to do. A dirty house like this needs a lot of work doing in it."

The large maid stiffened. "Why do you say this house is dirty?" she said. "Who are you to say that this house is dirty?"

"She . . ." began Mr J.L.B. Matekoni, but he was silenced by a glare from the maid and he stopped.

"I say that because I have seen it," said Mma Ramotswe. "I have seen all the dust in the dining room and all the rubbish in the garden. Mr J.L.B. Matekoni here is only a man. He cannot be expected to keep his own house clean."

The maid's eyes had opened wide and were staring at Mma Ramotswe with ill-disguised venom. Her nostrils were flared with anger, and her lips were pushed out in what seemed to be an aggressive pout.

"I have worked for this man for many years," she hissed. "Every day I have worked, worked, worked. I have made him good food and polished the floor. I have looked after him very well."

"I don't think so, Mma," said Mma Ramotswe calmly. "If you have been feeding him so well, then why is he thin? A man who is well looked-after becomes fatter. They are just like cattle. That is well-known."

The maid shifted her gaze from Mma Ramotswe to her employer. "Who is this woman?" she demanded. "Why is she coming into my kitchen and saying things like this? Please ask her to go back to the bar you found her in."

Mr J.L.B. Matekoni swallowed hard. "I have asked her to marry me," he blurted out. "She is going to be my wife."

At this, the maid seemed to crumple. "Aiee!" she cried. "Aiee! You cannot marry her! She will kill you! That is the worst thing you can do."

Mr J.L.B. Matekoni moved forward and placed a comforting hand on the maid's shoulder.

"Do not worry, Florence," he said. "She is a good woman, and I shall make sure that you will get another job. I have a cousin who has that hotel near the bus station. He needs maids and if I ask him to give you a job he will do so."

This did not pacify the maid. "I do not want to work in a hotel, where everyone is treated like a slave," she said. "I am not a do-this, do-that maid. I am a high-class maid, suitable for private houses. Oh! Oh! I am finished now. You are finished too if you marry this fat woman. She will break your bed. You will surely die very quickly. This is the end for you."

Mr J.LB. Matekoni glanced at Mma Ramotswe, signalling that they should leave the kitchen. It would be better, he thought, if the maid could recover in private. He had not imagined that the news would be well received, but he had certainly not envisaged her uttering such embarrassing and disturbing prophecies. The sooner he spoke to the cousin and arranged the transfer to the other job, the better.

They went back to the sitting room, closing the door firmly behind them.

"Your maid is a difficult woman," said Mma Ramotswe.

"She is not easy," said Mr J.L.B. Matekoni. "But I think that we have no choice. She must go to that other job."

Mma Ramotswe nodded. He was right. The maid would have to go, but so would they. They could not live in this house, she thought, even if it had a bigger yard. They would have to put in a tenant and move to Zebra Drive. Her own maid was infinitely better and would look after both of them extremely well. In no time at all, Mr J.L.B. Matekoni would begin to put on weight, and look more like the prosperous garage owner he was. She glanced about the room. Was there anything at all that they would need to move from this house to hers? The answer, she thought, was probably no. All that Mr J.L.B. Matekoni needed to bring was a suitcase containing his clothes and his bar of carbolic soap. That was all.

_____

A CLIENT ARRIVES

IT WOULD have to be handled tactfully. Mma Ramotswe knew that Mr J.L.B. Matekoni would be happy to live in Zebra Drive—she was sure of that—but men had their pride and she would have to be careful about how she conveyed the decision. She could hardly say: "Your house is a terrible mess; there are engines and car parts everywhere." Nor could she say: "I would not like to live that close to an old graveyard." Rather, she would approach it by saying: "It's a wonderful house, with lots of room. I don't mind old engines at all, but I am sure you will agree that Zebra Drive is very convenient for the centre of town." That would be the way to do it.

She had already worked out how the arrival of Mr J.L.B. Matekoni could be catered for in her house in Zebra Drive. Her house was not quite as large as his, but they would have more than enough room. There were three bedrooms. They would occupy the biggest of these, which was also the quietest, being at the back. She currently used the other two rooms for storage and for sewing, but she could clear out the storage room and put everything it contained in the garage. That would make a room for Mr J.L.B. Matekoni's private use. Whether he wished to use it to store car parts or old engines would be up to him, but a very strong hint would be given that engines should stay outside.

The living room could probably stay more or less unchanged. Her own chairs were infinitely preferable to the furniture she had seen in his sitting room, although he may well wish to bring the velvet picture of the mountain and one or two of his ornaments. These would complement her own possessions, which included the photograph of her father, her daddy, as she called him, Obed Ramotswe, in his favourite shiny suit, the photograph before which she stopped so often and thought of his life and all that it meant to her. She was sure that he would have approved of Mr J.L.B. Matekoni. He had warned her against Note Mokoti, although he had not tried to stop the marriage, as some parents might have done. She had been aware of his feelings but had been too young, and too infatuated with the plausible trumpet player, to take account of what her father thought. And, when the marriage had ended so disastrously, he had not spoken of his presentiment that this was exactly what would happen, but had been concerned only about her safety and her happiness—which is how he had always been. She was lucky to have had such a father, she thought; today there were so many people without a father, people who were being brought up by their mothers or their grandmothers and who in many cases did not even know who their father was. They seemed happy enough, it seemed, but there must always be a great gap in their lives. Perhaps if you don't know there's a gap, you don't worry about it. If you were a millipede, a *tshongololo,* crawling along the ground would you look at the birds and worry about not having wings? Probably not.

Mma Ramotswe was given to philosophical speculation, but only up to a point. Such questions were undoubtedly challenging, but they tended to lead to further questions which simply could not be answered. And at that point one ended up, as often as not, having to accept that things are as they are simply because that is the way they are. So everybody knew, for instance, that it was wrong for a man to be too close to a place where a woman is giving birth. That was something which was so obvious that it hardly needed to be stated. But then there were these remarkable ideas in other countries that suggested that men should actually attend the birth of their children. When Mma Ramotswe read about that in a magazine, her breath was taken away. But then she had asked herself why a father should not see his child being born, so that he could welcome it into the world and share the joy of the occasion, and she had found it difficult to find a reason. That is not to say it was not wrong—there was no question that it was profoundly wrong for a man to be there—but how could one justify the prohibition? Ultimately the answer must be that it was wrong because the old Botswana morality said that it was wrong, and the old Botswana morality, as everybody knew, was so plainly right. It just *felt* right.

Nowadays, of course, there were plenty of people who appeared to be turning away from that morality. She saw it in the behaviour of schoolchildren, who strutted about and pushed their way around with scant respect for older people. When she was at school, children respected adults and lowered their eyes when they spoke to them, but now children looked straight at you and answered back. She had recently told a young boy—barely thirteen, she thought—to pick up an empty can that he had tossed on the ground in the mall the other day. He had looked at her in amazement, and had then laughed and told her that she could pick it up if she liked as he had no intention of doing so. She had been so astonished by his cheek that she had been unable to think of a suitable riposte, and he had sauntered away, leaving her speechless. When she was young, a woman would have picked up a boy like that and spanked him on the spot. But today you couldn't spank other people's children in the street; if you tried to do so there would be an enormous fuss. She was a modern lady, of course, and did not approve of spanking, but sometimes one had to wonder. Would that boy have dropped the can in the first place if knew that somebody might spank him? Probably not.

THOUGHTS ABOUT marriage, and moving house, and spanking boys, were all very well but everyday life still required to be attended to, and for Mma Ramotswe, this meant that she had to open up the No. 1 Ladies' Detective Agency on Monday morning, as she did on every working morning, even if there was very little possibility of anybody coming in with an enquiry or telephoning. Mma Ramotswe felt that it was important to keep one's word, and the sign outside the agency announced that the opening hours were from nine in the morning until five in the afternoon, every day. In fact, no client had ever consulted her until well into the morning, and usually clients came in the late afternoon. Why this should be, she had no idea, although she sometimes reflected that it took people some time to build up the courage to cross her threshold and admit to whatever it was that was troubling them.

So Mma Ramotswe sat with her secretary, Mma Makutsi, and drank the large mug of bush tea which Mma Makutsi brewed for them both at the beginning of each day. She did not really need a secretary, but a business which wished to be taken seriously required somebody to answer the telephone or to take calls if she was out. Mma Makutsi was a highly skilled typist—she had scored 97 percent in her secretarial examinations—and was probably wasted on a small business such as this, but she was good company, and loyal, and, most important of all, had a gift for discretion.

"We must not talk about what we see in this business," Mma Ramotswe had stressed when she engaged her, and Mma Makutsi had nodded solemnly. Mma Ramotswe did not expect her to understand confidentiality—people in Botswana liked to talk about what was happening—and she was surprised when she found out that Mma Makutsi understood very well what the obligation of confidentiality entailed. Indeed, Mma Ramotswe had discovered that her secretary even refused to tell people where she worked, referring only to an office "somewhere over near Kgale Hill." This was somewhat unnecessary, but at least it was an indication that the clients' confidences would be safe with her.

Early morning tea with Mma Makutsi was a comforting ritual, but it was also useful from the professional point of view. Mma Makutsi was extremely observant, and she also listened attentively for any little snippet of gossip that could be useful. It was from her, for instance, that Mma Ramotswe had heard that a medium-ranking official in the planning department was proposing to marry the sister of the woman who owned Ready Now Dry Cleaners. This information may have seemed mundane, but when Mma Ramotswe had been engaged by a supermarket owner to discover why he was being denied a licence to build a dry-cleaning agency next to his supermarket, it was useful to be able to point out that the person making the decision may have an interest in another, rival dry-cleaning establishment. That information alone stopped the nonsense; all that Mma Ramotswe had needed to do was to point out to the official that there were people in Gaborone who were saying—surely without any justification—that he might allow his business connections to influence his judgement. Of course, when somebody had mentioned this to her, she had disputed the rumour vehemently, and had argued that there could be no possible connection between his dry-cleaning associations and the difficulty which anybody else might be having over getting a licence to open up such a business. The very thought was outrageous, she had said.

On that Monday, Mma Makutsi had nothing of significance to report. She had enjoyed a quiet weekend with her sister, who was a nurse at the Princess Marina Hospital. They had bought some material and had started to make a dress for the sister's daughter. On Sunday they had gone to church and a woman had fainted during one of the hymns. Her sister had helped to revive her and they had made her some tea in the hall at the side of the church. The woman was too fat, she said, and the heat had been too much for her, but she had recovered quickly and had drunk four cups of tea. She was a woman from the north, she said, and she had twelve children up in Francistown.

"That is too much," said Mma Ramotswe. "In these modern days, it is not a good thing to have twelve children. The Government should tell people to stop after six. Six is enough, or maybe seven or eight if you can afford to feed that many."

Mma Makutsi agreed. She had four brothers and two sisters and she thought that this had prevented her parents from paying adequate attention to the education of each of them.

"It was a miracle that I got 97 percent," she said.

'If there had only been three children, then you would have got over 100 percent," observed Mma Ramotswe.

"Impossible," said Mma Makutsi. "Nobody has ever got over 100 percent in the history of the Botswana Secretarial College. It's just not possible."

THEY WERE not busy that morning. Mma Makutsi cleaned her typewriter and polished her desk, while Mma Ramotswe read a magazine and wrote a letter to her cousin in Lobatse. The hours passed slowly, and by twelve o'clock Mma Ramotswe was prepared to shut the agency for lunch. But just as she was about to suggest that to Mma Makutsi, her secretary slammed a drawer shut, inserted a piece of paper into her typewriter and began to type energetically. This signalled the arrival of a client.

A large car, covered in the ubiquitous thin layer of dust that settled on everything in the dry season, had drawn up and a thin, white woman, wearing a khaki blouse and khaki trousers, had stepped out of the passenger seat. She glanced up briefly at the sign on the front of the building, took off her sunglasses, and knocked on the half-open door.

Mma Makutsi admitted her to the office, while Mma Ramotswe rose from her chair to welcome her.

"I'm sorry to come without an appointment," said the woman. "I hoped that I might find you in."

"You don't need an appointment," said Mma Ramotswe warmly, reaching out to shake her hand. "You are always welcome."

The woman took her hand, correctly, Mma Ramotswe noticed, in the proper Botswana way, placing her left hand on her right forearm as a mark of respect. Most white people shook hands very rudely, snatching just one hand and leaving their other hand free to perform all sorts of mischief. This woman had at least learned something about how to behave.

She invited the caller to sit down in the chair which they kept for clients, while Mma Makutsi busied herself with the kettle.

"I'm Mrs Andrea Curtin," said the visitor. "I heard from somebody in my embassy that you were a detective and you might be able to help me."

Mma Ramotswe raised an eyebrow. "Embassy?"

"The American Embassy," said Mrs Curtin. "I asked them to give me the name of a detective agency."

Mma Ramotswe smiled. "I am glad that they recommended me," she said. "But what do you need?"

The woman had folded her hands on her lap and now she looked down at them. The skin of her hands was mottled, Mma Ramotswe noticed, in the way that white people's hands were if they were exposed to too much sun. Perhaps she was an American who had lived for many years in Africa; there were many of these people. They grew to love Africa and they stayed, sometimes until they died. Mma Ramotswe could understand why they did this. She could not imagine why anybody would want to live anywhere else. How did people survive in cold, northern climates, with all that snow and rain and darkness?

"I could say that I am looking for somebody," said Mrs Curtin, raising her eyes to meet Mma Ramotswe's gaze. "But then that would suggest that there is somebody to look for. I don't think that there is. So I suppose I should say that I'm trying to find out what happened to somebody, quite a long time ago. I don't expect that that person is alive. In fact, I am certain that he is not. But I want to find out what happened."

Mma Ramotswe nodded. "Sometimes it is important to know," she said. "And I am sorry, Mma, if you have lost somebody."

Mrs Curtin smiled. "You're very kind. Yes, I lost somebody."

"When was this?" asked Mma Ramotswe.

"Ten years ago," said Mrs Curtin. "Ten years ago I lost my son."

For a few moments there was a silence. Mma Ramotswe glanced over to where Mma Makutsi was standing near the sink and noticed that her secretary was watching Mrs Curtin attentively. When she caught her employer's gaze, Mma Makutsi looked guilty and returned to her task of filling the teapot.

Mma Ramotswe broke the silence. "I am very sorry. I know what it is like to lose a child."

"Do you, Mma?"

She was not sure whether the question had an edge to it, as if it were a challenge, but she answered gently. "I lost my baby. He did not live."

Mrs Curtin lowered her gaze. "Then you know," she said.

Mma Makutsi had now prepared the bush tea and she brought over a chipped enamel tray on which two mugs were standing. Mrs Curtin took hers gratefully, and began to sip on the hot, red liquid.

"I should tell you something about myself," said Mrs Curtin. "Then you will know why I am here and why I would like you to help me. If you can help me I shall be very pleased, but if not, I shall understand."

"I will tell you," said Mma Ramotswe. "I cannot help everybody. I will not waste our time or your money. I shall tell you whether I can help."

Mrs Curtin put down her mug and wiped her hand against the side of her khaki trousers.

"Then let me tell you," she said, "why an American woman is sitting in your office in Botswana. Then, at the end of what I have to say, you can say either yes or no. It will be that simple. Either yes or no."

CHAPTER THREE

THE BOY WITH AN
AFRICAN HEART

CAME to Africa twelve years ago. I was forty-three and Africa meant nothing to me. I suppose I had the usual ideas about it—a hotchpotch of images of big game and savannah and Kilimanjaro rising out of the cloud. I also thought of famines and civil wars and potbellied, half-naked children staring at the camera, sunk in hopelessness. I know that all that is just one side of it—and not the most important side either—but it was what was in my mind.

My husband was an economist. We met in college and married shortly after we graduated; we were very young, but our marriage lasted. He took a job in Washington and ended up in the World Bank. He became quite senior there and could have spent his entire career in Washington, going up the ladder there. But he became restless, and one day he announced that there was a posting available to spend two years here in Botswana as a regional manager for World Bank activities in this part of Africa. It was promotion, after all, and if it was a cure for restlessness then I thought it preferable to his having an affair with another woman, which is the other way that men cure their restlessness. You know how it is, Mma, when men realize that they are no longer young. They panic, and they look for a younger woman who will reassure them that they are still men.

I couldn't have borne any of that, and so I agreed, and we came out here with our son, Michael, who was then just eighteen. He had been due to go to college that year, but we decided that he could have a year out with us before he started at Dartmouth. That's a very good college in America, Mma. Some of our colleges are not very good at all, but that one is one of the best. We were proud that he had a place there.

Michael took to the idea of coming out here and began to read everything he could find on Africa. By the time we arrived he knew far more than either of us did. He read everything that van der Post had written—all that dreamy nonsense—and then he sought out much weightier things, books by anthropologists on the San and even the Moffat journals. I think this is how he first fell in love with Africa—through all those books, even before he had set foot on African soil.

The Bank had arranged a house in Gaborone, just behind State House, where all those embassies and high commissions are. I took to it at once. There had been good rains that year and the garden had been well tended. There was bed after bed of cannas and arum lilies; great riots of bougainvillaea; thick kikuyu-grass lawns. It was a little square of paradise behind a high white wall.

Michael was like a child who has just discovered the key to the candy cupboard. He would get up early in the morning and take Jack's truck out onto the Molepolole Road. Then he would walk about in the bush for an hour or so before he came back for breakfast. I went with him once or twice, even though I don't like getting up early, and he would rattle on about the birds we saw and the lizards we found scuttling about in the dust; he knew all the names within days. And we would watch the sun come up behind us, and feel its warmth. You know how it is, Mma, out there, on the edge of the Kalahari. It's the time of day when the sky is white and empty and there is that sharp smell in the air, and you just want to fill your lungs to bursting.

Jack was busy with his work and with all the people he had to meet—Government people, US aid people, financial people and so on. I had no interest in any of that, and so I just contented myself in running the house and reading and meeting some of the people I liked to have coffee with in the mornings. I also helped with the Methodist clinic. I drove people between the clinic and their villages, which was a good way of seeing a bit of the country apart from anything else. I came to know a lot about your people that way, Mma Ramotswe.

I think that I can say that I had never been happier in my life. We had found a country where the people treated one another well, with respect, and where there were values other than the grab, grab, grab which prevails back home. I felt humbled, in a way. Everything about my own country seemed so shoddy and superficial when held up against what I saw in Africa. People suffered here, and many of them had very little, but they had this wonderful feeling for others. When I first heard African people calling others—complete strangers— their brother or their sister, it sounded odd to my ears. But after a while I knew exactly what it meant and I started to think the same way. Then one day, somebody called me her sister for the first time, and I started to cry, and she could not understand why I should suddenly be so upset. And I said to her: *It is nothing. I am just crying. I am just crying.* I wish I could have called my friends "my sisters," but it would have sounded contrived and I could not do it. But that is how I felt. I was learning lessons. I had come to Africa and I was learning lessons.

Michael started to study Setswana and he made good progress. There was a man called Mr Nogana who came to the house to give him lessons four days a week. He was a man in his late sixties, a retired schoolteacher, and a very dignified man. He wore small, round glasses, and one of the lenses was broken. I offered to buy him a replacement because I did not think that he had much money, but he shook his head and told me that he could see quite well and, thank you, it would not be necessary. They would sit on the verandah and Mr Nogana would go over Setswana grammar with him and give him the words for everything they saw: the plants in the garden, the clouds in the sky, the birds.

"Your son is learning quickly," he said to me. "He has got an African heart within him. I am just teaching that heart to speak."

Michael made his own friends. There were quite a few other Americans in Gaborone, some of whom were of a similar age to him, but he did not show much interest in these people, or in some of the other young expatriates who were there with diplomatic parents. He liked the company of local people, or of people who knew something about Africa. He spent a lot of time with a young South African exile and with a man who had been a medical volunteer in Mozambique. They were serious people, and I liked them too.

After a few months, he began to spend more and more time with a group of people who lived in an old farmhouse out beyond Molepolole. There was a girl there, an Afrikaner—she had come from Johannesburg a few years previously after getting into some sort of political trouble over the border. Then there was a German from Namibia, a lanky, bearded man who had ideas about agricultural improvement, and several local people from Mochudi who had worked in the Brigade movement there. I suppose that you might call it a commune of sorts, but then that would give the wrong idea. I think of communes as being the sort of place where hippies congregate and smoke *dagga*. This was not like that at all. They were all very serious, and what they really wanted to do was to grow vegetables in very dry soil.

The idea had come from Burkhardt, the German. He thought that agriculture in dry lands like Botswana and Namibia could be transformed by growing crops under shade-netting and irrigating them with droplets of water on strings. You will have seen how it works, Mma Ramotswe: the string comes down from a thin hosepipe and a droplet of water runs down the string and into the soil at the base of the plant. It really does work. I've seen it done.

Burkhardt wanted to set up a cooperative out there, based on that old farmhouse. He had managed to raise some money from somewhere or other and they had cleared a bit of bush and sunk a borehole. They had managed to persuade quite a number of local people to join the cooperative, and they were already producing a good crop of squash and cucumbers when

I first went out there with Michael. They sold these to the hotels in Gaborone and to the hospital kitchens too.

Michael began to spend more and more time with these people, and then eventually he told us that he wanted to go out there and live with them. I was a bit concerned at first—what mother wouldn't be—but we came round to the idea when we realised how much it meant to him to be doing something for Africa. So I drove him out there one Sunday afternoon and left him there. He said that he would come into town the following week and call in and see us, which he did. He seemed blissfully happy, excited even, at the prospect of living with his new friends.

We saw a lot of him. The farm was only an hour out of town and they came in virtually every day to bring produce or get supplies. One of the Botswana members had been trained as a nurse, and he had set up a clinic of sorts which dealt with minor ailments. They wormed children and put cream on fungal infections and things like that. The Government gave them a small supply of drugs, and Burkhardt got the rest from various companies that were happy to dispose of time-expired drugs which would still work perfectly well. Dr Merriweather was at the Livingstone Hospital then, and he used to call in from time to time to see that everything was in order. He told me once that the nurse was every bit as good as most doctors would be.

The time came for Michael to return to America. He had to be at Dartmouth by the third week of August, and in late July he told us that he did not intend to go. He wanted to stay in Botswana for at least another year, he said. He had contacted Dartmouth, without our knowing it, and they had agreed to defer his taking up his place for a year. I was alarmed, as you can imagine. You just have to go to college in the States, you see. If you don't, then you'll never get a job worth anything. And I had visions of Michael abandoning his education and spending the rest of his life in a commune. I suppose many parents have thought the same when their children have gone off to do something idealistic.

Jack and I discussed it for hours and he persuaded me that it would be best to go along with what Michael proposed. If we attempted to persuade him otherwise, then he could just dig in further and refuse to go at all. If we agreed to his plan, then he might be happier to leave when we did, at the end of the following year.

"It's good work that he's doing," Jack said. "Most people of his age are utterly selfish. He's not like that."

And I had to agree he was right. It seemed completely right to be doing what he was doing. Botswana was a place where people believed that work of that sort could make a difference. And remember that people had to do something to show that there was a real alternative to what was happening in South Africa. Botswana was a beacon in those days.

So Michael stayed where he was and of course when the time came for us to leave he refused to accompany us. He still had work to do, he said, and he wanted to spend a few more years doing it. The farm was thriving; they had sunk several more boreholes and they were providing a living for twenty families. It was too important to give up.

I had anticipated this—I think we both had. We tried to persuade him, but it was no use. Besides, he had now taken up with the South African woman, although she was a good six or seven years older than he was. I thought that she might be the real drawing factor, and we offered to help her come back with

us to the States, but he refused to entertain the notion. It was
Africa, he said, that was keeping him there; if we thought that
it was something as simple as a relationship with a woman
then we misunderstood the situation.

We left him with a fairly substantial amount of money. I am
in the fortunate position of having a fund which was set up for
me by my father and it meant very little to leave him with
money. I knew that there was a risk that Burkhardt would persuade him to give the money over to the farm, or use it to build
a dam or whatever. But I didn't mind. It made me feel more
secure to know that there were funds in Gaborone for him if
he needed them.

We returned to Washington. Oddly enough, when we got
back I realised exactly what it was that had prevented Michael
from leaving. Everything there seemed so insincere and, well,
aggressive. I missed Botswana, and not a day went past, not a
day, when I would not think about it. It was like an ache. I
would have given anything to be able to walk out of my house
and stand under a thorn tree or look up at that great white sky.
Or to hear African voices calling out to one another in the
night. I even missed the October heat.

Michael wrote to us every week. His letters were full of
news about the farm. I heard all about how the tomatoes were
doing and about the insects which had attacked the spinach
plants. It was all very vivid, and very painful to me, because I
would have loved to have been there doing what he was doing,
knowing that it made a difference. Nothing I could do in my
life made a difference to anybody. I took on various bits of
charitable work. I worked on a literacy scheme. I took library
books to housebound old people. But it was nothing by com-

parison with what my son was doing all those miles away in Africa.

Then the letter did not arrive one week and a day or two later there was a call from the American Embassy in Botswana. My son had been reported as missing. They were looking into the matter and would let me know as soon as they had any further information.

I came over immediately and I was met at the airport by somebody I knew on the Embassy staff. He explained to me that Burkhardt had reported to the police that Michael had simply disappeared one evening. They all took their meals together, and he had been at the meal. Thereafter nobody saw him. The South African woman had no idea where he had gone and the truck which he had bought after our departure was still in its shed. There was no clue as to what had happened.

The police had questioned everybody on the farm but had come up with no further information. Nobody had seen him and nobody had any idea what might have happened. It seemed that he had been swallowed up by the night.

I went out there on the afternoon of my arrival. Burkhardt was very concerned and tried to reassure me that he would soon turn up. But he was able to offer no explanation as to why he should have taken it into his head to leave without a word to anyone. The South African woman was taciturn. She was suspicious of me, for some reason, and said very little. She, too, could think of no reason for Michael to disappear.

I stayed for four weeks. We put a notice in the newspapers and offered a reward for information as to his whereabouts. I travelled backwards and forwards to the farm, going over every possibility in my mind. I engaged a game tracker to conduct a search of the bush in the area, and he searched for two weeks before giving up. There was nothing to be found.

Eventually they decided that one of two things had happened. He had been set upon by somebody, for whatever reason, possibly in the course of a robbery, and his body had been taken away. Or he had been taken by wild animals, perhaps by a lion that had wandered in from the Kalahari. It would have been quite unusual to find a lion that close to Molepolole, but it was just possible. But if that had happened, then the game tracker would have found some clue. Yet he had come up with nothing. No spoor. No unusual animal droppings. There was nothing.

I came back a month later, and again a few months after that. Everybody was sympathetic but eventually it became apparent that they had nothing more to say to me. So I left the matter in the hands of the Embassy here and every so often they contacted the police to find out if there was any fresh news. There never was.

Six months ago Jack died. He had been ill for a while with pancreatic cancer and I had been warned that there was no hope. But after he had gone, I decided that I should try one last time to see if there was anything I could do to find out what happened to Michael. It may seem strange to you, Mma Ramotswe, that somebody should go on and on about something that happened ten years ago. But I just want to know. I just want to find out what happened to my son. I don't expect to find him. I accept that he's dead. But I would like to be able to close that chapter and say goodbye. That is all I want. Will you help me? Will you try to find out for me? You say that you lost your child. You know how I feel then. You know that, don't you? It's a sadness that never goes away. Never.

FOR A few moments after her visitor had finished her story, Mma Ramotswe sat in silence. What could she do for this woman? Could she find anything out if the Botswana Police and the American Embassy had tried and failed? There was probably nothing she could do, and yet this woman needed help and if she could not obtain it from the No. 1 Ladies' Detective Agency then where would she be able to find it?

"I shall help you," she said, adding, "my sister."

CHAPTER FOUR

AT THE ORPHAN FARM

MR J.L.B. Matekoni contemplated the view from his office at Tlokweng Road Speedy Motors. There were two windows, one of which looked directly into the workshop, where his two young apprentices were busy raising a car on a jack. They were doing it the wrong way, he noticed, in spite of his constant reminders of the dangers involved. One of them had already had an accident with the blade of an engine fan and had been lucky not to lose a finger; but they persisted with their unsafe practices. The problem, of course, was that they were barely nineteen. At this age, all young men are immortal and imagine that they will live forever. They'll find out, thought Mr J.L.B. Matekoni grimly. They'll discover that they're just like the rest of us.

He turned in his chair and looked out through the other window. The view in this direction was more pleasing: across the backyard of the garage, one could see a cluster of acacia trees sticking up out of the dry thorn scrub and, beyond that, like islands rising from a grey-green sea, the isolated hills over towards Odi. It was mid-morning and the air was still. By mid-day there would be a heat haze that would make the hills seem to dance and shimmer. He would go home for his lunch then as it would be too hot to work. He would sit in his kitchen, which was the coolest room of the house, eat the maizemeal and stew which his maid prepared for him, and read the *Botswana Daily News*. After that, he inevitably took a short nap before he returned to the garage and the afternoon's work.

The apprentices ate their lunch at the garage, sitting on a couple of upturned oil drums that they had placed under one of the acacia trees. From this vantage point they watched the girls walk past and exchanged the low banter which seemed to give them such pleasure. Mr J.L.B. Matekoni had heard their conversation and had a poor opinion of it.

"You're a pretty girl! Have you got a car? I could fix your car for you. I could make you go much faster!"

This brought giggles and a quickening step from the two young typists from the Water Affairs office.

"You're too thin! You're not eating enough meat! A girl like you needs more meat so that she can have lots of children!"

"Where did you get those shoes from? Are those Mercedes-Benz shoes? Fast shoes for fast girls!"

Really! thought Mr J.L.B. Matekoni. He had never behaved like that when he was their age. He had served his apprentice-ship in the diesel workshops of the Botswana Bus Company and that sort of conduct would never have been tolerated. But this was the way young men behaved these days and there was nothing he could do about it. He had spoken to them about it, pointing out that the reputation of the garage depended on them just as it did on him. They had looked at him blankly, and he had realised then that they simply did not understand. They had not been taught what it was to have a reputation; the concept was completely beyond them. This realization had depressed him, and he had thought of writing to the Minister of Education about it and suggesting that the youth of Botswana be instructed in these basic moral ideas, but the letter, once composed, had sounded so pompous that he had decided not to send it. That was the difficulty, he realised. If you made any point about behaviour these days, you sounded old-fashioned and pompous. The only way to sound modern, it appeared, was to say that people could do whatever they wanted, whenever they wanted, and no matter what anybody else might think. That was the modern way of thinking.

MR J.L.B. Matekoni transferred his gaze to his desk and to the open page of his diary. He had noted down that today was his day to go to the orphan farm; if he left immediately he could do that before lunch and be back in time to check up on his apprentices' work before the owners came to collect their cars at four o'clock. There was nothing wrong with either car; all that they required was their regular service and that was well within the range of the apprentices' ability. He had to watch them, though; they liked to tweak engines in such a way that they ran at maximum capacity, and he would often have to tune the engines down before they left the garage.

"We are not meant to be making racing cars," he reminded them. "The people who drive these cars are not speedy types like you. They are respectable citizens."

"Then why are we called Speedy Motors?" asked one of the apprentices.

Mr J.LB. Matekoni had looked at his apprentice. There were times that he wanted to shout at him, and this perhaps was one, but he always controlled his temper.

"We are called Tlokweng Road Speedy Motors," he replied patiently, "because our *work* is speedy. Do you understand the distinction? We do not keep the customer waiting for days and days like some garages do. We turn the job round quickly, and carefully, too, as I keep having to tell you."

"Some people like speedy cars," chipped in the other apprentice. "There are some people who like to go fast."

"That may be so," said Mr J.L.B. Matekoni. "But not everyone is like that. There are some people who know that going fast is not always the best way of getting there, is it? It is better to be *late* than *the* late, is it not?"

The apprentices had stared at him uncomprehendingly, and he had sighed; again, it was the fault of the Ministry of Education and their modern ideas. These two boys would never be able to understand half of what he said. And one of these days they were going to have a bad accident.

HE DROVE out to the orphan farm, pressing vigorously on his horn, as he always did, when he arrived at the gate. He enjoyed his visits for more than one reason. He liked to see the children, of course, and he usually brought a fistful of sweets which he would distribute when they came flocking round him. But he also liked seeing Mrs Silvia Potokwane, who was the matron in charge. She had been a friend of his mother's, and he had known her all his life. For this reason it was natural that he should take on the task of fixing any machinery which needed attending to, as well as maintaining the two trucks and the battered old minibus which served as the farm's transport. He was not paid for this, but that was not to be expected. Everybody helped the orphan farm if they could, and he would not have accepted payment had it been pressed on him.

Mma Potokwane was in her office when he arrived. She leaned out of the window and beckoned him in.

"Tea is ready, Mr J.L.B. Matekoni," she called. "There will be cake too, if you hurry."

He parked his truck under the shady boughs of a monkey-bread tree. Several children had already appeared, and skipped along beside him as he made his way to the office block.

"Have you children been good?" asked Mr J.L.B. Matekoni, reaching into his pockets.

"We have been very good children," said the oldest child. "We have been doing good things all week. We are tired out now from all the good things we have been doing."

Mr J.L.B. Matekoni chuckled. "In that case, you may have some sweets."

He handed a fistful of sweets over to the oldest child, who received them politely, with both hands extended, in the proper Botswana fashion.

"Do not spoil those children," shouted Mma Potokwane from her window. "They are very bad children, those ones."

The children laughed and scampered off, while Mr J.L.B. Matekoni walked through the office door. Inside, he found Mma Potokwane, her husband, who was a retired policeman, and a couple of the housemothers. Each had a mug of tea and a plate with a piece of fruitcake on it.

Mr J.L.B. Matekoni sipped on his tea as Mma Potokwane told him about the problems they were having with one of their borehole pumps. The pump was overheating after less than half an hour's use and they were worried that it would seize up altogether.

"Oil," said Mr J.L.B. Matekoni. "A pump without oil gets hot. There must be a leak. A broken seal or something like that."

"And then there are the brakes on the minibus," said Mr Potokwane. "They make a very bad noise now."

"Brake pads," said Mr J.L.B. Matekoni. "It's about time we replaced them. They get so much dust in them in this weather and it wears them down. I'll take a look, but you'll probably have to bring it into the garage for the work to be done."

They nodded, and the conversation moved to events at the orphan farm. One of the orphans had just been given a job and would be moving to Francistown to take it up. Another orphan had received a pair of running shoes from a Swedish donor who sent gifts from time to time. He was the best runner on the farm and now he would be able to enter in competitions. Then there was a silence, and Mma Potokwane looked expectantly at Mr J.L.B. Matekoni.

"I hear that you have some news," she said after a while. "I hear that you're getting married."

Mr J.L.B. Matekoni looked down at his shoes. They had told nobody, as far as he knew, but that would not be enough to stop news getting out in Botswana. It must have been his maid, he thought. She would have told one of the other maids and they would have spread it to their employers. Everybody would know now.

"I'm marrying Mma Ramotswe," he began. "She is . . ."

"She's the detective lady, isn't she?" said Mma Potokwane. "I have heard all about her. That will make life very exciting for you. You will be lurking about all the time. Spying on people."

Mr J.L.B. Matekoni drew in his breath. "I shall be doing no such thing," he said. "I am not going to be a detective. That is Mma Ramotswe's business."

Mma Potokwane seemed disappointed. But then, she brightened up. "You will be buying her a diamond ring, I suppose," she said. "An engaged lady these days must wear a diamond ring to show that she is engaged."

Mr J.L.B. Matekoni stared at her. "Is it necessary?" he asked.

"It is very necessary," said Mma Potokwane. "If you read any of the magazines, you will see that there are advertisements for diamond rings. They say that they are for engagements."

Mr J.L.B. Matekoni was silent. Then: "Diamonds are rather expensive, aren't they?"

"Very expensive," said one of the housemothers. "One thousand pula for a tiny, tiny diamond."

"More than that," said Mr Potokwane. "Some diamonds cost two hundred thousand pula. Just one diamond."

Mr J.L.B. Matekoni looked despondent. He was not a mean man, and was as generous with presents as he was with his time, but he was against any waste of money and it seemed to him that to spend that much on a diamond, even for a special occasion, was entirely wasteful.

"I shall speak to Mma Ramotswe about it," he said firmly, to bring the awkward topic to a close. "Perhaps she does not believe in diamonds."

"No," said Mma Potokwane. "She will believe in diamonds. All ladies believe in diamonds. That is one thing on which all ladies agree."

MR J.L.B. Matekoni crouched down and looked at the pump. After he had finished tea with Mma Potokwane, he had followed the path that led to the pump-house. It was one of those peculiar paths that seemed to wander, but which eventually reached its destination. This path made a lazy loop round some pumpkin fields before it dipped through a *donga,* a deep eroded ditch, and ended up in front of the small lean-to that protected the pump. The pump-house was itself shaded by a stand of umbrella-like thorn trees, which, when Mr J.L.B. Matekoni arrived, provided a welcome circle of shade. A tin-roofed shack, like the pump-house was, could become impossibly hot in the direct rays of the sun and that would not help any machinery inside.

Mr J.L.B. Matekoni put down his tool box at the entrance to the pump-house and cautiously pushed the door open. He was careful about places like this because they were very well suited for snakes. Snakes seemed to like machinery, for some reason, and he had more than once discovered a somnolent snake curled around a part of some machine on which he was working. Why they did it, he had no idea; it might have been something to do with warmth and motion. Did snakes dream about some good place for snakes? Did they think that there was a heaven for snakes somewhere, where everything was down at ground level and there was nobody to tread on them?

His eyes took a few moments to accustom themselves to the dark of the interior, but after a while he saw that there was nothing untoward inside. The pump was driven by a large fly-wheel which was powered by an antiquated diesel engine. Mr J.L.B. Matekoni sighed. This was the trouble. Old diesel engines were generally reliable, but there came a point in their existence when they simply had to be pensioned off. He had hinted at this to Mma Potokwane, but she had always come up with reasons why money should be spent on other, more pressing projects.

"But water is the most important thing of all," said Mr J.L.B. Matekoni. "If you can't water your vegetables, then what are the children going to eat?"

"God will provide," said Mma Potokwane calmly. "He will send us a new engine one day."

"Maybe," said Mr J.L.B. Matekoni. "But then maybe not. God is sometimes not very interested in engines. I fix cars for quite a few ministers of religion, and they all have trouble. God's servants are not very good drivers."

Now, confronted with the evidence of diesel mortality, he retrieved his tool box, extracted an adjustable spanner, and began to remove the engine casing. Soon he was completely absorbed in his task, like a surgeon above the anaesthetised patient, stripping the engine to its solid, metallic heart. It had been a fine engine in its day, the product of a factory some-where unimaginably far away—a loyal engine, an engine of character. Every engine seemed to be Japanese these days, and made by robots. Of course these were reliable, because the parts were so finely turned and so obedient, but for a man like

Mr J.L.B. Matekoni those engines were as bland as sliced white bread. There was nothing in them, no roughage, no idiosyncracies. And as a result, there was no challenge in fixing a Japanese engine.

He had often thought how sad it was that the next generation of mechanics might never have to fix one of these old engines. They were all trained to fix the modern engines which needed computers to find out their troubles. When somebody came in to the garage with a new Mercedes-Benz, Mr J.L.B. Matekoni's heart sank. He could no longer deal with such cars as he had none of these new diagnostic machines that one needed. Without such a machine, how could he tell if a tiny silicon chip in some inaccessible part of the engine was sending out the wrong signal? He felt tempted to say that such drivers should get a computer to fix their car, not a live mechanic, but of course he did not, and he would do his best with the gleaming expanse of steel which nestled under the bonnets of such cars. But his heart was never in it.

Mr J.L.B. Matekoni had now removed the pump engine's cylinder heads and was peering into the cylinders themselves. It was exactly what he had imagined; they were both coked up and would need a rebore before too long. And when the pistons themselves were removed he saw that the rings were pitted and worn, as if affected by arthritis. This would affect the engine's efficiency drastically, which meant wasted fuel and less water for the orphans' vegetables. He would have to do what he could. He would replace some of the engine seals to staunch the oil loss and he would arrange for the engine to be brought in some time for a rebore. But there would come a time when none of this would help, and he thought they would then simply have to buy a new engine.

There was a sound behind him, and he was startled. The pump-house was a quiet place, and all that he had heard so far was the call of birds in the acacia trees. This was a human noise. He looked round, but there was nothing. Then it came again, drifting through the bush, a squeaking noise as if from an unoiled wheel. Perhaps one of the orphans was wheeling a wheelbarrow or pushing one of those toy cars which children liked to fashion out of bits of old wire and tin.

Mr J.L.B. Matekoni wiped his hands on a piece of rag and stuffed the rag back into his pocket. The noise seemed to be coming closer now, and then he saw it, emerging from the scrub bush that obscured the twists of the path: a wheelchair, in which a girl was sitting, propelling the chair herself. When she looked up from the path ahead of her and saw Mr J.L.B. Matekoni she stopped, her hands gripping the rims of the wheels. For a moment they stared at one another, and then she smiled and began to make her way over the last few yards of pathway.

She greeted him politely, as a well-brought-up child would do.

"I hope that you are well, Rra," she said, offering her right hand while her left hand laid across the forearm in a gesture of respect.

They shook hands.

"I hope that my hands are not too oily," said Mr J.L.B. Matekoni. "I have been working on the pump."

The girl nodded. "I have brought you some water, Rra. Mma Potokwane said that you had come out here without anything to drink and you might be thirsty."

She reached into a bag that was slung under the seat of the chair and extracted a bottle.

Mr J.L.B. Matekoni took the water gratefully. He had just

begun to feel thirsty and was regretting his failure to bring water with him. He took a swig from the bottle, watching the girl as he drank. She was still very young—about eleven or twelve, he thought—and she had a pleasant, open face. Her hair had been braided, and there were beads worked into the knots. She wore a faded blue dress, almost bleached to white by repeated washings, and a pair of scruffy *tackies* on her feet.

"Do you live here?" he asked. "On the farm?"

She nodded. "I have been here nearly one year," she answered. "I am here with my young brother. He is only five."

"Where did you come from?"

She lowered her gaze. "We came from up near Francistown. My mother is late. She died three years ago, when I was nine. We lived with a woman, in her yard. Then she told us we had to go."

Mr J.L.B. Matekoni said nothing. Mma Potokwane had told him the stories of some of the orphans, and each time he found that it made his heart smart with pain. In traditional society there was no such thing as an unwanted child; everybody would be looked after by somebody. But things were changing, and now there were orphans. This was particularly so now that there was this disease which was stalking through Africa. There were many more children now without parents and the orphan farm might be the only place for some of them to go. Is this what had happened to this girl? And why was she in a wheelchair?

He stopped his line of thought. There was no point in speculating about things which one could do little to help. There were more immediate questions to be answered, such as why was the wheelchair making such an odd noise.

"Your chair is squeaking," he said. "Does it always do that?"

She shook her head. "It started a few weeks ago. I think there is something wrong with it."

Mr J.L.B. Matekoni went down on his haunches and examined the wheels. He had never fixed a wheelchair before, but it was obvious to him what the problem was. The bearings were dry and dusty—a little oil would work wonders there—and the brake was catching. That would explain the noise.

"I shall lift you out," he said. "You can sit under the tree while I fix this chair for you."

He lifted the girl and placed her gently on the ground. Then, turning the chair upside down, he freed the brake block and readjusted the lever which operated it. Oil was applied to the bearings and the wheels were spun experimentally. There was no obstruction, and no noise. He righted the chair and pushed it over to where the girl was sitting.

"You have been very kind, Rra," she said. "I must get back now, or the housemother will think I'm lost."

She made her way down the path, leaving Mr J.L.B. Matekoni to his work on the pump. He continued with the repair and after an hour it was ready. He was pleased when it started the first time and appeared to run reasonably sweetly. The repair, however, would not last for long, and he knew that he would have to return to dismantle it completely. And how would the vegetables get water then? This was the trouble with living in a dry country. Everything, whether it was human life, or pumpkins, was on such a tiny margin.

JUDGMENT-DAY JEWELLERS

MMA POTOKWANE was right: Mma Ramotswe was, as she had predicted, interested in diamonds.

The subject came up a few days after Mr J.L.B. Matekoni had fixed the pump at the orphan farm.

"I think that people know about our engagement," said Mma Ramotswe, as she and Mr J.L.B. Matekoni sat drinking tea in the office of Tlokweng Road Speedy Motors. "My maid said that she had heard people talking about it in the town. She said that everybody knows."

"That is what this place is like," sighed Mr J.L.B. Matekoni. "I am always hearing about other people's secrets."

Mma Ramotswe nodded. He was right: there were no secrets in Gaborone. Everybody knew everybody else's business.

"For example," said Mr J.L.B. Matekoni, warming to the theme, "when Mma Sonqkwena ruined the gearbox of her son's new car by trying to change into reverse at thirty miles an hour, everybody seemed to hear about that. I told nobody, but they seemed to find out all the same."

Mma Ramotswe laughed. She knew Mma Sonqkwena, who was possibly the oldest driver in town. Her son, who had a profitable store in the Broadhurst Mall, had tried to persuade his mother to employ a driver or to give up driving altogether, but had been defeated by her indomitable sense of independence.

"She was heading out to Molepolole," went on Mr J.L.B. Matekoni, "and she remembered that she had not fed the chickens back in Gaborone. So she decided that she would go straight back by changing into reverse. You can imagine what that did to the gearbox. And suddenly everybody was talking about it. They assumed that I had told people, but I hadn't. A mechanic should be like a priest. He should not talk about what he sees."

Mma Ramotswe agreed. She appreciated the value of confidentiality, and she admired Mr J.L.B. Matekoni for understanding this too. There were far too many loose-tongued people about. But these were general observations, and there were more pressing matters still to be discussed, and so she brought the conversation round to the subject which had started the whole debate.

"So they are talking about our engagement," she said. "Some of them even asked to see the ring you had bought me." She glanced at Mr J.L.B. Matekoni before continuing. "So I told them that you hadn't bought it yet but that I'm sure that you would be buying it soon."

She held her breath. Mr J.L.B. Matekoni was looking at the ground, as he often did when he felt uncertain.

"A ring?" he said at last, his voice strained. "What kind of ring?"

Mma Ramotswe watched him carefully. One had to he circumspect with men, when discussing such matters. They had very little understanding of them, of course, but one had to be careful not to alarm them. There was no point in doing that. She decided to be direct. Mr J.L.B. Matekoni would spot subterfuge and it would not help.

"A diamond ring," she said. "That is what engaged ladies are wearing these days. It is the modern thing to do."

Mr J.L.B. Matekoni continued to look glumly at the ground.

"Diamonds?" he said weakly. "Are you sure this is the most modern thing?"

"Yes," said Mma Ramotswe firmly. "All engaged ladies in modern circles receive diamond rings these days. It is a sign that they are appreciated."

Mr J.L.B. Matekoni looked up sharply. If this was true—and it very much accorded with what Mma Potokwane had told him—then he would have no alternative but to buy a diamond ring. He would not wish Mma Ramotswe to imagine that she was not appreciated. He appreciated her greatly; he was immensely, humbly grateful to her for agreeing to marry him, and if a diamond were necessary to announce that to the world, then that was a small price to pay. He halted as the word "price" crossed his mind, recalling the alarming figures which had been quoted over tea at the orphan farm.

"These diamonds are very expensive," he ventured. "I hope that I shall have enough money."

"But of course you will," said Mma Ramotswe. "They have some very inexpensive ones. Or you can get terms . . ."

Mr J.L.B. Matekoni perked up. "I thought that they cost

thousands and thousands of pula," he said. "Maybe fifty thousand pula."

"Of course not," said Mma Ramotswe. "They have expensive ones, of course, but they also have very good ones that do not cost too much. We can go and take a look. Judgment-day Jewellers, for example. They have a good selection."

The decision was made. The next morning, after Mma Ramotswe had dealt with the mail at the detective agency, they would go to Judgment-day Jewellers and choose a ring. It was an exciting prospect, and even Mr J.L.B. Matekoni, feeling greatly relieved at the prospect of an affordable ring, found himself looking forward to the outing. Now that he had thought about it, there was something very appealing about diamonds, something that even a man could understand, if only he were to think hard enough about it. What was more important to Mr J.L.B. Matekoni was the thought that this gift, which was possibly the most expensive gift he would ever give in his life, was a gift from the very soil of Botswana. Mr J.L.B. Matekoni was a patriot. He loved his country, just as he knew Mma Ramotswe did. The thought that the diamond which he eventually chose could well have come from one of Botswana's own three diamond mines added to the significance of the gift. He was giving, to the woman whom he loved and admired more than any other, a tiny speck of the very land on which they walked. It was a special speck of course: a fragment of rock which had been burned to a fine point of brightness all those years ago. Then somebody had dug it out of the earth up at Orapa, polished it, brought it down to Gaborone, and set it in gold. And all of this to allow Mma Ramotswe to wear it on the second finger of her left hand and announce to the world that he, Mr J.L.B. Matekoni, the proprietor of Tlok-weng Road Speedy Motors, was to be her husband.

THE PREMISES of Judgment-day Jewellers were tucked away at the end of a dusty street, alongside the Salvation Bookshop, which sold Bibles and other religious texts, and Mothobani Bookkeeping Services: *Tell the Taxman to go away*. It was a rather unprepossessing shop, with a sloping verandah roof supported by whitewashed brick pillars. The sign, which had been painted by an amateur sign-writer of modest talent, showed the head and shoulders of a glamorous woman wearing an elaborate necklace and large pendant earrings. The woman was smiling in a lopsided way, in spite of the weight of the earrings and the evident discomfort of the necklace.

Mr J.L.B. Matekoni and Mma Ramotswe parked on the opposite side of the road, under the shade of an acacia tree. They were later than they had anticipated, and the heat of the day was already beginning to build up. By midday any vehicle left out in the sun would be almost impossible to touch, the seats too hot for exposed flesh, the steering wheel a rim of fire. Shade would prevent this, and under every tree there were nests of cars, nosed up against the trunks, like piglets to a sow, in order to enjoy the maximum protection afforded by the incomplete panoply of grey-green foliage.

The door was locked, but clicked open obligingly when Mr J.L.B. Matekoni sounded the electric bell. Inside the shop, standing behind the counter, was a thin man clad in khaki. He had a narrow head, and both his slightly slanted eyes and the golden tinge to his skin suggested some San blood—the blood of the Kalahari bushmen. But if this were so, then what would he be doing working in a jewellery shop? There was no real reason why he should not, of course, but it seemed inappropriate. Jewellery shops attracted Indian people, or Kenyans, who liked work of that sort; Basarwa were happier working with livestock—they made great cattlemen or ostrich hands.

The jeweller smiled at them. "I saw you outside," he said. "You parked your car under that tree."

Mr J.L.B. Matekoni knew that he was right. The man spoke correct Setswana, but his accent confirmed the visible signs. Underneath the vowels, there were clicks and whistles struggling to get out. It was a peculiar language, the San language, more like the sound of birds in the trees than people talking.

He introduced himself, as was polite, and then he turned to Mma Ramotswe.

"This lady is now engaged to me," he said. "She is Mma Ramotswe, and I wish to buy her a ring for this engagement." He paused. "A diamond ring."

The jeweller looked at him through his hooded eyes, and then shifted his gaze sideways to Mma Ramotswe. She looked back at him, and thought: *There is intelligence here. This is a clever man who cannot be trusted.*

"You are a fortunate man," said the jeweller. "Not every man can find such a cheerful, fat woman to marry. There are many thin, hectoring women around today. This one will make you very happy."

Mr J.L.B. Matekoni acknowledged the compliment. "Yes," he said. "I am a lucky man."

"And now you must buy her a very big ring," went on the jeweller. "A fat woman cannot wear a tiny ring."

Mr J.L.B. Matekoni looked down at his shoes.

"I was thinking of a medium-sized ring," he said. "I am not a rich man."

"I know who you are," said the jeweller. "You are the man who owns Tlokweng Road Speedy Motors. You can afford a good ring."

Mma Ramotswe decided to intervene. "I do not want a big ring," she said firmly. "I am not a lady to wear a big ring. I was hoping for a small ring."

The jeweller threw her a glance. He seemed almost annoyed by her presence—as if this were a transaction between men, like a transaction over cattle, and she was interfering.

"I'll show you some rings," he said, bending down to slide a drawer out of the counter below him. "Here are some good diamond rings."

He placed the drawer on the top of the counter and pointed to a row of rings nestling in velvet slots. Mr J.L.B. Matekoni caught his breath. The diamonds were set in the rings in clusters: a large stone in the middle surrounded by smaller ones. Several rings had other stones too—emeralds and rubies—and beneath each of them a small tag disclosed the price.

"Don't pay any attention to what the label says," said the jeweller, lowering his voice. "I can offer very big discounts."

Mma Ramotswe peered at the tray. Then she looked up and shook her head.

"These are too big," she said. "I told you that I wanted a smaller ring. Perhaps we shall have to go to some other shop."

The jeweller sighed. "I have some others," he said. "I have small rings as well."

He slipped the tray back into its place and extracted another. The rings on this one were considerably smaller. Mma Ramotswe pointed to a ring in the middle of the tray.

"I like that one," she said. "Let us see that one."

"It is not very big," said the jeweller. "A diamond like that may easily be missed. People may not notice it."

"I don't care," said Mma Ramotswe. "This diamond is going to be for me. It is nothing to do with other people."

Mr J.L.B. Matekoni felt a surge of pride as she spoke. This was the woman he admired, the woman who believed in the old Botswana values and who had no time for showiness.

"I like that ring too," he said. "Please let Mma Ramotswe try it on."

The ring was passed to Mma Ramotswe, who slipped it on her finger and held out her hand for Mr J.L.B. Matekoni to examine.

"It suits you perfectly," he said.

She smiled. "If this is the ring you would like to buy me, then I would be very happy."

The jeweller picked up the price tag and passed it to Mr J.L.B. Matekoni. "There can be no further discount on this one," he said. "It is already very cheap."

Mr J.L.B. Matekoni was pleasantly surprised by the price. He had just replaced the coolant unit on a customer's van and this, he noticed, was the same price, down to the last pula. It was not expensive. Reaching into his pocket, he took out the wad of notes which he had drawn from the bank earlier that morning and paid the jeweller.

"One thing I must ask you," Mr J.L.B. Matekoni said to the jeweller. "Is this diamond a Botswana diamond?"

The jeweller looked at him curiously.

"Why are you interested in that?" he asked. "A diamond is a diamond wherever it comes from."

"I know that," said Mr J.L.B. Matekoni. "But I would like to think that my wife will be wearing one of our own stones."

The jeweller smiled. "In that case, yes, it is. All these stones are stones from our own mines."

"Thank you," said Mr J.L.B. Matekoni. "I am happy to hear that."

THEY DROVE back from the jeweller's shop, past the Anglican Cathedral and the Princess Marina Hospital. As they passed the Cathedral, Mma Ramotswe said: "I think that perhaps we should get married there. Perhaps we can get Bishop Makhulu himself to marry us."

"I would like that," said Mr J.L.B. Matekoni. "He is a good man, the Bishop."

"Then a good man will be conducting the wedding of a good man," said Mma Ramotswe. "You are a kind man, Mr J.L.B. Matekoni."

Mr J.L.B. Matekoni said nothing. It was not easy to respond to a compliment, particularly when one felt that the compliment was undeserved. He did not think that he was a particularly good man. There were many faults in his character, he thought, and if anyone was good, it was Mma Ramotswe. She was far better than he was. He was just a mechanic who tried his best; she was far more than that.

They turned down Zebra Drive and drove into the short drive in front of Mma Ramotswe's house, bringing the car to a halt under the shade-netting at the side of her verandah. Rose, Mma Ramotswe's maid, looked out of the kitchen window and waved to them. She had done the day's laundry and it was hanging out on the line, white against the red-brown earth and blue sky.

Mr J.L.B. Matekoni took Mma Ramotswe's hand, touching, for a moment, the glittering ring. He looked at her, and saw that there were tears in her eyes.

"I'm sorry," she said. "I should not be crying, but I cannot help it."

"Why are you sad?" he asked. "You must not be sad."

She wiped away a tear and then shook her head.

"I'm not sad," she said. "It's just that nobody has ever given me anything like this ring before. When I married Note he gave me nothing. I had hoped that there would be a ring, but there was not. Now I have a ring."

"I will try to make up for Note," said Mr J.L.B. Matekoni. "I will try to be a good husband for you."

Mma Ramotswe nodded. "You will be," she said. "And I shall try to be a good wife for you."

They sat for a moment, saying nothing, each with the thoughts that the moment demanded. Then Mr J.L.B. Matekoni got out, walked round the front of the car, and opened her door for her. They would go inside for bush tea and she would show Rose the ring and the diamond that had made her so happy and so sad at the same time.

CHAPTER SIX

A DRY PLACE

SITTING IN her office at the No. 1 Ladies' Detective Agency, Mma Ramotswe reflected on how easy it was to find oneself committed to a course of action simply because one lacked the courage to say no. She did not really want to take on the search for a solution to what happened to Mrs Curtin's son; Clovis Andersen, the author of her professional bible, *The Principles of Private Detection,* would have described the enquiry as stale. "A stale enquiry," he wrote, "is unrewarding to all concerned. The client is given false hopes because a detective is working on the case, and the agent himself feels committed to coming up with something because of the client's expectations. This means that the agent will probably spend more time on the case than the circumstances should warrant. At the end of the day, nothing is likely to be achieved and one is left wondering whether there is not a case for allowing the past to be buried with decency. *Let the past alone* is sometimes the best advice that can be given."

Mma Ramotswe had reread this passage several times and had found herself agreeing with the sentiments it expressed. There was far too much interest in the past, she thought. People were forever digging up events that had taken place a long time ago. And what was the point in doing this if the effect was merely to poison the present? There were many wrongs in the past, but did it help to keep bringing them up and giving them a fresh airing? She thought of the Shona people and how they kept going on about what the Ndebele did to them under Mzilikazi and Lobengula. It is true that they did terrible things—after all, they were really Zulus and had always oppressed their neighbours—but surely that was no justification for continuing to talk about it. It would be better to forget all that once and for all.

She thought of Seretse Khama, Paramount Chief of the Bamgwato, First President of Botswana, Statesman. Look at the way the British had treated him, refusing to recognize his choice of bride and forcing him into exile simply because he had married an Englishwoman. How could they have done such an insensitive and cruel thing to a man like that? To send a man away from his land, from his people, was surely one of the cruellest punishments that could he devised. And it left the people leaderless; it cut at their very soul: *Where is our Khama? Where is the son of Kgosi Sekgoma II and the mohumagadi Tebogo?* But Seretse himself never made much of this later on. He did not talk about it and he was never anything but courteous to the British Government and to the Queen herself. A lesser man would have said: Look what you did to me, and now you expect me to be your friend!

Then there was Mr Mandela. Everybody knew about Mr
Mandela and how he had forgiven those who had imprisoned
him. They had taken away years and years of his life simply
because he wanted justice. They had set him to work in a
quarry and his eyes had been permanently damaged by the
rock dust. But at last, when he had walked out of the prison on
that breathless, luminous day, he had said nothing about
revenge or even retribution. He had said that there were more
important things to do than to complain about the past, and in
time he had shown that he meant this by hundreds of acts of
kindness towards those who had treated him so badly. That
was the real African way, the tradition that was closest to the
heart of Africa. We are all children of Africa, and none of us is
better or more important than the other. This is what Africa
could say to the world: it could remind it what it is to be
human.

She appreciated that, and she understood the greatness that
Khama and Mandela showed in forgiving the past. And yet,
Mrs Curtin's case was different. It did not seem to her that the
American woman was keen to find somebody to blame for her
son's disappearance, although she knew that there were many
people in such circumstances who became obsessed with
finding somebody to punish. And, of course, there was the
whole problem of punishment. Mma Ramotswe sighed. She
supposed that punishment was sometimes needed to make it
clear that what somebody had done was wrong, but she had
never been able to understand why we should wish to punish
those who repented for their misdeeds. When she was a girl in
Mochudi, she had seen a boy beaten for losing a goat. He had
confessed that he had gone to sleep under a tree when he
should have been watching the herd, and he had said that he

was truly sorry that he had allowed the goat to wander. What was the point, she wondered, in his uncle beating him with a mopani stick until he cried out for mercy? Such punishment achieved nothing and merely disfigured the person who exacted it.

But these were large issues, and the more immediate problem was where to start with the search for that poor, dead American boy. She imagined Clovis Andersen shaking his head and saying, "Well, Mma Ramotswe, you've landed yourself with a stale case in spite of what I say about these things. But since you've done so, then my usual advice to you is to go back to the beginning. Start there." The beginning, she supposed, was the farm where Burkhardt and his friends had set up their project. It would not be difficult to find the place itself, although she doubted whether she would discover anything. But at least it would give her a feeling for the matter, and that, she knew, was the beginning. Places had echoes—and if one were sensitive, one might just pick up some resonance from the past, some feeling for what had happened.

AT LEAST she knew how to find the village. Her secretary, Mma Makutsi, had a cousin who came from the village nearest to the farm and she had explained which road to take. It was out to the west, not far from Molepolole. It was dry country, verging on the Kalahari, covered with low bushes and thorn trees. It was sparsely populated, but in those areas where there was more water, people had established small villages and clusters of small houses around the sorghum and melon fields. There was not much to do here, and people moved to Lobatse or Gaborone for work if they were in a position to do so. Gaborone was full of people from places like this. They came to the city, but kept their ties with their lands and their cattle post. Places like this would always be home, no matter how long people spent away. At the end of the day, this is where they would wish to die, under these great, wide skies, which were like a limitless ocean.

She travelled down in her tiny white van on a Saturday morning, setting off early, as she liked to do on any trip. As she left the town, there were already streams of people coming in for a Saturday's shopping. It was the end of the month, which meant payday, and the shops would be noisy and crowded as people bought their large jars of syrup and beans, or splashed out on the coveted new dress or shoes. Mma Ramotswe liked shopping, but she never shopped around payday. Prices went up then, she was convinced, and went down again towards the middle of the month, when nobody had any money.

Most of the traffic on the road consisted of buses and vans bringing people in. But there were a few going in the opposite direction—workers from town heading off for a weekend back in their villages; men going back to their wives and children; women working as maids in Gaborone going back to spend their precious days of leisure with their parents and grandparents. Mma Ramotswe slowed down; there was a woman standing at the side of the road, waving her hand to request a lift. She was a woman of about Mma Ramotswe's age, dressed smartly in a black skirt and a bright red jersey. Mma Ramotswe hesitated, and then stopped. She could not leave her standing there; somewhere there would be a family waiting for her, counting on a motorist to bring their mother home.

She drew to a halt, and called out of the window of her van. "Where are you going, Mma?"

"I am going down that way," said the woman, pointing down the road. "Just beyond Molepolole. I am going to Silokwolela."

Mma Ramotswe smiled. "I am going there too," she said. "I can take you all the way."

The woman let out a whoop of delight. "You are very kind, and I am a very lucky person."

She reached down for the plastic bag in which she was carrying her possessions and opened the passenger door of Mma Ramotswe's van. Then, her belongings stored at her feet, Mma Ramotswe pulled out into the road again and they set off. From old habit, Mma Ramotswe glanced at her new travelling companion and made her assessment. She was quite well dressed—the jersey was new, and was real wool rather than the cheap artificial fibres that so many people bought these days; the skirt was a cheap one, though, and the shoes were slightly scuffed. This lady works in a shop, she thought. She has passed her standard six, and maybe even form two or three. She has no husband, and her children are living with the grandmother out at Silokwolela. Mma Ramotswe had seen the copy of the Bible tucked into the top of the plastic bag and this had given her more information. This lady was a member of a church, and was perhaps going to Bible classes. She would be reading her Bible to the children that night.

"Your children are down there, Mma?" asked Mma Ramotswe politely.

"Yes," came the reply. "They are staying with their grandmother. I work in a shop in Gaborone, New Deal Furnishers. You know them maybe?"

Mma Ramotswe nodded, as much for the confirmation of her judgement as in answer to the question.

"I have no husband," she went on. "He went to Francistown and he died of burps."

Mma Ramotswe gave a start. "Burps? You can die of burps?"

"Yes. He was burping very badly up in Francistown and they took him to the hospital. They gave him an operation and they found that there was something very bad inside him. This thing made him burp. Then he died."

There was a silence. Then Mma Ramotswe spoke. "I am very sorry."

"Thank you. I was very sad when this happened, as he was a very good man and he had been a good father to my children. But my mother was still strong, and she said that she would look after them. I could get a job in Gaborone, because I have my form two certificate. I went to the furniture shop and they were very pleased with my work. I am now one of the top salesladies and they have even booked me to go on a sales training course in Mafikeng."

Mma Ramotswe smiled. "You have done very well. It is not easy for women. Men expect us to do all the work and then they take the best jobs. It is not easy to be a successful lady."

"But I can tell that you are successful," said the woman. "I can tell that you are a business lady. I can tell that you are doing well."

Mma Ramotswe thought for a moment. She prided herself on her ability to sum people up, but she wondered whether this was not something that many women had, as part of the intuitive gift.

"You tell me what I do," she said. "Could you guess what my job is?"

The woman turned in her seat and looked Mma Ramotswe up and down.

"You are a detective, I think," she said. "You are a person who looks into other people's business."

The tiny white van swerved momentarily. Mma Ramotswe was shocked that this woman had guessed. Her intuitive powers must be even better than mine, she thought.

"How did you know that? What did I do to give you this information?"

The other woman shifted her gaze. "It was simple," she said. "I have seen you sitting outside your detective agency drinking tea with your secretary. She is that lady with very big glasses. The two of you sit there in the shade sometimes and I have been walking past on the other side of the road. That is how I knew."

They travelled in comfortable companionship, talking about their daily lives. She was called Mma Tsbago, and she told Mma Ramotswe about her work in the furniture shop. The manager was a kind man, she said, who did not work his staff too hard and who was always honest with his customers. She had been offered a job by another firm, at a higher wage, but had refused it. Her manager found out and had rewarded her loyalty with a promotion.

Then there were her children. They were a girl of ten and a boy of eight. They were doing well at school and she hoped that she might be able to bring them to Gaborone for their secondary education. She had heard the Gaborone Government Secondary School was very good and she hoped that she might be able to get a place for them there. She had also heard that there were scholarships to even better schools, and perhaps they might have a chance of one of those.

Mma Ramotswe told her that she was engaged to be married, and she pointed to the diamond on her finger. Mma

Tsbago admired it and asked who the fiancé was. It was a good thing to marry a mechanic, she said, as she had heard that they made the best husbands. You should try to marry a policeman, a mechanic or a minister of religion, she said, and you should never marry a politician, a barman, or a taxi driver. These people always caused a great deal of trouble for their wives.

"And you shouldn't marry a trumpeter," added Mma Ramotswe. "I made that mistake. I married a bad man called Note Mokoti. He played the trumpet."

"I'm sure that they are not good people to marry," said Mma Tsbago. "I shall add them to my list."

THEY MADE slow progress on the last part of the journey. The road, which was untarred, was pitted with large and dangerous potholes, and at several points they were obliged to edge dangerously out into the sandy verge to avoid a particularly large hole. This was perilous, as the tiny white van could easily become stuck in the sand if they were not careful and they might have to wait hours for rescue. But at last they arrived at Mma Tsbago's village, which was the village closest to the farm that Mma Ramotswe was seeking.

She had asked Mma Tsbago about the settlement, and had been provided with some information. She remembered the project, although she had not known the people involved in it. She recalled that there had been a white man and a woman from South Africa, and one or two other foreigners. A number of the people from the village had worked there, and people had thought that great things would come of it, but it had eventually fizzled out. She had not been surprised at that. Things fizzled out; you could not hope to change Africa. People lost interest, or they went back to their traditional way of doing things, or they simply gave up because it was all too much effort. And then Africa had a way of coming back and simply covering everything up again.

"Is there somebody in the village who can take me out there?" asked Mma Ramotswe.

Mma Tsbago thought for a moment.

"There are still some people who worked out there," she said. "There is a friend of my uncle. He had a job out there for a while. We can go to his place and you can ask him."

THEY WENT first to Mma Tsbago's house. It was a traditional Botswana house, made out of ochre mud bricks and surrounded by a low wall, a *lomotana*, which created a tiny yard in front of and alongside the house. Outside this wall there were two thatched grain bins, on raised legs, and a chicken house. At the back, made out of tin and leaning dangerously, was the privy, with an old plank door and a rope with which the door could be tied shut. The children ran out immediately, and embraced their mother, before waiting shyly to be introduced to the stranger. Then, from the dark interior of the house, there emerged the grandmother, wearing a threadbare white dress and grinning toothlessly.

Mma Tsbago left her bag in the house and explained that she would return within an hour. Mma Ramotswe gave sweets to the children, which they received with both palms upturned, thanking her gravely in the correct Setswana manner. These were children who would understand the old ways, thought Mma Ramotswe, approvingly—unlike some of the children in Gaborone.

They left the house and drove through the village in the white van. It was a typical Botswana village, a sprawling collection of one- or two-room houses, each in its own yard, each with a motley collection of thorn trees surrounding it. The houses were linked by paths, which wandered this way and that, skirting fields and crop patches. Cattle moved about listlessly, cropping at the occasional patch of brown, withered grass, while a pot-bellied herd-boy, dusty and be-aproned, watched them from under a tree. The cattle were unmarked, but everybody would know their owner, and their lineage. These were the signs of wealth, the embodied result of somebody's labours in the diamond mine at Jwaneng or the beef-canning factory at Lobatse.

Mma Tsbago directed her to a house on the edge of the village. It was a well-kept place, slightly larger than its immediate neighbours, and had been painted in the style of the traditional Botswana house, in reds and browns and with a bold, diamond pattern etched out in white. The yard was wellswept, which suggested that the woman of the house, who would also have painted it, was conscientious with her reed broom. Houses, and their decoration, were the responsibility of the woman, and this woman had evidently had the old skills passed down to her.

They waited at the gate while Mma Tsbago called out for permission to enter. It was rude to go up the path without first calling, and even ruder to go into a building uninvited.

"Ko, Ko!" called out Mma Tsbago. "Mma Potsane, I am here to see you!"

There was no response, and Mma Tsbago repeated her call. Again no answer came, and then the door of the house suddenly opened and a small, rotund woman, dressed in a long skirt and high-collared white blouse, came out and peered in their direction.

"Who is that?" she called out, shading her eyes with a hand. "Who are you? I cannot see you."

"Mma Tsbago. You know me. I am here with a stranger."

The householder laughed. "I thought it might be somebody else, and I quickly got dressed up. But I need not have bothered!"

She gestured for them to enter and they walked across to meet her.

"I cannot see very well these days," explained Mma Potsane. "My eyes are getting worse and worse. That is why I didn't know who you were."

They shook hands, exchanging formal greetings. Then Mma Potsane gestured across to a bench which stood in the shade of the large tree beside her house. They could sit there, she explained, because the house was too dark inside.

Mma Tsbago explained why they were there and Mma Potsane listened intently. Her eyes appeared to be irritating her, and from time to time she wiped at them with the sleeve of her blouse. As Mma Tsbago spoke, she nodded encouragement.

"Yes," she said. "We lived out there. My husband worked there. We both worked there. We hoped that we would be able to make some money with our crops and for a while it worked. Then . . ." She broke off, shrugging despondently.

"Things went wrong?" asked Mma Ramotswe. "Drought?"

Mma Potsane sighed. "There was a drought, yes. But there's always a drought, isn't there? No, it was just that people lost faith in the idea. There were good people living there, but they went away."

"The white man from Namibia? The German one?" asked Mma Ramotswe.

"Yes, that one. He was a good man, but he went away. Then there were other people, Batswana, who decided that they had had enough. They went too."

"And an American?" pressed Mma Ramotswe. "There was an American boy?"

Mma Potsane rubbed at her eyes. "That boy vanished. He disappeared one night. They had the police out here and they searched and searched. His mother came too, many times. She brought a Mosarwa tracker with her, a tiny little man, like a dog with his nose to the ground. He had a very fat bottom, like all those Basarwa have."

"He found nothing?" Mma Ramotswe knew the answer to this, but she wanted to keep the other woman talking. She had so far only heard the story from Mrs Curtin's viewpoint; it was quite possible that there were things which other people had seen which she did not know about.

"He ran round and round like a dog," said Mma Potsane, laughing. "He looked under stones and sniffed the air and muttered away in that peculiar language of theirs—you know how it is, all those sounds like trees in the wind and twigs breaking. But he found no sign of any wild animals which may have taken that boy."

Mma Ramotswe passed her a handkerchief to dab her eyes. "So what do you think happened to him, Mma? How can somebody just vanish like that?"

Mma Potsane sniffed and then blew her nose on Mma Ramotswe's handkerchief.

"I think that he was sucked up," she said. "There are sometimes whirlwinds here in the very hot season. They come in from the Kalahari and they suck things up. I think that maybe that boy got sucked up in a whirlwind and put down somewhere far, far away. Maybe over by Ghanzi way or in the middle of the Kalahari or somewhere. No wonder they didn't find him."

Mma Tsbago looked sideways at Mma Ramotswe, trying to catch her eye, but Mma Ramotswe looked straight ahead at Mma Potsane.

"That is always possible, Mma," she said. "That is an interesting idea." She paused. "Could you take me out there and show me round? I have a van here."

Mma Potsane thought for a moment. "I do not like to go out there," she said. "It is a sad place for me."

"I have twenty pula for your expenses," said Mma Ramotswe, reaching into her pocket. "I had hoped that you would be able to accept this from me."

"Of course," said Mma Potsane hurriedly. "We can go there. I do not like to go there at night, but in the day it is different."

"Now?" said Mma Ramotswe. "Could you come now?"

"I am not busy," said Mma Potsane. "There is nothing happening here."

Mma Ramotswe passed the money over to Mma Potsane, who thanked her, clapping both hands in a sign of gratitude. Then they walked back over her neatly swept yard and, saying goodbye to Mma Tsbago, they climbed into the van and drove off.

CHAPTER SEVEN

FURTHER PROBLEMS WITH THE
ORPHAN-FARM PUMP

ON THE day that Mma Ramotswe travelled out to Silok-wolela, Mr J.L.B. Matekoni felt vaguely ill at ease. He had become accustomed to meeting Mma Ramotswe on a Saturday morning to help her with her shopping or with some task about the house. Without her, he felt at a loose end: Gaborone seemed strangely empty; the garage was closed, and he had no desire to attend to the paperwork that had been piling up on his desk. He could call on a friend, of course, and perhaps go and watch a football match, but again he was not in the mood for that. Then he thought of Mma Silvia Potokwane, Matron in Charge of the Orphan Farm. There was inevitably something happening out there, and she was always happy to sit down and have a chat over a cup of tea. He would go out there and see how everything was. Then the rest of the day could take care of itself until Mma Ramotswe returned that evening.

Mma Potokwane spotted him, as usual, as he parked his car under one of the syringa trees.

"I see you!" she shouted from her window. "I see you, Mr J.L.B. Matekoni!"

Mr J.L.B. Matekoni waved in her direction as he locked the car. Then he strode towards the office, where the sound of cheerful music drifted out of one of the windows. Inside, Mma Potokwane was sitting beside her desk, a telephone receiver to her ear. She motioned for him to sit down and continued with her conversation.

"If you can give me some of that cooking oil," she said, "the orphans will be very happy. They like to have their potatoes fried in oil and it is good for them."

The voice at the other end said something, and she frowned, glancing up at Mr J.L.B. Matekoni, as if to share her irritation.

"But you cannot sell that oil if it is beyond its expiry date. So why should I pay you anything for it? It would be better to give it to the orphans than to pour it down the drain. I cannot give you money for it, and so I see no reason why you shouldn't give it to us."

Again something was said on the other end of the line, and she nodded patiently.

"I can make sure that the *Daily News* comes to photograph you handing the oil over. Everybody will know that you are a generous man. It will be there in the papers."

There was a further brief exchange and then she replaced the receiver.

"Some people are slow to give," she said. "It is something to do with how their mothers brought them up. I have read all about this problem in a book. There is a doctor called Dr

Freud who is very famous and has written many books about such people."

"Is he in Johannesburg?" asked Mr J.L.B. Matekoni.

"I do not think so," said Mma Potokwane. "It is a book from London. But it is very interesting. He says that all boys are in love with their mother."

"That is natural," said Mr J.L.B. Matekoni. "Of course boys love their mothers. Why should they not do so?"

Mma Potokwane shrugged. "I agree with you. I cannot see what is wrong with a boy loving his mother."

"Then why is Dr Freud worried about this?" went on Mr J.L.B. Matekoni. "Surely he should be worried if they did *not* love their mothers."

Mma Potokwane looked thoughtful. "Yes. But he was still very worried about these boys and I think he tried to stop them."

"That is ridiculous," said Mr J.L.B. Matekoni. "Surely he had better things to do with his time."

"You would have thought so," said Mma Potokwane. "But in spite of this Dr Freud, boys still go on loving their mothers, which is how it should be."

She paused, and then, brightening at the abandonment of this difficult subject, she smiled broadly at Mr J.L.B. Matekoni. "I am very glad that you came out today. I was going to phone you."

Mr J.L.B. Matekoni sighed. "Brakes? Or the pump?"

"The pump," said Mma Potokwane. "It is making a very strange noise. The water comes all right, but the pump makes a noise as if it is in pain."

"Engines do feel pain," said Mr J.L.B. Matekoni. "They tell us of their pain by making a noise."

"Then this pump needs help," said Mma Potokwane. "Can you take a quick look at it?"

"Of course," said Mr J.L.B. Matekoni.

IT TOOK him longer than he had expected, but at last he found the cause and was able to attend to it. The pump reassembled, he tested it, and it ran sweetly once more. It would need a total refit, of course, and that day would not be able to be put off for much longer, but at least the strange, moaning sound had stopped.

Back in Mma Potokwane's office, he relaxed with his cup of tea and a large slab of currant cake which the cooks had baked that morning. The orphans were well fed. The Government looked after its orphans well and gave a generous grant each year. But there were also private donors—a network of people who gave in money, or kind, to the orphan farm. This meant that none of the orphans actually wanted for anything and none of them was malnourished, as happened in so many other African countries. Botswana was a well-blessed country. Nobody starved and nobody languished in prison for their political beliefs. As Mma Ramotswe had pointed out to him, the Batswana could hold their heads up anywhere—anywhere.

"This is good cake," said Mr J.L.B. Matekoni. "The children must love it."

Mma Potokwane smiled. "Our children love cake. If we gave them nothing but cake, they would be very happy. But of course we don't. The orphans need onions and beans too."

Mr J.L.B. Matekoni nodded. "A balanced diet," he said widely. "They say that a balanced diet is the key to health."

There was silence for a moment as they reflected on his observation. Then Mma Potokwane spoke.

"So you will be a married man soon," she said. "That will make your life different. You will have to behave yourself, Mr J.L.B. Matekoni!"

He laughed, scraping up the last crumbs of his cake. "Mma Ramotswe will watch me. She will make sure that I behave myself well."

"Mmm," said Mma Potokwane. "Will you be living in her house or in yours?"

"I think it will be her house," said Mr J.L.B. Matekoni. "It is a bit nicer than mine. Her house is in Zebra Drive, you know."

"Yes," said the Matron. "I have seen her place. I drove past it the other day. It looks very nice."

Mr J.L.B. Matekoni looked surprised. "You drove past specially to take a look?"

"Well," said Mma Potokwane, grinning slightly. "I thought that I might just see what sort of place it was. It's quite big, isn't it?"

"It's a comfortable house," said Mr J.L.B. Matekoni. "I think that there will be enough room for us."

"Too much room," said Mma Potokwane. "There will be room for children."

Mr J.L.B. Matekoni frowned. "We had not been thinking of that. We are maybe a bit old for children. I am forty-five. And then . . . Well, I do not like to talk about it, but Mma Ramotswe has told me that she cannot have children. She had a baby, you know, but it died and now the doctors have said to her that . . ."

Mma Potokwane shook her head. "That is very sad. I am very sad for her."

"But we are very happy," said Mr J.L.B. Matekoni. "Even if we do not have children."

Mma Potokwane reached over to the teapot and poured her guest another cup of tea. Then she cut a further slice of cake—a generous helping—and slid it onto his plate.

"Of course, there is always adoption," she said, watching him as she spoke. "Or you could always just look after a child if you didn't want to adopt. You could take . . ." She paused, raising her teacup to her lips. "You could always take an orphan." Adding hurriedly: "Or even a couple of orphans."

Mr J.L.B. Matekoni stared at his shoes. "I don't know. I don't think I would like to adopt a child. But . . ."

"But a child could come and live with you. There's no need to go to all the trouble of adoption papers and magistrates," said Mma Potokwane. "Imagine how nice that would be!"

"Maybe . . . I don't know. Children are a big responsibility."

Mma Potokwane laughed. "But you're a man who takes responsibility easily. There you are with your garage, that's a responsibility. And those apprentices of yours. They're a responsibility too, aren't they? You are well used to responsibility." Mr J.L.B. Matekoni thought of his apprentices. They, too, had just appeared, sidling into the garage shortly after he had telephoned the technical trades college and offered to give two apprenticeships. He had entertained great hopes of them, but had been disappointed virtually from the beginning. When he was their age he had been full of ambition, but they seemed to take everything for granted. At first he had been unable to understand why they seemed so passive, but then all had been explained to him by a friend. "Young people these days cannot show enthusiasm," he had been told. "It's not considered smart to be enthusiastic." So this is what was wrong with the apprentices. They wanted to be thought smart.

On one occasion, when Mr J.L.B. Matekoni felt particularly irritated at seeing the two young men sitting unenthusiastically on their empty oil drums staring into the air he had raised his voice at them.

"So you think you're smart?" he shouted. "Is that what you think?"

The two apprentices had glanced at one another.

"No," said one, after a few moments. "No, we don't."

He had felt deflated and had slammed the door of his office. It appeared that they lacked the enthusiasm even to respond to his challenge, which just proved what he had thought anyway.

Now, thinking of children, he wondered whether he would have the energy to deal with them. He was approaching the point in life when he wanted a quiet and orderly time. He wanted to be able to fix engines in his own garage during the day and to spend his evenings with Mma Ramotswe. That would be bliss! Would children not introduce a note of stress into their domestic life? Children needed to be taken to school and put in the bathtub and taken to the nurse for injections. Parents always seemed so worn out by their children and he wondered whether he and Mma Ramotswe would really want that.

"I can tell that you're thinking about it," said Mma Potokwane. "I think your mind is almost made up."

"I don't know . . ."

"What you should do is just take the plunge," she went on. "You could give the children to Mma Ramotswe as a wedding present. Women love children. She will be very pleased. She'll be getting a husband and some children all on the same day! Any lady would love that, believe me."

"But . . ."

Mma Potokwane cut him short. "Now there are two children who would be very happy to go and live with you," she said. "Let them come on trial. You can decide after a month or so whether they can stay."

"Two children? There are two?" stuttered Mr J.L.B. Matekoni. "I thought . . ."

"They are a brother and sister," Mma Potokwane went on hurriedly. "We do not like to split up brothers and sisters. The girl is twelve and the boy is just five. They are very nice children."

"I don't know . . . I would have to . . ."

"In fact," said Mma Potokwane, rising to her feet. "I think that you have met one of them already. The girl who brought you water. The child who cannot walk."

Mr J.L.B. Matekoni said nothing. He remembered the child, who had been very polite and appreciative. But would it not be rather burdensome to look after a handicapped child? Mma Potokwane had said nothing about this when she had first raised the subject. She had slipped in an extra child—the brother—and now she was casually mentioning the wheelchair, as if it made no difference. He stopped himself. He could be in that chair himself.

Mma Potokwane was looking out of the window. Now she turned to address him.

"Would you like me to call that child?" she asked. "I am not trying to force you, Mr J.L.B. Matekoni, but would you like to meet her again, and the little boy?"

The room was silent, apart from a sudden creak from the tin roof, expanding in the heat. Mr J.L.B. Matekoni looked down at his shoes, and remembered, for a moment, how it was to be a child, back in the village, all those years ago. And remembered how he had experienced the kindness of the local mechanic, who had let him polish trucks and help with the mending of punctures, and who by this kindness had revealed and nurtured a vocation. It was easy to make a difference to other people's lives, so easy to change the little room in which people lived their life.

"Call them," he said. "I would like to see them."

Mma Potokwane smiled. "You are a good man, Mr J.L.B. Matekoni," she said. "I will send word for them to come. They will have to be fetched from the fields. But while we are waiting, I'm going to tell you their story. You listen to this."

CHAPTER EIGHT

THE CHILDREN'S TALE

YOU MUST understand, said Mma Potokwane, that although it is easy for us to criticize the ways of the Basarwa, we should think carefully before we do that. When you look at the life they lead, out there in the Kalahari, with no cattle of their own and no houses to live in; when you think about that and wonder how long you and I and other Batswana would be able to live like that, then you realize that these bushmen are remarkable people.

There were some of these people who wandered around on the edge of the Makadikadi Salt Pans, up on the road over to the Okavango. I don't know that part of the country very well, but I have been up there once or twice. I remember the first time I saw it: a wide, white plain under a white sky, with a few tall palm trees and grass that seemed to grow out of nothing. It was such a strange landscape that I thought I had wandered out of Botswana into some foreign land. But just a little bit farther on it changes back into Botswana and you feel comfortable again.

There was a band of Masarwa who had come up from the Kalahari to hunt ostriches. They must have found water in the salt pans and then wandered on towards one of the villages along the road to Maun. The people up there are sometimes suspicious of Basarwa, as they say that they steal their goats and will milk their cows at night if they are not watched closely.

This band had made a camp about two or three miles outside the village. They hadn't built anything, of course, but were sleeping under the bushes, as they often do. They had plenty of meat—having just killed several ostriches—and were happy to stay there until the urge came upon them to move.

There were a number of children and one of the women had just given birth to a baby, a boy. She was sleeping with him at her side, a little bit away from the others. She had a daughter, too, who was sleeping on the other side of her mother. The mother woke up, we assume, and moved her legs about to be more comfortable. Unfortunately there was a snake at her feet, and she rested her heel on its head. The snake bit her. That's how most snakebites occur. People are asleep on their sleeping mats and snakes come in for the warmth. Then they roll over onto the snake and the snake defends itself.

They gave her some of their herbs. They're always digging up roots and stripping bark off trees, but nothing like that can deal with a *lebolobolo* bite, which is what this must have been. According to the daughter, her mother died before the baby even woke up. Of course, they don't lose any time and they prepared to bury the mother that morning. But, as you might or might not know, Mr J.L.B. Matekoni, when a Mosarwa woman dies and she's still feeding a baby, they bury the baby too. There just isn't the food to support a baby without a mother. That's the way it is.

The girl hid in the bush and watched them take her mother and her baby brother. It was sandy there, and all they could manage was a shallow grave, in which they laid her mother, while the other women wailed and the men sang something. The girl watched as they put her tiny brother in the grave too, wrapped in an animal skin. Then they pushed the sand over them both and went back to the camp.

The moment they had gone, the child crept out and scrabbled quickly at the sand. It did not take her long, and soon she had her brother in her arms. There was sand in the child's nostrils, but he was still breathing. She turned on her heels and ran through the bush in the direction of the road, which she knew was not too far away. A truck came past a short time later, a Government truck from the Roads Department. The driver slowed, and then stopped. He must have been astonished to see a young Mosarwa child standing there with a baby in her arms. Of course he could hardly leave her, even though he could not make out what she was trying to tell him. He was going back to Francistown and he dropped her off at the Nyangabwe Hospital, handing her over to an orderly at the gate.

They looked at the baby, who was thin, and suffering badly from a fungal disease. The girl herself had tuberculosis, which is not at all unusual, and so they took her in and kept her in a TB ward for a couple of months while they gave her drugs. The baby stayed in the maternity nursery until the girl was better. Then, they let them go. Beds on the TB ward were needed for other sick people and it was not the hospital's job to look after a Mosarwa girl with a baby. I suppose they thought that she would go back to her people, which they usually do.

One of the sisters at the hospital was concerned. She saw the girl sitting at the hospital gate and she decided that she had nowhere to go. So she took her home and let her stay in her backyard, in a lean-to shack that they had used for storage but which could be cleared out to provide a room of sorts. This nurse and her husband fed the children, but they couldn't take them into the family properly, as they had two children of their own and they did not have a great deal of money.

The girl picked up Setswana quite quickly. She found ways of making a few pula by collecting empty bottles from the edge of the road and taking them back to the bottle store for the deposit. She carried the baby on her back, tied in a sling, and never let him leave her sight. I spoke to the nurse about her, and I understand that although she was still a child herself, she was a good mother to the boy. She made his clothes out of scraps that she found here and there, and she kept him clean by washing him under the tap in the nurse's backyard. Sometimes she would go and beg outside the railway station, and I think that people sometimes took pity on them and gave them money, but she preferred to earn it if she could.

This went on for four years. Then, quite without warning, the girl became ill. They took her back to the hospital and they found that the tuberculosis had damaged the bones very badly. Some of them had crumbled and this was making it difficult for her to walk. They did what they could, but they were unable to prevent her from ending up unable to walk. The nurse scrounged around for a wheelchair, which she was eventually given by one of the Roman Catholic priests. So now she looked after the boy from the wheelchair, and he, for his part, did little chores for his sister.

The nurse and her husband had to move. The husband worked for a meat-packing firm and they wanted him down in Lobatse. The nurse had heard of the orphan farm, and so she wrote to me. I said that we could take them, and I went up to Francistown to collect them just a few months ago. Now they are with us, as you have seen.

That is their story, Mr J.L.B. Matekoni. That is how they came to be here.

MR J.L.B. Matekoni said nothing. He looked at Mma Poto-kwane, who met his gaze. She had worked at the orphan farm for almost twenty years—she had been there when it had been started—and was inured to tragedy—or so she thought. But this story, which she had just told, had affected her profoundly when she had first heard it from the nurse in Francistown. Now it was having that effect on Mr J.L.B. Matekoni as well; she could see that.

"They will be here in a few moments," she said. "Do you want me to say that you might be prepared to take them?"

Mr J.L.B. Matekoni closed his eyes. He had not spoken to Mma Ramotswe about it and it seemed quite wrong to land her with something like this without consulting her first. Was this the way to start a marriage? To take a decision of such momentum without consulting one's spouse? Surely not.

And yet here were the children. The girl in her wheelchair, smiling up at him and the boy standing there so gravely, eyes lowered out of respect.

He drew in his breath. There were times in life when one had to act, and this, he suspected, was one of them.

"Would you children like to come and stay with me?" he said. "Just for a while? Then we can see how things go."

The girl looked to Mma Potokwane, as if for confirmation.

"Rra Matekoni will look after you well," she said. "You will be happy there."

The girl turned to her brother and said something to him, which the adults did not hear. The boy thought for a moment, and then nodded.

"You are very kind, Rra," she said. "We will be very happy to come with you."

Mma Potokwane clapped her hands.

"Go and pack, children," she said. "Tell your housemother that they are to give you clean clothes."

The girl turned her wheelchair round and left the room, accompanied by her brother.

"What have I done?" muttered Mr J.L.B. Matekoni, under his breath.

Mma Potokwane gave him his answer.

"A very good thing," she said.

CHAPTER NINE

THE WIND MUST COME
FROM SOMEWHERE

THEY DROVE out of the village in Mma Ramotswe's tiny white van. The dirt road was rough, virtually disappearing at points into deep potholes or rippling into a sea of corrugations that made the van creak and rattle in protest. The farm was only eight miles away from the village, but they made slow progress, and Mma Ramotswe was relieved to have Mma Potsane with her. It would be easy to get lost in the featureless bush, with no hills to guide one and each tree looking much like the next one. Though for Mma Potsane the landscape, even if dimly glimpsed, was rich in associations. Her eyes squeezed almost shut, she peered out of the van, pointing out the place where they had found a stray donkey years before, and there, by that rock, that was where a cow had died for no apparent reason. These were the intimate memories that made the land alive—that bound people to a stretch of baked earth, as valuable to them, and as beautiful, as if it were covered with sweet grass.

Mma Potsane sat forward in her seat. "There," she said. "Do you see it over there? I can see things better if they are far away. I can see it now."

Mma Ramotswe followed her gaze. The bush had become denser, thick with thorn trees, and these concealed, but not quite obscured, the shape of the buildings. Some of these were typical of the ruins to be found in southern Africa; white-washed walls that seemed to have crumbled until they were a few feet above the ground, as if flattened from above; others still had their roofs, or the framework of their roofs, the thatch having collapsed inwards, consumed by ants or taken by birds for nests.

"That is the farm?"

"Yes. And over there—do you see over there?—that is where we lived."

It was a sad homecoming for Mma Potsane, as she had warned Mma Ramotswe; this was where she had spent that quiet time with her husband after he had spent all those years away in the mines in South Africa. Their children grown up, they had been thrown back on each other's company and enjoyed the luxury of an uneventful life.

"We did not have much to do," she said. "My husband went every day to work in the fields. I sat with the other women and made clothes. The German liked us to make clothes, which he would sell in Gaborone."

The road petered out, and Mma Ramotswe brought the van to a halt under a tree. Stretching her legs, she looked through the trees at the building which must have been the main house. There must have been eleven or twelve houses at one time, judging from the ruins scattered about. It was so sad, she thought; all these buildings set down in the middle of the bush like this; all that hope, and now, all that remained were the mud foundations and the crumbling walls.

They walked over to the main house. Much of the roof had survived, as it, unlike the others, had been made of corrugated iron. There were doors too, old gauze-screened doors hanging off their jambs, and glass in some of the windows.

"That is where the German lived," said Mma Potsane. "And the American and the South African woman, and some other people from far away. We Batswana lived over there."

Mma Ramotswe nodded. "I should like to go inside that house."

Mma Potsane shook her head. "There will be nothing," she said. "The house is empty. Everybody has gone away."

"I know that. But now that we have come out here, I should like to see what it is like inside. You don't need to go in if you don't want to."

Mma Potsane winced. "I cannot let you go in by yourself," she muttered. "I shall come in with you."

They pushed at the screen which blocked the front doorway. The wood had been mined by termites, and it gave way at a touch.

"The ants will eat everything in this country," said Mma Potsane. "One day only the ants will be left. They will have eaten everything else."

They entered the house, feeling straightaway the cool that came with being out of the sun. There was a smell of dust in the air, the acrid mixed odour of the destroyed ceiling board and the creosote-impregnated timbers that had repelled the ants.

Mma Potsane gestured about the room in which they were standing. "You see. There is nothing here. It is just an empty house. We can leave now."

Mma Ramotswe ignored the suggestion. She was studying a piece of yellowing paper which had been pinned to a wall. It was a newspaper photograph—a picture of a man standing in front of a building. There had been a printed caption, but the paper had rotted and it was illegible. She beckoned for Mma Potsane to join her.

"Who is this man?"

Mma Potsane peered at the photograph, holding it close to her eyes. "I remember that man," she said. "He worked here too. He is a Motswana. He was very friendly with the American. They used to spend all their time talking, talking, like two old men at a *kgotla*."

"Was he from the village?" asked Mma Ramotswe.

Mma Potsane laughed. "No, he wasn't one of us. He was from Francistown. His father was headmaster there and he was a very clever man. This one too, the son; he was very clever. He knew many things. That was why the American was always talking to him. The German didn't like him, though. Those two were not friends."

Mma Ramotswe studied the photograph, and then gently took it off the wall and tucked it into her pocket. Mma Potsane had moved away, and she joined her, peering into the next room. Here, on the floor, there lay the skeleton of a large bird, trapped in the house and unable to get out. The bones lay where the bird must have fallen, picked clean by ants.

"This was the room they used as an office," said Mma Potsane. "They kept all the receipts and they had a small safe over there, in that corner. People sent them money, you know.

There were people in other countries who thought that this place was important. They believed that it could show that dry places like this could be changed. They wanted us to show that people could live together in a place like this and share everything."

Mma Ramotswe nodded. She was familiar with people who liked to test out all sorts of theories about how people might live. There was something about the country that attracted them, as if in that vast, dry country there was enough *air* for new ideas to breathe. Such people had been excited when the Brigade movement had been set up. They had thought it a very good idea that young people should be asked to spend time working for others and helping to build their country; but what was so exceptional about that? Did young people not work in rich countries? Perhaps they did not, and that is why these people, who came from such countries, should have found the whole idea so exciting. There was nothing wrong with these people—they were kind people usually, and treated the Batswana with respect. Yet somehow it could be *tiring* to be given advice. There was always some eager foreign organisation ready to say to Africans: this is what you do, this is how you should do things. The advice may be good, and it might work elsewhere, but Africa needed its own solutions.

This farm was yet another example of one of these schemes that did not work out. You could not grow vegetables in the Kalahari. That was all there was to it. There were many things that could grow in a place like this, but these were things that belonged here. They were not like tomatoes and lettuces. They did not belong in Botswana, or at least not in this part of it.

They left the office and wandered through the rest of the

house. Several of the rooms were open to the sky, and the floors in these rooms were covered in leaves and twigs. Lizards darted for cover, rustling the leaves, and tiny, pink and white geckoes froze where they clung to the walls, taken aback by the totally unfamiliar intrusion. Lizards; geckoes; the dust in the air; this was all it was—an empty house.

Save for the photograph.

MMA POTSANE was pleased once they were out again, and suggested that she show Mma Ramotswe the place where the vegetables had been grown. Again, the land had reasserted itself, and all that remained to show of the scheme was a pattern of wandering ditches, now eroded into tiny canyons. Here and there, it was possible to see where the wooden poles supporting the shade-netting had been erected, but there was no trace of the wood itself, which, like everything else, had been consumed by the ants.

Mma Ramotswe shaded her eyes with a hand.

"All that work," she mused. "And now this."

Mma Potsane shrugged her shoulders. "But that is always true, Mma," she said. "Even Gaborone. Look at all those buildings. How do we know that Gaborone will still be there in fifty years' time? Have the ants not got their plans for Gaborone as well?"

Mma Ramotswe smiled. It was a good way of putting it. All our human endeavours are like that, she reflected, and it is only because we are too ignorant to realize it, or are too forgetful to remember it, that we have the confidence to build something that is meant to last. Would the No. 1 Ladies' Detective

Agency be remembered in twenty years' time? Or Tlokweng
Road Speedy Motors? Probably not, but then did it matter all
that much?

The melancholy thought prompted her to remember. She
was not here to dream about archaeology but to try to find out
something about what happened all those years ago. She had
come to read a place, and had found that there was nothing, or
almost nothing, to be read. It was as if the wind had come and
rubbed it all out, scattering the pages, covering the footsteps
with dust.

She turned to Mma Potsane, who was silent beside her.

"Where does the wind come from, Mma Potsane?"

The other woman touched her cheek, in a gesture which
Mma Ramotswe did not understand. Her eyes looked empty,
Mma Ramotswe thought; one had dulled, and was slightly
milky; she should go to a clinic.

"Over there," said Mma Potsane, pointing out to the thorn
trees and the long expanse of sky, to the Kalahari. "Over there."

Mma Ramotswe said nothing. She was very close, she felt,
to understanding what had happened, but she could not
express it, and she could not tell why she knew.

CHAPTER TEN

CHILDREN ARE GOOD
FOR BOTSWANA

MR J.L.B. Matekoni's bad-tempered maid was slouching at the kitchen door, her battered red hat at a careless, angry angle. Her mood had become worse since her employer had revealed his unsettling news, and her waking hours had been spent in contemplating how she might avert catastrophe. The arrangement which she had with Mr J.L.B. Matekoni suited her very well. There was not a great deal of work to do; men never worried about cleaning and polishing, and provided they were well fed they were very untroublesome employers. And she did feed Mr J.L.B. Matekoni well, no matter what that fat woman might be saying to the contrary. She had said that he was too thin! Thin by her standards perhaps, but quite well built by the standards of any normal people. She could just imagine what she had in store for him—spoonfuls of lard for breakfast and thick slices of bread, which would puff him up like that fat chief from the north, the one who broke the chair when he went to visit the house where her cousin worked as a maid.

But it was not so much the welfare of Mr J.L.B. Matekoni that concerned her, it was her own threatened position. If she had to go off and work in a hotel she would not be able to entertain her men friends in that same way. Under the current arrangement, men were able to visit her in the house while her employer was at work—without his knowledge, of course— and they were able to go into Mr J.L.B. Matekoni's room where there was the large double bed which he had bought from Central Furnishers. It was very comfortable—wasted on a bachelor, really—and the men liked it. They gave her presents of money, and the gifts were always better if they were able to spend time together in Mr J.L.B. Matekoni's room. That would all come to an end if anything changed.

The maid frowned. The situation was serious enough to merit desperate action, but it was hard to see what she could do. There was no point trying to reason with him; once a woman like that had sunk her claws into a man then there would be no turning him back. Men became quite unreasonable in such circumstances and he simply would not listen to her if she tried to tell him of the dangers that lay ahead. Even if she found out something about that woman—something about her past—he would probably pay no attention to the disclosure. She imagined confronting Mr J.L.B. Matekoni with the information that his future wife was a murderess! That woman has already killed two husbands, she might say. She put something in their food. The are both dead now because of her.

But he would say nothing, and just smile. I do not believe you, he would retort; and he would continue to say that even if she waved the headlines from the *Botswana Daily News: Mma Ramotswe murders husband with poison. Police take porridge away and do tests. Porridge found to be full of poison.* No, he would not believe it.

She spat into the dust. If there was nothing that she could do to get him to change his mind, then perhaps she had better think about some way of dealing with Mma Ramotswe. If Mma Ramotswe were simply not there, then the problem would have been solved, if she could . . . No, it was a terrible thing to think, and then she probably would not be able to afford to hire a witch doctor. They were very expensive when it came to removing people, and it was far too risky anyway. People talked, and the police would come round, and she could imagine nothing worse than going to prison.

Prison! What if Mma Ramotswe were to be sent to prison for a few years? You can't marry somebody who is in prison, and they can't marry you. So if Mma Ramotswe were to be found to have committed a crime and be sent off for a few years, then all would stay exactly as it was. And did it really matter if she had not actually committed a crime, as long as the police thought that she had and they were able to find the evidence? She had heard once of how a man had been sent off to prison because his enemies had planted ammunition in his house and had informed the police that he was storing it for guerillas. That was back in the days of the Zimbabwe war, when Mr Nkomo had his men near Francistown and bullets and guns were coming into the country no matter how hard the police tried to stop them. The man had protested his innocence, but the police had just laughed, and the magistrate had laughed too.

There were few bullets and guns these days, but it might

still be possible to find something that could be hidden in her house. What did the police look for these days? They were very worried about drugs, she believed, and the newspapers sometimes wrote about this person or that person being arrested for trading in *dagga*. But they had to have a large amount before the police were interested and where would she be able to lay her hands on that? *Dagga* was expensive and she could probably afford no more than a few leaves. So it would have to be something else.

The maid thought. A fly had landed on her forehead and was crawling down the ridge of her nose. Normally she would have brushed it away, but a thought had crossed her mind and it was developing deliciously. The fly was ignored: a dog barked in the neighbouring garden; a truck changed gear noisily on the road to the old airstrip. The maid smiled, and pushed her hat back. One of her men friends could help her. She knew what he did, and she knew that it was dangerous. He could deal with Mma Ramotswe, and in return she would give him those attentions which he so clearly enjoyed but which were denied him at home. Everybody would be happy. He would get what he wanted. She would save her job. Mr J.L.B. Matekoni would be saved from a predatory woman, and Mma Ramotswe would get her just deserts. It was all very clear.

THE MAID returned to the kitchen and started to peel some potatoes. Now that the threat posed by Mma Ramotswe was receding—or shortly would—she felt quite positively disposed towards her wayward employer, who was just weak, like all men. She would cook him a fine lunch today. There was meat in the fridge—meat which she had earlier planned to take home with her, but which she would now fry up for him with a couple of onions and a good helping of mashed potatoes.

The meal was not quite ready when Mr J.L.B. Matekoni came home. She heard his truck and the sound of the gate slamming, and then the door opening. He usually called out when he came back—a simple "I'm home now" to let her know that she could put his lunch on the table. Today, though, there was no shout; instead, there was the sound of another voice. She caught her breath. The thought occurred to her that he might have come home with that woman, having asked her to lunch. In that case, she would hurriedly hide the stew and say that there was no food in the house. She could not bear the thought of Mma Ramotswe eating her food; she would rather feed it to a dog than lay it before the woman who had threatened her livelihood.

She moved towards the kitchen door and peered down the corridor. Just inside the front door, holding it open to let somebody follow him into the house, was Mr J.L.B. Matekoni.

"Careful," he said. "This door is not very wide."

Another voice answered, but she did not hear what it said. It was a female voice but not, she realised with a rush of relief, the voice of that terrible woman. Who was he bringing back to the house? Another woman? That would be good, because then she could tell that Ramotswe woman that he was not faithful to her and that might put an end to the marriage before it started.

But then the wheelchair came in and she saw the girl, pushed by her small brother, enter the house. She was at a loss what to think. What was her employer doing bringing these children into the house? They must be relatives; the children of some distant cousin. The old Botswana morality dictated that you had to provide for such people, no matter how distant the connection.

"I am here, Rra," she called out. "Your lunch is ready."

Mr J.L.B. Matekoni looked up. "Ah," he said. "There are some children with me. They will need to eat."

"There will be enough," she called out. "I have made a good stew."

She waited a few minutes before going into the living room, busying herself with the mashing of the overcooked potatoes. When she did go though, wiping her hands industriously on a kitchen rag, she found Mr J.L.B. Matekoni sitting in his chair. On the other side of the room, looking out of the window, was a girl, with a young boy, presumably her brother, standing beside her. The maid stared at the children, taking in at a glance what sort of children they were. Basarwa, she thought: unmistakable. The girl had that colour skin, the light brown, the colour of cattle dung; the boy had those eyes that those people have, a bit like Chinese eyes, and his buttocks stuck out in a little shelf behind him.

"These children have come to live here," said Mr J.L.B. Matekoni, lowering his eyes as he spoke. "They are from the orphan farm, but I am going to be looking after them."

The maid's eyes widened. She had not expected this. Masarwa children being brought into an ordinary person's house and allowed to live there was something no self-respecting person would do. These people were thieves—she never doubted that—and they should not be encouraged to come and live in respectable Batswana houses. Mr J.L.B. Matekoni may be trying to be kind, but there were limits to charity.

She stared at her employer. "They are staying here? For how many days?"

He did not look up at her. He was too ashamed, she thought.

"They are staying here for a long time. I am not planning to take them back."

She was silent. She wondered whether this had something to do with that Ramotswe woman. She might have decided that the children could come and stay as part of her programme to take over his life. First you move in some Masarwa children, and then you move in yourself. The moving in of the children may even have been part of a plot against herself, of course. Mma Ramotswe might well have expected that she would not approve of such children coming into the house and in this way she might force her out even before she moved in altogether. Well, if that was her plan, then she would do everything in her power to thwart it. She would show her that she liked these children and that she was happy to have them in the house. It would be difficult, but she could do it.

"You will be hungry," she said to the girl, smiling as she spoke. "I have some good stew. It is just what children like."

The girl returned the smile. "Thank you, Mma," she said respectfully. "You are very kind."

The boy said nothing. He was looking at the maid with those disconcerting eyes, and it made her shudder inwardly. She returned to the kitchen and prepared the plates. She gave the girl a good helping, and there was plenty for Mr J.L.B. Matekoni. But to the boy she gave only a small amount of stew, and covered most of that with the scrapings from the potato pot. She did not want to encourage that child, and the less he had to eat the better.

The meal was taken in silence. Mr J.L.B. Matekoni sat at the head of the table, with the girl at his right and the boy at the other end. The girl had to lean forward in her chair to eat,

as the table was so constructed that the wheelchair would not
fit underneath it. But she managed well enough, and soon finished her helping. The boy wolfed down his food and then sat
with his hands politely clasped together, watching Mr J.LB.
Matekoni.

Afterwards, Mr J.L.B. Matekoni went out to the truck and
fetched the suitcase which they had brought from the orphan
farm. The housemother had issued them with extra clothes
and these had been placed in one of the cheap brown cardboard suitcases which the orphans were given when they went
out into the world. There was a small, typed list taped to the
top of the case, and this listed the clothes issued under two
columns. *Boy: 2 pairs boys' pants, 2 pairs khaki shorts, 2 khaki
shirts, 1 jersey, 4 socks, 1 pair shoes, 1 Setswana Bible. Girl: 3
pairs girls' pants, 2 shirts, 1 vest, 2 skirts, 4 socks, 1 pair shoes, 1
Setswana Bible.*

He took the suitcase inside and showed the children to the
room they were to occupy, the small room he had kept for the
visitors who never seemed to arrive, the room with two mat-
tresses, a small pile of dusty blankets, and a chair. He placed
the suitcase on the chair and opened it. The girl wheeled herself over to the chair and looked in at the clothes, which were
new. She reached forward and touched them hesitantly, lovingly, as one would who had never before possessed new
clothes.

Mr J.L.B. Matekoni left them to unpack. Going out into the
garden, he stood for a moment under his shade-netting by the
front door. He knew that he had done something momentous
in bringing the children to the house, and now the full immensity of his action came home to him. He had changed the
course of the lives of two other people and now everything that

happened to them would be his responsibility. For a moment he felt appalled by the thought. Not only were there two extra mouths to feed, but there were schools to think about, and a woman to look after their day-to-day needs. He would have to find a nursemaid—a man could never do all the things that children need to have done for them. Some sort of house-mother, rather like the housemother who had looked after them at the orphan farm. He stopped. He had forgotten. He was almost a married man. Mma Ramotswe would be mother to these children.

He sat down heavily on an upturned petrol drum. These children were Mma Ramotswe's responsibility now, and he had not even asked her opinion. He had allowed himself to be bamboozled into taking them by that persuasive Mma Potok-wane, and he had hardly thought out all the implications. Could he take them back? She could hardly refuse to receive them as they were still, presumably, her legal responsibility. Nothing had been signed; there were no pieces of paper which could be waved in his face. But to take them back was unthinkable. He had told the children that he would look after them, and that, in his mind, was more important than any sig-nature on a legal document.

Mr J.L.B. Matekoni had never broken his word. He had made it a rule of his business life that he would never tell a customer something and then not stick to what he had said. Sometimes this had cost him dearly. If he told a customer that a repair to a car would cost three hundred pula, then he would never charge more than that, even if he discovered that the work took far longer. And often it did take longer, with those lazy apprentices of his taking hours to do even the simplest thing. He could not understand how it would be possible to take three hours to do a simple service on a car. All you had to do was to drain the old oil and pour it into the dirty oil container. Then you put in fresh oil, changed the oil filters, checked the brake fluid level, adjusted the timing, and greased the gearbox. That was the simple service, which cost two hundred and eighty pula. It could be done in an hour and a half at the most, but the apprentices managed to take much longer.

No, he could not go back on the assurance he had given those children. They were his children, come what may. He would talk to Mma Ramotswe and explain to her that children were good for Botswana and that they should do what they could to help these poor children who had no people of their own. She was a good woman, he knew, and he was sure that she would understand and agree with him. Yes, he would do it, but perhaps not just yet.

CHAPTER ELEVEN

THE GLASS CEILING

MMA MAKUTSI, Secretary of the No. 1 Ladies' Detective Agency and *cum laude* graduate of the Botswana Secretarial College, sat at her desk, staring out through the open door. She preferred to leave the door open when there was nothing happening in the agency (which was most of the time), but it had its drawbacks, as the chickens would sometimes wander in and strut about as if they were in a henhouse. She did not like these chickens, for a number of very sound reasons. To begin with, there was something unprofessional about having chickens in a detective agency, and then, quite apart from that, the chickens themselves irritated her profoundly. It was always the same group of chickens: four hens and a dispirited and, she imagined, impotent rooster, who was kept on by the hens out of charity. The rooster was lame and had lost a large proportion of the feathers on one of his wings. He looked defeated, as if he were only too well aware of his loss of status,

and he always walked several steps behind the hens themselves, like a royal consort relegated by protocol into a permanent second place.

The hens seemed equally irritated by Mma Makutsi's presence. It was as if she, rather than they, were the intruder. By
rights, this tiny building with its two small windows and its
creaky door should be a henhouse, not a detective agency. If
they outstared her, perhaps, she would go, and they would be
left to perch on the chairs and make their nests in the filing
cabinets. That is what the chickens wanted.

"Get out," said Mma Makutsi, waving a folded-up newspaper at them. "No chickens here! Get out!"

The largest of the hens turned and glared at her, while the
rooster merely looked shifty.

"I mean you!" shouted Mma Makutsi. "This is not a chicken
farm. Out!"

The hens uttered an indignant clucking and seemed to hesitate for a moment. But when Mma Makutsi pushed her chair
back and made to get up, they turned and began to move
towards the door, the rooster in the lead this time, limping
awkwardly.

The chickens dealt with, Mma Makutsi resumed her staring
out of the door. She resented the indignity of having to shoo
chickens out of one's office. How many first-class graduates of
the Botswana Secretarial College had to do that? she wondered. There were offices in town—large buildings with wide
windows and air-conditioning units where the secretaries sat
at polished desks with chrome handles. She had seen these
offices when the college had taken them for work-experience
visits. She had seen them sitting there, smiling, wearing
expensive earrings and waiting for a well-paid husband to step

forward and ask them to marry him. She had thought at the time that she would like a job like that, although she herself would be more interested in the work than in the husband. She had assumed, in fact, that such a job would be hers, but when the course had finished and they had all gone off for interviews, she had received no offers. She could not understand why this should be so. Some of the other women who got very much worse marks than she did—sometimes as low as 51 percent (the barest of passes) received good offers whereas she (who had achieved the almost inconceivable mark of 97 percent) received nothing. How could this be?

It was one of the other unsuccessful girls who explained it to her. She, too, had gone to interviews and been unlucky.

"It is men who give out these jobs, am I right?" she had said.

"I suppose so," said Mma Makutsi. "Men run these businesses. They choose the secretaries."

"So how do you think men choose who should get the job and who shouldn't? Do you think they choose by the marks we got? Is that how you think they do it?"

Mma Makutsi was silent. It had never occurred to her that decisions of this nature would be made on any other basis. Everything that she had been taught at school had conveyed the message that hard work helped you to get a good job.

"Well," said her friend, smiling wryly, "I can tell that you do think that. And you're wrong. Men choose women for jobs on the basis of their looks. They choose the beautiful ones and give them jobs. To the others, they say: We are very sorry. All the jobs have gone. We are very sorry. There is a world recession, and in a world recession there are only enough jobs for beautiful girls. That is the effect of a world recession. It is all economics."

Mma Makutsi had listened in astonishment. But she knew, even as the bitter remarks were uttered, that they were true. Perhaps she had known all along, at a subconscious level, and had simply not faced up to the fact. Good-looking women got what they wanted and women like her, who were perhaps not so elegant as the others, were left with nothing.

That evening she looked in the mirror. She had tried to do something about her hair, but had failed. She had applied hair-straightener and had pulled and tugged at it, but it had remained completely uncooperative. And her skin, too, had resisted the creams that she had applied to it, with the result that her complexion was far darker than that of almost every other girl at the college. She felt a flush of resentment at her fate. It was hopeless. Even with those large round glasses she had bought herself, at such crippling expense, she could not disguise the fact that she was a dark girl in a world where light-coloured girls with heavily applied red lipstick had everything at their disposal. That was the ultimate, inescapable truth that no amount of wishful thinking, no amount of expensive creams and lotions, could change. The fun in this life, the good jobs, the rich husbands, were not a matter of merit and hard work, but were a matter of brute, unshifting biology.

Mma Makutsi stood before the mirror and cried. She had worked and worked for her 97 percent at the Botswana Secretarial College, but she might as well have spent her time having fun and going out with boys, for all the good that it had done her. Would there be a job at all, or would she stay at home helping her mother to wash and iron her younger brothers' khaki pants?

The question was answered the next day when she applied

for and was given the job of Mma Ramotswe's secretary. Here was the solution. If men refused to appoint on merit, then go for a job with a woman. It may not be a glamorous office, but it was certainly an exciting thing to be. To be secretary to a private detective was infinitely more prestigious than to be a secretary in a bank or in a lawyer's office. So perhaps there was some justice after all. Perhaps all that work had been worthwhile after all.

But there was still this problem with the chickens.

"SO, MMA Makutsi," said Mma Ramotswe, as she settled herself down in her chair in anticipation of the pot of bush tea which her secretary was brewing for her. "So I went off to Molepolole and found the place where those people lived. I saw the farmhouse and the place where they tried to grow the vegetables. I spoke to a woman who had lived there at the time. I saw everything there was to see."

"And you found something?" asked Mma Makutsi, as she poured the hot water into the old enamel teapot and swirled it around with the tea leaves.

"I found a feeling," said Mma Ramotswe. "I felt that I knew something."

Mma Makutsi listened to her employer. What did she mean by saying that she felt she knew something? Either you know something or you don't. You can't think that you might know something, if you didn't actually know what it was that you were meant to know.

"I am not sure . . ." she began.

Mma Ramotswe laughed. "It's called an intuition. You can

read about it in Mr Andersen's hook. He talks about intuitions. They tell us things that we know deep inside, but which we can't find the word for."

"And this intuition you felt at that place," said Mma Makutsi hesitantly. "What did it tell you? Where this poor American boy was?"

"There," said Mma Ramotswe quietly. "That young man is there."

For a moment they were both silent. Mma Makutsi lowered the teapot onto the formica tabletop and replaced the lid.

"He is living out there? Still?"

"No," said Mma Ramotswe. "He is dead. But he is there. Do you know what I am talking about?"

Mma Makutsi nodded. She knew. Any sensitive person in Africa would know what Mma Ramotswe meant. When we die, we do not leave the place we were in when we were alive. We are still there, in a sense; our spirit is there. It never goes away. This was something which white people simply did not understand. They called it superstition, and said that it was a sign of ignorance to believe in such things. But they were the ones who were ignorant. If they could not understand how we are part of the natural world about us, then they are the ones who have closed eyes, not us.

Mma Makutsi poured the tea and handed Mma Ramotswe her mug.

"Are you going to tell the American woman this?" she asked. "Surely she will say: 'Where is the body? Show me the exact place where my son is.' You know how these people think. She will not understand you if you say that he is there somewhere, but you cannot point to the spot."

Mma Ramotswe raised the mug to her lips, watching her

secretary as she spoke. This was an astute woman, she thought. She understood exactly how the American woman would think, and she appreciated just how difficult it could be to convey these subtle truths to one who conceived of the world as being entirely explicable by science. The Americans were very clever; they sent rockets into space and invented machines which could think more quickly than any human being alive, but all this cleverness could also make them blind. They did not understand other people. They thought that everyone looked at things in the same way as Americans did, but they were wrong. Science was only part of the truth. There were also many other things that made the world what it was, and the Americans often failed to notice these things, although they were there all the time, under their noses.

Mma Ramotswe put down her mug of tea and reached into the pocket of her dress.

"I also found this," she said, extracting the folded newspaper photograph and passing it to her secretary. Mma Makutsi unfolded the piece of paper and smoothed it out on the surface of her desk. She gazed at it for a few moments before looking up at Mma Ramotswe.

"This is very old," she said. "Was it lying there?"

"No. It was on the wall. There were still some papers pinned on a wall. The ants had missed them."

Mma Makutsi returned her gaze to the paper.

"There are names," she said. "Cephas Kalumani. Oswald Ranta. Mma Soloi. Who are these people?"

"They lived there," said Mma Ramotswe. "They must have been there at the time."

Mma Makutsi shrugged her shoulders. "But even if we could find these people and talk to them," she said, "would that make any difference? The police must have talked to them at the time. Maybe even Mma Curtin talked to them herself when she first came back."

Mma Ramotswe nodded her head in agreement. "You're right," she said. "But that photograph tells me something. Look at the faces."

Mma Makutsi studied the yellowing image. There were two men in the front, standing next to a woman. Behind them was another man, his face indistinct, and a woman, whose back was half-turned. The names in the caption referred to the three in the front. Cephas Kalumani was a tall man, with slightly gangly limbs, a man who would look awkward and ill at ease in any photograph. Mma Soloi, who was standing next to him, was beaming with pleasure. She was a comfortable woman—the archetypical, hardworking Motswana woman, the sort of woman who supported a large family, whose life's labour, it seemed, would be devoted to endless, uncomplaining cleaning: cleaning the yard, cleaning the house, cleaning children. This was a picture of a heroine; unacknowledged, but a heroine nonetheless.

The third figure, Oswald Ranta, was another matter altogether. He was a well-dressed, dapper figure. He was wearing a white shirt and tie and, like Mma Soloi, was smiling at the camera. His smile, though, was very different.

"Look at that man," said Mma Ramotswe. "Look at Ranta."

"I do not like him," said Mma Makutsi. "I do not like the look of him at all."

"Precisely," said Mma Ramotswe. "That man is evil."

Mma Makutsi said nothing, and for a few minutes the two of them sat in total silence, Mma Makutsi staring at the photograph and Mma Ramotswe looking down into her mug of tea. Then Mma Ramotswe spoke.

"I think that if anything bad was done in that place, then it was done by that man. Do you think I am right?"

"Yes," said Mma Makutsi. "You are right." She paused. "Are you going to find him now?"

"That is my next task," said Mma Ramotswe. "I shall ask around and see if anybody knows this man. But in the meantime, we have some letters to write, Mma. We have other cases to think about. That man at the brewery who was anxious about his brother. I have found out something now and we can write to him. But first we must write a letter about that accountant."

Mma Makutsi inserted a piece of paper into her typewriter and waited for Mma Ramotswe to dictate. The letter was not an interesting one—it was all about the tracing of a company accountant who had sold most of the company's assets and then disappeared. The police had stopped looking for him but the company wanted to trace its property.

Mma Makutsi typed automatically. Her mind was not on the task, but her training enabled her to type accurately even if she was thinking about something else. Now she was thinking of Oswald Ranta, and of how they might trace him. The spelling of Ranta was slightly unusual, and the simplest thing would be to look the name up in the telephone directory. Oswald Ranta was a smart-looking man who could be expected to have a telephone. All she had to do was to look him up and write down the address. Then she could go and make her own enquiries, if she wished, and present Mma Ramotswe with the information.

The letter finished, she passed it over to Mma Ramotswe for signature and busied herself with addressing the envelope. Then, while Mma Ramotswe made a note in the file, she slipped open her drawer and took out the Botswana telephone directory. As she had thought, there was only one Oswald Ranta.

"I must make a quick telephone call," she said. "I shall only be a moment."

Mma Ramotswe grunted her assent. She knew that Mma Makutsi could be trusted with the telephone, unlike most secretaries, who she knew used their employers' telephones to make all sorts of long-distance calls to boyfriends in remote places like Maun or Orapa.

Mma Makutsi spoke in a low voice, and Mma Ramotswe did not hear her.

"Is Rra Ranta there, please?"

"He is at work, Mma. I am the maid."

"I'm sorry to bother you, Mma. I must phone him at work. Can you tell me where that is?"

"He is at the University. He goes there every day."

"I see. Which number there?"

She noted it down on a piece of paper, thanked the maid, and replaced the receiver. Then she dialled, and again her pencil scratched across paper.

"Mma Ramotswe," she said quietly. "I have all the information you need."

Mma Ramotswe looked up sharply.

"Information about what?"

"Oswald Ranta. He is living here in Gaborone. He is a lecturer in the Department of Rural Economics in the University. The secretary there says that he always comes in at eight o'clock every morning and that anybody who wishes to see him can make an appointment. You need not look any further."

Mma Ramotswe smiled.

"You are a very clever person," she said. "How did you find all this out?"

"I looked in the telephone directory," answered Mma Makutsi. "Then I telephoned to find out about the rest."

"I see," said Mma Ramotswe, still smiling. "That was very good detective work."

Mma Makutsi beamed at the praise. Detective work. She had done the job of a detective, although she was only a secretary.

"I am happy that you are pleased with my work," she said, after a moment. "I have wanted to be a detective. I'm happy being a secretary, but it is not the same thing as being a detective."

Mma Ramotswe frowned. "This is what you have wanted?"

"Every day," said Mma Makutsi. "Every day I have wanted this thing."

Mma Ramotswe thought about her secretary. She was a good worker, and intelligent, and if it meant so much to her, then why should she not be promoted? She could help her with her investigations, which would be a much better use of her time than sitting at her desk waiting for the telephone to ring. They could buy an answering machine to deal with calls if she was out of the office on an investigation. Why not give her the chance and make her happy?

"You shall have the thing you have wanted," said Mma Ramotswe. "You will be promoted to assistant detective. As from tomorrow."

Mma Makutsi rose to her feet. She opened her mouth to

speak, but the emotion within her strangled any words. She sat down.

"I am glad that you are pleased," said Mma Ramotswe. "You have broken the glass ceiling that stops secretaries from reaching their full potential."

Mma Makutsi looked up, as if to search for the ceiling that she had broken. There were only the familiar ceiling boards, fly-tracked and buckling from the heat. But the ceiling of the Sistine Chapel itself could not at that moment have been more glorious in her eyes, more filled with hope and joy.

CHAPTER TWELVE

AT NIGHT IN GABORONE

ALONE IN her house in Zebra Drive, Mma Ramotswe awoke, as she often did, in the small hours of the morning, that time when the town was utterly silent; the time of maximum danger for rats, and other small creatures, as cobras and mambas moved silently in their hunting. She had always suffered from broken sleep, but had stopped worrying about it. She never lay awake for more than an hour or so, and, since she retired to bed early, she always managed at least seven hours of sleep a night. She had read that people needed eight hours, and that the body eventually claimed its due. If that were so, then she made up for it, as she often slept for several hours on a Saturday and never got up early on Sunday. So an hour or so lost at two or three each morning was nothing significant.

Recently, while waiting to have her hair braided at the Make Me Beautiful Salon she had noticed a magazine article on sleep. There was a famous doctor, she read, who knew all about sleep and had several words of advice for those whose sleep was troubled. This Dr Shapiro had a special clinic just for people who could not sleep and he attached wires to their heads to see what was wrong. Mma Ramotswe was intrigued: there was a picture of Dr Shapiro and a sleepy-looking man and woman, in dishevelled pyjamas, with a tangle of wires coming from their heads. She felt immediately sorry for them: the woman, in particular, looked miserable, like somebody who was being forced to participate in an immensely tedious procedure but who simply could not escape. Or was she miserable because of the hospital pyjamas, in which she was being photographed; she may always have wished to have her photograph in a magazine, and now her wish was to be fulfilled—in hospital pyjamas.

And then she read on, and became outraged. "Fat people often have difficulty in sleeping well," the article went on. "They suffer from a condition called sleep apnoea, which means that their breathing is interrupted in sleep. Such people are advised to lose weight."

Advised to lose weight! What has weight to do with it? There were many fat people who seemed to sleep perfectly well; indeed, there was a fat person who often sat under a tree outside Mma Ramotswe's house and who seemed to be asleep most of the time. Would one advise that person to lose weight? It seemed to Mma Ramotswe as if such advice would be totally unnecessary and would probably simply lead to unhappiness. From being a fat person who was comfortably placed in the shade of a tree, this poor person would become a thin person, with not much of a bottom to sit upon, and probably unable to sleep as a result.

And what about her own case? She was a fat lady—*tradi-*

tionally built—and yet she had no difficulty in getting the required amount of sleep. It was all part of this terrible *attack* on people by those who had nothing better to do than to give advice on all sorts of subjects. These people, who wrote in newspapers and talked on the radio, were full of good ideas as to how to make people better. They poked their noses into other people's affairs, telling them to do this and do that. They looked at what you were eating and told you it was bad for you; then they looked at the way you raised your children and said that was bad too. And to make matters worse, they often said that if you did not heed their warnings, you would die. In this way they made everybody so frightened of them that they felt they had to accept the advice.

There were two main targets, Mma Ramotswe thought. First, there were fat people, who were now getting quite used to a relentless campaign against them; and then there were men. Mma Ramotswe knew that men were far from perfect— that many men were very wicked and selfish and lazy, and that they had, by and large, made rather a bad job of running Africa. But that was no reason to treat them badly, as some of these people did. There were plenty of good men about—people like Mr J.L.B. Matekoni, Sir Sereste Khama (First President of Botswana, Statesman, Paramount Chief of the Bangwato), and the late Obed Ramotswe, retired miner, expert judge of cattle, and her much-loved Daddy.

She missed the Daddy, and not a day went by, not one, that she did not think of him. Often when she awoke at this hour of the night, and lay alone in the darkness, she would search her memory to retrieve some recollection of him that had eluded her: some scrap of conversation, some gesture, some shared experience. Each memory was a precious treasure to her, fondly dwelt upon, sacramental in its significance. Obed Ramotswe, who had loved his daughter, and who had saved every rand, every cent, that he made in those cruel mines, and had built up that fine herd of cattle for her sake, had asked for nothing for himself. He did not drink, he did not smoke; he thought only of her and of what would happen to her.

If only she could erase those two awful years spent with Note Mokoti, when she knew that her Daddy had suffered so much, knowing, as he did, that Note would only make her unhappy. When she had returned to him, after Note's departure, and he had seen, even as he had embraced her, the scar of the latest beating, he had said nothing, and had stopped her explanation in its tracks.

"You do not have to tell me about it," he said. "We do not have to talk about it. It is over."

She had wanted to say sorry to him—to say that she should have asked his opinion of Note before she had married him, and listened, but she felt too raw for this and he would not have wanted it.

And she remembered his illness, when his chest had become more and more congested with the disease which killed so many miners, and how she had held his hand at his bedside and how, afterwards, she had gone outside, dazed, wanting to wail, as would be proper, but silent in her grief; and how she had seen a Go-Away bird staring at her from the bough of a tree, and how it had fluttered up, on to a higher branch, and turned round to stare at her again, before flying off; and of a red car that at that moment had passed in the road, with two children in the back, dressed in white dresses, with ribbons in their hair, who had looked at her too, and had waved. And of how the sky looked—heavy with rain, purple clouds stacked high atop one another, and of lightning in the distance, over the Kalahari, linking sky to earth. And of a woman who, not knowing that the world had just ended for her, called out to her from the verandah of the hospital: *Come inside, Mma. Do not stand there! There is going to be a storm. Come inside quickly!*

NOT FAR away, a small plane on its way to Gaborone flew low over the dam and then, losing height, floated down over the area known as the Village, over the cluster of shops on the Tlokweng Road, and finally, in the last minute of its journey, over the houses that dotted the bush on the airstrip boundary. In one of these, at a window, a girl sat watching. She had been up for an hour or so, as her sleep had been disturbed, and she had decided to get up from her bed and look out of the window. The wheelchair was beside the bed and she was able to manoeuvre herself into it without help. Then, propelling herself over to the open window, she had sat and looked out into the night.

She had heard the plane before she saw its lights. She had wondered what a plane was doing coming in at three in the morning. How could pilots fly at night? How could they tell where they were going in that limitless darkness? What if they took a wrong turn and went out over the Kalahari, where there were no lights to guide them and where it would be like flying within a dark cave?

She watched the plane fly almost directly above the house, and saw the shape of the wings and the cone of brightness which the landing light of the plane projected before it. The noise of the engine was loud now—not just a distant buzz—

but a heavy, churning sound. Surely it would wake the household, she thought, but when the plane had dropped down on to the airstrip and the engine faded, the house was still in silence.

The girl looked out. There was a light off in the distance somewhere, maybe at the airstrip itself, but apart from that there was only darkness. The house looked away from the town, not towards it, and beyond the edge of the garden there was only scrub bush, trees and clumps of grass, and thorn bushes, and the odd red mud outcrop of a termite mound.

She felt alone. There were two other sleepers in that house: her younger brother, who never woke up at night, and the kind man who had fixed her wheelchair and who had then taken them in. She was not frightened to be here; she trusted that man to look after them—he was like Mr Jameson, who was the director of the charity that ran the orphan farm. He was a good man, who thought only about the orphans and their needs. At first, she had been unable to understand how there should be people like that. Why did people care for others, who were not even their family? She looked after her brother, but that was her duty.

The housemother had tried to explain it to her one day.

"We must look after other people," she had said. "Other people are our brothers and sisters. If they are unhappy, then we are unhappy. If they are hungry, then we are hungry. You see."

The girl had accepted this. It would be her duty, too, to look after other people. Even if she could never have a child herself, she would look after other children. And she could try to look after this kind man, Mr J.L.B. Matekoni, and make sure that everything in his house was clean and tidy. That would be her job.

There were some people who had mothers to look after them. She was not one of those people, she knew. But why had her mother died? She remembered her only vaguely now. She remembered her death, and the wailing from the other women. She remembered the baby being taken from her arms and put in the ground. She had dug him out, she believed, but was not sure. Perhaps somebody else had done that and had passed the boy on to her. And then she remembered going away and finding herself in a strange place.

Perhaps one day she would find a place where she would stay. That would be good. To know that the place you were in was your own place—where you should be.

CHAPTER THIRTEEN

A PROBLEM IN
MORAL PHILOSOPHY

THERE WERE some clients who engaged Mma Ramotswe's sympathies on the first telling of their tale. Others one could not sympathise with because they were motivated by selfishness, or greed, or sometimes self-evident paranoia. But the genuine cases—the cases which made the trade of private detective into a real calling—could break the heart. Mma Ramotswe knew that Mr Letsenyane Badule was one of these.

He came without an appointment, arriving the day after Mma Ramotswe had returned from her trip to Molepolole. It was the first day of Mma Makutsi's promotion to assistant detective, and Mma Ramotswe had just explained to her that although she was now a private detective she still had secretarial duties.

She had realised that she would have to broach the subject early, to avoid misunderstandings.

"I can't employ both a secretary and an assistant," she said.

"This is a small agency. I do not make a big profit. You know that. You send out the bills."

Mma Makutsi's face had fallen. She was dressed in her smartest dress, and she had done something to her hair, which was standing on end in little pointed bunches. It had not worked.

"Am I still a secretary, then?" she said. "Do I still just do the typing?"

Mma Ramotswe shook her head. "I have not changed my mind," she said. "You are an assistant private detective. But somebody has to do the typing, don't they? That is a job for an assistant private detective. That, and other things."

Mma Makutsi's face brightened. "That is all right. I can do all the things I used to do, but I will do more as well. I shall have clients."

Mma Ramotswe drew in her breath. She had not envisaged giving Mma Makutsi her own clients. Her idea had been to assign her tasks to be performed under supervision. The actual management of cases was to be her own responsibility. But then she remembered. She remembered how, as girl she had worked in the Small Upright General Dealer Store in Mochudi and how thrilled she had been when she had first been allowed to do a stock-taking on her own. It was selfishness to keep the clients to herself. How could anybody be started on a career if those who were at the top kept all the interesting work for themselves?

"Yes," she said quietly. "You can have your own clients. But I will decide which ones you get. You may not get the very big clients . . . to begin with. You can start with small matters and work up."

"That is quite fair," said Mma Makutsi. "Thank you, Mma. I

do not want to run before I can walk. They told us that at the Botswana Secretarial College. Learn the easy things first and then learn the difficult things. Not the other way round."

"That's a good philosophy," said Mma Ramotswe. "Many young people these days have not been taught that. They want the big jobs right away. They want to start at the top, with lots of money and a big Mercedes-Benz."

"That is not wise," said Mma Makutsi. "Do the little things when you are young and then work up to doing the big things later."

"Mmm," mused Mma Ramotswe. "These Mercedes-Benz cars have not been a good thing for Africa. They are very fine cars, I believe, but all the ambitious people in Africa want one before they have earned it. That has made for big problems."

"The more Mercedes-Benzes there are in a country," offered Mma Makutsi, "the worse that country is. If there is a country without any Mercedes-Benzes, then that will be a good place. You can count on that."

Mma Ramotswe stared at her assistant. It was an interesting theory, which could be discussed at greater length later on. For the meantime, there were one or two matters which still needed to be resolved.

"You will still make the tea," she said firmly. "You have always done that very well."

"I am very happy to do that," said Mma Makutsi, smiling. "There is no reason why an assistant private detective cannot make tea when there is nobody more junior to do it."

IT HAD been an awkward discussion and Mma Ramotswe was pleased that it was over. She thought that it would be best if she gave her new assistant a case as soon as possible, to avoid the buildup of tension, and when, later that morning, Mr Letsenyane Badule arrived she decided that this would be a case for Mma Makutsi.

He drove up in a Mercedes-Benz, but it was an old one, and therefore morally insignificant, with signs of rust around the rear sills and with a deep dent on the driver's door.

"I am not one who usually comes to private detectives," he said, sitting nervously on the edge of the comfortable chair reserved for clients. Opposite him, the two women smiled reassuringly. The fat woman—she was the boss, he knew, as he had seen her photograph in the newspaper—and that other one with the odd hair and the fancy dress, her assistant perhaps.

"You need not feel embarrassed," said Mma Ramotswe. "We have all sorts of people coming through this door. There is no shame in asking for help."

"In fact," interjected Mma Makutsi. "It is the strong ones who ask for help. It is the weak ones who are too ashamed to come."

Mma Ramotswe nodded. The client seemed to be reassured by what Mma Makutsi had said. This was a good sign. Not everyone knows how to set a client at ease, and it boded well that Mma Makutsi had shown herself able to choose her words well.

The tightness of Mr Badule's grip on the brim of his hat loosened, and he sat back in his chair.

"I have been very worried," he said. "Every night I have been waking up in the quiet hours and have been unable to get back to sleep. I lie in my bed and I turn this way and that and cannot get this one thought out of my head. All the time it is there, going round and round. Just one question, which I ask myself time after time after time."

"And you never find an answer?" said Mma Makutsi. "The night is a very bad time for questions to which there are no answers."

Mr Badule looked at her. "You are very right, my sister. There is nothing worse than a nighttime question."

He stopped, and for a moment or two nobody spoke. Then Mma Ramotswe broke the silence.

"Why don't you tell us about yourself, Rra? Then a little bit later on, we can get to this question that is troubling you so badly. My assistant will make us a cup of tea first, and then we can drink it together."

Mr Badule nodded eagerly. He seemed close to tears for some reason, and Mma Ramotswe knew that the ritual of tea, with the mugs hot against the hand, would somehow make the story flow and would ease the mind of this troubled man.

I AM not a big, important man, began Mr Badule. I come from Lobatse originally. My father was an orderly at the High Court there and he served many years. He worked for the British, and they gave him two medals, with the picture of the Queen's head on them. He wore these every day, even after he retired. When he left the service, one of the judges gave him a hoe to use on his lands. The judge had ordered the hoe to be made in the prison workshop and the prisoners, on the judge's instructions, had burned an inscription into the wooden handle with a hot nail. It said: *First Class Orderly Badule, served Her Majesty and then the Republic of Botswana loyally for fifty years.*

Well done tried and trusty servant, from Mr Justice Maclean, Puisne Judge, High Court of Botswana.

That judge was a good man, and he was kind to me too. He spoke to one of the fathers at the Catholic School and they gave me a place in standard four. I worked hard at this school, and when I reported one of the other boys for stealing meat from the kitchen, they made me deputy-head boy.

I passed my Cambridge School certificate and afterwards I got a good job with the Meat Commission. I worked hard there too and again I reported other employees for stealing meat. I did not do this because I wanted promotion, but because I am not one who likes to see dishonesty in any form. That is one thing I learned from my father. As an orderly in the High Court, he saw all sorts of bad people, including murderers. He saw them standing in the court and telling lies because they knew that their wicked deeds had caught up with them. He watched them when the judges sentenced them to death and saw how big strong men who had beaten and stabbed other people became like little boys, terrified and sobbing and saying that they were sorry for all their bad deeds, which they had said they hadn't done anyway.

With such a background, it is not surprising that my father should have taught his sons to be honest and to tell the truth always. So I did not hesitate to bring these dishonest employees to justice and my employers were very pleased.

"You have stopped these wicked people from stealing the meat of Botswana," they said. "Our eyes cannot see what our employees are doing. Your eyes have helped us."

I did not expect a reward, but I was promoted. And in my new job, which was in the headquarters office, I found more people who were stealing meat, this time in a more indirect and clever way, but it was still stealing meat. So I wrote a letter to the General Manager and said: "Here is how you are losing meat, right under your noses, in the general office." And at the end I put the names, all in alphabetical order, and signed the letter and sent it off.

They were very pleased, and, as a result, they promoted me even further. By now, anybody who was dishonest had been frightened into leaving the company, and so there was no more work of that sort for me to do. But I still did well, and eventually I had saved enough money to buy my own butchery. I received a large cheque from the company, which was sorry to see me go, and I set up my butchery just outside Gaborone. You may have seen it on the road to Lobatse. It is called Honest Deal Butchery.

My butchery does quite well, but I do not have a lot of money to spare. The reason for this is my wife. She is a fashionable lady, who likes smart clothes and who does not like to work too much herself. I do not mind her not working, but it upsets me to see her spend so much money on braiding her hair and having new dresses made by the Indian tailor. I am not a smart man, but she is a very smart lady.

For many years after we got married there were no children. But then she became pregnant and we had a son. I was very proud, and my only sadness was that my father was not still alive so that he could see his fine new grandson.

My son is not very clever. We sent him to the primary school near our house and we kept getting reports saying that he had to try harder and that his handwriting was very untidy and full of mistakes. My wife said that he would have to be sent to a private school, where they would have better teachers and where they would force him to write more neatly, but I was worried that we could not afford that.

When I said that, she became very cross. "If you cannot pay for it," she said, "then I will go to a charity I know and get them to pay the fees."

"There are no such charities," I said. "If there were, then they would be inundated. Everyone wants his child to go to a private school. They would have every parent in Botswana lining up for help. It is impossible."

"Oh it is, is it?" she said. "I shall speak to this charity tomorrow, and you will see. You just wait and see."

She went off to town the next day and when she came back she said it had all been arranged. "The charity will pay all his school fees to go to Thornhill. He can start next term."

I was astonished. Thornhill, as you know, *Bomma,* is a very good school and the thought of my son going there was very exciting. But I could not imagine how my wife had managed to persuade a charity to pay for it, and when I asked her for the details so that I could write to them and thank them she replied that it was a secret charity.

"There are some charities which do not want to shout out their good deeds from the rooftops," she said. "They have asked me to tell nobody about this. But if you wish to thank them, you can write a letter, which I will deliver to them on your behalf."

I wrote this letter, but got no reply.

"They are far too busy to be writing to every parent they help," said my wife. "I don't see what you're complaining about. They're paying the fees, aren't they? Stop bothering them with all these letters."

There had only been one letter, but my wife always exaggerates things, at least when it concerns me. She accuses me of eating "hundreds of pumpkins, all the time," when I eat fewer pumpkins than she does. She says that I make more noise than an aeroplane when I snore, which is not true. She says that I am always spending money on my lazy nephew and sending him thousands of pula every year. In fact, I only give him one hundred pula on his birthday and one hundred pula for his Christmas box. Where she gets this figure of thousands of pula, I don't know. I also don't know where she gets all the money for her fashionable life. She tells me that she saves it, by being careful in the house, but I cannot see how it adds up. I will talk to you a little bit later about that.

But you must not misunderstand me, ladies. I am not one of these husbands who does not like his wife. I am very happy with my wife. Every day I reflect on how happy I am to be married to a fashionable lady—a lady who makes people look at her in the street. Many butchers are married to women who do not look very glamorous, but I am not one of those butchers. I am the butcher with the very glamorous wife, and that makes me proud.

I AM also proud of my son. When he went to Thornhill he was behind in all his subjects and I was worried that they would put him down a year. But when I spoke to the teacher, she said that I should not worry about this, as the boy was very bright and would soon catch up. She said that bright children could always manage to get over earlier difficulties if they made up their mind to work.

My son liked the school. He was soon scoring top marks in

mathematics and his handwriting improved so much that you would think it was a different boy writing. He wrote an essay which I have kept, "The Causes of Soil Erosion in Botswana," and one day I shall show that to you, if you wish. It is a very beautiful piece of work and I think that if he carries on like this, he will one day become Minister of Mines or maybe Minister of Water Resources. And to think that he will get there as the grandson of a High Court orderly and the son of an ordinary butcher.

You must be thinking: *What has this man got to complain about? He has a fashionable wife and a clever son. He has got a butchery of his own. Why complain?* And I understand why one might think that, but that does not make me any more unhappy. Every night I wake up and think the same thought. Every day when I come back from work and find that my wife is not yet home, and I wait until ten or eleven o'clock before she returns, the anxiety gnaws away at my stomach like a hungry animal. Because, you see, *Bomma,* the truth of the matter is that I think my wife is seeing another man. I know that there are many husbands who say that, and they are imagining things, and I hope that I am just the same—just imagining—but I cannot have any peace until I know whether what I fear is true.

WHEN MR Letsenyane Badule eventually left, driving off in his rather battered Mercedes-Benz, Mma Ramotswe looked at Mma Makutsi and smiled.

"Very simple," she said. "I think this is a very simple case, Mma Makutsi. You should be able to handle this case yourself with no trouble."

Mma Makutsi went back to her own desk, smoothing out the fabric of her smart blue dress. "Thank you, Mma. I shall do my best."

Mma Ramotswe nodded. "Yes," she went on. "A simple case of a man with a bored wife. It is a very old story. I read in a magazine that it is the sort of story that French people like to read. There is a story about a French lady called Mma Bovary, who was just like this, a very famous story. She was a lady who lived in the country and who did not like to be married to the same, dull man."

"It is better to be married to a dull man," said Mma Makutsi. "This Mma Bovary was very foolish. Dull men are very good husbands. They are always loyal and they never run away with other women. You are very lucky to be engaged to a . . ."

She stopped. She had not intended it, and yet it was too late now. She did not consider Mr J.L.B. Matekoni to be dull; he was reliable, and he was a mechanic, and he would be an utterly satisfactory husband. That is what she had meant; she did not mean to suggest that he was actually dull.

Mma Ramotswe stared at her. "To a what?" she said. "I am very lucky to be engaged to a what?"

Mma Makutsi looked down at her shoes. She felt hot and confused. The shoes, her best pair, the pair with the three glittering buttons stitched across the top, stared back at her, as shoes always do.

Then Mma Ramotswe laughed. "Don't worry," she said. "I know what you mean, Mma Makutsi. Mr J.L.B. Matekoni is maybe not the most fashionable man in town, but he is one of the best men there is. You could trust him with anything. He would never let you down. And I know he would never have any secrets from me. That is very important."

Grateful for her employer's understanding, Mma Makutsi was quick to agree.

'That is by far the best sort of man," she said. "If I am ever lucky enough to find a man like that, I hope he asks me to marry him."

She glanced down at her shoes again, and they met her stare. Shoes are realists, she thought, and they seemed to be saying: *No chance. Sorry, but no chance.*

"Well," said Mma Ramotswe. "Let's leave the subject of men in general and get back to Mr Badule. What do you think? Mr Andersen's book says that you must have a working supposition. You must set out to prove or disprove something. We have agreed that Mma Badule sounds bored, but do you think that there is more to it than that?"

Mma Makutsi frowned. "I think that there is something going on. She is getting money from somewhere, which means she is getting it from a man. She is paying the school fees herself with the money she has saved up."

Mma Ramotswe agreed. "So all you have to do is to follow her one day and see where she goes. She should lead you straight to this other man. Then you see how long she stays there, and you speak to the housemaid. Give her one hundred pula, and she will tell you the full story. Maids like to speak about the things that go on in their employers' houses. The employers often think that maids cannot hear, or see, even. They ignore them. And then, one day, they realise that the maid has been hearing and seeing all their secrets and is bursting to talk to the first person who asks her. That maid will tell you everything. You just see. Then you tell Mr Badule."

"That is the bit that I will not like," said Mma Makutsi. "All the rest I don't mind, but telling this poor man about this bad wife of his will not be easy."

Mma Ramotswe was reassuring. "Don't worry. Almost every time we detectives have to tell something like that to a client, the client already knows. We just provide the proof they are looking for. They know everything. We never tell them anything new."

"Even so," said Mma Makutsi. "Poor man. Poor man."

"Maybe," Mma Ramotswe added. "But remember, that for every cheating wife in Botswana, there are five hundred and fifty cheating husbands."

Mma Makutsi whistled. "That is an amazing figure," she said. "Where did you read that?"

"Nowhere," chuckled Mma Ramotswe. "I made it up. But that doesn't stop it from being true."

IT WAS a wonderful moment for Mma Makutsi when she set forth on her first case. She did not have a driving licence, and so she had to ask her uncle, who used to drive a Government truck and who was now retired, to drive her on the assignment in the old Austin which he hired out, together with his services as driver, for weddings and funerals. The uncle was thrilled to be included on such a mission, and donned a pair of darkened glasses for the occasion.

They drove out early to the house beside the butchery, where Mr Badule and his wife lived. It was a slightly down-at-heel bungalow, surrounded by pawpaw trees, and with a silver-painted tin roof that needed attention. The yard was virtually empty, apart from the pawpaws and a wilting row of cannas along the front of the house. At the rear of the house, backed up against a wire fence that marked the end of the property, were the servant quarters and a lean-to garage.

It was hard to find a suitable place to wait, but eventually Mma Makutsi concluded that if they parked just round the corner, they would be half-concealed by the small take-out stall that sold roast mealies, strips of fly-blown dried meat and, for those who wanted a real treat, delicious pokes of mopani worms. There was no reason why a car should not park there; it would be a good place for lovers to meet, or for somebody to wait for the arrival of a rural relative off one of the rickety buses that careered in from the Francistown Road.

The uncle was excited, and lit a cigarette.

"I have seen many films like this," he said. "I never dreamed that I would be doing this work, right here in Gaborone."

"Being a private detective is not all glamorous work," said his niece. "We have to be patient. Much of our work is just sitting and waiting."

"I know," said the uncle. "I have seen that on films too. I have seen these detective people sit in their cars and eat sandwiches while they wait. Then somebody starts shooting."

Mma Makutsi raised an eyebrow. "There is no shooting in Botswana," she said. "We are a civilized country."

They lapsed into a companionable silence, watching people set about their morning business. At seven o'clock the door of the Badule house opened and a boy came out, dressed in the characteristic uniform of Thornhill School. He stood for a moment in front of the house, adjusting the strap of his school satchel, and then walked up the path that led to the front gate. Then he turned smartly to the left and strode down the road.

"That is the son," said Mma Makutsi, lowering her voice, although nobody could possibly hear them. "He has a scholarship to Thornhill School. He is a bright boy, with very good handwriting."

The uncle looked interested.

"Should I write this down?" he asked. "I could keep a record of what happens."

Mma Makutsi was about to explain that this would not be necessary, but she changed her mind. It would give him something to do, and there was no harm in it. So the uncle wrote on a scrap of paper that he had extracted from his pocket: "Badule boy leaves house at 7 A.M. and proceeds to school on foot."

He showed her his note, and she nodded.

"You would make a very good detective, Uncle," she said, adding: "It is a pity you are too old."

Twenty minutes later, Mr Badule emerged from the house and walked over to the butchery. He unlocked the door and admitted his two assistants, who had been waiting for him under a tree. A few minutes later, one of the assistants, now wearing a heavily bloodstained apron, came out carrying a large stainless steel tray, which he washed under a standpipe at the side of the building. Then two customers arrived, one having walked up the street, another getting off a minibus which stopped just beyond the take-out stall.

"Customers enter shop," wrote the uncle. "Then leave, carrying parcels. Probably meat."

Again he showed the note to his niece, who nodded approvingly.

"Very good. Very useful. But it is the lady we are interested in," she said. "Soon it will be time for her to do something."

They waited a further four hours. Then, shortly before twelve, when the car had become stiflingly hot under the sun, and just at the point when Mma Makutsi was becoming irritated by her uncle's constant note-taking, they saw Mma Badule emerge from behind the house and walk over to the garage. There she got into the battered Mercedes-Benz and reversed out of the front drive. This was the signal for the uncle to start his car and, at a respectful distance, follow the Mercedes as it made its way into town.

Mma Badule drove fast, and it was difficult for the uncle to keep up with her in his old Austin, but they still had her in sight by the time that she drew into the driveway of a large house on Nyerere Drive. They drove past slowly, and caught a glimpse of her getting out of the car and striding towards the shady verandah. Then the luxuriant garden growth, so much richer than the miserable pawpaw trees at the butchery house, obscured their view.

But it was enough. They drove slowly round the corner and parked under a jacaranda tree at the side of the road.

"What now?" asked the uncle. "Do we wait here until she leaves?"

Mma Makutsi was uncertain. "There is not much point in sitting here," she said. "We are really interested in what is going on in that house."

She remembered Mma Ramotswe's advice. The best source of information was undoubtedly the maids, if they could be persuaded to talk. It was now lunchtime, and the maids would be busy in the kitchen. But in an hour or so, they would have their own lunch break, and would come back to the servants' quarters. And those could be reached quite easily, along the narrow sanitary lane that ran along the back of the properties. That would be the time to speak to them and to offer the crisp new fifty pula notes which Mma Ramotswe had issued her the previous evening.

The uncle wanted to accompany her, and Mma Makutsi had difficulty persuading him that she could go alone.

"It could be dangerous," he said. "You might need protection."

She brushed aside his objections. "Dangerous, Uncle? Since when has it been dangerous to talk to a couple of maids in the middle of Gaborone, in the middle of the day?"

He had had no answer to that, but he nonetheless looked anxious when she left him in the car and made her way along the lane to the back gate. He watched her hesitate behind the small, whitewashed building which formed the servants' quarters, before making her way round to the door, and then he lost sight of her. He took out his pencil, glanced at the time, and made a note: Mma Makutsi enters servants' quarters at 2:10 P.M.

THERE WERE two of them, just as she had anticipated. One of them was older than the other, and had crow's-feet wrinkles at the side of her eyes. She was a comfortable, large-chested woman, dressed in a green maid's dress and a pair of scuffed white shoes of the sort which nurses wear. The younger woman, who looked as if she was in her mid-twenties, Mma Makutsi's own age, was wearing a red housecoat and had a sultry, spoiled face. In other clothes, and made-up, she would not have looked out of place as a bar girl. Perhaps she is one, thought Mma Makutsi.

The two women stared at her, the younger one quite rudely.

"Ko ko," said Mma Makutsi, politely, using the greeting that could substitute for a knock when there was no door to be knocked upon. This was necessary, as although the women were not inside their house they were not quite outside either, being seated on two stools in the cramped open porch at the front of the building.

The older woman studied their visitor, raising her hand to shade her eyes against the harsh light of the early afternoon.

"Dumela, Mma. Are you well?"

The formal greetings were exchanged, and then there was silence. The younger woman poked at their small, blackened kettle with a stick.

"I wanted to talk to you, my sisters," said Mma Makutsi. "I want to find out about that woman who has come to visit this house, the one who drives that Mercedes-Benz. You know that one?"

The younger maid dropped the stick. The older one nodded. "Yes, we know that woman."

"Who is she?"

The younger retrieved her stick and looked up at Mma Makutsi. "She is a very important lady, that one! She comes to the house and sits in the chairs and drinks tea. That is who she is."

The other one chuckled. "But she is also a very tired lady," she said. "Poor lady, she works so hard that she has to go and lie down in the bedroom a lot, to regain her strength."

The younger one burst into a peal of laughter. "Oh yes," she said. "There is much resting done in that bedroom. He helps her to rest her poor legs. Poor lady."

Mma Makutsi joined in their laughter. She knew immediately that this was going to be much easier than she had imagined it would be. Mma Ramotswe was right, as usual; people liked to talk, and, in particular, they liked to talk about people who annoyed them in some way. All one had to do was to discover the grudge and the grudge itself would do all the work.

She felt in her pocket for the two fifty pula notes; it might not even be necessary to use them after all. If this were the case, she might ask Mma Ramotswe to authorise their payment to her uncle.

"Who is the man who lives in this house?" she said. "Has he no wife of his own?"

This was the signal for them both to giggle. "He has a wife all right," said the older one. "She lives out at their village, up near Mahalaype. He goes there at weekends. This lady here is his town wife."

"And does the country wife know about this town wife?"

"No," said the older woman. "She would not like it. She is a Catholic woman, and she is very rich. Her father had four shops up there and bought a big farm. Then they came and dug a big mine on that farm and so they had to pay that woman a lot of money. That is how she bought this big house for her husband. But she does not like Gaborone."

"She is one of those people who never likes to leave the village," the younger maid interjected. "There are some people like that. She lets her husband live here to run some sort of business that she owns down here. But he has to go back every Friday, like a schoolboy going home for the weekend."

Mma Makutsi looked at the kettle. It was a very hot day, and she wondered if they would offer her tea. Fortunately the older maid noticed her glance and made the offer.

"And I'll tell you another thing," said the younger maid as she lit the paraffin stove underneath the kettle. "I would write a letter to the wife and tell her about that other woman, if I were not afraid that I would lose my job."

"He told us," said the other. "He said that if we told his wife, then we would lose our jobs immediately. He pays us well, this man. He pays more than any other employer on this whole street. So we cannot lose this job. We just keep our mouths shut . . ."

She stopped, and at that moment both maids looked at one another in dismay.

"Aiee!" wailed the younger one. "What have we been doing? Why have we spoken like this to you? Are you from Maha-laype? Have you been sent by the wife? We are finished! We are very stupid women. Aiee!"

"No," said Mma Makutsi quickly. "I do not know the wife. I have not even heard of her. I have been asked to find out by that other woman's husband what she is doing. That is all."

The two maids became calmer, but the old one still looked worried. "But if you tell him what is happening, then he will come and chase this man away from his own wife and he might tell the real wife that her husband has another woman. That way we are finished too. It makes no difference."

"No," said Mma Makutsi. "I don't have to tell him what is going on. I might just say that she is seeing some man but I don't know who it is. What difference does it make to him? All he needs to know is that she is seeing a man. It does not matter which man it is."

The younger maid whispered something to the other, who frowned.

"What was that, Mma?" asked Mma Makutsi.

The older one looked up at her. "My sister was just wondering about the boy. You see, there is a boy, who belongs to that smart woman. We do not like that woman, but we do like the boy. And that boy, you see, is the son of this man, not of the other man. They both have very big noses. There is no doubt about it. You take a look at them and you will see it for yourself.

This one is the father of that boy, even if the boy lives with the other one. He comes here every afternoon after school. The mother has told the boy that he must never speak to his other father about coming here, and so the boy keeps this thing secret from him. That is bad. Boys should not be taught to lie like that. What will become of Botswana, Mma, if we teach boys to behave like that? Where will Botswana be if we have so many dishonest boys? God will punish us, I am sure of it. Aren't you?"

MMA MAKUTSI looked thoughtful when she returned to the Austin in its shady parking place. The uncle had dropped off to sleep, and was dribbling slightly at the side of his mouth. She touched him gently on the sleeve and he awoke with a start.

"Ah! You are safe! I am glad that you are back."

"We can go now," said Mma Makutsi. "I have found out everything I needed to know."

They drove directly back to the No. 1 Ladies' Detective Agency. Mma Ramotswe was out, and so Mma Makutsi paid her uncle with one of the fifty pula notes and sat down at her desk to type her report.

"The client's fears are confirmed," she wrote. "His wife has been seeing the same man for many years. He is the husband of a rich woman, who is also a Catholic. The rich woman does not know about this. The boy is the son of this man, and not the son of the client. I am not sure what to do, but I think that we have the following choices:

(a) We tell the client everything that we have found out.

That is what he has asked us to do. If we do not tell him this, then perhaps we would he misleading him. By taking on this case, have we not promised to tell him everything? If that is so, then we must do so, because we must keep our promises. If we do not keep our promises, then there will be no difference between Botswana and a certain other country in Africa which I do not want to name here but which I know you know.

(b) We tell the client that there is another man, but we do not know who it is. This is strictly true, because I did not find out the name of the man, although I know which house he lives in. I do not like to lie, as I am a lady who believes in God. But God sometimes expects us to think about what the results will be of telling somebody something. If we tell the client that that boy is not his son, he will be very sad. It will be like losing a son. Will that make him happier? Would God want him to be unhappy? And if we tell the client this, and there is a big row, then the father may not be able to pay the school fees, as he is doing at present. The rich woman may stop him from doing that and then the boy will suffer. He will have to leave that school.

For these reasons, I do not know what to do."

She signed the report and put it on Mma Ramotswe's desk. Then she stood up and looked out of the window, over the acacia trees and up into the broad, heat-drained sky. It was all very well being a product of the Botswana Secretarial College, and it was all very well having graduated with 97 percent. But they did not teach moral philosophy there, and she had no idea how to resolve the dilemma with which her successful investigation had presented her. She would leave that to Mma Ramotswe.

She was a wise woman, with far more experience of life than herself, and she would know what to do.

Mma Makutsi made herself a cup of bush tea and stretched out in her chair. She looked at her shoes, with their three twinkling buttons. Did they know the answer? Perhaps they did.

CHAPTER FOURTEEN

A TRIP INTO TOWN

ON THE morning of Mma Makutsi's remarkably success-ful, but nonetheless puzzling investigation into the affairs of Mr Letsenyane Badule, Mr J.L.B. Matekoni, proprietor of Tlokweng Road Speedy Motors, and undoubtedly one of the finest mechanics in Botswana, decided to take his newly acquired foster children into town on a shopping expedition. Their arrival in his house had confused his ill-tempered maid, Mma Florence Peko, and had plunged him into a state of doubt and alarm that at times bordered on panic. It was not every day that one went to fix a diesel pump and came back with two children, one of them in a wheelchair, saddled with an implied moral obligation to look after the children for the rest of their childhood, and, indeed, in the case of the wheelchair-bound girl, for the rest of her life. How Mma Silvia Potokwane, the ebullient matron of the orphan farm, had managed to persuade him to take the children was beyond him. There had been some sort of conversation about it, he knew, and he had said that he would do it, but how had he been pushed into committing himself there and then? Mma Potokwane was like a clever lawyer engaged in the examination of a witness: agreement would be obtained to some innocuous statement and then, before the witness knew it, he would have agreed to a quite different proposal.

But the children had arrived, and it was now too late to do anything about it. As he sat in the office of Tlokweng Road Speedy Motors and contemplated a mound of paperwork, he made two decisions. One was to employ a secretary—a decision which he knew, even as he took it, that he would never get round to implementing—and the second was to stop worrying about how the children had arrived and to concentrate on doing the right thing by them. After all, if one contemplated the situation in a calm and detached state of mind, it had many redeeming features. The children were fine children— you only had to hear the story of the girl's courage to realise that—and their life had taken a sudden and dramatic turn for the better. Yesterday they had been just two of one hundred and fifty children at the orphan farm. Today they were placed in their own house, with their own rooms, and with a father— yes, he was a father now!—who owned his own garage. There was no shortage of money; although not a conspicuously wealthy man, Mr J.L.B. Matekoni was perfectly comfortable. Not a single *thebe* was owed on the garage; the house was subject to no bond; and the three accounts in Barclays Bank of Botswana were replete with pula. Mr J.L.B. Matekoni could look any member of the Gaborone Chamber of Commerce in the eye and say: "I have never owed you a penny. Not one."

How many businessmen could do that these days? Most of them existed on credit, kowtowing to that smug Mr Timon Mothokoli, who controlled business credit at the bank. He had heard that Mr Mothokoli could drive to work from his house on Kaunda Way and would be guaranteed to drive past the doors of at least five men who would quake at his passing. Mr J.L.B. Matekoni could, if he wished, ignore Mr Mothokoli if he met him in the Mall, not that he would ever do that, of course.

So if there is all this liquidity, thought Mr J.L.B. Matekoni, then why not spend some of it on the children? He would arrange for them to go to school, of course, and there was no reason why they should not go to a private school, too. They would get good teachers there; teachers who knew all about Shakespeare and geometry. They would learn everything that they needed to get good jobs. Perhaps the boy . . . No, it was almost too much to hope for, but it was such a delicious thought. Perhaps the boy would demonstrate an aptitude for mechanical matters and could take over the running of Tlokweng Road Speedy Motors. For a few moments, Mr J.L.B. Matekoni indulged himself in the thought: his son, his *son,* standing in front of the garage, wiping his hands on a piece of oily rag, after having done a good job on a complicated gearbox. And, in the background, sitting in the office, himself and Mma Ramotswe, much older now, grey-haired, drinking bush tea.

That would be far in the future, and there was much to be done before that happy outcome could be achieved. First of all, he would take them into town and buy them new clothes. The orphan farm, as usual, had been generous in giving them going-away clothes that were nearly new, but it was not the same as having one's own clothes, bought from a shop. He imagined that these children had never had that luxury. They would never have unwrapped clothes from their factory packaging and put them on, with that special, quite unreproducible smell of new fabric rich in the nostrils. He would drive them in immediately, that very morning, and buy them all the clothes they needed. Then he would take them to the chemist shop and the girl could buy herself some creams and shampoo, and other things that girls might like for themselves. There was only carbolic soap at home, and she deserved better than that.

MR J.L.B. Matekoni fetched the old green truck from the garage, which had plenty of room in the back for the wheelchair. The children were sitting on the verandah when he arrived home; the boy had found a stick which he was tying up in string for some reason, and the girl was crocheting a cover for a milk jug. They taught them crochet at the orphan farm, and some of them had won prizes for their designs. She is a talented girl, thought Mr J.L.B. Matekoni; this girl will be able to do anything, once she is given the chance.

They greeted him politely, and nodded when he asked whether the maid had given them their breakfast. He had asked her to come in early so as to be able to attend to the children while he went off to the garage, and he was slightly surprised that she had complied. But there were sounds from the kitchen—the bangings and scrapings that she seemed to make whenever she was in a bad mood—and these confirmed her presence.

Watched by the maid, who sourly followed their progress

until they were out of sight near the old Botswana Defence Force Club, Mr J.L.B. Matekoni and the two children bumped their way into town in the old truck. The springs were gone, and could only be replaced with difficulty, as the manufacturers had passed into mechanical history, but the engine still worked and the bumpy ride was a thrill for the girl and boy. Rather to Mr J.L.B. Matekoni's surprise, the girl showed an interest in its history, asking him how old it was and whether it used a lot of oil.

"I have heard that old engines need more oil," she said. "Is this true, Rra?"

Mr J.L.B. Matekoni explained about worn engine parts and their heavy demands, and she listened attentively. The boy, by contrast, did not appear to be interested. Still, there was time. He would take him to the garage and get the apprentices to show him how to take off wheel nuts. That was a task that a boy could perform, even when he was as young as this one. It was best to start early as a mechanic. It was an art which, ideally, one should learn at one's father's side. Did not the Lord himself learn to be a carpenter in his father's workshop? Mr J.L.B. Matekoni thought. If the Lord came back today, he would probably be a mechanic, he reflected. That would be a great honour for mechanics everywhere. And there is no doubt but that he would choose Africa: Israel was far too dangerous these days. In fact, the more one thought about it, the more likely it was that he would choose Botswana, and Gaborone in particular. Now that would be a wonderful honour for the people of Botswana; but it would not happen, and there was no point in thinking about it any further. The Lord was not going to come back; we had had our chance and we had not made very much of it, unfortunately.

He parked the car beside the British High Commission, noting that His Excellency's white Range Rover was in front of the door. Most of the diplomatic cars went to the big garages, with their advanced diagnostic equipment and their exotic bills, but His Excellency insisted on Mr J.L.B. Matekoni.

"You see that car over there?" said Mr J.L.B. Matekoni to the boy. "That is a very important vehicle. I know that car very well."

The boy looked down at the ground and said nothing.

"It is a beautiful white car," said the girl, from behind him. "It is like a cloud with wheels."

Mr J.L.B. Matekoni turned round and looked at her.

"That is a very good way of talking about that car," he said. "I shall remember that."

"How many cylinders does a car like that have?" the girl went on. "Is it six?"

Mr J.L.B. Matekoni smiled, and turned back to the boy. "Well," he said. "How many cylinders do you think that car has in its engine?"

"One?" said the boy quietly, still looking firmly at the ground.

"One!" mocked his sister. "It is not a two-stroke!"

Mr J.L.B. Matekoni's eyes opened wide. "A two-stroke? Where did you hear about two-strokes?"

The girl shrugged. "I have always known about two-strokes," she said. "They make a loud noise and you mix the oil in with the petrol. They are mostly on small motorbikes. Nobody likes a two-stroke engine."

Mr J.L.B. Matekoni nodded. "No, a two-stroke engine is often very troublesome." He paused. "But we must not stand here and talk about engines. We must go to the shops and buy you clothes and other things that you need."

THE SHOP assistants were sympathetic to the girl, and went with her into the changing room to help her try the dresses which she had selected from the rack. She had modest tastes, and consistently chose the cheapest available, but these, she said, were the ones she wanted. The boy appeared more interested; he chose the brightest shirts he could find and set his heart on a pair of white shoes which his sister vetoed on the grounds of impracticality.

"We cannot let him have those, Rra," she said to Mr J.L.B. Matekoni. "They would get very dirty in no time and then he will just throw them to one side. This is a very vain boy."

"I see," mused Mr J.L.B. Matekoni thoughtfully. The boy was respectful, and presentable, but that earlier delightful image he had entertained of his son standing outside Tlokweng Road Speedy Motors seemed to have faded. Another image had appeared, of the boy in a smart white shirt and a suit . . . But that could not be right.

They finished their shopping and were making their way back across the broad public square outside the post office when the photographer summoned them.

"I can do a photograph for you," he said. "Right here. You stand under this tree and I can take your photograph. Instant. Just like that. A handsome family group."

"Would you like that?" asked Mr J.L.B. Matekoni. "A photograph to remind us of our shopping trip."

The children beamed up at him.

"Yes, please," said the girl, adding, "I have never had a photograph."

Mr J.L.B. Matekoni stood quite still. This girl, now in her early teens, had never had a photograph of herself. There was no record of her childhood, nothing which would remind her of what she used to be. There was nothing, no image, of which she could say: "That is me." And all this meant that there was nobody who had ever wanted her picture; she had simply not been special enough.

He caught his breath, and for a moment, he felt an overwhelming rush of pity for these two children; and pity mixed with love. He would give them these things. He would make it up to them. They would have everything that other children had been given, which other children took for granted; all that love, each year of lost love, would be replaced, bit by bit, until the scales were righted.

He wheeled the wheelchair into position in front of the tree where the photographer had established his outdoor studio. Then, his rickety tripod perched in the dust, the photographer crouched behind his camera and waved a hand to attract his subject's attention. There was a clicking sound, followed by a whirring, and with the air of a magician completing a trick, the photographer peeled off the protective paper and blew across the photograph to dry it.

The girl took it, and smiled. Then the photographer positioned the boy, who stood, hands clasped behind him, mouth wide open in a smile; again the theatrical performance with the print and the pleasure on the child's face.

"There," said Mr J.L.B. Matekoni. "Now you can put those in your rooms. And one day we will have more photographs."

He turned round and prepared to take control of the wheelchair, but he stopped, and his arms fell to his sides, useless, paralysed.

There was Mma Ramotswe, standing before him, a basket laden with letters in her right hand. She had been making her way to the post office when she saw him and she had stopped. What was going on? What was Mr J.L.B. Matekoni doing, and who were these children?

CHAPTER FIFTEEN

THE SULLEN, BAD MAID ACTS

FLORENCE PEKO, the sour and complaining maid of Mr J.L.B. Matekoni, had suffered from headaches ever since Mma Ramotswe had first been announced as her employer's future wife. She was prone to stress headaches, and anything untoward could bring them on. Her brother's trial, for instance, had been a season of headaches, and every month, when she went to visit him in the prison near the Indian supermarket she would feel a headache even before she took her place in the shuffling queue of relatives waiting to visit. Her brother had been involved in stolen cars, and although she had given evidence on his behalf, testifying to having witnessed a meeting at which he had agreed to look after a car for a friend—a skein of fabrication—she knew that he was every bit as guilty as the prosecution had made him out to be. Indeed, the crimes for which he received his five-year prison sentence were probably only a fraction of those he had committed. But that was not the point: she had been outraged at his conviction, and her outrage had taken the form of a prolonged shouting and gesturing at the police officers in the court. The magistrate, who was on the point of leaving, had resumed her seat and ordered Florence to appear before her.

"This is a court of law," she had said. "You must understand that you cannot shout at police officers, or anybody else in it. And moreover, you are lucky that the prosecutor has not charged you with perjury for all the lies you told here today."

Florence had been silenced, and had been allowed free. Yet this only increased her sense of injustice. The Republic of Botswana had made a great mistake in sending her brother to jail. There were far worse people than he, and why were they left untouched? Where was the justice of it if people like . . . The list was a long one, and, by curious coincidence, three of the men on it were known by her, two of them intimately.

And it was to one of these, Mr Philemon Leannye, that she now proposed to turn. He owed her a favour. She had once told the police that he was with her, when he was not, and this was after she had received her judicial warning for perjury and was wary of the authorities. She had met Philemon Leannye at a take-out stall in the African Mall. He was tired of bar girls, he had said, and he wanted to get to know some honest girls who would not take his money from him and make him buy drinks for them.

"Somebody like you," he had said, charmingly.

She had been flattered, and their acquaintance had blossomed. Months might go by when she would not see him, but he would appear from time to time and bring her presents—a silver clock once, a bag (with the purse still in it), a bottle of Cape Brandy. He lived over at Old Naledi, with a woman by whom he had had three children.

"She is always shouting at me, that woman," he complained. "I can't do anything right as far as she is concerned. I give her money every month but she always says that the children are hungry and how is she to buy the food? She is never satisfied."

Florence was sympathetic.

"You should leave her and marry me," she said. "I am not one to shout at a man. I would make a good wife for a man like you."

Her suggestion had been serious, but he had treated it as a joke, and had cuffed her playfully.

"You would be just as bad," he said. "Once women are married to men, they start to complain. It is a well-known fact. Ask any married man."

So their relationship remained casual, but, after her risky and rather frightening interview with the police—an interview in which his alibi was probed for over three hours—she felt that there was an obligation which one day could be called in.

"Philemon," she said to him, lying beside him on Mr. J.L.B. Matekoni's bed one hot afternoon. "I want you to get me a gun."

He laughed, but became serious when he turned over and saw her expression.

"What are you planning to do? Shoot Mr J.L.B. Matekoni? Next time he comes into the kitchen and complains about the food, you shoot him? Hah!"

"No. I am not planning to shoot anybody. I want the gun to put in somebody's house. Then I will tell the police that there is a gun there and they will come and find it."

"And so I don't get my gun back?"

"No. The police will take it. But they will also take the person whose house it was in. What happens if you are found with an illegal gun?"

Philemon lit a cigarette and puffed the air straight up towards Mr J.L.B. Matekoni's ceiling.

"They don't like illegal weapons here. You get caught with an illegal gun and you go to prison. That's it. No hanging about. They don't want this place to become like Johannesburg."

Florence smiled. "I am glad that they are so strict about guns. That is what I want."

Philemon extracted a fragment of tobacco from the space between his two front teeth. "So," he said. "How do I pay for this gun? Five hundred pula. Minimum. Somebody has to bring it over from Johannesburg. You can't pick them up here so easily."

"I have not got five hundred pula," she said. "Why not steal the gun? You've got contacts. Get one of your boys to do it." She paused before continuing. "Remember that I helped you. That was not easy for me."

He studied her carefully. "You really want this?"

"Yes," she said. "It's really important to me."

He stubbed his cigarette out and swung his legs over the edge of the bed.

"All right," he said. "I'll get you a gun. But remember that if anything goes wrong, you didn't get the gun from me."

"I shall say I found it," said Florence. "I shall say that it was lying in the bush over near the prison. Maybe it was something to do with the prisoners."

"Sounds reasonable," said Philemon. "When do you want it?"

"As soon as you can get it," she replied.

"I can get you one tonight," he said. "As it happens, I have a spare one. You can have that."

She sat up and touched the back of his neck gently. "You are a very kind man. You can come and see me anytime, you know. Anytime. I am always happy to see you and make you happy."

"You are a very fine girl," he said, laughing. "Very bad. Very wicked. Very clever."

HE DELIVERED the gun, as he had promised, wrapped in a wax-proof parcel, which he put at the bottom of a voluminous OK Bazaars plastic bag, underneath a cluster of old copies of *Ebony* magazine. She unwrapped it in his presence and he started to explain how the safety catch operated, but she cut him short.

"I'm not interested in that," she said. "All I'm interested in is this gun, and these bullets."

He had handed her, separately, nine rounds of stubby, heavy ammunition. The bullets shone, as if each had been polished for its task, and she found herself attracted to their feel. They would make a fine necklace, she thought, if drilled through the base and threaded through with nylon string or perhaps a silver chain.

Philemon showed her how to load bullets into the magazine and how to wipe the gun afterwards, to remove fingerprints. Then he gave her a brief caress, planted a kiss on her cheek, and left. The smell of his hair oil, an exotic rum-like smell, lingered in the air, as it always did when he visited her, and she felt a stab of regret for their languid afternoon and its pleasures. If she went to his house and shot his wife, would he marry her? Would he see her as his liberator, or the slayer of the mother of his children? It was difficult to tell.

Besides, she could never shoot anybody. She was a Christian, and she did not believe in killing people. She thought of herself as a good person, who was simply forced, by circumstances, to do things that good people did not do—or which they claimed they did not do. She knew better, of course. Everybody cut some corners, and if she was proposing to deal with Mma Ramotswe in this unconventional way, it was only because it was necessary to use such measures against somebody who was so patently a threat to Mr J.L.B. Matekoni. How could he defend himself against a woman as determined as that? It was clear that strong steps had to be taken, and a few years in prison would teach that woman to be more respectful of the rights of others. That interfering detective woman was the author of her own misfortune; she only had herself to blame.

NOW, THOUGHT Florence, I have obtained a gun. This gun must now be put into the place that I have planned for it, which is a certain house in Zebra Drive.

To do this, another favour had to be called in. A man known to her simply as Paul, a man who came to her for conversation and affection, had borrowed money from her two years previously. It was not a large sum, but he had never paid it back. He might have forgotten about it, but she had not, and now he would be reminded. And if he proved difficult, he, too, had a wife who did not know about the social visits that her husband paid to Mr J.L.B. Matekoni's house. A threat to reveal these might encourage compliance.

It was money, though, that had secured agreement. She mentioned the loan, and he stuttered out his inability to pay.

"Every pula I have has to be accounted for," he said. "We

have to pay the hospital for one of the children. He keeps getting ill. I cannot spare any money. I will pay you back one day."

She nodded her understanding. "It will be easy to forget," she said. "I shall forget this money if you do something for me."

He had stared at her suspiciously. "You go to an empty house—nobody will be there. You break a window in the kitchen and you get in."

"I am not a thief," he interrupted. "I do not steal."

"But I am not asking you to steal," she said. "What kind of thief goes into a house and puts something into it? That is not a thief!"

She explained that she wanted a parcel left in a cupboard somewhere, tucked away where it could not be found.

"I want to keep something safe," she said. "This thing will be safe there."

He had cavilled at the idea, but she mentioned the loan again, and he capitulated. He would go the following afternoon, at a time when everybody was at work. She had done her homework: there would not even be a maid at the house, and there was no dog.

"It couldn't be easier," she promised him. "You will get it done in fifteen minutes. In. Out."

She handed him the parcel. The gun had been replaced in its wax-proof paper and this had been itself wrapped in a further layer of plain brown paper. The wrapping disguised the nature of the contents, but the parcel was still weighty and he was suspicious.

"Don't ask," she said. "Don't ask and then you won't know."

It's a gun, he thought. She wants me to plant a gun in that house in Zebra Drive.

"I don't want to carry this thing about with me," he said. "It is very dangerous. I know that it's a gun and I know what happens to you if the police find you with a gun. I do not want to go to jail. I will fetch it from you at the Matekoni house tomorrow."

She thought for a moment. She could take the gun with her to work, tucked away in a plastic bag. If he wished to fetch it from her from there, then she had no objection. The important thing was to get it into the Ramotswe house and then, two days later, to make that telephone call to the police.

"All right," she said. "I will put it back in its bag and take it with me. You come at 2:30. He will have gone back to his garage by then."

He watched her replace the parcel in the OK Bazaars bag in which it had first arrived.

"Now," she said. "You have been a good man and I want to make you happy."

He shook his head. "I am too nervous to be happy. Maybe some other time."

THE FOLLOWING afternoon, shortly after two o'clock, Paul Monsopati, a senior clerk at the Gaborone Sun Hotel, and a man marked by the hotel management for further promotion, slipped into the office of one of the hotel secretaries and asked her to leave the room for a few minutes.

"I have an important telephone call to make," he said. "It is a private matter. To do with a funeral."

The secretary nodded, and left the room. People were always dying and funerals, which were eagerly attended by every distant relative who was able to do so, and by almost every casual acquaintance, required a great deal of planning.

Paul picked up the telephone receiver and dialled a number which he had written out on a piece of paper.

"I wish to speak to an Inspector," he said. "Not a sergeant. I want an Inspector."

"Who are you, Rra?"

"That is not important. You get me an Inspector, or you will be in trouble."

Nothing was said, and, after a few minutes, a new voice came on the line.

"Now listen to me, please, Rra," said Paul. "I cannot speak for long. I am a loyal citizen of Botswana. I am against crime."

"Good," said the Inspector. "That is what we like to hear."

"Well," said Paul. "If you go to a certain house you will find that there is a lady there who has an illegal firearm. She is one who sells these weapons. It will be in a white OK Bazaars bag. You will catch her if you go right now. She is the one, not the man who lives in that house. It is in her bag, and she will have it with her in the kitchen. That is all I have to say."

He gave the address of the house and then rang off. At the other end of the line, the Inspector smiled with satisfaction. This would be an easy arrest, and he would be congratulated for doing something about illegal weapons. One might complain about the public and about their lack of a sense of duty, but every so often something like this happened and a conscientious citizen restored one's faith in ordinary members of the public. There should be awards for these people. Awards and a cash prize. Five hundred pula at least.

CHAPTER SIXTEEN

FAMILY

MR J.L.B. Matekoni was aware of the fact that he was standing directly under the branch of an acacia tree. He looked up, and saw for a moment, in utter clarity, the details of the leaves against the emptiness of the sky. Drawn in upon themselves for the midday heat, the leaves were like tiny hands clasped in prayer; a bird, a common butcher bird, scruffy and undistinguished, was perched farther up the branch, claws clasped tight, black eyes darting. It was the sheer enormity of Mr J.L.B. Matekoni's plight that made this perception so vivid; as a condemned man might peep out of his cell on his last morning and see the familiar, fading world.

He looked down, and saw that Mma Ramotswe was still there, standing some ten feet away, her expression one of bemused puzzlement. She knew that he worked for the orphan farm, and she was aware of Mma Silvia Potokwane's persuasive ways. She would be imagining, he thought, that here was Mr J.L.B. Matekoni taking two of the orphans out for the day and arranging for them to have their photographs taken. She would not be imagining that here was Mr J.L.B. Matekoni with his two new foster children, soon to be her foster children too.

Mma Ramotswe broke the silence. "What are you doing?" she said simply. It was an entirely reasonable question—the sort of question that any friend or indeed fiancée may ask of another. Mr J.L.B. Matekoni looked down at the children. The girl had placed her photograph in a plastic carrier bag that was attached to the side of her wheelchair; the boy was clutching his photograph to his chest, as if Mma Ramotswe might wish to take it from him.

"These are two children from the orphan farm," stuttered Mr J.L.B. Matekoni. "This one is the girl and this one is the boy."

Mma Ramotswe laughed. "Well!" she said. "So that is it. That is very helpful."

The girl smiled and greeted Mma Ramotswe politely.

"I am called Motholeli," she said. "My brother is called Puso. These are the names that we have been given at the orphan farm."

Mma Ramotswe nodded. "I hope that they are looking after you well, there. Mma Potokwane is a kind lady."

"She is kind," said the girl. "Very kind."

She looked as if she was about to say something else, and Mr J.L.B. Matekoni broke in rapidly.

"I have had the children's photographs taken," he explained, and turning to the girl, he said: "Show them to Mma Ramotswe, Motholeli."

The girl propelled her chair forward and passed the photograph to Mma Ramotswe, who admired it.

"That is a very nice photograph to have," she said. "I have only one or two photographs of myself when I was your age. If ever I am feeling old, I go and take a look at them and I think that maybe I am not so old after all."

"You are still young," said Mr J.L.B. Matekoni. "We are not old these days until we are seventy—maybe more. It has all changed."

"That's what we like to think," chuckled Mma Ramotswe, passing the photograph back to the girl. "Is Mr J.L.B. Matekoni taking you back now, or are you going to eat in town?"

"We have been shopping," Mr J.L.B. Matekoni blurted out. "We may have one or two other things to do."

"We will go back to his house soon," the girl said. "We are living with Mr J.L.B. Matekoni now. We are staying in his house."

Mr J.L.B. Matekoni felt his heart thump wildly against his chest. I am going to have a heart attack, he thought. I am going to die now. And for a moment he felt immense regret that he would never marry Mma Ramotswe, that he would go to his grave a bachelor, that the children would be twice orphaned, that Tlokweng Road Speedy Motors would close. But his heart did not stop, but continued to beat, and Mma Ramotswe and all the physical world remained stubbornly there.

Mma Ramotswe looked quizzically at Mr J.L.B. Matekoni.

"They are staying in your house?" she said. "This is a new development. Have they just come?"

He nodded bleakly. "Yesterday," he said.

Mma Ramotswe looked down at the children and then back at Mr J.L.B. Matekoni.

"I think that we should have a talk," she said. "You children stay here for a moment. Mr J.L.B. Matekoni and I are going to the post office."

There was no escape. Head hanging, like a schoolboy caught in delinquency, he followed Mma Ramotswe to the corner of the post office, where before the stacked rows of private postal boxes, he faced the judgement and sentence that he knew were his lot. She would divorce him—if that was the correct term for the breakup of an engagement. He had lost her because of his dishonesty and stupidity—and it was all Mma Silvia Potokwane's fault. Women like that were always interfering in the lives of others, forcing them to do things; and then matters went badly astray and lives were ruined in the process.

Mma Ramotswe put down her basket of letters.

"Why did you not tell me about these children?" she asked. "What have you done?"

He hardly dared meet her gaze. "I was going to tell you," he said. "I was out at the orphan farm yesterday. The pump was playing up. It's so old. Then their minibus needs new brakes. I have tried to fix those brakes, but they are always giving problems. We shall have to try and find new parts, I have told them that, but . . ."

"Yes, yes," pressed Mma Ramotswe. "You have told me about those brakes before. But what about these children?"

Mr J.L.B. Matekoni sighed. "Mma Potokwane is a very strong woman. She told me that I should take some foster children. I did not mean to do it without talking to you, but she would not listen to me. She brought in the children and I really had no alternative. It was very hard for me."

He stopped. A man passed on his way to his postal box,

fumbling in his pocket for his key, muttering something to himself. Mma Ramotswe glanced at the man and then looked back at Mr J.L.B. Matekoni.

"So," she said, "you agreed to take these children. And now they think that they are going to stay."

"Yes, I suppose so," he mumbled.

"And how long for?" asked Mma Ramotswe.

Mr J.L.B. Matekoni took a deep breath. "For as long as they need a home," he said. "Yes, I offered them that."

Unexpectedly he felt a new confidence. He had done nothing wrong. He had not stolen anything, or killed anybody, or committed adultery. He had just offered to change the lives of two poor children who had had nothing and who would now be loved and looked after. If Mma Ramotswe did not like that, well there was nothing he could do about it now. He had been impetuous, but his impetuosity had been in a good cause.

Mma Ramotswe suddenly laughed. "Well, Mr J.L.B. Matekoni," she said. "Nobody could say of you that you are not a kind man. You are, I think, the kindest man in Botswana. What other man would do that? I do not know of one, not one single one. Nobody else would do that. Nobody."

He stared at her. "You are not cross?"

"I was," she said. "But only for a little while. One minute maybe. But then I thought: Do I want to marry the kindest man in the country? I do. Can I be a mother for them? I can. That is what I thought, Mr J.L.B. Matekoni."

He looked at her incredulously. "You are a very kind woman yourself, Mma. You have been very kind to me."

"We must not stand here and talk about kindness," she said. "There are those two children there. Let's take them back to Zebra Drive and show them where they are going to live. Then this afternoon I can come and collect them from your house and bring them to mine. Mine is more . . ."

She stopped herself, but he did not mind.

"I know that Zebra Drive is more comfortable," he said. "And it would be better for them to be looked after by you."

They walked back to the children, together, companionably.

"I'm going to marry this lady," announced Mr J.L.B. Matekoni. "She will be your mother soon."

The boy looked startled, but the girl lowered her eyes respectfully.

"Thank you, Mma," she said. "We shall try to be good children for you."

"That is good," said Mma Ramotswe. "We shall be a very happy family. I can tell it already."

Mma Ramotswe went off to fetch her tiny white van, taking the boy with her. Mr J.L.B. Matekoni pushed the girl's wheelchair back to the old truck, and they drove over to Zebra Drive, where Mma Ramotswe and Puso were already waiting for them by the time they arrived. The boy was excited, rushing out to greet his sister.

"This is a very good house," he cried out. "Look, there are trees, and melons. I am having a room at the back."

Mr J.L.B. Matekoni stood back as Mma Ramotswe showed the children round the house. Everything that he had felt about her was, in his mind, now confirmed beyond doubt. Obed Ramotswe, her father, who had brought her up after the death of her mother, had done a very fine job. He had given Botswana one of its finest ladies. He was a hero, perhaps without ever knowing it.

While Mma Ramotswe was preparing lunch for the children, Mr J.L.B. Matekoni telephoned the garage to check that the apprentices were managing to deal with the chores with which he had left them. The younger apprentice answered, and Mr J.L.B. Matekoni knew immediately from his tone that there was something seriously wrong. The young man's voice was artificially high and excited.

"I am glad that you telephoned, Rra," he said. "The police came. They wanted to speak to you about your maid. They have arrested her and she has gone off to the cells. She had a gun in her bag. They are very cross."

The apprentice had no further information, and so Mr J.L.B. Matekoni put down the receiver. His maid had been armed! He had suspected her of a great deal—of dishonesty, and possibly worse—but not of being armed. What was she up to in her spare time—armed robbery? Murder?

He went into the kitchen, where Mma Ramotswe was boiling up squares of pumpkin in a large enamel pot.

"My maid has been arrested and taken off to prison," he said flatly. "She had a gun. In a bag."

Mma Ramotswe put down her spoon. The pumpkin was boiling satisfactorily and would soon be tender. "I am not surprised," she said. "That was a very dishonest woman. The police have caught up with her at last. She was not too clever for them."

MR J.L.B. Matekoni and Mma Ramotswe decided that afternoon that life was becoming too complicated for both of them and that they should declare the rest of the day to be a day of simple activities, centred around the children. To this end, Mr

J.L.B. Matekoni telephoned the apprentices and told them to close the garage until the following morning.

"I have been meaning to give you time off to study," he said. "Well, you can have some study time this afternoon. Put up a sign and say that we shall reopen at eight tomorrow."

To Mma Ramotswe he said: "They won't study. They'll go off chasing girls. There is nothing in those young men's heads. Nothing."

"Many young people are like that," she said. "They think only of dances and clothes, and loud music. That is their life. We were like that too, remember?"

Her own telephone call to the No. 1 Ladies' Detective Agency had brought a confident Mma Makutsi to the line, who had explained to her that she had completed the investigation of the Badule matter and that all that required to be done was to determine what to do with the information she had gathered. They would have to talk about that, said Mma Ramotswe. She had feared that the investigation would produce a truth that would be far from simple in its moral implications. There were times when ignorance was more comfortable than knowledge.

The pumpkin, though, was ready, and it was time to sit down at the table, as a family for the first time.

Mma Ramotswe said grace.

"We are grateful for this pumpkin and this meat," she said. "There are brothers and sisters who do not have good food on their table, and we think of them, and wish pumpkin and meat for them in the future. And we thank the Lord who has brought these children into our lives so that we might be happy and they might have a home with us. And we think of what a happy day this is for the late mother and the late daddy of these children, who are watching this from above."

Mr J.L.B. Matekoni could add nothing to this grace, which he thought was perfect in every respect. It expressed his own feelings entirely, and his heart was too full of emotion to allow him to speak. So he was silent.

CHAPTER SEVENTEEN

SEAT OF LEARNING

THE MORNING is the best time to address a problem, thought Mma Ramotswe. One is at one's freshest in the first hours of the working day, when the sun is still low and the air is sharp. That is the time to ask oneself the major questions; a time of clarity and reason, unencumbered by the heaviness of the day.

"I have read your report," said Mma Ramotswe, when Mma Makutsi arrived for work. "It is a very full one, and very well written. Well done."

Mma Makutsi acknowledged the compliment graciously.

"I was happy that my first case was not a difficult one," she said. "At least it was not difficult to find out what needed to be found out. But those questions which I put at the end—they are the difficult bit."

"Yes," said Mma Ramotswe, glancing down at the piece of paper. "The moral questions."

"I don't know how to solve them," said Mma Makutsi. "If I

think that one answer is correct, then I see all the difficulties with that. Then I consider the other answer, and I see another set of difficulties."

She looked expectantly at Mma Ramotswe, who grimaced.

"It is not easy for me either," the older woman said. "Just because I am a bit older than you does not mean that I have the answer to every dilemma that comes along. As you get older, in fact, you see more sides to a situation. Things are more clear-cut at your age." She paused, then added: "Mind you, remember that I am not quite forty. I am not all that old."

"No," said Mma Makutsi. "That is just about the right age for a person to be. But this problem we have; it is all very troubling. If we tell Badule about this man and he puts a stop to the whole thing, then the boy's school fees will not be paid. That will be the end of this very good chance that he is getting. That would not be best for the boy."

Mma Ramotswe nodded. "I see that," she said. "On the other hand we can't lie to Mr Badule. It is unethical for a detective to lie to the client. You can't do it."

"I can understand that," said Mma Makutsi. "But there are times, surely, when a lie is a good thing. What if a murderer came to your house and asked you where a certain person was? And what if you knew where that person was, would it be wrong to say: 'I do not know anything about that person. I do not know where he is.' Would that not be a lie?"

"Yes. But then you have no duty to tell the truth to that murderer. So you can lie to him. But you do have a duty to tell the truth to your client, or to your spouse, or to the police. That is all different."

"Why? Surely if it is wrong to lie, then it is always wrong to lie. If people could lie when they thought it was the right thing to do, then we could never tell when they meant it." Mma Makutsi, stopped, and pondered for a few moments before continuing. "One person's idea of what is right may be quite different from another's. If each person can make up his own rule . . ." She shrugged, leaving the consequences unspoken.

"Yes," said Mma Ramotswe. "You are right about that. That's the trouble with the world these days. Everyone thinks that they can make their own decisions about what is right and wrong. Everybody thinks that they can forget the old Botswana morality. But they can't."

"But the real problem here," said Mma Makutsi, "is whether we should tell him everything. What if we say: 'You are right; your wife is unfaithful,' and leave it at that? Have we done our duty? We are not lying, are we? We are just not telling all the truth."

Mma Ramotswe stared at Mma Makutsi. She had always valued her secretary's comments, but she had never expected that she would make such a moral mountain out of the sort of little problem that detectives encountered every day. It was messy work. You helped other people with their problems; you did not have to come up with a complete solution. What they did with the information was their own affair. It was their life, and they had to lead it.

But as she thought about this, she realised that she had done far more than that in the past. In a number of her successful cases, she had gone beyond the finding of information. She had made decisions about the outcome, and these decisions had often proved to be momentous ones. For example, in the case of the woman whose husband had a stolen Mercedes-Benz, she had arranged for the return of the car to its owner. In the case of the fraudulent insurance claims by the man with thirteen fingers, she had made the decision not to report him to the police. That was a decision which had changed a life. He may have become honest after she had given him this chance, but he may not. She could not tell. But what she had done was to offer him a chance, and that may have made a difference. So she did interfere in other people's lives, and it was not true that all that she did was provide information.

In this case, she realised that the real issue was the fate of the boy. The adults could look after themselves; Mr Badule could cope with a discovery of adultery (in his heart of hearts he already knew that his wife was unfaithful); the other man could go back to his wife on his bended knees and take his punishment (perhaps be hauled back to live in that remote village with his Catholic wife), and as for the fashionable lady, well, she could spend a bit more time in the butchery, rather than resting on that big bed on Nyerere Drive. The boy, though, could not be left to the mercy of events. She would have to ensure that whatever happened, he did not suffer for the bad behaviour of his mother.

Perhaps there was a solution which would mean that the boy could stay at school. If one looked at the situation as it stood, was there anybody who was really unhappy? The fashionable wife was very happy; she had a rich lover and a big bed to lie about in. The rich lover bought her fashionable clothes and other things which fashionable ladies tend to enjoy. The rich lover was happy, because he had a fashionable lady and he did not have to spend too much time with his devout wife. The devout wife was happy because she was living where she wanted to live, presumably doing what she liked doing, and had a husband who came home regularly, but not so regularly as to be a nuisance to her. The boy was happy, because he had two fathers, and was getting a good education at an expensive school.

That left the Mr Letsenyane Badule. Was he happy, or if he was unhappy could he be made to be happy again without any change in the situation? If they could find some way of doing that, then there was no need for the boy's circumstances to change. But how might this be achieved? She could not tell Mr Badule that the boy was not his—that would be too upsetting, too cruel, and presumably the boy would be upset to learn this as well. It was probable that the boy did not realize who his real father was; after all, even if they had identical large noses, boys tend not to notice things like that and he may have thought nothing of it. Mma Ramotswe decided that there was no need to do anything about that; ignorance was probably the best state for the boy. Later on, with his school fees all paid, he could start to study family noses and draw his own conclusions.

"It's Mr Badule," Mma Ramotswe pronounced. "We have to make him happy. We have to tell him what is going on, but we must make him accept it. If he accepts it, then the whole problem goes away."

"But he's told us that he worries about it," objected Mma Makutsi.

"He worries because he thinks it is a bad thing for his wife to be seeing another man," Mma Ramotswe countered. "We shall persuade him otherwise."

Mma Makutsi looked doubtful, but was relieved that Mma Ramotswe had taken charge again. No lies were to be told, and, if they were, they were not going to be told by her. Anyway, Mma Ramotswe was immensely resourceful. If she believed that she could persuade Mr Badule to be happy, then there was a good chance that she could.

BUT THERE were other matters which required attention. There had been a letter from Mrs Curtin in which she asked whether Mma Ramotswe had unearthed anything. "I know it's early to be asking," she wrote, "but ever since I spoke to you, I have had the feeling that you would discover something for me. I don't wish to flatter you, Mma, but I had the feeling that you were one of these people who just *knew*. You don't have to reply to this letter; I know I should not be writing it at this stage, but I have to do something. You'll understand, Mma Ramotswe—I know you will."

The letter had touched Mma Ramotswe, as did all the pleas that she received from troubled people. She thought of the progress that had been made so far. She had seen the place and she had sensed that that was where that young man's life had ended. In a sense, then, she had reached the conclusion right at the beginning. Now she had to work backwards and find out why he was lying there—as she knew he was—in that dry earth, on the edge of the Great Kalahari. It was a lonely grave, so far away from his people, and he had been so young. How had it come to this? Wrong had been done at some point, and if one wanted to find out what wrong had occurred, then one had to find the people who were capable of doing that wrong. Mr Oswald Ranta.

THE TINY white van moved gingerly over the speed bumps which were intended to deter fast and furious driving by the university staff. Mma Ramotswe was a considerate driver and was ashamed of the bad driving which made the roads so perilous. Botswana, of course, was much safer than other countries in that part of Africa. South Africa was very bad; there were aggressive drivers there, who would shoot you if you crossed them, and they were often drunk, particularly after payday. If payday fell on a Friday night, then it was foolhardy to set out on the roads at all. Swaziland was even worse. The Swazis loved speed, and the winding road between Manzini and Mbabane, on which she had once spent a terrifying half hour, was a notorious claimant of motoring life. She remembered coming across a poignant item in an odd copy of *The Times of Swaziland,* which had displayed a picture of a rather mousy-looking man, small and insignificant, under which was printed the simple legend *The late Mr Richard Mavuso (46).* Mr Mavuso, who had a tiny head and a small, neatly trimmed moustache, would have been beneath the notice of most beauty queens and yet, unfortunately, as the newspaper report revealed, he had been run over by one.

Mma Ramotswe had been strangely affected by the report. *Local man, Mr Richard Mavuso (above) was run over on Friday night by the Runner-up to Miss Swaziland. The well-known Beauty Queen, Miss Gladys Lapelala, of Manzini, ran over Mr Mavuso as he was trying to cross the road in Mbabane, where he was a clerk in the Public Works Department.*

That was all that the report had said, and Mma Ramotswe wondered why she was so affected by it. People were being run over all the time, and not much was made of it. Did it make a difference that one was run over by a beauty queen? And was it sad because Mr Mavuso was such a small and insignificant man, and the beauty queen so big, and important? Perhaps such an event was a striking metaphor for life's injustices; the powerful, the glamorous, the fêted, could so often with impunity push aside the insignificant, the timorous.

She nosed the tiny white van into a parking space behind the Administration Buildings and looked about her. She passed the university grounds every day, and was familiar with the cluster of white, sun-shaded buildings that sprawled across the several hundred-acre site near the old airfield. Yet she had never had the occasion to set foot there, and now, faced with a rather bewildering array of blocks, each with its impressive, rather alien name, she felt slightly overawed. She was not an uneducated woman, but she had no BA. And this was a place where everybody one came across was either a BA or BSc or even more than that. There were unimaginably learned people here; scholars like Professor Tlou, who had written a history of Botswana and a biography of Seretse Khama. Or there was Dr Bojosi Otloghile, who had written a book on the High Court of Botswana, which she had bought, but not yet read. One might come across such a person turning a corner in one of these buildings and they would look just like anybody else. But their heads would contain rather more than the heads of the average person, which were not particularly full of very much for a great deal of the time.

She looked at a board which proclaimed itself a map of the campus. Department of Physics that way; Department of Theology that way; Institute of Advanced Studies first right. And then, rather more helpfully, Enquiries. She followed the arrow for Enquiries and came to a modest, prefabricated building, tucked away behind Theology and in front of African Languages. She knocked at the door and entered.

An emaciated woman was sitting behind a desk, trying to unscrew the cap of a pen.

"I am looking for Mr Ranta," she said. "I believe he works here."

The woman looked bored. "Dr Ranta," she said. "He is not just plain Mr Ranta. He is Dr Ranta."

"I am sorry," said Mma Ramotswe. "I would not wish to offend him. Where is he, please?"

"They seek him here, they seek him there," said the woman. "He is here one moment, the next moment, he is nowhere. That's Dr Ranta."

"But will he be here at this moment?" said Mma Ramotswe. "I am not worried about the next moment."

The woman arched an eyebrow. "You could try his office. He has an office here. But most of the time he spends in his bedroom."

"Oh," said Mma Ramotswe. "He is a ladies' man, this Dr Ranta?"

"You could say that," said the woman. "And one of these days the University Council will catch him and tie him up with rope. But in the meantime, nobody dares touch him."

Mma Ramotswe was intrigued. So often, people did one's work for one, as this woman was now doing.

"Why can people not touch him?" asked Mma Ramotswe.

"The girls themselves are too frightened to speak," said the woman. "And his colleagues all have something to hide themselves. You know what these places are like."

Mma Ramotswe shook her head. "I am not a BA," she said. "I do not know."

"Well," said the woman, "I can tell you. They have a lot of people like Dr Ranta in them. You'll find out. I can speak to you about this because I'm leaving tomorrow. I'm going to a better job."

Mma Ramotswe was given instructions as to how to find Dr Ranta's office and she took her leave of the helpful receptionist. It was not a good idea on the university's part, she thought, to put that woman in the enquiry office. If she greeted any enquiry as to a member of staff with the gossip on that person, a visitor might get quite the wrong impression. Yet perhaps it was just because she was leaving the next day that she was talking like this; in which case, thought Mma Ramotswe, there was an opportunity.

"One thing, Mma," she said, as she reached the door. "It may be hard for anybody to deal with Dr Ranta because he hasn't done anything wrong. It may not be a good thing to interfere with students, but that may not be grounds for sacking him, at least it may not be these days. So maybe there's nothing that can be done."

She saw immediately that it was going to work, and that her surmise, that the receptionist had suffered at the hands of Dr Ranta, was correct.

"Oh yes, he has," she retorted, becoming suddenly animated. "He showed an examination paper to a student if she would oblige him. Yes! I'm the only one who knows it. The student was my cousin's daughter. She spoke to her mother, but she would not report it. But the mother told me."

"But you have no proof?" said Mma Ramotswe, gently. "Is that the problem?"

"Yes," said the receptionist. "There is no proof. He would lie his way out of it."

"And this girl, this Margaret, what did she do?"

"Margaret? Who is Margaret?"

"Your cousin's daughter," said Mma Ramotswe.

"She is not called Margaret," said the receptionist. "She is called Angel. She did nothing, and he got away with it. Men get away with it, don't they? Every time."

Mma Ramotswe felt like saying *No. Not always,* but she was short of time, and so she said goodbye for the second time and began to make her way to the Department of Economics.

THE DOOR was open. Mma Ramotswe looked at the small notice before she knocked: *Dr Oswald Ranta, BSc (Econ.), (UB) PhD (Duke). If I am not in, you may leave a message with the Departmental Secretary. Students wishing to have essays returned should see their tutor or go to the Departmental Office.*

She listened for the sound of voices from within the room and none came. She heard the click of the keys of a keyboard. Dr Ranta was in.

He looked up sharply as she knocked and edged the door open.

"Yes, Mma," he said. "What do you want?"

Mma Ramotswe switched from English to Setswana. "I would like to speak to you, Rra. Have you got a moment?"

He glanced quickly at his watch.

"Yes," he said, not impolitely. "But I haven't got forever. Are you one of my students?"

Mma Ramotswe made a self-deprecating gesture as she sat down on the chair which he had indicated. "No," she said. "I am not that educated. I did my Cambridge Certificate, but nothing after that. I was busy working for my cousin's husband's bus company, you see. I could not go on with my education."

"It is never too late, Mma," he said. "You could study. We have some very old students here. Not that you are very old, of course, but the point is that anybody can study."

"Maybe," she said. "Maybe one day."

"You could study just about anything here," he went on. "Except medicine. We can't make doctors just yet."

"Or detectives."

He looked surprised. "Detectives? You cannot study detection at a university."

She raised an eyebrow. "But I have read that at American universities there are courses in private detection. I have a book by . . ."

He cut her short. "Oh that! Yes, at American colleges you can take a course in anything. Swimming, if you like. But that's only at some of them. At the good places, places that we call Ivy League, you can't get away with that sort of nonsense. You have to study real subjects."

"Like logic?"

"Logic? Yes. You would study that for a philosophy degree. They taught logic at Duke, of course. Or they did when I was there."

He expected her to look impressed, and she tried to oblige him with a look of admiration. This, she thought, is a man who needs constant reassurance—hence all the girls.

"But surely that is what detection is all about. Logic, and a bit of psychology. If you know logic, you know how things should work; if you know psychology, you should know how people work."

He smiled, folding his hands across his stomach, as if preparing for a tutorial. As he did so, his gaze was running down Mma Ramotswe's figure, and she sensed it. She looked back at him, at the folded hands, and the sharp dresser's tie.

"So, Mma," he said. "I would like to spend a long time discussing philosophy with you. But I have a meeting soon and I must ask you to tell me what you wanted to talk about. Was it philosophy after all?"

She laughed. "I would not waste your time, Rra. You are a clever man, with many committees in your life. I am just a lady detective. I . . ."

She saw him tense. The hands unfolded, and moved to the arms of the chair.

"You are a detective?" he asked. The voice was colder now.

She made a self-deprecating gesture. "It is only a small agency. The No. 1 Ladies' Detective Agency. It is over by Kgale Hill. You may have seen it."

"I do not go over there," he said. "I have not heard of you."

"Well, I wouldn't expect you to have heard of me, Rra. I am not well-known, unlike you."

His right hand moved uneasily to the knot of his tie.

"Why do you want to talk to me?" he asked. "Has somebody told you to come and speak to me?"

"No," she said. "It's not that."

She noticed that her answer relaxed him and the arrogance returned.

"Well then?" he said.

"I have come to ask you to talk about something that happened a long time ago. Ten years ago."

He stared at her. His look was guarded now, and she smelt off him that unmistakable, acrid smell of a person experiencing fear.

"Ten years is a long time. People do not remember."

"No," she conceded. "They forget. But there are some things that are not easily forgotten. A mother, for example, will not forget her son."

As she spoke, his demeanour changed again. He got up from his chair, laughing.

"Oh," he said. "I see now. That American woman, the one who is always asking questions, is paying you to go round digging up the past again. Will she never give up? Will she never learn?"

"Learn what?" asked Mma Ramotswe.

He was standing at the window, looking out on a group of students on the walkway below.

"Learn that there is nothing to be learned," he said. "That boy is dead. He must have wandered off into the Kalahari and got lost. Gone for a walk and never come back. It's easily done, you know. One thorn tree looks much like another, you know, and there are no hills down there to guide you. You get lost. Especially if you're a white man out of your natural element. What do you expect?"

"But I don't believe that he got lost and died," said Mma Ramotswe. "I believe that something else happened to him."

He turned to face her.

"Such as?" he snapped.

She shrugged her shoulders. "I am not sure exactly what. But how should I know? I was not there." She paused, before adding, almost under her breath. "You were."

She heard his breathing, as he returned to his chair. Down below, one of the students shouted something out, something about a jacket, and the others laughed.

"You say I was there. What do you mean?"

She held his gaze. "I mean that you were living there at the time. You were one of the people who saw him every day. You saw him on the day of his death. You must have some idea."

"I told the police at the time, and I have told the Americans who came round asking questions of all of us. I saw him that morning, once, and then again at lunchtime. I told them what we had for lunch. I described the clothes he was wearing. I told them everything."

As he spoke, Mma Ramotswe made her decision. He was lying. Had he been telling the truth, she would have brought the encounter to an end, but she knew now that her initial intuition had been right. He was lying as he spoke. It was easy to tell; indeed, Mma Ramotswe could not understand why everybody could not tell when another person was lying. In her eyes, it was so obvious, and Dr Ranta might as well have had an illuminated liar sign about his neck.

"I do not believe you, Rra," she said simply. "You are lying to me."

He opened his mouth slightly, and then closed it. Then, folding his hands over his stomach again, he leant back in his chair.

"Our talk has come to an end, Mma," he announced. "I am sorry that I cannot help you. Perhaps you can go home and study some more logic. Logic will tell you that when a person says he cannot help you, you will get no help. That, after all, is logical."

He spoke with a sneer, pleased with his elegant turn of phrase.

"Very well, Rra," said Mma Ramotswe. "You could help me, or rather you could help that poor American woman. She is a mother. You had a mother. I could say to you, *Think about that mother's feelings,* but I know that with a person like you that makes no difference. You do not care about that woman. Not just because she is a white woman, from far away; you wouldn't care if she was a woman from your own village, would you?"

He grinned at her. "I told you. We have finished our talk."

"But people who don't care about others can sometimes be made to care," she said.

He snorted. "In a minute I am going to telephone the Administration and tell them that there is a trespasser in my room. I could say that I found you trying to steal something. I could do that, you know. In fact, I think that is just what I might do. We have had trouble with casual thieves recently and they would send the security people pretty quickly. You might have difficulty explaining it all, Mrs Logician."

"I wouldn't do that, Rra," she said. "You see, I know all about Angel."

The effect was immediate. His body stiffened and again she smelled the acrid odour, stronger now.

"Yes," she said. "I know about Angel and the examination paper. I have a statement back in my office. I can pull the chair from under you now, right now. What would you do in Gaborone as an unemployed university lecturer, Rra? Go back to your village? Help with the cattle again?"

Her words, she noted, were like axe blows. Extortion, she thought. Blackmail. This is how the blackmailer feels when he has his victim at his feet. Complete power.

"You cannot do that . . . I will deny . . . There is nothing to show . . ."

"I have all the proof they will need," she said. "Angel, and another girl who is prepared to lie and say that you gave her exam questions. She is cross with you and she will lie. What she says is not true, but there will be two girls with the same story. We detectives call that corroboration, Rra. Courts like corroboration. They call it similar fact evidence. Your colleagues in the Law Department will tell you all about such evidence. Go and speak to them. They will explain the law to you."

He moved his tongue between his teeth, as if to moisten his lips. She saw that, and she saw the damp patch of sweat under his armpits; one of his laces was undone, she noted, and the tie had a stain, coffee or tea.

"I do not like doing this, Rra," she said. "But this is my job. Sometimes I have to be tough and do things that I do not like doing. But what I am doing now has to be done because there is a very sad American woman who only wants to say goodbye to her son. I know you don't care about her, but I do, and I think that her feelings are more important than yours. So I am going to offer you a bargain. You tell me what happened and I shall promise you—and my word means what it says, Rra—I shall promise you that we hear nothing more about Angel and her friend."

His breathing was irregular; short gasps, like that of a person with obstructive airways disease—a struggling for breath.

"I did not kill him," he said. "I did not kill him."

"Now you are telling the truth," said Mma Ramotswe. "I can tell that. But you must tell me what happened and where his body is. That is what I want to know."

"Are you going to go to the police and tell them that I withheld information? If you will, then I will just face whatever happens about that girl."

"No, I am not going to go to the police. This story is just for his mother. That is all."

He closed his eyes. "I cannot talk here. You can come to my house."

"I will come this evening."

"No," he said. "Tomorrow."

"I shall come this evening," she said. "That woman has waited ten years. She must not wait any longer."

"All right. I shall write down the address. You can come tonight at nine o'clock."

"I shall come at eight," said Mma Ramotswe. "Not every woman will do what you tell her to do, you know."

She left him, and as she made her way back to the tiny white van she listened to her own breathing and felt her own heart thumping wildly. She had no idea where she had found the courage, but it had been there, like the water at the bottom of a disused quarry—unfathomably deep.

CHAPTER EIGHTEEN

AT TLOKWENG ROAD
SPEEDY MOTORS

WHILE MMA Ramotswe indulged in the pleasures of black-mail—for that is what it was, even if in a good cause, and therein lay another moral problem which she and Mma Makutsi might chew over in due course—Mr J.L.B. Matekoni, *garagiste* to His Excellency, the British High Commissioner to Botswana, took his two foster children to the garage for the afternoon. The girl, Motholeli, had begged him to take them so that she could watch him work, and he, bemused, had agreed. A garage workshop was no place for children, with all those heavy tools and pneumatic hoses, but he could detail one of the apprentices to watch over them while he worked. Besides, it might be an idea to expose the boy to the garage at this stage so that he could get a taste for mechanics at an early age. An understanding of cars and engines had to be instilled early; it was not something that could be picked up later. One might become a mechanic at any age, of course, but not everybody

could have a feeling for engines. That was something that had
to be acquired by osmosis, slowly, over the years.

He parked in front of his office door so that Motholeli could
get into the wheelchair in the shade. The boy dashed off
immediately to investigate a tap at the side of the building and
had to be called back.

"This place is dangerous," cautioned Mr J.L.B. Matekoni.
"You must stay with one of these boys over there."

He called over the younger apprentice, the one who constantly tapped him on the shoulder with his greasy finger and
ruined his clean overalls.

"You must stop what you are doing," he said. "You watch over
these two while I am working. Make sure that they don't get
hurt."

The apprentice seemed to be relieved by his new duties and
beamed broadly at the children. He's the lazy one, thought
Mr J.L.B. Matekoni. He would make a better nanny than a
mechanic.

The garage was busy. There was a football team's minibus in
for an overhaul and the work was challenging. The engine had
been strained from constant overloading, but that was the case
with every minibus in the country. They were always overloaded as the proprietors attempted to cram in every possible
fare. This one, which needed new rings, had been belching
acrid black smoke to the extent that the players were complaining about shortness of breath.

The engine was exposed and the transmission had been
detached. With the help of the other apprentice, Mr J.L.B.
Matekoni attached lifting tackle to the engine block and began
to winch it out of the vehicle. Motholeli, watching intently
from her wheelchair, pointed something out to her brother. He

glanced briefly in the direction of the engine, but then looked away again. He was tracing a pattern in a patch of oil at his feet.

Mr J.L.B. Matekoni exposed the pistons and the cylinders. Then, pausing, he looked over at the children.

"What is happening now, Rra?" called the girl. "Are you going to replace those rings there? What do they do? Are they important?"

Mr J.L.B. Matekoni looked at the boy. "You see, Puso? You see what I am doing?"

The boy smiled weakly.

"He is a drawing a picture in the oil," said the apprentice. "He is drawing a house."

The girl said: "May I come closer, Rra?" she said. "I will not get in the way."

Mr J.L.B. Matekoni nodded and, after she had wheeled herself across, he pointed out to her where the trouble lay.

"You hold this for me," he said. "There."

She took the spanner, and held it firmly.

"Good," he said. "Now you turn this one here. You see? Not too far. That's right."

He took the spanner from her and replaced it in his tray. Then he turned and looked at her. She was leaning forward in her chair, her eyes bright with interest. He knew that look; the expression of one who loves engines. It could not be faked; that younger apprentice, for example, did not have it, and that is why he would never be more than a mediocre mechanic. But this girl, this strange, serious child who had come into his life, had the makings of a mechanic. She had the art. He had never before seen it in a girl, but it was there. And why not? Mma Ramotswe had taught him that there is no reason why women should not do anything they wanted. She was undoubtedly right. People had assumed that private detectives would be men, but look at how well Mma Ramotswe had done. She had been able to use a woman's powers of observation and a woman's intuition to find out things that could well escape a man. So if a girl might aspire to becoming a detective, then why should she not aspire to entering the predominantly male world of cars and engines?

Motholeli raised her eyes, meeting his gaze, but still respectfully.

"You are not cross with me, Rra?" she said. "You do not think I am a nuisance?"

He reached forward and laid a hand gently on her arm.

"Of course I am not cross," he said. "I am proud. I am proud that now I have a daughter who will be a great mechanic. Is that what you want? Am I right?"

She nodded modestly. "I have always loved engines," she said. "I have always liked to look at them. I have loved to work with screwdrivers and spanners. But I have never had the chance to do anything."

"Well," said Mr J.L.B. Matekoni. "That changes now. You can come with me on Saturday mornings and help here. Would you like that? We can make a special workbench for you—a low one—so that it is the right height for your chair."

"You are very kind, Rra."

For the rest of the day, she remained at his side, watching each procedure, asking the occasional question, but taking care not to intrude. He tinkered and coaxed, until eventually the minibus engine, reinvigorated, was secured back in place and, when tested, produced no acrid black smoke.

"You see," said Mr J.L.B. Matekoni proudly, pointing to the

clear exhaust. "Oil won't burn off like that if it's kept in the right place. Tight seals. Good piston rings. Everything in its proper place."

Motholeli clapped her hands. "That van is happier now," she said.

Mr J.L.B. Matekoni smiled. "Yes," he agreed. "It is happier now."

He knew now, beyond all doubt, that she had the talent. Only those who really understood machinery could conceive of happiness in an engine; it was an insight which the non-mechanically minded simply lacked. This girl had it, while the younger apprentice did not. He would kick an engine, rather than talk to it, and he had often seen him forcing metal. You cannot force metal, Mr J.L.B. Matekoni had told him time after time. If you force metal, it fights back. Remember that if you remember nothing else I have tried to teach you. Yet the apprentice would still strip bolts by turning the nut the wrong way and would bend flanges if they seemed reluctant to fall into proper alignment. No machinery could be treated that way.

This girl was different. She understood the feelings of engines, and would be a great mechanic one day—that was clear.

He looked at her proudly, as he wiped his hands on cotton lint. The future of Tlokweng Road Speedy Motors seemed assured.

CHAPTER NINETEEN

WHAT HAPPENED

MA RAMOTSWE felt afraid. She had experienced fear only once or twice before in her work as Botswana's only lady private detective (a title she still deserved; Mma Makutsi, it had to be remembered, was only an *assistant* private detective). She had felt this way when she had gone to see Charlie Gotso, the wealthy businessman who still cultivated witch doctors, and indeed on that meeting she had wondered whether her calling might one day bring her up against real danger. Now, faced with going to Dr Ranta's house, the same cold feeling had settled in her stomach. Of course, there were no real grounds for this. It was an ordinary house in an everyday street near Maru-a-Pula School. There would be neighbours next door, and the sound of voices; there would be dogs barking in the night; there would be the lights of cars. She could not imagine that Dr Ranta would pose any danger to her. He was an accomplished seducer perhaps, a manipulator, an opportunist, but not a murderer.

On the other hand, the most ordinary people can be murderers. And if this were to be the manner of one's death, then one was very likely to know one's assailant and meet him in very ordinary circumstances. She had recently taken out a subscription to the *Journal of Criminology* (an expensive mistake, because it contained little of interest to her) but among the meaningless tables and unintelligible prose she had come across an arresting fact: the overwhelming majority of homicide victims know the person who kills them. They are not killed by strangers, but by friends, family, work acquaintances. Mothers killed their children. Husbands killed their wives. Wives killed their husbands. Employees killed their employers. Danger, it seemed, stalked every interstice of day-to-day life. Could this be true? Not in Johannesburg, she thought, where people fell victim to *tsostis* who prowled about at night, to car thieves who were prepared to use their guns, and to random acts of indiscriminate violence by young men with no sense of the value of life. But perhaps cities like that were an exception; perhaps in more normal circumstances homicide happened in just this sort of surrounding—a quiet talk in a modest house, while people went about their ordinary business just a stone's throw away.

Mr J.L.B. Matekoni sensed that something was wrong. He had come to dinner, to tell her of his visit earlier that evening to his maid in prison, and had immediately noticed that she seemed distracted. He did not mention it at first; there was a story to tell about the maid, and this, he thought, might take Mma Ramotswe's mind off whatever it was that was preoccupying her.

"I have arranged for a lawyer to see her," he said. "There is a man in town who knows about this sort of case. I have arranged for him to go and see her in her cell and to speak for her in court."

Mma Ramotswe piled an ample helping of beans on Mr J.L.B. Matekoni's plate.

"Did she explain anything?" she asked. "It can't look good for her. Silly woman."

Mr J.L.B. Matekoni frowned. "She was hysterical when I first arrived. She started to shout at the guards. It was very embarrassing for me. They said: 'Please control your wife and tell her to keep her big mouth shut.' I had to tell them twice that she was not my wife."

"But why was she shouting?" asked Mma Ramotswe. "Surely she understands that she can't shout her way out of there."

"She knows that, I think," said Mr J.L.B. Matekoni. "She was shouting because she was so cross. She said that somebody else should be there, not her. She mentioned your name for some reason."

Mma Ramotswe placed the beans on her own plate. "Me? What have I got to do with this?"

"I asked her that," Mr J.L.B. Matekoni went on. "But she just shook her head and said nothing more about it."

"And the gun? Did she explain the gun?"

"She said that the gun didn't belong to her. She said that it belonged to a boyfriend and that he was coming to collect it. Then she said that she didn't know that it was there. She thought the parcel contained meat. Or so she claims."

Mma Ramotswe shook her head. "They won't believe that. If they did, then would they ever be able to convict anybody found in possession of an illegal weapon?"

"That's what the lawyer said to me over the telephone," said Mr J.L.B. Matekoni. "He said that it was very hard to get somebody off one of these charges. The courts just don't believe them if they say that they didn't know there was a gun. They assume that they are lying and they send them to prison for at least a year. If they have previous convictions, and there usually are, then it can be much longer."

Mma Ramotswe raised her teacup to her lips. She liked to drink tea with her meals, and she had a special cup for the purpose. She would try to buy a matching one for Mr J.L.B. Matekoni, she thought, but it might be difficult, as this cup had been made in England and was very special.

Mr J.L.B. Matekoni looked sideways at Mma Ramotswe. There was something on her mind. In a marriage, he thought, it would be important not to keep anything from one's spouse, and they might as well start that policy now. Mind you, he recalled that he had just kept the knowledge of two foster children from Mma Ramotswe, which was hardly a minor matter, but that was over now and a new policy could begin.

"Mma Ramotswe," he ventured. "You are uneasy tonight. Is it something I have said?"

She put down her teacup, glancing at her watch as she did so.

"It's nothing to do with you," she said. "I have to go and speak to somebody tonight. It's about Mma Curtin's son. I am worried about this person I have to see."

She told him of her fears. She explained that although she knew that it was highly unlikely that an economist at the University of Botswana would turn to violence, nonetheless she felt convinced of the evil in his character, and this made her profoundly uneasy.

"There is a word for this sort of person," she explained. "I read about them. He is called a psychopath. He is a man with no morality."

He listened quietly, his brow furrowed with concern. Then, when she had finished speaking, he said: "You cannot go. I cannot have my future wife walking into danger like that."

She looked at him. "It makes me very pleased to know that you are worried about me," she said. "But I have my calling, which is that of a private detective. If I was going to be frightened, I should have done something else."

Mr J.L.B. Matekoni looked unhappy. "You do not know this man. You cannot go to his house, just like that. If you insist, then I shall come too. I shall wait outside. He need not know I am there."

Mma Ramotswe pondered. She did not want Mr J.L.B. Matekoni to fret, and if his presence outside would relieve his anxiety, then there was no reason why he should not come. "Very well," she said. "You wait outside. We'll take my van. You can sit there while I am talking to him."

"And if there is any emergency," he said, "you can shout. I shall be listening."

They both finished the meal in a more relaxed frame of mind. Motholeli was reading to her brother in his bedroom, the children having had their evening meal earlier. Dinner over, while Mr J.L.B. Matekoni took the plates through to the kitchen, Mma Ramotswe went down the corridor to find the girl half-asleep herself, the book resting on her knee. Puso was still awake, but drowsy, one arm across his chest, the other hanging down over the edge of the bed. She moved his arm back onto the bed and he smiled at her sleepily.

"It is time for you to go to bed too," she said to the girl. "Mr J.L.B. Matekoni tells me that you have had a busy day repairing engines."

She wheeled Motholeli back to her own room, where she helped her out of the chair and onto the side of the bed. She liked to have her independence, and so she allowed her to undress herself unaided and to get into the new nightgown that Mr J.L.B. Matekoni had bought for her on the shopping trip. It was the wrong colour, thought Mma Ramotswe, but then it had been chosen by a man, who could not be expected to know about these things.

"Are you happy here, Motholeli?" she asked.

"I am so happy," said the girl. "And every day my life is getting happier."

Mma Ramotswe tucked the sheet about her and planted a kiss on her cheek. Then she turned out the light and left the room. *Every day I am getting happier.* Mma Ramotswe wondered whether the world which this girl and her brother would inherit would be better than the world in which she and Mr J.L.B. Matekoni had grown up. They had grown happier, she thought, because they had seen Africa become independent and take its own steps in the world. But what a troubled adolescence the continent had experienced, with its vainglorious dictators and their corrupt bureaucracies. And all the time, African people were simply trying to lead decent lives in the midst of all the turmoil and disappointment. Did the people who made all the decisions in this world, the powerful people in places like Washington and London, know about people like Motholeli and Puso? Or care? She was sure that they would care, if only they knew. Sometimes she thought that people overseas had no room in their heart for Africa, because nobody had ever told them that African people were just the same as they were. They simply did not know about people like her Daddy, Obed Ramotswe, who stood, proudly attired in his shiny suit, in the photograph in her living room. You had no grandchildren, she said to the photograph, but now you have. Two. In this house.

The photograph was mute. He would have loved to have met the children, she thought. He would have been a good grandfather, who would have shown them the old Botswana morality and brought them to an understanding of what it is to live an honourable life. She would have to do that now; she and Mr J.L.B. Matekoni. One day soon she would drive out to the orphan farm and thank Mma Silvia Potokwane for giving them the children. She would also thank her for everything that she did for all those other orphans, because, she suspected, nobody ever thanked her for that. Bossy as Mma Potokwane might be, she was a matron, and it was a matron's job to be like that, just as detectives should be nosy, and mechanics . . . Well, what should mechanics be? Greasy? No, greasy was not quite right. She would have to think further about that.

"I WILL be ready," said Mr J.L.B. Matekoni, his voice lowered, although there was no need. "You will know that I am here. Right here, outside the house. If you shout out, I will hear you."

They studied the house, in the dim light of the streetlamp, an undistinguished building with a standard red-tiled roof and unkempt garden.

"He obviously does not employ a gardener," observed Mma Ramotswe. "Look at the mess."

It was inconsiderate not to have a gardener if, like Dr Ranta, you were in a well-paid white-collar job. It was a social duty to employ domestic staff, who were readily available and desperate for work. Wages were low—unconscionably so, thought Mma Ramotswe—but at least the system created jobs. If everybody with a job had a maid, then that was food going into the mouths of the maids and their children. If everybody did their own housework and tended their own gardens, then what were the people who were maids and gardeners to do?

By not cultivating his garden, Dr Ranta showed himself to be selfish, which did not surprise Mma Ramotswe at all.

"Too selfish," remarked Mr J.L.B. Matekoni.

"That's exactly what I was thinking," said Mma Ramotswe.

She opened the door of the van and manoeuvred herself out. The van was slightly too small for a lady like herself, of traditional build, but she was fond of it and dreaded the day when Mr J.L.B. Matekoni would be able to fix it no longer. No modern van, with all its gadgets and sophistication, would be able to take the place of the tiny white van. Since she had acquired it eleven years previously, it had borne her faithfully on her every journey, putting up with the heights of the October heat, or the fine dust which at certain times of year drifted in from the Kalahari and covered everything with a red-brown blanket. Dust was the enemy of engines, Mr J.L.B. Matekoni had explained—on more than one occasion—the enemy of engines, but the friend of the hungry mechanic.

Mr J.L.B. Matekoni watched Mma Ramotswe approach the front door and knock. Dr Ranta must have been waiting for her, as she was quickly admitted and the door was closed behind her.

"Is it just yourself, Mma?" said Dr Ranta. "Is your friend out there coming in?"

"No," she said. "He will wait for me outside."

Dr Ranta laughed. "Security? So you feel safe?"

She did not answer his question. "You have a nice house," she said. "You are fortunate."

He gestured for her to follow him into the living room. Then he pointed to a chair and he himself sat down.

"I don't want to waste my time talking to you," he said. "I will speak only because you have threatened me and I am experiencing some difficulty with some lying women. That is the only reason why I am talking to you."

His pride was hurt, she realised. He had been cornered—and by a woman, too; a stinging humiliation for a womaniser. There was no point in preliminaries, she thought, and so she went straight to the point.

"How did Michael Curtin die?" she asked.

He sat in his chair, directly opposite her, his lips pursed.

"I worked there," he said, appearing to ignore her question. "I was a rural economist and they had been given a grant by the Ford Foundation to employ somebody to do studies of the economics of these small-scale agricultural ventures. That was my job. But I knew that things were hopeless. Right from the start. Those people were just idealists. They thought that you could change the way things had always been. I knew it wouldn't work."

"But you accepted the money," said Mma Ramotswe.

He stared at her contemptuously. "It was a job. I am a professional economist. I study things that work and things that don't work. Maybe you don't understand that."

"I understand," she said.

"Well," he went on. "We—the management, so to speak—lived in one large house. There was a German who was in charge of it—a man from Namibia, Burkhardt Fischer. He had a wife, Marcia, and then there was a South African woman, Carla Smit, the American boy and myself.

"We all got on quite well, except that Burkhardt did not like me. He tried to get rid of me shortly after I arrived, but I had a contract from the Foundation and they refused. He told lies about me, but they didn't believe him.

"The American boy was very polite. He spoke reasonable Setswana and people liked him. The South African woman took to him and they started to share the same room. She did everything for him—cooked his food, washed his clothes, and made a great fuss of him. Then she started to get interested in me. I didn't encourage her, but she had an affair with me, while she was still with that boy. She said to me that she was going to tell him, but that she didn't want to hurt his feelings. So we saw one another secretly, which was difficult to do out there, but we managed.

"Burkhardt suspected what was happening and he called me into his office and threatened that he would tell the American boy if I did not stop seeing Carla. I told him that it was none of his business, and he became angry. He said that he was going to write to the Foundation again and say that I was disrupting the work of the collective. So I told him that I would stop seeing Carla.

"But I did not. Why should I? We met one another in the evenings. She said that she liked going for walks in the bush in the dark; he did not like this, and he stayed. He warned her about going too far and about looking out for wild animals and snakes.

"We had a place where we went to be alone together. It was a hut beyond the fields. We used it for storing hoes and string and things like that. But it was also a good place for lovers to meet.

"That night we were in the hut together. There was a full moon, and it was quite light outside. I suddenly realised that somebody was outside the hut and I got up. I crept to the door and opened it very slowly. The American boy was outside. He was wearing just a pair of shorts and his veldschoens. It was a very hot night.

"He said: 'What are you doing here?' I said nothing, and he suddenly pushed past me and looked into the hut. He saw Carla there, and of course he knew straightaway.

"At first he did not say anything. He just looked at her and then he looked at me. Then he began to run away from the hut. But he did not run back towards the house, but in the opposite direction, out into the bush.

"Carla shouted for me to go after him, and so I did. He ran quite fast, but I managed to catch up with him and I grabbed him by the shoulder. He pushed me off, and got away again. I followed him, even through thorn bushes, which were scratching at my legs and arms. I could easily have caught one of those thorns in my eye, but I did not. It was very dangerous.

"I caught him again, and this time he could not struggle so hard. I put my arms around him, to calm him down so that we could get him back to the house, but he fell away from me and he stumbled.

"We were at the edge of a deep ditch, a *donga,* that ran

through the bush there. It was about six feet deep, and as he stumbled he fell down into the ditch. I looked down and saw him lying there on the ground. He did not move at all and he was making no sound.

"I climbed down and looked at him. He was quite still, and when I tried to look at his head to see if he had hurt it, it lolled sideways in my hand. I realised that he had broken his neck in the fall and that he was no longer breathing.

"I ran back to Carla and told her what had happened. She came with me back to the *donga* and we looked at him again. He was obviously dead, and she started to scream.

"When she had stopped screaming, we sat down there in the ditch and wondered what to do. I thought that if we went back and reported what had happened, nobody would believe that he had slipped by accident. I imagined that people would say that he and I had had a fight after he discovered that I was seeing his girlfriend. I knew, in particular, that if the police spoke to Burkhardt, he would say bad things about me and would tell them that I had probably killed him. It would have looked very bad for me.

"So we decided to bury the body and to say that we knew nothing about it. I knew that there were anthills nearby; the bush there is full of them, and I knew that this was a good place to get rid of a body. I found one quite easily, and I was lucky. An anteater had made quite a large hole in the side of one of the mounds, and I was able to enlarge this slightly and then put the body in. Then I stuffed in stones and earth and swept around the mound with a branch of a thorn tree. I think that I must have covered all traces of what had happened, because the tracker that they got in picked up nothing. Also, there was rain the next day, and that helped to hide any signs.

"The police asked us questions over the next few days, and there were other people, too. I told them that I had not seen him that evening, and Carla said the same thing. She was shocked, and became very quiet. She did not want to see me anymore, and she spent a lot of her time crying.

"Then Carla left. She spoke to me briefly before she went, and she told me that she was sorry that she had become involved with me. She also told me that she was pregnant, but that the baby was his, not mine because she must already have been pregnant by the time she and I started seeing one another.

"She left, and then I left one month later. I was given a scholarship to Duke; she left the country. She did not want to go back to South Africa, which she didn't like. I heard that she went up to Zimbabwe, to Bulawayo, and that she took a job running a small hotel there. I heard the other day that she is still there. Somebody I know was in Bulawayo and he said that he had seen her in the distance."

He stopped and looked at Mma Ramotswe. "That is the truth, Mma," he said. "I didn't kill him. I have told you the truth."

Mma Ramotswe nodded. "I can tell that," she said. "I can tell that you were not lying." She paused. "I am not going to say anything to the police. I told you that, and I do not go back on my word. But I am going to tell the mother what happened, provided that she makes the same promise to me—that she will not go to the police, and I think that she will give me that promise. I do not see any point in the police reopening the case."

It was clear that Dr Ranta was relieved. His expression of hostility had gone now, and he seemed to be seeking some sort of reassurance from her.

"And those girls," he said. "They won't make trouble for me?"

Mma Ramotswe shook her head. "There will be no trouble from them. You need not worry about that."

"What about that statement?" he asked. "The one from that other girl? Will you destroy it?"

Mma Ramotswe rose to her feet and moved towards the door.

"That statement?"

"Yes," he said. "The statement about me from the girl who was lying."

Mma Ramotswe opened the front door and looked out. Mr J.L.B. Matekoni was sitting in the car and looked up when the front door was opened.

She stepped down onto the pathway.

"Well, Dr Ranta," she said quietly. "I think that you are a man who has lied to a lot of people, particularly, I think, to women. Now something has happened which you may not have had happen to you before. A woman has lied to you and you have fallen for it entirely. You will not like that, but maybe it will teach you what it is to be manipulated. There was no girl."

She walked down the path and out of the gate. He stood at the door watching her, but she knew that he would not dare do anything. When he got over the anger which she knew he would be feeling, he would reflect that she had let him off lightly, and, if he had the slightest vestige of a conscience he might also be grateful to her for setting to rest the events of ten years ago. But she had her doubts about his conscience, and she thought that this, on balance, might be unlikely.

As for her own conscience: she had lied to him and she had resorted to blackmail. She had done so in order to obtain information which she otherwise would not have got. But again that troubling issue of means and ends raised its head. Was it right to do the wrong thing to get the right result? Yes, it must be. There were wars which were just wars. Africa had been obliged to fight to liberate itself, and nobody said that it was wrong to use force to achieve that result. Life was messy, and sometimes there was no other way. She had played Dr Ranta at his own game, and had won, just as she had used deception to defeat that cruel witch doctor in her earlier case. It was regrettable, but necessary in a world that was far from perfect.

CHAPTER TWENTY

BULAWAYO

LEAVING EARLY, with the town barely stirring and the sky still in darkness, she drove in the tiny white van out onto the Francistown Road. Just before she reached the Mochudi turnoff, where the road ambled down to the source of the Limpopo, the sun began to rise above the plains, and for a few minutes, the whole world was a pulsating yellow-gold—the *kopjes,* the panoply of the treetops, last season's dry grass beside the road, the very dust. The sun, a great red ball, seemed to hang above the horizon and then freed itself and floated up over Africa; the natural colours of the day returned, and Mma Ramotswe saw in the distance the familiar roofs of her childhood, and the donkeys beside the road, and the houses dotted here and there among the trees.

This was a dry land, but now, at the beginning of the rainy season, it was beginning to change. The early rains had been good. Great purple clouds had stacked up to the north and east, and the rain had fallen in white torrents, like a waterfall covering the land. The land, parched by months of dryness, had swallowed the shimmering pools which the downpour had created, and, within hours, a green tinge had spread over the brown. Shoots of grass, tiny yellow flowers, spreading tentacles of wild ground vines, broke through the softened crust of the earth and made the land green and lush. The waterholes, baked-mud depressions, were suddenly filled with muddy-brown water, and riverbeds, dry passages of sand, flowed again. The rainy season was the annual miracle which allowed life to exist in these dry lands—a miracle in which one had to believe, or the rains might never come, and the cattle might die, as they had done in the past.

She liked the drive to Francistown, although today she was going a further three hours north, over the border and into Zimbabwe. Mr J.L.B. Matekoni had been unwilling for her to go, and had tried to persuade her to change her mind, but she had insisted. She had taken on this enquiry, and she would have to see it through.

"It is more dangerous than Botswana," he had said. "There's always some sort of trouble up there. There was the war, and then the rebels, and then other troublemakers. Roadblocks. Holdups. That sort of thing. What if your van breaks down?"

It was a risk she had to take, although she did not like to worry him. Apart from the fact that she felt that she had to make the trip, it was important for her to establish the principle that she would make her own decisions on these matters. You could not have a husband interfering with the workings of the No. 1 Ladies' Detective Agency; otherwise they might as well change the name to the No. 1 Ladies' (and Husband) Detective Agency. Mr J.L.B. Matekoni was a good mechanic, but not a detective. It was a question of . . . What was it? Subtlety? Intuition?

So the trip to Bulawayo would go ahead. She considered that she knew how to look after herself; so many people who got into trouble had only themselves to blame for it. They ventured into places where they had no business to be; they made provocative statements to the wrong people; they failed to read the social signals. Mma Ramotswe knew how to merge with her surroundings. She knew how to handle a young man with an explosive sense of his own importance, which was, in her view, the most dangerous phenomenon one might encounter in Africa. A young man with a rifle was a landmine; if you trod on his sensitivities—which was not hard to do—dire consequences could ensue. But if you handled him correctly—with the respect that such people crave—you might defuse the situation. But at the same time, you should not be too passive, or he would see you as an opportunity to assert himself. It was all a question of judging the psychological niceties of the situation.

She drove on through the morning. By nine o'clock she was passing through Mahalapye, where her father, Obed Ramotswe, had been born. He had moved south to Mochudi, which was her mother's village, but it was here that his people had been, and they were still, in a sense, her people. If she wandered about the streets of this haphazard town and spoke to old people, she was sure that she would find somebody who knew exactly who she was; somebody who could slot her into some complicated genealogy. There would be second, third, fourth cousins, distant family ramifications, that would bind her to people she had never met and among whom she would find an immediate sense of kinship. If the tiny white van were to break down, then she could knock on any one of those doors and expect to receive the help that distant relatives can claim among the Batswana.

Mma Ramotswe found it difficult to imagine what it would be like to have no people. There were, she knew, those who had no others in this life, who had no uncles, or aunts, or distant cousins of any degree; people who were *just themselves.* Many white people were like that, for some unfathomable reason; they did not seem to want to have people and were happy to be just themselves. How lonely they must be—like spacemen deep in space, floating in the darkness, but without even that silver, unfurling cord that linked the astronauts to their little metal womb of oxygen and warmth. For a moment, she indulged the metaphor, and imagined the tiny white van in space, slowly spinning against a background of stars and she, Mma Ramotswe, of the No. 1 Ladies' Space Agency, floating weightless, head over heels, tied to the tiny white van with a thin washing line.

SHE STOPPED at Francistown, and drank a cup of tea on the verandah of the hotel overlooking the railway line. A diesel train tugged at its burden of coaches, crowded with travellers from the north, and shunted off; a goods train, laden with copper from the mines of Zambia, stood idle, while its driver stood and talked with a railways official under a tree. A dog, exhausted by the heat, lame from a withered leg, limped past. A child, curious, nose streaming, peeped round a table at Mma Ramotswe, and then scuttled off giggling when she smiled at him.

Now came the border crossing, and the slow shuffling

queue outside the white block in which the uniformed officials shuffled their cheaply printed forms and stamped pass-
ports and permissions, bored and officious at the same time.
The formalities over, she set out on the last leg of the journey,
past granite hills that faded into soft blue horizons, through an
air that seemed cooler, higher, fresher than the oppressive heat
of Francistown. And then into Bulawayo, into a town of wide
streets and jacaranda trees, and shady verandahs. She had a
place to stay here; the house of a friend who visited her from
time to time in Gaborone, and there was a comfortable room
awaiting her, with cold, polished red floors and a thatch roof
that made the air within as quiet and as cool as the atmosphere
in a cave.

"I am always happy to see you," said her friend. "But why are
you here?"

"To find somebody," said Mma Ramotswe. "Or rather, to
help somebody else to find somebody."

"You're talking in riddles," laughed her friend.

"Well, let me explain," said Mma Ramotswe. "I'm here to
close a chapter."

SHE FOUND her, and the hotel, without difficulty. Mma
Ramotswe's friend made a few telephone calls and gave her
the name and address of the hotel. It was an old building, in
the colonial style, on the road to the Matopos. It was not clear
who might stay there, but it seemed well kept and there was a
noisy bar somewhere in the background. Above the front door,
painted in small white lettering on black was a sign: *Carla
Smit, Licensee, licensed to sell alcoholic beverages*. This was the
end of the quest, and, as the end of a quest so often was, it was

a mundane setting, quite unexceptionable; yet it was surprising nonetheless that the person sought should actually exist, and be there.

"I AM Carla."

Mma Ramotswe looked at the woman, sitting behind her desk, an untidy pile of papers in front of her. On the wall behind her, pinned above a filing cabinet, was a year-chart with blocks of days marked up in bright colours; a gift from its printers, in heavy Bodoni type: *Printed by the Matabeleland Printing Company (Private) Limited: You think, we ink!* It occurred to her that she might issue a calendar to her own clients: *Suspicious? Call the No. 1 Ladies' Detective Agency. You ask, we answer!* No, that was too lame. *You cry, we spy!* No. Not all the clients felt miserable. *We find things out.* That was better: it had the necessary *dignity.*

"You are?" the woman enquired, politely, but with a touch of suspicion in her voice. She thinks that I have come for a job, thought Mma Ramotswe, and she is steeling herself to turn me down.

"My name is Precious Ramotswe," she said. "I'm from Gaborone. And I have not come to ask for a job."

The woman smiled. "So many people do," she said. "There is such terrible unemployment. People who have done all sorts of courses are desperate for a job. Anything. They'll do anything. I get ten, maybe twelve enquiries every week; many more at the end of the school year."

"Conditions are bad?"

The woman sighed. "Yes, and have been for some time. Many people suffer."

"I see," said Mma Ramotswe. "We are lucky down there in Botswana. We do not have these troubles."

Carla nodded, and looked thoughtful. "I know. I lived there for a couple of years. It was some time ago, but I hear it hasn't changed too much. That's why you are lucky."

"You preferred the old Africa?"

Carla looked at her quizzically. This was a political question, and she would need to be cautious.

She spoke slowly, choosing her words. "No. Not in the sense of preferring the colonial days. Of course not. Not all white people liked that, you know. I may have been a South African, but I left South Africa to get away from apartheid. That's why I went to Botswana."

Mma Ramotswe had not meant to embarrass her. Her question had not been a charged one, and she tried to set her at her ease. "I didn't mean that," she said. "I meant the old Africa, when there were fewer people without jobs. People had a place then. They belonged to their village, to their family. They had their lands. Now a lot of that has gone and they have nothing but a shack on the edge of a town. I do not like that Africa."

Carla relaxed. "Yes. But we cannot stop the world, can we? Africa has these problems now. We have to try to cope with them."

There was a silence. This woman has not come to talk politics, thought Carla; or African history. Why is she here?

Mma Ramotswe looked at her hands, and at the engagement ring, with its tiny point of light. "Ten years ago," she began, "you lived out near Molepolole, at that place run by Burkhardt Fischer. You were there when an American called Michael Curtin disappeared in mysterious circumstances."

She stopped. Carla was staring at her, glassy-eyed.

"I am nothing to do with the police," said Mma Ramotswe, hurriedly. "I have not come here to question you."

Carla's expression was impassive. "Then why do you want to talk about that? It happened a long time ago. He went missing. That's all there is to it."

"No," said Mma Ramotswe. "That is not all there is to it. I don't have to ask you what happened, because I know exactly what took place. You and Oswald Ranta were there, in that hut, when Michael turned up. He fell into a *donga* and broke his neck. You hid the body because Oswald was frightened that the police would accuse him of killing Michael. That is what happened."

Carla said nothing, but Mma Ramotswe saw that her words had shocked her. Dr Ranta had told the truth, as she had thought, and now Carla's reaction was confirming this.

"You did not kill Michael," she said. "It had nothing to do with you. But you did conceal the body, which meant that his mother never found out what happened to him. That was the wrong thing to do. But that's not the point. The point is that you can do something to cancel all that out. You can do that thing quite safely. There is no risk to you."

Carla's voice was distant, barely audible. "What can I do? We can't bring him back."

"You can bring an end to his mother's search," she said. "All she wants to do is to say goodbye to her son. People who have lost somebody are often like that. There may be no desire for revenge in their hearts; they just want to know. That's all."

Carla leaned back in her chair, her eyes downcast. "I don't know . . . Oswald would be furious if I talked about . . ."

Mma Ramotswe cut her short. "Oswald knows, and agrees."

"Then why can't he tell her?" retorted Carla, suddenly angry. "He did it. I only lied to protect him."

Mma Ramotswe nodded her understanding. "Yes," she said. "It's his fault, but he is not a good man. He cannot give anything to that woman, or to anybody else for that matter. Such people cannot say sorry to another. But you can. You can meet this woman and tell her what happened. You can seek her forgiveness."

Carla shook her head. "I don't see why . . . After all these years . . ."

Mma Ramotswe stopped her. "Besides," she said. "You are the mother of her grandchild. Is that not so? Would you deny her that little bit of comfort? She has no son now. But there is a . . ."

"Boy," said Carla. "He is called Michael too. He is nine, almost ten."

Mma Ramotswe smiled. "You must bring the child to her, Mma," she said. "You are a mother. You know what that means. You have no reason now not to do this. Oswald cannot do anything to you. He is no threat."

Mma Ramotswe rose to her feet and walked over to the desk, where Carla sat, crumpled, uncertain.

"You know that you must do this," she said.

She took the other woman's hand and held it gently. It was sun-specked, from exposure to high places and heat, and hard work.

"You will do it, won't you, Mma? She is ready to come out to Botswana. She will come in a day or two if I tell her. Can you get away from here? Just for a few days?"

"I have an assistant," said Carla. "She can run the place."

"And the boy? Michael? Will he not be happy to see his grandmother?"

Carla looked up at her.

"Yes, Mma Ramotswe," she said. "You are right."

SHE RETURNED to Gaborone the following day, arriving late at night. Her maid, Rose, had stayed in the house to look after the children, who were fast asleep when Mma Ramotswe arrived home. She crept into their rooms and listened to their soft breathing and smelled the sweet smell of children sleeping. Then exhausted from the drive, she tumbled into her bed, mentally still driving, her eyes moving behind heavy, closed lids.

She was in the office early the following morning, leaving the children in Rose's care. Mma Makutsi had arrived even earlier than she had, and was sitting efficiently behind her desk, typing a report.

"Mr Letsenyane Badule," she announced. "I am reporting on the end of the case."

Mma Ramotswe raised an eyebrow. "I thought that you wanted me to sort that out."

Mma Makutsi pursed her lips. "To begin with, I was not brave enough," she said. "But then he came in yesterday and I had to speak to him. If I had seen him coming, I could have locked the door and put up a closed sign. But he came in before I could do anything about it."

"And?" prompted Mma Ramotswe.

"And I told him about his wife's being unfaithful."

"What did he say?"

"He was upset. He looked very sad."

Mma Ramotswe smiled wryly. "No surprise there," she said.

"Yes, but then I told him that he should not do anything about this as his wife was not doing it for herself, but was doing it for her son's sake. She had taken up with a rich man purely to make sure that his son would get a good education. I said that she was being very selfless. I said that it might be best to leave things exactly as they are."

Mma Ramotswe looked astounded. "He believed that?" she said, incredulously.

"Yes," said Mma Makutsi. "He is not a very sophisticated man. He seemed quite pleased."

"I'm astonished," said Mma Ramotswe.

"Well, there you are," said Mma Makutsi. "He remains happy. The wife also continues to be happy. The boy gets his education. And the wife's lover and the wife's lover's wife are also happy. It is a good result."

Mma Ramotswe was not convinced. There was a major ethical flaw in this solution, but to define it exactly would require a great deal more thought and discussion. She would have to talk to Mma Makutsi about this at greater length, once she had more time to do so. It was a pity, she thought, that the *Journal of Criminology* did not have a problem page for just such cases. She could have written and asked for advice in this delicate matter. Perhaps she could write to the editor anyway and suggest that an agony aunt be appointed; it would certainly make the journal very much more readable.

Several quiet days ensued, in which, once again, they were without clients, and could bring the administrative affairs of the agency up to date. Mma Makutsi oiled her typewriter and went out to buy a new kettle, for the preparation of bush tea.

Mma Ramotswe wrote letters to old friends and prepared accounts for the impending end of the financial year. She had not made a lot of money, but she had not made a loss, and she had been happy and entertained. That counted for infinitely more than a vigorously healthy balance sheet. In fact, she thought, annual accounts should include an item specifically headed *Happiness,* alongside expenses and receipts and the like. That figure in her accounts would be a very large one, she thought.

But it would be nothing to the happiness of Andrea Curtin, who arrived three days later and who met, late that afternoon, in the office of the No. 1 Ladies' Detective Agency, the mother of her grandson and her grandson himself. While Carla was left alone to give the account of what happened on that night ten years ago, Mma Ramotswe took the boy for a walk, and pointed out to him the granite slopes of Kgale Hill and the distant smudge of blue which was the waters of the dam. He was a courteous boy, rather grave in his manner, who was interested in stones, and kept stopping to scratch at some piece of rock or to pick up a pebble.

"This one is quartz," he said, showing her a piece of white rock. "Sometimes you find gold in quartz."

She took the rock and examined it. "You are very interested in rocks?"

"I want to be a geologist," he said solemnly. "We have a geologist who stays in our hotel sometimes. He teaches me about rocks."

She smiled encouragingly. "It would be an interesting job, that," she said. "Rather like being a detective. Looking for things."

She handed the piece of quartz back to him. As he took it,

his eye caught her engagement ring, and for a moment he held her hand, looking at the gold band and its twinkling stone.

"Cubic zirconium," he said. "They make them look like diamonds. Just like the real thing."

WHEN THEY returned, Carla and the American woman were sitting side by side and there was a peacefulness, even joy, in the older woman's expression which told Mma Ramotswe that what she had intended had indeed been achieved.

They drank tea together, just looking at one another. The boy had a gift for his grandmother, a small soapstone carving, which he had made himself. She took it, and kissed him, as any grandmother would.

Mma Ramotswe had a gift for the American woman, a basket which on her return journey from Bulawayo she had bought, on impulse, from a woman sitting by the side of the road in Francistown. The woman was desperate, and Mma Ramotswe, who did not need a basket, had bought it to help her. It was a traditional Botswana basket, with a design worked into the weaving.

"These little marks here are tears," she said. "The giraffe gives its tears to the women and they weave them into the basket."

The American woman took the basket politely, in the proper Botswana way of receiving a gift—with both hands. How rude were people who took a gift with one hand, as if snatching it from the donor; she knew better.

"You are very kind, Mma," she said. "But why did the giraffe give its tears?"

Mma Ramotse shrugged; she had never thought about it. "I

suppose that it means that we can all give something," she said. "A giraffe has nothing else to give—only tears." Did it mean that? she wondered. And for a moment she imagined that she saw a giraffe peering down through the trees, its strange, stilt-borne body camouflaged among the leaves; and its moist velvet cheeks and liquid eyes; and she thought of all the beauty that there was in Africa, and of the laughter, and the love.

The boy looked at the basket. "Is that true, Mma?"

Mma Ramotswe smiled.

"I hope so," she said.

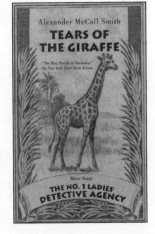

MORALITY FOR BEAUTIFUL GIRLS

While trying to resolve some financial problems for her business, Mma Ramotswe finds herself investigating the alleged poisoning of a government official as well as the moral character of the four finalists of the Miss Beauty and Integrity contest. Other difficulties arise at her fiancé's Tlokweng Road Speedy Motors, as Mma Ramotswe discovers he is more complicated than he seems.

Volume 3
1-4000-3136-2 (pbk)

The mysteries are "smart and sassy . . . [with] the power to amuse or shock or touch the heart, sometimes all at once."
—*Los Angeles Times*

THE KALAHARI TYPING SCHOOL FOR MEN

Mma Precious Ramotswe is content. But, as always, there are troubles. Mr J.L.B. Matekoni has not set the date for their wedding, her assistant Mma Makutsi wants a husband, and worst of all, a rival detective agency has opened up in town. Of course, Precious will manage these things, as she always does, with her uncanny insight and good heart.

Volume 4
1-4000-3180-X (pbk)
0-375-42217-X (hc)

THE FULL CUPBOARD OF LIFE

Mma Ramotswe has weighty matters on her mind. She has been approached by a wealthy lady to check up on several suitors. Are these men interested in her or just her money? This may be difficult to find out, but it's just the kind of case Mma Ramotswe likes.

Volume 5
1-4000-3181-8 (pbk)
0-375-42218-8 (hc)

IN THE COMPANY OF CHEERFUL LADIES

Precious Ramotswe is busier than usual at the No. 1 Ladies' Detective Agency when the appearance of a strange intruder in her house and a mysterious pumpkin in her yard add to her concerns. But what finally rattles Mma Ramotswe's normally unshakable composure is the visitor who forces her to confront a painful secret from her past.

Volume 6
0-375-42271-4 (hc)
Paperback available Spring 2006

A New Series Begins

THE SUNDAY PHILOSOPHY CLUB

THE SUNDAY PHILOSOPHY CLUB
Isabel Dalhousie is fond of problems, and sometimes she becomes interested in problems that are, quite frankly, none of her business— including some that are best left to the police. Filled with endearingly thorny characters and a Scottish atmosphere as thick as a highland mist, *The Sunday Philosophy Club* is an irresistible pleasure.

Volume 1
1-4000-7709-5 (pbk)
0-375-42298-6 (hc)

FRIENDS, LOVERS, CHOCOLATE
While taking care of her niece Cat's delicatessen, Isabel meets a heart transplant patient who has had some strange experiences in the wake of surgery. Against the advice of her housekeeper, Isabel is intent on investigating. Matters are further complicated when Cat returns from vacation with a new boyfriend, and Isabel's fondness for him lands her in another muddle.

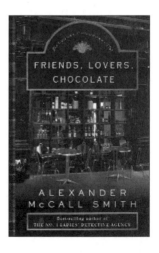

Volume 2
0-375-42299-4 (hc)
Paperback available Fall 2006

The Official Home of Alexander McCall Smith on the Web

WWW.ALEXANDERMCCALLSMITH.COM

A comprehensive Web site for new readers and longtime fans alike, with five exclusive content areas:

• THE NO. 1 LADIES' DETECTIVE AGENCY

The original site for McCall Smith's bestselling series. Explore Precious Ramotswe's Botswana through book descriptions, a photo gallery, advice from Mma Ramotswe, and more.

• THE SUNDAY PHILOSOPHY CLUB

Enter a Scottish atmosphere as thick as a highland mist, complete with a photo tour of Isabel Dalhousie's Edinburgh.

• PROFESSOR DR VON IGELFELD ENTERTAINMENTS

Three original paperback novellas introducing the eccentric and ever-likable Professor Dr von Igelfeld, his colleagues, and their comic adventures.

• ABOUT THE AUTHOR

Read about Alexander McCall Smith and get updates on tour events and other author activities.

• JOIN THE COMMUNITY

Share the world of Alexander McCall Smith with friends, family, and fellow book club members. Print our free Reading Group Guides and sign up for the Alexander McCall Smith Fan Club and e-Newsletter.

ALEXANDER McCALL SMITH

MORALITY FOR BEAUTIFUL GIRLS

In addition to the huge international phenomenon The No. 1 Ladies' Detective Agency series, Alexander McCall Smith is the author of The Sunday Philosophy Club series, the Portuguese Irregular Verbs series, *The Girl Who Married a Lion*, and *44 Scotland Street*. He was born in what is now Zimbabwe and taught law at the University of Botswana and Edinburgh University. He lives in Scotland and returns regularly to Botswana.

MORALITY

FOR BEAUTIFUL

GIRLS

MORALITY

FOR BEAUTIFUL

GIRLS

Alexander McCall Smith

Anchor Books

A Division of Random House, Inc.

New York

FIRST ANCHOR BOOKS EDITION, NOVEMBER 2002

Library of Congress Cataloging-in-Publication Data
McCall Smith, R. A.
Morality for beautiful girls / Alexander McCall Smith.
p.   cm.
1. Ramotswe, Precious (Fictitious character)—Fiction.   2. Women private
investigators—Botswana—Fiction.   3. Beauty contests—Fiction.
4. Botswana—Fiction.   I. Title.

PR6063.C326 M67 2002
823'.914—dc21   2002071712

Anchor ISBN 10: 1-4000-3136-2
Anchor ISBN 13: 978-1-4000-3136-8

www.anchorbooks.com

Printed in the United States of America
23   25   27   29   30   28   26   24

This book is for
Jean Denison
and
Richard Denison

MORALITY

FOR BEAUTIFUL

GIRLS

CHAPTER ONE

THE WORLD AS SEEN BY
ANOTHER PERSON

MA RAMOTSWE, the daughter of the late Obed Ramotswe of Mochudi, near Gaborone, Botswana, Africa, was the announced fiancée of Mr J.L.B. Matekoni, son of the late Pumphamilitse Matekoni, of Tlokweng, peasant farmer and latterly chief caretaker of the Railway Head Office. It was a fine match, everybody thought; she, the founder and owner of The No. 1 Ladies' Detective Agency, Botswana's only detective agency for the concerns of both ladies and others; he, the proprietor of Tlokweng Road Speedy Motors, and by general repute one of the finest mechanics in Botswana. It was always a good thing, people said, to have independent interests in a marriage. Traditional marriages, in which the man made all the decisions and controlled most of the household assets, were all very well for women who wanted to spend their time cooking and looking after children, but times had changed, and for educated women who wanted to make something of their lives, it was undoubtedly better for both spouses to have something to do.

There were many examples of such marriages. There was that of Mma Maketetse, for example, who had set up a small factory specialising in the making of khaki shorts for schoolboys. She had started with a cramped and ill-ventilated sewing room at the back of her house, but by employing her cousins to cut and sew for her she had built up one of Botswana's best businesses, exporting khaki shorts to Namibia in the face of stiff competition from large clothing factories in the Cape. She had married Mr Cedric Maketetse, who ran two bottle stores in Gaborone, the capital, and had recently opened a third in Francistown. There had been a faintly embarrassing article about them in the local paper, with the catchy headline: *Shorts manufacturing lady buttons it up with drink merchant.* They were both members of the Chamber of Commerce, and it was clear to all that Mr Maketetse was immensely proud of his wife's business success.

Of course, a woman with a successful business had to be careful that a man who came courting her was not merely looking for a way of spending the rest of his days in comfort. There had been plenty of cases of that happening, and Mma Ramotswe had noticed that the consequences of such unions were almost inevitably dire. The man would either drink or gamble away the profits of his wife's enterprise, or he would try to run the business and destroy it in the process. Men were good at business, thought Mma Ramotswe, but women were just as good. Women were thriftier by nature; they had to be, trying to run households on a tight budget and feed the ever-open mouths of children. Children ate so much, it seemed, and one could never cook enough pumpkin or porridge to fill their hungry bellies. And as for men, they never seemed happier than when eating large quantities of expensive meat. It was all rather discouraging.

"That will be a good marriage," people said, when they heard of her engagement to Mr J.L.B. Matekoni. "He is a reliable man, and she is a very good woman. They will be very happy running their businesses and drinking tea together."

Mma Ramotswe was aware of this popular verdict on her engagement and shared the sentiment. After her disastrous marriage to Note Mokoti, the jazz trumpeter and incorrigible ladies' man, she had decided that she would never remarry, in spite of frequent offers. Indeed, she had initially turned down Mr J.L.B. Matekoni when he had first proposed, only to accept him some six months later. She had realised that the best test of a prospective husband involves no more than the asking of a very simple question, which every woman—or at least every woman who has had a good father—can pose and to which she will know the answer in her bones. She had asked herself this question in respect of Mr J.L.B. Matekoni, and the answer had been unambiguous.

"And what would my late Daddy have thought of him?" she said to herself. She posed the question after she had accepted Mr J.L.B. Matekoni, as one might ask oneself whether one had taken the right turning at a road junction. She remembered where she had been when she asked it. She was taking an evening walk near the dam, along one of those paths that led this way and that through the thorn bushes. She had suddenly stopped, and looked up at the sky, into that faint, washed out blue that would suddenly, at the approach of sunset, become streaked with copper-red. It was a quiet time of the

day, and she was utterly alone. And so she spoke the question
out loud, as if there were somebody there to hear it.

She looked up at the sky, half-expecting the answer to be
there. But of course it was not, and she knew it anyway, without the need to look. There was no doubt in her mind that
Obed Ramotswe, who had seen every sort of man during the
time he had worked in those distant mines, and who knew the
foibles of all of them, would have approved of Mr J.L.B.
Matekoni. And if that were the case, then she should have no
fears about her future husband. He would be kind to her.

NOW, SITTING in the office of the No. 1 Ladies' Detective
Agency with her assistant, Mma Makutsi, the most distinguished graduate of her year at the Botswana Secretarial College, she reflected on the decisions which her impending
marriage to Mr J.L.B. Matekoni would oblige her to take.
The most immediate issue, of course, had been where they
might live. That had been decided rather quickly; Mr J.L.B.
Matekoni's house near the old Botswana Defence Club,
attractive though it undoubtedly was, with its old colonial
verandah and its shiny tin roof, was not as suitable as her own
house in Zebra Drive. His garden was sparse; little more than
a swept yard, in fact; whereas she had a good collection of
paw-paw trees, some very shady acacias, and a well-established
melon patch. Moreover, when it came to the interiors, there
was little to recommend Mr J.L.B. Matekoni's spartan corridors and unlived-in rooms, especially when compared with the
layout of her own house. It would be a great wrench, she felt,
to abandon her living room, with its comfortable rug on the

red-polished concrete floor, her mantelpiece with her commemorative plate of Sir Sereste Khama, Paramount Chief,
Statesman, and first President of Botswana, and, in the corner,
her treadle sewing machine that still worked so well, even in a
power cut when more modern sewing machines would fall
silent.

She had not had to say very much about it. In fact, the decision in favour of Zebra Drive did not even have to be spelled
out. After Mr J.L.B. Matekoni had been persuaded by Mma
Potokwane, the matron at the orphan farm, to act as foster
father to an orphaned boy and his crippled sister, the children
had moved into her house and immediately settled in. After
that, it was accepted that the whole family would, in due
course, live in Zebra Drive. For the time being, Mr J.L.B.
Matekoni would continue to live in his own house, but would
take his evening meal at Zebra Drive.

That was the easy part of the arrangement. Now there
remained the issue of the business. As Mma Ramotswe sat at
her desk, watching Mma Makutsi shuffling papers in the filing
cabinet of their small office, her thoughts were taken up with
the difficult task that lay ahead of her. It had not been an easy
decision to make, but she had now made it and she would have
to steel herself and put it into effect. That was what business
was all about.

One of the most elementary rules of running a business was
that facilities should not be needlessly duplicated. After she
and Mr J.L.B. Matekoni married, they would have two businesses with two offices. They were very different concerns,
of course, but Tlokweng Road Speedy Motors had a large
amount of office space and it would make a great deal of sense

for Mma Ramotswe to run her agency from there. She had made a close inspection of Mr J.L.B. Matekoni's building and had even obtained advice from a local builder.

"There will be no difficulty," he had said after inspecting the garage and its office. "I can put in a new door on that side over there. Then the clients for your business can come in and not have anything to do with all those greasy goings-on in the workshop."

Combining the two offices would enable Mma Ramotswe to let out her own office and the income derived from that would make all the difference. At present, the uncomfortable truth about the No. 1 Ladies' Detective Agency was that it was simply not making enough money. It was not that there were no clients—there had been a ready supply of those—it was just that detective work was immensely time-consuming and people were simply unable to pay for her services if she charged at a realistic hourly rate. A couple of hundred pula for the resolution of uncertainty or for the finding of a missing person was affordable, and usually well worth it, but several thousand pula for the same job was another matter altogether. Doubt could be preferable to sure knowledge if the difference between the two was a large sum of money.

The business might have broken even if it were not for the wages which Mma Ramotswe had to pay Mma Makutsi. She had originally employed her as a secretary, on the grounds that every business which wished to be taken seriously had to have a secretary, but had soon realised the talents that lay behind those large spectacles. Mma Makutsi had been promoted to assistant detective, a position that gave her the status she so craved. But Mma Ramotswe had felt obliged to raise her pay at the same time, thus plunging the agency's current account further into the red.

She had discussed the matter with Mr J.L.B. Matekoni, who had agreed with her that she had very little choice.

"If you continue like this," he said gravely, "you'll end up bankrupt. I've seen that happen to businesses. They appoint somebody called a judicial manager. He is like a vulture, circling, circling. It is a very bad thing to happen to a business."

Mma Ramotswe clicked her tongue. "I do not want that," she said. "It would be a very sad end to the business."

They had looked at one another glumly. Then Mr J.L.B. Matekoni spoke. "You'll have to sack her," he said. "I've had to sack mechanics in the past. It is not easy, but that is what business is about."

"She was so happy when I promoted her," said Mma Ramotswe quietly. "I can't suddenly tell her that she is no longer a detective. She has no people here in Gaborone. Her people are up in Bobonong. They are very poor, I think."

Mr J.L.B. Matekoni shook his head. "There are many poor people," he said. "Many of these people are suffering badly. But you cannot keep a business going on air. That is well-known. You have to add what you get in and then take away what you spend. The difference is your profit. In your case, there is a minus sign in front of that figure. You cannot . . ."

"I cannot," broke in Mma Ramotswe. "I cannot sack her now. I am like her mother. She wants so much to be a detective and she is hardworking."

Mr J.L.B. Matekoni looked down at his feet. He suspected that Mma Ramotswe was expecting him to propose something, but he was not quite sure what it was. Did she expect him to give her money? Did she want him to meet the bills of the No. 1 Ladies' Detective Agency, even though she had made it so clear that she expected him to keep to his garage business while she attended to her clients and their unsettling problems?

"I do not want you to pay," said Mma Ramotswe, looking at him with a firmness that made him both fear and admire her.

"Of course not," he said hurriedly. "I was not thinking that at all."

"On the other hand," went on Mma Ramotswe, "you do need a secretary at the garage. Your bills are always in a mess, are they not? You never keep a note of what you pay those useless apprentices of yours. I should imagine that you make loans to them, too. Do you keep a record?"

Mr J.L.B. Matekoni looked shifty. How had she found out that the apprentices each owed him over six hundred pula and had shown no signs of being able to repay it?

"Do you want her to come and work for me?" he asked, surprised at the suggestion. "What about her detective position?"

Mma Ramotswe did not answer for a moment. She had not worked anything out, but a plan was now beginning to take shape. If they moved her office to the garage, then Mma Makutsi could keep her job as assistant detective while at the same time she could do the secretarial work that the garage needed. Mr J.L.B. Matekoni could pay her a wage for that, which would mean that the agency's accounts would be relieved of a large part of that burden. This, coupled with the rent which she would receive for the existing offices, would make the financial position look considerably healthier.

She explained her proposal to Mr J.L.B. Matekoni. Although he had always expressed doubts as to Mma Makutsi's usefulness, he could see the attractions of Mma Ramotswe's scheme, not the least of which was that it would keep her happy. And that, he knew, was what he wanted above all else.

MMA RAMOTSWE cleared her throat.

"Mma Makutsi," she began. "I have been thinking about the future."

Mma Makutsi, who had finished her rearranging of the filing cabinet, had made them both a cup of bush tea and was settling down to the half-hour break that she usually took at eleven in the morning. She had started to read a magazine—an old copy of the *National Geographic*—which her cousin, a teacher, had lent her.

"The future? Yes, that is always interesting. But not as interesting as the past, I think. There is a very good article in this magazine, Mma Ramotswe," she said. "I will lend it to you after I have finished reading it. It is all about our ancestors up in East Africa. There is a Dr Leakey there. He is a very famous doctor of bones."

"Doctor of bones?" Mma Ramotswe was puzzled. Mma Makutsi expressed herself very well—both in English and Setswana—but occasionally she used rather unusual expressions. What was a doctor of bones? It sounded rather like a witch doctor, but surely one could not describe Dr Leakey as a witch doctor?

"Yes," said Mma Makutsi. "He knows all about very old bones. He digs them up and tells us about our past. Here, look at this one."

She held up a picture, printed across two pages. Mma Ramotswe squinted to make it out. Her eyes were not what they once were, she had noticed, and she feared that sooner or later she would end up like Mma Makutsi, with her extraordinary, large glasses.

"Is that Dr Leakey?"

Mma Makutsi nodded. "Yes, Mma," she said, "that is him. He is holding a skull which belonged to a very early person. This person lived a long time ago and is very late."

Mma Ramotswe found herself being drawn in. "And this very late person," she said. "Who was he?"

"The magazine says that he was a person when there were very few people about," explained Mma Makutsi. "We all lived in East Africa then."

"Everybody?"

"Yes. Everybody. My people. Your people. All people. We all come from the same small group of ancestors. Dr Leakey has proved that."

Mma Ramotswe was thoughtful. "So we are all brothers and sisters, in a sense?"

"We are," said Mma Makutsi. "We are all the same people. Eskimos, Russians, Nigerians. They are the same as us. Same blood. Same DNA."

"DNA?" asked Mma Ramotswe. "What is that?"

"It is something which God used to make people," explained Mma Makutsi. "We are all made up of DNA and water."

Mma Ramotswe considered the implications of these revelations for a moment. She had no views on Eskimos and Russians, but Nigerians were a different matter. But Mma Makutsi was right, she reflected: if universal brotherhood—and sisterhood—meant anything, it would have to embrace the Nigerians as well.

"If people knew this," she said, "if they knew that we were all from the same family, would they be kinder to one another, do you think?"

Mma Makutsi put down the magazine. "I'm sure they would," she said. "If they knew that, then they would find it very difficult to do unkind things to others. They might even want to help them a bit more."

Mma Ramotswe was silent. Mma Makutsi had made it difficult to go on, but she and Mr J.L.B. Matekoni had taken the decision and she had no alternative but to break the bad news.

"That is all very interesting," she said, trying to sound firm. "I must read more about Dr Leakey when I have more time. At the moment I am having to spend all my time on working out how to keep this business going. The accounts are not good, you know. Our accounts are not like those accounts you see published in the newspapers—you know the ones, where they have two columns, income and expenditure, and the first is always bigger than the second. With this business it is the other way round."

She paused, watching the effect of her words on Mma Makutsi. It was difficult to tell what she was thinking, with those glasses.

"So I am going to have to do something," she went on. "If I do nothing, then we shall be put under judicial management or the bank manager will come and take the office from us. That is what happens to businesses that do not make a profit. It is very bad."

Mma Makutsi was staring at her desk. Then she looked up at Mma Ramotswe and for a moment the branches of the thorn tree outside the window were reflected in her glasses.

Mma Ramotswe found this disconcerting; it was as if one were looking at the world as seen by another person. As she thought this, Mma Makutsi moved her head, and Mma Ramotswe saw, for a moment, the reflection of her own red dress.

"I am doing my best," said Mma Makutsi quietly. "I hope that you will give me a chance. I am very happy being an assistant detective here. I do not want to be just a secretary for the rest of my life."

She stopped and looked at Mma Ramotswe. What was it like, thought Mma Ramotswe, to be Mma Makutsi, graduate of the Botswana Secretarial College with 97 percent in the final examination, but with nobody, except for some people far away up in Bobonong? She knew that Mma Makutsi sent them money, because she had seen her once in the Post Office, buying a postal order for one hundred pula. She imagined that they had been told about the promotion and were proud of the fact that their niece, or whatever she was to them, was doing so well in Gaborone. Whereas the truth was that the niece was being kept as an act of charity and it was really Mma Ramotswe supporting those people up in Bobonong.

Her gaze shifted to Mma Makutsi's desk, and to the still-exposed picture of Dr Leakey holding the skull. Dr Leakey was looking out of the photograph, directly at her. Well Mma Ramotswe? he seemed to be saying. What about this assistant of yours?

She cleared her throat. "You must not worry," she said. "You will still be assistant detective. But we will need you to do some other duties as well when we move over to Tlokweng Road Speedy Motors. Mr J.L.B. Matekoni needs help with his paperwork. Half of you will be a secretary, but half of you will be an assistant detective." She paused, and then added hurriedly, "But you can call yourself assistant detective. That will be your official title."

For the rest of the day, Mma Makutsi was quieter than usual. She made Mma Ramotswe her afternoon tea in silence, handing the mug over to her without saying anything, but at the end of the day she seemed to have accepted her fate.

"I suppose that Mr J.L.B. Matekoni's office is a mess," she said. "I cannot see him doing his paperwork properly. Men do not like that sort of thing."

Mma Ramotswe was relieved by the change of tone. "It is a real mess," she said. "You will be doing him a very good service if you sort it out."

"We were taught how to do that at college," said Mma Makutsi. "They sent us one day to an office that was in a very bad way, and we had to sort it out. There were four of us—myself and three pretty girls. The pretty girls spent all their time talking to the men in the office while I did the work."

"Ah!" said Mma Ramotswe. "I can imagine that."

"I worked until eight o'clock at night," went on Mma Makutsi. "The other girls all went off with the men to a bar at five o'clock and left me there. The next morning, the Principal of the College said that we had all done a very good job and that we were all going to get a top mark for the assignment. The other girls were very pleased. They said that although I had done most of the tidying they had had the more difficult part of the job, which was keeping the men from getting in the way. They really thought that."

Mma Ramotswe shook her head. "They are useless girls, those girls," she said. "There are too many people like that in

Botswana these days. But at least you know that you have succeeded. You are an assistant detective and what are they?
Nothing, I should think."

Mma Makutsi took off her large spectacles and polished the
lenses carefully with the corner of a handkerchief.

"Two of them are married to very rich men," she said. "They
have big houses over near the Sun Hotel. I have seen them
walking about in their expensive sunglasses. The third went off
to South Africa and became a model. I have seen her picture
in a magazine. She has got a husband who is a photographer
for that magazine. He has plenty of money too and she is very
happy. They call him Polaroid Khumalo. He is very handsome
and well-known."

She replaced her glasses and looked at Mma Ramotswe.

"There will be a husband for you some day," said Mma
Ramotswe. "And that man will be a very fortunate man."

Mma Makutsi shook her head. "I do not think there will be
a husband," she said. "There are not enough men in Botswana.
That is a well-known fact. All the men are married now and
there is nobody left."

"Well, you don't have to get married," said Mma Ramotswe.
"Single girls can have a very good life these days. I am single. I
am not married."

"But you are marrying Mr J.L.B. Matekoni," said Mma
Makutsi. "You will not be single for long. You could . . ."

"I didn't have to marry him," interrupted Mma Ramotswe. "I
was happy by myself. I could have stayed that way."

She stopped. She noticed that Mma Makutsi had taken her
spectacles off again and was polishing them once more. They
had misted over.

Mma Ramotswe thought for a moment. She had never been

able to see unhappiness and not do something about it. It was a difficult quality for a private detective to have, as there was so much unhappiness entailed in her work, but she could not harden her heart, however much she tried. "Oh, and there's another thing," she said. "I didn't tell you that in this new job of yours you will be described as Assistant Manager of Tlokweng Road Speedy Motors. It is not just a secretarial job."

Mma Makutsi looked up and smiled.

"That is very good," she said. "You are very kind to me, Mma."

"And there will be more money," said Mma Ramotswe, throwing caution aside. "Not much more, but a little bit more. You will be able to send a bit more up to those people of yours up in Bobonong."

Mma Makutsi appeared considerably cheered by this information, and there was a zest in the way in which she performed the last tasks of the day, the typing of several letters which Mma Ramotswe had drafted in longhand. It was Mma Ramotswe who now seemed morose. It was Dr Leakey's fault, she decided. If he had not come into the conversation, then she might have been firmer. As it was, not only had she promoted Mma Makutsi again, but she had given her, without consulting Mr J.L.B. Matekoni, a pay raise. She would have to tell him about that, of course, but perhaps not just yet. There was always a time for the breaking of difficult news, and one had to wait for one's moment. Men usually let their defences down now and then, and the art of being a successful woman, and beating men at their own game, was to wait your moment. When that moment arrived, you could manipulate a man with very little difficulty. But you had to wait.

CHAPTER TWO

———

A BOY IN THE NIGHT

THEY WERE camped in the Okavango, outside Maun, under a covering of towering mopani trees. To the north, barely half a mile away, the lake stretched out, a ribbon of blue in the brown and green of the bush. The savannah grass here was thick and rich, and there was good cover for the animals. If you wanted to see elephant, you had to be watchful, as the lushness of the vegetation made it difficult to make out even their bulky grey shapes as they moved slowly through their forage.

The camp, which was a semipermanent collection of five or six large tents pitched in a semicircle, belonged to a man they knew as Rra Pula, Mr Rain, owing to the belief, empirically verified on many an occasion, that his presence brought much-needed rain. Rra Pula was happy to allow this belief to be perpetuated. Rain was good luck; hence the cry Pula! Pula! Pula! when good fortune was being celebrated or invoked. He was a thin-faced man with the leathery, sun-speckled skin of the white person who has spent all his life under an African sun. The freckles and sun-spots had now become one, which had made him brown all over, like a pale biscuit put into the oven.

"He is slowly becoming like us," one of his men said as they sat round the fire one night. "One day he will wake up and he will be a Motswana, same colour as us."

"You cannot make a Motswana just by changing his skin," said another. "A Motswana is a Motswana inside. A Zulu is the same as us outside, but inside he is always a Zulu. You can't make a Zulu into a Motswana either. They are different."

There was silence round the fire as they mulled over this issue.

"There are a lot of things that make you what you are," said one of the trackers at last. "But the most important thing is your mother's womb. That is where you get the milk that makes you a Motswana or a Zulu. Motswana milk, Motswana child. Zulu milk, Zulu child."

"You do not get milk in the womb," said one of the younger men. "It is not like that."

The older man glared at him. "Then what do you eat for the first nine months, Mr Clever, Mr BSc? Are you saying that you eat the mother's blood? Is that what you are saying?"

The younger man shook his head. "I am not sure what you eat," he said. "But you do not get milk until you are born. I am certain of that."

The older man looked scornful. "You know nothing. You have no children, have you? What do you know about it? A man with no children talking about children as if he had many. I have five children. Five."

He held up the fingers of one hand. "Five children," he repeated. "And all five were made by their mother's milk."

They fell silent. At the other fire, on chairs rather than logs, were sitting Rra Pula and his two clients. The sound of their voices, unintelligible mumbling, had drifted across to the men, but now they were silent. Suddenly Rra Pula stood up.

"There's something out there," he said. "A jackal maybe. Sometimes they come quite close to the fire. The other animals keep their distance."

One of the clients, a middle-aged man wearing a wide-brimmed slouch hat, stood up and stared into the darkness.

"Would a leopard come in this close?" he asked.

"Never," said Rra Pula. "Very shy creatures."

A woman sitting on a canvas folding stool now turned her head sharply.

"There's definitely something there," she said. "Listen."

Rra Pula put down the mug he had been holding and called across to his men.

"Simon! Motopi! One of you bring me a torch. Double quick!"

The younger man stood up and walked quickly over to the equipment tent. As he walked across to give it to his employer, he too heard the noise and he switched on the powerful light, sweeping its beam through the circle of darkness around the camp. They saw the shapes of the bushes and small trees, all curiously flat and one-dimensional in the probing beam of light.

"Won't that scare it away?" asked the woman.

"Might do," said Rra Pula. "But we don't want any surprises, do we?"

The light swung round and briefly moved up to illuminate

the leaves of a thorn tree. Then it dropped to the base of the tree, and that is where they saw it.

"It's a child," said the man in the slouch hat. "A child? Out here?"

The child was on all fours. Caught in the beam of light, he was like an animal in the headlights of a car, frozen in indecision.

"Motopi!" called Rra Pula. "Fetch that child. Bring him here."

The man with the torch moved quickly through the grass, keeping the beam of light on the small figure. When he reached him, the child suddenly moved sharply back into the darkness, but something appeared to slow him down, and he stumbled and fell. The man reached forward, dropping the torch as he did so. There was a sharp sound as it hit a rock and the light went out. But the man had the child by then, and had lifted him up, kicking and wriggling.

"Don't fight me, little one," he said in Setswana. "I'm not going to hurt you. I'm not going to hurt you."

The child kicked out and his foot caught the man in his stomach.

"Don't do that!" He shook the child, and, holding him with one hand, slapped him hard across the shoulder.

"There! That's what you'll get if you try to kick your uncle! And there'll be more if you don't watch out!"

The child, surprised by the blow, stopped resisting, and went limp.

"And here's another thing," muttered the man, as he walked over towards Rra Pula's fire. "You smell."

He put the boy down on the ground, beside the table where the Tilley lamp stood; but he still held on to the child's wrist, in case he should try to run away or even to kick one of the white people.

"So this is our little jackal," said Rra Pula, looking down at the boy.

"He's naked," said the woman. "He hasn't got a scrap of clothing."

"What age is he?" asked one of the men. "He can't be more than six or seven. At the most."

Rra Pula now lifted up the lamp and held it closer to the child, playing the light over a skin which seemed criss-crossed with tiny scars and scratches, as if he had been dragged through a thorn bush. The stomach was drawn in, and the ribs showed; the tiny buttocks contracted and without flesh; and on one foot, stretching right across the arch, an open sore, white rimmed about a dark centre.

The boy looked up into the light and seemed to draw back from the inspection.

"Who are you?" asked Rra Pula in Setswana. "Where have you come from?"

The child stared at the light, but did not react to the question.

"Try in Kalanga," Rra Pula said to Motopi. "Try Kalanga, then try Herero. He could be Herero. Or a Mosarwa. You can make yourself understood in these languages, Motopi. You see if you can get anything out of him."

The man dropped to his haunches so as to be at the child's level. He started in one language, enunciating the words carefully, and then, getting no reaction, moved to another. The boy remained mute.

"I do not think this child can speak," he said. "I think that he does not know what I am saying."

The woman moved forward and reached out to touch the child's shoulder.

"You poor little thing," she said. "You look as if . . ."

She gave a cry and withdrew her hand sharply. The boy had bitten her.

The man snatched at the child's right arm and dragged him to his feet. Then, leaning forward, he struck him sharply across the face. "No," he shouted. "Bad child!"

The woman, outraged, pushed the man away. "Don't hit him," she cried. "He's frightened. Can't you see? He didn't mean to hurt me. I shouldn't have tried to touch him."

"You cannot have a child biting people, Mma," said the man quietly. "We do not like that."

The woman had wrapped a handkerchief around her hand, but a small blood stain had seeped through.

"I'll get you some penicillin for that," said Rra Pula. "A human bite can go bad."

They looked down at the child, who had now lain down, as if preparing for sleep, but was looking up at them, watching them.

"The child has a very strange smell," said Motopi. "Have you noticed that, Rra Pula?"

Rra Pula sniffed. "Yes," he said. "Maybe it's that wound. It's suppurating."

"No," said Motopi. "I have a very good nose. I can smell that wound, but there is another smell too. It is a smell that you do not find on a child."

"What's that?" asked Rra Pula. "You recognise that smell?"

Motopi nodded. "Yes," he said. "It is the smell of a lion. There is nothing else that has that smell. Only lion."

For a moment nobody said anything. Then Rra Pula laughed.

"Some soap and water will sort all that out," he said. "And something on that sore on his foot. Sulphur powder should dry it out."

Motopi picked up the child, gingerly. The boy stared at him, and cowered, but did not resist.

"Wash him and then keep him in your tent," said Rra Pula. "Don't let him escape."

The clients returned to their seats about the fire. The woman exchanged glances with the man, who lifted an eyebrow and shrugged.

"Where on earth has he come from?" she asked Rra Pula, as he poked at the fire with a charred stick.

"One of the local villages, I expect," he said. "The nearest one is about twenty miles over that way. He's probably a herd boy who got lost and wandered off into the bush. That happens from time to time."

"But why has he got no clothes?"

He shrugged. "Sometimes the herd boys just wear a small apron. He probably lost his to a thorn bush. Perhaps he left it lying somewhere."

He looked up at the woman. "These things happen a lot in Africa. There are plenty of children who go missing. They turn up. No harm comes to them. You aren't worried about him, are you?"

The woman frowned. "Of course I am. Anything could have happened to him. What about the wild animals? He could have been taken by a lion. Anything could have happened to him."

"Yes," said Rra Pula. "It could. But it didn't. We'll take him tomorrow into Maun and leave him with the police down there. They can sort it out. They'll work out where he's come from and get him home."

The woman seemed thoughtful. "Why did your man say that he smelled like a lion? Wasn't that rather an odd thing to say?"

Rra Pula laughed. "People say all sorts of odd things up here. They see things differently. That man, Motopi, is a very good tracker. But he tends to talk about animals as if they were human beings. He says that they say things to him. He claims that he can smell an animal's fear. That's the way he talks. It just is."

They sat in silence for a while, and then the woman announced that she was going to bed. They said good-night, and Rra Pula and the man sat by the fire for another half hour or so, saying very little, watching the logs slowly burn out and the sparks fly up into the sky. Inside his tent, Motopi lay still, stretched out across the entrance so that the child could not get out without disturbing him. But the child was not likely to do that; he had fallen asleep more or less immediately after being put into the tent. Now Motopi, on the verge of drifting off to sleep, watched him through one, heavy-lidded eye. The child, a light kaross thrown over him, was breathing deeply. He had eaten the piece of meat they had given him, ripping at it greedily, and had eagerly drunk the large cup of water which they had offered him, licking at the water as an animal might do at a drinking hole. There was still that strange smell, he thought, that musty-acrid smell which reminded him so strongly of the smell of a lion. But why, he wondered, would a child smell of a lion?

CHAPTER THREE

GARAGE AFFAIRS

ON HER way to Tlokweng Road Speedy Motors, Mma Ramotswe had decided that she would simply have to make a clean breast of it to Mr J.L.B. Matekoni. She knew that she had exceeded her authority by promoting Mma Makutsi to be Assistant Manager of the garage—she would have resented it greatly if he had attempted to promote her own staff—and she realised that she would just have to tell him exactly what had happened. He was a kind man, and although he had always thought that Mma Makutsi was a luxury whom Mma Ramotswe could ill afford, he would surely understand how important it was for her to have a position. After all, it would make no difference if Mma Makutsi called herself Assistant Manager, provided that she was doing the work that she was meant to do. But then there was the problem of the raise in pay. That would be more difficult.

Later that afternoon, driving in the tiny white van which Mr J.L.B. Matekoni had recently fixed for her, Mma Ramotswe made her way to Tlokweng Road Speedy Motors. The van was performing well now that Mr J.L.B. Matekoni spent so much of his spare time tinkering with its engine. He had replaced many of its parts with brand new spares which he had ordered from over the border. There was a new carburettor, for example, and an entirely new set of brakes. Mma Ramotswe now had to do no more than touch the brake pedal and the van would screech to a halt. In the past, before Mr J.L.B. Matekoni had taken such an interest in her van, Mma Ramotswe had been obliged to pump the brake pedal three or four times before she even began to slow down.

"I think I shall never again go into the back of somebody," said Mma Ramotswe gratefully when she tried the new brakes for the first time. "I shall be able to stop exactly when I want to."

Mr J.L.B. Matekoni looked alarmed. "It is very important to have good brakes," he said. "You mustn't let your brakes get like that again. Just you ask me, and I shall make sure that they are in tip-top order."

"I shall do that," Mma Ramotswe promised. She had very little interest in cars, although she dearly loved her tiny white van, which had served her so faithfully. She could not understand why people spent so much time hankering after a Mercedes-Benz when there were many other cars which safely transported one to one's destination, and back again, without requiring a fortune to do so. This interest in cars was a male problem, she thought. One saw it develop in small boys, with the little wire models they made of cars, and it never really went away. Why should men find cars so interesting? A car was no more than a machine, and one might think that men would be interested in washing machines or irons, for that matter. Yet they were not. You never saw men standing around talking about washing machines.

She drove up to the front of Tlokweng Road Speedy Motors and alighted from the tiny white van. Through the small window that gave on to the forecourt, she could see that there was nobody in the office, which meant that Mr J.L.B. Matekoni would probably be under a car in the workshop, or standing over his two difficult apprentices while he attempted to convey to them some difficult point of mechanics. He had confessed to Mma Ramotswe his despair of making anything of these boys, and she had sympathised with him. It was not easy trying to persuade young people of the need to work; they expected everything to be handed to them on a plate. None of them seemed to understand that everything they had in Botswana—and it was a great deal—had been acquired through hard work and self-denial. Botswana had never borrowed money and then sunk into debt as had happened in so many other countries in Africa. They had saved and saved and spent money very carefully; every cent, every thebe, had been accounted for; none had gone into the pockets of politicians. We can be proud of our country, thought Mma Ramotswe; and I am. I'm proud of what my father, Obed Ramotswe did; I'm proud of Seretse Khama and of how he invented a new country out of a place that had been ignored by the British. They may not have cared much about us, she reflected, but now they know what we can do. They admired us for that; she had read what the American Ambassador had said. "We salute the people of Botswana for what they have done," he had announced. The words had made her glow with pride. She knew that people overseas, people in those distant, rather frightening countries, thought highly of Botswana.

It was a good thing to be an African. There were terrible things that happened in Africa, things that brought shame and despair when one thought about them, but that was not all there was in Africa. However great the suffering of the people of Africa, however harrowing the cruelty and chaos brought about by soldiers—small boys with guns, really—there was still so much in Africa from which one could take real pride. There was the kindness, for example, and the ability to smile, and the art and the music.

She walked round to the workshop entrance. There were two cars inside, one up on the ramp, and the other parked against a wall, its battery connected to a small charger by the front wheel. Several parts had been left lying on the floor—an exhaust pipe and another part which she did not recognise—and there was an open toolbox underneath the car on the ramp. But there was no sign of Mr J.L.B. Matekoni.

It was only when one of them stood up that Mma Ramotswe realised that the apprentices were there. They had been sitting on the ground, propped up against an empty oil drum, playing the traditional stone game. Now one of them, the taller boy whose name she could never remember, rose and wiped his hands on his dirty overall.

"Hallo, Mma," he said. "He is not here. The boss. He's gone home."

The apprentice grinned at her in a way which she found slightly offensive. It was a familiar grin, of the sort that one might imagine him giving a girl at a dance. She knew these young men. Mr J.L.B. Matekoni had told her that all they were interested in was girls, and she could well believe it. And the distressing thing was that there would be plenty of girls who would be interested in these young men, with their heavily pomaded hair and their flashing white grins.

"Why has he gone home so early?" she asked. "Is the work all finished? Is that why you two are sitting about?"

The apprentice smiled. He had the air, she thought, of somebody who knew something, and she wondered what it was. Or was it just his sense of superiority, the condescending manner that he probably adopted towards all women?

"No," he replied, glancing down at his friend. "Anything but finished. We still have to deal with that vehicle up there." He gestured casually towards the car on the ramp.

Now the other apprentice arose. He had been eating something and there was a thin line of flour about his mouth. What would the girls think of that? thought Mma Ramotswe mischievously. She imagined him turning on his charm for some girl, blissfully unaware of the flour round his mouth. He may be good-looking, but a white outline around the lips would bring laughter rather than any racing of the heart.

"The boss is often away these days," said the second apprentice. "Sometimes he goes off at two o'clock. He leaves us to do all the work."

"But there's a problem," chipped in the other apprentice. "We can't do everything. We're pretty good with cars, you know, but we haven't learned everything, you know."

Mma Ramotswe glanced up at the car on the ramp. It was one of those old French station wagons which were so popular in parts of Africa.

"That one's an example," said the first apprentice. "It's making steam out of its exhaust. It comes up in a big cloud. That means that a gasket has gone and that the coolant's getting into the piston chamber. So that makes steam. Hiss. Lots of steam."

"Well," said Mma Ramotswe, "why don't you fix it? Mr J.L.B. Matekoni can't hold your hand all the time, you know."

The younger apprentice pouted. "You think that it's simple, Mma? You think it's simple? You ever tried to take the cylinder head off a Peugeot? Have you done that, Mma?"

Mma Ramotswe made a calming gesture. "I was not criticising you," she said. "Why don't you get Mr J.L.B. Matekoni to show you what to do?"

The older apprentice looked irritated. "That's all very well, Mma. But the trouble is that he won't. And then he goes off home and leaves us to explain to the customers. They don't like it. They say: Where's my car? How do you expect me to get around if you're going to take days and days to fix my car? Am I to walk, like a person with no car? That's what they say, Mma."

Mma Ramotswe said nothing for a moment. It seemed so unlikely that Mr J.L.B. Matekoni, who was normally so punctilious, would allow this to happen in his own business. He had built his reputation on getting repairs done well, and speedily. If anybody was dissatisfied with a job that he had done, they were fully entitled to bring the car back and he would do the whole thing again without charge. That was the way that he had always worked, and it seemed inconceivable that he would leave a car up on the ramp in the care of these two apprentices who seemed to know so little about engines and who could not be trusted not to take shortcuts.

She decided to press the older apprentice a bit further. "Do you mean to tell me," she said, her voice lowered, "do you mean to tell me that Mr J.L.B. Matekoni doesn't *care* about these cars?"

The apprentice stared at her, rudely allowing their eyes to lock. If he knew anything about proper behaviour, thought Mma Ramotswe, he wouldn't keep eye contact with me; he would look down, as befits a junior in the presence of a senior.

"Yes," said the apprentice simply. "For the last ten days or so, Mr J.L.B. Matekoni seems to have lost interest in this garage. Only yesterday he told me that he thought he would go away to his village and that I should be left in charge. He said I should do my best."

Mma Ramotswe drew in her breath. She could tell that the young man was telling the truth, but it was a truth which was very difficult to believe.

"And here's another thing," said the apprentice, wiping his hands on a piece of oil rag. "He hasn't paid the spare parts supplier for two months. They telephoned the other day, when he had gone away early, and I took the call, didn't I, Siletsi?"

The other apprentice nodded.

"Anyway," he went on. "Anyway, they said that unless we paid within ten days they would not provide us with any further spare parts. They said that I should tell that to Mr J.L.B. Matekoni and get him to buck up his ways. That's what they said. Me tell the boss. That's what they said I should do."

"And did you?" asked Mma Ramotswe.

"I did," he said. "I said: A word in your ear, Rra. Just a word. Then I told him."

Mma Ramotswe watched his expression. It was clear that he was pleased to be cast in the role of the concerned employee, a role, she suspected, which he had not had occasion to occupy before.

"And then? What did he say to your advice?"

The apprentice sniffed, wiping his hand across his nose.

"He said that he would try to do something about it. That's what he said. But you know what I think? You know what I think is happening, Mma?"

Mma Ramotswe looked at him expectantly.

He went on, "I think that Mr J.L.B. Matekoni has stopped caring about this garage. I think that he has had enough. I think he wants to hand it over to us. Then he wants to go off to his lands out there and grow melons. He is an old man now, Mma. He has had enough."

Mma Ramotswe drew in her breath. The sheer effrontery of the suggestion astonished her: here was this . . . this *useless* apprentice, best known for his ability to pester the girls who walked past the garage, the very apprentice whom Mr J.L.B. Matekoni had once seen using a hammer on an engine, now saying that Mr J.L.B. Matekoni himself was ready to retire.

It took her the best part of a minute to compose herself sufficiently to reply.

"You are a very rude young man," she said at last. "Mr J.L.B. Matekoni has not lost interest in his garage. And he is not an old man. He is just in his early forties, which is not old at all, whatever you people think. And finally, he has no intention of handing the garage over to you two. That would be the end of the business. Do you understand me?"

The older of the apprentices looked for reassurance from his friend, but the other was staring fixedly at the ground.

"I understand you, Mma. I am sorry."

"As well you should be," said Mma Ramotswe. "And here's a bit of news for you. Mr J.L.B. Matekoni has just appointed an assistant manager for this garage. This new manager will be starting here very soon, and you two had better look out."

Her remarks had the desired effect on the older apprentice, who dropped his oily piece of cloth and looked anxiously at the other.

"When does he start?" he asked nervously.

"Next week," said Mma Ramotswe. "And it's a she."

"A she? A woman?"

"Yes," said Mma Ramotswe, turning to leave. "It is a woman called Mma Makutsi, and she is very strict with apprentices. So there will be no more sitting around playing stones. Do you understand?"

The apprentices nodded glumly.

"Then get on with trying to fix that car," said Mma Ramotswe. "I shall come back in a couple of hours and see how it's going."

She walked back to the van and climbed into the driving seat. She had succeeded in *sounding* very determined when she gave the apprentices their instructions, but she felt far from certain inside. In fact, she felt extremely concerned. In her experience, when people began to behave out of character it was a sign that something was very wrong. Mr J.L.B. Matekoni was a thoroughly conscientious man, and thoroughly conscientious men did not let their customers down unless there was a very good reason. But what was it? Was it something to do with their impending marriage? Had he changed his mind? Did he wish to escape?

*   *   *

MMA MAKUTSI locked the door of the No. 1 Ladies' Detective Agency. Mma Ramotswe had gone off to the garage to talk to Mr J.L.B. Matekoni and had left her to finish the letters and get them to the post. No request made of her would have seemed excessive, so great was Mma Makutsi's joy at her promotion and the news of her increase in wages. It was a Thursday, and tomorrow was payday, even if it would be a payday at the old rate. She would treat herself to something in anticipation, she thought—perhaps a doughnut on the way home. Her route took her past a small stall that sold doughnuts and other fried foods and the smell was tantalising. Money was the problem, though. A large, fried doughnut cost two pula, which made it an expensive treat, especially if one thought what the evening meal would cost. Living in Gaborone was expensive; everything seemed to cost twice as much as it did at home. In the country, ten pula would get one a long way; here in Gaborone ten pula notes seemed to melt in one's hand.

Mma Makutsi rented a room in the backyard of a house off the Lobatse Road. The room formed half of a small, breeze-block shack which looked out to the back fence and a meandering lane, the haunt of thin-faced dogs. The dogs were loosely attached to the people who lived in the houses, but seemed to prefer their own company and roamed about in packs of two or three. Somebody must have fed them, at irregular intervals, but their rib cages still showed and they seemed constantly to be scavenging for scraps from the rubbish bins. On occasion, if Mma Makutsi left her door open, one of these dogs would wander in and gaze at her with mournful, hungry eyes until she shooed it out. This was perhaps a greater indignity than that which befell her at work, when the chickens came into the office and started pecking about her feet.

She bought her doughnut at the stall and ate it there and then, licking the sugar off her fingers when she had finished. Then, her hunger assuaged, she began the walk home. She could have ridden home in a minibus—it was a cheap enough form of transport—but she enjoyed the walk in the cool of the evening, and she was usually in no hurry to reach home. She wondered how he was; whether it had been a good day for her brother, or whether his coughing would have tired him out. He had been quite comfortable over the last few days, although he was very weak now, and she had enjoyed one or two nights of unbroken sleep.

He had come to live with her two months earlier, making the long journey from their home by bus. She had gone to meet him at the bus station down by the railway, and for a brief moment she had looked at him without recognising him. The last time she had seen him he had been well-built, even bulky; now he was stooped and thin and his shirt flapped loosely about his torso. When she realised that it was him, she had run up and taken his hand, which had shocked her, for it was hot and dry and the skin was cracked. She had lifted his suitcase for him, although he had tried to do that himself, and had carried it all the way to the minibus that plied its trade down the Lobatse Road.

After that, he had settled in, sleeping on the mat which she had set up on the other side of her room. She had strung a wire from wall to wall and hung a curtain over it, to give him privacy and some sense of having his own place, but she heard every rasping breath he drew and was often woken by his mumbling in his dreams.

"You are a kind sister to take me in," he said. "I am a lucky man to have a sister like you."

She had protested that it was no trouble, and that she liked having him with her, and that he could stay with her when he was better and found a job in Gaborone, but she knew that this was not going to happen. He knew too, she was sure, but neither spoke about it or the cruel disease which was ending his life, slowly, like a drought dries up a landscape.

Now, coming home, she had good news for him. He was always very interested to hear what had happened at the agency, as he always asked her for all the details of her day. He had never met Mma Ramotswe—Mma Makutsi did not want her to know about his illness—but he had a very clear picture of her in his head and he always asked after her.

"I will meet her one day, maybe," he said. "And I will be able to thank her for what she has done for my sister. If it hadn't been for her, then you would never have been able to become an assistant detective."

"She is a kind woman."

"I know she is," he said. "I can see this nice woman with her smile and her fat cheeks. I can see her drinking tea with you. I am happy just to think about it."

Mma Makutsi wished that she had thought to buy him a doughnut, but often he had no appetite and it would have been wasted. His mouth was painful, he said, and the cough made it difficult for him to eat very much. So often he would take only a few spoonfuls of the soup which she prepared on her small paraffin stove, and even then he would sometimes have difficulty in keeping these down.

Somebody else was in the room when she got home. She heard a strange voice and for a moment she feared that something terrible had happened in her absence, but when she entered the room she saw that the curtain had been drawn back and that there was a woman sitting on a small folding stool beside his mat. When she heard the door open, the woman stood up and turned to face her.

"I am the nurse from the Anglican hospice," she said. "I have come to see our brother. My name is Sister Baleje."

The nurse had a pleasant smile, and Mma Makutsi took to her immediately.

"You are kind to come and see him," Mma Makutsi said. "I wrote that letter to you just to let you know that he was not well."

The nurse nodded. "That was the right thing to do. We can call in to see him from time to time. We can bring food if you need it. We can do something to help, even if it's not a great deal. We have some drugs we can give him. They are not very strong, but they can help a bit."

Mma Makutsi thanked her, and looked down at her brother.

"It is the coughing that troubles him," she said. "That is the worst thing, I think."

"It is not easy," said the nurse.

The nurse sat down on her stool again and took the brother's hand.

"You must drink more water, Richard," she said. "You must not let yourself get too thirsty."

He opened his eyes and looked up at her, but said nothing. He was not sure why she was here, but thought that she was a friend of his sister, perhaps, or a neighbour.

The nurse looked at Mma Makutsi and gestured for her to sit on the floor beside them. Then, still holding his hand, she reached forward and gently touched his cheek.

"Lord Jesus," she said, "who helps us in our suffering. Look down on this poor man and have mercy on him. Make his days joyful. Make him happy for his good sister here, who looks after him in his illness. And bring him peace in his heart."

Mma Makutsi closed her eyes, and put her hand on the shoulder of the nurse, where it rested, as they sat in silence.

CHAPTER FOUR

A VISIT TO DR MOFFAT

As MMA Makutsi sat at her brother's side, Mma Ramotswe was driving her tiny white van up to the gate of Mr J.L.B. Matekoni's house near the old Botswana Defence Force Club. She could see that he was in; the green truck which he inevitably drove—in spite of his having a rather better vehicle which he left parked at the garage—stood outside his front door, which he had left half open for the heat. She left the van outside, to save herself from getting in and out to open and shut the gate, and walked up to the house past the few scruffy plants which Mr J.L.B. Matekoni called his garden.

"Ko! Ko!" she called at the door. "Are you there, Mr J.L.B. Matekoni?"

A voice came from the living room. "I am here. I am in, Mma Ramotswe."

Mma Ramotswe walked in, noticing immediately how dusty

and unpolished was the floor of the hall. Ever since Mr J.L.B. Matekoni's sullen and unpleasant maid, Florence, had been sent to prison for harbouring an unlicensed gun, the house had been allowed to get into an unkempt state. She had reminded Mr J.L.B. Matekoni on several occasions to engage a replacement maid, at least until they got married, and he had promised to do so. But he had never acted, and Mma Ramotswe had decided that she would simply have to bring her maid in one day and attempt a spring clean of the whole place.

"Men will live in a very untidy way, if you let them," she had remarked to a friend. "They cannot keep a house or a yard. They don't know how to do it."

She made her way through the hall and into the living room. As she entered, Mr J.L.B. Matekoni, who had been lying full length on his uncomfortable sofa, rose to his feet and tried to make himself look less dishevelled.

"It is good to see you, Mma Ramotswe," he said. "I have not seen you for several days."

"That is true," said Mma Ramotswe. "Perhaps that is because you have been so busy."

"Yes," he said, sitting down again, "I have been very busy. There is so much work to be done."

She said nothing, but watched him as he spoke. There was something wrong; she had been right.

"Are things busy at the garage?" she asked.

He shrugged his shoulders. "Things are always busy at the garage. All the time. People keep bringing their cars in and saying Do this, do that. They think I have ten pairs of hands. That's what they think."

"But do you not expect people to bring their cars to the garage?" she asked gently. "Is that not what a garage is for?"

Mr J.L.B. Matekoni looked at her briefly and then shrugged. "Maybe. But there is still too much work."

Mma Ramotswe glanced about the room, noticing the pile of newspapers on the floor and the small stack of what looked like unopened letters on the table.

"I went to the garage," she said. "I expected to see you there, but they said that you had left early. They said you often left early these days."

Mr J.L.B. Matekoni looked at her, and then transferred his gaze to the floor. "I find it hard to stay there all day, with all that work," he said. "It will get done sooner or later. There are those two boys. They can do it."

Mma Ramotswe gasped. "Those two boys? Those apprentices of yours? But they are the very ones you always said could do nothing. How can you say now that they will do everything that needs to be done? How can you say that?"

Mr J.L.B. Matekoni did not reply.

"Well, Mr J.L.B. Matekoni?" pressed Mma Ramotswe. "What's your answer to that?"

"They'll be all right," he said, in a curious, flat voice. "Let them get on with it."

Mma Ramotswe stood up. There was no point talking to him when he was in this sort of mood—and it certainly was a mood that he seemed to be in. Perhaps he was ill. She had heard that a bout of flu could leave one feeling lethargic for a week or two; perhaps that was the simple explanation of this out-of-character behaviour. In which case, she would just have to wait until he came out of it.

"I've spoken to Mma Makutsi," she said as she prepared to leave. "I think that she can start at the garage sometime in the

next few days. I have given her the title of Assistant Manager.
I hope that you don't mind."

His reply astonished her.

"Assistant Manager, Manager, Managing Director, Minister
of Garages," he said. "Whatever you like. It makes no difference, does it?"

Mma Ramotswe could not think of a suitable reply, so she
said goodbye and started to walk out of the door.

"Oh, by the way," said Mr J.L.B. Matekoni as she started to
leave the house, "I thought that I might go out to the lands for
a little while. I want to see how the planting is going. I might
stay out there for a while."

Mma Ramotswe stared at him. "And in the meantime, what
happens to the garage?"

Mr J.L.B. Matekoni sighed. "You run it. You and that secretary
of yours, the Assistant Manager. Let her do it. It'll be all right."

Mma Ramotswe pursed her lips. "All right," she said. "We'll
look after it, Mr J.L.B. Matekoni, until you start to feel better."

"I'm fine," said Mr J.L.B. Matekoni. "Don't worry about me.
I'm fine."

SHE DID not drive home to Zebra Drive, although she knew
that the two foster children would be waiting there for her.
Motholeli, the girl, would have prepared their evening meal by
now, and she needed little supervision or help, in spite of her
wheelchair. And the boy, Puso, who was inclined to be rather
boisterous, would perhaps have expended most of his energy
and would be ready for his bath and his bed, both of which
Motholeli could prepare for him.

Instead of going home, she turned left at Kudu Road and made her way down past the flats to the house in Odi Way where her friend Dr Moffat lived. Dr Moffat, who used to run the hospital out at Mochudi, had looked after her father and had always been prepared to listen to her when she was in difficulties. She had spoken to him about Note before she had confided in anybody else, and he had told her, as gently as he could, that in his experience such men never changed.

"You must not expect him to become a different man," he had said. "People like that rarely change."

He was a busy man, of course, and she did not wish to intrude on his time, but she decided that she would see if he was in and whether he could throw any light on the way in which Mr J.L.B. Matekoni was behaving. Was there some strange infection doing the rounds which made people all tired and listless? If this were the case, then how long might one expect it to last?

Dr Moffat had just returned home. He welcomed Mma Ramotswe at the door and led her into his study.

"I am worried about Mr J.L.B. Matekoni," she explained. "Let me tell you about him."

He listened for a few minutes and then stopped her.

"I think I know what the trouble might be," he said. "There's a condition called depression. It is an illness like any other illness, and quite common too. It sounds to me as if Mr J.L.B. Matekoni could be depressed."

"And could you treat that?"

"Usually quite easily," said Dr Moffat. "That is, provided that he has depression. If he has, then we have very good antidepressants these days. If all went well, which it probably would, we could have him starting to feel quite a bit better in three weeks or so, maybe even a little bit earlier. These pills take some time to act."

"I will tell him to come and see you straightaway," said Mma Ramotswe.

Dr Moffat looked doubtful. "Sometimes they don't think there's anything wrong with them," he said. "He might not come. It's all very well my telling you what the trouble probably is; he's the one who has to seek treatment."

"Oh, I'll get him to you," said Mma Ramotswe. "You can count on that. I'll make sure that he seeks treatment."

The doctor smiled. "Be careful, Mma Ramotswe," he said. "These things can be difficult."

CHAPTER FIVE

THE GOVERNMENT MAN

THE FOLLOWING morning Mma Ramotswe was at the No. 1 Ladies' Detective Agency before Mma Makutsi arrived. This was unusual, as Mma Makutsi was normally first to arrive and already would have opened the mail and brewed the tea by the time that Mma Ramotswe drove up in her tiny white van. However, this was going to be a difficult day, and she wanted to make a list of the things that she had to do.

"You are very early, Mma," said Mma Makutsi. "Is there anything wrong?"

Mma Ramotswe thought for a moment. In a sense there was a great deal wrong, but she did not want to dishearten Mma Makutsi, and so she put a brave face on it.

"Not really," she said. "But we must start preparing for the move. And also, it will be necessary for you to go and get the garage sorted out. Mr J.L.B. Matekoni is feeling a bit unwell and might be going away for a while. This means that you will not only be Assistant Manager, but Acting Manager. In fact, that is your new title, as from this morning."

Mma Makutsi beamed with pleasure. "I shall do my best as Acting Manager," she said. "I promise that you will not be disappointed."

"Of course I won't be," said Mma Ramotswe. "I know that you are very good at your job."

For the next hour they worked in companionable silence. Mma Ramotswe drafted her list of things to do, then scratched some items out and added others. The early morning was the best time to do anything, particularly in the hot season. In the hot months, before the rains arrived, the temperature soared as the day wore on until the very sky seemed white. In the cool of the morning, when the sun barely warmed the skin and the air was still crisp, any task seemed possible; later, in the full heat of day, both body and mind were sluggish. It was easy to think in the morning—to make lists of things to do—in the afternoon all that one could think about was the end of the day and the prospect of relief from the heat. It was Botswana's one drawback, thought Mma Ramotswe. She knew that it was the perfect country—all Batswana knew that—but it would be even more perfect if the three hottest months could be cooled down.

At nine o'clock Mma Makutsi made a cup of bush tea for Mma Ramotswe and a cup of ordinary tea for herself. Mma Makutsi had tried to accustom herself to bush tea, loyally drinking it for the first few months of her employment, but had eventually confessed that she did not like the taste. From that time on there were two teapots, one for her and one for Mma Ramotswe.

"It's too strong," she said. "And I think it smells of rats."

"It does not," protested Mma Ramotswe. "This tea is for people who really appreciate tea. Ordinary tea is for anyone."

Work stopped while tea was served. This tea break was traditionally a time for catching up on small items of gossip rather than for the broaching of any large subjects. Mma Makutsi enquired after Mr J.L.B. Matekoni, and received a brief report of Mma Ramotswe's unsatisfactory meeting with him.

"He seemed to have no interest in anything," she said. "I could have told him that his house was on fire and he probably wouldn't have bothered very much. It was very strange."

"I have seen people like that before," said Mma Makutsi. "I had a cousin who was sent off to that hospital in Lobatse. I visited her there. There were plenty of people just sitting and staring up at the sky. And there were also people shouting out at the visitors, shouting strange things, all about nothing."

Mma Ramotswe frowned. "That hospital is for mad people," she said. "Mr J.L.B. Matekoni is not going mad."

"Of course not," said Mma Makutsi hurriedly. "He would never go mad. Of course not."

Mma Ramotswe sipped at her tea. "But I still have to get him to a doctor," she said. "I was told that they can treat this sort of behaviour. It is called depression. There are pills which you can take."

"That is good," said Mma Makutsi. "He will get better. I am sure of it."

Mma Ramotswe handed over her mug for refilling. "And what about your family up in Bobonong?" she asked. "Are they well?"

Mma Makutsi poured the rich red tea into the mug. "They are very well, thank you, Mma."

Mma Ramotswe sighed. "I think that it is easier to live in

Bobonong than here in Gaborone. Here we have all these troubles to think about, but in Bobonong there is nothing. Just a whole lot of rocks." She stopped herself. "Of course, it's a very good place, Bobonong. A very nice place."

Mma Makutsi laughed. "You do not have to be polite about Bobonong," she said. "I can laugh about it. It is not a good place for everybody. I would not like to go back, now that I have seen what it is like to live in Gaborone."

"You would be wasted up there," said Mma Ramotswe. "What's the use of a diploma from the Botswana Secretarial College in a place like Bobonong? The ants would eat it."

Mma Makutsi cast an eye up to the wall where her diploma from the Botswana Secretarial College was framed. "We must remember to take that to the new office when we move," she said. "I would not like to leave it behind."

"Of course not," said Mma Ramotswe, who had no diplomas. "That diploma is important for the clients. It gives them confidence."

"Thank you," said Mma Makutsi.

The tea break over, Mma Makutsi went to wash the cups under the standpipe at the back of the building, and it was just as she returned that the client arrived. It was the first client for over a week, and neither of them was prepared for the tall, well-built man who knocked at the door, in the proper Botswana manner, and politely awaited his invitation to enter. Nor were they prepared for the fact that the car which brought him there, complete with smartly attired Government driver, was an official Mercedes-Benz.

*   *   *

YOU KNOW who I am, Mma?" he said, as he took up the invitation to seat himself in the chair before Mma Ramotswe's desk.

"Of course, I do, Rra," said Mma Ramotswe courteously. "You are something to do with the Government. You are a Government Man. I have seen you in the newspapers many times."

The Government Man made an impatient gesture with his hand. "Yes, there's that, of course. But you know who I am when I am not being a Government Man?"

Mma Makutsi coughed politely, and the Government Man half-turned to face her.

"This is my assistant," explained Mma Ramotswe. "She knows many things."

"You are also the relative of a chief," said Mma Makutsi. "Your father is a cousin of that family. I know that, as I come from that part too."

The Government Man smiled. "That is true."

"And your wife," went on Mma Ramotswe, "she is some relative of the King of Lesotho, is she not? I have seen a photograph of her, too."

The Government Man whistled. "My! My! I can see that I have come to the right place. You people seem to know everything."

Mma Ramotswe nodded to Mma Makutsi and smiled. "It is our business to know things," she said. "A private detective who knows nothing would be no use to anybody. Information is what we deal in. That is our job. Just as your job is giving orders to civil servants."

"I don't just give orders," the Government Man said peevishly. "I have to make policy. I have to make decisions."

"Of course," said Mma Ramotswe hurriedly. "It must be a very big job being a Government Man."

The Government Man nodded. "It is not easy," he said. "And it is not made any easier if one is worried about something. Every night I wake up at two, three and these worries make me sit up in my bed. And then I don't sleep, and when it comes to making decisions in the morning my head is all fuzzy and I cannot think. That is what happens when you are worried."

Mma Ramotswe knew that they were now coming to the reason for the consultation. It was easier to reach it this way, to allow the client to bring the matter up indirectly rather than to launch straight into an enquiry. It seemed less rude, somehow, to allow the matter to be approached in this way.

"We can help with worries," she said. "Sometimes we can make them vanish altogether."

"So I have heard," said the Government Man. "People say that you are a lady who can work miracles. I have heard that."

"You are very kind, Rra." She paused, running over in her mind the various possibilities. It was probably unfaithfulness, which was the most common problem of all the clients who consulted her, particularly if, as in the Government Man's case, they were in busy jobs that took them away from home a great deal. Or it could be something political, which would be new terrain for her. She knew nothing about the workings of political parties, other than that they involved a great deal of intrigue. She had read all about American presidents and the difficulties that they had with this scandal and that scandal, with ladies and burglars and the like. Could there be something like that in Botswana? Surely not, and if there were, she would not choose to get involved. She could not see herself meeting informants on dark corners in the dead of night, or talking in whispers to journalists in bars. On the other hand, Mma Makutsi might appreciate the opportunity . . .

The Government Man raised his hand, as if to command silence. It was an imperious gesture, but then he was the scion of a well-connected family and perhaps these things came naturally.

"I take it that I can speak in complete confidence," he said, glancing briefly at Mma Makutsi.

"My assistant is very confidential," said Mma Ramotswe. "You can trust her."

The Government Man narrowed his eyes. "I hope so," he said. "I know what women are like. They like to talk."

Mma Makutsi's eyes opened wide with indignation.

"I can assure you, Rra," said Mma Ramotswe, her tone steely, "that the No. 1 Ladies' Detective Agency is bound by the strictest principle of confidentiality. The strictest principle. And that goes not only for me but also for that lady over there, Mma Makutsi. If you are in any doubt as to this, then you should find some other detectives. We would not object to that." She paused. "And another thing, Rra. There is a lot of talking that goes on in this country, and most of it, in my opinion, is done by men. The women are usually too busy to talk."

She folded her hands on her desk. She had said it now, and she should not be surprised if the Government Man walked out. A man in his position would not be used to being spoken to in that way and he presumably would not take well to it.

For a moment the Government Man said nothing, but simply stared at Mma Ramotswe.

"So," he said at last. "So. You are quite right. I am sorry that I suggested that you would not be able to keep a secret." Then, turning to Mma Makutsi, he added, "I am sorry that I suggested that thing about you, Mma. It was not a good thing to say."

Mma Ramotswe felt the tension ebb away. "Good," she said. "Now why don't you tell us about these worries? My assistant will boil the kettle. Would you like bush tea or ordinary tea?"

"Bush," said the Government Man. "It's good for worries, I think."

"BECAUSE YOU know who I am," said the Government Man, "I don't have to start at the beginning, or at least at the beginning of the beginning. You know that I am the son of an important man. You know that. And I am the firstborn, which means that I shall be the one to head the family when God calls my father to join him. But I hope that will not be for a long time.

"I have two brothers. One had something wrong with his head and does not talk to anybody. He never talked to anybody and took no interest in anything from the time he was a little boy. So we have sent him out to a cattle post and he is happy there. He stays there all the time and he is no trouble. He just sits and counts the cattle and then, when he has finished, he starts again. That is all that he wants to do in life, even though he is thirty-eight now.

"Then there is my other brother. He is much younger than I am. I am fifty-four, and he is only twenty-six. He is my brother by another mother. My father is old-fashioned and he had two wives and his mother was the younger. There were many girl children—I have nine sisters by various mothers, and many of them have married and have their own children. So we are a big family, but small in the number of important boys, who are really only myself and this brother of twenty-six. He is called Mogadi.

"I am very fond of my brother. Because I am so much older

than he is, I remember him very well from when he was baby. When he grew a bit, I taught him many things. I showed him how to find mopani worms. I showed him how to catch flying ants when they come out of their holes at the first rains. I told him which things you can eat in the bush and which you cannot.

"Then one day he saved my life. We were staying out at the cattle post where our father keeps some of his herds. There were some Basarwa there, because my father's cattle post is not far from the place where these people come in from the Kalahari. It is a very dry place, but there is a windmill which my father set up to pump water for the cattle. There is a lot of water deep underground and it tastes very good. These Basarwa people liked to come and drink this water while they were wandering around and they would do some work for my father in return for some milk from the cows and, if they were lucky, a bit of meat. They liked my father because he never beat them, unlike some people who use sjamboks on them. I have never approved of beating these people, never.

"I took my brother out to see some Basarwa, who were living under a tree not far away. They had some slingshots out of ostrich leather and I wanted to get one for my brother. I took some meat to give to them in exchange. I thought that they might also give us an ostrich egg.

"It was just after the rains, and there was fresh grass and flowers. You know, Mma, what it is like down there when the first rains come. The land is suddenly soft and there are flowers, flowers all around. It is very beautiful, and for a while you forget just how hot and dry and hard it has been. We walked along a path which the animals had made with their hooves, myself in the front and my little brother just behind me. He had a long stick which he was trailing along the ground beside him. I was very happy to be there, with my little brother, and with the fresh grass that I knew would make the cattle fat again.

"He suddenly called out to me, and I stopped. There in the grass beside us was a snake, with its head up off the ground and its mouth open, hissing. It was a big snake, about as long as I am tall, and it had raised about an arm's length of its body off the ground. I knew immediately what sort of snake this was and my heart stopped within me.

"I was very still, because I knew that a movement could make the snake strike and it was only this far from me. It was very close. The snake was looking at me, with those angry eyes that those mambas have, and I thought that it was going to strike me and there was nothing I could do.

"At that moment there was a scraping noise and I saw that my little brother, who was only eleven or twelve at the time, was moving the stick towards the snake, pushing its tip along the ground. The snake moved its head, and before we could make out what was happening, it had struck at the end of the stick. That gave me time to turn round, pick up my brother, and run down the path. The snake disappeared. It had bitten the stick and perhaps it had broken a fang. Whatever happened, it did not choose to follow us.

"He saved my life. You know, Mma, what happens if a person is bitten by a mamba. There is no chance. So from that day I knew that I owed my life to this little brother of mine.

"That was fourteen years ago. Now we do not walk through the bush together very often, but I still love my brother very much and that is why I was unhappy when he came to see me here in Gaborone and told me that he was going to marry a girl he had met when he was a student here at the university. He was doing a BSc there and while he was doing this he came across a girl from Mahalapye. I know her father because he is a clerk in one of the ministries here. I have seen him sitting under the trees with other clerks at lunchtime, and now he waves to me every time he sees my car go past. I waved back at the beginning, but now I cannot be bothered. Why should I wave to this clerk all the time just because his daughter has met my brother?

"My brother is staying down at the farm that we have up north of Pilane. He runs it very well and my father is very content with what he is doing. My father has given him the farm, in fact, and it is now his. This makes him a wealthy man. I have another farm which also belonged to my father, so I am not jealous of that. Mogadi married this girl about three months ago and she moved into the farmhouse that we have. My father and my mother live there. My aunts come and stay for much of the year. It is a very big house and there is room for everybody.

"My mother did not want this woman to marry my brother. She said that she would not make a good wife and that she would only bring unhappiness to the family. I also thought that it was not a good idea, but in my case it was because I thought I knew why she wanted to marry my brother. I did not think that it was because she loved him, or anything like that; I think that she was being encouraged by her father to marry my brother because he came from a rich and important family. I shall never forget, Mma, how her father looked about the place when he came to talk about the marriage with my father. His eyes were wide with greed, and I could see him adding up the value of everything. He even asked my brother how many cattle he had—that from a man who has no cattle himself, I should imagine!

"I accepted my brother's decision, although I thought it was a bad one, and I tried to be as welcoming as possible to this new wife. But it was not easy. This was because all the time I could see that she was plotting to turn my brother against his family. She obviously wants my mother and father out of that house and has made herself very unpleasant to my aunts. It is like a house in which a wasp is trapped, always buzzing away and trying to sting the others.

"That would have been bad enough, I suppose, but then something happened which made me even more concerned. I was down there a few weeks ago and I went to see my brother at the house. When I arrived, I was told that he was not well. I went through to his room and he was lying in bed holding his stomach. He had eaten something very bad, he said; perhaps it was rotten meat.

"I asked him whether he had seen a doctor and he said that it was not serious enough for that. He would get better soon, he thought, even if he felt very ill at that point. I then went and spoke to my mother, who was sitting by herself on the verandah.

"She beckoned me to sit beside her and, having checked to see that there was nobody else about, she told me what was on her mind.

"'That new wife is trying to poison your brother,' she said. 'I saw her go into the kitchen before his meal was served. I saw her. I told him not to finish his meat as I thought it was rotten. If I hadn't told him that, he would have eaten the whole helping and would have died. She's trying to poison him.'

"I asked her why she would do this. 'If she has just married a nice rich husband,' I said, 'why should she want to get rid of him so quickly?'

"My mother laughed. 'Because she'll be much richer as a widow than as a wife,' she said. 'If he dies before she has children, then he has made a will which gives everything to her. The farm, this house, everything. And once she has that, then she can throw us out and all the aunts. But first she has to kill him.'

"I thought at first that this was ridiculous, but the more I pondered it, the more I realised that it provided a very clear motive for this new wife and that it could well be true. I could not talk to my brother about it, as he refuses to hear anything said against his wife, and so I thought that I had better get somebody from outside the family to look into this matter and see what was happening."

Mma Ramotswe raised a hand to interrupt him. "There's the police, Rra. This sounds like something for the police. They are used to dealing with poisoners and people like that. We are not that sort of detective. We help people with the problems in their lives. We are not here to solve crimes."

As Mma Ramotswe spoke, she noticed Mma Makutsi look crestfallen. She knew that her assistant had a different vision of their role; that was the difference, thought Mma Ramotswe between being almost forty and being twenty-eight. At almost forty—or even forty, if one were fussy about dates—one was not on the lookout for excitement; at twenty-eight, if any excitement was to be had, then one wanted to have it. Mma Ramotswe understood, of course. When she had married Note Mokoti, she had yearned for all the glamour that went with being the wife of a well-known musician, a man who turned the heads of all when he entered a room, a man whose very voice seemed redolent of the thrilling notes of jazz that he coaxed out of his shining Selmer trumpet. When the marriage ended, after a pitifully short time, with its only memorial being that minute, sad stone that marked the short life of their premature baby, she had yearned for a life of stability and order. Certainly, excitement was not what she sought, and, indeed Clovis Andersen, author of her professional bible, *The Principles of Private Detection,* had clearly warned, on page two if not on page one itself, that those who became private detectives to find a more exciting life were gravely mistaken as to the nature of the work. *Our job,* he wrote, in a paragraph which had stuck in Mma Ramotswe's mind and which she had quoted in its entirety to Mma Makutsi when she had first engaged her, *is to help people in need to resolve the unresolved questions in their lives. There is very little drama in our calling; rather a process of patient observation, deduction, and analysis. We are sophisticated watchmen, watching and reporting; there is nothing romantic in our job and those who are looking for romance should lay down this manual at this point and do something else.*

Mma Makutsi's eyes had glazed over when Mma Ramotswe had quoted this to her. It was obvious, then, that she thought of the job in a very different way. Now, with no less a person than the Government Man sitting before them talking about family intrigue and possible poisonings, she felt that at last here was an investigation which could allow them to get their teeth into something worthwhile. And, just as this arose, Mma Ramotswe seemed intent on putting off the client!

The Government Man stared at Mma Ramotswe. Her intervention had annoyed him, and it seemed that he was making an effort to control his displeasure. Mma Makutsi noticed that the top of his lip quivered slightly as he listened.

"I cannot go to the police," he said, struggling to keep his voice normal. "What could I say to the police? The police would ask for some proof, even from me. They would say that they could hardly go into that house and arrest a wife who would say that she had done nothing, with the husband there, too, saying *This woman has not done anything. What are you talking about?*"

He stopped and looked at Mma Ramotswe as if he had made out his case.

"Well?" he said abruptly. "If I cannot go to the police, then it becomes the job of a private detective. That's what you people are for, isn't it? Well, Mma?"

Mma Ramotswe returned his gaze, which in itself was a gesture. In traditional society, she should not have looked so hard into the eyes of a man of his rank. That would have been very rude. But times had changed, and she was a citizen of the modern Republic of Botswana, where there was a constitution which guaranteed the dignity of all citizens, lady private detectives among them. That constitution had been upheld from the very day in 1966 when the Union Jack had been taken down in the stadium and that wonderful blue flag had been raised to the ululating of the crowd. It was a record which no other country in Africa, not one, could match. And she was, after all, Precious Ramotswe, daughter of the late Obed Ramotswe, a man whose dignity and worth was the equal of any man, whether he was from a chiefly family or not. He had been able to look into the eye of anyone, right to the day of his death, and she should be able to do so too.

"It is for me to decide whether I take a case, Rra," she said. "I cannot help everybody. I try to help people as much as I can, but if I cannot do a thing, then I say that I am sorry but I cannot help that person. That is how we work in the No. 1 Ladies' Detective Agency. In your case, I just do not see how we could find out what we need to find out. This is a problem inside a family. I do not see how a stranger could find out anything about it."

The Government Man was silent. He glanced at Mma Makutsi, but she dropped her eyes.

"I see," he said after a few moments. "I think you do not want to help me, Mma. Well now, that is very sad for me." He paused. "Do you have a licence for this business, Mma?"

Mma Ramotswe caught her breath. "A licence? Is there a law which requires a licence to be a private detective?"

The Government Man smiled, but his eyes were cold. "Probably not. I haven't checked. But there could be. Regulation, you know. We have to regulate business. That's why we have things like hawkers' licences or general dealers' licences, which we can take away from people who are not suitable to be hawkers or general dealers. You know how that works."

It was Obed Ramotswe who answered; Obed Ramotswe through the lips of his daughter, his Precious.

"I cannot hear what you are saying, Rra. I cannot hear it."

Mma Makutsi suddenly noisily shuffled the papers on her desk.

"Of course, you're right, Mma," she said. "You could not simply go up to that woman and ask her whether she was planning to kill her husband. That would not work."

"No," said Mma Ramotswe. "That is why we cannot do anything here."

"On the other hand," said Mma Makutsi quickly. "I have an idea. I think I know how this might be done."

The Government Man twisted round to face Mma Makutsi. "What is your idea, Mma?"

Mma Makutsi swallowed. Her large glasses seemed to shine with brightness at the force of the idea.

"Well," she began. "It is important to get into the house and listen to what those people are talking about. It is important to watch that woman who is planning to do these wicked things. It is important to look into her heart."

"Yes," said the Government Man. "That is what I want you people to do. You look into that heart and find the evil. Then you shine a torch on the evil and say to my brother: *See! See this bad heart in your wife. See how she is plotting, plotting all the time!*"

"It wouldn't be that simple," said Mma Ramotswe. "Life is not that simple. It just isn't."

"Please, Mma," said the Government Man. "Let us listen to this clever woman in glasses. She has some very good ideas."

Mma Makutsi adjusted her glasses and continued. "There are servants in the house, aren't there?"

"Five," said the Government Man. "Then there are servants for outside. There are men who look after the cattle. And there are the old servants of my father. They cannot work anymore, but they sit in the sun outside the house and my father feeds them well. They are very fat."

"So you see," said Mma Makutsi. "An inside servant sees everything. A maid sees into the bed of the husband and wife, does she not? A cook sees into their stomachs. Servants are always there, watching, watching. They will talk to another servant. Servants know everything."

"So you will go and talk to the servants?" asked the Government Man. "But will they talk to you? They will be worried about their jobs. They will just be quiet and say that there is nothing happening."

"But Mma Ramotswe knows how to talk to people," countered Mma Makutsi. "People talk to her. I have seen it. Can you not get her to stay in your father's house for a few days? Can you not arrange that?"

"Of course I can," said the Government Man. "I can tell my parents that there is a woman who has done me a political favour. She needs to be away from Gaborone for a few days because of some troubles here. They will take her."

Mma Ramotswe glanced at Mma Makutsi. It was not her assistant's place to make suggestions of this sort, particularly when their effect would be to railroad her into taking a case which she did not wish to take. She would have to speak to Mma Makutsi about this, but she did not wish to embarrass her in front of this man with his autocratic ways and his pride. She would accept the case, not because his thinly veiled threat had worked—that she had clearly stood up to by saying that she could not hear him—but because she had been presented with a way of finding out what needed to be found out.

"Very well," she said. "We will take this on, Rra. Not because of anything you have said to me, particularly those things that I did not hear." She paused, allowing the effect of her words to be felt. "But I will decide what to do once I am there. You must not interfere."

The Government Man nodded enthusiastically. "That is fine, Mma. I am very happy with that. And I am sorry that I

said things which I should not have said. You must know that
my brother is very important to me. I would not have said anything if it had not been for my fears for my brother. That is all."

Mma Ramotswe looked at him. He did love his brother. It
could not be easy to see him married to a woman whom he
mistrusted so strongly. "I have already forgotten what was said,
Rra," she said. "You need not worry."

The Government Man rose to his feet. "Will you start
tomorrow?" he said. "I shall make the arrangements."

"No," said Mma Ramotswe. "I will start in a few days' time.
I have much to do here in Gaborone. But do not worry, if there
is anything that can be done for your poor brother, I shall do it.
Once we take on a case, we do not treat it lightly. I promise you
that."

The Government Man reached across the desk and took her
hand in his. "You are a very kind woman, Mma. What they say
about you is true. Every word."

He turned to Mma Makutsi. "And you, Mma. You are a
clever lady. If you ever decide that you are tired of being a private detective, come and work for the Government. The Government needs women like you. Most of the women we have
working in Government are no good. They sit and paint their
nails. I have seen them. You would work hard, I think."

Mma Ramotswe was about to say something, but the Government Man was already on his way out. From the window,
they saw his driver open the car door smartly and slam it shut
behind him.

"If I did go to work for the Government," said Mma
Makutsi, adding quickly, "and I'm not going to do that, of
course. But I wonder how long it would be before I had a car
like that, and a driver."

Mma Ramotswe laughed. "Don't believe everything he says," she said. "Men like that can make all sorts of promises. And he is a very stupid man. Very proud too."

"But he was telling the truth about the brother's wife?" asked Mma Makutsi anxiously.

"Probably," said Mma Ramotswe. "I don't think he made that up. But remember what Clovis Andersen says. Every story has two sides. So far, we've only heard one. The stupid side."

LIFE WAS becoming complicated, thought Mma Ramotswe. She had just agreed to take on a case which could prove far from simple, and which would take her away from Gaborone. That in itself was problematic enough, but the whole situation became much more difficult when one thought about Mr J.L.B. Matekoni and Tlokweng Road Speedy Motors. And then there was the question of the children; now that they had settled into her house at Zebra Drive she would have to establish some sort of routine for them. Rose, her maid, was a great help in that respect, but she could not shoulder the whole burden herself.

The list she had begun to compose earlier that morning had been headed by the task of preparing the office for a move. Now she thought that she should promote the issue of the garage to the top of the list and put the office second. Then she could fit the children in below that: she wrote SCHOOL in capital letters and a telephone number beneath that. This was followed by GET MAN TO FIX FRIDGE. TAKE ROSE'S SON TO THE DOCTOR FOR HIS ASTHMA, and finally she wrote: DO SOMETHING ABOUT BAD WIFE.

"Mma Makutsi," she said. "I think that I am going to take

you over to the garage. We cannot let Mr J.L.B. Matekoni down, even if he is behaving strangely. You must start your duties as Acting Manager right now. I will take you in the van."

Mma Makutsi nodded. "I am ready, Mma," she said. "I am ready to manage."

UNDER NEW MANAGEMENT

T LOKWENG ROAD Speedy Motors stood a short distance off the road, half a mile beyond the two big stores that had been built at the edge of the district known as the Village. It was in a cluster of three buildings: a general dealer's shop that stocked everything from cheap clothing to paraffin and golden syrup, and a builder's yard which dealt in timber and sheets of corrugated iron for roofs. The garage was at the eastern end, with several thorn trees around it and an old petrol pump to the front. Mr J.L.B. Matekoni had been promised a more modern pump, but the petrol company was not keen for him to sell petrol in competition with their more modern outlets and they conveniently forgot this promise. They continued to deliver petrol, as they were contractually bound to do, but they did it without enthusiasm and tended to forget when they had agreed to come. As a result, the fuel storage tanks were frequently empty.

None of that mattered very much. Clients came to Tlokweng Road Speedy Motors because they wanted their cars to be fixed by Mr J.L.B. Matekoni rather than to buy petrol. They were people who understood the difference between a good mechanic and one who merely fixed cars. A good mechanic understood cars; he could diagnose a problem just by listening to an engine running, in much the same way as an experienced doctor may see what is wrong just by looking at the patient.

"Engines talk to you," he explained to his apprentices. "Listen to them. They are telling you what is wrong with them, if only you listen."

Of course, the apprentices did not understand what he meant. They had an entirely different view of machinery and were quite incapable of appreciating that engines might have moods, and emotions, that an engine might feel stressed or under pressure, or relieved and at ease. The presence of the apprentices was an act of charity on the part of Mr J.L.B. Matekoni, who was concerned that there should be enough properly trained mechanics in Botswana to replace his generation when it eventually retired.

"Africa will get nowhere until we have mechanics," he once remarked to Mma Ramotswe. "Mechanics are the first stone in the building. Then there are other people on top. Doctors. Nurses. Teachers. But the whole thing is built on mechanics. That is why it is important to teach young people to be mechanics."

Now, driving up to Tlokweng Road Speedy Motors, Mma Ramotswe and Mma Makutsi saw one of the apprentices at the wheel of a car while the other was pushing it slowly forward into the workshop. As they approached, the apprentice who was doing the pushing abandoned his task to look at them and the car rolled backwards.

Mma Ramotswe parked her tiny white van under a tree and she and Mma Makutsi walked over to the office entrance.

"Good morning, Bomma," the taller of the two apprentices said. "Your suspension on that van of yours is very bad. You are too heavy for it. See how it goes down on one side. We can fix it for you."

"There is nothing wrong with it," retorted Mma Ramotswe. "Mr J.L.B. Matekoni himself looks after that van. He has never said anything about suspension."

"But he is saying nothing about anything these days," said the apprentice. "He is quite silent."

Mma Makutsi stopped and looked at the boy. "I am Mma Makutsi," she said, staring at him through her large glasses. "I am the Acting Manager. If you want to talk about suspension, then you can come and talk to me in the office. In the meantime, what are you doing? Whose car is that and what are you doing to it?"

The apprentice looked over his shoulder for support from his friend.

"It is the car of that woman who lives behind the police station. I think she is some sort of easy lady." He laughed. "She uses this car to pick up men and now it will not start. So she can get no men. Ha!"

Mma Makutsi bristled with anger. "It would not start, would it?"

"Yes," said the apprentice. "It would not start. And so Charlie and I had to drive over with the truck and tow it in. Now we are pushing it into the garage to look at the engine. It will be a big job, I think. Maybe a new starter motor. You know these things. They cost a lot of money and it is good that the men give that woman all that money so she can pay. Ha!"

Mma Makutsi moved her glasses down on her nose and stared at the boy over the top of them.

"And what about the battery?" she said. "Maybe it's the battery. Did you try to jump-start it?"

The apprentice stopped smiling.

"Well?" asked Mma Ramotswe. "Did you take the leads? Did you try?"

The apprentice shook his head. "It is an old car. There will be something else wrong with it."

"Nonsense," said Mma Makutsi. "Open the front. Have you got a good battery in the workshop? Put the leads on that and try."

The apprentice looked at the other, who shrugged.

"Come on," said Mma Makutsi. "I have a lot to do in the office. Get going please."

Mma Ramotswe said nothing, but watched with Mma Makutsi as the apprentices moved the car the last few yards into the workshop and then linked the battery leads to a fresh battery. Then, sullenly, one of them climbed into the driver's seat and tried the ignition. The engine started immediately.

"Charge it up," said Mma Makutsi. "Then change the oil for that woman and take the car back to her. Tell her that you are sorry it has taken longer than necessary to fix, but that we have given her an oil change for nothing to make up for it." She turned to Mma Ramotswe, who was standing smiling beside her. "Customer loyalty is very important. If you do something for the customer, then the customer is going to stay with you forever. That is very important in business."

"Very," agreed Mma Ramotswe. She had harboured doubts about Mma Makutsi's ability to manage the garage, but these were well on their way to being allayed.

"Do you know much about cars?" she asked her assistant casually, as they began to sort out the crowded surface of Mr J.L.B. Matekoni's desk.

"Not very much," answered Mma Makutsi. "But I am good with typewriters, and one machine is very much like another, don't you think?"

THEIR IMMEDIATE task was to find out what cars were waiting to be attended to and which were booked in for future attention. The elder of the two apprentices, Charlie, was summoned into the office and asked to give a list of outstanding work. There were eight cars, it transpired, which were parked at the back of the garage waiting for parts. Some of these had been ordered and others had not. Once a list had been made, Mma Makutsi telephoned each supplier in turn and enquired about the part.

"Mr J.L.B. Matekoni is very cross," she said sharply. "And we will not be able to pay you for past orders if you do not let us get on with new work. Do you understand that?"

Promises were made, and, for the most part, kept. Parts began to arrive several hours later, brought round by the suppliers themselves. These were duly labelled—something which had not happened before, said the apprentices—and placed on a bench, in order of urgency. In the meantime, their work coordinated by Mma Makutsi, the apprentices busily fitted parts, tested engines, and eventually handed over each vehicle to Mma Makutsi for testing. She interrogated them as to what had been done, sometimes asking to inspect the work itself, and then, being unable to drive, she handed the vehicle over to Mma Ramotswe for a test run before she telephoned the owner to tell them that the work was finished. Only half the bill would be charged, she explained, to compensate for the length of the delay. This mollified every owner, except one, who announced that he would be going elsewhere in future.

"Then you will not be able to take advantage of our free service offer," said Mma Makutsi quietly. "That is a pity."

This brought the necessary change of mind, and at the end of the day Tlokweng Road Speedy Motors had returned six cars to their owners, all of whom had appeared to have forgiven them.

"It has been a good first day," said Mma Makutsi, as she and Mma Ramotswe watched the exhausted apprentices walking off down the road. "Those boys worked very hard and I have rewarded them with a bonus of fifty pula each. They are very happy and I'm sure that they will become better apprentices. You'll see."

Mma Ramotswe was bemused. "I think you may be right, Mma," she said. "You are an exceptional manager."

"Thank you," said Mma Makutsi. "But we must go home now, as we have a lot to do tomorrow."

Mma Ramotswe drove her assistant home in the tiny white van, along the roads that were crowded with people returning from work. There were minibuses, overloaded and listing alarmingly to one side with their burden, bicycles with passengers perched on the carriers, and people simply walking, arms swinging, whistling, thinking, hoping. She knew the road well, having driven Mma Makutsi home on many occasions, and was familiar with the ramshackle houses with their knots of staring, inquisitive children who seemed to populate such areas. She dropped her assistant at her front gate and watched her walk round to the back of the building and the breeze-block shack in which she lived. She thought she saw a figure in the doorway, a shadow perhaps, but then Mma Makutsi turned round and Mma Ramotswe, who could not be seen to be watching her, had to drive off.

CHAPTER SEVEN

THE GIRL WITH THREE LIVES

NOT EVERYBODY had a maid, of course, but if you were in a well-paid job and had a house of the size which Mma Ramotswe did, then not to employ a maid—or indeed not to support several domestic servants—would have been seen as selfishness. Mma Ramotswe knew that there were countries where people had no servants, even when they were well enough off to do so. She found this inexplicable. If people who were in a position to have servants chose not to do so, then what were the servants to do?

In Botswana, every house in Zebra Drive—or indeed every house with over two bedrooms—would be likely to have a servant. There were laws about how much domestic servants should be paid, but these were often flouted. There were people who treated their servants very badly, who paid them very little and expected them to work all hours of the day, and these people, as far as Mma Ramotswe knew, were probably in

the majority. This was Botswana's dark secret—this exploita-
tion—which nobody liked to talk about. Certainly nobody
liked to talk about how the Masarwa had been treated in the
past, as slaves effectively, and if one mentioned it, people
looked shifty and changed the subject. But it had happened,
and it was still happening here and there for all that anybody
knew. Of course, this sort of thing happened throughout
Africa. Slavery had been a great wrong perpetrated against
Africa, but there had always been willing African slavers, who
sold their own people, and there were still vast legions of
Africans working for a pittance in conditions of near-slavery.
These people were quiet people, weak people, and the domestic servants were amongst them.

Mma Ramotswe was astonished that people could behave
so callously to their servants. She herself had been in the
house of a friend who had referred, quite casually, to the fact
that her maid was given five days holiday a year, and unpaid at
that. This friend boasted that she had managed to cut the
maid's wages recently because she thought her lazy.

"But why doesn't she go, if you do such a thing?" asked Mma
Ramotswe.

The friend had laughed. "Go where? There are plenty of
people wanting her job, and she knows it. She knows that I
could get somebody to do her job for half the wages she's getting."

Mma Ramotswe had said nothing, but had mentally ended
the friendship at that point. This had given her cause for
thought. Can one be the friend of a person who behaves
badly? Or is the case that bad people can only have bad
friends, because only other bad people will have sufficient in
common with them to be friends? Mma Ramotswe thought of

notoriously bad people. There was Idi Amin, for example, or Henrik Verwoerd. Idi Amin, of course, had something wrong with him; perhaps he was not bad in the same way as Mr Verwoerd, who had seemed quite sane, but who had a heart of ice. Had anybody loved Mr Verwoerd? Had anybody held his hand? Mma Ramotswe assumed that they had; there had been people at his funeral, had there not, and did they not weep, just as people weep at the funerals of good men? Mr Verwoerd had his people, and perhaps not all of his people were bad. Now that things had changed over the border in South Africa, these people still had to go on living. Perhaps they now understood the wrong they had done; even if they did not, they had been forgiven, for the most part. The ordinary people of Africa tended not to have room in their hearts for hatred. They were sometimes foolish, like people anywhere, but they did not bear grudges, as Mr Mandela had shown the world. As had Seretse Khama, thought Mma Ramotswe; though nobody outside Botswana seemed to remember him anymore. Yet he was one of Africa's great men, and had shaken the hand of her father, Obed Ramotswe, when he had visited Mochudi to talk to the people. And she, Precious Ramotswe, then a young girl, had seen him step out of his car and the people had flocked about him and among them, holding his old battered hat in his hand, was her father. And as the Khama had taken her father's hand, her own heart had swelled with pride; and she remembered the occasion every time she looked at the photograph of the great statesman on her mantelpiece.

Her friend who treated her maid badly was not a wicked person. She behaved well towards her family and she had always been kind to Mma Ramotswe, but when it came to her maid—and Mma Ramotswe had met this maid, who seemed an agreeable, hardworking woman from Molepolole—she seemed to have little concern for her feelings. It occurred to Mma Ramotswe that such behaviour was no more than ignorance; an inability to understand the hopes and aspirations of others. That understanding, thought Mma Ramotswe, was the beginning of all morality. If you knew how a person was feeling, if you could imagine yourself in her position, then surely it would be impossible to inflict further pain. Inflicting pain in such circumstances would be like hurting oneself.

Mma Ramotswe knew that there was a great deal of debate about morality, but in her view it was quite simple. In the first place, there was the old Botswana morality, which was simply right. If a person stuck to this, then he would be doing the right thing and need not worry about it. There were other moralities, of course; there were the Ten Commandments, which she had learned by heart at Sunday School in Mochudi all those years ago; these were also right in the same, absolute way. These codes of morality were like the Botswana Penal Code; they had to be obeyed to the letter. It was no good pretending you were the High Court of Botswana and deciding which parts you were going to observe and which you were not. Moral codes were not designed to be selective, nor indeed were they designed to be questioned. You could not say that you would observe this prohibition but not that. *I shall not commit theft—certainly not—but adultery is another matter: wrong for other people, but not for me.*

Most morality, thought Mma Ramotswe, was about doing the right thing because it had been identified as such by a long process of acceptance and observance. You simply could not create your own morality because your experience would never be enough to do so. What gives you the right to say that you know better than your ancestors? Morality is for everybody, and this means that the views of more than one person are needed to create it. That was what made the modern morality, with its emphasis on individuals and the working out of an individual position, so weak. If you gave people the chance to work out their morality, then they would work out the version which was easiest for them and which allowed them to do what suited them for as much of the time as possible. That, in Mma Ramotswe's view, was simple selfishness, whatever grand name one gave to it.

Mma Ramotswe had listened to a World Service broadcast on her radio one day which had simply taken her breath away. It was about philosophers who called themselves existentialists and who, as far as Mma Ramotswe could ascertain, lived in France. These French people said that you should live in a way which made you feel real, and that the real thing to do was the right thing too. Mma Ramotswe had listened in astonishment. You did not have to go to France to meet existentialists, she reflected; there were many existentialists right here in Botswana. Note Mokoti, for example. She had been married to an existentialist herself, without even knowing it. Note, that selfish man who never once put himself out for another—not even for his wife—would have approved of existentialists, and they of him. It was very existentialist, perhaps, to go out to bars every night while your pregnant wife stayed at home, and even more existentialist to go off with girls—young existentialist girls—you met in bars. It was a good life being an existentialist, although not too good for all the other, nonexistentialist people around one.

*   *   *

MMA RAMOTSWE did not treat her maid, Rose, in an existential-ist way. Rose had worked for her from the day that she first moved in to Zebra Drive. There was a network of unemployed people, Mma Ramotswe discovered, and this sent out word of anybody who was moving into a new house and who might be expected to need a servant. Rose had arrived at the house within an hour of Mma Ramotswe herself.

"You will need a maid, Mma," she had said. "And I am a very good maid. I will work very hard and will not be a trouble to you for the rest of your life. I am ready to start now."

Mma Ramotswe had made an immediate judgement. She saw before her a respectable-looking woman, neatly presented, of about thirty. But she saw, too, a mother, one of whose chil-dren was waiting by the gate, staring at her. And she wondered what the mother had said to her child. *We shall eat tonight if this woman takes me as her maid. Let us hope. You wait here and stand on your toe.* Stand on your toe. That is what one said in Setswana if one hoped that something would happen. It was the same as the expression which white people used: cross your fingers.

Mma Ramotswe glanced towards the gate and saw that the child was indeed standing on her toe, and she knew then that there was only one answer she could give.

She looked at the woman. "Yes," she said. "I need a maid, and I will give the job to you, Mma."

The woman clapped her hands together in gratitude and waved to the child. I am lucky, thought Mma Ramotswe. I am lucky that I can make somebody so happy just by saying some-thing.

Rose moved in immediately and rapidly proved her worth. Zebra Drive had been left in a bad way by its previous owners,

who had been untidy people, and there was dust in every corner. Over three days she swept and polished, until the house
smelled of floor wax and every surface shone. Not only that,
but she was an expert cook and a magnificent ironer. Mma
Ramotswe was well dressed, but she always found it difficult
to find the energy to iron her blouses as much as she might
have wished. Rose did this with a passion that was soon
reflected in starched seams and expanses to which creases
were quite alien.

Rose took up residence in the servants' quarters in the back
yard. This consisted of a small block of two rooms, with a
shower and toilet to one side and a covered porch under which
a cooking fire might be made. She slept in one of the rooms,
while her two small children slept in the other. There were
other, older children, including one who was a carpenter and
earning a good wage. But even with that, the expenses of living
were such as to leave very little over, particularly since her
younger son had asthma and needed expensive inhalers to
help him breathe.

NOW, COMING home after dropping off Mma Makutsi, Mma
Ramotswe found Rose in the kitchen, scouring a blackened
cooking pot. She enquired politely after the maid's day and was
told that it had been a very good one.

"I have helped Motholeli with her bath," she said. "And now
she is through there, reading to her little brother. He has been
running round all day and is tired, tired. He will be asleep very
soon. Only the thought of his supper is keeping him awake, I
think."

Mma Ramotswe thanked her and smiled. It had been a

month since the children had arrived from the orphanage, by
way of Mr J.L.B. Matekoni, and she was still getting used to
their presence in the house. They had been his idea—and
indeed he had not consulted her before he had agreed to act as
their foster father—but she had accepted the situation and
had quickly taken to them. Motholeli, who was in a wheelchair, had proved herself useful about the house and had
expressed an interest in mending cars—much to Mr J.L.B.
Matekoni's delight. Her brother, who was much younger, was
more difficult to fathom. He was active enough, and spoke
politely when spoken to, but seemed to be keener on his own
company, or that of his sister, than on that of other children.
Motholeli had made some friends already, but the boy seemed
shy of doing so.

She had started at Gaborone Secondary School, which was
not far away, and was happy there. Each morning, one of the
other girls from her class would arrive at the door and volunteer to push the wheelchair to school.

Mma Ramotswe had been impressed.

"Do the teachers tell you to do this?" she asked one of them.

"They do not, Mma," came the reply. "We are the friends of
this girl. That is why we do this."

"You are kind girls," said Mma Ramotswe. "You will be kind
ladies in due course. Well done."

The boy had been found a place at the local primary school,
but Mma Ramotswe hoped that Mr J.L.B. Matekoni would pay
to send him to Thornhill. This cost a great deal of money, and
now she wondered whether it would ever be possible. That
was just one of the many things which would have to be sorted
out. There was the garage, the apprentices, the house near the
old Botswana Defence Force Club, and the children. There

was also the wedding—whenever that would be—although Mma Ramotswe hardly dared think of that at present.

She went through to the living room, to see the boy seated beside his sister's wheelchair, listening to her as she read.

"So," said Mma Ramotswe. "You are reading a story to your little brother. Is it a good one?"

Motholeli looked round and smiled.

"It is not a story, Mma," she said. "Or rather, it is not a proper story from a book. It is a story I have written at school, and I am reading it to him."

Mma Ramotswe joined them, perching on the arm of the sofa.

"Why don't you start off again?" she said. "I would like to hear your story."

MY NAME is Motholeli and I am thirteen years old, almost fourteen. I have a brother, who is seven. My mother and father are late. I am very sad about this, but I am happy that I am not late too and that I have my brother.

I am a girl who has had three lives. My first life was when I lived with my mother and my aunts and uncles, up in the Makadikadi, near Nata. That was long ago, and I was very small. They were bush people and they moved from place to place. They knew how to find food in the bush by digging for roots. They were very clever people, but nobody liked them.

My mother gave me a bracelet made out of ostrich skin, with pieces of ostrich eggshell stitched into it. I still have that. It is the only thing I have from my mother, now that she is late.

After she died, I rescued my little brother, who had been buried in the sand with her. He was just under the sand, and so I scraped it off his face and saw that he was still breathing. I remember picking him up and running through the bush until I found a road. A man came down the road in a truck and when he saw me he stopped and took me to Francistown. I do not remember what happened there, but I was given to a woman who said that I could live in her yard. They had a small shed, which was very hot when the sun was on it, but which was cool at night. I slept there with my baby brother.

I fed him with the food that I was given from that house. I used to do things for those kind people. I did their washing and hung it out on the line. I cleaned some pots for them too, as they did not have a servant. There was a dog who lived in the yard too, and it bit me one day, sharply, in my foot. The woman's husband was very cross with the dog after that and he beat it with a wooden pole. That dog is late now, after all that beating for being wicked.

I became very sick, and the woman took me to the hospital. They put needles into me and they took out some of my blood. But they could not make me better, and after a while I could not walk anymore. They gave me crutches, but I was not very good at walking with them. Then they found a wheelchair; which meant that I could go home again. But the woman said that she could not have a wheelchair girl living in her yard, as that would not look good and people would say: *What are you doing having a girl in a wheelchair in your yard? That is very cruel.*

Then a man came by who said that he was looking for orphans to take to his orphan farm. There was a lady from the Government with him who told me that I was very lucky to get a place on such a fine orphan farm. I could take my brother, and we would be very happy living there. But I must always remember to love Jesus, this woman said. I replied that I was ready to love Jesus and that I would make my little brother love him too.

That was the end of my first life. My second life started on the day that I arrived at the orphan farm. We had come down from Francistown in a truck, and I was very hot and uncomfortable in the back. I could not get out, as the truck driver did not know what to do with a girl in a wheelchair. So when I arrived at the orphan farm, my dress was wet and I was very ashamed, especially since all the other orphans were standing there watching us come to their place. One of the ladies there told the other children to go off and play, and not to stare at us, but they only went a little way and they watched me from behind the trees.

All the orphans lived in houses. Each house had about ten orphans in it and had a mother who looked after them. My housemother was a kind lady. She gave me new clothes and a cupboard to keep my things in. I had never had a cupboard before and I was very proud of it. I was also given some special clips which I could put in my hair. I had never had such beautiful things, and I would keep them under my pillow, where they were safe. Sometimes at night I would wake up and think how lucky I was. But I would also cry sometimes, because I was thinking of my first life and I would be thinking about my uncles and aunts and wondering where they were now. I could see the stars from my bed, through a gap in the curtain, and I thought: if they looked up, they would see the same stars, and we would be looking at them at the same time. But I wondered if they remembered me, because I was just a girl and I had run away from them.

I was very happy at the orphan farm. I worked hard, and Mma Potokwane, who was the matron, said that one day, if I was lucky, she would find somebody who would be new parents for us. I did not think that this was possible, as nobody would want to take a girl in a wheelchair when there were plenty of first-class orphan girls who could walk very well and who would be looking for a home too.

But she was right. I did not think that it would be Mr J.L.B. Matekoni who took us, but I was very pleased when he said that we could go to live in his house. That is how my third life began.

They made us a special cake when we left the orphan farm, and we ate it with the housemother. She said that she always felt very sad when one of the orphans went, as it was like a member of the family leaving. But she knew Mr J.L.B. Matekoni very well, and she told me that he was one of the best men in Botswana. I would be very happy in his house, she said.

So I went to his house, with my small brother, and we soon met his friend, Mma Ramotswe, who is going to be married to Mr J.L.B. Matekoni. She said that she would be my new mother, and she brought us to her house, which is better for children than Mr J.L.B. Matekoni's house. I have a very good bedroom there, and I have been given many clothes. I am very happy that there are people like this in Botswana. I have had a very fortunate life and I thank Mma Ramotswe and Mr J.L.B. Matekoni from my heart.

I would like to be a mechanic when I grow up. I shall help Mr J.L.B. Matekoni in his garage and at night I will mend Mma Ramotswe's clothes and cook her meals. Then, when they are very old, they will be able to be proud of me and say that I have been a good daughter for them and a good citizen of Botswana.

That is the story of my life. I am an ordinary girl from Botswana, but it is very lucky to have three lives. Most people only have one life.

This story is true. I have not made any of it up. It is all true.

AFTER THE girl had finished, they were all silent. The boy looked up at his sister and smiled. He thought: I am a lucky boy to have such a clever sister. I hope that God will give her back her legs one day. Mma Ramotswe looked at the girl and laid a hand gently on her shoulder. She thought: I will look after this child. I am now her mother. Rose, who had been listening from the corridor, looked down at her shoes and thought: What a strange way of putting it: three lives.

LOW SEROTONIN LEVELS

THE FIRST thing that Mma Ramotswe did the following morning was to telephone Mr J.L.B. Matekoni in his house near the old Botswana Defence Force Club. They often telephoned one another early in the morning—at least since they had become engaged—but it was usually Mr J.L.B. Matekoni who called. He would wait until the time Mma Ramotswe would have had her cup of bush tea, which she liked to drink out in the garden, before he would dial her number and declare himself formally, as he always liked to do: "This is Mr J.L.B. Matekoni, Mma. Have you slept well?"

The telephone rang for over a minute before it was picked up.

"Mr J.L.B. Matekoni? This is me. How are you? Have you slept well?"

The voice at the other end of the line sounded confused, and Mma Ramotswe realised that she had woken him up.

"Oh. Yes. Oh. I am awake now. It is me."

Mma Ramotswe persisted with the formal greeting. It was important to ask a person if he had slept well; an old tradition, but one which had to be maintained.

"But have you slept well, Rra?"

Mr J.L.B. Matekoni's voice was flat when he replied. "I do not think so. I spent all night thinking and there was no sleep. I only went to sleep when everybody else was waking up. I am very tired now."

"That is a pity, Rra. I'm sorry that I woke you up. You must go back to bed and get some sleep. You cannot live without sleep."

"I know that," said Mr J.L.B. Matekoni irritably. "I am always trying to sleep these days, but I do not succeed. It is as if there is some strange animal in my room which does not want me to sleep and keeps nudging me."

"Animal?" asked Mma Ramotswe. "What is this animal?"

"There is no animal. Or at least there is no animal when I turn on the light. It's just that I think there is one there who does not want me to sleep. That is all I said. There is really no animal."

Mma Ramotswe was silent. Then she asked, "Are you feeling well, Rra? Maybe you are ill."

Mr J.L.B. Matekoni snorted. "I am not ill. My heart is thumping away inside me. My lungs are filling up with air. I am just fed up with all the problems that there are. I am worried that they will find out about me. Then everything will be over."

Mma Ramotswe frowned. "Find out about you? Who will find out about what?"

Mr J.L.B. Matekoni dropped his voice. "You know what I'm talking about. You know very well."

"I know nothing, Rra. All I know is that you are saying some very strange things."

"Ha! You say that, Mma, but you know very well what I am talking about. I have done very wicked things in my life and now they are going to find out about me and arrest me. I will be punished, and you will be very ashamed of me, Mma. I can tell you that."

Mma Ramotswe's voice was small now as she struggled to come to terms with what she had heard. Could it be true that Mr J.L.B. Matekoni had committed some terrible crime which he had concealed from her? And had he now been found out? It seemed impossible that this could be true; he was a fine man, incapable of doing anything dishonourable, but then such people sometimes had a murky secret in their past. Everybody has done at least one thing to be ashamed of, or so she had heard. Bishop Makhulu himself had given a talk about this once to the Women's Club and he had said that he had never met anybody, even in the Church, who had not done something which he or she later regretted. Even the saints had done something bad; St Francis, perhaps, had stamped on a pigeon—no, surely not—but perhaps he had done something else which caused him regret. For her own part, there were many things which she would rather she had not done, starting from the time that she had put treacle on the best dress of another girl when she was six because she did not have such a dress herself. She still saw that person from time to time— she lived in Gaborone and was married to a man who worked at the diamond-sorting building. Mma Ramotswe wondered whether she should confess, even over thirty years later, and tell this woman what she had done, but she could not bring herself to do so. But every time that this woman greeted her in a friendly manner, Mma Ramotswe remembered how she had taken the tin of treacle and poured it over the pink material when the girl had left the dress in their classroom one day. She would have to tell her one day; or perhaps she could ask Bishop Makhulu to write a letter on her behalf. *One of my flock seeks your forgiveness, Mma. She is grievously burdened with a wrong which she committed against you many years ago. Do you remember your favourite pink dress . . .*

If Mr J.L.B. Matekoni had done something like that—perhaps poured engine oil over somebody—then he should not worry about it. There were few wrongs, short of murder, which could not be put right again. Many of them, indeed, were more minor than the transgressor imagined, and could be safely left where they lay in the past. And even the more serious ones might be forgiven once they were acknowledged. She should reassure Mr J.L.B. Matekoni; it was easy to inflate some tiny matter if one spent the night worrying about it.

"We have all done something wrong in our lives, Rra," she said. "You, me, Mma Makutsi, the Pope even. None of us can say that we have been perfect. That is not how people are. You must not worry about it. Just tell me what it was. I'm sure that I'll be able to set your mind at rest."

"Oh, I cannot do that, Mma. I cannot even start to tell you. You would be very shocked. You would never want to see me again. You see, I am not worthy of you. You are too good for me, Mma."

Mma Ramotswe felt herself becoming exasperated. "You are not talking sense. Of course you are worthy of me. I am just an ordinary person. You are a perfectly good man. You are good at your job and people think a great deal of you. Where does the British High Commissioner take his car to be serviced? To you. Where does the orphan farm turn when it needs somebody to fix something? To you. You have a very good garage and I am honoured that I am going to marry you. That is all there is to it."

Her remarks were greeted with silence. Then: "But you do not know how bad I am. I have never told you of these wicked things."

"Then tell me. Tell me now. I am strong."

"Oh I cannot do that, Mma. You would be shocked."

Mma Ramotswe realised that the conversation was getting nowhere, and so she changed her tack.

"And speaking of your garage," she said. "You were not there yesterday, or the day before. Mma Makutsi is running it for you. But that cannot go on forever."

"I am pleased that she is running it," said Mr J.L.B. Matekoni flatly. "I am not feeling very strong at the moment. I think that I should stay here in my house. She will look after everything. Please thank her for me."

Mma Ramotswe took a deep breath. "You are not well, Mr J.L.B. Matekoni. I think that I can arrange for you to see a doctor. I have spoken to Dr Moffat. He says that he will see you. He thinks it is a good idea."

"I am not broken," said Mr J.L.B. Matekoni. "I do not need to see Dr Moffat. What can he do for me? Nothing."

IT HAD not been a reassuring call, and Mma Ramotswe spent an anxious few minutes pacing about her kitchen after she had rung off. It was clear to her that Dr Moffat had been right;

that Mr J.L.B. Matekoni was suffering from an illness—depression, he had called it—but now she was more worried about the terrible thing that he said he had done. There was no less likely murderer than Mr J.L.B. Matekoni, but what if it transpired that this was what he was? Would it change her feelings for him if she discovered that he had killed somebody, or would she tell herself that it was not really his fault, that he was defending himself when he hit his victim over the head with a spanner? This is what the wives and girlfriends of murderers inevitably did. They never accepted that their man could be capable of being a murderer. Mothers were like that, too. The mothers of murderers always insisted that their sons were not as bad as people said. Of course, for a mother, the man remained a small boy, no matter how old he became, and small boys can never be guilty of murder.

Of course, Note Mokoti could have been a murderer. He was quite capable of killing a man in cold blood, because he had no feelings. It was easy to imagine Note stabbing somebody and walking away as casually as if he had done no more than shake his victim's hand. When he had beaten her, as he had on so many occasions before he left, he had shown no emotion. Once, when he had split the skin above her eyebrow with a particularly savage blow, he had stopped to examine his handiwork as if he were a doctor examining a wound.

"You will need to take that to the hospital," he had said, his voice quite even. "That is a bad cut. You must be more careful."

The one thing that she was grateful for in the whole Note episode was that her Daddy was still alive when she left him. At least he had the pleasure of knowing that his daughter was no longer with that man, even if he had had almost two years of suffering while she was with him. When she had gone to

him and told him that Note had left, he had said nothing about
her foolishness in marrying him, even if he might have thought
about it. He simply said that she must come back to his house,
that he would always look after her, and that he hoped that her
life would be better now. He had shown such dignity, as he
always did. And she had wept, and gone to him and he had told
her that she was safe with him and that she need not fear that
man again.

But Note Mokoti and Mr J.L.B. Matekoni were totally different men. Note was the one who had committed the crimes,
not Mr J.L.B. Matekoni. And yet, why did he insist that he had
done something terrible if he had not? Mma Ramotswe found
this puzzling, and, as ever when puzzled, she decided to turn
to that first line of information and consolation on all matters
of doubt or dispute: the Botswana Book Centre.

She breakfasted quickly, leaving the children to be cared for
by Rose. She would have liked to give them some attention,
but her life now seemed unduly complicated. Dealing with Mr
J.L.B. Matekoni had moved to the top of her list of tasks, followed by the garage, the investigation into the Government
Man's brother's difficulties, and the move to the new office. It
was a difficult list: every task on it had an element of urgency
and yet there was a limited number of hours in her day.

She drove the short distance into town and found a good
parking place for the tiny white van behind the Standard Bank.
Then, greeting one or two known faces in the square, she
made her way to the doors of the Botswana Book Centre. It
was her favourite shop in town, and she usually allowed herself a good hour for the simplest purchase, which gave plenty
of time for browsing the shelves; but this morning, with such a
clear and worrying mission on her mind, she set her face firmly

against the temptations of the magazine shelves with their pictures of improved houses and glamorous dresses.

"I would like to speak to the Manager," she said to one of the staff.

"You can speak to me," a young assistant said.

Mma Ramotswe was adamant. The assistant was polite, but very young and it would be better to speak to a man who knew a lot about books. "No," said Mma Ramotswe. "I wish to speak to the manager, Mma. This is an important matter."

The Manager was summoned, and greeted Mma Ramotswe politely.

"It is good to see you," he said. "Are you here as a detective, Mma?"

Mma Ramotswe laughed. "No, Rra. But I would like to find a book which will help me deal with a very delicate matter. May I speak to you in confidence?"

"Of course you may, Mma," he said. "You will never find a bookseller talking about the books that his customers are reading if they wish to keep it private. We are very careful."

"Good," said Mma Ramotswe. "I am looking for a book about an illness called depression. Have you heard of such a book?"

The Manager nodded. "Do not worry, Mma. I have not only heard of such book, but I have one in the shop. I can sell that to you." He paused. "I am sorry about this, Mma. Depression is not a happy illness."

Mma Ramotswe looked over her shoulder. "It is not me," she said. "It is Mr J.L.B. Matekoni. I think that he is depressed."

The Manager's expression conveyed his sympathy as he led her to a shelf in the corner and extracted a thin red-covered book.

"This is a very good book on that illness," he said, handing her the book. "If you read what is written on the back cover, you will see that many people have said that this book has helped them greatly in dealing with this illness. I am very sorry about Mr J.L.B. Matekoni, by the way. I hope that this book makes him feel better."

"You are a very helpful man, Rra," she said. "Thank you. We are very lucky to have your good book shop in this country. Thank you."

She paid for the book and walked back to the tiny white van, leafing through the pages as she did so. One sentence in particular caught her eye and she stopped in her tracks to read it.

A characteristic feature of acute depressive illness is the feeling that one has done some terrible thing, perhaps incurred a debt one cannot honour or committed a crime. This is usually accompanied by a feeling of lack of worth. Needless to say, the imagined wrong was normally never committed, but no amount of reasoning will persuade the sufferer that this is so.

Mma Ramotswe reread the passage, her spirits rising gloriously as she did so. A book on depression might not normally be expected to have that effect on the reader, but it did now. Of course Mr J.L.B. Matekoni had done nothing terrible; he was, as she had known him to be, a man of unbesmirched honour. Now all that she had to do was to get him to see a doctor and be treated. She closed the book and glanced at the synopsis on the back cover. *This very treatable disease* . . . it said. This cheered her even further. She knew what she had to do, and her list, even if it had appeared that morning to be a long and complicated one, was now less mountainous, less daunting.

*   *   *

SHE WENT straight from the Botswana Book Centre to Tlok-weng Road Speedy Motors. To her relief, the garage was open and Mma Makutsi was standing outside the office, drinking a cup of tea. The two apprentices were sitting on their oil drums, the one smoking a cigarette and the other drinking a soft drink from a can.

"It's rather early for a break," said Mma Ramotswe, glancing at the apprentices.

"Oh, Mma, we all deserve a break," said Mma Makutsi. "We have been here for two and half hours already. We all came in at six and we have been working very hard."

"Yes," said one of the apprentices. "Very hard. And we have done some very fine work, Mma. You tell her, Mma. You tell her what you did."

"This Acting Manager is a No. 1 mechanic," interjected the other apprentice. "Even better than the boss, I think."

Mma Makutsi laughed. "You boys are too used to saying nice things to women. That will not work with me. I am here as an acting manager, not as a woman."

"But it's true, Mma," said the elder apprentice. "If she won't tell you, then I will. We had a car here, one which had been sitting for four, five days. It belongs to a senior nurse at the Princess Marina Hospital. She is a very strong woman and I would not like to have to dance with her. Ow!"

"That woman would never dance with you," snapped Mma Makutsi. "What would she be doing dancing with a greasy boy like you, when she can dance with surgeons and people like that?"

The apprentice laughed off the insult. "Anyway, when she brought the car in she said that it stopped from time to time in the middle of the traffic and she would have to wait for a while and then start it again. Then it would start again and go for a while and then stop.

"We looked at it. I tried it and it started. I drove it over to the old airport and even out on the Lobatse Road. Nothing. No stopping. But this woman said that it was always stopping. So I replaced the spark plugs and tried it again. This time it stopped right at the circle near the Golf Club. Just stopped. Then it started again. And a very funny thing happened, which that woman had told us about. The windscreen wipers came on when the car stopped. I didn't touch them.

"So, early this morning I said to Mma Makutsi here: 'This is a very strange car, Mma. It stops and then starts.'

"Mma Makutsi came and looked at the car. She looked in the engine and saw that the plugs were new and there was a new battery too. Then she opened the door and got in, and she made a face like this, see. Just like this, with her nose all turned up. And she said: 'This car smells of mice. I can tell that it has a mouse smell.'

"She began to look about. She peered under the seats and she found nothing there. Then she looked under the dash and she started to shout out to me and my brother here. She said: 'There is a nest of mice in this car. And they have eaten the insulation off the wires right here. Look.'

"So we looked at those wires, which are very important wires for a car—the ones which are connected to the ignition, and we saw that two of them were touching, or almost touching, just where the mice had gnawed off the covering. This would mean that the engine would think that the ignition was off when the wires touched and power would go to the wipers. So that is what happened. In the meantime, the mice had run out of the car because they had been found. Mma Makutsi took out their nest and threw it away. Then she bound the wires with some tape that we gave her and now the car is fixed. It has a mouse problem no longer, all because this woman is such a good detective."

"She is a mechanic detective," said the other apprentice. "She would make a man very happy, but very tired, I think. Ow!"

"Quiet," said Mma Makutsi, playfully. "You boys must get back to work. I am the Acting Manager here. I am not one of the girls you pick up in bars. Get back to your work."

Mma Ramotswe laughed. "You obviously have a talent for finding things out, Mma. Perhaps being a detective and being a mechanic are not so different after all."

They went into the office. Mma Ramotswe immediately noticed that Mma Makutsi had made a great impression on the chaos. Although Mr J.L.B. Matekoni's desk was still covered with papers, these appeared to have been sorted into piles. Bills to be sent out had been placed in one pile, while bills to be paid had been put in another. Catalogues from suppliers had been stacked on top of a filing cabinet, and car manuals had been replaced on the shelf above his desk. And at one end of the room, leaning against the wall, was a shiny white board on which Mma Makutsi had drawn two columns headed CARS IN and CARS OUT.

"They taught us at the Botswana Secretarial College," said Mma Makutsi, "that it is very important to have a system. If you have a system which tells you where you are, then you will never be lost."

"That is true," agreed Mma Ramotswe. "They obviously knew how to run a business there."

Mma Makutsi beamed with pleasure. "And there is another

thing," she said. "I think that it would be helpful if I made you a list."

"A list?"

"Yes," said Mma Makutsi, handing her a large red file. "I have put your list in there. Each day I shall bring this list up to date. You will see that there are three columns. URGENT, NOT URGENT, and FUTURE SOMETIME."

Mma Ramotswe sighed. She did not want another list, but equally she did not want to discourage Mma Makutsi, who certainly knew how to run a garage.

"Thank you, Mma," she said, opening the file. "I see that you have already started my list."

"Yes," said Mma Makutsi. "Mma Potokwane telephoned from the orphan farm. She wanted to speak to Mr J.L.B. Matekoni, but I told her that he was not here. So she said that she was going to get in touch with you anyway and could you telephone her. You'll see that I have put it in the NOT URGENT column."

"I shall phone her," said Mma Ramotswe. "It must be something to do with the children. I had better phone her straightaway."

Mma Makutsi went back to the workshop, where Mma Ramotswe heard her calling out some instructions to the apprentices. She picked up the telephone—covered, she noticed, with greasy fingerprints, and dialled the number which Mma Makutsi had written on her list. While the telephone rang, she placed a large red tick opposite the solitary item on the list.

Mma Potokwane answered.

"Very kind of you to telephone, Mma Ramotswe. I hope that the children are well?"

"They are very settled," said Mma Ramotswe.

"Good. Now, Mma, could I ask you a favour?"

Mma Ramotswe knew that this is how the orphan farm operated. It needed help, and of course everybody was prepared to help. Nobody could refuse Mma Silvia Potokwane.

"I will help you, Mma. Just tell me what it is."

"I would like you to come and drink tea with me," said Mma Potokwane. "This afternoon, if possible. There is something you should see."

"Can you not tell me what it is?"

"No, Mma," said Mma Potokwane. "It is difficult to describe over the telephone. It would be better to see for yourself."

CHAPTER NINE

AT THE ORPHAN FARM

THE ORPHAN farm was some twenty minutes' drive out of town. Mma Ramotswe had been there on several occasions, although not as frequently as Mr J.L.B. Matekoni, who paid regular visits to deal with bits and pieces of machinery that seemed always to be going wrong. There was a borehole pump in particular that required his regular attention, and then there was their minibus, the brakes of which constantly needed attention. He never begrudged them his time, and they thought highly of him, as everybody did.

Mma Ramotswe liked Mma Potokwane, to whom she was very distantly connected through her mother's side of the family. It was not uncommon to be connected to somebody in Botswana, a lesson which foreigners were quick to learn when they realised that if they made a critical remark of somebody they were inevitably speaking to that person's distant cousin.

Mma Potokwane was standing outside the office, talking to one of the staff, when Mma Ramotswe arrived. She directed the tiny white van to a visitors' parking place under a shady syringa tree, and then invited her guest inside.

"It is so hot these days, Mma Ramotswe," she said. "But I have a very powerful fan in my office. If I turn it on to its highest setting, it can blow people out of the room. It is a very useful weapon."

"I hope that you will not do that to me," said Mma Ramotswe. For a moment she had a vision of herself being blown out of Mma Potokwane's office, her skirts all about her, up into the sky where she could look down on the trees and the paths and the cattle staring up at her in astonishment.

"Of course not," said Mma Potokwane. "You're the sort of visitor I like to receive. The sort I don't like are interfering people. People who try to tell me how to be the matron of an orphan farm. Sometimes we get these people. People who stick their noses in. They think they know about orphans, but they don't. The people who know the most about orphans are those ladies out there." She pointed out of her window, to where two of the housemothers, stout women in blue housecoats, were taking two toddlers for a walk along a path, the tiny hands firmly grasped, the hesitant, wobbly steps gently encouraged.

"Yes," went on Mma Potokwane. "Those ladies know. They can deal with any sort of child. A very sad child, who cries for its late mother all the time. A very wicked child, who has been taught to steal. A very cheeky child who has not learned to respect its elders and who uses bad words. Those ladies can deal with all those children."

"They are very good women," said Mma Ramotswe. "The

two orphans whom Mr J.L.B. Matekoni and I took say that they were very happy here. Only yesterday, Motholeli read me a story which she had written at school. The story of her life. She referred to you, Mma."

"I am glad that she was happy here," said Mma Potokwane. "She is a very brave girl, that one." She paused. "But I did not ask you out here to talk about those children, Mma. I wanted to tell you about a very strange thing that has happened here. It is so strange that even the housemothers cannot deal with it. That is why I thought that I would ask you. I was phoning Mr J.L.B. Matekoni to get your number."

She reached across her desk and poured Mma Ramotswe a cup of tea. Then she cut into a large fruitcake which was on a plate to the side of the tea tray. "This cake is made by our senior girls," she said. "We train them to cook."

Mma Ramotswe accepted her large slice of cake and looked at the rich fruit within it. There were at least seven hundred calories in that, she thought, but it did not matter; she was a traditionally built lady and she did not have to worry about such things.

"You know that we take all sorts of children," continued Mma Potokwane. "Usually they are brought to us when the mother dies and nobody knows who the father is. Often the grandmother cannot cope, because she is too ill or too poor, and then the children have nobody. We get them from the social work people or from the police sometimes. Sometimes they might just be left somewhere and a member of the public gets in touch with us."

"They are lucky to get here," said Mma Ramotswe.

"Yes. And usually, whatever has happened to them in the past, we have seen something like it before. Nothing shocks us. But every now and then a very unusual case comes in and we don't know what to do."

"And there is such a child now?"

"Yes," said Mma Potokwane. "After you have finished eating that big piece of cake I will take you and show you a boy who arrived with no name. If they have no name, we always give them one. We find a good Botswana name and they get that. But that is usually only with babies. Older children normally tell us their names. This boy didn't. In fact, he doesn't seem to have learned how to speak at all. So we decided to call him Mataila."

Mma Ramotswe finished her cake and drained the dregs of her tea. Then, together with Mma Potokwane, she walked over to one of the houses at the very edge of the circle of buildings in which the orphans lived. There were beans growing there, and the small yard in front of the door was neatly swept. This was a housemother who knew how to keep a house, thought Mma Ramotswe. And if that was the case, then how could she be defeated by a mere boy?

The housemother, Mma Kerileng, was in the kitchen. Drying her hands on her apron, she greeted Mma Ramotswe warmly and invited the two women into the living room. This was a cheerfully decorated room, with pictures drawn by the children pinned up on a large notice board. A box in one corner was filled with toys.

Mma Kerileng waited until her guests were seated before she lowered herself into one of the bulky armchairs which were arranged around a low central table.

"I have heard of you, Mma," she said to Mma Ramotswe. "I have seen your picture in the newspaper. And of course I have met Mr J.L.B. Matekoni when he has been out here fixing all the machines that are always breaking. You are a lucky lady to be marrying a man who can fix things. Most husbands just break things."

Mma Ramotswe inclined her head at the compliment. "He is a good man," she said. "He is not well at the moment, but I am hoping that he will be better very soon."

"I hope so too," said Mma Kerileng. She looked expectantly at Mma Potokwane.

"I wanted Mma Ramotswe to see Mataila," she said. "She may be able to advise us. How is he today?"

"It is the same as yesterday," said Mma Kerileng. "And the day before that. There is no change in that boy."

Mma Potokwane sighed. "It is very sad. Is he sleeping now? Can you open the door?"

"I think that he's awake," said the housemother. "Let us see anyway."

She arose from her chair and led them down a highly polished corridor. Mma Ramotswe noticed, with approval, how clean the house was. She knew how much hard work there would be in this woman; throughout the country there were women who worked and worked and who were rarely given any praise. Politicians claimed the credit for building Botswana, but how dare they? How dare they claim the credit for all the hard work of people like Mma Kerileng, and women like her.

They stopped outside a door at the end of the corridor and Mma Kerileng took a key out of her housecoat pocket.

"I cannot remember when we last locked a child in a room," she said. "In fact, I think it has never happened before. We have never had to do such a thing."

The observation seemed to make Mma Potokwane feel

uncomfortable. "There is no other way," she said. "He would run off into the bush."

"Of course," said Mma Kerileng. "It just seems very sad."

She pushed the door open, to reveal a room furnished only with a mattress. There was no glass in the window, which was covered with a large latticework wrought-iron screen of the sort used as burglar bars. Sitting on the mattress, his legs splayed out before him, was a boy of five or six, completely naked.

The boy looked at the women as they entered and for a brief moment Mma Ramotswe saw an expression of fear, of the sort one might see in the eyes of a frightened animal. But this lasted only for a short time before it was replaced by a look of vacancy, or absence.

"Mataila," said Mma Potokwane, speaking very slowly in Setswana. "Mataila, how are you today? This lady here is called Mma Ramotswe. Ramotswe. Can you see her?"

The boy looked up at Mma Potokwane as she spoke, and his gaze remained with her until she stopped speaking. Then he looked down at the floor again.

"I don't think he understands," said Mma Potokwane. "But we speak to him anyway."

"Have you tried other languages?" asked Mma Ramotswe.

Mma Potokwane nodded. "Everything we can think of. We had somebody come out from the Department of African Languages at the university. They tried some of the rarer ones, just in case he had wandered down from Zambia. We tried Herero. We tried San, although he's obviously not a Mosarwa to look at. Nothing. Absolutely nothing."

Mma Ramotswe took a step forward to get a closer look at

the boy. He raised his head slightly, but did nothing else. She stepped forward again.

"Be careful," said Mma Potokwane. "He bites. Not always, but quite often."

Mma Ramotswe stood still. Biting was a not uncommon method of fighting in Botswana, and it would not be surprising to find a child that bit. There had been a recent case reported in Mmegi of assault by biting. A waiter had bitten a customer after an argument over shortchanging, and this had led to a prosecution in the Lobatse Magistrate's Court. The waiter had been sentenced to one month's imprisonment and had immediately bitten the policeman who was leading him off to the cells; a further example, thought Mma Ramotswe, of the shortsightedness of violent people. This second bite had cost him another three months in prison.

Mma Ramotswe looked down at the child.

"Mataila?"

The boy did nothing.

"Mataila?" She stretched out towards the boy, ready to withdraw her hand sharply if necessary.

The boy growled. There was no other word for it, she thought. It was a growl, a low, guttural sound that seemed to come from his chest.

"Did you hear that?" asked Mma Potokwane. "Isn't that extraordinary? And if you're wondering why he's naked, it's because he ripped up the clothes we gave him. He ripped them with his teeth and threw them down on the ground. We gave him two pairs of shorts, and he did the same thing to both of them."

Mma Potokwane now moved forward.

"Now, Mataila," she said. "You get up and come outside. Mma Kerileng will take you out for some fresh air."

She reached down and took the boy, gingerly, by the arm. His head turned for a moment, and Mma Ramotswe thought that he was about to bite, but he did not and he meekly rose to his feet and allowed himself to be led out of the room.

Outside the house, Mma Kerileng took the boy's hand and walked with him towards a clump of trees at the edge of the compound. The boy walked with a rather unusual gait, observed Mma Ramotswe, between a run and a walk, as if he might suddenly bound off.

"So that's our Mataila," said Mma Potokwane, as they watched the housemother walk off with her charge. "What do you think of that?"

Mma Ramotswe grimaced. "It is very strange. Something terrible must have happened to that child."

"No doubt," said Mma Potokwane. "I said that to the doctor who looked at him. He said maybe yes, maybe no. He said that there are some children who are just like that. They keep to themselves and they never learn to talk."

Mma Ramotswe watched as Mma Kerileng briefly let go of the child's hand.

"We have to watch him all the time," said Mma Potokwane. "If we leave him, he runs off into the bush and hides. He went missing for four hours last week. They eventually found him over by the sewerage ponds. He does not seem to know that a naked child running as fast as he can is likely to attract attention."

Mma Potokwane and Mma Ramotswe began to walk back together towards the office. Mma Ramotswe felt depressed. She wondered how one would make a start with a child like

that. It was easy to respond to the needs of appealing orphans—
of children such as the two who had come to live in Zebra
Drive—but there were so many other children, children who
had been damaged in some way or other, and who would need
patience and understanding. She contemplated her life, with
its lists and its demands, and she wondered how she would
ever find the time to be the mother of a child like that. Surely
Mma Potokwane could not be planning that she and Mr J.L.B.
Matekoni should take this child too? She knew that the
matron had a reputation for determination and for not taking
no for an answer—which of course made her a powerful advo-
cate for her orphans—but she could not imagine that she
would try to impose in this way, for in any view it would be a
great imposition to foist this child off on her.

"I am a busy woman," she started to say, as they neared the
office. "I'm sorry, but I cannot take . . ."

A group of orphans walked past them and greeted the
matron politely. They had with them a small, undernourished
puppy, which one of them was cradling in her arms; one
orphan helps another, thought Mma Ramotswe.

"Be careful with that dog," warned Mma Potokwane. "I am
always telling you that you should not pick up these strays.
Will you not listen . . ."

She turned to Mma Ramotswe. "But Mma Ramotswe! I
hope that you did not think . . . Of course I did not expect you
to take that boy! We can barely manage him here, with all our
resources."

"I was worried," said Mma Ramotswe. "I am always prepared to help, but there is a limit to what I can do."

Mma Potokwane laughed, and touched her guest reassuringly on the forearm. "Of course you are. You are already help-

ing us by taking those two orphans. No, I wanted only to ask your advice. I know that you have a very good reputation for finding missing people. Could you tell us—just tell us—how we might find out about this boy? If we could somehow discover something about his past, about where he came from, we might be able to get through to him."

Mma Ramotswe shook her head. "It will be too difficult. You would have to talk to people near where he was found. You would have to ask a lot of questions, and I think that people will not want to talk. If they did, they would have said something."

"You are right about that," said Mma Potokwane sadly. "The police asked a lot of questions up there, outside Maun. They asked in all the local villages, and nobody knew of a child like that. They showed his photograph and people just said no. They knew nothing of him."

Mma Ramotswe was not surprised. If anybody wanted the child, then somebody would have said something. The fact that there was a silence probably meant that the child had been deliberately abandoned. And there was always the possibility of some sort of witchcraft with a child like that. If a local spirit doctor had said that the child was possessed, or was a tokolosi, then nothing could be done for him: he was probably fortunate to be alive. Such children often met a quite different fate.

They were now standing beside the tiny white van. The tree had shed a frond on the vehicle's top, and Mma Ramotswe picked it up. They were so delicate, the leaves of this tree; with their hundreds of tiny leaves attached to the central stem, like the intricate tracing of a spider's web. Behind them was the sound of children's voices; a song which Mma Ramotswe remembered from her own childhood, and which made her smile.

> *The cattle come home, one, two, three,*
> *The cattle come home, the big one, the small one, the one*
>   *with one horn,*
> *I live with the cattle, one, two, three,*
> *Oh mother, look out for me.*

She looked into Mma Potokwane's face; a face which said, in every line and in every expression: I am the matron of an orphan farm.

"They are still singing that song," said Mma Ramotswe.

Mma Potokwane smiled. "I sing it too. We never forget the songs of our childhood, do we?"

"Tell me," said Mma Ramotswe. "What did they say about that boy? Did the people who found him say anything?"

Mma Potokwane thought for a moment. "They told the police that they found him in the dark. They said that he was very difficult to control. And they said that he had a strange smell about him."

"What strange smell?"

Mma Potokwane made a dismissive gesture with a hand. "One of the men said that he smelled of lion. The policeman remembered it because it was such a strange thing to say. He wrote it down in his report, which came to us eventually when the tribal administration people up there sent the boy down to us."

"Like lion?" asked Mma Ramotswe.

"Yes," said Mma Potokwane. "Ridiculous."

Mma Ramotswe said nothing for a moment. She climbed

into the tiny white van and thanked Mma Potokwane for her hospitality.

"I shall think about this boy," she said. "Maybe I shall be able to come up with an idea."

They waved to one another as Mma Ramotswe drove down the dusty road, through the orphanage gates, with their large ironwork sign proclaiming: Children live here.

She drove slowly, as there were donkeys and cattle on the road, and the herd boys who looked after them. Some of the herd boys were very young, no more than six or seven, like that poor, silent boy in his little room.

What if a young herd boy got lost, thought Mma Ramotswe. What if he got lost in the bush, far from the cattle post? Would he die? Or might something else happen to him?

CHAPTER TEN

THE CLERK'S TALE

MMA RAMOTSWE realised that something would have to be done about the No. 1 Ladies' Detective Agency. It did not take long to move the contents of the old office to the new quarters at the back of Tlokweng Road Speedy Motors; there was not much more than one filing cabinet and its contents, a few metal trays in which papers awaiting filing could be placed, the old teapot and its two chipped mugs, and of course the old typewriter—which had been given to her by Mr J.L.B. Matekoni and was now going home. These were manhandled into the back of the tiny white van by the two apprentices, after only the most token complaint that this was not part of their job. It would appear that they would do anything requested of them by Mma Makutsi, who had only to whistle from the office to find one of them running in to find out what she needed.

This compliance was a surprise to Mma Ramotswe, and she
wondered what it was that Mma Makutsi had over these two
young men. Mma Makutsi was not beautiful in a conventional
sense. Her skin was too dark for modern tastes, thought Mma
Ramotswe, and the lightening cream that she used had left
patches. Then there was her hair, which was often braided,
but braided in a very strange way. And then there were her
glasses, of course, with their large lenses that would have
served the needs of at least two people, in Mma Ramotswe's
view. Yet here was this person who would never have got into
round one of a beauty competition, commanding the slavish
attentions of these two notoriously difficult young men. It was
very puzzling.

It could be, of course, that there was something more than
mere physical appearance behind this. Mma Makutsi may not
have been a great beauty, but she certainly had a powerful personality, and perhaps these boys recognised that. Beauty
queens were often devoid of character, and men must surely
tire of that after a while. Those dreadful competitions which
they held—the *Miss Lovers Special Time Competition* or the
Miss Cattle Industry Competition—brought to the fore the
most vacuous of girls. These vacuous girls then attempted to
pronounce on all sorts of issues, and to Mma Ramotswe's utter
incomprehension, they were often listened to.

She knew that these young men followed the beauty competitions, for she had heard them talking about them. But now
their main concern seemed to be to impress Mma Makutsi,
and to flatter her. One had even attempted to kiss her, and had
been pushed away with amused indignation.

"Since when does a mechanic kiss the manager?" asked

Mma Makutsi. "Get back to work before I beat your useless bottom with a big stick."

The apprentices had made short work of the move, loading the entire contents within half an hour. Then, with the two young men travelling in the back to hold the filing cabinet in place, the No. 1 Ladies' Detective Agency, complete with painted sign, made its way to its new premises. It was a sad moment, and both Mma Ramotswe and Mma Makutsi were close to tears as they locked the front door for the last time.

"It is just a move, Mma," said Mma Makutsi, in an attempt to comfort her employer. "It is not as if we are going out of business."

"I know," said Mma Ramotswe, looking, for the last time perhaps, at the view from the front of the building, over the rooftops of the town and the tops of the thorn trees. "I have been very happy here."

We are still in business. Yes, but only just. Over the last few days, with all the turmoil and the lists, Mma Ramotswe had devoted very little time to the affairs of the agency. In fact, she had devoted no time at all, when she came to think about it. There was only one outstanding case, and nothing else had come in, although it undoubtedly would. She would be able to charge the Government Man a proper fee for her time, but that would depend on a successful outcome. She could send him an account even if she found nothing, but she always felt embarrassed asking for payment when she was unable to help the client. Perhaps she would just have to steel herself to do this in the Government Man's case, as he was a wealthy man and could well afford to pay. It must be very easy, she thought, to have a detective agency that catered only to the needs of rich people, the No. 1 Rich Person's Detective Agency, as the charging of fees would always be painless. But that was not what her business was, and she was not sure that she would be happy with that. Mma Ramotswe liked to help everybody, no matter what their station was in life. She had often been out of pocket on a case, simply because she could not refuse to help a person in need. This is what I am called to do, she said to herself. I must help whomsoever asks for my help. That is my duty: to help other people with the problems in their lives. Not that you could do everything. Africa was full of people in need of help and there had to be a limit. You simply could not help everybody; but you could at least help those who came into your life. That principle allowed you to deal with the suffering you saw. That was your suffering. Other people would have to deal with the suffering that they, in their turn, came across.

BUT WHAT to do, here and now, with the problems of the business? Mma Ramotswe decided that she would have to revise her list and put the Government Man's case at the top. This meant that she should start making enquiries immediately, and where better to start than with the suspect wife's father? There were several reasons for this, the most important being that if there really were a plot to dispose of the Government Man's brother, then this would probably not be the wife's idea, but would have been dreamed up by the father. Mma Ramotswe was convinced that people who got up to really serious mischief very rarely acted entirely on their own initiative. There was usually somebody else involved, somebody who would stand to benefit in some way, or somebody close to the perpetrator of the deed who was brought in for moral support. In this case, the most likely person would be the wife's father. If, as the Government Man had implied, this man was aware of the social betterment which the marriage entailed, and made much of it, then he was likely to be socially ambitious himself. And in that case, it would be highly convenient for him to have the son-in-law out of the way, so that he could, through his daughter, lay hands on a substantial part of the family assets. Indeed, the more Mma Ramotswe thought about it, the more likely it seemed that the poisoning attempt was the clerk's idea.

She could imagine his thoughts, as he sat at his small government desk and reflected on the power and authority which he saw all about him and of which he had only such a small part. How galling it must be for a man of this stripe to see the Government Man drive past him in his official car; the Government Man who was, in fact, the brother-in-law of his own daughter. How difficult it must be for him not to have the recognition that he undoubtedly felt that he would get if only more people knew that he was connected in such a way with such a family. If the money and the cattle came to him—or to his daughter, which amounted to the same thing—then he would be able to give up his demeaning post in the civil service and pursue the life of a rich farmer; he, who now had no cattle, would have cattle aplenty. He, who now had to scrimp and save in order to afford a trip up to Francistown each year, would be able to eat meat every day and drink Lion Lager with his friends on Friday evenings, generously buying rounds for all. And all that stood between him and all this was one small, beating heart. If that heart could be silenced, then his entire life would be transformed.

The Government Man had given Mma Ramotswe the wife's

family name and had told her that the father liked to spend his lunch hour sitting under a tree outside the Ministry. This gave her all the information she needed to find him: his name and his tree.

"I am going to begin this new case," she said to Mma Makutsi, as the two of them sat in their new office. "You are busy with the garage. I shall get back to being a detective."

"Good," said Mma Makutsi. "It is a demanding business running a garage. I shall continue to be very busy."

"I am glad to see that the apprentices are working so hard," said Mma Ramotswe. "You have them eating out of your hand."

Mma Makutsi smiled conspiratorially. "They are very silly young men," she said. "But we ladies are used to dealing with silly young men."

"So I see," said Mma Ramotswe. "You must have had many boyfriends, Mma. These boys seem to like you."

Mma Makutsi shook her head. "I have had almost no boyfriends. I cannot understand why these boys are like this to me when there are all these pretty girls in Gaborone."

"You underestimate yourself, Mma," said Mma Ramotswe. "You are obviously an attractive lady to men."

"Do you think so?" asked Mma Makutsi, beaming with pleasure.

"Yes," said Mma Ramotswe. "Some ladies become more attractive to men the older they get. I have seen this happen. Then, while all the young girls, the beauty queens, get less and less attractive as they get older, these other ladies become more and more so. It is a very interesting thing."

Mma Makutsi looked thoughtful. She adjusted her glasses, and Mma Ramotswe noticed her glancing surreptitiously at her reflection in the window pane. She was not sure if what she had said was true, but even if it were not, she would be glad that she had said it if it had the effect of boosting Mma Makutsi's confidence. It would do her no harm at all to be admired by these two feckless boys, as long as she did not get involved with them, and it was clear to Mma Ramotswe that there was little chance of that—at least for the time being.

She left Mma Makutsi in the office and drove off in the tiny white van. It was now half past twelve; the drive would take ten minutes, which would give her time to find a parking place and to make her way to the Ministry and to start looking for the wife's father, Mr Kgosi Sipoleli, ministry clerk and, if her intuitions were correct, would-be murderer.

She parked the tiny white van near the Catholic church, as the town was busy and there were no places to be had any closer. She would have a walk—a brief one—and she did not mind this, as she was bound to see people whom she knew and she had a few minutes in hand for a chat on her way.

She was not disappointed. Barely had she turned the corner from her parking place than she ran into Mma Gloria Bopedi, mother of Chemba Bopedi, who had been at school with Mma Ramotswe in Mochudi. Chemba had married Pilot Matanyani, who had recently become headmaster of a school at Selibi-Pikwe. She had seven children, the oldest of whom had recently become champion under-fifteen sprinter of Botswana.

"How is your very fast grandson, Mma?" asked Mma Ramotswe.

The elderly woman beamed. She had few teeth left, noticed Mma Ramotswe, who thought that it would be better for her to have the remaining ones out and be fitted with false teeth.

"Oh! He is fast, that one," said Mma Bopedi. "But he is a naughty boy too. He learned to run fast so that he could get out of trouble. That is how he came to be so fast."

"Well," said Mma Ramotswe, "something good has come out of it. Maybe he will be in the Olympics one day, running for Botswana. That will show the world that the fast runners are not all in Kenya."

Again she found herself reflecting on the fact that what she said was not true. The truth of the matter was that the best runners did all come from Kenya, where the people were very tall and had long legs, very suitably designed for running. The problem with the Batswana was that they were not very tall. Their men tended to be stocky, which was fine for looking after cattle, but which did not lend itself to athleticism. Indeed, most Southern Africans were not very good runners, although the Zulus and the Swazis sometimes produced somebody who made a mark on the track, such as that great Swazi runner, Richard "Concorde" Mavuso.

Of course, the Boers were quite good at sports. They produced these very large men with great thighs and thick necks, like Brahman cattle. They played rugby and seemed to do very well at it, although they were not very bright. She preferred a Motswana man, who may not be as big as one of those rugby players, nor as swift as one of those Kenyan runners, but at least he would be reliable and astute.

"Don't you think so, Mma?" she said to Mma Bopedi.

"Don't I think what, Mma?" asked Mma Bopedi.

Mma Ramotswe realised that she had included the other woman in her reverie, and apologised.

"I was just thinking about our men," she said.

Mma Bopedi raised an eyebrow. "Oh, really, Mma? Well, to tell you the truth, I also think about our men from time to time. Not very often, but sometimes. You know how it is."

Mma Ramotswe bade Mma Bopedi farewell and continued with her journey. Now, outside the optician's shop, she came across Mr Motheti Pilai, standing quite still, looking up at the sky.

"Dumela, Rra," she said politely. "Are you well?"

Mr Pilai looked down. "Mma Ramotswe," he said. "Please let me look at you. I have just been given these new spectacles, and I can see the world clearly for the first time in years. Ow! It is a wonderful thing. I had forgotten what it was like to see clearly. And there you are, Mma. You are looking very beautiful, very fat."

"Thank you, Rra."

He moved the spectacles to the end of his nose. "My wife was always telling me that I needed new glasses, but I was always afraid to come here. I do not like that machine that he has which shines light into your eyes. And I do not like that machine which puffs air into your eyeball. So I put it off and put it off. I was very foolish."

"It is never a good thing to put something off," said Mma Ramotswe, thinking of how she had put off the Government Man's case.

"Oh, I know that," said Mr Pilai. "But the problem is that even if you know that is the best thing to do, you often don't do it."

"That is very puzzling," said Mma Ramotswe. "But it is true. It's as if there were two people inside you. One says: do this. Another says: do that. But both these voices are inside the same person."

Mr Pilai stared at Mma Ramotswe. "It is very hot today," he said.

She agreed with him, and they both went about their business. She would stop no more, she resolved; it was now almost one o'clock and she wanted to have enough time to locate Mr Sipoleli and to have the conversation with him that would start her enquiry.

THE TREE was easily identified. It stood a short distance from the main entrance to the Ministry, a large acacia tree with a wide canopy that provided a wide circle of shade on the dusty ground below. Immediately beside the trunk were several strategically placed stones—comfortable seats for anyone who might wish to sit under the tree and watch the daily business of Gaborone unfold before him. Now, at five minutes to one, the stones were unoccupied.

Mma Ramotswe chose the largest of the stones and settled herself upon it. She had brought with her a large flask of tea, two aluminum mugs, and four corned beef sandwiches made with thickly cut slices of bread. She took out one of the mugs and filled it with bush tea. Then she leaned back against the trunk of the tree and waited. It was pleasant to be seated there in the shade, with a mug of tea, watching the passing traffic. Nobody paid the slightest attention to her, as it was an entirely normal thing to see: a well-built woman under a tree.

Shortly after ten past one, when Mma Ramotswe had finished her tea and was on the point of dozing off in her comfortable place, a figure emerged from the front of the Ministry and walked over towards the tree. As he drew near, Mma

Ramotswe jolted herself to full wakefulness. She was on duty now, and she must make the most of the opportunity to talk to Mr Sipoleli, if that, as she expected, was the person now approaching her.

The man was wearing a pair of neatly pressed blue trousers, a short-sleeved white shirt, and a dark brown tie. It was exactly what one would expect a junior civil servant, in the clerical grade, to wear. And as if to confirm the diagnosis, there was a row of pens tucked neatly into his shirt pocket. This was clearly the uniform of the junior clerk, even if it was being worn by a man in his late forties. This, then, was a clerk who was stuck where he was and was not going any further.

The man approached the tree cautiously. Staring at Mma Ramotswe, it seemed as if he wanted to say something but could not quite bring himself to speak.

Mma Ramotswe smiled at him. "Good afternoon, Rra," she said. "It is hot today, is it not? That is why I am under this tree. It is clearly a good place to sit in the heat."

The man nodded. "Yes," he said. "I normally sit here."

Mma Ramotswe affected surprise. "Oh? I hope that I am not sitting on your rock, Rra. I found it here and there was nobody sitting on it."

He made an impatient gesture with his hands. "My rock? Yes it is, as a matter of fact. That is my rock. But this is a public place and anybody can sit on it, I suppose."

Mma Ramotswe rose to her feet. "But Rra, you must have this rock. I shall sit on that one over on that side."

"No, Mma," he said hurriedly, his tone changing. "I do not want to inconvenience you. I can sit on that rock."

"No. You sit on this rock here. It is your rock. I would not have sat on it if I had thought that it was another person's rock. I can sit on this rock, which is a good rock too. You sit on that rock."

"No," he said firmly. "You go back where you were, Mma. I can sit on that rock any day. You can't. I shall sit on this rock."

Mma Ramotswe, with a show of reluctance, returned to her original rock, while Mr Sipoleli settled himself down.

"I am drinking tea, Rra," she said. "But I have enough for you. I would like you to have some, since I am sitting on your rock."

Mr Sipoleli smiled. "You are very kind, Mma. I love to drink tea. I drink a lot of tea in my office. I am a civil servant, you see."

"Oh?" said Mma Ramotswe. "That is a good job. You must be important."

Mr Sipoleli laughed. "No," he said. "I am not at all important. I am a junior clerk. But I am lucky to be that. There are people with degrees being recruited into my level of job. I have my Cambridge Certificate, that is all. I feel that I have done well enough."

Mma Ramotswe listened to this as she poured his tea. She was surprised by what she had heard; she had expected a rather different sort of person, a minor official puffed up with his importance and eager for greater status. Here, by contrast, was a man who seemed to be quite content with what he was and where he had got himself.

"Could you not be promoted, Rra? Would it not be possible to go further up?"

Mr Sipoleli considered her question carefully. "I suppose it would," he said after a few moments' thought. "The problem is that I would have to spend a lot of time getting on the right side of more senior people. Then I would have to say the right things and write bad reports on my juniors. That is not what I would like to do. I am not an ambitious man. I am happy where I am, really I am."

Mma Ramotswe's hand faltered in the act of passing him his tea. This was not at all what she had expected, and suddenly she remembered Clovis Andersen's words of advice. Never make any prior assumptions, he had written. Never decide in advance what's what or who's who. This may set you off on the wrong track altogether.

She decided to offer him a sandwich, which she pulled out of her plastic bag. He was pleased, but chose the smallest of the sandwiches; another indication, she thought, of a modest personality. The Mr Sipoleli of her imagining would have taken the largest sandwich without hesitation.

"Do you have family in Gaborone, Rra?" she asked innocently.

Mr Sipoleli finished his mouthful of corned beef before answering. "I have three daughters," he said. "Two are nurses, one at the Princess Marina and the other out at Molepolole. Then there is my firstborn, who did very well at school and went to the university. We are very proud of her."

"She lives in Gaborone?" asked Mma Ramotswe, passing him another sandwich.

"No," he replied. "She is living somewhere else. She married a young man she met while she was studying. They live out that way. Over there."

"And this son-in-law of yours," said Mma Ramotswe. "What about him? Is he good to her?"

"Yes," said Mr Sipoleli. "He is a very good man. They are very happy, and I hope that they have many children. I am looking forward to being a grandfather."

Mma Ramotswe thought for a moment. Then she said: "The best thing about seeing one's children married must be the thought that they will be able to look after you when you are old."

Mr Sipoleli smiled. "Well, that is probably true. But in my case, my wife and I have different plans. We intend to go back to Mahalapye. I have some cattle there—just a few—and some lands. We will be happy up there. That is all we want."

Mma Ramotswe was silent. This patently good man was obviously telling the truth. Her suspicion that he could be behind a plot to kill his son-in-law was an absurd conclusion to have reached, and she felt thoroughly ashamed of herself. To hide her confusion, she offered him another cup of tea, which he accepted gratefully. Then, after fifteen minutes of further conversation about matters of the day, she stood up, dusted down her skirt, and thanked him for sharing his lunch hour with her. She had found out what she wanted to know, at least about him. But the meeting with the father also threw some doubt on her surmises as to the daughter. If the daughter was at all like the father, then she could not possibly be a poisoner. This good unassuming man was unlikely to have raised a daughter who would do a thing like that. Or was he? It was always possible for bad children to spring from the loins of good parents; it did not require much experience of life to realise that. Yet, at the same time, it tended to be unlikely, and this meant that the next stage of the investigation would require a considerably more open mind than had characterised the initial stage.

I have learned a lesson, Mma Ramotswe told herself as she walked back to the tiny white van. She was deep in thought, and she barely noticed Mr Pilai, still standing outside the optician's shop, gazing at the branches of the tree above his head.

"I have been thinking about what you said to me, Mma," he remarked, as she walked past. "It was a very thought-provoking remark."

"Yes," said Mma Ramotswe, slightly taken aback. "And I am afraid I do not know what the answer is. I simply do not."

Mr Pilai shook his head. "Then we shall have to think about it some more," he said.

"Yes," said Mma Ramotswe. "We shall."

CHAPTER ELEVEN

MMA POTOKWANE OBLIGES

THE GOVERNMENT Man had given Mma Ramotswe a telephone number which she could use at any time and which would circumvent his secretaries and assistants. That afternoon she tried the number for the first time, and got straight through to her client. He sounded pleased to hear from her, and expressed his pleasure that the investigation had begun.

"I would like to go down to the house next week," said Mma Ramotswe. "Have you contacted your father?"

"I have done that," said the Government Man. "I have told him that you will be coming to stay for a rest. I told him that you have found many votes for me amongst the women and that I must repay you. You will be well looked after."

Details were agreed, and Mma Ramotswe was given directions to the farm, which lay off the Francistown Road, to the north of Pilane.

"I am sure that you will find evidence of wickedness," said the Government Man. "Then we can save my poor brother."

Mma Ramotswe was noncommittal. "We shall see. I can't guarantee anything. I shall have to see."

"Of course, Mma," the Government Man said hurriedly. "But I have complete confidence in your ability to find out what is happening. I know that you will be able to find evidence against that wicked woman. Let's just hope that you are in time."

After the telephone call, Mma Ramotswe sat at her desk and stared at the wall. She had just taken a whole week out of her diary, and that meant that all the other tasks on her list were consigned to an uncertain future. At least she need not worry about the garage for the time being, nor indeed need she worry about dealing with enquiries at the agency. Mma Makutsi could do all that and if, as was increasingly often the case these days, she was under a car at the time, then the apprentices had been trained to answer the telephone on her behalf.

But what about Mr J.L.B. Matekoni? That was the one really difficult issue which remained untouched, and she realised that she would have to do something quickly. She had finished reading the book on depression and she now felt more confident in dealing with its puzzling symptoms. But there was always a danger with that illness that the sufferer might do something rash—the book had been quite explicit about that—and she dreaded the thought of Mr J.L.B. Matekoni being driven to such extremes by his feelings of lowness and self-disesteem. She would have to get him to Dr Moffat somehow, so that treatment could begin. But when she had told him that he was to see a doctor, he had flatly refused. If she tried again, she would probably get the same response.

She wondered whether there was any way of getting him to take the pills by trickery. She did not like the idea of using underhand methods with Mr J.L.B. Matekoni, but when a person's reason was disturbed, then she thought that any means were justified in getting them better. It was as if a person had been kidnapped by some evil being and held ransom. You would not hesitate, she felt, to resort to trickery to defeat the evil being. In her view, that was perfectly in line with the old Botswana morality, or indeed with any other sort of morality.

She had wondered whether she could conceal the tablets in his food. This might have been possible if she had been attending to his every meal, but she was not. He had stopped coming round to her house for his evening meal, and it would look very strange if she suddenly arrived at his house to cater for him. Anyway, she suspected that he was not eating very much in his state of depression—the book had warned about this—as he appeared to be losing weight quite markedly. It would be impossible, then, to administer the drugs to him in this way, even if she decided that this was the proper thing to do.

She sighed. It was unlike her to sit and stare at a wall, and for a moment the thought crossed her mind that she, too, might be becoming depressed. But the thought passed quickly; it would be out of the question for Mma Ramotswe to become ill. Everything depended on her: the garage, the agency, the children, Mr J.L.B Matekoni, Mma Makutsi—not to mention Mma Makutsi's people up in Bobonong. She simply could not afford the time to be ill. So she rose to her feet, straightened her dress, and made her way to the telephone on the other side of the room. She took out the small book in which she noted down telephone numbers. Potokwane, Silvia. Matron. Orphan Farm.

MMA POTOKWANE was interviewing a prospective foster parent when Mma Ramotswe arrived. Sitting in the waiting room, Mma Ramotswe watched a small, pale gecko stalk a fly on the ceiling above her head. Both the gecko and the fly were upside down; the gecko relying on minute suction pads on each of its toes, the fly on its spurs. The gecko suddenly darted forward, but was too slow for the fly, which launched itself into a victory roll before settling on the windowsill.

Mma Ramotswe turned to the magazines that littered the table. There was a Government brochure with a picture of senior officials. She looked at the faces—she knew many of these people, and in one or two cases knew rather more about them than would be published in Government brochures. And there was the face of her Government Man, smiling confidently into the camera, while all the time, as she knew, he was eaten up by anxiety for his younger brother and imagining plots against his life. "Mma Ramotswe?"

Mma Potokwane had ushered the foster parent out and now stood looking down on Mma Ramotswe. "I'm sorry to have kept you waiting, Mma, but I think I have found a home for a very difficult child. I had to make sure that the woman was the right sort of person."

They went into the matron's room, where a crumb-littered plate bore witness to the last serving of fruitcake.

"You have come about the boy?" asked Mma Potokwane. "You must have had an idea."

Mma Ramotswe shook her head. "Sorry, Mma. I have not had time to think about that boy. I have been very busy with other things."

Mma Potokwane smiled. "You are always a busy person."

"I've come to ask you a favour," said Mma Ramotswe.

"Ah!" Mma Potokwane was beaming with pleasure. "Usually it is I who do that. Now it is different, and I am pleased."

"Mr J.L.B. Matekoni is ill," explained Mma Ramotswe. "I think that he has an illness called depression."

"Ow!" interrupted Mma Potokwane. "I know all about that. Remember that I used to be a nurse. I spent a year working at the mental hospital at Lobatse. I have seen what that illness can do. But at least it can be treated these days. You can get better from depression."

"I have read that," said Mma Ramotswe. "But you have to take the drugs. Mr J.L.B. Matekoni won't even see a doctor. He says he's not ill."

"That's nonsense," said Mma Potokwane. "He should go to the doctor immediately. You should tell him."

"I tried," said Mma Ramotswe. "He said there was nothing wrong with him. I need to get somebody to take him to the doctor. Somebody . . ."

"Somebody like me?" cut in Mma Potokwane.

"Yes," said Mma Ramotswe. "He has always done what you have asked him to do. He wouldn't dare refuse you."

"But he'll need to take the drugs," said Mma Potokwane. "I wouldn't be there to stand over him."

"Well," mused Mma Ramotswe, "if you brought him here, you could nurse him. You could make sure that he took the drugs and became better."

"You mean that I should bring him to the orphan farm?"

"Yes," said Mma Ramotswe. "Bring him here until he's better."

Mma Potokwane tapped her desk. "And if he says that he does not want to come?"

"He would not dare to contradict you, Mma," said Mma Ramotswe. "He would be too scared."

"Oh," said Mma Potokwane. "Am I like that, then?"

"A little bit," said Mma Ramotswe, gently. "But only to men. Men respect a matron."

Mma Potokwane thought for a moment. Then she spoke. "Mr J.L.B. Matekoni has been a good friend to the orphan farm. He has done a great deal for us. I will do this thing for you, Mma. When shall I go to see him?"

"Today," said Mma Ramotswe. "Take him to Dr Moffat. Then bring him right back here."

"Very well," said Mma Potokwane, warming to her task. "I shall go and find out what all this nonsense is about. Not wanting to go to the doctor? What nonsense! I shall sort all this out for you, Mma. You just trust me."

Mma Potokwane showed Mma Ramotswe to her car.

"You won't forget the boy, will you, Mma?" she asked. "You will remember to think about him?"

"Don't worry, Mma," she replied. "You have taken a big weight off my mind. Now I shall try to take one off yours."

DR MOFFAT saw Mr J.L.B. Matekoni in the study at the end of his verandah, while Mma Potokwane drank a cup of tea with Mrs Moffat in the kitchen. The doctor's wife, who was a librarian, knew a great deal, and Mma Potokwane had occasionally consulted her for pieces of information. It was evening, and in the doctor's study insects which had penetrated the fly screens were drunkenly circling the bulb of the desk lamp, throwing themselves against the shade and then, singed by the heat, fluttering wing-injured away. On the desk were a stethoscope and a sphygmomanometer, with its rubber bulb hanging over the edge; on the wall, an old engraving of Kuruman Mission in the mid-nineteenth century.

"I have not seen you for some time, Rra," Dr Moffat said. "My car has been behaving itself well."

Mr J.L.B. Matekoni started to smile, but the effort seemed to defeat him. "I have not . . ." He tailed off. Dr Moffat waited, but nothing more came.

"You have not been feeling very well?"

Mr J.L.B. Matekoni nodded. "I am very tired. I cannot sleep."

"That is very hard. If we do not sleep, then we feel bad." He paused. "Are you troubled by anything in particular? Are there things that worry you?"

Mr J.L.B. Matekoni thought. His jaws worked, as if he was trying to articulate impossible words, and then he replied. "I am worried that bad things I did a long time ago will come back. Then I shall be in disgrace. They will all throw stones at me. It will be the end."

"And these bad things? What are they? You know that you can speak to me about them and I shall not tell anybody."

"They are bad things I did a long time ago. They are very bad things. I cannot speak to anybody about them, not even you."

"And is that all you want to tell me about them?"

"Yes."

Dr Moffat watched Mr J.L.B. Matekoni. He noticed the collar, fastened at the wrong button; he saw the shoes, with their broken laces; he saw the eyes, almost lachrymose in their anguish, and he knew.

"I am going to give you some medicine that will help you to get well," he said. "Mma Potokwane out there says that she will look after you while you are getting better."

Mr J.L.B. Matekoni nodded dumbly.

"And you will promise me that you will take this medicine," Dr Moffat went on. "Will you give me your word that you will do that?"

Mr J.L.B. Matekoni's gaze, firmly fixed on the floor, did not move up. "My word is worth nothing," he said quietly.

"That is the illness speaking," Dr Moffat said gently. "Your word is worth a great deal."

MMA POTOKWANE led him to her car and opened the passenger door for him. She looked at Dr Moffat and his wife, who were standing at the gate, and she waved to them. They waved back before returning to the house. Then she drove off, back to the orphan farm, passing Tlokweng Road Speedy Motors as she did so. The garage, deserted and forlorn in the darkness, got no glance from its proprietor, its begetter, as he rode past.

CHAPTER TWELVE

FAMILY BUSINESS

SHE LEFT in the cool of the morning, although the journey would take little more than an hour. Rose had prepared breakfast, and she ate it with the children, sitting on the verandah of her house on Zebra Drive. It was a quiet time, as little traffic passed along their road before seven, when people would start to go to work. There were a few people walking by—a tall man, with shabby trousers, eating a fire-charred corn cob, a woman carrying a baby, strapped to her back with its shawl, the baby's head nodding in sleep. One of her neighbour's yellow dogs, lean and undernourished, slunk by, occupied in some mysterious, but quite purposeful canine business. Mma Ramotswe tolerated dogs, but she had a strong distaste for the foul-smelling yellow creatures that lived next door. Their howling at night disturbed her—they would bark at shadows, at the moon, at gusts of wind—and she was sure that they deterred birds, which she did like, from coming to her garden. Every house, except hers, seemed to have its quota of dogs, and occasionally these dogs, overcoming the restrictions of imposed loyalties, would rise above their mutual animosity and walk down the street in a pack, chasing cars and frightening cyclists.

Mma Ramotswe poured bush tea for herself and Motholeli; Puso refused to get used to tea and had a glass of warm milk, into which Mma Ramotswe had stirred two generous spoons of sugar. He had a sweet tooth, possibly as a result of sweet foods which his sister had given him when she was caring for him in that yard up in Francistown. She would try to wean him onto healthier things, but that change would require patience. Rose had made them porridge, which stood in bowls, dark molasses trailed across its surface, and there were sections of paw-paw on a plate. It was a healthy breakfast for a child, thought Mma Ramotswe. What would these children have eaten had they stayed with their people, she wondered? Those people survived on next to nothing; roots dug up from the ground, grubs, the eggs of birds; yet they could hunt as nobody else could, and there would have been ostrich meat and duiker, which people in towns could rarely afford.

She remembered how, when travelling north, she had stopped beside the road to enjoy a flask of tea. The stopping place was a clearing at the side of the road, where a battered sign indicated that one was at that point crossing the Tropic of Capricorn. She had thought herself alone, and had been surprised when there emerged from behind a tree a Mosarwa, or Bushman, as they used to be called. He was wearing a small leather apron and carrying a skin bag of some sort; and had approached her, whistling away in that curious language they use. For a moment she had been frightened; although she was twice his size, these people carried arrows, and poisons, and were naturally very quick.

She had risen uncertainly to her feet, ready to abandon her flask and seek the safety of the tiny white van, but he had simply pointed to his mouth in supplication. Understanding, Mma Ramotswe had passed her cup to him, but he had indicated that it was food, not drink, that he wanted. All that Mma Ramotswe had with her was a couple of egg sandwiches, which he took greedily when offered and bit into hungrily. When he had finished, he licked his fingers and turned away. She watched him as he disappeared into the bush, merging with it as naturally as would a wild creature. She wondered what he had made of the egg sandwich and whether it tasted better to him, or worse, than the offerings of the Kalahari; the rodents and tubers.

The children had belonged to that world, but there could be no going back. That was a life to which one simply could not return, because what had been taken for granted then would seem impossibly hard, and the skills would have gone. Their place now was with Rose, and Mma Ramotswe, in the house on Zebra Drive.

"I am going to have to be away for four or five days," she explained to them over breakfast. "Rose will be looking after you. You will be all right."

"That is fine, Mma," said Motholeli. "I will help her."

Mma Ramotswe smiled at her encouragingly. She had brought up her little brother, and it was in her nature to help those who were younger than she was. She would be a fine mother eventually, she thought, but then she remembered. Could she be a mother in a wheelchair? It would probably be impossible to bear a child if one could not walk, Mma Ramotswe thought, and even if it were possible, she was not sure that any man would want to marry a woman in a wheelchair. It was very unfair, but you could not hide your face from the truth. It would always be more difficult for that girl, always. Of course there were some good men around who would not think that such a thing mattered, and who would want to marry the girl for the fine, plucky person that she was, but such men were very rare, and Mma Ramotswe had trouble in thinking of many. Or did she? There was Mr J.L.B. Matekoni, of course, who was a very good man—even if temporarily a little bit odd—and there was the Bishop, and there had been Sir Seretse Khama, statesman and Paramount Chief. Dr Merriweather, who ran the Scottish Hospital at Molepolole; he was a good man. And there were others, who were less well-known, now that she came to think of it. Mr Potolani, who helped very poor people and gave away most of the money he had made from his stores; and the man who fixed her roof and who repaired Rose's bicycle for nothing when he saw that it needed fixing. There were many good men, in fact, and perhaps there would be a good man in due course for Motholeli. It was possible.

That is, of course, if she wanted to find a husband. It was perfectly possible to be happy without a husband, or at least a bit happy. She herself was happy in her single state, but she thought, on balance, that it would be preferable to have a husband. She looked forward to the day when she would be able to make sure that Mr J.L.B. Matekoni was properly fed. She looked forward to the day when, if there was a noise in the night—as there often was these days—it would be Mr J.L.B.

Matekoni who would get up to investigate, rather than herself. We do need somebody else in this life, thought Mma Ramotswe; we need a person whom we can make our little god on this earth, as the old Kgatla saying had it. Whether it was a spouse, or a child, or a parent, or anybody else for that matter, there must be somebody who gives our lives purpose. She had always had the Daddy, the late Obed Ramotswe, miner, cattle farmer, and gentleman. It had given her pleasure to do things for him in his lifetime, and now it was a pleasure to do things for his memory. But the memory of a father went only so far.

Of course, there were those who said that none of this required marriage. They were right, to an extent. You did not have to be married to have somebody in your life, but then you would have no guarantee of permanence. Marriage itself did not offer that, but at least both people said that they wanted a lifelong union. Even if they proved to be wrong, at least they had tried. Mma Ramotswe had no time for those who decried marriage. In the old days, marriage had been a trap for women, because it gave men most of the rights and left women with the duties. Tribal marriage had been like that, although women acquired respect and status as they grew older, particularly if they were the mothers of sons. Mma Ramotswe did not support any of that, and thought that the modern notion of marriage, which was meant to be a union of equals, was a very different thing for a woman. Women had made a very bad mistake, she thought, in allowing themselves to be tricked into abandoning a belief in marriage. Some women thought that this would be a release from the tyranny of men, and in a way it had been that, but then it had also been a fine chance for men to behave selfishly. If you were a man and you were told that you could be with one woman until you got tired of her and then you could easily go on to a younger one, and all the time nobody would say that your behaviour was bad—because you were not committing adultery and so what wrong were you doing?—then that would suit you very well indeed.

"Who is doing all the suffering these days?" Mma Ramotswe had asked Mma Makutsi one day, as they sat in their office and waited for a client to appear. "Is it not women who have been left by their men going off with younger girls? Is that not what happens? A man gets to forty-five and decides that he has had enough. So he goes off with a younger woman."

"You are right, Mma," said Mma Makutsi. "It is the women of Botswana who are suffering, not the men. The men are very happy. I have seen it with my own eyes. I saw it at the Botswana Secretarial College."

Mma Ramotswe waited for more details.

"There were many glamorous girls at the College," went on Mma Makutsi. "These were the ones who did not do very well. They got fifty percent, or just over. They used to go out three or four nights a week, and many of them would meet older men, who would have more money and a nice car. These girls did not care that these men were married. They would go out with these men and dance in the bars. Then, what would happen, Mma?"

Mma Ramotswe shook her head. "I can imagine."

Mma Makutsi took off her glasses and polished them on her blouse. "They would tell these men to leave their wives. And the men would say that this was a good idea, and they would go off with these girls. And there would be many unhappy women who now would not be able to get another man because the men only go for young glamorous girls and they do not want an older woman. That is what I saw happening, Mma, and I could give you a list of names. A whole list."

"You do not need to," said Mma Ramotswe. "I have got a very long list of unhappy ladies. Very long."

"And how many unhappy men do you know?" went on Mma Makutsi. "How many men do you know who are sitting at home and thinking what to do now that their wife has gone off with a younger man? How many, Mma?"

"None," said Mma Ramotswe. "Not one."

"There you are," said Mma Makutsi. "Women have been tricked. They have tricked us, Mma. And we walked into their trap like cattle."

THE CHILDREN dispatched to school, Mma Ramotswe packed her small brown suitcase and began the drive out of town, out past the breweries and the new factories, the new low-cost suburb, with its rows of small, breeze-block houses, over the railway line which led to Francistown and Bulawayo, and onto the road that would lead her to the troubled place that was her destination. The first rains had come, and the parched brown veld was turning green, giving sweet grass to the cattle and the wandering herds of goats. The tiny white van had no radio—or no radio that worked—but Mma Ramotswe knew songs that she could sing, and she sang them, the window open, the crisp air of morning in her lungs, the birds flying up from the side of the road, plumage glistening; and above her, empty beyond emptiness, that sky that went on for miles and miles, the palest of blues.

She had felt uneasy about her mission, largely because what

she was about to do, she felt, was a breach of the fundamental principles of hospitality. You do not go into a house, as a guest, under false colours; and this was precisely what she was doing. Certainly, she was the guest of the father and mother, but even they did not know the true purpose of her visit. They were receiving her as one to whom their son owed a favour; whereas she was really a spy. She was a spy in a good cause, naturally, but that did not change the fact that her goal was to penetrate the family to find out a secret.

But now, in the tiny white van, she decided to put moral doubts aside. It was one of those situations where there were sound points to be made on both sides. She had decided that she would do it, because it was, on balance, better to act out a lie than to allow a life to be lost. Doubts should now be put away and the goal pursued wholeheartedly. There was no point in agonising over the decision you had made and wondering whether it was the right one. Besides, moral scruples would prevent the part from being played with conviction, and this might show. It would be like an actor questioning the part that he was playing mid-role.

She passed a man driving a mule cart, and waved. He took a hand from the rein and waved back, as did his passengers on the cart, two elderly women, a younger woman, and a child. They would be going out to the lands, thought Mma Ramotswe; a little bit late, perhaps, as they should have ploughed by the time that the first rains came, but they would sow their seed in time and they would have corn, and melons, and beans, perhaps by harvest time. There were several sacks on the cart, and these would contain the seed and the family's food, as well, while they were out on the lands. The women would make porridge and if the boys were lucky they might catch something for the pot—a guinea fowl would make a delicious stew for the whole family.

Mma Ramotswe saw the cart and the family retreating in the rearview mirror, as if they were going back into the past, getting smaller and smaller. One day people would no longer do this; they would no longer go out to the lands for the planting, and they would buy their food in stores, as people did in town. But what a loss for the country that would be; what friendship, and solidarity, and feeling for the land would be sacrificed if that were to happen. She had gone out to the lands as a girl, travelling with her aunts, and had stayed there while the boys had been sent to the cattle posts, where they would live for months in almost complete isolation, supervised by a few old men. She had loved the time at the lands, and had not been bored. They had swept the yards and woven grass; they had weeded the melon patches and told one another long stories about events that never happened, but could happen, perhaps, in another Botswana, somewhere else.

And then, when it had rained, they had cowered in the huts and heard the thunder roll above the land and smelled the lightning when it came too close, that acrid smell of burned air. When the rains had let up, they had gone outside and waited for the flying ants, which would emerge from their holes in the moistened ground and which could be picked up before they took flight, or plucked from the air as they began their journey, and eaten there and then, for the taste of butter.

She passed Pilane, and glanced down the road to Mochudi, to her right. This was a good place for her, and a bad one too. It was a good place, because it was the village of her girlhood; a bad place because right there, not far from the turnoff, was the place where a path crossed the railroad and her mother had died on that awful night, when the train had struck her. And although Precious Ramotswe was only a baby, that had been the shadow across her life; the mother whom she could not remember.

Now she was getting close to her destination. She had been given exact directions, and the gate was there, in the cattle fence, exactly where she had been told it would be. She drew off the road and got out to deal with the gate. Then, setting off on the dirt track that led west, she made her way to the small compound of houses that she could see about a mile or so distant, tucked amongst a cover of bush and overlooked by the tower of a metal windmill. This was a substantial farm, thought Mma Ramotswe, and she felt a momentary pang. Obed Ramotswe would have loved to have had a place like this, but although he had done well with his cattle, he had never been quite rich enough to have a large farm of this type. This would be six thousand acres, at least; maybe more.

The farm compound was dominated by a large, rambling house, topped by a red tin roof and surrounded on all sides by shady verandahs. This was the original farmhouse, and it had been encircled, over the years, by further buildings, two of which were houses themselves. The farmhouse was framed on either side by a luxuriant growth of purple-flowered bougainvillaea, and there were paw-paw trees behind it and to one side. An effort had been made to provide as much shade as possible—for not far to the west, perhaps just a bit farther than the eye could see, the land changed and the Kalahari began. But here, still, there was water, and the bush was good for cattle. Indeed, not too far to the east, the Limpopo began, not much of a river at that point, but capable of flowing in the rainy season.

There was a truck parked up against an outbuilding, and Mma Ramotswe left the tiny white van there. There was an enticing place under the shade of one of the largest trees, but it would have been rude of Mma Ramotswe to choose such a spot, which would be likely to be the parking place of a senior member of the family.

She left her suitcase on the passenger seat beside her and walked towards the gate that gave access to the front yard of the main house. She called out; it would have been discourteous to barge in without an invitation. There was no reply, and so she called out again. This time, a door opened and a middle-aged woman came out, drying her hands on her apron. She greeted Mma Ramotswe politely and invited her to come into the house.

"She is expecting you," she said. "I am the senior maid here. I look after the old woman. She has been waiting for you."

It was cool under the eaves of the verandah, and even cooler in the dim interior of the house. It took Mma Ramotswe's eyes a moment or two to get accustomed to the change in light, and at first there seemed to be more shadows that shapes; but then she saw the straight-backed chair on which the old woman was sitting, and the table beside her with the jug of water and the teapot.

They exchanged greetings, and Mma Ramotswe curtsied to the old woman. This pleased her hostess, who saw that here was a woman who understood the old ways, unlike those cheeky modern women from Gaborone who thought they knew everything and paid no attention to the elders. Ha! They thought they were clever; they thought they were this and that, doing men's jobs and behaving like female dogs when it came to men. Ha! But not here, out in the country, where the old ways still counted for something; and certainly not in this house.

"You are very kind to have me to stay here, Mma. Your son is a good man, too."

The old woman smiled. "No, Mma. That is all right. I am sorry to hear that you are having troubles in your life. These troubles that seem big, big in town are small troubles when you are out here. What matters out here? The rain. The grass for the cattle. None of the things that people are fretting over in town. They mean nothing when you are out here. You'll see."

"It is a nice place," said Mma Ramotswe. "It is very peaceful."

The old woman looked thoughtful. "Yes, it is peaceful. It has always been peaceful, and I would not want that to change." She poured out a glass of water and passed it to Mma Ramotswe.

"You should drink that, Mma. You must be very thirsty after your journey."

Mma Ramotswe took the glass, thanked her, and put it to her lips. As she did so, the old woman watched her carefully.

"Where are you from, Mma?" she said. "Have you always lived in Gaborone?"

Mma Ramotswe was not surprised by the question. This was a polite way of finding out where allegiances lay. There were eight main tribes in Botswana—and some smaller ones—and although most younger people did not think these things should be too important, for the older generation they counted a great deal. This woman, with her high status in tribal society, would be interested in these matters.

"I am from Mochudi," she said. "That is where I was born."

The old woman seemed visibly to relax. "Ah! So you are Kgatla, like us. Which ward did you live in?"

Mma Ramotswe explained her origins, and the old woman nodded. She knew that headman, yes, and she knew his cousin, who was married to her brother's wife's sister. Yes, she thought that she had met Obed Ramotswe a long time ago, and then, dredging into memory, she said, "Your mother is late, isn't she? She was the one who was killed by a train when you were a baby."

Mma Ramotswe was mildly surprised, but not astonished, that she should know this. There were people who made it their business to remember the affairs of the community, and this was obviously one. Today they called them oral historians, she believed; whereas in reality, they were old women who liked to remember the things that interested them most: marriages, deaths, children. Old men remembered cattle.

Their conversation went on, the old woman slowly and subtly extracting from Mma Ramotswe the full story of her life. She told her about Note Mokoti, and the old woman shook her head in sympathy, but said that there were many men like that and that women should look out for them.

"My family chose my husband for me," she said. "They started negotiations, although they would not have pressed the matter if I had said that I didn't like him. But they did the choosing and they knew what sort of man would be good for me. And they were right. My husband is a very fine husband, and I have given him three sons. There is one who is very interested in counting cattle, which is his hobby; he is a very clever man, in his way. Then there is the one you know, Mma, who is a very big man in the Government, and then there is the one who lives here. He is a very good farmer and has won prizes for his bulls. They are all fine men. I am proud."

"And have you been happy, Mma?" asked Mma Ramotswe. "Would you change your life at all if somebody came and said: here is some medicine to change your life. Would you do it?"

"Never," said the old woman. "Never. Never. God has given me everything a person could ask for. A good husband. Three strong sons. Strong legs that even today can take me walking five, six miles without any complaint. And you see here, look. All my teeth are still in my head. Seventy-six years and no teeth gone. My husband is the same. Our teeth will last until we are one hundred. Maybe longer."

"That is very lucky," said Mma Ramotswe. "Everything is very good for you."

"Almost everything," said the old woman.

Mma Ramotswe waited. Was she due to say something more? Perhaps she might reveal something she had seen her daughter-in-law do. Perhaps she had seen her preparing the poison, or had word of it somehow, but all she said was: "When the rains come, I find that my arms ache in the wet air. Here, and just here. For two months, three months, I have very sore arms that make it difficult to do any sewing. I have tried every medicine, but nothing works. So I think, if this is all that God has sent me to carry in this life, then I am still a very lucky woman."

THE MAID who had shown Mma Ramotswe in was summoned to take her to her room, which was at the back of the house. It was simply furnished, with a patchwork bedcover and a framed picture of Mochudi Hill on the wall. There was a table, with a crocheted white doily, and a small chest of drawers in which clothes could be stored.

"There is no curtain in this room," said the maid. "But nobody ever goes past this window and you will be private here, Mma."

She left Mma Ramotswe to unpack her clothes. There would be lunch at twelve o'clock, the maid explained, and until then she should entertain herself.

"There is nothing to do here," said the maid, adding, wistfully, "This is not Gaborone, you know."

The maid started to leave, but Mma Ramotswe prolonged the conversation. In her experience, the best way of getting somebody to talk was to get them to speak about themselves. This maid would have views, she felt; she was clearly not a stupid woman, and she spoke good, well-enunciated Setswana.

"Who else lives here, Mma?" she asked. "Are there other members of the family?"

"Yes," said the maid. "There are other people. There is their son and his wife. They have three sons, you see. One who has got a very small head and who counts cattle all day, all the time. He is always out at the cattle post and he never comes here. He is like a small boy, you see, and that is why he stays with the herdboys out there. They treat him like one of them, although he is a grown man. That is one. Then there is the one in Gaborone, where he is very important, and the one here. Those are the sons."

"And what do you think of those sons, Mma?"

It was a direct question and probably posed prematurely, which was risky; the woman could become suspicious at such prying. But she did not; instead she sat down on the bed.

"Let me tell you, Mma," she began. "That son who is out at

the cattle post is a very sad man. But you should hear the way that his mother talks about him. She says he is clever! Clever! Him! He is a little boy, Mma. It is not his fault, but that is what he is. The cattle post is the best place for him, but they should not say that he is clever. That is just a lie, Mma. It is like saying that there is rain in the dry season. There isn't."

"No," said Mma Ramotswe. "That is true."

The maid barely acknowledged her intervention before continuing. "And then that one in Gaborone; when he comes out here he makes trouble for everybody. He asks us all sorts of questions. He pokes his nose into everything. He even shouts at his father, would you believe it? But then the mother shouts at him and puts him in his place. He may be a big man in Gaborone, but here he is just the son and he should not shout at his elders."

Mma Ramotswe was delighted. This was exactly the sort of maid she liked to interview.

"You are right, Mma," she said. "There are too many people shouting at other people these days. Shout. Shout. You hear it all the time. But why do you think he shouts? Is it just to clear his voice?"

The maid laughed. "He has a big voice, that one! No, he shouts because he says that there is something wrong in this place. He says that things are not being done properly. And then he says . . ." She lowered her voice. "And then he says that the wife of his brother is a bad woman. He said that to the father, in so many words. I heard him. People think that maids don't hear, but we have ears the same as anybody. I heard him say that. He said wicked things about her."

Mma Ramotswe raised an eyebrow. "Wicked things?"

"He says that she is sleeping with other men. He says that

when they have their firstborn it will not be of this house. He says that their sons will belong to other men and different blood will get this farm. That's what he says."

Mma Ramotswe was silent. She looked out of her window. There was bougainvillaea directly outside, and its shadow was purple. Beyond it, the tops of the thorn trees, stretching out to the low hills on the horizon; a lonely land, at the beginning of the emptiness.

"And do you think that's true, Mma? Is there any truth in what he says about that woman?"

The maid crumpled up her features. "Truth, Mma? Truth? That man does not know what truth means. Of course it is not true. That woman is a good woman. She is the cousin of my mother's cousin. All the family, all of them, are Christians. They read the Bible. They follow the Lord. They do not sleep with other men. That is one thing which is true."

CHAPTER THIRTEEN

THE CHIEF JUSTICE OF BEAUTY

MA MAKUTSI, Acting Manager of Tlokweng Road Speedy Motors and assistant detective at the No. 1 Ladies' Detective Agency, went to work that day in some trepidation. Although she welcomed responsibility and had delighted in her two promotions, she had nonetheless always had Mma Ramotswe in the background, a presence to whom she could turn if she found herself out of her depth. Now, with Mma Ramotswe away, she realised that she was solely responsible for two businesses and two employees. Even if Mma Ramotswe was planning to be no more than four or five days on the farm, that was long enough for things to go wrong and, since Mma Ramotswe could not be contacted by telephone, Mma Makutsi would have to handle everything. As far as the garage was concerned, she knew that Mr J.L.B. Matekoni was now being looked after at the orphan farm and that she should not attempt to contact him until he was better. Rest and a complete break from the worries of work had been advised by the doctor, and Mma Potokwane, not accustomed to contradicting doctors, would be fiercely protective of her patient.

Mma Makutsi secretly hoped that the agency would get no clients until Mma Ramotswe came back. This was not because she did not want to work on a case—she certainly did—but she did not wish to be solely and completely responsible. But, of course, a client did come in, and, what was worse, it was a client with a problem that required immediate attention.

Mma Makutsi was sitting at Mr J.L.B. Matekoni's desk, preparing garage bills, when one of the apprentices put his head round the door.

"There is a very smart-looking man wanting to see you, Mma," he announced, wiping his greasy hands on his overalls. "I have opened the agency door and told him to wait."

Mma Makutsi frowned at the apprentice. "Smart-looking?"

"Big suit," said the apprentice. "You know. Handsome, same as me but not quite. Shiny shoes. A very smart man. You watch yourself, Mma. Men like that try to charm ladies like you. You just see."

"Don't wipe your hands on your overalls," snapped Mma Makutsi, as she rose from her chair. "We pay for the laundering. You don't. We give you cotton waste to use for that purpose. That is what it's for. Has Mr J.L.B. Matekoni not told you that?"

"Maybe," said the apprentice. "Maybe not. The boss said lots of things to us. We can't remember everything he says."

Mma Makutsi brushed past him on her way out. These boys are impossible, she thought, but at least they were proving to be harder workers than she expected. Perhaps Mr J.L.B. Matekoni had been too soft on them in the past; he was such a kind man and it was not in his nature to criticise people unduly. Well, it was in her nature at least. She was a graduate of the Botswana Secretarial College, and the College teachers had always said: Do not be afraid to criticize—in a constructive way, of course—your own performance and, if necessary, the performance of others. Well, Mma Makutsi had criticised, and it had borne fruit. The garage was doing well and there seemed to be more and more work each day.

She paused at the door of the agency, just round the corner of the building, and looked at the car parked under the tree behind her. This man—this smart man, as the apprentice had described him—certainly drove an attractive car. She ran her eye for a moment over the smooth lines of the vehicle and its double aerials, front and back. Why would somebody need so many aerials? It would be impossible to listen to more than one radio station at a time, or make more than one telephone call while driving. But whatever the explanation, they certainly added to the air of glamour and importance which surrounded the car.

She pushed the door open. Inside, seated in the chair facing Mma Ramotswe's desk, knees crossed in relaxed elegance, was Mr Moemedi "Two Shots" Pulani, immediately recognisable to any reader of the *Botswana Daily News*, across whose columns his handsome, self-assured face had so often been printed. Mma Makutsi's immediate thought was that the apprentice should have recognised him, and she felt momentarily annoyed at his failure to do so, but then she reminded herself that the apprentice was an apprentice mechanic and not an apprentice detective, and, furthermore, she had never seen the apprentices reading the newspapers anyway. They read a South African motorcycle magazine, which they pored over in fascination, and a publication called *Fancy Girls* which they attempted to hide from Mma Makutsi whenever she came across them peering at it during their lunch hour. So there was no reason, she realised, for them to know about Mr Pulani, his fashion empire, and his well-known work for local charities.

Mr Pulani rose to his feet as she entered and greeted her politely. They shook hands, and then Mma Makutsi walked round the desk and sat in Mma Ramotswe's chair.

"I am glad that you could see me without an appointment, Mma Ramotswe," said Mr Pulani, taking a silver cigarette case out of his breast pocket.

"I am not Mma Ramotswe, Rra," she said, declining his offer of a cigarette. "I am the Assistant Manager of the agency." She paused. It was not strictly true that she was the Assistant Manager of the agency; in fact, it was quite untrue. But she was certainly managing it in Mma Ramotswe's absence, and so perhaps the description was justified.

"Ah," said Mr Pulani, lighting his cigarette with a large gold-plated lighter. "I would like to speak to Mma Ramotswe herself, please."

Mma Makutsi flinched as the cloud of smoke drifted over the table to her.

"I'm sorry," she said. "That will not be possible for some days. Mma Ramotswe is investigating a very important case abroad." She paused again. The exaggeration had come so easily, and without any thought. It sounded more impressive that Mma Ramotswe should be abroad—it gave the agency an international feel—but she should not have said it.

"I see," said Mr Pulani. "Well, Mma, in that case I shall speak to you."

"I am listening, Rra."

Mr Pulani leaned back in his seat. "This is very urgent. Will you be able to look into something today, straightaway?"

Mma Makutsi took a deep breath before the next cloud of smoke engulfed her.

"We are at your disposal," she said. "Of course, it is more expensive to handle things urgently. You'll understand that, Rra."

He brushed her warning aside. "Expense is not the issue," he said. "What is at issue is the whole future of the Miss Beauty and Integrity contest."

He paused for the effect of his words to be felt. Mma Makutsi obliged.

"Oh! That is a very serious matter."

Mr Pulani nodded. "Indeed it is, Mma. And we have three days to deal with this issue. Just three days."

"Tell me about it, Rra. I am ready to listen."

"THERE IS an interesting background to this, Mma," began Mr Pulani. "I think that the story begins a long time ago, a long time. In fact, the story begins in the Garden of Eden, when God made Adam and Eve. You will remember that Eve tempted Adam because she was so beautiful. And women have continued to be beautiful in the eyes of men since that time, and they still are, as you know.

"Now, the men of Botswana like pretty ladies. They are always looking at them, even when they are elders, and thinking that is a pretty woman, or that this woman is prettier than that woman, and so on."

"They are like that with cattle, too," interjected Mma Makutsi. "They say this cow is a good cow and this one is not so good. Cattle. Women. It's all the same to men."

Mr Pulani cast her a sideways glance. "Maybe. That is one way of looking at it. Perhaps." He paused briefly before continuing. "Anyway, it is this interest of men in pretty ladies that makes beauty competitions so popular here in Botswana. We like to find the most beautiful ladies in Botswana and give them titles and prizes. It is a very important form of entertainment for men. And I am one such man, Mma. I have been involved in the beauty queen world for fifteen years, nonstop. I am maybe the most important person in the beauty side of things."

"I have seen your picture in the papers, Rra," said Mma Makutsi. "I have seen you presenting prizes."

Mr Pulani nodded. "I started the Miss Glamorous Botswana competition five years ago, and now it is the top one. The lady who wins our competition always gets into the Miss Botswana competition and sometimes into the Miss Universe competition. We have sent ladies to New York and Palm Springs; they have been given high marks for beauty. Some say that they are our best export after diamonds."

"And cattle," added Mma Makutsi.

"Yes, and cattle," Mr Pulani agreed. "But there are some people who are always sniping at us. They write to the newspapers and tell us that it is wrong to encourage ladies to dress up and walk in front of a lot of men like that. They say that it encourages false values. Pah! False values? These people who write these letters are just jealous. They are envious of the beauty of these girls. They know that they would never be able to enter a competition like that. So they complain and complain and they are very happy when something goes wrong for

a beauty competition. They forget, by the way, that these competitions raise a lot of money for charity. Last year, Mma, we
raised five thousand pula for the hospital, twenty thousand
pula for drought relief—twenty thousand, Mma—and almost
eight thousand pula for a nursing scholarship fund. Those are
big sums, Mma. How much money have our critics raised? I
can tell you the answer to that. Nothing.

"But we have to be careful. We get a lot of money from sponsors, and if sponsors withdraw, then we are in trouble. So if
something goes wrong for our competition, then the sponsors
may say that they do not want to have anything more to do
with us. They say that they do not want to be embarrassed by
bad publicity. They say that they are paying for good publicity,
not for bad."

"And has something gone wrong?"

Mr Pulani tapped his fingers on the desk. "Yes. Some very
bad things have happened. Last year, two of our beauty queens
were found to be bad girls. One was arrested for prostitution in
one of the big hotels. That was not good. Another was shown
to have obtained goods under false pretences and to have used
a credit card without authorisation. There were letters in the
paper. There was much crowing. They said things like: Are
these girls the right sort of girls to be ambassadors for
Botswana? Why not go straight to the prison and pick some of
the women prisoners and make them beauty queens? They
thought that was very funny, but it was not. Some of the companies saw this and said that if this happened again, they
would withdraw sponsorship. I had four letters, all saying the
same thing.

"So I decided that this year the theme of our competition
would be Beauty and Integrity. I told our people that we must

choose beauty queens who are good citizens, who will not
embarrass us in this way. It is the only way that we are going to
keep our sponsors happy.

"So for the first round, all the ladies had to fill in a form
which I designed myself. This asked all sorts of questions
about their views. It asked things like: Would you like to work
for charity? Then it asked: What are the values which a good
citizen of Botswana should uphold? And: Is it better to give
than receive?

"All the girls filled in these questions, and only those who
showed that they understood the meaning of good citizenship
were allowed to go on to the finals. From these girls we made
a shortlist of five. I went to the papers and told them that we
had found five very good citizens who believed in the best values. There was an article in the *Botswana Daily News* which
said: *Good girls seek beauty title*.

"I was very happy, and there was silence from our critics,
who had to sit on their hands because they could not come out
and criticise these ladies who wanted to be good citizens. The
sponsors telephoned me and said that they were content to be
identified with the values of good citizenship and that if all
went well they would continue to provide their sponsorship
next year. And the charities themselves said to me that this was
the way of the future."

Mr Pulani paused. He looked at Mma Makutsi, and for a
moment his urbane manner deserted him and he looked crestfallen. "Then, yesterday I heard the bad news. One of our
short-listed girls was arrested by the police and charged with
shoplifting. I heard about it through one of my employees and
when I checked with a friend who is an inspector of police, he
said that it was true. This girl had been found shoplifting in

the Game store. She tried to steal a large cooking pot by slipping it under her blouse. But she did not notice that the handle was sticking out of the side and the store detective stopped her. Fortunately it has not got into the newspapers, and with any luck it will not, at least until the case comes up in the Magistrate's Court."

Mma Makutsi felt a pang of sympathy for Mr Pulani. In spite of his flashiness, there was no doubt that he did a great deal for charity. The fashion world was inevitably flashy, and he was probably no worse than any of the others, but at least he was doing his best for people in trouble. And beauty competitions were a fact of life, which you could not wish out of existence. If he was trying to make his competition more acceptable, then he deserved support.

"I am sorry to hear that, Rra," she said. "That must have been very bad news for you."

"Yes," he said, miserably. "And it is made much worse by the fact that the finals are in three days. There are now only four girls on the list, but how do I know that they are not going to embarrass me? That one must have lied when she filled in her questionnaire and made out that she was a good citizen. How do I know that the rest of them aren't lying when they say that they would like to do things for charity? How do I know that? And if we choose a girl who is a liar, then she may well prove to be a thief or whatever. And that means that we are bound to face embarrassment once she gets going."

Mma Makutsi nodded. "It is very difficult. You really need to be able to look into the hearts of the remaining four. If there is a good one there . . ."

"If there is such a lady," said Mr Pulani forcefully, "then she will win. I can arrange for her to win."

"But what about the other judges?" asked Mma Makutsi.

"I am the chief judge," he said. "You might call me the Chief Justice of Beauty. My vote is the one that counts."

"I see."

"Yes. That is the way it works."

Mr Pulani stubbed out his cigarette on the sole of his shoe. "So you see, Mma. That is what I want you to do. I will give you the names and addresses of the four ladies. I would like you to find out if there is one really good lady there. If you can't find that, then at least tell me which is the most honest of the lot. That would be second best."

Mma Makutsi laughed. "How can I look into the hearts of these girls that quickly?" she asked. "I would have to talk to many, many people to find out about them. It could take weeks."

Mr Pulani shrugged. "You haven't got weeks, Mma. You've got three days. You did say that you could help me."

"Yes, but . . ."

Mr Pulani reached into a pocket and took out a piece of paper. "This is a list of the four names. I have written the address of each lady after her name. They all live in Gaborone." He slipped the piece of paper across the desk and then extracted a thin leather folder from another pocket. As he opened it, Mma Makutsi saw that it contained a chequebook. He opened it and began to write. "And here, Mma, is a cheque for two thousand pula, made payable to the No. 1 Ladies' Detective Agency. There. It's postdated. If you can give me the information I need the day after tomorrow, you can present this at the bank the next day."

Mma Makutsi stared at the cheque. She imagined how it would feel to be able to say to Mma Ramotswe when she returned, "I earned the agency two thousand pula in fees, Mma, already paid." She knew that Mma Ramotswe was not a greedy woman, but she also knew that she worried about the financial viability of the agency. A fee of that size would help a great deal, and would be a reward, thought Mma Makutsi, for the confidence that Mma Ramotswe had shown in her.

She slipped the cheque into a drawer. As she did so, she saw Mr Pulani relax.

"I am counting on you, Mma," he said. "Everything that I have heard about the No. 1 Ladies' Detective Agency has been good. I hope that I shall see that for myself."

"I hope so too, Rra," said Mma Makutsi. But she was already feeling doubtful about how she could possibly find out which of the four short-listed ladies were honest. It seemed an impossible task.

She escorted Mr Pulani to the door, noticing for the first time that he was wearing white shoes. She observed, too, his large gold cuff links and his tie with its sheen of silk. She would not like to have a man like that, she thought. One would have to spend all one's time at a beauty parlour in order to keep up the appearance he would no doubt expect. Of course, reflected Mma Makutsi, that would suit some ladies perfectly well.

CHAPTER FOURTEEN

GOD DECIDED THAT BOTSWANA
WOULD BE A DRY PLACE

THE MAID had said that the midday meal would be at one o'clock, which was several hours away. Mma Ramotswe decided that the best way of spending this time would be to familiarise herself with her surroundings. She liked farms—as most Batswana did—because they reminded her of her childhood and of the true values of her people. They shared the land with cattle, and with birds and the many other creatures that could be seen if one only watched. It was easy perhaps not to think about this in the town, where there was food to be had from shops and where running water came from taps, but for many people this was not how life was.

After her revealing conversation with the maid, she left her room and made her way out of the front door. The sun was hot overhead, and shadows were short. To the east, over the low, distant hills, blue under their heat haze, heavy rain clouds were building up. There could be rain later on if the clouds built up further, or at least there would be rain for somebody, out there, along the border. It looked as if the rains would be good this year, which is what everybody was praying for. Good rains meant full stomachs; drought meant thin cattle and wilted crops. They had experienced a bad drought a few years previously, and the Government, its heart heavy, had instructed people to start slaughtering their cattle. That was the worst thing for anybody to have to do, and the suffering had cut deep.

Mma Ramotswe looked about her. There was a paddock some distance off, and cattle were crowded around a drinking trough. A pipe ran from the creaking windmill and its concrete storage tank over the surface of the ground to the trough and the thirsty cattle. Mma Ramotswe decided that she would go and take a look at the cattle. She was, after all, the daughter of Obed Ramotswe, whose eye for cattle was said by many to have been one of the best in Botswana. She could tell a good beast when she saw one, and sometimes, when she drove past a particularly handsome specimen on the road, she would think of what the Daddy would have said about it. Good shoulders, perhaps; or, that is a good cow; look at the way she is walking; or, that bull is all talk, I do not think that he would make many calves.

This farm would have a large number of cattle, perhaps five or six thousand. For most people, that was riches beyond dreaming; ten or twenty cattle were quite enough to make one feel that one had at least some wealth, and she would be happy with that. Obed Ramotswe had built up his herd by judicious buying and selling and had ended up with two thousand cattle at the end of his life. It was this that had provided her with her legacy and with the means to buy the house in Zebra Drive and start the agency. And there were cattle left over, some which she had decided not to sell and which were looked after by herdboys at a distant cattle post which a cousin visited for her. There were sixty of them, she thought; all fine descendants of the lumbering Brahman bulls which her father had so painstakingly selected and bred. One day she would go out there, travelling on the ox-wagon, and see them; it would be an emotional occasion, because they were a link with the Daddy and she would miss him acutely, she knew, and she would probably weep and they would wonder why this woman still wept for her father who had died long ago now.

We still have tears to shed, she thought. We still have to weep for those mornings when we went out early and watched the cows amble along the cattle paths and the birds flying high in the thermal currents.

"What are you thinking of, Mma?"

She looked up. A man had appeared beside her, a stock whip in his hand, a battered hat on his head.

Mma Ramotswe greeted him. "I am thinking of my late father," she said. "He would have liked to see these cattle here. Do you look after them, Rra? They are fine beasts."

He smiled in appreciation. "I have looked after these cattle all their lives. They are like my children. I have two hundred children, Mma. All cattle."

Mma Ramotswe laughed. "You must be a busy man, Rra."

He nodded, and took a small paper packet out of his pocket. He offered Mma Ramotswe a piece of dried beef, which she accepted.

"You are staying at the house?" he asked. "They often have people coming up here and staying. Sometimes the son who is in Gaborone brings his friends from the Government. I have seen them with my own eyes. Those people."

"He is very busy that one," said Mma Ramotswe. "Do you know him well?"

"Yes," said the man, chewing on a piece of beef. "He comes out here and tells us what to do. He worries about the cattle all the time. He says this one is sick, that one is lame. Where is that other one? All the time. Then he goes away and things get back to normal."

Mma Ramotswe frowned sympathetically. "That cannot be easy for his brother, the other one, can it?"

The cattleman opened his eyes wide. "He stands there like a dog and lets his brother shout at him. He is a good farmer, that younger one, but the firstborn still thinks that he is the one who is running this farm. But we know that their father had spoken to the chief and it had been agreed that the younger one would get most of the cattle and the older one could have money. That is what was decided."

"But the older one doesn't like it?"

"No," said the cattleman. "And I suppose I can see how he feels. But he has done very well in Gaborone and he has another life. The younger one is the farmer. He knows cattle."

"And what about the third one?" asked Mma Ramotswe. "The one who is out that way?" She pointed towards the Kalahari.

The cattleman laughed. "He is just a boy. It is very sad. There is air in his head, they say. It is because of something that the mother did when he was in her womb. That is how these things happen."

"Oh?" said Mma Ramotswe. "What did she do?" She knew of the belief which people in the country had that a handicapped child was the result of some bad act on the parents' part. If a woman had an affair with another man, for example, then that could lead to the birth of a simpleton. If a man rejected his wife and went off with another woman while she was expecting his child, that, too, could lead to disaster for the baby.

The cattleman lowered his voice. But who was there to hear, thought Mma Ramotswe, but the cattle and the birds?

"She is the one to watch," said the man. "She is the one. The old woman. She is a wicked woman."

"Wicked?"

He nodded. "Watch her," he said. "Watch her eyes."

THE MAID came to her door shortly before two o'clock and told her that the meal was ready.

"They are eating in the porch on that side," she said, pointing to the other side of the house.

Mma Ramotswe thanked her and left her room. The porch was on the cooler side of the house, shaded by an awning of netting and a profusion of creepers that had been trained across a rough wooden trellis. Two tables had been drawn up alongside one another and covered with a starched white tablecloth. At one end of the large table, several dishes of food had been placed in a circle: steaming pumpkin, a bowl of maize meal, a plate of beans and other greens, and a large tureen of heavy meat stew. Then there was a loaf of bread and a dish of butter. It was good food, of the type which only a wealthy family could afford every day.

Mma Ramotswe recognised the old woman, who was sitting slightly back from the table, a small gingham cloth spread over her lap, but other members of the family were there too:

a child of about twelve, a young woman in a smart green skirt and a white blouse—the wife, Mma Ramotswe assumed—and a man at her side, dressed in long khaki trousers and a short-sleeved khaki shirt. The man stood up when Mma Ramotswe appeared and came out from behind the table to welcome her.

"You are our guest," he said, smiling as he spoke. "You are very welcome in this house, Mma."

The old woman nodded at her. "This is my son," she said. "He was with the cattle when you arrived."

The man introduced her to his wife, who smiled at her in a friendly way.

"It is very hot today, Mma," said the young woman. "But it is going to rain, I think. You have brought us this rain, I think."

It was a compliment, and Mma Ramotswe acknowledged it. "I hope so," she said. "The land is still thirsty."

"It is always thirsty," said the husband. "God decided that Botswana would be a dry place for dry animals. That is what he decided."

Mma Ramotswe sat down between the wife and the old woman. While the wife started to serve the meal, the husband poured water into the glasses.

"I saw you looking at the cattle," said the old woman. "Do you like cattle, Mma?"

"What Motswana does not like cattle?" replied Mma Ramotswe.

"Perhaps there are some," said the old woman. "Perhaps there are some who do not understand cattle. I don't know."

She turned away as she gave her answer and was now looking out through the tall, unglazed windows of the porch, out across the expanse of bush that ran away to the horizon.

"They tell me that you are from Mochudi," said the young woman, handing Mma Ramotswe her plate. "I am from there, too."

"That was some time ago," said Mma Ramotswe. "I am in Gaborone now. Like so many people."

"Like my brother," said the husband. "You must know him well if he is sending you out here."

There was a moment of silence. The old woman turned to look at her son, who looked away from her.

"I do not know him well," said Mma Ramotswe. "But he invited me to this house as a favour. I had helped him."

"You are very welcome," said the old woman quickly. "You are our guest."

The last remark was aimed at her son, but he was busy with his plate and affected not to notice what his mother had said. The wife, though, had caught Mma Ramotswe's eye when this exchange took place, and had then quickly looked away again.

They ate in silence. The old woman had her plate on her lap, and was busy excavating a pile of maize meal soaked in gravy. She placed the mixture in her mouth and chewed slowly on it, her rheumy eyes fixed on the view of the bush and the sky. For her part, the wife had helped herself only to beans and pumpkin, which she picked at halfheartedly. Looking down at her plate, Mma Ramotswe noticed that she and the husband were the only people who were eating stew. The child, who had been introduced as a cousin of the wife's, was eating a thick slice of bread onto which syrup and gravy had been ladled.

Mma Ramotswe looked at her food. She sank her fork into the pile of stew which nestled between a large helping of pumpkin and a small mound of maize meal. The stew was thick and glutinous, and when she took up her fork it trailed a thin trail of glycerine-like substance across the plate. But when she put the fork into her mouth, the food tasted normal, or almost normal. There was slight flavour, she thought, a flavour which she might have described as metallic, like the taste of the iron pills which her doctor had once given her, or perhaps bitter, like the taste of a split lemon pip.

She looked at the wife, who smiled at her.

"I am not the cook," the young woman said. "If this food tastes good, it is not because I cooked it. There is Samuel in the kitchen. He is a very good cook, and we are proud of him. He is trained. He is a chef."

"It is woman's work," said the husband. "That is why you do not find me in the kitchen. A man should be doing other things."

He looked at Mma Ramotswe as he spoke, and she sensed the challenge.

She took a moment or two to answer. Then: "That is what many people say, Rra. Or at least, that is what many men say. I am not sure whether many women say it, though."

The husband put down his fork. "You ask my wife," he said, quietly. "You ask her whether she says it. Go on."

The wife did not hesitate. "What my husband says is right," she said.

The old woman turned to Mma Ramotswe. "You see?" she said. "She supports her husband. That is how it is here in the country. In the town it may be different, but in the country that is how it is."

SHE RETURNED to her room after the meal and lay down on her bed. The heat had got no better, although the clouds had continued to build up in the east. It was clear now that there was going to be rain, even if it would not come until nighttime. There would be a wind soon, and with it would come that wonderful, unmistakable smell of rain, that smell of dust and water meeting that lingered for a few seconds in the nostrils and then was gone, and would be missed, sometimes for months, before the next time that it caught you and made you stop and say to the person with you, any person: That is the smell of rain, there, right now.

She lay on her bed and stared up at the white ceiling boards. They had been well dusted, which was a sign of good house-keeping. In many houses, the ceilings were fly-spotted or marked, at the edges, with the foundations of termite trails. Sometimes large spiders could be seen looping across what must have seemed to them upside-down white tundras. But here, there was nothing, and the paintwork was unsullied.

Mma Ramotswe was puzzled. All that she had learned today was that the staff had views, but that they all disliked the Government Man. He threw his weight around, it seemed, but was there anything untoward in that? Of course the older brother would have views on how the cattle should be handled, and of course it was natural for him to give these views to his younger brother. Of course the old woman would think that her handicapped son was clever; and of course she would believe that city people lost interest in cattle. Mma Ramotswe realised that she knew very little about her. The cattleman thought she was wicked, but he gave no reason to back up his assessment. He had told her to watch her eyes, which she had done, to no effect. All that she had noticed was that she looked away, into the distance, while they all had lunch together. What did this mean?

Mma Ramotswe sat up. There was something to be learned there, she thought. If somebody looked away, into the distance, then it meant that he or she did not want to be there. And the most common reason for not wanting to be somewhere was because one did not like the company one was in. That was always true. Now, if she was always looking away, that meant that she did not like somebody there. She does not dislike me, thought Mma Ramotswe, because she gave no indication of this when I saw her earlier and she has not had the chance to develop a dislike. The child would hardly have given rise to that sort of reaction, and indeed she had treated him quite fondly, patting his head on one or two occasions during the meal. That left the son and his wife.

No mother dislikes her son. Mma Ramotswe understood that there were women who were ashamed of their sons, and there were also women who were angry with their sons. But no mother actually disliked a son at heart. A son could do anything, and would be forgiven by his mother. This old woman, therefore, disliked her daughter-in-law and disliked her intensely enough to want to be somewhere else when she was in her company.

Mma Ramotswe lay back on her bed, the immediate excitement of her conclusion having passed. Now she had to establish why the old woman disliked the daughter-in-law, and if it was because her other son, the Government Man, had said something to her about his suspicions. Perhaps more important, though, was the question of whether the woman knew that her mother-in-law disliked her. If she did, then she would have a motive for doing something about it, but if she were a poisoner—and she did not look like it, and there were also the contrary views of the maid to be taken into account—then surely she would have attempted to poison the old woman rather than her husband.

Mma Ramotswe felt drowsy. She had not slept well the previous evening, and the drive and the heat and the heavy lunch were having their effect. The stew had been very rich; rich and viscous, with that glutinous trail. She closed her eyes, but did not see darkness. There was a white aura, a faint luminous line, that seemed to cross her inner vision. The bed moved slightly, as if with the wind that had now started to blow from over the border, far away. The rain smell came, and then the hot, urgent drops, punishing the ground, stinging it, and bouncing back up like tiny grey worms.

Mma Ramotswe slept, but her breathing was shallow, and her dreams were fevered. When she awoke and felt the pain in her stomach, it was almost five o'clock. The main storm had passed, but there was still rain, beating on the tin roof of the house like a troop of insistent drummers. She sat up, and then lay down again from the nausea. She turned on the bed and dropped her feet to the floor. Then she rose, unsteadily, and stumbled on her way to the door and the bathroom at the end of the corridor outside. There she was sick, and almost immediately felt better. By the time she had reached her room, the worst of the nausea had passed and she was able to reflect on her situation. She had come to the home of a poisoner and had been poisoned herself. She should not be surprised at that. Indeed it was entirely and completely predictable.

CHAPTER FIFTEEN

WHAT DO YOU WANT TO
DO WITH YOUR LIFE?

MMA MAKUTSI had only three days. It was not a long time, and she wondered whether she could possibly find out enough about each of the four finalists to enable her to advise Mr Pulani. She looked at the neatly typed list which he had provided, but neither the names, nor the addresses which followed them, told her anything. She knew that there were people who claimed that they could judge people on their names, that girls called Mary were inevitably honest and home-loving, that you should never trust a Sipho, and so on. But this was an absurd notion, very much less helpful than the notion that you could tell whether a person was a criminal by looking at the shape of his head. Mma Ramotswe had shown her an article about that theory and she had joined her in her laughter. But the idea—even if clearly not a very appropriate one for a modern person like herself to hold—had intrigued her and she had discreetly embarked on her own researches.

The ever-helpful librarian of the British Council Library had produced a book within minutes and had pressed it into her hands. *Theories of Crime* was a considerably more scholarly work than Mma Ramotswe's professional bible, *The Principles of Private Detection* by Clovis Andersen. That was perfectly adequate for tips on dealing with clients, but it was weak on theory. It was obvious to Mma Makutsi that Clovis Andersen was no reader of *The Journal of Criminology;* whereas the author of *Theories of Crime* was quite familiar with the debates which took place as to what caused crime. Society was one possible culprit, Mma Makutsi read; bad housing and a bleak future made criminals of young men, and we should remember, the book warned, that those to whom evil was done *did evil in return*.

Mma Makutsi read this with astonishment. It was absolutely correct, she reflected, but she had never thought about it in those terms. Of course those who did wrong had been wronged themselves—that very much accorded with her own experience. In her third year at school, all those years ago in Bobonong, she remembered a boy who had bullied the smaller boys and had delighted in their terror. She had never been able to understand why he had done it—perhaps he was just evil—but then, one evening, she had passed by his house and had seen him being beaten by his drunken father. The boy wriggled and cried out, but had been unable to escape the blows. The following day, on the way to school, she had seen him striking a smaller boy and push him into a painful wagenbikkie bush with its cruel thorns. Of course she had not linked cause and effect at that age, but now it came back to her and she reflected on the wisdom revealed in the text of *Theories of Crime*.

Sitting alone in the office of the No. 1 Ladies' Detective Agency, it took her several hours of reading to reach what she was looking for. The section on biological explanations of crime was shorter than the other sections, largely because the author was clearly uncomfortable with them.

"The nineteenth century Italian criminologist, Cesare Lombroso," she read, "although liberal in his views of prison reform, was convinced that criminality could be detected by the shape of the head. Thus he expended a great deal of energy on charting the physiognomy of criminals, in a misguided attempt to identify those facial and cranial features that were indicative of criminality. These quaint illustrations (reproduced below) are a testament to the misplaced enthusiasm which could so easily have been directed into more fruitful lines of research."

Mma Makutsi looked at the illustrations taken from Lombroso's book. An evil-looking man with a narrow forehead and fiery eyes looked out at the reader. Underneath this picture was the legend: *Typical murderer (Sicilian type)*. Then there was a picture of another man, elaborately moustachioed but with narrow, pinched eyes. This, she read, was a *Classic thief (Neapolitan type)*. Other criminal "types" stared out at the reader, all of them quite unambiguously malign. Mma Makutsi gave a shudder. These were clearly extremely unpleasant men and nobody would trust any of them. Why, then, describe the theories of Lombroso as "misguided"? Not only was that rude, in her opinion, but it was patently wrong. Lombroso was right; you *could* tell (something which women had known for a very long time—they could tell what men were like just by looking at them, but they did not need to be Italian to do so; they could do it right here in Botswana). She was puzzled; if the theory was so clearly right, then why should the author of this criminological work deny it? She thought for a moment and then the explanation came to her: he was *jealous!* That must be the reason. He was jealous because Lombroso had thought about this before he had and he wanted to develop his own ideas about crime. Well! If that were the case, then she would bother no more with *Theories of Crime.* She had found out a bit more about this sort of criminology, and now all she had to do was apply it. She would use the theories of Lombrosan criminology to detect who, of the four girls on the list, was trustworthy and who was not. Lombroso's illustration had simply confirmed that she should trust her intuition. A brief time with these girls, and perhaps a discreet inspection of their cranial structures—she would not want to stare—would be enough to provide her with an answer. It would have to suffice; there was nothing else that she could do in the short time available and she was particularly keen that the matter should be satisfactorily resolved by the time of Mma Ramotswe's return.

FOUR NAMES, none of them known to Mma Makutsi: Motlamedi Matluli, Gladys Tlhapi, Makita Phenyonini, and Patricia Quatleneni; and beneath them, their ages and their addresses. Motlamedi was the youngest, at nineteen, and the most readily accessible—she was a student at the university. Patricia was the oldest at twenty-four, and possibly the most difficult to contact, at her vague address in Tlokweng (plot 2456). Mma Makutsi decided that she would visit Motlamedi first, as it would be a simple matter to find her in her students' hall on the neatly laid-out university campus. Of course, it would not necessarily be easy to interview her; Mma Makutsi knew that girls like that, with their place at the university and a good job virtually guaranteed for them, tended to look down on people who had not had their advantages, particularly those who had attended the Botswana Secretarial College. Her own 97 percent in the final examinations, the result of such hard work, would be mocked by one such as Motlamedi. But she would speak to her and treat any condescension with dignity. She had nothing to be ashamed of; she was now the Acting Manager of a garage, was she not, and an assistant detective as well. What official titles did this beautiful girl have? She was not even Miss Beauty and Integrity, even if she was in the running for that particular honour.

She would go to see her. But what would she say? She could hardly seek out this girl and then say to her: Excuse me, *I have come to look at your head.* That would invite a hostile response, even if it had the merits of being completely true. And then the idea came to her. She could pretend to be doing a survey of some sort, and while the girls were answering, she could look closely at their head and facial features to see if any of the telltale signs of dishonesty was present. And the idea became even better. The survey need not be some meaningless marketing survey of the sort which people were used to responding to; it could be a survey of moral attitudes. It could pose certain questions which, in a very subtle way, would uncover the girls' attitudes. The questions would be carefully phrased, so that the girls would not suspect a trap, but they would be as revealing as searchlights. *What do you really want to do with your life?* for example. Or: *Is it better to make a lot of money than to help others?*

The ideas fell neatly into place, and Mma Makutsi smiled

with delight as each new possibility revealed itself to her. She would claim to be a journalist, sent by the *Botswana Daily News* to write a feature article on the competition—small deceptions are permissible, Clovis Andersen had written, provided that the ends justified the means. Well, the ends in this case were clearly important, as the reputation of Botswana itself could be in the balance. The girl who won Miss Beauty and Integrity could find herself in the running for the title of Miss Botswana, and that post was every bit as important as being an ambassador. Indeed, a beauty queen was a sort of ambassador for her country, and people would judge the country on how she conducted herself. If she had to tell a small lie in order to prevent a wicked girl from seizing the title and bringing shame to the country, then that was a small price to pay. Clovis Andersen would undoubtedly have agreed with her, even if the author of *Theories of Crime*, who seemed to take a very high moral tone on all issues, might have had some misplaced reservations.

Mma Makutsi set to typing out the questionnaire. The questions were simple, but probing:

1. What are the main values which Africa can show to the world?

This question was designed to establish whether the girls knew what morality was all about. A morally aware girl would answer something along the lines: *Africa can show the world what it is to be human. Africa recognises the humanity of all people.*

Once they had negotiated this or, rather *if* they negotiated this, the next question would become more personal:

2. What do you want to do with your life?

This was where Mma Makutsi would trap any dishonest girl. The standard answer which any beauty contestant gave to this question was this: *I should like to work for charity, possibly with children. I would like to leave the world a better place than it was when I came into it.*

That was all very well, but they had all learned that answer from a book somewhere, possibly a book by somebody like Clovis Andersen. *Good Practice for Beauty Queens,* perhaps, or *How to Win in the World of Beauty Competitions.*

An honest girl, thought Mma Makutsi, would answer in something like the following fashion: *I wish to work for charity, possibly with children. If no children are available, I shall be happy to work with old people; I do not mind. But I am also keen to get a good job with a large salary.*

3. Is it better to be beautiful than to be full of integrity?

There was no doubt, again, that the answer which was expected of a beauty contestant was that integrity was more important. All the girls would probably feel that they had to say that, but there was a remote possibility that honesty would propel one into saying that being beautiful had its advantages. This was something that Mma Makutsi had noticed about secretarial jobs; beautiful girls were given all the jobs and there was very little left over for the rest, even if one had achieved 97 percent in the final examination. The injustice of this had always rankled, although in her own case, hard work had eventually paid off. How many of her contemporaries who may have had a better complexion than herself were now acting managers? The answer was undoubtedly none. Those beautiful girls married rich men, and lived in comfort thereafter, but they could hardly have claimed to have had careers—unless wearing expensive clothes and going to parties could be described as a career.

Mma Makutsi typed her questionnaire. There was no photocopier in the office, but she had used carbon paper and there were now four copies of the question sheet, with *Botswana Daily News Features Department* meretriciously typed at the top of the page. She looked at her watch; it was noon, and the day had warmed up uncomfortably. There had been some rain a few days previously, but this had rapidly been soaked up by the earth and the ground was crying out for more. If rain came, as it probably would, the temperatures would fall and people would feel comfortable again. Tempers became frayed in the hot season and arguments broke out about little things. Rain brought peace between people.

She went out of the office and closed the door behind her. The apprentices were busy with an old van which had been driven in by a woman who brought vegetables up from Lobatse to sell to the supermarkets. She had heard about the garage from a friend, who had said that it was a good place for a woman to take her vehicle.

"It is a ladies' garage, I think," the friend had said. "They understand ladies and they look after them well. It is the best place for a lady to take her car."

The acquisition of a reputation for looking after ladies' cars had kept the apprentices busy. Under Mma Makutsi's management, they had responded well to the challenge, working late hours and taking much greater care with their work. She checked up on them from time to time, and insisted that they explain to her exactly what they were doing. They enjoyed this, and it also helped to focus their thoughts on the problem before them. Their diagnostic power—so important a weapon in the armoury of any good mechanic—had improved greatly and they also wasted less time in idle chatter about girls.

"We like working for a woman," the older apprentice had said to her one morning. "It is a good thing to have a woman watching you all the time."

"I am very happy about that," said Mma Makutsi. "Your work is getting better and better all the time. One day you may be a famous mechanic like Mr J.L.B. Matekoni. That is always possible."

Now she walked over to the apprentices and watched them manipulating an oil filter.

"When you have finished that," she said, "I would like one of you to drive me over to the university."

"We are very busy, Mma," complained the younger one. "We have two more cars to see to today. We cannot go off here and there all the time. We are not taxi drivers."

Mma Makutsi sighed. "In that case I shall have to get a taxi. I have this important business to do with a beauty competition. I have to speak to some of the girls."

"I can drive you," said the older apprentice hurriedly. "I am almost ready. My brother here can finish this off."

"Good," said Mma Makutsi. "I knew that I could call on your finer nature."

THEY PARKED under a tree on the university campus, not far from the large, white-painted block to which Mma Makutsi had been directed when she showed the address to the man on the gate. A small group of female students stood chatting beneath a sun shelter that shaded the front door to the three-storey building. Leaving the apprentice in the van, Mma Makutsi made her way over to this group and introduced herself.

"I am looking for Motlamedi Matluli," she said. "I have been told she lives here."

One of the students giggled. "Yes, she lives here," she said. "Although I think that she would like to live somewhere a bit grander."

"Like the Sun Hotel," said another, causing them all to laugh.

MMA MAKUTSI smiled. "She is a very important girl, then?"

This brought forth more laughter. "She thinks she is," said one. "Just because she has all the boys running after her she thinks she owns Gaborone. You should just see her!"

"I would like to see her," said Mma Makutsi simply. "That is why I am here."

"You will find her in front of her mirror," said another. "She is on the first floor, in room 114."

Mma Makutsi thanked her informants and made her way up the concrete staircase to the first floor. She noticed that somebody had scribbled something uncomplimentary on the wall of the staircase, a remark about one of the girls. One of the male students, no doubt, had been rebuffed and had vented his feelings in graffiti. She felt annoyed; these people were privileged—ordinary people in Botswana would never have the chance to get this sort of education, which was all paid for by the Government, every pula and thebe of it—and all they could think of doing was writing on walls. And what was Motlamedi doing, spending time preening herself and entering beauty competitions when she should have been working on her books? If she were the Rector of the university she would tell people like that to make up their minds. You can be one thing or the other. You can cultivate your mind, or you can cultivate your hairstyle. But you cannot do both.

She found room 114 and knocked loudly on the door. There were sounds of a radio within and so she knocked again, louder this time.

"All right!" shouted a voice from within. "I'm coming."

The door was opened and Motlamedi Matluli stood before her. The first thing that struck Mma Makutsi about her was her eyes, which were extraordinarily large. They dominated the face, giving it a gentle, innocent quality, rather like the face of those small night creatures they called bush babies.

Motlamedi looked her visitor up and down.

"Yes Mma?" she asked casually. "What can I do for you?"

This was very rude, and Mma Makutsi smarted at the insult. If this girl had any manners, she would have invited me in, she thought. She is too busy with her mirror which, as the students below had predicted, was propped up on her desk and was surrounded by creams and lotions.

"I am a journalist," said Mma Makutsi. "I am writing an article about the finalists for Miss Beauty and Integrity. I have some questions I would like you to answer."

The change in Motlamedi's attitude was immediately apparent. Quickly, and rather effusively asking Mma Makutsi in, she cleared some clothes off a chair and invited her visitor to sit down.

"My room is not often this untidy," she laughed, gesturing to the piles of clothes that had been tossed down here and there.

"But I am just in the middle of sorting things out. You know how it is."

Mma Makutsi nodded. Taking the questionnaire out of her briefcase, she passed it over to the young woman who looked at it and smiled.

"These questions are very easy," she said. "I have seen questions like this before."

"Please fill them in," asked Mma Makutsi. "Then I would like to talk to you for a very short time before I leave you to get on with your studies."

The last remark was made as she looked about the room; it was, as far as she could make out, devoid of books.

"Yes," said Motlamedi, applying herself to the questionnaire, "we students are very busy with our studies."

While Motlamedi wrote out her answers, Mma Makutsi glanced discreetly at her head. Unfortunately the style in which the finalist had arranged her hair was such that it was impossible to see the shape of the head. Even Lombroso himself, thought Mma Makutsi, might have found it difficult to reach a view on this person. Yet this did not really matter; everything she had seen of this person, from her rudeness at the door to her look of near-disdain (concealed at the moment when Mma Makutsi had declared herself to be a journalist), told her that this woman would be a bad choice for the post of Miss Beauty and Integrity. She was unlikely to be charged with theft, of course, but there were other ways in which she could bring disgrace to the competition and to Mr Pulani. The most likely of these was involvement in some scandal with a married man; girls of this sort were no respecters of matrimony and could be expected to seek out any man who could advance her career, irrespective of whether he already had a wife. What sort of example would that be to the youth of Botswana? Mma Makutsi asked herself. The mere thought of it made her feel angry and she found herself involuntarily shaking her head with disapproval.

Motlamedi looked up from her form.

"What are you shaking your head about, Mma?" she asked. "Am I writing the wrong thing?"

"No, you are not." Her reply came hurriedly. "You must write the truth. That is all I am interested in."

Motlamedi smiled. "I always tell the truth," she said. "I have told the truth since I was a child. I cannot stand people who tell lies."

"Oh yes?"

She finished writing and handed the form to Mma Makutsi.

"I hope I have not written too much," she said. "I know that you journalists are very busy people."

Mma Makutsi took the form and ran her eye down the responses.

Question 1: Africa has a very great history, although many people pay no attention to it. Africa can teach the world about how to care for other people. There are other things, too, that Africa can teach the world.

Question 2: It is my greatest ambition to work for the benefit of other people. I look forward to the day when I can help more people. That is one of the reasons why I deserve to win this competition: I am a girl who likes to help people. I am not one of these selfish girls.

Question 3: It is better to be a person of integrity. An honest girl is rich in her heart. That is the truth. Girls who worry about their looks are not as happy as girls who think about other people first. I am one of these latter girls, and that is how I know this thing.

Motlamedi watched as Mma Makutsi read.

"Well, Mma?" she said. "Would you like to ask me about anything I have written?"

Mma Makutsi folded the sheet of paper and slipped it into her briefcase.

"No thank you, Mma," she said. "You have told me everything I need to know. I do not need to ask you any other questions."

Motlamedi looked anxious.

"What about a photograph?" she said. "If the paper would like to send a photographer I think that I could let a photograph be taken. I shall be here all afternoon."

Mma Makutsi moved towards the door.

"Perhaps," she said. "But I do not know. You have given me very useful answers here and I shall be able to put them into the newspaper. I feel I know you quite well now."

Motlamedi felt that she could now afford to be gracious.

"I am glad that we have met," she said. "I look forward to our next meeting. Maybe you will be at the competition . . . you could bring the photographer."

"Perhaps," said Mma Makutsi, as she left.

THE APPRENTICE was talking to a couple of young women when Mma Makutsi emerged. He was explaining something about the car and they were listening to him avidly. Mma Makutsi did not hear the entire conversation, but she did pick up the end: ". . . at least eighty miles an hour. And the engine is very quiet. If a boy is sitting with a girl in the back and wants to kiss her in that car he has to be very quiet because they will hear it in the front."

The students giggled.

"Do not listen to him, ladies," said Mma Makutsi. "This young man is not allowed to see girls. He already has a wife and three children and his wife gets very cross if she hears that girls are talking to him. Very cross."

The students moved back. One of them now looked at the apprentice reproachfully.

"But that is not true," protested the young man. "I am not married."

"That's what all you men say," said one of the students, angry now. "You come round here and talk to girls like us while all the time you are thinking of your wives. What sort of behaviour is that?"

"Very bad," chipped in Mma Makutsi, as she opened the passenger door and prepared to get in. "Anyway, it is time for us to go. This young man has to drive me somewhere else."

"You be careful of him, Mma," said one of the students. "We know about boys like that."

The apprentice started the car, tight-lipped, and drove off.

"You should not have said that, Mma. You made me look foolish."

Mma Makutsi snorted. "You made yourself look foolish. Why are you always running after girls? Why are you always trying to impress them?"

"Because that's how I enjoy myself," said the apprentice defensively. "I like talking to girls. We have all these beautiful girls in this country and there is nobody to talk to them. I am doing a service to the country."

Mma Makutsi looked at him scornfully. Although the young men had been working hard for her and had responded well to her suggestions, there seemed to be a chronic weakness in their character—this relentless womanising. Could anything be done about it? She doubted it, but it would pass in time, she thought, and they would become more serious. Or perhaps they would not. People did not change a great deal. Mma Ramotswe had said that to her once and it had stuck in her mind. People do not change, but that does not mean that they will always remain the same. What you can do is find out the good side of their character and then bring that out. Then it might seem that they had changed, which they had not; but they would be different afterwards, and better. That's what Mma Ramotswe had said—or something like that. And if there was one person in Botswana—one person—to whom one should listen very carefully, it was Mma Ramotswe.

CHAPTER SIXTEEN

THE COOK'S TALE

MMA RAMOTSWE lay on her bed and gazed up at the whiteboards of the ceiling. Her stomach felt less disturbed now, and the worst of the dizziness had passed. But when she shut her eyes, and then opened them again fairly shortly thereafter, there was a white ring about everything, a halo of light which danced for a moment and then dimmed. In other circumstances it might have been a pleasant sensation, but here, at the mercy of a poisoner, it was alarming. What substance would produce such a result? Poisons could attack eyesight, Mma Ramotswe knew that well. As a child they had been taught about the plants which could be harvested in the bush, the shrubs that could produce sleep, the tree bark which could bring an unwanted pregnancy to a sudden end, the roots that cured itching. But there were others, plants that produced the muti used by the witch doctors, innocent-looking plants which could kill at a touch, or so they were told. It was one of these, no doubt, that had been slipped onto her plate by her host's wife, or, more likely, put into an entire dish of food, indiscriminately, but avoided by the poisoner herself. If a person was wicked enough to poison a husband, then she would not stop at taking others with him.

Mma Ramotswe looked at her watch. It was past seven, and the windows were dark. She had slept through the sunset and now it was time for the evening meal, not that she felt like eating. They would be wondering where she was, though, and so she should tell them that she was unwell and could not join them for supper.

She sat up in her bed and blinked. The white light was still there, but was fading now. She put her feet over the edge of the bed and wriggled her toes into her shoes, hoping that no scorpions had crawled into them during her rest. She had always checked her shoes for scorpions since, as a child, she had put her foot into her school shoes one morning and had been badly stung by a large brown scorpion which had sheltered there for the night. Her entire foot had swollen up, so badly, in fact, that they had carried her to the Dutch Reformed Hospital at the foot of the hill. A nurse there had put on a dressing and given her something for the pain. Then she had warned her always to check her shoes and the warning had remained with her.

"We live up here," said the nurse, holding her hand at chest height. "They live down there. Remember that."

Later, it had seemed to her that this was a warning that could apply in more senses than one. Not only did it refer to scorpions and snakes—about which it was patently true—but it could apply with equal force to people. There was a world beneath the world inhabited by ordinary, law-abiding people; a world of selfishness and mistrust occupied by scheming and manipulative people. One had to check one's shoes.

She withdrew her toes from the shoes before they had reached the end. Reaching down, she picked up the right shoe and tipped it up. There was nothing. She picked up the left shoe and did the same. Out dropped a tiny glistening creature, which danced on the floor for a moment, as if in defiance, and then scuttled off into the dark of a corner.

Mma Ramotswe made her way down the corridor. As she reached the end, where the corridor became a living room, the maid came out of a doorway and greeted her.

"I was coming to find you, Mma," said the maid. "They have made food and it is almost ready."

"Thank you, Mma. I have been sleeping. I have not been feeling well, although I am better now. I do not think that I could eat tonight, but I would like some tea. I'm very thirsty."

The maid's hands shot up to her mouth. "Aiee! That is very bad, Mma! All of the people have been ill. The old lady has been sick, sick, all the time. The man and his wife have been shouting out and holding their stomachs. Even the boy was sick, although he was not so bad. The meat must have been bad."

MMA RAMOTSWE stared at the maid. "Everybody?"

"Yes. Everybody. The man was shouting that he would go and chase the butcher who sold that meat. He was very cross."

"And the wife? What was she doing?"

The maid looked down at the floor. These were intimate matters of the human stomach and it embarrassed her to talk about them so openly.

"She could keep nothing down. She tried to take water—I brought it to her—but it came straight up again. Her stomach is now empty, though, and I think she is feeling better. I have been a nurse all afternoon. Here, there. I even looked in through your door to see that you were all right and I saw you sleeping peacefully. I did not know that you had been sick too."

Mma Ramotswe was silent for a moment. The information which the maid had given her changed the situation entirely. The principal suspect, the wife, had been poisoned, as had the old woman, who was also a suspect. This meant either that there had been an accident in the distribution of the poison, or that neither of these had anything to do with it. Of the two possibilities, Mma Ramotswe thought that the second was the more likely. When she had been feeling ill she imagined that she had been deliberately poisoned, but was this likely? On sober reflection, beyond the waves of nausea that had engulfed her, it seemed ridiculous to think that a poisoner would strike so quickly, and so obviously, on the arrival of a guest. It would have been suspicious and unsubtle, and poisoners, she had read, were usually extremely subtle people.

The maid looked at Mma Ramotswe expectantly, as if she thought that the guest might now take over the running of the household.

"None of them needs a doctor, do they?" asked Mma Ramotswe.

"No. They are all getting better, I think. But I do not know what to do. They shout at me a lot and I cannot do anything when they are all shouting."

"No," said Mma Ramotswe. "That would not be easy for you."

She looked at the maid. They shout at me a lot. Here was

another with a motive, she reflected, but the thought was absurd. This was an honest woman. Her face was open and she smiled as she spoke. Secrets left shadows on the face, and there were none there.

"Well," said Mma Ramotswe, "you could make me some tea, perhaps. Then, after that, I think you should go off to your room and leave them to get better. Perhaps they will shout less in the morning."

The maid smiled appreciatively. "I will do that, Mma. I will bring you your tea in your room. Then you can go back to sleep."

SHE SLEPT, but fitfully. From time to time she awoke, and heard voices from within the house, or the sounds of movement, a door slamming, a window being opened, the creaking noises of an old house by night. Shortly before dawn, when she realised that she would not fall asleep, she arose, slipped on her house-coat, and made her way out of the house. A dog at the back door rose to its feet, still groggy with sleep, and sniffed suspiciously at her feet; a large bird, which had been perched on the roof, launched itself with an effort and flew away.

Mma Ramotswe looked about her. The sun would not be up for half an hour or so, but there was enough light to make things out and it grew stronger and clearer every moment. The trees were still indistinct, dark shapes, but the branches and the leaves would soon appear in detail, like a painting revealed. It was a time of day that she loved, and here, in this lonely spot, away from roads and people and the noise they made, the loveliness of her land appeared distilled. The sun would come before too long and coarsen the world; for the moment, though, the bush, the sky, the earth itself, seemed modest and understated.

Mma Ramotswe took a deep breath. The smell of the bush, the smell of the dust and the grass, caught at her heart, as it always did; and now there was added a whiff of wood smoke, that marvellous, acrid smell that insinuates itself through the still air of morning as people make their breakfast and warm their hands at the flames. She turned around. There was a fire nearby; the morning fire to heat the hot water boiler, or the fire, perhaps, of a watchman who had spent the night hours around a few burning embers.

She walked round to the back of the house, following a small path which had been marked out with whitewashed stones, a habit picked up from the colonial administrators who had whitewashed the stones surrounding their encampments and quarters. They had done this throughout Africa, even whitewashing the lower trunks of the trees they had planted in long avenues. Why? Because of Africa.

She turned the corner of the house and saw the man crouched before the old brick-encased boiler. Such boilers were common features of older houses, which had no electricity, and of course they were still necessary out here, where there was no power apart from that provided by the generator. It would be far cheaper to heat the household's water in such a boiler than to use the diesel-generated current. And here was the boiler being stoked up with wood to make hot water for the morning baths.

The man saw her approaching and stood up, wiping his khaki trousers as he did so. Mma Ramotswe greeted him in the traditional way and he replied courteously. He was a tall man in his early forties, well-built, and he had strong, good-looking features.

"You are making a good fire there, Rra," she observed, pointing to the glow that came from the front of the boiler.

"The trees here are good for burning," he said simply. "There are many of them. We never lack for firewood."

Mma Ramotswe nodded. "So this is your job?"

He frowned. "That and other things."

"Oh?" The tone of his remark intrigued her. These "other things" were clearly unwelcome. "What other things, Rra?"

"I am the cook," he said. "I am in charge of the kitchen and I make the food."

He looked at her defensively, as if expecting a response.

"That is good," said Mma Ramotswe. "It is a good thing to be able to cook. They have got some very fine men cooks down in Gaborone. They call them chefs and they wear peculiar white hats."

The man nodded. "I used to work in a hotel in Gaborone," he said. "I was a cook there. Not the head cook, but one of the junior ones. That was a few years ago."

"Why did you come here?" asked Mma Ramotswe. It seemed an extraordinary thing to have done. Cooks like that in Gaborone would have been paid far more, she assumed, than cooks in the farmhouses.

The cook stretched out a leg and pushed a piece of wood back into the fire with his foot.

"I never liked it," he said. "I did not like being a cook then, and I do not like it now."

"Then why do it, Rra?"

He sighed. "It is a difficult story, Mma. To tell it would take a long time, and I have to get back to work when the sun comes up. But I can tell you some of it now, if you like. You sit down there, Mma, on that log. Yes. That is fine. I shall tell you since you ask me.

"I come from over that way, by that hill, over there, but behind it, ten miles behind it. There is a village there which nobody knows because it is not important and nothing ever happens there. Nobody pays attention to it because the people there are very quiet. They never shout and they never make a fuss. So nothing ever happens.

"There was a school in the village with a very wise teacher. He had two other teachers to help him, but he was the main one, and everybody listened to him rather than the other teachers. He said to me one day, 'Samuel, you are a very clever boy. You can remember the names of all the cattle and who the mothers and fathers of the cattle were. You are better than anybody else at that. A boy like you could go to Gaborone and get a job.'

"I did not find it strange that I should remember cattle as I loved cattle more than anything else. I wanted to work with cattle one day, but there was no work with cattle where we were and so I had to think of something else. I did not believe that I was good enough to go to Gaborone, but when I was sixteen the teacher gave me some money which the Government had given him and I used it to buy a bus ticket to Gaborone. My father had no money, but he gave me a watch which he had found one day lying beside the edge of the tarred road. It was his prize possession, but he gave it to me and told me to sell it for money to buy food once I reached Gaborone.

"I did not want to sell that watch, but eventually, when my

stomach was so empty that it was sore, I had to do so. I was given one hundred pula for it, because it was a good watch, and I spent that on food to make me strong.

"It took me many days to find work, and my money for food would not last forever. At last I found work in a hotel, where they made me carry things and open doors for guests. Sometimes these guests came from very far away, and they were very rich. Their pockets were full of money. They gave me tips sometimes, and I saved the money in the post office. I wish I still had that money.

"After a while, they transferred me to the kitchen, where I helped the chefs. They found out that I was a good cook and they gave me a uniform. I cooked there for ten years, although I hated it. I did not like those hot kitchens and all those smells of food, but it was my job, and I had to do it. And it was while I was doing that, working in that hotel, that I met the brother of the man who lives here. You may know the one I am talking about—he is the important one who lives in Gaborone. He said that he would give me a job up here, as Assistant Manager of the farm, and I was very happy. I told him that I knew all about cattle, and that I would look after the farm well.

"I came up here with my wife. She is from this part, and she was very happy to be back. They gave us a nice place to live, and my wife is now very contented. You will know, Mma, how important it is to have a wife or a husband who is contented. If you do not, then you will never have any peace. Never. I also have a contented mother-in-law. She moved in and lives at the back of the house. She is always singing because she is so happy that she has her daughter and my children there.

"I was looking forward to working with the cattle, but as

soon as I met the brother who lives up here, he asked me what I had done and I said that I had been a cook. He was very pleased to hear this and he said that I should be the cook in the house. They were always having big, important people up from Gaborone and it would impress them if there was a real cook in the house. I said that I did not want to do this, but he forced me. He spoke to my wife and she took his side. She said that this was such a good place to be that only a fool would not do what these people wanted me to do. My mother-in-law started to wail. She said that she was an old woman and she would die if we had to move. My wife said to me: 'Do you want to kill my mother? Is that what you are wanting to do?'

"So I have had to be the cook in this place, and I am still surrounded by cooking smells when I would rather be out with the cattle. That is why I am not contented, Mma, when all my family is very contented. It is a strange story, do you not think?"

HE FINISHED the story and looked mournfully at Mma Ramotswe. She met his gaze, and then looked away. She was thinking, her mind racing ahead of itself, the possibilities jostling one another until a hypothesis emerged, was examined, and a conclusion reached.

She looked at him again. He had risen to his feet and was closing the door of the boiler. Within the water tank, an old petrol drum converted for the purpose, she heard the bubbling of heating water. Should she speak, or should she remain silent? If she spoke, she could be wrong and he could take violent exception to what she said. But if she held back, then she would have lost the moment. So she decided.

"There's something that I've been wanting to ask you, Rra," she said.

"Yes?" He glanced up at her briefly, and then busied himself again with the tidying of the wood stack.

"I saw you putting something into the food yesterday. You didn't see me, but I saw you. Why did you do it?"

He froze. He was on the point of lifting up a large log, his hands stretched around it, his back bent, ready to take the weight. Then, quite slowly, his hands unclasped and he straightened himself up.

"You saw me?" His voice was strained, almost inaudible.

Mma Ramotswe swallowed. "Yes. I saw you. You put something in the food. Something bad."

He looked at her now, and she saw that the eyes had dulled. The face, animated before, was devoid of expression.

"You are not trying to kill them, are you?"

He opened his mouth to answer, but no sound came.

Mma Ramotswe felt emboldened. She had made the right decision and now she had to finish what she had begun.

"You just wanted them to stop using you as a cook, didn't you? If they felt that your food tasted bad, then they would just give up on you as a cook and you could get back to the work that you really wanted to do. That's right, isn't it?"

He nodded.

"You were very foolish, Rra," said Mma Ramotswe. "You could have harmed somebody."

"Not with what I used," he said. "It was perfectly safe."

Mma Ramotswe shook her head. "It is never safe."

The cook looked down at his hands.

"I am not a murderer," he said. "I am not that sort of man."

Mma Ramotswe snorted. "You are very lucky that I worked out what you were doing," she said. "I didn't see you, of course, but your story gave you away."

"And now?" said the cook. "You will tell them and they will call the police. Please, Mma, remember that I have a family. If I cannot work for these people it will be hard for me to find another job now. I am getting older. I cannot . . ."

Mma Ramotswe raised a hand to stop him. "I am not that sort of person," she said. "I am going to tell them that the food you used was bad, but that you could not tell it. I am going to tell the brother that he should give you another job."

"He will not do that," said the cook. "I have asked him."

"But I am a woman," said Mma Ramotswe. "I know how to make men do things."

The cook smiled. "You are very kind, Mma."

"Too kind," said Mma Ramotswe, turning to go back towards the house. The sun was beginning to come up and the trees and the hills and the very earth were golden. It was a beautiful place to be, and she would have liked to have stayed. But now there was nothing more to do. She knew what she had to tell the Government Man and she might as well return to Gaborone to do it.

CHAPTER SEVENTEEN

AN EXCELLENT TYPE OF GIRL

T HAD not been difficult to identify Motlamedi as unsuitable for the important office of Miss Beauty and Integrity. There were three further names on the list, though, and each of them would have to be interviewed for a judgement to be made. They might not be so transparent; it was rare for Mma Makutsi to feel sure about somebody on a first meeting, but there was no doubt in her mind that Motlamedi was, quite simply, a *bad girl*. This description was very specific; it had nothing to do with *bad women* or *bad ladies*—they were quite different categories. Bad women were prostitutes; bad ladies were manipulative older ladies, usually married to older men, who interfered in the affairs of others for their own selfish ends. The expression *bad girl*, by contrast, referred to somebody who was usually rather younger (certainly under thirty) and whose interest was in having a good time. That was the essence of it, in fact—a good time. Indeed there was a subcategory of bad girls, that of *good-time girls*. These were girls who were mainly to be found in bars with flashy men, having what appeared to be a good time. Some of these flashy men, of course, saw themselves as merely being *one of the boys,* which they thought gave them an excuse for all sorts of selfish behaviour. But not in Mma Makutsi's book.

At the other end of the spectrum, there were *good girls*. These were girls who worked hard and who were appreciated by their families. They were the ones who visited the elders; who looked after the smaller children, sitting for hours under a tree watching the children play; and who in due course trained to be nurses or, as in Mma Makutsi's case, undertook a general secretarial training at the Botswana Secretarial College. Unfortunately, these good girls, who carried half the world upon their shoulders, did not have much fun.

There was no doubt that Motlamedi was not a good girl, but was there any possibility, Mma Makutsi now glumly asked herself, that any of the others might prove to be much better? The difficulty was that good girls were unlikely to enter a beauty competition in the first place. It was, in general, not the sort of thing that good girls thought of doing. And if her pessimism were to prove justified, then what would she be able to say to Mr Pulani when he came to her for her report? It would not be very useful to say that all the girls were as bad as one another, that none of them was worthy of the title. That would be singularly unhelpful, and she suspected that she would not even be able to put in a fee note for that sort of information.

She sat in her car with the apprentice and looked despairingly at her list of names.

"Where to now?" asked the apprentice. His tone was surly,

but only just so; he realised that she was, after all, still Acting Manager, and both he and his colleague had a healthy respect for this remarkable woman who had come to the garage and turned their working practices upside down.

Mma Makutsi sighed. "I have three girls to see," she said. "And I cannot decide which one to go to next."

The apprentice laughed. "I know a lot about girls," he said. "I could tell you."

Mma Makutsi cast a scornful glance in his direction. "You and your girls!" she said. "That's all you think of, isn't it? You and that lazy friend of yours. Girls, girls, girls . . ."

She stopped herself. Yes, he was an expert in girls—it was well-known—and Gaborone was not such a large place. There was a chance, probably quite a good chance, that he actually knew something about these girls. If they were bad girls, as they almost certainly were, or, more specifically, good-time girls, then he would probably have encountered them on his rounds of the bars. She signalled for him to draw over to the side of the road.

"Stop. Stop here. I want to show you this list."

The apprentice drew in and took the list from Mma Makutsi. As he read it, he broke into a smile.

"This is a fine list of girls!" he said enthusiastically. "These are some of the best girls in town. Or at least three of them are the best girls in town. Big girls, you know what I mean, big, excellent girls. These are girls that we boys are very appreciative of. We approve of these girls. Oh yes! Too much!"

Mma Makutsi's heart skipped a beat. Her intuition had been right; he had the answer to her quest and now all that she had to do was to coax it out of him.

"So which girls do you know?" she asked. "Which are the three you know?"

The apprentice laughed. "This one here," he said. "This one who is called Makita. I know her. She is very good fun, and she laughs a lot, especially when you tickle her. Then this one, Gladys, my, my! Ow! One, two, three! And I also know this one here, this girl called Motlamedi, or rather my brother knows her. He says that she is a very clever girl who is a student at the university but she doesn't waste too much time on her books. Lots of brains, but also a very big bottom. She is more interested in being glamorous."

Mma Makutsi nodded. "I have just been speaking to that girl," she said. "Your brother is right about her. But what about that other girl, Patricia, the one who lives in Tlokweng? Do you know that girl?"

The apprentice shook his head. "She is an unknown girl that one," he said, adding quickly, "But I am sure that she is a very charming girl, too. You never know."

Mma Makutsi took the piece of paper away from him and tucked it into the pocket of her dress. "We are going to Tlokweng," she said. "I need to meet this Patricia."

They drove out to Tlokweng in silence. The apprentice appeared to be lost in thought—possibly thinking about the girls on the list—while Mma Makutsi was thinking about the apprentice. It was very unfair—but entirely typical of the injustice of the relations between the sexes—that there was no expression quite like *good-time girl* that could be applied to boys like this ridiculous apprentice. They were every bit as bad—if not worse—as the *good-time girls* themselves, but nobody seemed to blame them for it. Nobody spoke of *bar boys,* for example, and nobody would describe any male over twelve as a *bad boy*. Women, as usual, were expected to behave better than men, and inevitably attracted criticism for doing things that men were licensed to do with impunity. It was not fair; it had never been fair, and it would probably never be fair in the future. Men would wriggle out of it somehow, even if you tied them up in a constitution. Men judges would find that the constitution really said something rather different from what was written on the page and interpret it in a favour of men. *All people, both men and women, are entitled to equal treatment in the workplace* became *Women can get some jobs, but they cannot do certain jobs (for their own protection) as men will do these jobs better anyway.*

Why did men behave like this? It had always been a mystery to Mma Makutsi although latterly she had begun to glimpse the makings of an explanation. She thought that it might have something to do with the way in which mothers treated their sons. If the mothers allowed the boys to think that they were special—and all mothers did that, as far as Mma Makutsi could make out—then that encouraged boys to develop attitudes which never left them. If young boys were allowed to think that women were there to look after them, then they would continue to think this when they grew up—and they did. Mma Makutsi had seen so many examples of it that she could not imagine anybody seriously challenging the theory. This very apprentice was an example. She had seen his mother come to the garage once with a whole watermelon for her son and she had seen her cut it for him and give it to him in the way in which one would feed a small child. That mother should not be doing that; she should be encouraging her son to buy his own watermelons and cut them up himself. It was exactly this sort of treatment which made him so immature in his treatment of women. They were playthings to him; hewers of watermelon; eternal substitute mothers.

THEY ARRIVED at plot 2456, at the gate of the neat, mud-brown little house with its outhouse for the chickens and, unusually, two traditional grain bins at the back. The chicken food would be kept there, she thought; the sorghum grain that would be scattered each morning on the neatly swept yard, to be pecked at by the hungry birds on their release from the coop. It was obvious to Mma Makutsi that an older woman lived here, as only an older woman would take the trouble to keep the yard in such a traditional and careful way. She would be Patricia's grandmother, perhaps—one of those remarkable African women who worked and worked into her eighties, and beyond, and who were the very heart of the family.

The apprentice parked the car while Mma Makutsi made her way up the path that led to the house. She had called out, as was polite, but she thought that they had not heard her; now a woman appeared at the door, wiping her hands on a cloth and greeting her warmly.

Mma Makutsi explained her mission. She did not say that she was a journalist, as she had done on the visit to Motlamedi; it would have been wrong to do that here, in this traditional home, to the woman who had revealed herself to be Patricia's mother.

"I want to find out about the people in this competition," she said. "I have been asked to talk to them."

The woman nodded. "We can sit at the doorway," she said. "It is shady. I will call my daughter. That is her room there."

She pointed to a door at the side of the house. The green paint which had once covered it was peeling off and the hinges looked rusty. Although the yard appeared well kept, the house itself seemed to be in need of repair. There was not a great deal of money about, thought Mma Makutsi, and pondered, for a moment, what the cash prize for the eventually elected Miss Beauty and Integrity could mean in circumstances such as these. That prize was four thousand pula, and a voucher to spend in a clothing store. Not much of the money would be wasted, thought Mma Makutsi, noticing the frayed hem of the woman's skirt.

She sat down and took the mug of water which the woman had offered her.

"It is hot today," said the woman. "But there will be rain soon. I am sure of that."

"There will be rain," agreed Mma Makutsi. "We need the rain."

"We do need it, Mma," said the woman. "This country always needs rain."

"You are right, Mma. Rain."

They were silent for a moment, thinking about rain. When there was no rain, you thought about it, hardly daring to hope for the miracle to begin. And when the rain came, all you could think about was how long it would last. *God is crying. God is crying for this country. See, children, there are his tears. The rain is his tears.* That is what the teacher at Bobonong had said one day, when she was young, and she had remembered her words.

"Here is my daughter."

Mma Makutsi looked up. Patricia had appeared silently and was standing before her. She smiled at the younger woman, who dropped her eyes and gave a slight curtsey. *I am not that old!* thought Mma Makutsi, but she was impressed by the gesture.

"You can sit down," said her mother. "This lady wants to talk to you about the beauty competition."

Patricia nodded. "I am very excited about it, Mma. I know that I won't win, but I am still very excited."

Don't be too sure about that, thought Mma Makutsi, but did not say anything.

"Her aunt has made her a very nice dress for the competition," said the mother. "She has spent a lot of money on it and it is very fine material. It is a very good dress."

"But the other girls will be more beautiful," said Patricia. "They are very smart girls. They live in Gaborone. There is even one who is a student at the university. She is a very clever girl that one."

And bad, thought Mma Makutsi.

"You must not think that you will lose," interjected the mother. "That is not the way to go into a competition. If you think that you will lose, then you will never win. What if Seretse Khama had said: We will never get anywhere. Then where would Botswana be today? Where would it be?"

Mma Makutsi nodded her agreement. "That is no way to set out," she said. "You must think: I can win. Then you may win. You never know."

Patricia smiled. "You are right. I shall try to be more determined. I shall do my best."

"Good," said Mma Makutsi. "Now tell me, what would you like to do with your life?"

There was a silence. Both Mma Makutsi and the mother looked expectantly at Patricia.

"I would like to go to the Botswana Secretarial College," replied Patricia.

Mma Makutsi looked at her, watching her eyes. She was not lying. This was a wonderful girl, a truthful girl, one of the finest girls in Botswana, quite beyond any doubt.

"That is a very fine college," she said. "I am a graduate of it myself." She paused, and then decided to go ahead. "In fact, I got 97 percent there."

Patricia sucked in her breath. "Ow! That is a very high mark, Mma. You must be very clever."

Mma Makutsi laughed dismissively. "Oh no, I worked hard. That was all."

"But it is very good," said Patricia. "You are very lucky, Mma, to be pretty and clever too."

Mma Makutsi was at a loss for words. She had not been called pretty before, or not by a stranger. Her aunts had said that she should try to make something of what looks she had, and her mother had made a similar remark; but nobody had called her pretty, except this young woman, still in her late teens, who was herself so obviously pretty.

"You are very kind," she said.

"She is a kind girl," said the mother. "She has always been a kind girl."

Mma Makutsi smiled. "Good," she said. "And do you know something? I think that she has a very good chance of winning that competition. In fact, I am sure that she is going to win. I am sure of it."

CHAPTER EIGHTEEN

THE FIRST STEP

MMA RAMOTSWE returned to Gaborone on the morning of her conversation with the cook. There had been further conversations—prolonged in one case—with other members of the household. She had talked to the new wife, who had listened gravely, and had hung her head. She had spoken to the old woman, who had been proud at first, and unbending, but who had eventually acknowledged the truth of what Mma Ramotswe had told her and had agreed with her in the end. And then she had confronted the brother, who had stared at her open-mouthed, but who had taken his cue from his mother, who had intruded into the conversation and told him sharply where his duty lay. At the end of it Mma Ramotswe felt raw; she had taken such risks, but her intuition had proved her correct and her strategy had paid off. There was only one more person to speak to now, and that person was back in Gaborone and he, she feared, might not be so easy.

The drive back was a pleasant one. The previous day's rains had already had an effect and there was a tinge of green across the land. In one or two places, there were puddles of water in which the sky was reflected in patches of silver blue. And the dust had been laid, which was perhaps most refreshing of all; that omnipresent, fine dust that towards the end of the dry season would get everywhere, clogging everything up and making one's clothes stiff and uncomfortable.

She drove straight back to Zebra Drive, where the children greeted her excitedly, the boy rushing round the tiny white van with whoops of delight and the girl propelling her wheelchair out onto the drive to meet her. And in the kitchen window, staring out at her, the face of Rose, her maid, who had looked after the children over her brief absence.

Rose made tea while Mma Ramotswe heard the children tell her of what had happened at school. There had been a competition and a classmate had won a prize of a fifty pula book token. One of the teachers had broken his arm and had appeared with the injured limb in a sling. A girl in one of the junior classes had eaten a whole tube of toothpaste and had been sick, which was only to be expected, was it not?

But there was other news. Mma Makutsi had telephoned from the office and had asked Mma Ramotswe to call back the moment she arrived home, which she had thought would be the following day.

"She sounded very excited," said Rose. "She said there was something important she wanted to talk to you about."

A steaming cup of bush tea before her, Mma Ramotswe dialled the number of Tlokweng Road Speedy Motors, the number shared by the two offices. The telephone rang for some time before she heard the familiar voice of Mma Makutsi.

"The No. 1 Tlokweng Road . . ." she began. "No. The No. 1 Speedy Ladies' . . ."

"It's just me, Mma," said Mma Ramotswe. "And I know what you mean."

"I am always getting the two mixed up," said Mma Makutsi, laughing. "That's what comes of trying to run two businesses at the same time."

"I am sure that you have been running both very well," said Mma Ramotswe.

"Well, yes," said Mma Makutsi. "In fact, I telephoned you to tell you that I have just collected a very large fee. Two thousand pula for one case. The client was very happy."

"You have done very well," said Mma Ramotswe. "I shall come in later and see just how well you have done. But first I would like you to arrange an appointment for me. Telephone that Government Man and tell him that he must come and see me at four o'clock."

"And if he's busy?"

"Tell him that he cannot be busy. Tell him that this matter is too important to wait."

She finished her tea and then ate a large meat sandwich which Rose had prepared for her. Mma Ramotswe had got out of the habit of a cooked lunch, except at weekends, and was happy with a snack or a glass of milk. She had a taste for sugar, however, and this meant that a doughnut or a cake might follow the sandwich. She was a traditionally built lady, after all, and she did not have to worry about dress size, unlike those poor, neurotic people who were always looking in mirrors and thinking that they were too big. What was too big, anyway? Who was to tell another person what size they should be? It was a form of dictatorship, by the thin, and she was not having any of it. If these thin people became any more insistent, then the more generously sized people would just have to sit on them. Yes, that would teach them! Hah!

It was shortly before three when she arrived at the office. The apprentices were busy with a car, but greeted her warmly and with none of the sullen resentment which had so annoyed her in the past.

"You're very busy," she said. "That is a very nice car that you're fixing there."

The older apprentice wiped his mouth with his sleeve. "It is a wonderful car. It belongs to a lady. Do you know that all the ladies are bringing their cars here now? We are so busy that we will need to take on apprentices ourselves! That will be a fine thing! We shall have desks and an office and there will be apprentices running round doing what we tell them to do."

"You are a very amusing young man," said Mma Ramotswe, smiling. "But do not get too big for your boots. Remember that you are just an apprentice and that the lady in there with the glasses is the boss now."

The apprentice laughed. "She is a good boss. We like her." He paused for a moment, looking intently at Mma Ramotswe. "But what about Mr J.L.B. Matekoni? Is he getting better?"

"It is too early to say," Mma Ramotswe replied. "Dr Moffat said that these pills could take two weeks. We have a few days to wait before we can tell."

"He is being well looked after?"

Mma Ramotswe nodded. The fact that the apprentice had asked that question was a good sign. It suggested that he was beginning to take an interest in the welfare of others. Perhaps he was growing up. Perhaps it was something to do with Mma Makutsi, who might have been teaching them a bit about morality as well as a bit about hard work.

She entered the office, to find Mma Makutsi on the telephone. She finished the conversation quickly and rose to greet her employer.

"Here it is," said Mma Makutsi, handing a piece of paper to Mma Ramotswe.

Mma Ramotswe looked at the cheque. Two thousand pula, it seemed, awaited the No. 1 Ladies' Detective Agency at the Standard Bank. And at the bottom of the cheque was the well-known name that made Mma Ramotswe draw in her breath.

"The beauty contest man . . . ?"

"That's him," said Mma Makutsi. "He was the client."

Mma Ramotswe tucked the cheque safely away in her bodice. Modern business methods were all very well, she thought, but when it came to the safeguarding of money there were some places which had yet to be bettered.

"You must have worked very quickly," said Mma Ramotswe. "What was the problem? Wife difficulties?"

"No," said Mma Makutsi. "It was all about beautiful girls and the finding of a beautiful girl who could be trusted."

"Very intriguing," said Mma Ramotswe. "And you obviously found one."

"Yes," said Mma Makutsi. "I found the right one to win his competition."

Mma Ramotswe was puzzled, but there was not enough time to go into it as she had to prepare herself for her four o'clock appointment. Over the next hour, she dealt with the mail, helped Mma Makutsi file papers relating to the garage, and drank a quick cup of bush tea. By the time that the large black car drew up outside the office and disgorged the Government Man, the office was tidy and organised and Mma Makutsi, seated primly behind her desk, was pretending to type a letter.

"SO!" SAID the Government Man, leaning back in the chair and folding his hands across his stomach. "You didn't stay very long up there. I take it that you managed to catch that poisoner. I very much hope that you did!"

Mma Ramotswe glanced at Mma Makutsi. They were used to male arrogance, but this far surpassed the normal such display.

"I spent exactly as much time up there as I needed to, Rra," she said calmly. "Then I came back to discuss the case with you."

The Government Man's lip curled. "I want an answer, Mma. I have not come to conduct a long conversation."

The typewriter clicked sharply in the background. "In that case," said Mma Ramotswe, "you can go back to your office. You either want to hear what I have to say, or you don't."

The Government Man was silent. Then he spoke, his voice lowered. "You are a very insolent woman. Perhaps you do not have a husband who can teach you how to speak to men with respect."

The noise from the typewriter rose markedly.

"And perhaps you need a wife who can teach you how to speak to women with respect," said Mma Ramotswe. "But do not let me hold you up. The door is there, Rra. It is open. You can go now."

The Government Man did not move.

"Did you hear what I said, Rra? Am I going to have to throw you out? I have got two young men out there who are very strong from all that work with engines. Then there is Mma Makutsi, whom you didn't even greet by the way, and there is me. That makes four people. Your driver is an old man. You are outnumbered, Rra."

Still the Government Man did not move. His eyes now were fixed on the floor.

"Well, Rra?" Mma Ramotswe drummed her fingers on the table.

The Government Man looked up.

"I am sorry, Mma. I have been rude."

"Thank you," said Mma Ramotswe. "Now, after you have greeted Mma Makutsi properly, in the traditional way, please, then we shall begin."

"I AM going to tell you a story," said Mma Ramotswe to the Government Man. "This story begins when there was a family with three sons. The father was very pleased that his firstborn was a son and he gave him everything that he wanted. The mother of this boy was also pleased that she had borne a boy for her husband, and she also made a fuss of this boy. Then another boy was born, and it was very sad for them when they realised that this boy had something wrong with his head. The mother heard what people were saying behind her back, that the reason why the boy was like that was that she had been with another man while she was pregnant. This was not true, of course, but all those wicked words cut and cut at her and she was ashamed to be seen out. But that boy was happy; he liked to be with cattle and to count them, although he could not count very well.

"The firstborn was very clever and did well. He went to Gaborone and he became well-known in politics. But as he became more powerful and well-known, he became more and more arrogant.

"But another son had been born. The firstborn was very happy with this, and he loved that younger boy. But underneath the love, there was fear that this new boy would take away the love that he himself had in the family and that the father would prefer him. Everything that the father did was seen as a sign that he preferred this youngest son, which was not true, of course, because the old man loved all his sons.

"When the youngest son took a wife, the firstborn was very angry. He did not tell anybody that he was angry, but that anger was bubbling away inside him. He was too proud to talk to anybody about it, because he had become so important and so big. He thought that this new wife would take his brother away from him, and then he would be left with nothing. He thought that she would try to take away their farm and all their cattle. He did not bother to ask himself whether this was true.

"He began to believe that she was planning to kill his brother, the brother whom he loved so much. He could not sleep for thinking of this, because there was so much hate growing up within him. So at last he went to see a certain lady—and I am that lady—and asked her to go and find proof that this was what was happening. He thought in this way that she might help him to get rid of the brother's wife.

"The lady did not know then what lay behind all this, and so she went up to stay with this unhappy family on their farm.

She spoke to them all and she found out that nobody was trying to kill anybody and that all this talk about poison had come up only because there was an unhappy cook who got his herbs mixed up. This man had been made unhappy by the brother because he had been forced to do things that he did not want to do. So the lady from Gaborone spoke to all the members of the family, one by one. Then she came back to Gaborone and spoke to the brother. He was very rude to her, because he had developed habits of rudeness and because he always got his own way. But she realised that under the skin of a bully there is always a person who is frightened and unhappy. And this lady thought that she would speak to that frightened and unhappy person.

"She knew, of course, that he would be unable to speak to his own family himself, and so she had done so for him. She told the family how he felt, and how his love for his brother had made him act jealously. The wife of his brother understood and she promised that she would do everything in her power to make him feel that she had not taken his beloved brother away from him. Then the mother understood too; she realised that she and her husband had made him feel anxious about losing his share of the farm and that they would attend to that. They said that they would make sure that everything was divided equally and that he need have no fear for what would happen in the future.

"Then this lady said to the family that she would talk to the brother in Gaborone and that she was sure that he would understand. She said that she would pass on to him any words that they might wish to say. She said that the real poison within families is not the poison that you put in your food, but the poison that grows up in the heart when people are jealous of one another and cannot speak these feelings and drain out the poison that way.

"So she came back to Gaborone with some words that the family wanted to say. And the words of the youngest brother were these: *I love my brother very much. I will never forget him. I would never take anything from him. The land and the cattle are for sharing with him.* And the wife of this man said: *I admire the brother of my husband and I would never take away from him the brother's love that he deserves to have.* And the mother said: *I am very proud of my son. There is room here for all of us. I have been worried that my sons will grow apart and that their wives will come between them and break up our family. I am not worried about that anymore. Please ask my son to come and see me soon. I do not have much time.* And the old father did not say very much except: *No man could ask for better sons.*"

THE TYPEWRITER was silent. Now Mma Ramotswe stopped speaking and watched the Government Man, who sat quite still, only his chest moving slightly as he breathed in and out. Then he raised a hand slowly to his face, and leant forward. He raised his other hand to his face.

"Do not be ashamed to cry, Rra," said Mma Ramotswe. "It is the way that things begin to get better. It is the first step."

CHAPTER NINETEEN

THE WORDS FOR AFRICA

T HERE WAS rain over the next four days. Every afternoon the clouds built up and then, amid bolts of lightning and great clashes of thunder, the rain fell upon the land. The roads, normally so dry and dusty, were flooded and the fields were shimmering expanses. But the thirsty land soon soaked up the water and the ground reappeared; but at least the people knew that the water was there, safely stored in the dam, and percolating down into the soil into which their wells were sunk. Everybody seemed relieved; another drought would have been too much to bear, although people would have put up with it, as they always had. The weather, they said, was changing and everybody felt vulnerable. In a country like Botswana, where the land and the animals were on such a narrow margin, a slight change could be disastrous. But the rains had come, and that was the important thing.

Tlokweng Road Speedy Motors became busier and busier,

and Mma Makutsi decided that the only thing to do, as Acting Manager, was to employ another mechanic for a few months, to see how things developed. She placed a small advertisement in the newspaper, and a man who had worked on the diamond mines as a diesel mechanic, but who had now retired, came forward and offered to work three days a week. He was started immediately, and he got on well with the apprentices.

"Mr J.L.B. Matekoni will like him," said Mma Ramotswe, "when he comes back and meets him."

"When will he come back?" asked Mma Makutsi. "It is over two weeks now."

"He'll be back one day," said Mma Ramotswe. "Let's not rush him."

That afternoon, she drove out to the orphan farm, parking her tiny white van directly outside Mma Potokwane's window. Mma Potokwane, who had seen her coming up the drive, had already put on the kettle by the time that Mma Ramotswe knocked at her door.

"Well, Mma Ramotswe," she said. "We have not seen you for a little while."

"I have been away," said Mma Ramotswe. "Then the rains came and the road out here has been very muddy. I did not want to get stuck in the mud."

"Very wise," said Mma Potokwane. "We had to get the bigger orphans out to push one or two trucks that got stuck just outside our drive. It was very difficult. All the orphans were covered in red mud and we had to hose them down in the yard."

"It looks like we will get good rains this year," said Mma Ramotswe. "That will be a very good thing for the country."

The kettle in the corner of the room began to hiss and Mma Potokwane arose to make tea.

"I have no cake to give you," she said. "I made a cake yesterday, but people have eaten every last crumb of it. It is as if the locusts had been here."

"People are very greedy," said Mma Ramotswe. "It would have been nice to have some cake. But I am not going to sit here and think about it."

They drank their tea in comfortable silence. Then Mma Ramotswe spoke.

"I thought I might take Mr J.L.B. Matekoni out for a run in the van," she ventured. "Do you think he might like that?"

Mma Potokwane smiled. "He would like it very much. He has been very quiet since he came here, but I have found out that there is something that he has been doing. I think it is a good sign."

"What is that?"

"He has been helping with that little boy," said Mma Potokwane. "You know the one that I asked you to find out something about? You remember that one?"

"Yes," said Mma Ramotswe, hesitantly. "I remember that little boy."

"Did you find out anything?" asked Mma Potokwane.

"No," said Mma Ramotswe. "I do not think that there is much that I can find out. But I do have an idea about that boy. It is just an idea."

Mma Potokwane slipped a further spoon of sugar into her tea and stirred it gently with a teaspoon.

"Oh yes? What's your idea?"

Mma Ramotswe frowned. "I do not think that my idea would help," she said. "In fact, I think it would not be helpful."

Mma Potokwane raised her teacup to her lips. She took a

long sip of tea and then replaced the cup carefully on the table.

"I think I know what you mean, Mma," she said. "I think that I have had the same idea. But I cannot believe it. Surely it cannot be true."

Mma Ramotswe shook her head. "That is what I have said to myself. People talk about these things, but they have never proved it, have they? They say that there are these wild children and that every so often somebody finds one. But do they ever actually prove that they have been brought up by animals? Is there any proof?"

"I have never heard of any," said Mma Potokwane.

"And if we told anybody what we think about this little boy, then what would happen? The newspapers would be full of it. There would be people coming from all over the world. They would probably try to take the boy off to live somewhere where they could look at him. They would take him outside Botswana."

"No," said Mma Potokwane. "The Government would never allow that."

"I don't know about that," said Mma Ramotswe. "They might. You can't be sure."

They sat silently. Then Mma Ramotswe spoke. "I think that there are some matters that are best left undisturbed," she said. "We don't want to know the answer to everything."

"I agree," said Mma Potokwane. "It is sometimes easier to be happy if you don't know everything."

Mma Ramotswe thought for a moment. It was an interesting proposition, and she was not sure if it was always true; it would require further thought, but not just then. She had a more immediate task in hand, and that was to drive Mr J.L.B. Matekoni out to Mochudi, where they could climb the kopje and look out over the plains. She was sure that he would like the sight of all that water; it would cheer him up.

"Mr J.L.B. Matekoni has been helping a bit with that boy," said Mma Potokwane. "It has been good for him to have something to do. I have seen him teaching him how to use a catapult. And I also hear that he has been teaching him words—teaching him how to speak. He is being very kind to him, and that, I think, is a good sign."

Mma Ramotswe smiled. She imagined Mr J.L.B. Matekoni teaching the wild boy the words for the things that he saw about him; teaching him the words for his world, the words for Africa.

MR J.L.B. Matekoni was not very communicative on the way up to Mochudi, sitting in the passenger seat of the tiny white van, staring out of the window at the unfolding plains and the other travellers on the road. He made a few remarks, though, and he even asked about what was happening at the garage, which he had not done at all when she had last gone to see him in his quiet room at the orphan farm.

"I hope that Mma Makutsi is controlling those apprentices of mine," he said. "They are such lazy boys. All they think about is women."

"There are still those problems with women," she said. "But she is making them work hard and they are doing well."

They reached the Mochudi turnoff and soon they were on the road that ran straight up towards the hospital, the kgotla, and the boulder-strewn kopje behind it.

"I think we should climb up the kopje," said Mma Ramotswe. "There is a good view from up there. We can see the difference that the rains have made."

"I am too tired to climb," said Mr J.L.B. Matekoni. "You go up. I shall stay down here."

"No," said Mma Ramotswe, firmly. "We shall both go up. You take my arm."

The climb did not take long, and soon they were standing on the edge of a large expanse of elevated rock, looking down on Mochudi: on the church, with its red tin roof, on the tiny hospital, where the heroic daily battle was fought, with small resources against such powerful enemies, and out, over the plains to the south. The river was flowing now, broadly and lazily, winding its way past clumps of trees and bush and the clusters of compounds that made up the straggling village. A small herd of cattle was being driven along a path near the river, and from where they stood the cattle looked tiny, like toys. But the wind was in their direction, and the sound of their bells could be made out, a distant, soft sound, so redolent of the Botswana bushland, so much the sound of home. Mma Ramotswe stood quite still; a woman on a rock in Africa, which was who, and where, she wanted to be.

"Look," said Mma Ramotswe. "Look down there. That is the house where I lived with my father. That is my place."

Mr J.L.B. Matekoni looked down and smiled. He smiled; and she noticed.

"I think you are feeling a bit better now, aren't you," she said.

Mr J.L.B. Matekoni nodded his head.

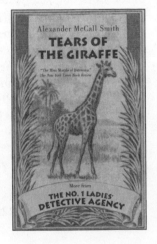

MORALITY FOR BEAUTIFUL GIRLS

While trying to resolve some financial problems for her business, Mma Ramotswe finds herself investigating the alleged poisoning of a government official as well as the moral character of the four finalists of the Miss Beauty and Integrity contest. Other difficulties arise at her fiancé's Tlokweng Road Speedy Motors, as Mma Ramotswe discovers he is more complicated than he seems.

Volume 3
1-4000-3136-2 (pbk)

The mysteries are "smart and sassy . . . [with] the power to amuse or shock or touch the heart, sometimes all at once."
—*Los Angeles Times*

THE KALAHARI TYPING SCHOOL FOR MEN

Mma Precious Ramotswe is content. But, as always, there are troubles. Mr J.L.B. Matekoni has not set the date for their wedding, her assistant Mma Makutsi wants a husband, and worst of all, a rival detective agency has opened up in town. Of course, Precious will manage these things, as she always does, with her uncanny insight and good heart.

Volume 4
1-4000-3180-X (pbk)
0-375-42217-X (hc)

THE FULL CUPBOARD OF LIFE

Mma Ramotswe has weighty matters on her mind. She has been approached by a wealthy lady to check up on several suitors. Are these men interested in her or just her money? This may be difficult to find out, but it's just the kind of case Mma Ramotswe likes.

Volume 5
1-4000-3181-8 (pbk)
0-375-42218-8 (hc)

IN THE COMPANY OF CHEERFUL LADIES

Precious Ramotswe is busier than usual at the No. 1 Ladies' Detective Agency when the appearance of a strange intruder in her house and a mysterious pumpkin in her yard add to her concerns. But what finally rattles Mma Ramotswe's normally unshakable composure is the visitor who forces her to confront a painful secret from her past.

Volume 6
0-375-42271-4 (hc)
Paperback available Spring 2006

A New Series Begins
THE SUNDAY PHILOSOPHY CLUB

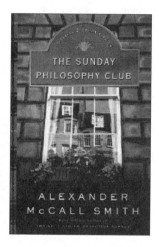

**THE SUNDAY
PHILOSOPHY CLUB**
Isabel Dalhousie is fond of problems,
and sometimes she becomes
interested in problems that are,
quite frankly, none of her business—
including some that are best left to
the police. Filled with endearingly
thorny characters and a Scottish
atmosphere as thick as a highland
mist, *The Sunday Philosophy Club* is
an irresistible pleasure.

**Volume 1
1-4000-7709-5 (pbk)
0-375-42298-6 (hc)**

**FRIENDS, LOVERS,
CHOCOLATE**
While taking care of her niece Cat's
delicatessen, Isabel meets a heart
transplant patient who has had some
strange experiences in the wake of
surgery. Against the advice of her
housekeeper, Isabel is intent on
investigating. Matters are further
complicated when Cat returns from
vacation with a new boyfriend, and
Isabel's fondness for him lands her in
another muddle.

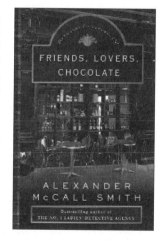

**Volume 2
0-375-42299-4 (hc)
Paperback available Fall 2006**

The Official Home of Alexander McCall Smith on the Web

WWW.ALEXANDERMCCALLSMITH.COM

A comprehensive Web site for new readers and longtime fans alike, with five exclusive content areas:

- **THE NO. 1 LADIES' DETECTIVE AGENCY**
  The original site for McCall Smith's bestselling series. Explore Precious Ramotswe's Botswana through book descriptions, a photo gallery, advice from Mma Ramotswe, and more.

- **THE SUNDAY PHILOSOPHY CLUB**
  Enter a Scottish atmosphere as thick as a highland mist, complete with a photo tour of Isabel Dalhousie's Edinburgh.

- **PROFESSOR DR VON IGELFELD ENTERTAINMENTS**
  Three original paperback novellas introducing the eccentric and ever-likable Professor Dr von Igelfeld, his colleagues, and their comic adventures.

- **ABOUT THE AUTHOR**
  Read about Alexander McCall Smith and get updates on tour events and other author activities.

- **JOIN THE COMMUNITY**
  Share the world of Alexander McCall Smith with friends, family, and fellow book club members. Print our free Reading Group Guides and sign up for the Alexander McCall Smith Fan Club and e-Newsletter.

Acclaim for Alexander McCall Smith and

THE KALAHARI TYPING SCHOOL FOR MEN

"An affectionate portrait of Africa. The appeal . . . lies in [its] very decency . . . as Mma Ramotswe would say, that 'old Botswana morality.'"　　　　　　　　　　　—*U.S. News & World Report*

"Spare and neatly crafted. . . . Sparkles with African sunshine and Mma Ramotswe's wit."　　　　　　　　—*The Dallas Morning News*

"A side of Africa too rarely seen on the news, and Smith's old-fashioned storytelling gifts make Precious a treasure."　—*People*

"Charming."　　　　　　　　　　　　　　　　　—*Newsday*

"[Precious Ramotswe's] heart and moxie have captivated readers worldwide."　　　　　　　　　　　　　—*Associated Press*

"What with the touching flashbacks to Mma Ramotswe's younger days and the rich supporting cast of friends, associates and unexpectedly acquired foster children, Mr. McCall Smith's saga is evolving into a tapestry of extraordinary nuance and richness."
　　　　　　　　　　　　　　　　　—*The Wall Street Journal*

"Wise and charming."　　　　　　　　　　　—*The Plain Dealer*

Alexander McCall Smith

THE KALAHARI TYPING SCHOOL FOR MEN

In addition to the huge international phenomenon The No. 1 Ladies'
Detective Agency series, Alexander McCall Smith is the author of
The Sunday Philosophy Club series, the Portuguese Irregular Verbs
series, *The Girl Who Married a Lion*, and *44 Scotland Street*. He
was born in what is now Zimbabwe and taught law at the University
of Botswana and Edinburgh University. He lives in Scotland and
returns regularly to Botswana.

THE KALAHARI TYPING SCHOOL FOR MEN

THE KALAHARI

TYPING SCHOOL FOR MEN

Alexander McCall Smith

ANCHOR BOOKS

A Division of Random House, Inc.

New York

FIRST ANCHOR BOOKS EDITION, MARCH 2004

The Library of Congress has cataloged the Pantheon edition as follows:
McCall Smith, R. A.
The Kalahari typing school for men / Alexander McCall Smith.
p. cm.
1. Ramotswe, Precious (Fictitious character)—Fiction.
2. Women private investigators—Botswana—Fiction.
3. Botswana—Fiction. I. Title.
PR6063.C326 K35 2003
823'.914—dc21   2002030709

Anchor ISBN 10: 1-4000-3180-X
Anchor ISBN 13: 978-1-4000-3180-1

www.anchorbooks.com

Printed in the United States of America
20   19   18   17   16   15   14   13

This book is for
Amy Moore
Florence Christie
and
Elaine Gadd

THE KALAHARI TYPING SCHOOL FOR MEN

HOW TO FIND A MAN

MUST REMEMBER, thought Mma Ramotswe, how fortunate I am in this life; at every moment, but especially now, sitting on the verandah of my house in Zebra Drive, and looking up at the high sky of Botswana, so empty that the blue is almost white. Here she was then, Precious Ramotswe, owner of Botswana's only detective agency, The No. 1 Ladies' Detective Agency—an agency which by and large had lived up to its initial promise to provide satisfaction for its clients, although some of them, it must be said, could never be satisfied. And here she was too, somewhere in her late thirties, which as far as she was concerned was the very finest age to be; here she was with the house in Zebra Drive and two orphan children, a boy and a girl, bringing life and chatter into the home. These were blessings with which anybody should be content. With these things in one's life, one might well say that nothing more was needed.

But there was more. Some time ago, Mma Ramotswe had become engaged to Mr. J.L.B. Matekoni, proprietor of Tlokweng Road Speedy Motors, and by all accounts the finest mechanic in Botswana, a kind man, and a gentle one. Mma Ramotswe had been married once before, and the experience had been disastrous. Note Mokoti, the smartly dressed jazz trumpeter, might have been a young girl's dream, but he soon turned out to be a wife's nightmare. There had been a daily diet of cruelty, of hurt given out like a ration, and when, after her fretful pregnancy, their tiny, premature baby had died in her arms, so few hours after it had struggled into life, Note had been off drinking in a shebeen somewhere. He had not even come to say good-bye to the little scrap of humanity that had meant so much to her and so little to him. When at last she left Note, Mma Ramotswe would never forget how her father, Obed Ramotswe, whom even today she called the Daddy, had welcomed her back and had said nothing about her husband, not once saying *I knew this would happen*. And from that time she had decided that she would never again marry unless—and this was surely impossible—she met a man who could live up to the memory of the late Daddy, that fine man whom everybody respected for his knowledge of cattle and for his understanding of the old Botswana ways.

Naturally there had been offers. Her old friend Hector Mapondise had regularly asked her to marry him, and although she had just as regularly declined, he had always taken her refusals in good spirit, as befitted a man of his status (he was a cousin of a prominent chief). He would have made a perfectly good husband, but the problem was that he was rather dull and, try as she might, Mma Ramotswe could scarcely prevent herself from nodding off in his company. It would be very difficult being married to him; a somnolent experience, in fact, and Mma Ramotswe enjoyed life too much to want to sleep through it. Whenever she saw Hector Mapondise driving past in his large green car, or walking to the post office to collect his mail, she remembered the occasion on which he had taken her to lunch at the President Hotel and she had fallen asleep at the table, halfway through the meal. It had given a new meaning, she reflected, to the expression *sleeping with a man.* She had woken, slumped back in her chair, to see him staring at her with his slightly rheumy eyes, still talking in his low voice about some difficulty he was having with one of the machines at his factory.

"Corrugated iron is not easy to handle," he was saying. "You need very special machines to push the iron into that shape. Do you know that, Mma Ramotswe? Do you know why corrugated iron is the shape it is?"

Mma Ramotswe had not thought about this. Corrugated iron was widely used for roofing: was it, then, something to do with providing ridges for the rain to run off? But why would that be necessary in a dry country like Botswana? There must be some other reason, she imagined, although it was not immediately apparent to her. The thought of it, however, made her feel drowsy again, and she struggled to keep her eyes open.

No, Hector Mapondise was a worthy man, but far too dull. He should seek out a dull woman, of whom there were legions throughout the country, women who were slow-moving and not very exciting, and he should marry one of these bovine ladies. But the problem was that dull men often had no interest in such women and fell for people like Mma Ramotswe. That was the trouble with people in general: they were surprisingly unrealistic in their expectations. Mma Ramotswe smiled at the thought, remembering how, as a young woman, she had had a very tall friend who had been loved by an extremely short man. The short man looked up at the face of his beloved, from almost below her waist, and she looked down at him, almost squinting over the distance that separated them. That distance could have been one thousand miles or more—the breadth of the Kalahari and back; but the short man was not to realise that, and was to desist, heartsore, only when the tall girl's equally tall brother stooped down to look into his eyes and told him that he was no longer to look at his sister, even from a distance, or he would face some dire, unexpressed consequence. Mma Ramotswe felt sorry for the short man, of course, as she could never find it in herself to dismiss the feelings of others; he should have realised how impossible were his ambitions, but people never did.

Mr. J.L.B. Matekoni was a very good man, but, unlike Hector Mapondise, he could not be described as dull. That was not to say that he was exciting, in the way in which Note had seemed exciting; he was just easy company. You could sit with Mr. J.L.B. Matekoni for hours, during which he might say nothing very important, but what he said was never tedious. Certainly he talked about cars a great deal, as most men did, but what he had to say about them was very much more interesting than what other men had to say on the subject. Mr. J.L.B. Matekoni regarded cars as having personalities, and he could tell just by looking at a car what sort of owner it had.

"Cars speak about people," he had once explained to her. "They tell you everything you need to know."

It had struck Mma Ramotswe as a strange thing to say, but Mr. J.L.B. Matekoni had gone on to illustrate his point with a number of telling examples. Had she ever seen the inside of the car belonging to Mr. Motobedi Palati, for example? He was an untidy man, whose tie was never straight and whose shirt was permanently hanging out of his trousers. Not surprisingly, the inside of his car was a mess, with unattached wires sticking out from under the dashboard and a hole underneath the driver's seat—so that dust swirled up into the car and covered everything with a brown layer. Or what about that rather intimidating nursing sister from the Princess Marina Hospital, the one who had humiliated a well-known politician when she had heckled him at a public meeting, raising questions about nurses' pay that he simply could not answer? Her car, as one might expect, was in pristine condition and smelled vaguely of antiseptic. He could come up with further examples if she wished, but the point was made, and Mma Ramotswe nodded her head in understanding.

It was Mma Ramotswe's tiny white van that had brought them together. Even before she had taken it for repair at Tlokweng Road Speedy Motors, she had been aware of Mr. J.L.B. Matekoni, as a rather quiet man who lived by himself in a house near the old Botswana Defence Force Club. She had wondered why he was by himself, which was so unusual in Botswana, but had not thought much about him until he had engaged her in conversation after he had serviced the van one day, and had warned her about the state of her tyres. Thereafter she had taken to dropping in to see him in the garage from time to time, exchanging views about the day's events and enjoying the tea which he brewed on an old stove in the corner of his office.

Then there had come that extraordinary day when the tiny white van had choked and refused to start, and he had spent an entire afternoon in the yard at Zebra Drive, the van's engine laid out in what seemed like a hundred pieces, its very heart exposed. He had put everything together and had come into the house as evening fell and they had sat together on her verandah. He had asked her to marry him, and she had said that she would, almost without thinking about it, because she realised that here was a man who was as good as her father, and that they would be happy together.

Mma Ramotswe had not been prepared for Mr. J.L.B. Matekoni to fall ill, or at least to fall ill in the way in which he had done. It would have been easier, perhaps, if his illness had been one of the body, but it was his mind which was affected, and it seemed to her that the man she had known had simply vacated his body and gone somewhere else. Thanks to Mma Silvia Potokwane, matron of the orphan farm, and to the drugs which Dr. Moffat gave to Mma Potokwane to administer to Mr. J.L.B. Matekoni, the familiar personality returned. The obsessive brooding, the air of defeat, the lassitude—all these faded away and Mr. J.L.B. Matekoni began to smile again and take an interest in the business he had so uncharacteristically neglected.

Of course, during his illness he had been unable to run the garage, and it had been Mma Ramotswe's assistant, Mma Makutsi, who had managed to keep that going. Mma Makutsi had done wonders with the garage. Not only had she made major steps in reforming the lazy apprentices, who had given Mr. J.L.B. Matekoni such trouble with their inconsiderate way with cars (one had even been seen to use a hammer on an engine), but she had attracted a great deal of new customers to the garage. An increasing number of women had their own cars now, and they were delighted to take them to a garage run by a lady. Mma Makutsi may not have known a great deal about engines when she first started to run the garage, but she had learned quickly and was now quite capable of carrying out service and routine repairs on most makes of car, provided that they were not too modern and too dependent on temperamental devices of the sort which German car manufacturers liked to hide in cars to confuse mechanics elsewhere.

"What are we going to do to thank her?" asked Mma Ramotswe. "She's put so much work into the garage, and now here you are back again, and she is just going to be an assistant manager and assistant private detective once more. It will be hard for her."

Mr. J.L.B. Matekoni frowned. "I would not like to upset her," he said. "You are right about how hard she has worked. I can see it in the books. Everything is in order. All the bills are paid, all the invoices properly numbered. Even the garage floor is cleaner, and there is less grease all over the place."

"And yet her life is not all that good," mused Mma Ramotswe. "She is living in that one room over at Old Naledi with a sick brother. I cannot pay her very much. And she has no husband to look after her. She deserves better than that."

Mr. J.L.B. Matekoni agreed. He would be able to help her by allowing her to continue as assistant manager of Tlokweng Road Speedy Motors, but it was difficult to see what he could do beyond that. Certainly the question of husbands had nothing to do with him. He was a man, after all, and the problems which single girls had in their lives were beyond him. It was women's business, he thought, to help their friends when it came to meeting people. Surely Mma Ramotswe could advise her on the best tactics to adopt in that regard? Mma Ramotswe was a popular woman who had many friends and admirers. Was there not something that Mma Makutsi could do to find a husband? Surely she could be told how to go about it?

Mma Ramotswe was not at all sure about this. "You have to be careful what you say," she warned Mr. J.L.B. Matekoni. "People don't like you to think that they know nothing. Especially somebody like Mma Makutsi, with her ninety-seven percent or whatever it was. You can't go and tell somebody like that that they don't know a basic thing, such as how to find a husband."

"It's nothing to do with ninety-seven percent," said Mr. J.L.B. Matekoni. "You could get one hundred percent for typing and still not know how to talk to men. Getting married is different from being able to type. Quite different."

The mention of marriage had made Mma Ramotswe wonder about when they were going to get married themselves, and she almost asked him about this but stopped. Dr. Moffat had explained to her that it was important that Mr. J.L.B. Matekoni should not be subjected to too much stress, even if he had recovered from the worst of his depression. It would undoubtedly be stressful for him if she started to ask about wedding dates, and so she said nothing about that and even agreed—for the sake of avoiding stress—to speak to Mma Makutsi at some time in the near future with a view to finding out whether the issue of husbands could be helped in any way with a few well-chosen words of advice.

DURING MR. J.L.B. Matekoni's illness they had moved the No. 1 Ladies' Detective Agency into the back office at Tlokweng Road Speedy Motors. It had proved to be a successful arrangement: the affairs of the garage could be easily supervised from the back of the building, and there was a separate entrance for agency clients. Each business benefited in other ways. Those who brought their cars in for repair sometimes realised that there was a matter which might benefit from investigation—an errant husband, for example, or a missing relative—while others who came with a matter for the agency would arrange at the same time for their cars to be serviced or their brakes to be checked.

Mma Ramotswe and Mma Makutsi had arranged their desks in such a way that they could engage in conversation if they wished, without staring at one another all the time. If Mma Ramotswe turned in her chair, she could address Mma Makutsi on the other side of the room without having to twist her neck or talk over her shoulder, and Mma Makutsi could do the same if she needed to ask Mma Ramotswe for anything.

Now, with the day's post of four letters attended to and filed, Mma Ramotswe suggested to her assistant that it was time for a cup of bush tea. This was a little earlier than normal, but it was a warm day and she always found that the best way of dealing with the heat was a cup of tea, accompanied by an Ouma's rusk dipped into the liquid until it was soft enough to be eaten without hurting the teeth.

"Mma Makutsi," Mma Ramotswe began after her assistant had delivered the cup of freshly made tea to her desk, "are you happy?"

Mma Makutsi, who was halfway back to her desk, stopped where she stood. "Why do you ask, Mma?" she said. "Why do you ask me if I'm happy?" The question had stopped her heart, as she lived in fear of losing her job and this question, she thought, could only be a preliminary to suggesting that she move on to another job. But there would be no other job, or at least no other job remotely like this one. Here she was an assistant detective and previously, possibly still, an acting garage manager. If she had to go somewhere else, then she would revert to being a junior clerk, at best, or a junior secretary at somebody else's beck and call. And she would never be as well paid as she was here, with the extra money that came to her for her garage work.

"Why don't you sit down, Mma?" went on Mma Ramotswe. "Then we can drink our tea together and you can tell me if you are happy."

Mma Makutsi made her way back to her desk. She picked up her cup, but her hand shook and she put it down again. Why was life so unfair? Why did all the best jobs go to the beautiful girls, even if they barely got fifty percent in the examinations at the Botswana Secretarial College while she, with her results, had experienced such difficulty in finding a job at all? There was no obvious answer to that question. Unfairness seemed to be an inescapable feature of life, at least if you were Mma Makutsi from Bobonong in northern Botswana, daughter of a man whose cattle had always been thin. Everything, it seemed, was unfair.

"I am very happy," said Mma Makutsi miserably. "I am happy with this job. I do not want to go anywhere else."

Mma Ramotswe laughed. "Oh, the job. Of course you're happy with that. We know that. And we're very happy with you. Mr. J.L.B. Matekoni and I are very happy. You are our right-hand woman. Everybody knows that."

It took Mma Makutsi a few moments to absorb this compliment, but when she did, she felt relief flood through her. She picked up her teacup, with a steady hand now, and took a deep draught of the hot red liquid.

"What I'm really wanting to find out," went on Mma Ramotswe, "is whether you're happy in your . . . in yourself. Are you getting what you want out of life?"

Mma Makutsi thought for a moment. "I'm not sure what I want out of life," she said after a while. "I used to think that I would like to be rich, but now that I've met some rich people I'm not so sure about that."

"Rich people are just people," said Mma Ramotswe. "I have not met a rich person yet who isn't just the same as us. Being happy or unhappy has nothing to do with being rich."

Mma Makutsi nodded. "So now I think that happiness comes from somewhere else. It comes from somewhere inside."

"Somewhere inside?"

Mma Makutsi adjusted her large spectacles. She was an avid reader and enjoyed a serious conversation of this sort, in which she would be able to bring up snippets that she had garnered from old issues of the *National Geographic* or the *Mail and Guardian*.

"Happiness is found in the head," she said, warming to the subject. "If the head is full of happiness, then the person is definitely happy. That is clearly true."

"And the heart?" ventured Mma Ramotswe. "Does the heart not come into it?"

There was a silence. Mma Makutsi looked down, tracing a pattern with her finger on a dusty corner of her desktop. "The heart is the place where love happens," she said quietly.

Mma Ramotswe took a deep breath. "Would you not like to have a husband, Mma Makutsi?" she said gently. "Would it not make you happier to have a husband to look after you?" She paused and then added, "I was just wondering, that's all."

Mma Makutsi looked at her. Then she took off her glasses and polished them with a corner of her handkerchief. It was a favourite handkerchief of hers—with lace at the edges—but now it was threadbare from so much use and could not last much longer. But she loved it still and would buy another one just like it when she had the money.

"I would like to have a husband," she said. "But there are many beautiful girls. They are the ones who are getting the husbands. There is nobody left over for me."

"But you are a very good-looking lady," said Mma Ramotswe stoutly. "I am sure that there are many men who will agree with me."

Mma Makutsi shook her head. "I do not think so, Mma," she said. "Although you are very kind to say that to me."

"Perhaps you should try to find a man," said Mma Ramotswe. "Maybe you should be doing a bit more about it if no men are coming your way. Try to find them."

"Where?" asked Mma Makutsi. "Where are these men you are talking about?"

Mma Ramotswe waved a hand in the direction of the door, and of Africa outside. "Out there," she said. "There are men out there. You have to meet them."

"Where exactly?" asked Mma Makutsi.

"In the middle of the town," said Mma Ramotswe. "You see them sitting about at lunchtime. Men. Plenty of them."

"All married," said Mma Makutsi.

"Or in bars," said Mma Ramotswe, feeling that the conversation was not taking the turn she had planned for it.

"But you know what they are like in bars," said Mma Makutsi. "Bars are full of men who are looking for bad girls."

Mma Ramotswe had to agree. Bars were full of men like Note Mokoti and his friends, and she would never wish anybody like that on Mma Makutsi. It would be far better to be single than to become involved with somebody who would only make you unhappy.

"It is kind of you to think of me like this," said Mma Makutsi after a while. "But you and Mr. J.L.B. Matekoni mustn't worry about me. I am happy enough, and if there is going to be somebody for me, then I am sure that I shall meet him. Then everything will change."

Mma Ramotswe grasped at the opportunity to bring the conversation to an end. "I'm sure that you are right," she said.

"Perhaps," said Mma Makutsi.

Mma Ramotswe busied herself with a sheaf of papers on her desk. She felt saddened by the air of defeat which seemed to descend upon her assistant whenever the conversation turned to her personal circumstances. There was no real need for Mma Makutsi to feel like this. She might have had difficulties in her life until now—certainly one should not underestimate what it must be like to grow up in Bobonong, that rather dry and distant place from where Mma Makutsi had come—but there were plenty of people who came from places like that and made something of their lives in spite of their origins. If you went through life thinking, *I'm just a local girl from somewhere out in the bush,* then what was the point of making any effort? We all had to come from somewhere, and most of us came from somewhere not particularly impressive. Even if you were born in Gaborone, you had to come from a particular house in Gaborone, and ultimately that meant that you came from just a small patch of the earth; and that was no different from any other patch of the earth anywhere else.

Mma Makutsi should make more of herself, thought Mma Ramotswe. She should remember who she was—which was a citizen of Botswana, of the finest country in Africa, and one of the most distinguished graduates of the Botswana Secretarial College. Both of those were matters of which one could be justly proud. You could be proud to be a Motswana, because your country had never done anything of which to feel ashamed. It had conducted itself with complete integrity, even in times when it had to contend with neighbours in a state of civil war. It had always been honest, too, without that ruinous corruption that had shamed so many other countries in Africa, and which had bled away the wealth of an entire continent. They had never stooped to that, because Sir Seretse Khama, that great man whom her father had once greeted personally at Mochudi, had made it clear to every single citizen that there was to be no taking or giving of bribes, no dipping into money that belonged to the country. And everyone had listened to him and obeyed this precept because they could recognise in him the qualities of chiefly greatness which his forebears, the Khamas, had always possessed. Those qualities could not be acquired overnight, but they took generations to mature (whatever people said). That was why when Queen Elizabeth II met Seretse Khama, she knew immediately what sort of man he was. She knew because she could tell that he was the same sort of person as she was: a person who had been brought up to serve. Mma Ramotswe knew all this, but she sometimes wondered whether people who were slightly younger—people like Mma Makutsi—were aware of what a great man the first president of Botswana had been and of how he had been admired by the queen herself. Or would it mean anything to her? Would she *understand*?

Mma Ramotswe was a royalist, of course. She admired monarchs, as long as they were respectable and behaved in the correct way. She admired the king of Lesotho, because he was a direct descendant of Moshoeshoe I, who had saved his country from the Boers and who had been a good, wise man (and modest, too—had he not described himself as the flea in the blanket of Queen Victoria?). She admired the old king of Swaziland, King Sobhuza II, who had had one hundred and forty-one wives, all at the same time. She admired him in spite of his having all those wives, which, after all, was a very traditional approach to life; she admired him because he loved his people and because he consistently refused to allow the death penalty to be exacted, always— with only one exception in his long reign, a most serious case of witchcraft murder—granting mercy at the last moment. (What sort of man, she wondered, could coldly say to another who was begging for his life: *no, you must die?*) There were other kings and queens, of course, not just African ones. There was the late queen of Tonga, who was a very special queen, because she was so fat. Mma Ramotswe had seen a picture of her in an encyclopaedia, and it had covered two pages, so wide was the queen. And there was the Dutch queen, of whom she had seen a photograph in a magazine, enigmatically described in the caption below the picture as the Orange Queen. And indeed she had been wearing a dark orange outfit and two-tone orange-and-brown shoes. Mma Ramotswe thought that she might like to meet that queen, who looked so cheerful and smiled so warmly (and what, she wondered, was this House of Orange in which this queen was said to live?). Maybe she would come to Botswana one day, in her two-tone shoes perhaps; but one should not hope too much. Nobody came to Botswana, because people just did not know about it. They had not heard. They just had not heard.

Mma Makutsi might do well to reflect on the example of this Orange Queen, with her pleasant smile and self-evidently optimistic outlook. She should remind herself that even if she did come from Bobonong, she had put that behind her and was now a person who lived in the capital, in Gaborone itself. She should also remind herself that even if she thought that her complexion was too dark, there were plenty of men who were very happy with women who looked that way rather than those pallid creatures one sometimes saw who had made their skins look blotchy with lightening creams. And as for those large glasses which Mma Makutsi wore, there might be some who would find them a little bit intimidating, but many other men simply would fail to notice them, in much the same way as they failed to notice what women were wearing in general, no matter what efforts women made with their clothing.

The trouble with men, of course, was that they went about with their eyes half closed for much of the time. Sometimes Mma Ramotswe wondered whether men actually wanted to see anything, or whether they decided that they would notice only the things that interested them. That was why women were so good at tasks which required attention to the way people felt. Being a private detective, for example, was exactly the sort of job at which a woman could be expected to excel (and look at the success of the No. 1 Ladies' Detective Agency). That was because women watched and tried to understand what was going on in people's minds. Of course there were some men who could do this—one thought immediately of Clovis Andersen, author of *The Principles of Private Detection,* Mma Ramotswe's well-thumbed copy of which occupied pride of place on the shelf behind her desk. Clovis Andersen must be a most sympathetic man, Mma Ramotswe thought; more like a woman, in many ways, with his advice to study people's clothing carefully. (*There are many clues in what people wear,* he wrote. *Our clothes reveal a great deal about us. They talk. A man who wears no tie does not dress that way because he has no tie—he probably has an appreciable number of ties in his wardrobe at home—he is wearing no tie because he has chosen to do so. That means that he wishes to appear casual.*) Mma Ramotswe had found that a puzzling passage and had wondered where it was leading. She was not sure what one could deduce from the fact that a man wished to appear casual, but she was sure that, like all the observations of Clovis Andersen, this was in some way important.

She looked up from her desk and glanced at Mma Makutsi, who was busying herself with the typing of a letter which Mma Ramotswe had drafted, in pencil, earlier on. *We must try to help her,* she thought. *We must try to persuade her to value herself more than she does at present.* She was a fine woman, with great talents, and it was absurd that she should go through life thinking less of herself because she had no husband. That was such a waste. Mma Makutsi deserved to be happy. She deserved to have something to look forward to other than a bleak existence in one room in Old Naledi; a room that she shared with her sick brother, and into which no light came. Everybody deserved more than that, even in this unlucky world, a world which had brought such rewards to Mma Ramotswe but which seemed to be grudging in its appreciation of Mma Makutsi. *We shall change all that,* thought Mma Ramotswe, *because it is possible to change the world, if one is determined enough, and if one sees with sufficient clarity just what it is that has to be changed.*

CHAPTER TWO

LEARN TO DRIVE WITH JESUS

LIFE AT Tlokweng Road Speedy Motors (and, indeed, at the No. 1 Ladies' Detective Agency) was returning to normal. Mr. J.L.B. Matekoni had resumed his old practice of coming in to work shortly before seven in the morning, and would already be prostrate on his inspection board shining a torch up into a car's underbelly by the time the two apprentices arrived at eight o'clock. Their contract of apprenticeship stipulated that they should work eight hours a day, with time off for study every three months, but Mr. J.L.B. Matekoni had given up expecting them to comply with this. Certainly they arrived at eight and left at five, which made nine hours each day, but from this total there was deducted an hour for lunch, and two tea breaks of forty-five minutes each. It was the tea breaks that were the problem, but any attempt to insist on a far shorter break had been met with sullen resistance.

Eventually he had given up; he was a generous man and did not like conflict.

"You may have it easy here," he had warned them on more than one occasion, "but don't think that all bosses are like this. When you finish your apprenticeship—*if you finish*—then you'll have to find another job, a real job, and you'll learn all about it then."

"Learn about what, boss?" asked the older apprentice, smiling conspiratorially at his friend.

"About the working world," said Mr. J.L.B. Matekoni. "About what it's like to be kept really hard at it."

The older apprentice rolled his eyes in mock horror. "But you'll keep us on here, won't you, boss? You couldn't do without us, could you?"

The arrival of Mma Makutsi as acting manager of the garage had brought about a change, even if the long tea breaks survived. She had quickly shown that she would take no nonsense from the two apprentices, and they had rapidly abandoned their slovenly ways. Mma Ramotswe had been unable to work out what lay behind the change, so dramatic was it; she had assumed that it was something to do with working for a woman, which may have encouraged them to show what they could do, but she had eventually thought that it was something deeper than that. Certainly the two boys had wanted to impress her, but it seemed, too, that she had instilled in them a real pride in their work. Now, with Mr. J.L.B. Matekoni back in the garage, both Mma Ramotswe and Mma Makutsi were anxious to see whether the change would prove to be permanent.

"Those two boys are much better," remarked Mr. J.L.B. Matekoni shortly after his return. "They're still a bit lazy, which is probably just their nature, and they still talk endlessly about girls, which may also be their nature, come to think of it. But I think that their work is much neater . . . much less . . . less . . ."

"Greasy?" prompted Mma Ramotswe.

"Yes," agreed Mr. J.L.B. Matekoni. "That's it. They used to be so messy, as you know, but now that's all changed. And they're also not so brutal with the engines. They seem to have learned something while I was away."

And there were further changes—changes of which Mr. J.L.B. Matekoni as yet had no inkling. It was Mma Ramotswe, in fact, who first became aware that something had happened, and she sought confirmation from Mma Makutsi before she made any remark to Mr. J.L.B. Matekoni. Mma Makutsi was astonished; she had been too busy to have noticed, she remarked in her defence, otherwise she would surely have picked up something like that. Now, after she had spoken discreetly to Charlie, the elder of the two apprentices, she was able to confirm Mma Ramotswe's suspicions.

"You're right," she said. "The younger one has heard about the Lord. And he was the one who was by far the worst with the girls—always going on about them, remember—and now there he is, joined up to one of those marching churches. The Lord told him to do it, Charlie said. He's surprised, too. He's very disappointed that he doesn't seem to be too keen to talk about girls anymore. Charlie doesn't like that."

The news was passed on to Mr. J.L.B. Matekoni, who sighed. These apprentices were a mystery to him, and he looked forward to the day when they would be off his hands, if that day were ever to come. Life had become much more complicated for him, and he was not sure whether he liked it that way. In the past it had been simple: he had been alone at the garage and had only himself to worry about. Now there were Mma Makutsi, the two apprentices, and Mma Ramotswe, and that was even before one took into account the two orphans whose fostering he had arranged. That had been a very rash act on his part, although it was not one which he really regretted. The children were so happy staying in Mma Ramotswe's house on Zebra Drive that it would have been churlish beyond measure to begrudge them that. But, even then, to go from being responsible for one person, himself, to being responsible for seven was a step which might daunt any man, no matter how broad his shoulders.

While Mr. J.L.B. Matekoni imagined that he was responsible for others, they imagined that they were responsible for him. Mma Makutsi, for example, had taken her role within the garage with immense seriousness. She had changed the system of book-keeping and had improved the flow of cash; she had conducted a full inventory of stock and had listed all spare parts held in the storeroom, and she had sorted out the fuel receipts, which had been allowed to get into a terrible state. All of this was an achieve-ment, she knew, but she was still worried. The No. 1 Ladies' Detective Agency did not make a large profit, even if it did at least make some money. The garage did better, but the apprentices' wages were a major drain on that side of the business. If they wanted to prosper, particularly when bank charges were going up, they would just have to find more business, or—and this she found an intriguing possibility—they would have to diversify. It had been a challenge to take on responsibility for a garage; why not take on something else as well? For a moment she felt quite dizzy, contemplating the possibility of a sprawling business. Fac-tories, farms, stores—all of these were possible if one only tried. But where would one start? The marriage of the No. 1 Ladies' Detective Agency to Tlokweng Road Speedy Motors had been a natural development, following on the engagement of the owners of the two concerns; finding something entirely new might be rather more difficult.

The idea came to Mma Makutsi one morning when she was preparing a cup of bush tea. Mma Ramotswe was out shopping and Mr. J.L.B. Matekoni had driven off to look at a car which he had offered to sell on behalf of an old client. It was not much of a car, he had told her, but he regarded himself as responsible for his clients' cars from birth to death, so to speak, as an old-fashioned doctor would see his patients through life's journey. She took the freshly brewed tea into the garage workshop, where the two apprentices were sitting on a couple of upturned oil drums, watching a thin stray dog nose about the entrance to the garage.

"You look very busy," said Mma Makutsi.

The older apprentice looked up at her resentfully. "It's our tea break, Mma. Same as yours. We can't work all the time."

Mma Makutsi nodded. She was not interested in giving the apprentices one of the periodic dressings-down that had proved to be so effective while Mr. J.L.B. Matekoni was away; she wanted their reaction to her idea.

"I've thought of a new thing for the business to do," she announced, taking a sip of her bush tea. "I wondered what you would think."

"You are a lady who is full of ideas," said the younger apprentice. "Your head must hurt, Mma."

Mma Makutsi smiled. "Only hard ideas make your head hurt. My ideas are always simple."

"I have simple ideas, too," said the older apprentice. "I have ideas of girls. Those are my ideas. Simple. Girls, and then more girls."

Mma Makutsi ignored this, addressing her next remark to the younger apprentice. "There are many people wanting to learn how to drive, are there not?"

The younger apprentice shrugged. "They can learn. There are lots of bush roads for them to practise on."

"But that won't help them drive in town," said Mma Makutsi quickly. "There are too many things happening in town. There are cars going this way and that. There are people crossing the road."

"And lots of girls," interjected the older apprentice. "Lots of girls walking about. All the time."

The younger apprentice turned to look at his friend. "What is wrong with you? You are always thinking of girls."

"So are you," snapped the other. "Anyone who says he does not think of girls is a liar. All men think of girls. That is what men like to do."

"Not all the time," said the younger one. "There are other things to think about."

"That is not true," the older one retorted. "If you didn't think about girls, then it is a sign that you are about to die. That is a well-known fact."

"I am not interested in any of this," said Mma Makutsi. "And, anyway, I'd heard that one of you has changed." She paused, looking at the younger one for confirmation; but he merely lowered his eyes.

"So," she continued, "I will tell you of an idea that I have had. I think that it is a good idea and I would like to hear what you think of it."

"You can tell us," said the older apprentice. "We are listening to what you have to say."

Mma Makutsi dropped her voice, as if there were eavesdroppers in the darker corners of the garage. The apprentices leaned forward to catch her words. "I have decided that we should open a driving school," she announced. "I will make some enquiries, but I do not think that there are enough driving schools. We could start a new one and give people a lesson after work. We could charge forty pula a time. Twenty pula could go to the teacher and twenty pula to Mr. J.L.B. Matekoni for the garage and for using his car. It would be a great success."

The apprentices stared at her, and for a few moments nothing was said. Then the older one spoke.

"I do not want to have anything to do with it," he said. "After work I like to go to see my friends. I do not have time to take people for driving lessons."

Mma Makutsi looked at his friend. "And you?"

The younger apprentice smiled back at her. "You are a very clever lady, Mma. I think that this is a good idea."

"There!" said Mma Makutsi, turning to the older apprentice. "You see, your friend here has a more positive way of looking at things. You are just useless. Look what all that thinking about girls has done to your brain."

The younger apprentice smirked. "You hear that? Mma Makutsi is right. You should listen to her." He turned to Mma Makutsi. "What will you call this driving school, Mma?"

"I have not thought about it," she said. "I will think of something. The name you give to a business is very important. That is why the No. 1 Ladies' Detective Agency has been a success. The name says everything you need to know about the business."

The younger apprentice looked up at her hopefully. "I have a good idea for the name," he said. "We could call it *Learn to Drive with Jesus.*"

There was a silence. The older apprentice cast a glance in the direction of his friend and then turned away.

"I am not sure about that," said Mma Makutsi. "I will think about it, but I am not sure."

"It is a very good name," said the younger apprentice. "It will attract a careful class of driver, and it will mean that we have no accidents. The Lord will look after us.

"I hope so," said Mma Makutsi. "I shall talk to Mr. J.L.B. Matekoni about it and see what he thinks. Thank you for the suggestion."

CHAPTER THREE

TO KILL A HOOPOE

MMA RAMOTSWE completed her shopping. Before the two orphans had come to stay, shopping had been an easy task and she found that she rarely had to get supplies more than once a week. Now it seemed that everything ran out shortly after she had replenished stocks. Only two days ago she had bought flour—a large bag, too—and now the flour was finished and the cake baked by the girl, Motholeli, had been all but consumed by her brother, Puso. That was a good sign, of course: boys should have good appetites, and it was natural for them to want to eat large amounts of cake and sweet things. As they grew older, they would move to meat, which was very important for a man. But all this food that was being consumed cost money, and had it not been for the generous contributions made by Mr. J.L.B. Matekoni—contributions which in fact covered the entire cost of keeping the children—Mma Ramotswe would have begun to feel the pinch.

It was Mr. J.L.B. Matekoni's idea to foster the children in the first place, and although she never regretted taking them in, she wished that he had consulted her first. It was not that she resented the fact that Motholeli was confined to a wheelchair and that she was now responsible for a handicapped child, it was just that she had imagined that something quite as important as this would have been the subject of some discussion. But it was not in Mr. J.L.B. Matekoni's heart to say no—that was the problem. And she loved him all the more for that. Mma Silvia Potokwane, matron of the orphan farm, had understood that very well and, as usual, had been able to ensure the best possible arrangements for her orphans. She must have been planning for months to place the orphans with him, and of course she must have realised that they would end up living in Mma Ramotswe's house in Zebra Drive rather than in Mr. J.L.B. Matekoni's house near the old Botswana Defence Club. Of course, after the marriage (whenever that would be), they would all live together under one roof. The children had already been asking about that, and she had told them that she was waiting for Mr. J.L.B. Matekoni to decide on a date.

"He does not rush things," she had explained. "Mr. J.L.B. Matekoni is a very careful man. He likes to do things slowly."

Puso had seemed impatient, and she had realised that his need was for a father. Mr. J.L.B. Matekoni would be that in due course, but in the meantime the boy, who had never had a parent, would be wondering whether he ever would. At the age of six, a week was a long time; a month would be interminable.

Motholeli, who had suffered so much and who had been so brave, understood. She had been used to waiting and of course it took her much longer to do anything, manoeuvring her wheel-chair with difficulty through doorways that always seemed too small or along corridors that ended in awkward steps. Only now and then did she seem to register disappointment, and that was never for more than a few moments. So when Mma Ramotswe returned from her shopping and struggled into the kitchen, laden with brown paper bags, she was surprised to find that there was no cheerful greeting from Motholeli, only a downcast look.

She lowered her parcels onto the table. "So much shopping," she said. "Lots of meat. A sort of chicken." She paused. She knew that Motholeli liked pumpkins. "And a pumpkin," she said, adding: "A big one. Very yellow."

At first the girl said nothing. Then, when she replied, her voice was flat: "That is good."

Mma Ramotswe looked at her. Motholeli had left that morning in good spirits, and so it must have been something which had happened at school. She remembered her own school days and the ups and downs which she had experienced. They had been such little dramas—at least when looked at from her current perspective—but they had seemed so grave and frightening at the time. She remembered the occasion when the head teacher of her school at Mochudi had tried to flush out a thief. One of the children had been stealing, and the teacher had summoned every child into his office and had insisted that he or she place a hand on the large Setswana Bible which he kept on his table. Then each child had been asked to say, beneath the head teacher's piercing gaze: *I swear that I am not a thief.*

"Nobody who is innocent has anything to fear," the teacher had announced before the whole school, assembled on the dusty playing field. "But the person who lies with his hand on the Bible will be struck down. That is one thing that is sure. Maybe not straightaway, but later, when you are not expecting it. That is when the Lord will strike you down."

The silence had been complete. She had looked up into the sky but had seen only utter emptiness. It was undoubtedly true, of course; people were struck by lightning, and it must have been because they deserved it: thieves, perhaps, or even worse. She had no doubt but that the thief, whoever it was, would know this just as she did and would falter before he uttered the fateful words. But when the last pupil had filed out of the office and the head teacher had come out looking angry, she realised that she had been wrong and that one of their number was now in mortal danger. Who could it be? She had her suspicions, of course; everybody knew that Elijah Sebekedi could not be trusted, and although nobody had actually seen him stealing anything, how could he afford to buy those tins of condensed milk which he drank so conspicuously on his way home from school? His father, as was well known, was a drunkard and spent all his money on traditional beer, leaving nothing for his family. The children survived on handouts; the shoes they wore, the clothes, were recognised by the other children as those which they had abandoned, thinking that no more wear could be extracted from them. So there was only one explanation for Elijah's tins of condensed milk.

She thought about him that night as she lay on her sleeping mat, watching the square of moonlight move slowly across the wall opposite her bedroom window. The rainy season was not far away, and there would be storms. Elijah Sebekedi should be worried about that; there would be lightning about. She closed her eyes, and then, her heart pounding, she opened them again. She herself had lied! Only a week ago she had helped herself to a doughnut which she had found in the kitchen. She had been unable to resist it and had felt immediately guilty after she had finished licking the last of the sugar off her fingers. She had said *I swear that I am not a thief,* blatantly, falsely, and had repeated it as the head teacher had not heard her the first time that she had uttered those fateful, damning words. And now she would be struck by lightning; there was no escape.

SHE DID not sleep well, and the next morning she was silent as she ate her breakfast in the kitchen. Mma Ramotswe had lost her mother when she was still young and was looked after by her father and several of his female relatives who took it in turns to keep house for them. There was a seemingly endless supply of these relatives—competent, cheerful women who appeared to look forward to their turn to come to Mochudi and to rearrange and reverse everything which their predecessor had done in the house. These were house-proud women, who kept the yard spotless, the sand brushed and raked every day, the chicken manure cleared away and deposited on the melon patch; women who understood the importance of scouring your pans until the black was scraped away and the metal below was shining. These were not small things. These were the things which showed children growing up in the house how they should live their lives as clean, upright people.

Now, sitting at the kitchen table with her father and his aunt from Palapye, watching the soft rays of the early morning sun streaming in through the door, Precious Ramotswe was aware that if it clouded over—as it might—and if there were lightning—as there might be—then she might not be sitting here the next morning. Of course there was only one thing to do, which was to confess, which she did, there and then to her father and the aunt, and Obed Ramotswe, after listening to her with astonishment, had turned to his aunt, and she had laughed and said: "But that was meant for you, that doughnut. You did not steal it." And at this, overcome with relief, Precious had burst into tears and told the adults of the fate that awaited Elijah. Obed Ramotswe exchanged glances with his aunt.

"That is a very unkind thing to do to children," he said. "That poor boy will not be struck by lightning. Maybe he will learn one day not to be a thief. It is for his father to teach him that, but he is always drinking." He paused. It was a grave thing to criticise a teacher, especially in front of a child, but the words came out before he could stop them: "The Lord is more likely to strike the head teacher than that boy."

Mma Ramotswe had not thought of this incident for years, and now, looking at Motholeli, she wondered what local torment was causing her unhappiness. People said that school days were happy, but they often were not. Often it was like being in prison; wary of older children and terrified of teachers, unable to talk to anybody about troubles because you thought that there would be nobody who would understand. Perhaps things had changed for the better, and in some ways they had. Teachers were not allowed to beat children as they did in the past, although, Mma Ramotswe reflected, there were some boys—and indeed some young men— who might have been greatly improved by moderate physical correction. The apprentices, for example: would it help if Mr. J.L.B. Matekoni resorted to physical chastisement—nothing severe, of course—but just an occasional kick in the seat of the pants while they were bending over to change a tyre or something like that? The thought made her smile. She would even offer to administer the kick herself, which she imagined might be oddly satisfying, as one of the apprentices, the one who still kept on about girls, had a largeish bottom which she thought would be quite comfortable to kick. How enjoyable it would be to creep up behind him and kick him when he was least expecting it, and then to say: *Let that be a lesson!* That was all one would have to say, but it would be a blow for women everywhere.

But those were not serious thoughts and would not help the immediate problem, which was to find out what was troubling Motholeli and making her so palpably miserable.

Mma Ramotswe put away the last of her groceries and then put on the kettle to make a pot of red bush tea. Then she sat down.

"You're unhappy," she said simply. "And it's something at school, isn't it?"

Motholeli shook her head. "No," she said. "I am not."

"That is not true," said Mma Ramotswe. "You are a happy girl normally. You are famous for your happiness. And now you are almost crying. I do not have to be a detective to know that."

The girl looked down at the ground.

"I have no mother," she said quietly. "I am a girl who has no mother."

Something caught at Mma Ramotswe's throat: a feeling of sudden, overwhelming sympathy. So that was it. She was missing her mother; of course she was. She was missing her mother in exactly the same way in which she, Precious Ramotswe, had missed her own mother, whom she had never known, and in the same way, too, that she missed her father, every day of her life, every day, her good, kind father, Obed Ramotswe, of whom she was so proud. Mma Ramotswe rose to her feet and crossed the kitchen floor. Now she crouched down and embraced the girl.

"Of course you have a mother, Motholeli," she whispered. "Your mummy is there, in heaven, and she is watching you, watching you every day. And I'll tell you what she's thinking: she's thinking, *I am very proud of that fine girl, my daughter. I am very proud of how hard she is working and how she is looking after her little brother.* That is what she is thinking."

She felt the girl's shoulder heave beneath her and she felt the warm tears of the child against her own skin.

"You mustn't cry," she said. "You mustn't be unhappy. She would not want you to be unhappy, would she?"

"She doesn't care. She doesn't care what happens to me."

Mma Ramotswe caught her breath. "But you mustn't say that. That is not true. It is not. Of course she cares."

"That is not what this girl is telling me at school," said Motholeli. "She says that I am a girl who has no mother because my mother did not like me and left. That is what she says."

"And who is this girl?" asked Mma Ramotswe angrily. "Who is she to tell you these lies?"

"She is a very popular girl at school. She is a rich girl. She has many friends, and they all believe what she says."

"Her name?" said Mma Ramotswe. "What is the name of this popular girl?"

Motholeli gave the name, and Mma Ramotswe immediately knew. For a moment she said nothing, then, wiping the tears away from Motholeli's cheek, she spoke to her.

"We will talk about this more later on," she said. "For now, you just remember that everything that this girl has said to you—everything—is just not true. It doesn't matter who she is. It doesn't matter one little bit. You lost your mother because she was sick. She was a good woman, I know that. I have asked about her, and that is what Mma Potokwane told me. She said she was a strong woman who was kind to people. You remember that. You remember that and be proud of it. Do you understand what I am saying?"

The girl looked up. Then she nodded.

"And there is something else you must remember," Mma Ramotswe said. "There is something else that you must remember for the rest of your life. Sir Seretse Khama said that every person in Botswana, every person, is of equal value. The same. That means you, too. Everyone. You may be an orphan girl, but you are as good as anybody else. There is nobody who can look at you and say, *I am better than you.* Do you understand that?"

Mma Ramotswe waited until Motholeli had nodded before

she rose to her feet. "And in the meantime," she said, "we should start cooking this fine pumpkin so that when Mr. J.L.B. Matekoni comes to have dinner with us this evening, we shall have a good meal ready for him on the table. Would you like that?"

Motholeli smiled. "I would like that very much, Mma."

"Good," said Mma Ramotswe.

MR. J.L.B. Matekoni left the garage at five o'clock and drove straight to the house in Zebra Drive. He liked the early evening, when the heat had gone out of the sun and it was pleasant to walk about in the last hour or so before dusk set in. This evening he was planning to spend some time clearing Mma Ramotswe's vegetable garden at the back of the house before he would join her for a cup of bush tea on the verandah. There they would catch up on the day's events before going in for dinner. There was always something to discuss; information which Mma Ramotswe had picked up while doing her shopping or items from that day's *Botswana Daily News* (except for football news, in which Mma Ramotswe had no interest). They always agreed with one another; Mr. J.L.B. Matekoni trusted Mma Ramotswe's judgement on matters of human nature and local politics, while she deferred to him on business issues and agriculture. Was the price of cattle too low at the moment, or was it reasonable enough, given the price that the canning factory and the butchers were prepared to pay? Mr. J.L.B. Matekoni would know the answer to that, and in Mma Ramotswe's experience he was always right on these issues. What about that new politician, the one who had just been made a junior minister; was he to be trusted, or was he interested only in himself or, at a pinch, in the welfare of his own people in the town he came from? Only in himself, Mma Ramotswe would say without hesitation; look at him, just look at the way that he holds his hands clasped in front of him when he talks. That's always a sign; always.

Mr. J.L.B. Matekoni parked his car just inside the gate. He liked to leave it there, allowing ample room for Mma Ramotswe to drive past in her tiny white van, if she needed to go out. Then, changing from his garage shoes, which were always covered in oil, to the scuffed and dusty suede veldschoens that he liked to wear outside, Mr. J.L.B. Matekoni made his way to the back of the yard where he had planted several rows of beans under an awning of shade netting. In a dry country like Botswana, shade netting made all the difference to a plant's chances, keeping the drying rays of the sun off the vulnerable green leaves and allowing the earth to retain a little of any precious moisture left over from watering. The ground was always so thirsty; water poured upon it was soaked up with a parched eagerness that left little trace. But people persisted in spite of this and tried to make small patches of green amid the brown.

The yard in Zebra Drive was considerably larger than neighbouring plots. Mma Ramotswe had always intended to clear it entirely but had never got round to cutting back the tangle of bush—stunted thorn trees, high grass, and sundry shrubs—which overgrew the back section of her plot. Behind it was a small stretch of wasteland, also overgrown, across which an informal path wound its way. People liked to use this as a shortcut to town, and in the morning one might hear whistling or singing from men on bicycles as they rode along the path. Babies were conceived here, too, especially on Saturday evenings, and Mma Ramotswe had often thought that at least some of the children whom she saw playing games there had been drawn back by some strange homing instinct to revisit the place where they had started out.

Mr. J.L.B. Matekoni filled an old watering can from the standpipe at the side of the house. Inside the kitchen, Mma Ramotswe heard the tap running and looked out of the window. She waved to her fiancé, who waved back, mouthing a few words of greeting to her, before he carried the can off to the vegetable plot. Mma Ramotswe smiled to herself, and thought, *Here I am at last, with a good man, who is prepared to work in the garden and grow beans for me.* It was a comforting thought, and it made her feel warm with pleasure as she watched his retreating form disappear behind the clump of acacias that masked the rear portion of the yard.

Mr. J.L.B. Matekoni stooped under the shade netting and began to pour water, gently, almost dribbling it, against the lower stem of each bean plant. Every drop of water was precious in Botswana, and one would have to be foolhardy to use a hose to splash water all over the place. It was even more effective, if one had the resources, to set up a drip feed system, in which the water would travel down from a central reservoir on a thin line of cotton thread which would dip down into the ground at the plant's roots. That was the best water husbandry of all: tiny trickles of water delivered to the roots, minuscule drop by minuscule drop. *Perhaps one day I shall do that,* thought Mr. J.L.B. Matekoni. *Perhaps I shall do that when I am too old to fix cars anymore and have sold Tlokweng Road Speedy Motors. Then I shall be a farmer, as all my people have been before me. I shall go back to my lands, way out there on the edge of the Kalahari, and sit under a tree and watch my melons grow in the sun.*

He bent down to examine one of the bean plants, which had become entangled in the string up which it grew. As he gently redirected the plant's stem, there was a sudden noise behind him; a little thud, as of a stone hitting something, and then a dry, scrabbling noise, and he spun round immediately. A noise like that could easily be a snake; one had to be constantly on the watch for snakes, which might be lying anywhere and might suddenly rear up and strike. A cobra would be bad enough—and he had experienced several rather-too-close encounters with them—but what if it was a mamba, angered by a disturbance? Mambas were aggressive snakes which did not like people treading on their ground, and which would attack with real anger. A bite from a mamba was rarely survivable, as their poison travelled so quickly through the body and paralysed the lungs and the heart.

It was not a snake but a bird, which had fluttered down from the bough of a tree and had flown, at a strange angle, down against the shade netting. Now it had fallen to the ground and was beating its wings against the sand, raising a small cloud of dust. After a few struggling movements, it lay still, a hoopoe, with its gorgeous striped plumage and its tiny crown of black and white feathers sticking up like the headdress of some miniature chieftain.

Mr. J.L.B. Matekoni reached down to the bird, which watched his approaching hand with a liquid stare, but which seemed unable to move any longer. Its breast rose under the feathers, almost imperceptibly, and then was still. He picked it up still warm but now limp, and he turned it over. On its other side, the tiny eye—a black speck like the pip of a papaw—was hanging out of its socket, and there was a red patch in the plumage where the bird had been struck by a stone.

"Oh," said Mr. J.L.B. Matekoni, and then again, "oh."

He laid the bird down on the ground and looked about him, out into the scrub bush.

"You skellums," he shouted. "I saw this! I saw you kill this bird!"

Boys, he thought. It would be boys with their catapults, hiding in the bushes and killing birds, not to eat, of course, but just killing them. Killing doves or pigeons was one thing; they could be eaten, but nobody could eat a hoopoe, and who could possibly wish to kill such a friendly little bird? You simply did not kill hoopoes.

Of course it would be impossible to catch the boys in question; they would have run away by now, or they would be hiding in the bush laughing at him behind their hands. There was nothing to be done but to toss the little carcass away. Rats would find it, or maybe a snake, and make a meal of it. This little death would be a windfall for somebody.

WHEN MR. J.L.B. Matekoni went back to the house, discouraged by the hoopoe's death, and by the condition of the beans, and by everything, he found Mma Ramotswe waiting for him at the kitchen door.

"Have you seen Puso?" she asked. "He was playing out in the yard. But now it is dinnertime and he has not come back. You may have heard me calling him."

"I have not seen him," said Mr. J.L.B. Matekoni. "I have been out at the back. . . ." He stopped.

"And?" said Mma Ramotswe. "Is he back there?"

Mr. J.L.B. Matekoni hesitated for a moment.

"I think he is," he said gravely. "I think he is using a catapult out there."

They both went out to the vegetable patch and peered into the bush on the other side of the fence.

"Puso," called out Mma Ramotswe. "We know that you are hiding. You come out or I shall come and get you myself."

They waited for a few moments. Then Mma Ramotswe called out again.

"Puso! You are there! We know you are there!"

Mr. J.L.B. Matekoni thought he saw a movement in the high grass. It was a good place for a boy to hide, but it would be easy enough to go and get him out if they had to.

"Puso!" shouted Mma Ramotswe. "You are there! Come out!"

"I am not here." The boy's voice was very clear. "I am not."

"You are a rascal," said Mma Ramotswe. "How can you say you are not there? Who is speaking if it is not you?"

There was a further silence, and then the branches of a bush parted and the small boy crawled out.

"He killed a hoopoe with his catapult," whispered Mr. J.L.B. Matekoni. "I saw it."

Mma Ramotswe drew in her breath as the boy approached her, his head down, looking steadfastly at the ground.

"Go to your room, Puso," she said. "Go to your room and stay there until we call you."

The boy looked up. His face was streaked with tears.

"I hate you," he said. Then he turned to Mr. J.L.B. Matekoni. "And I hate you, too."

The words seemed to hang in the air between them, but the boy now dashed past the two astonished adults, running back towards the house, not looking back at Mma Ramotswe and Mr. J.L.B. Matekoni as he ran.

CHAPTER FOUR

TRUST YOUR AFFAIRS TO A MAN

NOTHING SEEMED to be going well for Mma Ramotswe. Firstly, there was that distressing evening with the children—Motholeli being bullied and the boy behaving in that troubling way, shooting a hoopoe and then remaining mute for the rest of the evening. There were matters still to be sorted out for Motholeli, of course, but at least she had cheered up after their talk; with the boy it had been different. He had just shut them out, refusing to eat, and it seemed that nothing they could say would make any difference. They had not attempted to punish him over the hoopoe, and one might have thought that he would be grateful for that, but he was not. Did he really hate them? And, if he did, why should he do so when all they had offered him was love and support? Was this how orphan children behaved? Mma Ramotswe knew that children who were damaged in their early years could be very difficult; and this boy, when all was said and done, had actually been buried alive as a baby. Something like that could leave a mark; indeed, it would have been surprising had it not. But why should he suddenly turn on them like that when he had seemed to be quite happy before? That was puzzling. She would have to go and see Mma Potokwane at the orphan farm and seek her advice. There was nothing that Mma Potokwane did not know about children and their behaviour.

But that was not all. There had been a development which could threaten the No. 1 Ladies' Detective Agency itself, unless something was done; and nothing, it seemed, could be done. It was Mma Makutsi who broke the news on the morning after the disturbing events at Zebra Drive.

"I have very bad news," said Mma Makutsi when Mma Ramotswe arrived at the office. "I have been sitting here for the last hour, wanting to cry."

Mma Ramotswe looked at her assistant. She was not sure if she could take more trauma after last night; she felt raw from her engagement with the children's problems, and she had been looking forward to a quiet day. It would not matter if there were no clients that day; in fact, it would be better if there were no clients at all. It was difficult enough having one's own problems to sort out, let alone having to attend to the problems of others.

"Do you really have to tell me?" asked Mma Ramotswe. "I am not in a mood for problems."

Mma Makutsi pursed her lips. "This is very important, Mma," she said severely, as if lecturing one who was being completely irresponsible. "I cannot pretend that I have not seen what I have seen."

Mma Ramotswe sat down at her desk and looked across at Mma Makutsi.

"In that case," she said, "you had better tell me. What has happened?"

Mma Makutsi took off her spectacles and polished them on the hem of her skirt.

"Well," she said, "yesterday afternoon, as you may remember, Mma, I left a little bit early. At four o'clock."

Mma Ramotswe nodded. "You said that you had to go shopping."

"Yes," said Mma Makutsi. "And I did go shopping. I went up to the Broadhurst shops. There is a shop there that sells stockings very cheaply. I wanted to go there."

Mma Ramotswe smiled. "It is always best to go after bargains. I always do that."

Mma Makutsi acknowledged the remark but pressed on. "There is a shop there—or there used to be a shop there—that sold cups and saucers. You may remember it. The owner went away and they closed it down. Do you remember?"

Mma Ramotswe did. She had bought a birthday present for somebody there, a large cup with a picture of a horse on it, and the handle had fallen off almost immediately.

"That place was empty for a while," said Mma Makutsi. "But when I went up there yesterday afternoon and walked past it, just before half past four, I saw a new person putting up a sign outside the shop. And I saw some new furniture through the window. Brand-new office furniture."

She glanced around at the shabby furniture with which their own office was filled: the old grey filing cabinet with one drawer that did not work properly; the desks with their uneven surfaces; the rickety chairs. Mma Ramotswe intercepted the glance and anticipated what was coming. There was going to be a request for new furniture. Mma Makutsi must have spoken to somebody up there at Broadhurst and had been told of bargains to be had. But it would be impossible. The business was losing money as it was; it was only because of the connection with Tlokweng Road Speedy Motors and the paying of Mma Makutsi's salary through that side of the business that they managed to continue trading at all. If it were not for Mr. J.L.B. Matekoni, they would have had to close down some months ago.

Mma Ramotswe raised a hand. "I'm sorry, Mma Makutsi," she said. "We cannot buy new equipment here. We simply don't have the money."

Mma Makutsi stared at her. "That was not what I was going to say," she protested. "I was going to say something quite different." She paused, so that Mma Ramotswe might feel suitably guilty for her unwarranted assumption.

"I'm sorry," said Mma Ramotswe. "Tell me what you saw."

"A new detective agency," said Mma Makutsi. "As large as life. It calls itself the Satisfaction Guaranteed Detective Agency."

Mma Makutsi folded her arms, watching the effect of her words upon her employer. Mma Ramotswe narrowed her eyes. This was dramatic news indeed. She had become so used to being the only private detective in town, indeed in the whole country, that it had never occurred to her there would be competition. This was the news that she least wished to hear, and for a moment she was tempted to throw her hands in the air and announce that she was giving up. But that was a passing thought, and no more than that. Mma Ramotswe was not one to give up that easily, and even if it was discouraging to have orphan problems at home and a shortage of work at the agency, this was no reason to abandon the business. So she squared her shoulders and smiled at Mma Makutsi.

"Every business must expect competition," she said. "We are no different. We cannot expect to have it all our own way forever, can we?"

Mma Makutsi looked doubtful. "No," she said at last. "We learned about that at the Botswana Secretarial College. It's called the principle of competition."

"Oh," said Mma Ramotswe. "And what does this principle say?"

Mma Makutsi looked momentarily flustered. She had received ninety-seven percent in the final examinations at the Botswana Secretarial College—that was well-known—but she had never been examined on the principle of competition, as far as she could recall.

"It means that there is competition," she pronounced. "You don't just have one business. There will always be more than one business."

"That is true," said Mma Ramotswe.

"So that means that if one business does well, then there will be other businesses which will try to do well, too," Mma Makutsi went on, warming to her theme. "There is nothing that can be done about it. In fact, it is healthy."

Mma Ramotswe was not convinced. "Healthy enough to take away all our business," she said.

Mma Makutsi nodded. "But we also learned that you have to know what the competition is. I remember them saying that."

Mma Ramotswe agreed, and, encouraged, Mma Makutsi continued. "We need to do some detective work for ourselves," she said. "We need to go and take a look at these new people and see what they are up to. Then we will know what the competition is."

Mma Ramotswe reached for the key to her tiny white van.

"You are right, Mma Makutsi," she said. "We need to go and introduce ourselves to these new detectives. Then we'll know just how clever they are."

"Yes," said Mma Makutsi. "And there's one other thing. These new detectives are not ladies, like ourselves. These are men."

"Ah," said Mma Ramotswe. "That is a good thing, and a bad thing, too."

IT WAS not hard to find the Satisfaction Guaranteed Detective Agency. A large sign, very similar to the one which had appeared outside the original premises of the No. 1 Ladies' Detective Agency, announced the name of the business and showed a picture of a smiling man behind a desk, hands folded, and clearly satisfied. Then, underneath this picture, was painted in large red letters: Experienced staff. Ex-CID. Ex–New York. Ex-cellent!

Mma Ramotswe parked the tiny white van on the opposite side of the street, under a convenient acacia tree.

"So!" she said, her voice lowered, although nobody could possibly hear them. "So that is the competition."

Mma Makutsi, who was sitting in the passenger seat, leaned forward to be able to see past Mma Ramotswe. Her employer was a large lady—traditionally built, as she described herself—and it was not easy to get a good view of the offending sign.

"Ex-CID," said Mma Ramotswe. "A retired policeman then. That is not good news for us. People will love the idea of taking their problems to a retired policeman."

"And ex–New York," said Mma Makutsi admiringly. "That will impress people a great deal. They have seen films about New York detectives and they know how good they are."

Mma Ramotswe cast a glance at Mma Makutsi. "Do you mean Superman?" she asked.

"Yes," said Mma Makutsi. "That sort of thing. Superman."

Mma Ramotswe opened her mouth to say something to her assistant but then stopped. She was well aware of Mma Makutsi's academic achievements at the Botswana Secretarial College—she could hardly avoid the framed certificate to that effect hanging above Mma Makutsi's desk—but sometimes she thought her extraordinarily naive. Superman indeed! Why anybody above, well, the age of six or seven *at the most* should be interested in such nonsense quite escaped her. And yet they did show an interest; when films like that came to the cinema in town, the one owned by the rich man with a house near Nyerere Drive, there were always crowds of people who were prepared to pay for the seats. Of course some of these were courting couples, who would not necessarily be interested in what was happening on the screen, but others appeared to go for the films themselves.

There was no point in arguing about Superman with Mma Makutsi. Whoever had opened this agency, even if they were really ex–New York, would hardly be Superman.

"We'll go in and introduce ourselves," said Mma Ramotswe. "I can see somebody inside. They are already at work."

"On some big important case," observed Mma Makutsi rue-fully.

"Perhaps," said Mma Ramotswe. "But then again, perhaps not. When people drive past the No. 1 Ladies' Detective Agency and see us inside, they may think that we're working on a big important case. Yet most of the time, as you know, we are only sit-ting there drinking bush tea and reading the *Botswana Daily News*. So you see that appearances can be deceptive."

Mma Makutsi thought that this was rather too self-effacing. It was true that they were not particularly busy at present, and it was also true that a fair amount of bush tea was consumed in the office, but it was not always like that. There were times when they were very busy and the passerby would have been quite correct in making the assumption that the office was a hive of activity. So Mma Ramotswe was wrong; but there was no point in arguing with Mma Ramotswe, who seemed to be in a rather defeatist mood. Something was happening at home, thought Mma Makutsi, because it was so unlike her to be anything but optimistic.

They crossed the road and approached the door of the small shop which now housed the Satisfaction Guaranteed Detective Agency. The front was largely taken up by a glass display window, behind which a screen prevented the passerby from seeing more than the heads of the people working within. In the window was a framed picture of a group of men standing together outside a rather impressive-looking official building. The men were all wearing wide-brimmed hats which shaded their faces and made it impossible to distinguish their features.

"Not a good photograph," muttered Mma Ramotswe to Mma Makutsi. "Worse than useless."

The door itself, which was half glass-fronted, bore a handwritten sign: Please Enter. No Need to Knock. But Mma Ramotswe, who believed in the traditional values—one of which was always to knock and call out *Ko Ko!* before one entered—knocked at the door before pushing it open.

"No need to knock, Mma," said a man sitting behind a desk. "Just come in."

"I always knock, Rra," said Mma Ramotswe. "It is the right thing to do."

The man smiled. "In my business," he said, "it's not always a good idea to knock. It warns people to stop whatever they're doing."

Mma Ramotswe laughed at the joke. "And one would not want that!"

"No, indeed," said the man. "But as you see, I am doing nothing bad. What a pity! I am just sitting here waiting for two beautiful ladies like you to come in and see me."

Mma Ramotswe glanced very quickly at Mma Makutsi before she replied. "You are a very kind man, Rra," she said. "I am not called beautiful every day. It is nice when that happens."

The man behind the desk made a self-deprecating gesture. "When you are a detective, Mma, you get used to observing things. I saw you coming in, and the first thing I said to myself was: *Two very, very beautiful ladies coming in the door. This is your lucky day. . . .*" He stopped, and then, rising to his feet and sitting down again almost immediately, he put the palm of a hand to his forehead.

"But, Mma, what am I saying! You are Mma Ramotswe, aren't you? The No. 1 Ladies' Detective Agency? I have seen your picture in the newspaper, and here I am telling you all about being a detective! And all the time it is you and Mma . . . Mma . . ."

"Makutsi," said Mma Makutsi. "I am an assistant detective at the No. 1 Ladies' Detective Agency. I was at the Botswana Secretarial College before—"

The man nodded, cutting her short. "Oh, that place. Yes."

Mma Ramotswe noticed the effect which this had on Mma Makutsi. It was as if somebody had applied an electric wire to her skin.

"It is a fine college," said Mma Ramotswe quickly, and then, to change the subject, "But what is your name, Rra?"

"I am Mr. Buthelezi," said the man, reaching out to shake hands. "Cephas Buthelezi. Ex-CID."

Mma Ramotswe took his hand and shook it, as did Mma Makutsi, reluctantly in her case. Then, invited to sit down by Mr. Buthelezi, they lowered themselves gingerly onto the shiny new chairs in front of his desk.

"Buthelezi is a famous name," said Mma Ramotswe. "Are you of the same family as he is?"

Mr. Buthelezi laughed. "Or might one say, is he of the same family as I am? Ha, ha!"

Mma Ramotswe waited a moment. "Well, is he?" she asked.

Mr. Buthelezi reached for a packet of cigarettes on his desk and extracted one.

"Many people are called Buthelezi," he said. "And many people are not. People are also called Nkomo or Ramaphosa or whatever.

That does not make them a real Nkomo or a real Ramaphosa, does it? There are many names, are there not?"

Mma Ramotswe nodded her agreement. "That is true, Rra. There are many names."

Mr. Buthelezi lit his cigarette. He had not offered his guests one—not that they smoked—but the lack of consideration had been noted, at least by Mma Makutsi, who, after the slighting reference to the Botswana Secretarial College, was looking for reasons to damn their newly discovered competitor.

Mma Ramotswe had been waiting for an answer to her question but now realised that one would not be forthcoming. "Of course," she said, "that is a Zulu name, is it not? You are from that part of the world, Rra?"

Mr. Buthelezi picked a fragment of tobacco from his front teeth.

"My late father was a Zulu from Natal," he said. "But my late mother was from here, a Motswana. She met my father when she was working over the border, in South Africa. She sent me to school in Botswana, and then, when I had finished school, I went back to live with them in South Africa. That is when I joined the CID in Johannesburg. Now I am back in my mother's country."

"And I see on your sign that you have lived in New York, too," said Mma Ramotswe. "You have had a busy life, Rra!"

Mr. Buthelezi looked away, as if remembering a rich and varied life. "Yes, New York. I have been in New York."

"Did you like living there, Rra?" asked Mma Makutsi. "I have always wanted to go to New York."

"New York is a very large city," said Mr. Buthelezi. "My God! Wow! There are many buildings there."

"But how long did you live there?" asked Mma Makutsi. "Were you there for many years?"

"Not many years," said Mr. Buthelezi.

"How long?" asked Mma Makutsi.

"You are very interested in New York, Mma," said Mr. Buthelezi. "You should go there yourself. Don't just get my view of it. See the place with your own eyes. Wow!"

For a few moments there was a silence, with Mma Makutsi's unanswered question hanging in the air: how long? Mr. Buthelezi drew on his cigarette and blew the smoke up towards the ceiling. He seemed comfortable enough with the silence, but after a while he reached forward and passed a small leaflet to Mma Ramotswe.

"This is my brochure, Mma," he said. "I am happy for you to see it. I do not mind that there is more than one detective agency in this town. It's growing so quickly, isn't it? There is work for two of us." *And what about me?* thought Mma Makutsi. *What about me? Are there not three of us, or am I just a nothing in your eyes?*

Mma Ramotswe took the cheaply printed brochure. There was a picture of Mr. Buthelezi on the front, sitting at a different desk and looking rather formal. She turned the page. Again there was a picture of Mr. Buthelezi, this time standing beside a black car, with indistinct tall buildings in the background. The middle ground, which was oddly hazy, appeared to be waste ground of some sort, and there were no other figures in the photograph, which was labelled underneath, *New York*.

She looked at the text opposite the picture. *Is something troubling you?* it read. *Is your husband coming home late and smelling of ladies' perfume? Is one of your employees stealing your business secrets? Don't take any chances! Entrust your enquiries to a MAN!*

The effect of this on Mma Ramotswe was similar to the effect which the earlier remark about the Botswana Secretarial College had produced on Mma Makutsi. Silently she passed the brochure to her assistant, who adjusted her glasses to read it.

"It has been very good to meet you, Rra," said Mma

Ramotswe, struggling with the words. Insincerity had never come easily to her, but good manners required it on occasion, even if a superhuman effort was needed. "We must meet again soon so that we can discuss our cases together."

Mr. Buthelezi beamed with pleasure. "That would be very good, Mma," he said. "You and me talking about professional matters . . ."

"And Mma Makutsi," said Mma Ramotswe.

"Of course," said Mr. Buthelezi, glancing quickly, and dismissively, at his other visitor.

Mma Makutsi had handed the brochure back to Mr. Buthelezi, who insisted that they keep it. Then the two women stood up, took their leave politely, if rather coldly, and left the shop, closing the door perhaps rather too firmly behind them. Once outside, they crossed the road in complete silence, and it was not until Mma Ramotswe had turned the tiny white van round and started to head for home that anything was said.

"So!" said Mma Ramotswe.

Mma Makutsi searched for something to say but could think of nothing that fitted the occasion; nothing that summed up her outrage at the way in which the Botswana Secretarial College had been referred to as *that place.* So she said, "So," too, and left it at that.

CHAPTER FIVE

THE TALKING CURE

THEY RETURNED to the office in silence. Mma Makutsi wanted to talk, but one look at Mma Ramotswe, sitting behind the wheel of the tiny white van, her face set in an uncharacteristic scowl, persuaded her that if there was to be any discussion of their encounter with Mr. Buthelezi, then this would have to come later. There could be no doubt, of course, of what Mma Ramotswe thought about their new colleague—if one could call him that. How dare he sit there and speak to Mma Ramotswe, the doyenne of the profession of private enquiry agent in Botswana, in that condescending fashion, as if he had all the experience and she were the newcomer. And then there was the boastful brochure, which Mma Makutsi now clutched in her hands, resisting all temptation to crunch it into a ball and throw it out of the window of the tiny white van. It was reasonable enough, of course, for people to wish to speak to a man, if that is what they wanted, but that did not mean that a man would be better. Trust your enquiries to a man indeed! The No. 1 Ladies' Detective Agency, as they had made abundantly clear from the very beginning, was not merely a service provided for ladies by ladies; it was a service for everybody, men and women equally. And the title made no claim to the special talents of ladies in private detection (although one could make that case if one sat down to it); all it implied was that this was a detective agency that happened to be run by ladies.

Mma Ramotswe parked the tiny white van directly behind the garage, outside the back door of the building that they shared with Tlokweng Road Speedy Motors. Mr. J.L.B. Matekoni was busy in the inspection pit, peering up at the chassis of a battered blue minibus and showing something to one of the apprentices beside him. He waved cheerfully, and Mma Ramotswe acknowledged his greeting, but she did not walk over to chat with him, as she normally would have done. Instead, both she and Mma Makutsi went directly into the agency and sat down at their desks in indignant silence.

Mma Makutsi had garage bills to attend to, and she busied herself with these. Mma Ramotswe, who sat on the committee of the Anglican Cathedral Women's League for Better Housing, had the minutes of a meeting to read through and a draft to prepare of a letter to the Ministry of Housing. She immersed herself in these tasks, but she found it difficult to concentrate, and after twenty minutes or so of saying the wrong thing to the deputy minister, and being unable to find the right words, she rose to her feet and went outside.

It was a comfortable time of year, immediately after the worst of the heat and before the winter set in. Not that the country had much of a winter. The nights could get chilly, of course, with that dry cold that could penetrate to the very bones, but the winter days were usually sunny and clear, with air that one could almost

drink, so pure and fresh it was; air with a hint of wood smoke; air
that filled one with gratitude that one was here, in this place, and
nowhere else. This time of year, when the grass was already turning brown but there were still patches of green, was perfect, in
Mma Ramotswe's view. Now she stood outside, under one of the
acacia trees, looking towards Tlokweng, watching a small group
of donkeys cropping the grass beside the road. Her anger had
largely passed, and watching the patient, unassuming donkeys
helped restore her sense of perspective. The children's difficulties were not really serious; small boys could behave in peculiar
ways (just like men), and as for Motholeli, bullying was an
inevitable, universal problem. She would discuss this with Mma
Potokwane, who would tell her exactly what to do.

Mr. Buthelezi was a rather more serious matter, but then
again, was he really that much of a threat? He was bombastic and
pleased with himself, but that did not mean he would take business away from her. People did not want bluster when they were
worried about something; they wanted good sense and caution.
Those ridiculous photographs of him would surely put people
off. People could tell the difference, could they not, between fantasy and reality? As Clovis Andersen pointed out in *The Principles
of Private Detection,* anybody who went into the profession thinking that it was glamorous because they had read books or seen
films about it was fundamentally misguided. Of course Mr.
Buthelezi would never have read Clovis Andersen (*I should have
asked him directly,* thought Mma Ramotswe; *that would have put him
in place*).

She turned away from the road and looked away, down to the
stand of eucalyptus trees that had been planted years ago, when
Gaborone was still called Chief Gaborone's Place, and which had
established itself as a forest. She was fearful of this forest, for
some reason, and never walked there alone. It was a sad place,

she thought, with its tall red-brown termite mounds and its paths that went to nobody's house but merely petered out in bark-littered clearings. Cattle moved through the trees, and she could hear their bells now but turned away with a shiver. That was not a good place.

The donkeys had wandered onto the road and were standing still, wondering whether to cross or not. A boy shouted at them and threw a stone to move them on, calling out their names: Broken Ear, Broken Ear! Thin One, Thin One! Come on, come on, move!

Which was Broken Ear, she wondered, as they all seemed to have fine ears, and none, now that one came to think of it, looked particularly thin. She was thinking of this, of the names which people give their animals, when a car turned off the road, circled Tlokweng Road Speedy Motors twice, and then drew up next to the tiny white van. Mma Ramotswe watched as the driver, a tall, well-built man in his early forties, got out.

"Dumela, Mma," he said as he walked over towards her. "Can you help me? I am looking for the No. 1 Ladies' Detective Agency."

Mma Ramotswe realised that she must seem somewhat dreamy to him, standing there, staring at the donkeys; a woman who was perhaps not all there in the head. "That is me, Rra. I am sorry, I was thinking of something else." She pointed to the don-keys. "I was listening to the herd boy calling out the names of those donkeys. I was not paying attention."

The man chuckled. "And why should you? There's nothing wrong with watching donkeys, or cattle, for that matter. I love to watch cattle myself. I can look at them for hours."

"Who can't?" replied Mma Ramotswe. "My father had a good eye for cattle. He could tell you a lot about a cow's owner just by looking at her."

"There are people like that," he agreed. "It is a great talent.

Perhaps you can do it. You could be a cattle detective, asking the cattle to tell you things."

Mma Ramotswe laughed. She had immediately taken to this man, whoever he was; he was the opposite of Mr. Buthelezi. You could not imagine this man being photographed in a wide-brimmed hat.

"I must tell you my name," said the man. "I am Molefelo, and I come from Lobatse. I am a civil engineer, but I have a hotel down there, too. I used to build things, but now I just sit in an office and run them. It is not as much fun, I'm afraid."

Mma Ramotswe listened politely. She had heard vaguely of Mr. Molefelo, she thought. She knew Lobatse, and she had probably been to his hotel once or twice with Mr. J.L.B. Matekoni when they had gone down there together to visit her cousin. In fact, the last time she had been there, she had eaten a meal which had made her very ill; but this was not the time to mention that, she thought.

"We can go into the office," she said, pointing to the door. "It will be more comfortable to sit down. My assistant will make us tea and we can talk."

Mr. Molefelo glanced towards the door of the agency, where Mma Makutsi could be seen, peering out at them.

"I wonder if we could stay outside," he said hesitantly. "It is such a pleasant day and. . . ." He paused before continuing. "Actually, Mma, what I have to say is very private. Very, very private. I wonder if we could talk about it outside? We could take a walk, perhaps. I could talk to you while we were walking."

Mma Ramotswe had encountered embarrassment before in her clients and understood that it was often no use trying to reassure them. If there was something which was really private, the presence of another often inhibited them. Of course, there was nothing—or almost nothing—that she had not heard. Nothing would astonish her, although there were occasions on which she marvelled at the ability people had to complicate their lives.

"I'm happy to go for a walk," she said to Mr. Molefelo. "I will just tell my assistant that I am going, and then I am ready."

THEY WALKED along a path that led back from the garage in the direction of the dam. There were thorn bushes and the sweet smell of grazing cattle. As they walked, Mr. Molefelo talked, and Mma Ramotswe listened.

"You may wonder, Mma, why I am telling you this, but I think you should know that I am a man who has changed. Something happened to me two months ago which has made me think about everything, about my whole life and how I've led it, and about how I should lead the rest of it. Do you know what I'm talking about?

"You are not talking to a particularly bad man, or anything like that. You are talking to a man who is probably much like other men. Just an average sort of man. There are thousands of men like me in Botswana. Ordinary men. Not very clever and not very stupid. Just ordinary men."

"You are being modest," interrupted Mma Ramotswe. "You are an engineer, aren't you? That is a clever thing to be."

"Not really. You have to be able to do mathematics and technical drawing, maybe. But beyond that, it's mostly common sense." He was silent for a moment before continuing. "But that's not the point about being ordinary. The point about being ordinary is that the average man does some bad things in his life and some good things. There are probably no men who have done no bad things. Probably not one."

"Nor women," said Mma Ramotswe. "Women are just as bad as men. Sometimes they are worse."

"I wouldn't know about that," said Mr. Molefelo. "I do not know many women very well. I do not know how women behave. But that is not the point. I was talking about men, and I think I do know how men behave."

"You have done a bad thing?" asked Mma Ramotswe bluntly. "Is that what you're trying to say?"

Mr. Molefelo nodded. "I have. But don't worry, it was not too bad—I haven't killed anybody or anything like that. I'll tell you about the bad thing I did—although I haven't told anybody else, you know. But first I should like to tell you about what happened a few months ago. Then you will understand why I want to talk to you.

"As I told you, I have a hotel down in Lobatse. This has done quite well—it is a good place for weddings—and I have used the money I made from it to buy land. I bought land down near the border with Namibia, right down there. It takes me four hours' driving from Lobatse to get there, and so I can't go down every week. I have a man, though, who looks after it for me, and there are some families who live on the land and do work for me."

"And this man, is he good with cattle? That is very important," said Mma Ramotswe.

"Yes, he is good with cattle. But he is also good with ostriches. I have a good flock of ostriches down there and some fine birds. Big ones. Strong. It's a good place for ostriches."

Mma Ramotswe did not know about ostriches. She had seen them, of course, and she knew that many people were keen on them. But in her mind, they were a poor substitute for cattle. She imagined a Botswana covered with ostriches rather than cattle. What a strange place that would be; undignified, really.

"My ostriches are well known for their good meat," Mr. Molefelo went on. "But they are also good breeders. I have one who is very kind to the hens and has many children. He is a very fine ostrich, and I keep him in a special paddock so that he does not fight. I have seen him kick, you know. Ow! If he kicked a man, he would divide him in two. I'm not exaggerating. Two pieces. Down the middle."

"I shall be very careful," said Mma Ramotswe.

"I saw a man kicked by an ostrich once. He was the brother of one of the men who works on my farm, and he was not very strong. A long time ago, when he was a child, he was trodden upon by some cattle and hurt his back. He did not grow up straight, because his spine was twisted. So he could not do much work. Then he got TB, and that made him even worse. All that coughing, I suppose, makes you very weak.

"He came to see his brother one day, and they gave him some beer, although this weak man was not used to drinking. He liked the beer, and it made him feel brave for once in his life. So he went over to the ostrich pen and climbed over the tall fence that we use to keep the ostriches in. There was an ostrich nearby who was watching him, and he was very surprised when a man ran up to him waving his arms. The ostrich tried to run away, but he caught his wing in the fence and was slow. So the man caught him, and that was when the ostrich kicked him.

"I had heard all this shouting when the man climbed over the fence, and I came to see what was happening. I saw him trying to seize the ostrich's tail feathers, and then I saw him going up in the air and landing down with a thump. He never got up, but lay there while the ostrich looked at him. And that was the end of that man."

Mma Ramotswe looked down at the ground, thinking of this poor man with his twisted spine. "I am sorry to hear about that man," she said. "There are many sad things that happen, and sometimes we do not hear about them. All the time, there are these sad things that God sends Africa."

"Yes," said Mr. Molefelo. "You are right, Mma. The world is very cruel to us sometimes."

They walked on a few paces, thinking about what Mma Ramotswe had said. Then Mr. Molefelo continued. "I must now tell you what happened to me just a few months ago. This is not just a story that I am telling you; it is so that you can understand why I have come to see you.

"I went down to my farm with my wife and my two sons. They are strong boys—one is this high and one is this high." He gestured with the palm of his hand held upwards; it was never a good idea to show the height of a person with the palm facing downwards, as this could push the spirit down. "We were going to stay there for a week, but something happened on the second night which changed that. Some men came to the farm from over the border. They came at night, riding on their horses. They were ostrich rustlers."

Mma Ramotswe stopped and looked at Mr. Molefelo in astonishment.

"There are ostrich rustlers? They steal your ostriches?"

Mr. Molefelo nodded. "They are very dangerous men. They come in bands with their guns, and they chase the ostriches back over the border into Namibia. The Namibians say that they are trying to catch them, but there are never enough policemen. Never. They say they will look for them, but how do you find men like that who live out in the bush, in camps? They are like ghosts. They come and go at night, and you will find a ghost more easily than you will find those men. They are men who have no names, no family, nothing. They are like leopards.

"I was sleeping in the house when they came. I am not a heavy sleeper, and I heard a noise down in the ostrich paddocks. So I got out of bed to see whether there was some creature coming to eat the ostriches—a lion, perhaps, or a hyena. I took a big torch and my rifle, and I walked down the path that led from the house to the paddocks. I did not need to switch on the torch, as there was a very large moon, which made shadows on the ground.

"I had almost reached the paddock when I was suddenly knocked to the ground. I dropped my rifle and my torch, and my face was in the dirt. I remember breathing the dust and coughing, and then I was kicked in the side, painfully, and a man pulled my head up and looked at me. He had a rifle in his hand—not my rifle—and he put the barrel at my head and said something to me. I did not understand him, as he was not speaking in Setswana. It may have been Hereto or one of the languages they speak over there. It could even have been Afrikaans, which quite a lot of them use down there, not just the Boers.

"I thought I was going to die, and so I thought of my sons. I wondered what would happen to them when they no longer had a father. Then I thought of my own father, for some reason, and I remembered walking with him through the bush, just as we are doing now, Mma, and talking to him about cattle. I thought that I would like to do that with my own sons, but I had been too busy, and now it was too late. These were strange thoughts. I was not thinking of myself but of other people."

Mma Ramotswe stooped down to pick up an interesting-looking stick. "I can understand that," she said, examining the stick, "I'm sure that I would think the same."

But would she? She had never been in that position; she had never been in danger at all, really, and she had no idea what would go through her mind. She would like to imagine that she would think of her father, Obed Ramotswe, the Daddy, that great man; but perhaps if matters came to such a pass, the mind would do the wrong thing and start thinking about mundane issues, like the electricity bill. It would be sad to leave this life on such a note, worrying about whether the Botswana Electricity Corporation had been paid. The Botswana Electricity Corporation would never think about her, she was sure.

"This man was very rough. He pulled my head back. Then he made me sit up, with the gun still pointing at my head, while he called out to one of his friends. They came out of the shadows, on their horses, and they stood about me, with the horses breathing against me. They talked among themselves, and I realised that they were discussing whether or not to shoot me. I am sure that they were talking about this, although I could not understand their language.

"Then I saw a light and heard somebody in the distance call out in Setswana. It was one of my men, who must now have woken up and had shouted out to the others. This made the man who was holding me hit me on the side of the head with his rifle. Then he stood up and ran over to a tree where he had tied his horse. There was more shouting from my men, and I heard them start the engine of the truck. One of the men who had surrounded me shouted out something to the others, and they rode off. I was left alone, feeling the blood run down the side of my face. I still have a scar, which you can see, look, just here between my cheek and my ear. That is my reminder of what happened."

"You were a lucky man to have escaped," said Mma Ramotswe. "They could easily have shot you. If you weren't here talking to me, I would have thought the story ended quite differently."

Mr. Molefelo smiled. "I thought that, too. But it did not. And I was able to go back to see my wife and my sons, who started to cry when they saw their father with blood streaming down his face. And I was crying, too, I think, and shaking all over like a dog who's been thrown in the water. And I was like this for more than a day, I think. I was very ashamed. A man should not behave like that. But I was like a frightened little boy.

"We went back to Lobatse so that I could see one of the doctors there who knew how to stitch up faces. He gave me injections and drew the wound together. Then I went back to work and tried to forget about what had happened. But I could not, Mma. I kept thinking about what this meant for my life. I know that this may sound strange to you, but it made me think about everything I had done. It made me weigh up my life. And it made me want to tie things up, so that next time—and I hope there will not be a next time—the next time I faced death like that, I could think: *I have set my life in order.*"

"That is a very good idea," said Mma Ramotswe. "We should all do that, I think. But we never do. For example, my electricity bill—"

"Those are small things," Mr. Molefelo interjected. "Bills and debts are nothing, really. What really counts are the things that you have done to people. That is what counts. And that is why I've come to see you, Mma. I want to confess. I do not go to the Catholic Church, where you can sit in a box and tell the priest all about the things you have done. I cannot do that. But I want to talk to somebody, and that is why I have come to see you."

Mma Ramotswe nodded. She understood. Shortly after opening the No. 1 Ladies' Detective Agency, she had discovered that part of her role would be to listen to people and to help them unburden themselves of their past. And indeed her subsequent reading of Clovis Andersen had confirmed this. *Be gentle,* he had written. *Many of the people who will come to see you are injured in spirit. They need to talk about things that have hurt them, or about things that they have done. Do not sit in judgement on them, but listen. Just listen.*

They had reached a place where the path dipped down into a dried-up watercourse. There was a termite mound to one side of it, and on the other, a small expanse of rock rising out of the red earth. There was the chewed-up pith of sugarcane lying to the side of the path and a fragment of broken blue glass, which caught the sun. Not far away a goat was standing on its hind legs, nibbling at the less accessible leaves of a shrub. It was a good place to sit and listen, under a sky that had seen so much and heard so much that one more wicked deed would surely make no difference. Sins, thought Mma Ramotswe, are darker and more powerful when contemplated within confining walls. Out in the open, under such a sky as this, misdeeds were reduced to their natural proportions—small, mean things that could be faced quite openly, sorted, and folded away.

CHAPTER SIX

OLD TYPEWRITERS, GATHERING DUST

MA MAKUTSI watched Mma Ramotswe set off for her walk with Mr. Molefelo and said to herself: "This is one of the limitations of being only an assistant detective. I miss the important things. I hear about the clients at one remove. I am really just a secretary, not an assistant detective." And, turning to the pile of garage bills which was now ready for dispatch, she thought: "I am not really an assistant garage manager, either; I am a garage secretary, which is a different thing altogether."

She rose from her desk to make herself a cup of bush tea. Even if a client had arrived—and there was no guarantee that the consultation taking place on the walk would mature into a full-scale, paid investigation—the future of the agency, and of her job, looked doubtful. There was also the question of money. She knew that Mma Ramotswe and Mr. J.L.B. Matekoni paid her as generously as they could, but after she had paid her increasingly expensive rent and sent money home to her parents and aunts in Bobonong, there was virtually nothing left for her to spend on herself. She was aware of the fact that some of her dresses were wearing thin and that her shoes would need resoling before too long. She did her best to keep her appearance smart, but it was difficult on a tight budget. At the moment, all that she had in her savings account was two hundred and thirty-eight pula and forty-five thebe. That would not be enough for a pair of good new shoes or a couple of dresses. And once she had spent that, there would be nothing left to buy the medicines that she might need for her brother.

Mma Makutsi realised that the only way of improving her situation was to take on extra work in her spare time. The driving school had been a good idea, but the more she thought about it, the more she realised that it would not work. She imagined what would happen if she were to speak about it to Mr. J.L.B. Matekoni. He would be supportive, of course, but she could hear his response, even before he made it.

"The insurance will be too expensive," he would point out. "If you are going to let learners drive a car, you have to pay a very high premium. The insurance companies know that they will crash."

He would tell her what the extra premium was likely to be, and she would be shocked by the figure. If that was what she would have to pay, then her earlier calculations were all wrong. They would have to charge very much more for each lesson, and that would cut out any advantage they might have over the large driving schools, which could use economies of scale. So the idea, which had seemed to offer a real prospect of extra money, would have to be abandoned, and she would have to start thinking of alternatives.

It was while she was typing a letter to one of the garage's recalcitrant debtors that the idea occurred to her. It was such a strikingly good idea that it took over her train of thought and became incorporated in the letter itself:

"Dear Sir," she typed, "We have written to you before on 25/11 and 18/12 and 14/2 about the outstanding sum of five hundred and twenty-two pula in respect of the repair of your vehicle. We note that you have not paid this sum and we have therefore no alternative but to. . . . Isn't it an interesting thing that most typists are women? When I was at the Botswana Secretarial College, it was only women, and yet men have to type if they want to use computers, which they do if they are engineers or businessmen or work in banks. I have seen them sitting in banks trying to type with one finger and wasting a lot of time. Why do they not learn to type properly? The answer to that is that they are ashamed to say they cannot type and they do not want to go and have to learn with a class full of girls. They are worried that the girls would be better at typing than they are! And they would be! Even those useless girls who only got fifty percent at the college. Even they would be better than men. So why not have a special class for men—a typing school for men? They could come after work and learn to type with other men. We could hold this class in a church hall, perhaps, so that when the men came to it, people would think that they were just going to a church meeting. I could teach it myself. I would be the principal and would give the men a special certificate at the end of the course. This is to certify that Mr. So-and-So completed the course on typing for men and is now a proficient typist. Signed, Grace P. Makutsi, Principal, Kalahari Typing School for Men."

She finished typing the letter and drew it from the machine with a flourish. She was astonished at the way in which the words had flowed from her, and by the completeness, the utter rightness, of the business plan which the letter contained. Reading over it again, she reflected on the fundamental insight into male psychology which had sprung, unannounced, from the typewriter keys. Of course it was right that men did not like to see women doing things better than they did; this was something which every girl learned at an early age. She remembered how her brothers had been unable to bear losing any game to her or one of her sisters. They had to win, and if there was any sign that they might lose, the game would be abandoned on some pretext or other. And this was no different from adult life.

Typing, of course, was a special case. Not only was there male anxiety about being bettered by women in the operation of a machine (men liked to think that they were the ones who understood how to use machines), but there was the additional embarrassment for them of being seen to do something which many people viewed as a woman's activity. Men did not like to be secretaries and had invented a special word for men who had to do any of that sort of work. They called themselves clerks. But what was the difference between a clerk and a secretary? One wore trousers and one wore a dress.

Mma Makutsi was convinced of the workability of her idea but realised there were many obstacles that would need to be overcome. First and foremost of these was a fundamental issue of what she had been taught at the Botswana Secretarial College to call capitalisation, but which, in simple language, meant money. Her capital was the grand total of two hundred and thirty eight pula and forty-five thebe, and that would buy, at the most, one secondhand typewriter. For a class of ten, she would need ten typewriters, which, at four hundred pula each, came to four thousand pula. This was a fabulous sum which would take her years to save. And even if she were able to borrow it from the bank, interest rates were such that all the fees from the students would go into payments. Not that the bank would lend to her in the first place, with no track record of profit and no security, not even one cow, for the loan.

There seemed no way round this brute fact of economic existence. To make money, one needed to have money in the first place. That was why those who had came by more and more. Mma Ramotswe was an example of this. Although she was always very modest about her circumstances, she had started with the great advantage of being able to sell all those cattle left to her by her father, just at a time when the price of cattle had shot up. And she had inherited his savings, too, which had been wisely placed in a part share of a store and a piece of ground. The piece of ground, it turned out, had been exactly where a company needed to build a depot on the edge of Gaborone, and that had driven the price up to unimaginable levels. All this had enabled Mma Ramotswe to buy the house in Zebra Drive and to set up the No. 1 Ladies' Detective Agency. That was why Mma Ramotswe was the owner and she was the employee, and nothing, it seemed, would change that. Of course, she could marry a man with money, but what man with money would even look at her when there were all those glamorous girls around? Really, it was all very bleak.

Typewriters! Who had a large supply of old, partly unworkable typewriters gathering dust in a storeroom? The Botswana Secretarial College!

Mma Makutsi picked up the telephone. There was a rule that personal calls from the garage and the agency were not allowed. ("This is not directed against you," Mma Ramotswe had said, "it's those apprentices. Imagine if they were able to speak on the phone from work to all those girls. We would not be able to pay the bill, or even half of it.") This was different. This was work, even if a sideline.

She dialled the number of the college and politely enquired

after the health of the telephonist at the other end before she asked to speak to the assistant principal, Mma Manapotsi. She knew Mma Manapotsi well and often chatted with her if they met in town.

"We have always been so proud of you," said Mma Manapotsi. "Ninety-seven percent! I shall never forget that. We still haven't had any other girl, not a single one, who has managed more than eighty-five percent. Your name is secure in the annals of the college! We are so proud."

"But you must also be proud of your son," Mma Makutsi would remind her. Mma Manapotsi's son, Harry, was a successful footballer, a member of the Zebras team and famous for scoring a crucial goal in a match against the Bulawayo Dynamos the previous year. He was an inveterate ladies' man, as many of these footballers were, and his hair was always covered with a curious sticky gel, for the benefit of ladies, Mma Makutsi assumed. But his mother was proud of him, as any mother would be of a son who was capable of bringing crowds to their feet.

When Mma Manapotsi was put on the line, they exchanged warm greetings before Mma Makutsi broached the subject of the typewriters. As she spoke, she stood on her toe under the desk, just for luck. They might have thrown the old typewriters out by now, or had them repaired and put back into service.

She explained that she was hoping to start a small typing class and that she would be prepared to pay for the rental of the typewriters, even if they did not work perfectly.

"But of course," said Mma Manapotsi. "Why not? Those old machines are useless, and we need to clear the space. You could have them in exchange for . . ."

Mma Makutsi thought of her savings and imagined the savings book with a row of noughts in every column.

"For an offer to come and talk to the girls now and then," went on Mma Manapotsi. "I was thinking of introducing a new part of the curriculum. Talks from distinguished graduates on what to expect in the working world. You could be the first speaker."

Mma Makutsi accepted the offer with alacrity.

"There are a dozen machines or so," said Mma Manapotsi. "They don't work properly, you know. They go qwertyui** rather than qwertyuiop. Some of them even go qop."

"I don't mind," said Mma Makutsi. "They're only for men."

"Well, that's all right then," said Mma Manapotsi.

MMA MAKUTSI replaced the receiver on its cradle and then rose from her desk. She glanced through the open door that led into the garage; nobody was watching. Slowly, she began to gyrate round the office in celebratory dance, ululating quietly as she did so, her right hand moving back and forward before her mouth. It was a victory dance. The Kalahari Typing School for Men had just been born; her first business, her very own idea. It would work—she had no doubt of that—and it would solve all her problems. The men would come flocking, all eager to learn the vital skill, and the money would flow into her account.

She adjusted her glasses, which had slipped down to the end of her nose during the dance, and looked out of the window. She could hardly wait to tell Mma Ramotswe all about it, as she knew that she would approve. Mma Ramotswe had Mma Makutsi's real interests at heart—she knew that very well. It would be a relief to her to hear that her employee had come up with such a sound project for her spare time. This was exactly the spirit of enterprise which Mma Ramotswe had spoken about on a number of occasions. Enterprise with compassion. Those poor men, desperate to know how to type, but too ashamed to ask how to do it, had relief in store.

CHAPTER SEVEN

WHAT MR. MOLEFELO DID

MR. MOLEFELO sat on his rock, under the empty sky, watched by a small herd of cattle that had gathered not far off, and told Mma Ramotswe, his confessor, of what he had done all those years ago.

"I came to Gaborone when I was eighteen. I had grown up in a small village outside Francistown, where my father was the clerk of the village council. It was an important job in the village, but not important outside. I found out when I came to Gaborone that being a village clerk was nothing and that nobody had heard of him down here.

"I had always been good with my hands, and I had been entered by my school for a place in the Botswana Technical College, which was much smaller then than it is today. I had done well at school in all the science subjects, and I think my father hoped that I would end up designing rockets or something like that. He had no idea that this sort of work is not done in Gaborone; in his eyes, Gaborone was a place where anything could happen.

"My family did not have much money, but I was given a government scholarship to help me in my studies at the college. This was meant to provide you with just enough money to pay the fees and to live simply for the rest of the term. That was not easy, and there were many days when I was hungry. But that does not matter so much when you are young. It is easy to have no money then because you think that it will change and there will be money, and food, tomorrow.

"The college arranged for students to stay with families in Gaborone. These were people who had a spare room, or even in some cases just a shed, which they wanted to rent out. Some of us had to live in uncomfortable places, far from the college. Others were lucky and had rooms in houses where they gave you good food and looked after you like one of the family. I was one of these. I had half a room in a house near the prison, staying with the family of one of the senior officials in the prison service. There were three bedrooms in this house, and I shared one of them with another boy from the college. He was always studying and made no noise. He was also very kind to me, and shared the loaves of bread which he got for nothing from his uncle, who worked in a bakery. He also had an uncle who worked in a butchery, and we got free sausages from him. This boy seemed to get everything free, in fact. His clothes were all free, too—they were given to him by an aunt who worked in a shop which sold clothes.

"The woman of the house was called Mma Tsolamosese. She was a very fat lady—a bit like yourself, Mma—and she was very kind to us. She used to make sure that my shirts were washed and ironed, because she said that my mother would expect that. 'I am your mother in Gaborone,' she said. 'There is one mother up there in Francistown and one mother down here. The one down here is me.'

"The husband was a very quiet man. He did not like his work, I think, because when she asked him what had happened in the prison that day, he simply shook his head and said: 'Prisons are full of bad men. They do bad things all day. That is what happens.' I do not remember him saying much more than that.

"I was very happy living in this house and studying at the college. I was happy, too, because I had found a girlfriend at long last. When I was at home I had tried and tried to find a girl who would talk to me, but there was nobody. Now, when I came to Gaborone, I found that there were many girls who were eager to get to know students at the college because they knew that we would be getting good jobs one day, and if they could get us to marry them, that would mean an easy life for them. I know, I know, Mma, it's not as simple as that, but I think that many of these girls did think that way.

"I met a girl who was hoping to train as a nurse. She had been working very hard at school and had already passed most of the examinations that she would need to get into the nurse training programme. She was very kind to me, and I was very happy that she was my girlfriend. We went together to the dances that they had at the college, and she was always dressed very smartly for these. I was proud that the other boys at the college should see me with this girl.

"Then, Mma, I have to tell you, we were so friendly, this girl and myself, that she found out she was expecting a baby. I was the father, she said. I did not know what to say about this. I think that I just looked at her when she told me. I was shocked, I think, because I was just a student and I could not be a father to a baby just yet.

"I told her that I would not be able to help with this baby and that she should send the baby off to her grandmother, who lived at Molepolole. I think I said that grandmothers were used to looking after such babies. She said that she did not think her grandmother was strong enough to do this, as she had been ill, and all her teeth had fallen out. I said that perhaps there was an aunt who could do this.

"I went back to my room in Mma Tsolamosese's house and did not sleep that night. The boy I shared the room with asked me what was troubling me, and I told him. He said that this was all my fault and that if I spent more time at my books then I would not get into trouble like that. This did not help me very much, and so I asked him what he would do if he were in my shoes. He said that he had an aunt who worked in a nursery school and that he would give the baby to her, and she would look after it for free.

"I saw my girlfriend the next day and asked her whether she was still expecting a baby. I hoped that she had made some sort of mistake, but she replied that the baby was still there and was growing bigger every day. She would have to tell her mother soon, she said, and her mother would tell her father. When that happened, I should have to look out, she said, as her father would probably come and kill me, or he would get somebody else to do that for him. She said that she thought he had already killed somebody in an argument over cattle, although he did not like to talk about it very much. This did not make me feel any happier. I imagined that I would have to leave the college and try to find work somewhere far away from Gaborone, where this man would not be able to find me.

"My girlfriend was now becoming angry with me. The next time I saw her, she shouted at me and told me that I had let her down. She said that because of me, she would have to try to get rid of the baby before it was born. She said that she knew a woman up in Old Naledi who would do this thing, but that because it was illegal, it would cost one hundred pula, which was a lot of money in those days. I said that I did not have one hundred pula, but I would think about ways of getting it.

"I went home and sat in my room, thinking. I had no idea of how I would get the money to pay for her to get rid of the baby. I had no savings, and I could not ask my father for it. He had no money to spare, and he would just be very cross with me if he knew why I wanted such a large sum. It was while I was thinking of this that I heard Mma Tsolamosese turn on her radio in the room next door. It was a very fine radio, which had taken them a long time to save for. I suddenly thought: *That is something that is worth at least one hundred pula.*

"You will guess what happened, Mma. Yes. That very night, when everybody had gone to bed, I went into that room and took the radio. I went outside and hid it in the bush near the house, in a place where I knew that nobody would find it. Then I went back to the house and I opened the window in that room, so the next morning it would look as if somebody had managed to force the window and had stolen the radio.

"Everything worked exactly as I had planned it. The next morning, when Mma Tsolamosese went into the room, she started to shout. Her husband got up and he started to shout, too, which was very unusual for a quiet man like that. 'Those bad men have stolen it. They have taken our radio. Oh! Oh!'

"I pretended to be as shocked as everybody else. When the police came, they asked me if I had heard anything that night, and I lied. I said that I had heard a noise, but that I had thought it was just Rra Tsolamosese getting up in the middle of the night.

The police wrote this down in their book, and then they went away. They told Mma Tsolamosese that it was very unlikely she would get the radio back. 'These people take them over the border and sell them. It will be far away by now. We are very sorry, Mma.'

"I waited until all the fuss had died down, and then I went out to the place where I had hidden the radio. I was very careful to make sure that nobody saw me, which they did not. I then hid the radio under my coat, and I went off to a place near the railway station where I had heard there were people who would buy things without asking any questions. I sat down under a tree, with the radio on my knee, and waited for something to happen. Sure enough, after only about ten minutes, a man came up to me and said that it was a beautiful radio and that it would be worth at least one hundred and fifty pula, if I ever wanted to sell it. I said that I was happy to sell it, and so he said to me: 'In that case, I will give you one hundred pula, because I can tell that you have stolen this radio and it is more risky for me.'

"I tried to argue, but all the time I was worried that the police would suddenly arrive, and so I sold it to him for one hundred pula. I gave the money to my girlfriend that night, and she just cried and cried when she took it from me. She said, though, that she would see me that weekend, after she had been out to Old Naledi to have the baby got rid of.

"I said that I would see her, but I am sorry to say, Mma, that I did not. We used to meet outside a café in the African Mall. She would wait for me, and then we would go for a walk together and look at the shops. She was waiting for me, as normal, but I stood under a tree, some distance away, and watched. I did not have the courage to go up to her and tell her that I no longer wanted to see her. It would have been a simple thing for me to walk up and talk to her, but I did not do this. I just watched from under the tree. After about half an hour, she went away. I saw her walking off, looking down at the ground, as if she was ashamed.

"She sent a letter to me through one of the other boys, whose sister she knew. She said that I should not send her away after everything that had happened. She said that she was crying for the baby, and that I should not have made her go to the woman in Old Naledi. She said, though, that she forgave me and that she would come to see me at the Tsolamoseses' house.

"I sent her a letter through the same boy. In it, I told her that I was now too busy with my studies to see her again and that she should not come to the house, even to say good-bye. I said that I was sorry she was unhappy, but that once she started to train as a nurse she would be very busy and would forget about me. I told her that there were many other boys, and that she would find one quickly if she looked hard enough.

"I know that she received this letter, as the sister who delivered it told her brother that she had done so. A week or so later, though, she came to the house, while we were sitting down for the dinner which Mma Tsolamosese had cooked for us. One of the Tsolamosese children looked out of the window and said that there was a girl standing at the gate. Mma Tsolamosese sent the child out to discover what this girl wanted, and the answer came back that she wanted to see me. I had been looking down at my plate, pretending that this thing had nothing to do with me, but now I had to go out and speak to her. 'Maybe Molefelo is a secret heartbreaker,' said Mma Tsolamosese as I left the room.

"I was very cross with her for coming, and I think that I raised my voice. She just stood there and cried and said that she still loved me, even though I was being cruel to her. She said that she would not disturb my studies and that she would only expect to see me once a week. She also said that she would try to find ways of paying back the one hundred pula that I had given her.

"I said: 'I don't want your money. I am no longer in love with you because I have found out that you are one of those girls who always nag men and make them feel bad about themselves. Boys have to watch out for girls like you.'

"This made her cry even more, and then she said: 'I will wait for you forever. I will think of you every day, and one day you will come back to me. I will write you a letter and then you will know how much I love you.'

"She reached forward and tried to hold my arm, but I pushed her away and turned to go back into the house. She started to follow me, but I pushed her away again, and this time she left. But all the time that this was happening, the Tsolamosese family was watching from the front window of the house.

"When I came back, they had returned to their seats at the table.

" 'You should not treat girls like that,' said Mma Tsolamosese. 'I am speaking to you now as your mother in this place. No mother would like to see her son behaving like that.'

"The father looked at me, too. Then he said: 'You are behaving like one of the bad men in the prison. They are always pushing and shoving other people. You be careful, or you may find yourself in that place one day. You just be careful.'

"And their son, who had also been watching, said: 'Yes. One day somebody will come and push you. That could happen.'

"I felt very embarrassed over what had happened, and so I lied. I told them that this girl was trying to get me to help her cheat in her examinations and that I was refusing to do this. They were astonished to hear this, and they said that they were sorry they had misjudged me. 'It is a good thing for Botswana that we have honest people like you,' said the father. 'If everybody were like you, then I would be out of a job. There would be no more need for the Botswana Prisons Department.'

"I sat there and said nothing. I was thinking of how I had stolen from these people, and how I had lied to them. I was thinking of how sad I had made my girlfriend and how I had forced her to get rid of our baby. I was thinking of the baby itself. But I just sat there and said nothing while I ate the food of the people whose kindness I had abused. Only the boy who shared my room seemed to know how I was feeling. He looked at me carefully and then he turned away. I realised then that he knew I had done some very bad things.

"There is not much more to say, Mma. After a few weeks, I forgot all about it. I still thought of the radio from time to time, and felt cold inside when I did so, but I never thought of the girl. Then, when I had finished at the college and I had found a job, I began to be too busy to think much about my past. I was lucky. I did very well in business, and I was able to buy the hotel at a very good price. I found a good wife to marry me, and I had the two fine sons I told you about. There are also three daughters. I have everything I need, but after what happened to me when those men came to my farm, I want to clear up my bad conscience. I want to make good the bad deeds that I did."

Mr. Molefelo stopped talking and looked at Mma Ramotswe, who had been twisting a long blade of grass around her finger as she listened to him speaking.

"Is that everything, Rra?" she asked after a while. "Have you told me everything?"

Mr. Molefelo nodded. "I have not hidden anything. That is what happened. I remember it very clearly, and I have told you everything."

Mma Ramotswe stared at him. He was telling the truth, she knew, because the truth was in his eyes.

"That cannot have been easy to say," she said. "You have been very brave. Most people never tell these stories about themselves. Most people make themselves sound better than they really are."

"There would have been no point doing that," said Mr. Molefelo. "The whole point of talking to you was to tell somebody the truth."

"And now?" she asked. "What do you want to do now?"

Mr. Molefelo frowned. "I want you to help me. That is why I have come to see you."

"But what can I do?" asked Mma Ramotswe. "I cannot change the past. I cannot take you back all those years."

"Of course not. I did not expect you to be able to do that. I just want you to sort this thing out for me."

"How can I do that? I can't bring back that baby. I can't find that radio. I can't prevent the sadness which that girl felt. All these are things which are long dead and buried. How many years is it? Nearly twenty years? That is a long time."

"I know it is a long time. But it might be possible to do something. I would like to pay the Tsolamosese family back. I would like to give some money to the girl. I would like to sort these things out."

Mma Ramotswe sighed. "Do you think that money can change things? Do you think that just by giving somebody money, you can undo what you did?"

"No," said Mr. Molefelo. "I do not think that. I am not stupid. I would also like to give them an apology. I would like to apologise and also to give them money."

For a few moments there was silence as Mma Ramotswe pondered this. What would she do herself, she wondered, in these circumstances? If she had the courage, she would go to the people involved and confess what had happened. Then she would try to make amends. This was what he was doing, except for the fact that he was expecting her to do it for him. An indirect apology of that sort was no apology at all, she thought.

"Don't you think," she began, "don't you think that you are just asking me to do your dirty work—or should I call it your hard work—for you? Don't you think that this means you are not really ready to apologise?"

Mr. Molefelo stared at her. He seemed upset, and she wondered whether she was being too direct. It had been difficult enough for him to talk about this without her now making it worse by effectively accusing him of cowardice. And who was she to accuse anybody of cowardice? How did anybody know how brave he would be?

"I'm sorry," she said, reaching out to touch his arm. "I did not mean to be unkind. I understand how hard this is for you."

There was anguish in his expression as he replied. "All I want you to do, Mma, is to find these people. I do not know where they are. Then, when you have found them, I promise you that I shall be brave. I will go to them and I will speak to them directly."

"That is good," said Mma Ramotswe. "Nobody could ask more of you."

"But will you help?" asked Mr. Molefelo. "Will you help me by coming with me when I go to see them? I do not know whether I will fail at the last moment if you do not come with me."

"Of course I'll come with you," she said. "I will come with you, and I will be saying to myself: *This a brave man. Only a brave man can look at his past wrongs and then face up to them like this.*"

Mr. Molefelo smiled, his relief quite apparent. "You are a very kind lady, Mma Ramotswe."

"I don't know about that," said Mma Ramotswe, rising to her

feet and dusting off her dress. "But now it is time for us to walk back. And on the walk back, I shall tell you about a little problem I have. It is all about a boy who killed a hoopoe, and I want to hear from you what you think. You are a man with two boys, and maybe you can give me some advice."

CHAPTER EIGHT

THE TYPEWRITERS, AND A PRAYER MEETING

WHENEVER SHE walked past the Botswana Secretarial College, Mma Makutsi felt a surge of pride. She had spent six months of her life at the college, during which time she had scraped an existence, working part-time as a night waitress in a hotel (a job which she hated) and struggling to stay awake during the day. Her resolve and her persistence had paid off, and she would never forget the strength of the applause at the graduation ceremony when, before the proud eyes of her parents, who had sold a sheep to pay for the journey down to Gaborone, she had crossed the stage to receive her secretarial diploma as the leading graduate of the year. Her life, she suspected, would involve no greater triumph than that.

"Do you see that?" she said to the elder apprentice, whom Mr. J.L.B. Matekoni had instructed to help her in the task of fetching the typewriters. "That motto on the notice board up there? *Be accurate.* That's the motto of the college."

"Yes," said the apprentice. "That's a good motto. You don't want to be inaccurate if you are a typist. Otherwise you have to do everything twice. That would not be good."

Mma Makutsi looked at him sideways. "A good motto for every walk of life, would you not think?"

The apprentice said nothing, and they continued to walk down the corridor that led to the office.

"All the students here are girls, are they not, Mma?" asked the apprentice.

"Yes," she said. "There is no reason why that should be. But that is how it was in my day."

"I would like to study here, then," said the apprentice. "That would suit me. I should like to sit in a classroom with all those girls."

Mma Makutsi smiled. "Some of them would like that, too, I think. The wrong sort of girl."

"There are no wrong sort of girls," countered the apprentice. "All girls have their uses. All girls are welcome."

They had arrived at the office, and Mma Makutsi was announcing herself to the assistant principal's receptionist.

"Mma Manapotsi will be pleased to see you, Mma," said the receptionist, glancing appreciatively at the apprentice, who was smiling at her. "She remembers you well."

Mma Makutsi was shown into Mma Manapotsi's office while the apprentice remained outside, perched on the edge of the receptionist's desk. He was amusing her by pressing a finger on a blank sheet of paper and leaving a fingerprint of black grease outlined on the surface.

"My trademark," he said. "If I hold hands with a pretty girl— like you—I leave a trademark! It says: My property! Keep off!"

Inside, Mma Manapotsi greeted Mma Makutsi warmly. There were enquiries about her current job, and a delicate question as to the salary she was commanding.

"It sounds very important being an assistant detective and assistant manager," said Mma Manapotsi. "I hope that they are paying you what you deserve. We like our graduates to be properly rewarded."

"They are paying me as much as they can," said Mma Makutsi. "Very few people get paid what they really deserve, though, do they? Even the president does not get the salary he deserves, I think. We should pay him more, I think."

"That may be so," said Mma Manapotsi. "I have always thought that the assistant principals of colleges should get more, too. But we must not complain, must we, Mma? If everybody complained all the time, then there would be no time for anything else but complaints. We do not complain here at the Botswana Secretarial College. We get on with the job."

"That is what I think, too," said Mma Makutsi.

The conversation continued in this way for a few minutes. From beyond the door that led into the receptionist's room, there was a murmur of voices and an occasional giggle. At length, they reached the subject of the old typewriters, and Mma Manapotsi confirmed her offer.

"We can fetch them now," she said. "Your young man out there can carry them for you, if he is not too busy with that girl of mine."

"He is always like that with girls," said Mma Makutsi. "Every girl he meets. It is a sad thing, but that is the way he is."

"We would not want men to ignore us altogether," said Mma Manapotsi. "But sometimes it would be better if they ignored us a bit."

They made their way to the storeroom where, amid piles of papers and books, the disused typewriters were stacked.

"They are very old," said Mma Manapotsi, "but most of them could probably be made to work, or almost work. They will need oiling."

"Plenty of that in the garage," remarked the apprentice, turning a roller experimentally.

"Perhaps," said Mma Manapotsi. "But remember, these machines are not like cars. They are much more delicate."

They returned to Tlokweng Road Speedy Motors, where Mr. J.L.B. Matekoni had agreed the typewriters could be stored and worked upon until Mma Makutsi had found a place for the classes to be held. Mma Ramotswe, who had endorsed the plan in spite of some misgivings about whether there would be enough pupils, offered to pay for the placing of a press advertisement drawing attention to the classes, and also expressed an interest in helping with the restoration of the typewriters.

"Motholeli would like to help, too," she said. "She is very keen on machines, that girl, and she has very nimble fingers."

"This business will be a great success," said Mr. J.L.B. Matekoni. "I have a feeling for businesses. I think that this one will do well."

Mma Makutsi was buoyed by his prediction. She was awed by the thought that she was about to embark on a venture of her own, and the warm words of her employers encouraged her greatly. "Do you really think so, Rra?"

"I have no doubt of it," said Mr. J.L.B. Matekoni.

IT WAS, it transpired, a time of mutual support. The No. 1 Ladies' Detective Agency supported Tlokweng Road Speedy Motors, providing secretarial and bookkeeping services in the shape of Mma Makutsi, who still occasionally helped with the servicing of cars as well. In return, Tlokweng Road Speedy Motors paid most of Mma Makutsi's salary, thus making it possible for her to serve as assistant detective. For her part, Mma Ramotswe supported Mr. J.L.B. Matekoni, making his evening meal for him and laundering his overalls and those of the apprentices as well. The apprentices, nurtured and trained by Mr. J.L.B. Matekoni, who was tolerant of their foibles as most employers would not be, repaid in their own way. When it came to the restoration of the typewriters, it was they who did most of the work, giving up a great deal of their spare time over the next two weeks in an effort to coax the old machines into serviceability.

It was in this spirit of mutual assistance that everybody agreed to attend a religious meeting at which the younger apprentice was speaking. He had asked them whether they would care to come and hear him speak, as it would be the first time that he had addressed the entire brotherhood of his church, and it was, he said, a very important occasion for him.

"We shall have to go," said Mr. J.L.B. Matekoni. "I don't think we can refuse."

"You are right," said Mma Ramotswe. "It is very important to him. It is a bit like a prize-giving. If he were getting a prize, we would have to go."

"These things can go on for many hours," warned Mma Makutsi. "Don't expect to get away in less than three hours. You must eat a big piece of meat before you go, otherwise you will feel weak."

The meeting took place the following Sunday, in a small church near the diamond-sorting building. Mma Ramotswe and Mr. J.L.B. Matekoni arrived in good time and had been sitting there, contemplating the ceiling, for at least twenty minutes before Mma Makutsi arrived.

"Now we are all here," whispered Mr. J.L.B. Matekoni. "Only his brother, Charlie, is not coming."

"He'll be with some girl," said Mma Makutsi. "That is where he is."

Mma Ramotswe said nothing. She was watching the congregation coming in, waving discreetly to one or two, and smiling at the children. At last the platform party entered—the minister, dressed in a flowing blue gown, and the choir, also in blue, in whose ranks the apprentice was to be seen, smiling encouragingly at his guests.

There were hymns and prayers, and then the minister rose to speak.

"There are sinners all about us," he warned. "They are wearing ordinary clothes, and they walk and talk like any other person. But their hearts are full of sin, and they are plotting more sin as we sit here."

Mr. J.L.B. Matekoni glanced at Mma Ramotswe. Was his heart full of sin? Was hers?

"Fortunately we can be saved," continued the minister. "All we have to do is to look into our hearts and see what sins are there. Then we can do something about it."

There were murmurs of agreement from the congregation. One man groaned softly, as if in pain, but it was only sin, thought Mma Ramotswe. Sin makes one groan. The weight of sin. Its mark. Its stain.

"And those who come into this church," said the minister. "They bring their sins in, too. They bring sins into the midst of God's people. They come straight from Babylon."

Mr. J.L.B. Matekoni, who had been looking at his folded

hands as the minister spoke, now looked up and saw that people were staring at him, as well as at Mma Ramotswe and Mma Makutsi. He nudged Mma Ramotswe discreetly.

"Yes," said the minister. "There are strangers here. You are very welcome, but you must declare your sins before God's people. We shall help you. We shall make you strong."

There was now complete silence. Mma Makutsi looked around anxiously. Surely this was no way to welcome visitors. Usually congregations greeted strangers warmly and clapped when you stood up. This must be a strange religion to which the apprentice had subscribed.

The minister now pointed at Mr. J.L.B. Matekoni. "Speak, my brother," he said. "We are listening."

Mr. J.L.B. Matekoni looked frantically at Mma Ramotswe.

"I . . ." he began. "I am a sinner. Yes—I suppose . . ."

Suddenly Mma Ramotswe stood up. "Oh my!" she called out. "I am the sinner here. I am the one! I have committed so many sins that I cannot count them. They are weighty. They are making me sink. Oh! Oh!"

The minister raised his right arm. "The power of the Lord be upon you, my sister! He will release you from these sins! Tell the sins! Speak their awful name!"

"Oh, they are so numerous," said Mma Ramotswe. "Oh! I cannot bear these sins. They are making me hot. I am feeling the fire of hell! Oh, the fire of hell is consuming me! I am so hot! Oh!"

She sank back on the pew, fanning herself with the hymn sheet.

"The fires!" she shouted. "The fires are all about me. Take me out!"

Mr. J.L.B. Matekoni felt the dig in his ribs.

"I must take her outside," he said to the congregation at large. "The fire—"

Mma Makutsi rose to her feet. "I will help you. The poor lady. All those sins. Oh! Oh!"

Once outside, they walked as quickly as they could to Mr. J.L.B. Matekoni's car, which was parked alongside a row of believers' cars, outwardly no different from any of them.

"You are a very good actress," said Mr. J.L.B. Matekoni as they drove away. "I was very embarrassed there. I was having to think of sins."

"Maybe I wasn't acting," said Mma Ramotswe dryly.

CHAPTER NINE

THE CIVIL SERVICE

MR. MOLEFELO had given Mma Ramotswe very little information. All she knew about the people for whom she was to look was that Mr. Tsolamosese had been a senior officer at the prison; that the Tsolamosese family had lived in a government house near the old airfield; and that the girlfriend, whose name was Tebogo Bathopi, came from Molepolole and was hoping to train as a nurse. This was not a great deal to go on: much would have happened in the course of twenty years; Tebogo would probably have married and changed her name; Mr. Tsolamosese would surely have retired and the family would have left the house. But it was hard to disappear completely in Botswana, where there were fewer than two million people and where people had a healthy curiosity as to who was who and where people had come from. It was very difficult to be anonymous, even in Gaborone, as there would always be neighbours who would want to know exactly what one was doing and who one's people had been. If you wanted anonymity, you had to leave the country altogether and go somewhere like Johannesburg, where nobody knew, nor cared very much, it would seem.

Tracking down the Tsolamosese family would be relatively easy, thought Mma Ramotswe. Even if Mr. Tsolamosese had retired from the prison service, there was bound to be somebody at the prison who would know where he had gone. Prison officials were a close-knit community; they lived cheek by jowl with one another in the prison lines, and their families often intermarried. They had to be protective of one another, as there was always the danger that a released prisoner might try to settle a score, which had happened on one or two occasions, as Mma Ramotswe had read. In one case, a prisoner who succeeded in escaping hid in the house of a warder, under his bed, and waited for him to go off to sleep before he crawled out and stabbed him through his blankets. It had been a chilling incident, although the warder had survived the attack relatively unscathed, and the prisoner had been rearrested and beaten. Such evil was difficult to contemplate, thought Mma Ramotswe. How could anybody do that sort of thing to a fellow human being? The answer, of course, was that such people were cold inside. They had no feelings, and it was easy for them to do things like that and worse. God would judge them, she knew, but in the meantime they could do a great deal of damage. Worst of all, these people destroyed trust. You used to be able to trust people, but now you had to be so careful, even in a good country like Botswana. It was unimaginably worse in other places, of course, but even in Botswana you had to hold on to your handbag if you walked out at night, in case a young man with a knife came and took it from you. What could be further from the old Botswana ways of courtesy and respect? What, she wondered, would Obed Ramotswe make of it if he were to come back and see what had happened; her father, who, if he found so much as a one-pula note on the roadway, would hand it over to the police, oblivious to their surprise at his honesty.

Mma Ramotswe decided to divide her task into two. First she would find the Tsolamosese family and propose the reparation which she had discussed with Mr. Molefelo. Then, that piece of the past set to rest, she would set about the more difficult task of tracing Tebogo. The first step, though, was a telephone call to the prison, and an enquiry as to whether Mr. Tsolamosese still worked there. As she had anticipated, the official who answered the telephone had not heard the name. Mma Ramotswe asked then to speak to the oldest person in the office.

"Why do you want to speak to an old person, Mma?" she had been asked politely.

"Because they know more, Rra," she had replied.

There was a silence at the other end of the line. Then, after a few moments of hesitation, the oldest official was fetched.

"I am fifty-eight, Mma," he said, introducing himself over the line. "Is that old enough for you, or do you want somebody who is eighty or ninety?"

"Fifty-eight is very good, Rra," she said. "A person who is fifty-eight will know what he is talking about."

This remark was well received. "I shall try to help you, if I can. What is it you wish to know?"

"I would like to know if you remember Mr. Tsolamosese," she said. "He worked in the prison some years ago. Perhaps he is no longer working."

"Ah," said the voice. "I was here when he was working here. He was a very quiet man. He did not say very much, but he did well in the service and was very senior."

"He is no longer working, then?" Mma Ramotswe pressed.

"No, he is not working. In fact, I am sorry to tell you he is late."

Mma Ramotswe's heart sank. But perhaps Mma Tsolamosese was still alive, and Mr. Molefelo would be able to make it up to her.

"He had a heart attack, I think," said the voice. "About eight years ago. He was still here then, but he was very ill and he became late."

"And the widow?" asked Mma Ramotswe.

"She went away. I don't think anybody here knows anything about her. She must have gone back to her village. You could ask the pensions people, of course. She will be getting her widow's pension if she is still alive. That will mean that they will have her address somewhere. You could try them."

"You have been very kind, Rra," said Mma Ramotswe. "I have something to give that lady, and you have helped me to find her. You are very kind."

"It is my job to help," said the voice.

"That is very good."

"Yes," said the voice.

"I hope that you are very happy," said Mma Ramotswe. "You have been very helpful."

"I am very happy," said the voice. "I shall be retiring next year and I shall be growing sorghum."

"I hope it grows well," said Mma Ramotswe.

"You are very kind, Mma. Thank you."

They said farewell, and Mma Ramotswe put down the telephone with a smile. In spite of everything, in spite of all the change, with all the confusion and uncertainty which it brought; in spite of the casual disregard with which people were increasingly treating one another these days, there were still people who spoke to others with the proper courtesy, who treated others, whom they did not know, in the way which was proper according to the standards of the old Botswana morality. And whenever that happened, whenever one encountered such behaviour, one was reminded that all was by no means lost.

Her next task was not a telephone call but a visit. She knew the office which dealt with pensions, and she would call there to find out whether Mma Tsolamosese was still receiving her pension. If she was, then she would have to try to get the address from them. That might be difficult, but not impossible. There was a tendency in government offices to treat everything as confidential, even if it clearly was not, but Mma Ramotswe had found that there were usually ways round this.

The government pensions office, when she arrived there shortly after lunchtime, was still shut, but Mma Ramotswe was happy to wait under the shade of a nearby tree until a tired-looking clerk opened the door and peered outside.

The public office to which she was admitted had that typical look and smell of government offices. The furniture, such as it was, was completely functional—straight-backed chairs and simple two-drawer desks. On the wall at the back there was a picture of His Excellency, the president of the Republic of Botswana, and on the other walls there was a map of Botswana, broken down into administrative districts, a calendar supplied by the *Botswana Gazette,* and a fly-spotted framed picture of cattle gathered round a borehole-fed watering tank.

The clerk behind the desk looked at Mma Ramotswe in a sleepy way.

"I am looking for the widow of a government pensioner," she said, noting the spoiled collar of the clerk's shirt. He would not go far in the civil service, she thought; civil servants were usually proud of their appearance, and this man was not.

"Name?" he said.

"Mine?"

"Pensioner."

Mma Ramotswe had written the name on a piece of paper, and she passed it to the clerk. Underneath the name she had written: *Prisons Department*, and after that the date of Mr. Tso-lamosese's death.

The clerk looked at the piece of paper and made his way out of the room into a corridor which Mma Ramotswe could see was lined with lever-arch files. She watched him walk down the shelves until he stopped, extracted a file, and ruffled through some papers. Then he returned to the desk.

"Yes," he said. "There is a widow of that name. She receives a pension from the Prisons Department."

Mma Ramotswe smiled. "Thank you, Rra. Could you give me her address? I have something to deliver to her."

The clerk shook his head. "No, I cannot do that. The details of the pensioners are confidential. We could not have the whole world coming in here and finding out where these people live. That is not possible."

Mma Ramotswe took a deep breath. This was precisely what she had feared would happen, and she knew that she would have to be extremely careful. This clerk was not bright, and people like that could show a remarkable tenacity when it came to rules. Because they could not distinguish between meritorious and unmeritorious requests, they could refuse to budge from the let-ter of the regulations. And there would be no point in trying to reason with them. The best tactic was to undermine their cer-tainty as to the rule. If they could be persuaded that the rule was otherwise, then it might be possible to get somewhere. But it would be a delicate task.

"But that is not the rule," said Mma Ramotswe. "I would

never tell you your job—a clever man like you does not need to be told by a woman how to do his job—but I think that you have got the rule wrong. The rule says that you must not give the name of a pensioner. It says nothing about the address. That you can tell."

The clerk shook his head. "I do not think you can be right, Mma. I am the one who knows the rules. You are the public."

"Yes, Rra. I am sure that you are very good when it comes to rules. I am sure that this is the case. But sometimes, when one has to know so many rules, one can get them mixed up. You are thinking of rule 25. This rule is really rule 24(b), subsection (i). That is the rule that you are thinking of. That is the rule which says that no names of pensioners must be revealed, but which does not say anything about addresses. The rule which deals with addresses is rule 18, which has now been cancelled."

The clerk shifted on his feet. He felt uneasy now and was not sure what to make of this assertive woman with her rule numbers. Did rules have numbers? Nobody had told him about them, but it was quite possible, he supposed.

"How do you know about these rules?" he asked. "Who told you?"

"Have you not read the *Government Gazette?*" asked Mma Ramotswe. "The rules are usually printed out in the *Gazette,* for everybody to see. Everybody is allowed to see the rules, as they are there for the protection of the public, Rra. That is important."

The clerk said nothing. He was biting his lip now, and Mma Ramotswe saw him throw a quick glance over his shoulder.

"Of course," she pressed on, "if you are too junior to deal with these matters, then I would be very happy to deal with a more senior person. Perhaps there is somebody in the back office who is senior enough to understand these rules."

The clerk's eyes narrowed, and Mma Ramotswe knew at that

moment that her judgement had been correct: if he called somebody else, he would lose face.

"I am quite senior enough," he said haughtily. "And what you say about the rules is quite correct. I was just waiting to see if you knew. It is very good that you did. If only more members of the public knew about these rules, then our job would be easier."

"You are doing your job very well, Rra," said Mma Ramotswe. "I am glad that I found you and not some junior person who would know nothing about the rules."

The clerk nodded sagely. "Yes," he said. "Anyway, this is the address of the woman you mention. Here, I'll write it down for you. It is a small village on the way to Lobatse. Maybe you know it. She is living there."

Mma Ramotswe took the piece of paper from the clerk and tucked it into the pocket of her dress. Then, having thanked him for his help, she went outside, reflecting on how bureaucracy was very rarely an obstruction, provided that one applied to it the insights of ordinary, everyday psychology, insights with which Mma Ramotswe, more than many, had always been well endowed.

CHAPTER TEN

THE KALAHARI TYPING SCHOOL FOR MEN
THROWS OPEN ITS DOORS (TO MEN)

LOOKING BACK, as she later would do, on the early days of the Kalahari Typing School for Men, Mma Makutsi, assistant detective at the No. 1 Ladies' Detective Agency and formerly acting manager of Tlokweng Road Speedy Motors, would marvel at just how easy it was to start the school. If all businesses were as easy, she reflected, then the road to plutocracy would be simple indeed. What made it all so simple and so painless? The answers might form the kernel of a business school essay: a good idea; a niche in the market; low start-up costs; and, what is perhaps most important of all, a willingness to work hard. All of these were present in ample measure in the case of the Kalahari Typing School for Men.

The easiest task—potentially the most difficult—had been the finding of a place to hold the classes. This issue had been quickly resolved by the younger apprentice, who offered to speak to the minister about the possible use of the meeting room attached to his church.

"It is never used during the week," he had said. "The minister is always saying that we must share. This is a chance for us to do just that."

The minister was amenable, under the condition that the religious pamphlets be left in the hall so that those attending the classes might have the chance to be saved.

"There will be many sinners wishing to learn to type," he said. "They will see the pamphlets and some of them will realise what sinners they are."

Mma Makutsi had readily agreed and had taken the typewriters, most of which were now in basic working order even if not all the keys worked, over to the hall, where they were stored in two padlocked cupboards. There were already tables and chairs in the hall, and these could seat over thirty, although the number of pupils would be limited by the ten typewriters available.

Within a few days, everything was prepared. A small advertisement had been inserted in the *Botswana Daily News,* worded in such a way as to appeal to exactly the audience which Mma Makutsi had in mind.

Men: do you know that it is very important these days to be able to type? If you cannot type, you will be overtaken. There is no room in the modern world for those who cannot type. You can now learn, in confidential conditions, at the Kalahari Typing School for Men, under the supervision of Mma Grace Makutsi, Dip. Sec. (magna cum laude) (Bw. Sec. Coll.).

Prospective students were then referred to the telephone number of the No. 1 Ladies' Detective Agency and instructed to ask for the Typing School Department.

On the day of publication, Mma Makutsi was at work earlier than usual. She had obtained an early copy of the paper from the printers and had read and reread the text of the advertisement. It gave her considerable pleasure to see her name in print. It was the first time that she had ever seen this, and she sat and stared at it for some time, thinking, *That's me, that's my name, in print, in the newspaper, me.*

The first call came half an hour later, and one followed another throughout the day. By four o'clock in the afternoon, there were twenty-two firm bookings for a place in the class; ten would start that week, a further ten would be admitted to the second course some two months later, and two were placed on a waiting list.

Mma Ramotswe shared Mma Makutsi's pleasure.

"You were right," she said. "There must be many men who are desperate to learn how to type. It is very sad."

"I told you it would work out," said Mr. J.L.B. Matekoni. "I told you."

THE FIRST class took place on a Wednesday evening. Mma Ramotswe had given Mma Makutsi the afternoon off so that she could prepare for the occasion, and Mma Makutsi had spent some time setting out sheets of paper at each desk and distributing the exercise booklet which she had herself typed out and duplicated. On a makeshift blackboard at one end of the room she had drawn, in chalk, the layout of the keyboard, dissected with wavy lines for the domain of each finger and each thumb. This was the basic knowledge of the typist, the foundation stone of the skill that would send the fingers racing across the keyboard and the keys clattering against the roller.

There had never been any doubt about the pedagogical philosophy which would underpin the efforts of the Kalahari Typing

School for Men. This was the same as the philosophy of the Botswana Secretarial College, and it held that every finger must be taught to know its place. There would be no shortcuts; there would be no leeway for sloppy habits. The little finger must *think* q; the thumb must *think* space bar. That is how they had put it at the Botswana Secretarial College, and Mma Makutsi had never heard the philosophy of typing put so succinctly and so truly.

On the basis of this instinctive positioning of fingers, the students would be taught, by sheer repetition, to bridge the gap between perception of the word to be typed (or its imagination) and the movement of the muscles. That was something that could be acquired only through practice, and through the constant performance of standard exercises. Within a few weeks, if the student had any aptitude at all, words could be typed slowly but accurately, even making allowances for the fact that men have larger, more ungainly fingers.

The class was due to begin at six, which gave time for the students to make their way from their workplaces to the hall. Well before that time, however, they had all assembled, and Mma Makutsi found herself confronted with ten expectant faces. She looked at her watch, counted the students, and announced that the class would begin.

The hour went very quickly. The students were instructed in the insertion of sheets of paper and in the function of the various keys. Then they were asked to type, in unison, on the command of Mma Makutsi, the word "hat."

"All together," called out Mma Makutsi, "*h* and *a* and *t*. Now stop."

A hand went up.

"My *h* does not work, Mma," said a puzzled-looking, smartly dressed man. "I pressed it twice, but it has not worked. I have typed 'at.'"

Mma Makutsi was prepared for this. "Some keys are not in working order," she said. "This does not matter. You must still press them, because you will find that these keys will work in the office. It does not matter at this stage."

She looked at the man, who had his hair parted down the middle and a neatly trimmed moustache. He was smiling up at her, his lips parted slightly, as if he was about to say something. But he did not, and they moved on to new but equally unchallenging words.

"Cat," shouted Mma Makutsi. "And mat. Hat cat mat."

At the end of the hour, Mma Makutsi made her way round the desks and inspected the results. She had learned at the Botswana Secretarial College the importance of encouragement, and she made sure that she had a word of praise for each student.

"You will be a very good typist, Rra," she would say. "You have good finger control." Or: "You have typed 'mat' very clearly. That is very good."

Once the class was over, the men made their way out of the hall, talking enthusiastically amongst themselves. Mma Makutsi, tidying up in the background, overheard a remark which one of the students passed to another.

"She is a good teacher, that woman," he said. "She does not make me feel stupid. She is good at her job."

Alone in the hall, she smiled to herself. She had enjoyed the class and had discovered a new talent: an ability to teach. And what was more, she had in the small cash box on her desk the first week's fees, in carefully counted notes of the Bank of Botswana. It was a comfortable sum, and there were virtually no overheads to pay. This money was hers to dispose of, although she planned to give a small portion of it to Mma Ramotswe to cover the cost of the telephone and as a recognition of her contribution to the business. Once she had done that, she would put the balance in her savings account. The days of poverty were over.

After she had locked up, she tucked the cash box into her bag of papers and started the walk back home. She walked along an untarred back road, past small houses from which light spilled, and in which she witnessed, framed in the windows, scenes of everyday domesticity. Children sat at tables, some upright, attentive, while others stared up at the ceiling; parents ladled the evening meal into their bowls; bare lightbulbs in some rooms, coloured lamp shades in others; music drifted from kitchens, a young girl sat on the kitchen step, singing a snatch of song which Mma Makutsi remembered from her own childhood, and which made her stop for a moment, there in the shadows, and remember.

CHAPTER ELEVEN

_____

MMA RAMOTSWE GOES TO A SMALL VILLAGE TO THE SOUTH OF GABORONE

SHE DROVE down in the tiny white van, the morning sun streaming through the open window, the air warm against her skin, the grey-green trees, the browning grass, the plains stretching out on both sides of the road. The traffic was light; an occasional van, minibuses crowded and swaying on their ruined suspensions, a truck full of green-uniformed soldiers, the men calling out to any girl walking along the edge of the road, private cars speeding down to Lobatse and beyond on their unknown business. Mma Ramotswe liked the Lobatse road. Many trips in Botswana were daunting in their length, particularly the trip up to Francistown, in the north, which seemed to go on forever, along a straight ribbon of a road. Lobatse, by contrast, was little more than an hour away, and there was always just enough activity on the way to keep boredom at bay.

Roads, thought Mma Ramotswe, were a country's showcase.

How people behaved on roads told you everything you needed to know about the national character. So the Swazi roads, on which she had driven on one frightening occasion some years earlier, were fraught with danger, full of those who overtook on the wrong side and those who had a complete disregard for speed limits. Even the Swazi cattle were more foolhardy than Botswana cattle. They seemed to lurch in front of cars as if inviting collision, challenging drivers at the very last moment. All of this was because the Swazis were an ebullient, devil-may-care people. That was how they were, and that was how they drove. Batswana were more careful; they did not boast, as the Swazis tended to do, and they drove more carefully.

Of course, cattle were always a problem on the roads, even in Botswana, and there was nobody in Botswana who did not know somebody, or know of somebody who knew somebody, who had collided with a cow. This could be disastrous, and each year people were killed by cattle which were knocked into the car itself, sometimes impaling drivers on their horns. It was for this reason that Mma Ramotswe did not like to drive at night, if she could possibly avoid it, and when she had to do so, she crawled along, peering into the darkness ahead, ready to brake sharply if the black shape of a cow or a bull should suddenly emerge from the darkness.

A journey was a good time to think, and as she drove, Mma Ramotswe mulled over in her mind the possible outcomes of this rather unusual affair. The more she thought about Mr. Molefelo, the more she admired what he had done in coming to see her. Most do not bother with the really old wrongs; many forget them entirely, whether deliberately—if you can make a deliberate effort to forget—or by allowing the past to fade of its own accord. Mma Ramotswe wondered whether people have a duty to keep memories alive, and had decided that they have. Certainly the old beliefs were that those who had gone before should be remembered. There were rituals to this effect, the purpose of which was to remind you of your duties to grandparents and great-grandparents, and the parents of great-grandparents and their parents, too. If you did not remember them, then they might pine and die, not here, of course, but in those other places where the ancestors lived; somewhere over there, where you could not see. Half of Botswana thought that way, and the other half thought the church way, which held that when you died you went to heaven, if you deserved it, of course, and once you were there you were looked after by saints and angels and people like that. Some people said that there were cattle in heaven, too, which was probably true; white cattle, with sweet breath, and watery brown eyes; saintly cattle who moved slowly and allowed children, the late children, to ride on their backs. What fun for those poor children, who had never known their mothers and fathers perhaps, because they had died too young; what a consolation that they should have these gentle cattle to be their companions. Mma Ramotswe thought this, and then, for a moment, she felt tears well in her eyes. She had lost her baby, and where was she? She hoped that her baby was happy and would be waiting for her when she herself left Botswana and went to heaven. Would Mr. J.L.B. Matekoni get round to naming a wedding date before then? She hoped so, although he certainly seemed to be taking his time. Perhaps they could get married in heaven, if he left it too late. That would certainly be cheaper.

To return to Mr. Molefelo and Mma Tsolamosese. It was difficult to anticipate what Mma Tsolamosese would say when the truth was revealed to her about what had happened all those years ago. She would be angry, no doubt, and she might even talk of going to the police. Mr. Molefelo had presumably not thought of that possibility when he came to her with the request to trace Mma Tsolamosese. He had assumed that the matter could be cleared up informally, but if Mma Tsolamosese made a complaint at the local police station, then they might feel obliged to press charges. It would be surprising if they did that, after all those years, but Mma Ramotswe imagined that there was nothing in the Botswana Penal Code to prevent that happening. She had not read the Botswana Penal Code from cover to cover; in fact she had not read it at all, but it could be bought from the Government Printer for a few pula; she had seen copies lying about and had paged through one of these, but it had not been immediately obvious to her what the Code was trying to say. This was the difficulty with laws and with legal language: they used language which very few people, apart from lawyers, understood. Penal Codes, then, were all very well, but she wondered whether it might not be simpler to rely on something like the Ten Commandments, which, with a bit of modernisation, seemed to give a perfectly good set of guidelines for the conduct of one's life, or so Mma Ramotswe thought. Everybody knew that it was particularly wrong to kill; everybody knew that it was wrong to steal; everybody knew that it was wrong to commit adultery and to covet one's neighbour's goods. . . . She hesitated. No they did not. They did not know that at all, or at least not anymore. There were children, horrible, cheeky children being brought up with precisely the opposite message ringing in their ears, and that was the problem, she thought grimly. People were far too ready to abandon their husbands and wives because they had tired of them. If you woke up one day and thought that you might find somebody more exciting than the person you had, then you could walk out! Just like that! And you could take it even further, could you not, and just walk out on all sorts of people. If you decide that your parents are beginning to bore you, then just walk out! And friends, too. They could become very demanding, but all you had to do was to walk out. Where had all this come from, she wondered. It was not African, she thought, and it certainly had nothing to do with the old Botswana morality. So it must have come from somewhere else.

To return to Mr. Molefelo and Mma Tsolamosese once again. Mma Ramotswe hoped that Mma Tsolamosese would not be inclined to go to the police, to rake over these very old coals; in which case she would inform her that Mr. Molefelo wished to make an apology and buy her a new radio. She had not discussed with him the precise terms of his amends, but he had said to her that money would be no object. "I shall pay whatever it takes," he had said. "My conscience is more important to me than money. You can get lots of money out of the bank. You cannot get peace of mind out of the bank."

Well, she would have to see what happened and handle matters accordingly. It would not be long now, with the turning to the village coming up, badly signposted, and a bumpy track to be negotiated up the hillside to Mma Tsolamosese's house, which, if her directions were correct, she could just make out at the edge of the village.

An elderly woman was sitting on a stool outside the house, pounding corn in a traditional wooden mortar. She stopped as the tiny white van drew up, and rose to her feet to greet Mma Ramotswe.

They exchanged greetings in the traditional way.

"Dumela, Mma," Mma Ramotswe said. "Have you slept well?"

"Yes, Mma. I have slept well."

Mma Ramotswe introduced herself and asked whether the woman was Mma Tsolamosese.

The woman smiled. She had a pleasant, open expression, and Mma Ramotswe warmed to her immediately. "I am Mma Tsolamosese. This is my place."

Mma Ramotswe accepted the invitation to sit down on a wooden chair, strung with strips of leather. It was not strong-looking, but she knew that these traditional chairs were well made and could bear her weight. The woman then went inside and fetched a mug of water for her visitor, which Mma Ramotswe accepted gratefully.

The house was of average size for such a village. It was square, neatly thatched, and had mud-daub walls of a warm ochre colour. The front door was painted white but had been scratched at the base by a dog. From inside the house, which was dark, as the curtains were drawn, there came the sound of two childish voices.

"There are two children who live here," said Mma Tsolamosese. "There is the daughter of one of my sons, whose wife has gone to look after her mother in Shashe. Then there is the daughter of my daughter, who is late. I am looking after both of these children."

"That is the work of so many women," said Mma Ramotswe. "Children and more children, all the time until we die. That seems to be what women have to do."

Mma Tsolamosese nodded her agreement. She was looking very carefully at Mma Ramotswe, her intelligent gaze moving over her visitor's face and clothes, going off to the tiny white van and then back.

"I have looked after children all my life," said Mma Tsolamosese. "It started when I was fourteen and had to look after my older sister's child. Then it carried on when I had my own children, and now I am a grandmother and the task is not finished." She paused for a moment and then continued: "Why have you come to see me, Mma? I am very happy to see you, but I wonder why you have come."

Mma Ramotswe laughed. "I have not come all this way to discuss children with you," she said. "I have come to talk to you about something which happened a long time ago."

Mma Tsolamosese opened her mouth to say something, but stopped. She was puzzled, and eager to find out, but she would wait for her visitor to explain herself.

"I believe your late husband worked for the Prison Department," Mma Ramotswe said.

"He did," said Mma Tsolamosese. "He was a good man. He worked for the department for many years and was quite senior. Thanks to that, I get a pension today."

"And you lived near the old airfield in Gaborone?" went on Mma Ramotswe. "And you let students live in your spare room?"

"We always did that," said Mma Tsolamosese. "It helped with housekeeping money. Not that they could pay much rent."

"There was a student called Molefelo," said Mma Ramotswe. "He was studying at the Botswana Technical College. Do you remember him?"

Mma Tsolamosese smiled. "I remember that boy well. He was a very nice boy. He was always clean."

Mma Ramotswe hesitated. It was not going to be easy to tell her; even now, at this distance in time, it would be news of a gross betrayal. But she had to do it; it was part of her job to be the bearer of bad news, and she would have to steel herself.

"When he was staying with you," she said, watching Mma Tsolamosese's face closely, "you had a burglary. A man forced a window and stole a radio. Did that happen?"

Mma Tsolamosese frowned. "Yes, it did happen. I would not forget a thing like that. It was a very fine radio."

Mma Ramotswe drew a deep breath. She would have to do it. "Molefelo took it," she said. "He stole the radio."

At first, Mma Tsolamosese looked confused. Then she reached down and dipped her fingers into the maize flour in the mortar.

"No," she said. "He did not do it. He was living with us when it happened. You have got it wrong. Somebody else stole it. One of the prisoners, I think. That is always a danger when you live near a prison."

"No, Mma," said Mma Ramotswe, her voice gentle. "It was not a prisoner. It was Molefelo. He needed money urgently for some . . . something he had to do. So he stole your radio and made it look like a burglary. He sold it for one hundred pula to a man near the railway station. That is what happened."

Mma Tsolamosese looked up sharply. "How do you know this, Mma? How can you talk about this thing if you weren't even there?"

Mma Ramotswe sighed. "He told me himself. Molefelo. He is feeling very bad—he has felt bad about it for years—and now he wants to come and apologise. He wants to buy you a new radio. He wants to make it up."

"I do not want a radio," said Mma Tsolamosese. "I do not like the music they play all the time now. Clank, clank. They do not play good music anymore."

"It is important to him," said Mma Ramotswe. She paused. "Have you ever done anything bad yourself, Mma?"

Mma Tsolamosese stared at her. "Everybody has," she said.

"Yes," said Mma Ramotswe. "Everybody has. But do you ever remember wanting to set right some bad thing you have done? Do you remember that at all?"

There was a silence between them. Mma Tsolamosese looked away, out across the hillside. Seated on her stool, she was now hugging her knees. When she spoke, her voice was quiet.

"Yes, I do. I remember that."

Mma Ramotswe lost no time. "Well, that is how Molefelo feels. And should you not give him the chance to say sorry?"

The reply was not immediate, but it did come. "Yes," she said. "It was a long time ago. It is good that he is thinking this now. I would not want him to suffer in his heart."

"You are right, Mma," said Mma Ramotswe. "What you are doing is the right thing."

They sat together in the sunlight. There were beans to be shelled, and Mma Ramotswe did this while Mma Tsolamosese continued to crush maize, a gnarled hand on the pestle, the other on the rim of the wooden mortar. They had drunk a mug of heavily sweetened tea and felt relaxed and comfortable in one another's company. Mma Tsolamosese was now quite happy about the apology, and had agreed that Mma Ramotswe should bring Molefelo out so that they could meet.

"He was just a young boy then," said Mma Tsolamosese. "What he did then is nothing to do with the man he has become."

"Yes," said Mma Ramotswe. "He is a different person."

A young teenage girl, barefoot and wearing a shabby green dress, appeared at the door and bobbed politely to Mma Ramotswe.

"This is the daughter of my son," said Mma Tsolamosese. "She is very helpful with the little one. Bring her out to see, Koketso. Bring her out to see Mma."

The girl went back into the house and came out carrying a toddler of two. She placed the child on its legs and held its hand while it took a few tentative steps.

"This is the child of my late daughter," said Mma Tsolamosese. "I am looking after her, as I told you."

Mma Ramotswe reached across and took the child's hand in her own.

"She is a very pretty child, Mma," she said. "She will grow into a very pretty lady in time."

Mma Tsolamosese looked at her and turned her head away. Mma Ramotswe thought that she had offended her in some way but could not work out why this should be. It was perfectly polite to compliment a grandmother on the prettiness of her grand-daughter; indeed, not to do so would have been unfeeling.

"Take her off now, Koketso," said Mma Tsolamosese. "I think that she might be hungry. There is some pap near the stove. You can give that to her."

The teenage girl came forward to pick up the child and retreated into the house. Mma Ramotswe continued with her shelling of the beans but sneaked a glance at Mma Tsolamosese, who had renewed her pounding of the maize.

"I'm sorry if I upset you," said Mma Ramotswe. "I did not mean to."

Mma Tsolamosese put down her pestle. Her voice, when she spoke, sounded tired: "It is not your fault, Mma. You were not to know. That child . . . the mother, who is late, had that disease which has run this way and that way through the country, and everywhere. That is what took her. And the child . . ."

Mma Ramotswe could tell what was coming.

"The doctor said that the child will become ill, too, sooner or later," said Mma Tsolamosese. "She will not live. That is why I was upset. You did not mean it, but you were talking about something that will never be."

Mma Ramotswe pushed aside her half-filled bowl of shelled beans and went over to Mma Tsolamosese's side, putting an arm about her shoulder.

"I am sorry, Mma," she said. "I am so sorry, sorry."

There was nothing more that could be said, but as she stood there, sharing the moments of private grief, the idea had come to her of what Mr. Molefelo could do.

CHAPTER TWELVE

THE MIRACLE THAT WAS WROUGHT AT TLOKWENG ROAD SPEEDY MOTORS

THE STUDENTS of the Kalahari Typing School for Men met at the church hall every weekday night, with the exception of Fridays. Their progress was rapid; indeed Mma Makutsi had to revise her estimates of how long it would take them to become proficient typists and was able to announce to them that the course would last five weeks, rather than six.

"You will get the same diploma," she announced, making a mental note to do something about the printing of the certificates. "It will be the same course, but you people will have finished it one week early."

"Will we get some money back?" asked one of the men, causing a ripple of laughter amongst the others.

"No," said Mma Makutsi. "Certainly not. You will get the same amount of knowledge. So that costs the same amount. That is only fair."

They appeared to accept this without complaint, and she moved on, with relief, to the next assignment. To give them a change from copy typing, they were all invited to compose a short essay in the remaining half hour of the class. They would need to produce only half a page at the most, but they should try to do this with as few mistakes as possible. There would be fifty marks for a perfect essay, with two marks being subtracted for each mistake. The topic, she announced, was to be "The Important Things in My Life" and the essay should be written anonymously and claimed back later. This would avoid embarrassment: people could write about what really mattered to them without feeling awkward. The title was not an original idea; at school she herself had written a prizewinning essay on the subject, and it had remained with her as the perfect essay topic. Nobody would be stuck for something to say: everybody had something in which they were interested.

The students set to the essay with vigour. At the end of the class, the essays were all left on the table and collected by Mma Makutsi. She intended to take them home and read them there, but a glance at the topmost essay so absorbed her that she sat down and read through them all. All of life seemed to be laid out before her: mothers, wives, football teams, ambitions at work, cherished motor cars; everything that men liked.

This one was typical: "There are so many things that are important to me in my life. I find it difficult to chose which things are the most important, but I think that the Zebras Football Team is one of them. Ever since I was a little boy I wanted to play for the Zebras, but I was never much good at football. So I watched from the stands and shouted very loudly for the Zebras to win. When that happens, I feel very happy and I spend the night celebrating with my friends, who are also Zebra fans. I cannot imagine Botswana without the Zebras. It would not be the same country, and we would all feel that something was missing from our lives."

This was almost perfectly typed, and Mma Makutsi was impressed with the clarity of expression. "The reader," she wrote in the margin, "is left in no doubt of the importance of the Zebras in your life." She paged through another couple of essays; there was another hymn of praise to the Zebras and a touching tribute to a young son and his doings. Then, almost at the bottom of the heap, she found: "I have discovered something very important in my life. I did not expect to find it, but it came to me suddenly, like lightning. I am not a man who has had much excitement in his life, but this thing is very exciting and my heart has been racing for more than one week. It is a lady I have met. She is one of the most beautiful ladies I have ever seen, and I think that she must be one of the kindest, nicest ladies in Botswana. She always smiles at me and does not mind if I make mistakes. She has walked past me, and has made my heart sing, although she does not know it. I do not know whether to tell her that she is filling my head with ideas of love. If I tell her, she might say that I am not good enough for her. But if I do not tell her, then she may never know how I feel. She is the most important thing in my life. I cannot stop thinking of her, even when she is teaching me typing."

Mma Makutsi stood stock-still, as anybody would do on coming across so unambiguous a declaration of love. One of her students, one of these men, was in love with her! She thought that nobody could fall in love with her, and one of these men had done just that. Oh! Oh!

She looked at the essay. Of course, there was no name on it, but there was no doubt about the author. She had been so engrossed in the sense that she had paid little attention to the typing. Every letter *h* was missing. "S e is t e most important t ing in my life," the essay read. "I cannot stop t inking of er."

Her heart beating with excitement, she took out a pencil and wrote at the bottom of the essay: "This is a very moving essay, which is well typed. You should tell this lady, though, or she might never know. You should ask her to go out with you after the class. That is what you should do."

THAT AFTERNOON, Tlokweng Road Speedy Motors had been left in the hands of the two apprentices. Both Mr. J.L.B. Matekoni and Mma Ramotswe had gone out to the orphan farm to fix a pump—in the case of Mr. J.L.B. Matekoni—and to talk to the matron, Mma Silvia Potokwane—in the case of Mma Ramotswe. Mma Makutsi, who was allowed three afternoons off a month, had decided that afternoon to go downtown to deposit money in her savings account, which had grown considerably with the income from the typing school, and to purchase a new pair of shoes. Her current pair, with their bright red buttons, would be left for resoling, and she had her eye on a new pair which she had spotted in the window of a shop in the town. The shoes themselves were light green, with lowish heels (which were very important for comfort and walking; high heels were always a temptation, but, like all temptations, one paid for them later). On each toe there was a large leather bow, also in green, and the linings were sky blue. It was the sky-blue linings that particularly appealed to her, and she imagined the pleasure that would come from putting one's feet into such surroundings each morning. They were rather more expensive than her normal shoes, but such footwear could not be expected to come cheaply, especially with linings like that. She had seen them and known immediately that they must be hers. With these green shoes, the good fortune which had entered her life with the successful setting up of the Kalahari Typing School for Men would surely continue. They were also shoes that would give the wearer confidence: a person could speak with authority in such shoes.

The apprentices enjoyed being left by themselves. They assured Mr. J.L.B. Matekoni that they would not give any repair estimates, although it was agreed that they could get on with existing work. There was a troublesome mud-coloured French station wagon parked in front of the garage, and they would work on that, trying to fix two doors that would not shut properly and to deal with an overheating engine. They were familiar with the car, which they had tried to fix before on at least two occasions, and its problems were something of a personal challenge to them.

"That French car will keep you busy," said Mr. J.L.B. Matekoni. "But be careful with it. That car is a liar."

"A liar, Rra?" asked the younger apprentice. "How can a car be a liar?"

"Its instruments do not tell the truth," said Mr. J.L.B. Matekoni. "You can adjust them, but they go back to their old ways. A car that does that is a liar. You can do very little about it."

Left to themselves, the apprentices made a cup of tea and sat on their oil drums for half an hour. Charlie, the older apprentice, called out to any girls who were passing, shouting out invitations to come and see inside the garage.

"Lots going on in this garage," he called out. "Come on. Come and take a look. There's lots for a girl like you to do in here!"

The younger apprentice tried to look the other way as the girls went past, but usually failed, sneaking a glance, but not calling out. After they had finished their tea, they drove the mud-coloured French station wagon onto the new hydraulic ramp which Mr. J.L.B. Matekoni had recently had installed. This was the first disobedience, the apple in Eden, as they had been given strict instructions that the only person to operate this was Mr. J.L.B. Matekoni himself. But now, faced with the chance to elevate the French car, they could not resist.

The ramp worked magnificently, lifting the car with consummate ease. But then it stopped, the extended central steel piston shining with oil, the car perched precariously above the mechanism. The older apprentice pushed the deflation switch, but nothing happened. He tried again and then turned the power on and off. Nothing happened.

"Broken," said the younger apprentice. "Your fault."

They sat down on their oil drums and stared miserably at the elevated car.

"What is Mr. J.L.B. Matekoni going to say?" said the younger apprentice.

"I'm going to say that we had nothing to do with it," said the older apprentice. "I'm going to say it was an accident. We parked the car above the ramp and then it went off by itself. We didn't touch it."

The younger apprentice looked at him. "I cannot tell lies anymore," he said. "Now that I am saved, I cannot lie."

The older one met his stare. "Then you will get both of us into bad trouble. Really bad trouble." He paused. "So I'm going to say that you did it. I'll tell him that it was you."

"You would not do that to me," said the younger apprentice. "And anyway, I would tell him the truth. The boss can tell when somebody is lying. Mma Ramotswe can, too. You would never be able to fool her." He paused. "But there is something we can do."

"Oh yes," said the older apprentice, mocking him. "Pray?"

"Yes," the younger one said as he slid off the oil drum and went down on his knees. "Oh Lord," he said. "Release this car," adding, "please."

There was silence. Outside, a large truck went past, grinding its gears. A cicada began to screech in the scrub bush at the back; a grey dove fluttered its wings briefly in the bough of the acacia tree beside the garage. And there was heat over the land.

Suddenly there was a hissing sound. They looked up, both surprised. The trapped air in the hydraulic system was clearing, allowing the column and its burden to descend gracefully towards the ground.

CHAPTER THIRTEEN

TEA AT THE ORPHAN FARM

MA SILVIA Potokwane was the matron of the orphan farm, which lay twenty minutes' drive to the east of the town. She had worked there for fifteen years, as deputy matron and then as matron, and it was said that she remembered the name of every orphan who had passed through her hands. This was never put to the test, but if one of the staff ever asked her: "I was trying to remember the name of that boy who came from Maun, the one with the sticking-out ears who was such a quick runner, can you remind me, Mma?" she would reply, without hesitation, "Cedric Motoposipe. He had a brother who was no good at athletics but became a very good cook and is now working at the Sun Hotel as a chef. Good boys, both of them." Or somebody might ask: "That girl who went to live in Lobatse when she left us and married a policeman, what was her name?" and Mma Potokwane would reply: "Memedi Gafetsili."

Not only did Mma Potokwane remember the names of all the orphans, but she also knew anybody of any consequence in Botswana. Once she met anybody, she filed away their details in her mind and, in particular, she remembered in what way they might help the orphan farm; those who had money would be asked for donations; butchers would be asked for spare offcuts; bakers would be asked for surplus doughnuts and cakes. These requests were rarely refused; it would take a degree of courage that few possessed to turn Mma Potokwane down, and as a result the orphans very seldom wanted for anything.

Mr. J.L.B. Matekoni, who had known Mma Potokwane for over twenty years, was called out regularly to deal with any mechanical problems which arose. He kept alive the old van which they used to transport orphans—this involved much scouring of the country for spare parts, as the van was an old one—and he also attended to the borehole pump, which lost a certain amount of oil and tended to overheat. It would have been possible to recommend that their old machinery, including this pump, be scrapped, but he knew that Mma Potokwane would never accede to such a suggestion. She believed in getting as much use as possible from everything, and thought that as long as machinery, or anything else, could be cajoled into operation, it should be kept; to do otherwise, she thought, was wasteful. Indeed, the last time that Mma Ramotswe had drunk tea with her in the office at the orphan farm, she had noticed that her china cup had been repaired several times, once on the handle and twice elsewhere.

Now, parking Mr. J.L.B. Matekoni's truck in a place under an old frangipani tree specially reserved for visitors, they saw Mma Potokwane waving to them out of her window. By the time they had alighted from the truck and Mr. J.L.B. Matekoni had taken out the tool kit that he would need to repair the pump, Mma

Potokwane had emerged from the front door of the office and was advancing towards them.

She greeted them warmly. "My two very good friends," she said, "both arriving at the same time! Mma Ramotswe and her fiancé, Mr. J.L.B. Matekoni!"

"He is my driver now," joked Mma Ramotswe. "I do not have to drive anymore."

"And I do not have to cook anymore," added Mr. J.L.B. Matekoni.

"But you never did cook, Rra," said Mma Potokwane. "What is this talk about cooking?"

"I sometimes cooked," said Mr. J.L.B. Matekoni.

"When did you cook?" asked Mma Potokwane.

"Sometimes," said Mr. J.L.B. Matekoni. "But we must not stand around and talk about cooking. I must go and fix this pump of yours. What is it doing now?"

"It is making a very strange noise," said Mma Potokwane. "It is unlike the other times when it has made a strange noise. This time it sounds like an elephant when it trumpets. That is the sort of noise it makes. Not all the time, but every now and then. It is also shaking like a dog. That is what it is doing."

Mr. J.L.B. Matekoni shook his head. "It is a very old pump," he said. "Machinery doesn't last forever, you know. It is just like us. It has to die sometime."

He could tell that Mma Potokwane was not prepared to entertain such defeatist talk.

"It may be old," she said, "but it is still working, isn't it? If I have to go out and buy a new pump, then that will take money which could be used for other things. The children need shoes. They need clothes. I have to pay the housemothers and the cooks and everybody. There is no money for new pumps."

"I was just pointing out the truth about machines," said Mr. J.L.B. Matekoni. "I did not say I would not try to fix it."

"Good," said Mma Potokwane, bringing the pump discussion to a close. "We are all fond of that pump. We do not want it to go just yet. One day, maybe, but not yet."

She turned to Mma Ramotswe. "While Mr. J.L.B. Matekoni is fixing the pump," she said, "we shall go and have tea. Then, when he has finished, his tea will be ready. I also have a fruitcake, and there will be a very big piece set aside for him."

THE PUMP house was at the other end of a wide field that bordered the row of cottages in which the orphans lived. There was a large vegetable patch at the side of this field, and then the field itself, which had been used for maize and which was still covered by the withered stalks of the last year's crop. The borehole which the pump served was a good one, tapping into an underground stream which was fed, Mr. J.L.B. Matekoni suspected, by waters that seeped down from the dam. He had always found it surprising that there should be so much underground water in a dry country; that underneath these great brown plains, which could get so parched in the dry season, there could still be deep lakes of sweet, fresh water. Of course you could not rely on there being water underground. When they had built the big stone house out at Mokolodi, they had found it very difficult to get any water at all. They had consulted the best water diviners there were, and these men had walked this way and that with their sticks in their hands, and nothing had happened; there had simply been no movement. For some reason, the underground water was not there. Eventually they had been obliged to use an old water tanker to bring water for the house.

Mr. J.L.B. Matekoni walked across the field, the dust on his shoes, the dried mealie stalks cracking under his feet. The earth was generous, he thought: sand and soil could be persuaded, with a little water, to yield such life, and to make such good things for the table. Everything depended on that simple generosity: trees, cattle, pumpkin vines, people—everything. And this soil, the soil on which he walked, was special soil. It was Botswana. It was his soil. It had made the very bodies of his people; of his father, Mr. P.Z. Matekoni, and his grandfather, Mr. T. Matekoni, before him. All of them, down the generations, were linked by this bond with this particular part of Africa, which they loved, and cherished, and which gave them so much in return.

He looked up. Mr. J.L.B. Matekoni always wore a hat when he was outside; a brown hat with no hatband, made of thin felt of some description, and very old, like the orphan-farm pump. He tilted his hat back slightly, so that he could see the sky more clearly. It was so empty, so dizzying in its height, so unconcerned by the man who was crossing a field beneath it, and thinking as he did so.

He walked on and reached the pump house. The pump, which was controlled by an automatic switch attached to the water storage tank, was in action as he reached it. It sounded as if it was working normally, and Mr. J.L.B. Matekoni wondered whether Mma Potokwane had been imagining the problem. But even as he stood there, before the pump house door, thinking of the large slice of fruitcake to which he could now return, the pump issued the strange sound which Mma Potokwane had described. It did indeed sound like the trumpeting of an elephant, but to Mr. J.L.B. Matekoni's ears it meant something much more worrying: it was the pump's death rattle.

He sighed and entered the pump house, taking care to look out for snakes, which liked to lie in such places. He reached out and flicked the manual override switch. The pump groaned and then stopped. Now there was silence, and Mr. J.L.B. Matekoni put down his toolbox and extracted a spanner. He felt weary. Life was a battle against wear; the wear of machinery and the wear of the soul. Oil. Grease. Wear.

He laid down his spanner. No. He would not fix this pump anymore. Mma Potokwane was always telling him to do this and do that, and he had always done it. How many times had he fixed this pump? At least twenty times, probably more. And he had never charged a single thebe for his time, and of course he never would. But there came a time when one had to stand up to somebody like Mma Potokwane. She had been so kind to him when he was ill—although now he remembered so little of that strange time of confusion and sadness—and he would always be loyal to her. But he was the mechanic, not she. He was the one who knew when a pump had come to the end of its life and needed to be replaced. She knew nothing about pumps and cars, although sometimes she behaved as if she did. She would have to listen to him for a change. He would say: "Mma Potokwane, I have examined the pump, and it can no longer be fixed. It is broken beyond all repair. You must telephone one of your donors and tell them that a new pump is needed."

He closed the door behind him, taking one last look at the pump. It was an old friend, in a way. No modern pump would look like that, with its wheel and its beautiful heavy casing; no modern pump would make a noise like the trumpeting of an elephant. This pump had come from far away and could be given back to the British now. *Here is your pump, which you left in Africa. It is finished now.*

"SUCH GOOD cake," said Mma Ramotswe, accepting the second slice which Mma Potokwane had placed on her plate. "These days

I find I do not have the time for baking. I should like to make cakes, but where is the time?"

"This cake," said Mma Potokwane, licking crumbs off her fingers, "is made by one of the housemothers who is a very good cook, Mma Gotofede. Whenever I am expecting visitors, she makes a cake. And all the time she is looking after the children in her cottage. And you know how much work that entails."

"They are good women, these housemothers," said Mma Ramotswe, looking out of the window to where a couple of the women were enjoying a break from their labours, chatting on the verandah of one of the neat cottages in which groups of ten or twelve orphans lived.

Mma Potokwane followed her gaze. "That is Mma Gotofede over there," she said. "The lady with the green apron. She is the one who is such a good cook."

"I knew somebody of that name once," said Mma Ramotswe. "They lived in Mochudi. They were a big family. Many children."

"She is married to one of the sons of that family," said Mma Potokwane. "He works for the Roads Department. He drives a steamroller. She told me that he ran over a dog with his steamroller last week, by mistake, of course. It was a very old dog, apparently, who did not hear the steamroller coming."

"That is very sad," said Mma Ramotswe. "But the late dog would not have suffered. At least there is that."

Mma Potokwane thought for a moment. "I suppose not," she said.

"This cake is delicious," said Mma Ramotswe. "Perhaps Mma Gotofede would teach me how to make it one day. Motholeli and Puso would like it."

Mma Potokwane smiled at the mention of the children. "I hope that they are doing well," she said. "It is very kind of you and Mr. J.L.B. Matekoni to adopt them like that."

Mma Ramotswe lifted her teacup and looked at Mma Potokwane over the rim. There had never been any mention of adoption before this; the agreement had been to foster them, had it not? Not that it made much difference, but you had to watch Mma Potokwane: she would do anything to benefit the orphans.

"We are happy to have them," said Mma Ramotswe. "They can live with us until they are grown up. Motholeli wants to be a mechanic, by the way. Did you know that? She is very good with machines, and Mr. J.L.B. Matekoni is going to teach her."

Mma Potokwane clapped her hands with delight. She was ambitious for the orphans, and nothing gave her greater pleasure than to hear that one of the children was doing well in life. "That is such good news," she said. "Why can't a girl become a mechanic? Even if she is in a wheelchair. I am very happy to hear that news. She'll be able to help Mr. J.L.B. Matekoni fix our pump."

"He is going to make a ramp for her wheelchair," said Mma Ramotswe. "Then she will be able to get at the engines."

Mma Potokwane nodded her approval of the plan. "And her brother?" she said. "Is he doing well, too?"

She knew from Mma Ramotswe's hesitation that something was wrong.

"What's the matter? Is he not well?"

"It's not that," said Mma Ramotswe. "He is eating well and he is growing. Already I have bought him new shoes. There is nothing wrong there. It's just that . . ."

"Behaviour?" prompted Mma Potokwane.

Mma Ramotswe nodded. "I didn't want to bother you with it, but I thought that you might be able to advise me. You have seen every sort of child there is. You know all about children."

"They are all different," agreed Mma Potokwane. "Brother and sister—it makes no difference. The recipe for each child is just for that child, even if it is the same mother and father. One child is fat, one child is thin. One child is clever, one is not that clever. So it goes on. Every child is different."

"He started off as a good little boy," said Mma Ramotswe. "He was polite and he did nothing wrong. And then, suddenly, he started to do bad things. We have not smacked him or anything like that, but he has become very sullen and resentful. He glowers at me sometimes and I do not know what to do."

Mma Potokwane listened attentively as Mma Ramotswe went on to describe some of the incidents which had taken place, including the killing of the hoopoe with the catapult.

"He did not learn to kill birds here," said Mma Potokwane firmly. "We do not allow the children to kill animals. They are taught that the animals are their brothers and sisters. That is what we do."

"And when Mr. J.L.B. Matekoni spoke to him about it, he said that he hated him."

"Hated?" exclaimed Mma Potokwane. "Nobody should hate Mr. J.L.B. Matekoni, and certainly not a little boy who has been given a home by him, and by you."

"It is as if somebody has poured poison into his ear," said Mma Ramotswe.

Mma Potokwane reached forward and refilled Mma Ramotswe's teacup, frowning as she did so. "That is probably more true than you think, Mma. Poison in the ear. It happens to all children."

"I do not understand," said Mma Ramotswe. "When could this have happened?"

"He goes to school now, doesn't he? Children go to school and they discover that there are other children. Not all these children behave well. Some of them are bad children. They are the ones with the poison."

Mma Ramotswe remembered what Motholeli had told her about the bullying. Puso was much younger, of course, but could be experiencing the same thing.

"I think that he doesn't know where he stands," said Mma Potokwane. "He will know that he is different from the other boys at school—because he's an orphan—but he will have no idea how to make up for that. So he's blaming you because he's lost."

Mma Ramotswe thought that this sounded reasonable, but then what could they do? They had tried to be kind to him and give him more attention, but that seemed to have no effect.

"I think," said Mma Potokwane, "that it is time for Mr. J.L.B. Matekoni to start giving him some rules to live by. He needs to show him limits. Other boys will have fathers or uncles to do that. They need it." She paused, watching the effect of her words on Mma Ramotswe. "He needs to be more of a father, I suspect. He needs to be stronger. His trouble is that he is such a gentle, kind man. We all know that. But that might not be what that little boy needs."

Mma Ramotswe became very thoughtful. "Mr. J.L.B. Matekoni must be firmer?"

Mma Potokwane smiled. "A bit. But what he needs to do is to take the boy out with him in his truck. Take him out to the lands, to see the cattle. Things like that."

"I shall tell him," said Mma Ramotswe.

Mma Potokwane put her teacup down and looked out of the window again. A group of children was playing under a shady jacaranda tree. "You can find out everything you want about children by watching them play," she said. "Look at those children over there. You'll see that the boys are playing together, pushing one another over, and the girls are watching. They will want to join in, but they won't know how to do it, and they're not very keen on that rough game. See? Can you see what's happening?"

Mma Ramotswe looked out. She saw the boys—a group of five or six of them—engaged in their physical play. She saw one of the girls pointing at the boys and then stepping forward to say something to them. The boys ignored her.

"See," said Mma Potokwane. "If you want to understand the world, just look out there. Those boys are just playing, but it's very serious to them. They're finding out who the leader is going to be. That tall boy there, you see him, he's the leader. He'll be doing the same thing in ten, twenty years' time."

"And the girls?" asked Mma Ramotswe. "Why are they just standing there?"

Mma Potokwane laughed. "They think the game is silly, but they would like to join in. They are watching the boys. Then they will work out some way of spoiling the boys' fun. They will get better and better at that."

"I am sure that you are right," said Mma Ramotswe.

"I think I am," Mma Potokwane said. "We had somebody out from the university, you know. This person called herself a psychologist. She had studied in America, and she had read many books about how children grow up. I said: just look out of the window. She did not know what I meant, but I think that you do, Mma Ramotswe."

"Yes," said Mma Ramotswe. "I do."

"You don't have to read a book to understand how the world works," Mma Potokwane continued. "You just have to keep your eyes open."

"That's true," agreed Mma Ramotswe. But she had her reservations about Mma Potokwane's assertions. She had a great respect for books herself, and she wished that she had read more. One could never read enough. Never.

CHAPTER FOURTEEN

MR. BERNARD SELELIPENG

YOU WERE very brave back there," said Mma Ramotswe to Mr. J.L.B. Matekoni as they travelled back from the orphan farm. "It is not easy to stand up to Mma Potokwane, and you did it."

Mr. J.L.B. Matekoni smiled. "I didn't think I would have the courage. But when I looked at the old pump, and heard it make those strange sounds, I decided that I just would not do it again. After all those repairs. There is a time to let a machine go."

"I watched her face as you told her," said Mma Ramotswe. "She was very surprised. It was as if one of the children had spoken back to her. She had not expected it."

In spite of her surprise, though, Mma Potokwane had given in remarkably quickly. There had been a halfhearted attempt to persuade Mr. J.L.B. Matekoni to change his mind and to fix the pump—"just for one last time"—but when she realised that he was adamant, she had switched to the question of who could be persuaded to pay for a new one. There was a general-purpose fund, of course, which was more than capable of footing the bill, but this would be drawn upon only when there was no other way of meeting the cost. Somewhere there would be somebody who might be persuaded that it would be an honour to have a pump named after them; that was always a good way of getting funds. Some people liked to do good by stealth, discreetly and anonymously providing funds, but others liked to do their charitable works in the glare of as much publicity as Mma Potokwane could arrange. This did not matter, of course: the important thing was to get the pump.

Mr. J.L.B. Matekoni had not left the orphan farm without making a positive contribution. Although he had brought bad tidings about the pump, he had nonetheless spent an hour attending to a timing problem in the engine of the old blue minivan used to transport the orphans. Again, this could not be kept going indefinitely, and he wondered when he would have to announce its end to Mma Potokwane, but for the time being he could keep it on the road with judicious tinkering.

While he worked on the van, Mma Ramotswe and Mma Potokwane had occupied themselves by visiting some of the housemothers. Mma Gotofede had been consulted about her recipe for fruitcake and had written it out for Mma Ramotswe and given her one or two tips on how to ensure the right consistency and moisture level. Then they had seen the new laundry, and Mma Potokwane had demonstrated the efficiency of the steam irons which they had recently acquired.

"The children must always look neat," she had explained. "A neat child is happier than a scruffy child. That is a well-known fact."

It had been a good visit, and in the truck on the way back, after they had discussed the pump, Mma Ramotswe judged the time right to raise with Mr. J.L.B. Matekoni the issue of Puso's behaviour. It would be a difficult message to convey. She did not want Mr. J.L.B. Matekoni to think that she was criticising him, or that Mma Potokwane had done so, but she had to encourage him to play a greater role in the boy's life.

"I talked to her about Puso," she ventured. "She was sorry to hear that he had been difficult."

"Was she surprised?" he asked.

Mma Ramotswe shook her head. "Not at all. She said that boys are difficult to raise. She said that men need to spend time with boys, to help them. If they do not, then boys can be confused and difficult. Somebody must spend more time with Puso."

"Me?" he said. "She must mean me."

Mma Ramotswe wondered whether he was angry; it was hard to tell with Mr. J.L.B. Matekoni. She had seen him angry on one or two occasions, but he had controlled himself so well that one might have missed it.

"I suppose so," she said. "She suggested that you could do more things with him. In that way he would think of you more as his father. It would be good for him."

"Oh," said Mr. J.L.B. Matekoni. "I see. She must think that I am not a good father, then."

Mma Ramotswe did not like to lie. She was a stout defender of the truth, but there were occasions on which a slight embroidering of reality was necessary in order to save another from hurt.

"Not at all," she said. "Mma Potokwane said that you were the best father that boy could ever wish for. That's what she said."

It was not, but it could have been said by Mma Potokwane. If she did not think this, then why had she been so keen to send the children to him in the first place? No, this was not a lie; it was an *interpretation*.

It had the hoped-for effect. Mr. J.L.B. Matekoni beamed with pleasure and scratched his head. "That was a kind thing for her to say. But I shall try to do more with him, as she suggests. I shall take him for rides in the truck."

"A good idea," said Mma Ramotswe quickly. "And maybe you can play some games with him. Football, perhaps."

"Yes," said Mr. J.L.B. Matekoni. "I shall do all these things, starting this very evening. I shall do them."

When they returned to Zebra Drive, while Mma Ramotswe prepared the evening meal, Mr. J.L.B. Matekoni took Puso for a ride in his truck to look at the dam, taking him onto his lap and allowing him to steer the wheel as they bumped along a back track. On the way home, they stopped at a café for potato chips, which they ate in the cab of the truck. Then they returned, and Mma Ramotswe noticed that both were smiling.

THE NEXT day at the shared premises of the No. 1 Ladies' Detective Agency and Tlokweng Road Speedy Motors, everybody's mood, if not elevated, was at least buoyant. Mr. J.L.B. Matekoni felt considerable satisfaction at having prompted the purchase of a new pump at the orphan farm, and was happy, too, with the progress he had made in communicating with Puso. Mma Ramotswe shared his pleasure in this and was further cheered when the morning post brought three cheques from clients who had been stalling in their payments. The younger apprentice had about him an air of quiet serenity, as if he had seen a vision, thought Mma Ramotswe, although she could not work out what could have made him look so pleased with himself. The older apprentice was strangely silent—although in no sense grumpy. Something had happened to him, too, thought Mma Ramotswe, although again she could not imagine what it was, unless, in his case, it had been the discovery of some breathtakingly beautiful girl who had stunned him into silence and contemplation.

The younger apprentice would very much have liked to spread the good news of the miracle which they had witnessed at Tlokweng Road Speedy Motors the previous afternoon. He could not do this—not at the garage at least—because of the compromising circumstances in which the miracle had occurred. To announce that prayer had caused the malfunctioning hydraulics to work would entail admitting that they had wrongfully used the equipment in the first place. Mr. J.L.B. Matekoni would probably not be so interested in how the car came down as he would be in how it came to be up in the air, and this would lead to a reprimand, at the very least, or possibly to a docking of pay, which he was entitled to do under their apprenticeship contract in the event of serious wrongdoing. So the apprentice could not announce that something special had happened, nor claim the credit for having caused this event. He would have to wait until the following Sunday, when he would be able to reveal to the congregation at the church, to the brothers and sisters who would be interested in this sort of thing, that prayer had brought immediate and concrete results.

The older apprentice was naturally sceptical about such things, but he had been astonished by what appeared to be a clear connection between a prayed-for event and the event itself. If his younger colleague could do this, then did it mean that everything else that he did was equally valid? This had alarming implications, as it meant that he would have to pay some attention to his predictions of divine wrath should he, Charlie, not change his ways. That was a sobering thought.

Mma Ramotswe also noticed that there was something different about Mma Makutsi. It could have been that she had new shoes and a new dress, both of which could do a great deal for a person's mood, but she thought that there was something more to it than that. What struck her was a certain demureness that appeared to have crept into her manner, and for this there was usually only one explanation.

"You are happy today, Mma," she said casually, as she entered the details of the cheques in her cash-received book.

Mma Makutsi made an airy movement with her right hand. "It is a nice day. We have received those cheques."

Mma Ramotswe smiled. "Yes," she said. "But we have received cheques before, and they have not had this effect on you. There is something more, isn't there?"

"You're the detective," said Mma Makutsi playfully. "You tell me what it is."

"You have met a man," said Mma Ramotswe plainly. "That is how people behave when they have met a man."

Mma Makutsi seemed deflated. "Oh," she said.

"There," said Mma Ramotswe. "I knew it. I am very pleased, Mma. I hope that he is a nice man."

"Oh he is," enthused Mma Makutsi. "He is a very handsome man. With a moustache. He has a moustache and his hair is parted in the middle."

"That is interesting," said Mma Ramotswe. "I like moustaches, too." She wondered whether Mr. J.L.B. Matekoni would be persuaded to grow a moustache, but decided that it was unlikely. She had heard him talking to the apprentices about the need for mechanics to be clean-shaven; it was something to do with grease, she imagined.

She waited for Mma Makutsi to enlarge on her description, but she sat at her desk, busying herself with a sheaf of garage bills. So she returned to her cash book.

"He has a very nice smile, too," Mma Makutsi suddenly added. "That is one of the nice things about him."

"Oh yes?" said Mma Ramotswe. "And have you been out dancing with him? Men with moustaches can be good dancers."

Mma Makutsi lowered her voice. "We haven't actually been out together yet," she said. "But that will happen soon. Maybe tonight."

MR. BERNARD Selelipeng was the first student to arrive that evening, knocking at the door of the hall a good twenty minutes before the class was due to start. Mma Makutsi had already been there for half an hour, setting out the papers for the evening's exercises and touching up the chalked-in finger diagram on the blackboard. A group of Boy Scouts had met in the hall that afternoon, and one of the Scouts had traced finger marks over Mma Makutsi's drawing of the typewriter keyboard, necessitating some repairs to the third finger on the right hand and the little finger on the left.

"It's only me, Mma," he said on entering the room. "Bernard Selelipeng."

She looked up and smiled at him. She noticed the gleaming parting in his hair and the neat buttoned-down collar. She saw, too, his highly polished shoes; another good sign, in her view, and one which suggested that he would appreciate her own new green shoes.

She smiled at him as he made his way over to his desk, to which she had earlier returned his essay. As he picked up the piece of paper and began to read her pencilled-in comment, she purported to concentrate on the pile of papers on her table, but she was watching for his reaction.

He looked up, and she knew immediately that she had done the right thing. Folding up his essay, he crossed the room to stand before her.

"I hope that you did not think I was being rude, Mma," he said. "I wanted to write the truth, and that was the truth."

"Of course I did not think you rude," she said. "I was happy to read what you had written."

"And your reply is just what I was hoping for," he said. "I would like to ask you to come for a drink with me after the class tonight. Will you be free?"

Of course she would, and for the rest of the class, although she was outwardly occupied with the teaching of typing, she could not think of anything other than Mr. Bernard Selelipeng, and it was difficult to address questions to the class as a whole rather than to the smiling, elegant man seated in the middle of the second row. There were so many questions that had to be answered. What was his job, for example? Where was he from? How old was he? She guessed that he was in his mid- to late thirties, but it was always difficult to tell with men.

At the end, when the class had been dismissed and everybody except for Bernard Selelipeng and Mma Makutsi had dispersed, he helped her to tidy up and to lock the hall. Then he showed her to his car, the possession of which was another good sign, and they drove off in the direction of a bar which he said he knew at the edge of the town, on the Francistown Road. It was an intensely pleasurable feeling for her, sitting in the passenger seat of his car, like any other of those fortunate women who were driven about by their husbands and lovers with such an air of security and possession. It seemed to her to feel completely right, that she should be transported in this way, a handsome, moustachioed man at the wheel. How quickly, too, one might become accustomed to this; no long walk to work across dusty paths, trodden by so many other feet, nor any frustrating wait for the crowded and stuffy minibuses which would ferry one about in bone-shaking discomfort for a pula or two.

Bernard Selelipeng glanced at her and flashed his smile in her direction. The smile, she thought, was his most attractive feature. It was a warm, inviting smile, of the sort that one could imagine living with. A husband who scowled all the time would be worse than no husband at all, but a man who smiled like that would turn his wife weak at the knees every day.

They arrived at the bar. Mma Makutsi had seen it before, from the road, but had never been in. It was an expensive place, she had heard, where you could have a meal, too, if you wished. There was music playing in the background as they went in, and a waiter quickly appeared to take their order. Bernard Selelipeng ordered a beer, and Mma Makutsi, who never drank alcohol, ordered a soft drink with ice.

Bernard Selelipeng knocked his glass gently against hers and smiled again. They had not made much conversation in the car, and now he asked her politely where she lived and what she did for a living during the day. Mma Makutsi was not sure whether she should tell him about the No. 1 Ladies' Detective Agency, as she was not certain whether he would be inhibited by her being a detective, even if only an assistant detective, and so she confined herself to mentioning her role as the assistant manager of Tlokweng Road Speedy Motors.

"And what about you, Rra?" she asked. "What do you do yourself?"

"I work in the diamond office," he said. "I am a personnel manager there."

This impressed Mma Makutsi. Jobs with the diamond company were well paid and secure, and it was a good thing, she thought, to be a personnel manager, which had a modern ring to it. But even as she thought this, she wondered why a personnel manager, handsome, of an interesting age, and in possession of his own car, should be unattached. He must be one of the most eligible men in Gaborone, and yet he was paying attention to her, Mma Makutsi, who was not necessarily the most glamorous of ladies. He could go to the Botswana Secretarial College, park out-side the drive, and pick up any number of fashionable girls much younger than herself. And yet he did not. She glanced at his left hand as he lifted his glass of beer to his mouth. There was no ring.

"I live by myself," said Bernard Selelipeng. "I have a flat in one of those blocks at the edge of the village. That's not far from your garage. That's where I live."

"They are very nice flats," said Mma Makutsi.

"I would like to show you my place someday," said Bernard Selelipeng. "I think you would like it."

"But why do you live by yourself?" asked Mma Makutsi. "Most people would get lonely living by themselves."

"I am divorced," said Bernard Selelipeng. "My wife went away with another man and took our children with her. That is why I am by myself."

Mma Makutsi was astonished that any woman could leave a man like this, but of course she might well have been the flashy type, and they were notorious. She imagined that such a wife could have her head turned by a richer, more successful man—although Bernard Selelipeng was clearly successful.

They made easy conversation for several hours. He was witty and entertaining, and she laughed at his descriptions of some of his colleagues in the diamond office. She told him about the apprentices, and he laughed at them. Then, shortly before ten o'clock, he looked at his watch and announced that he would be happy to run her home, as he had to be at an early meeting the following morning and did not wish to be too late. So they went back to the car and drove back through the night. Outside the house in which she rented her room, he stopped the car but did not turn off the engine. Again this was a good sign.

"Good night," he said, touching her gently on the shoulder. "I will see you at the class tomorrow."

She smiled at him encouragingly. "You have been very kind," she said. "Thank you for this evening."

"I cannot wait for us to go out again," he said. "There is a film I would like to see at the cinema. Perhaps we can go to that."

"I would like that very much," said Mma Makutsi.

She watched him drive down the road, the rear red lights of his car disappearing in the darkness. She sighed; he was so kind, so gentlemanly, rather like a glamorous version of Mr. J.L.B. Matekoni. What a coincidence it was that she and Mma Ramotswe should both have found such good men, when there were so many charlatans and deceivers about.

CHAPTER FIFTEEN

A DISGRUNTLED CLIENT

ITH SUCH a profusion of positive developments, they had given little thought to the rival agency, and perhaps they would have forgotten about it completely had it not been for two developments which reminded them of Mr. Buthelezi. The first of these was an interview published in the *Botswana Gazette,* an interview which took up the entire features page and was headed by a picture of Mr. Buthelezi sitting at his desk, a cigarette in one hand and the telephone hand-piece in the other. The article was spotted by Mma Ramotswe, who read it out to Mma Makutsi while the latter sipped thoughtfully, but with increasing astonishment, at a mug of bush tea.

"From New York to Gaborone, via Johannesburg," ran the caption at the top of the page. "A detective from different worlds: we spoke to the charming Mr. Buthelezi in his well-appointed office, and asked him what it was like to be a private detective in Gaborone.

"'It is quite hard being the first proper detective,' he said. 'There are, as people know, one or two ladies who have been dabbling in this for a little while, but they have no background in detection. I am not saying that there is not a job for them to do. There will always be jobs relating to children and the like. I am sure that they will do those very well. But for the real work, you need a proper detective.

"'I was trained with the CID in Johannesburg. That was a very tough training, with all those gangsters and all those murders, but I soon learned to be tough. You have to be tough in this business. That's why men are best at it. They're tougher than women.

"'I had many cases in the CID. Well-known murders. Jewel thefts. Ow! Millions of rands gone, just like that! Kidnappings, too. All of that was my daily bread, and I soon found that I understood the criminal mind very well. That's experience for you.

"'I have been very busy since I opened up. There are obviously many problems here in this city, and so if any readers have something that needs looking into, I am their man. I repeat, I am their man.

"'You ask what are the best qualities for a private detective? I would say that an understanding of how human psychology works is one of the best. Then a good eye for detail. We have to notice things—often very little things—in order to find out the truth for our clients. So a private detective is like a camera, always taking photographs in his mind and always trying to understand what is going on. That is the secret.

"'You ask how you become a private detective? The answer is that you have to be trained, preferably in the CID. You cannot just set up your sign and say that you are a private detective.

Some people have tried that, even here in Gaborone, but that will never work. You have to have been trained.

"It's also helpful if you've been to London or New York, or to some of those places. If you've done that, then you know the world, and nobody will be able to pull the wool over your eyes. I have been in New York, and I know all about the private detection side of things there. I know many of the men working in this area. They are very clever men, these New York detectives, and we were close friends.

"But at the end of the day, I always say, East West, Home's Best! That is why I am back here in Gaborone, which was my mother's place and which was where I went to school. I am a Motswana detective with a strange name. I know a lot, and what I don't know, I'll soon find out. Give me a call. Anytime!'"

Mma Ramotswe finished reading and then tossed the newspaper down with disgust. She was used to bragging men, and was tolerant of them, but these words from Mr. Buthelezi went too far. All those references to the superiority of men over women in detection were unambiguously aimed at her and her agency, and while it was obvious that an attack of this sort could only be the result of insecurity on his part, it could hardly be left unanswered. And yet an answer was probably what he wanted, as it would merely draw further attention to his business. Moreover—and this was worrying—what he said would probably strike a chord with many of the newspaper's readers. She suspected that there were plenty of people who did believe that the work which she did was better done by a man. They believed this of driving and flying aeroplanes, in spite of the fact that she had read—and others surely had read, too—of the evidence that women are simply safer drivers and pilots than men. The reason for this, apparently, is that they are more cautious and less given to flamboyant risk-taking. That is why women, on the whole, drive more slowly than men. Yet many men refused to acknowledge this fact and made belittling remarks about women's driving.

"I'm going to do a little bit of research," she said to Mma Makutsi. "Could you go and fetch Charlie, Mma. I want him to read this."

Mma Makutsi looked puzzled. "Why?" she asked. "You know that he's only interested in girls. He won't be interested in this."

"An experiment," said Mma Ramotswe. "You wait and see."

Mma Makutsi left the office and came back a few minutes later with the older apprentice, who was wiping his hands on the cotton lint that Mr. J.L.B. Matekoni provided in his battle against grease.

"Yes, Mma," said the apprentice. "Mma Makutsi says you need my advice. I am always happy to give advice. Ha!"

Mma Ramotswe ignored the comment.

"You read this, please," she said. "I would like to get your opinion on it."

She handed him the newspaper, pointing to the article, and the apprentice sat down on the chair in front of her desk. As he read, his lips moved, and Mma Ramotswe watched the look of concentration on his face. *He never reads a newspaper,* she thought. *There really is nothing in that head but thoughts of girls and cars.*

When he had finished, the apprentice looked up at Mma Ramotswe.

"I have read it now, Mma," he said, handing the paper back to her. She saw the greasy fingerprints on the edges and delicately avoided touching them.

"What do you think of it, Charlie?" she asked.

He shrugged. "I am sorry, Mma," he said. "I am sorry for you."

"Sorry?"

"Yes," he expanded. "I am sorry that this is going to make it difficult for your business. Everybody will go to that man now."

"So you were impressed?"

He smiled. "Of course. That is a very clever man there. New York. Did you see that? And Johannesburg. All those places. He knows what is happening, and he will deal with many things. I am sorry, because I do not want the business to go to him."

"You are very loyal," said Mma Ramotswe. And then, as the apprentice rose to his feet and left the room, she thought: *Exactly!*

"Well, Mma," said Mma Ramotswe. "That shows us something, doesn't it?"

Mma Makutsi made a dismissive gesture. "That boy is stupid. We all know that. Don't believe anything he says."

"He's not that stupid," said Mma Ramotswe. "To get the apprenticeship, he had to pass exams. He is probably a fairly average young man. So, you see, many, many people will be impressed by this Mr. Buthelezi. We cannot change that fact."

MANY PEOPLE, perhaps, but not all. That afternoon, when Mma Makutsi had been dispatched to the births, deaths, and marriages registry to pursue some routine enquiries on behalf of a client, Mma Ramotswe was visited, unannounced, by a woman whose view of the Satisfaction Guaranteed Agency and its boastful proprietor was quite the opposite of the view held by the apprentice. She arrived in a smart new car, which she parked directly outside the agency door, and waited politely for Mma Ramotswe to acknowledge her presence before she entered the office. This always pleased Mma Ramotswe; she could not abide the modern habit of entering a room before being asked to do so, or, even worse, the assumption that some people made that they could come into your office uninvited and actually sit on your desk while they spoke. If that happened to her, she would refrain from speaking at all but would look pointedly at the bottom planted upon her desk until her disapproval registered and it was removed.

Her visitor was a woman somewhere in her late thirties, about Mma Ramotswe's own age, even slightly younger. She was dressed well but not flashily, and her clothing, together with the new car outside, told Mma Ramotswe all that she needed to know about her economic circumstances. This woman, she imagined, was a well-paid senior civil servant, or even a business-woman.

"I have no appointment, Mma," said the woman, "but I hoped that you would be able to see me anyway."

Mma Ramotswe smiled. "I am always happy to see people, Mma. An appointment is not necessary. I am happy to talk at any time," adding: "within reason."

The woman accepted Mma Ramotswe's invitation to sit down. She had not given her name, although she had used the correct greeting; doubtless, the name would emerge later.

"I must be truthful, Mma," she said. "I have no confidence in private detectives. I must tell you that."

Mma Ramotswe raised an eyebrow. If she had no confidence in private detectives, then why would she come to the No. 1 Ladies' Detective Agency, the name of which was sufficiently self-explanatory, she would have thought.

"I am sorry to hear that, Mma," she said. "Maybe you would tell me why."

The woman now looked slightly apologetic. "Not that I mean to be rude, Mma. It's just that I have had a very unpleasant experience with a detective agency. That is why I feel as I do."

Mma Ramotswe nodded. "The Satisfaction Guranteed Agency? Mr. Buthele—"

She did not have the time to finish. "Yes," said the woman. "That man! How he thinks that he can call himself a private detective, I do not know."

Mma Ramotswe was intrigued. She wished that Mma Makutsi had been present, as it would have been good to share with her whatever was about to be disclosed. And it was going to be choice, she thought. But before she allowed her visitor to explain, the idea occurred to her that she should make an offer, on behalf of the entire profession. Yes, it was just the right thing to do in the circumstances.

"Let me say one thing, Mma," she said, raising her hand. "If you have suffered at the hands of a fellow member of my profession—and I must say that I am not surprised to hear this—then the No. 1 Ladies' Detective Agency will undertake to complete the enquiry which Mr. Buthe . . . which that man has obviously not done properly. That is my offer."

The woman was clearly impressed. "You are very good, Mma. I did not come expecting that, but I am happy to accept your offer. I can tell that things are different in this place."

"They are," said Mma Ramotswe quietly. "We do not make claims that we cannot live up to. We are not like that."

"Good," said the woman. "Now, let me tell you what happened."

SHE HAD gone to see Mr. Buthelezi after seeing his advertisement in the newspaper. He had been very polite to her, although she had found his manner rather overwhelming.

"But I thought that this might be something to do with the name," she said, glancing at Mma Ramotswe, who nodded, almost imperceptibly. One had to be careful about what one said, but people understood, and they knew what Zulu people could be like. Perhaps the word was . . . well, *pushy* or, if one were a bit more charitable, *self-confident*. Not that one liked to make such remarks openly, of course. Mr. Buthelezi said that he was a Motswana and not a Zulu, but you could not ignore paternal ancestry that easily, especially if you were a man. It stood to reason, Mma Ramotswe thought, that boys took more after their father than their mother; could people seriously doubt that? Some did, apparently, but they were obviously wrong.

The woman went on to explain why she had been to see Mr. Buthelezi in the first place.

"I live in Mochudi," she said, "although I am originally from Francistown. I am a physiotherapist at the hospital there. I work with people who have broken limbs or who have been very ill and need help in getting back on their feet. That is one of the things we do, but there are others. It is a very good job."

"And very important," said Mma Ramotswe. "You must be proud to be a physiotherapist, Mma."

The woman nodded. "I am. Anyway, I live up there because that is where the job is. I also have four children, and they are happy at the school there. The only problem is that my husband has a job in town here and he did not like driving in from Mochudi every morning and back again. We put our savings into a small flat. I get my house in Mochudi with the job, so this seemed like a good thing to do."

It was at this point that Mma Ramotswe realised what was coming. Ever since she had opened the No. 1 Ladies' Detective Agency, she had received a regular stream of requests to deal with errant husbands, or husbands suspected of being errant. These wifely fears were usually well founded, and Mma Ramotswe had been obliged to be the bearer of news of infidelity rather more often than she might have wished. But that was part of the job, and she did it with dignity and compassion. She was sure that this was what her new client was about to disclose; husbands working away from home rarely behaved themselves, although some, a small number, did.

Mma Ramotswe was right. The woman now described her fears about her husband and how she was sure that he was seeing somebody else.

"I usually telephone him in the evenings," she said. "We talk about things that have happened during the day, and the children also speak to him. It is expensive, but it is important for the children to talk to their daddy. But now he is never in when I call. He says that this is because he is now enjoying walking, and he goes for a lot of walks, but that is nonsense. I can tell that this is a lie."

"It sounds like it," said Mma Ramotswe. "Some men cannot lie very well."

The woman had consulted Mr. Buthelezi about her concerns, and he had promised to look into the matter, telling her to get back in touch with him after a day or so. He said that he would follow the husband and let her know what he was up to.

"And did he?" asked Mma Ramotswe. She was eager to hear how her rival operated.

"He says that he did," said the woman. "But I do not believe him. He says that he followed him and that he is going to church. That is just ridiculous. My husband does not go to church. I have tried and tried to make him go, but he is lazy about it. And when he came home last weekend, I said to him on Sunday: 'Let's go to church.' And he said that he did not want to go. Now, if he had become a great churchgoer, then surely he would want to go on a Sunday. But he did not. That proves it, in my mind."

Mma Ramotswe had to agree.

"But there is something more," said the woman. "I had paid a very large fee in advance, and when I said that I thought I should get some of it back, Mr. Buthe . . . that man just refused. He said that the money was his now. So I came to you."

Mma Ramotswe smiled. "I will do my best. I will see whether this churchgoing is true, and, if it isn't—and I agree with you that it does not sound likely—then I shall find out what he really is doing, and I shall tell you all about it."

They discussed one or two further details, including the name and address of the husband, and the address of the place where he worked.

"I have brought you a photograph, too," the woman said. "It will help you to recognize him."

She passed over a black-and-white photograph of a man looking into the camera. Mma Ramotswe glanced at it and saw a neatly attired man with an engaging smile, a carefully tended centre parting, and a moustache. She had never seen him before, but he would be easily picked out from a crowd.

"This will be very useful, Mma," she said. "When clients do not provide photographs, our work can be more difficult."

Mma Selelipeng rose to her feet.

"I am very cross with him," she said. "But I know that once I find this lady who is trying to steal my husband, I shall be able to deal with her. I shall teach her a lesson."

Mma Ramotswe frowned.

"You must not do anything illegal," she said. "I will not help you if that is what you are planning."

Mma Selelipeng raised her hands in horror. "No, nothing like that, Mma. I would just be planning to speak to her. To warn her. That is all. Don't you think that any woman has a right to do that?"

Mma Ramotswe nodded. She had no time for husband stealers, and no time for deceiving men. People had the right to protect what was theirs, but she was a kind woman and understood human weakness. This Mr. Bernard Selelipeng probably needed no more than a gentle reminder of his duties as a husband and a father. Looking at the photograph again, she suspected that this would suffice. It was not a strong face, she thought; it was not the face of a man who would leave his wife for good. He would go back like a naughty boy who has been caught stealing melons. She was sure of it.

MMA RAMOTSWE GETS A FLAT TYRE; MMA MAKUTSI GOES TO THE CINEMA WITH MR. BERNARD SELELIPENG

MMA RAMOTSWE was driving back to Zebra Drive that evening, taking her normal route from the Tlokweng Road and turning off into Odi Drive, when the tiny white van began to pull over to the left. She wondered for a moment whether the steering was faulty, and she shifted her weight in the seat towards the right, but this made no difference. Now there was a strange sound coming from the back of the van, a grinding sound, as of metal on stone, and she realised that she had a flat tyre. This was both an annoyance and a relief at the same time, the relief coming from the fact that it was an easily tackled problem. If one had a spare wheel, that is, and she did not. She had asked one of the apprentices to take it out for inflating, and she had seen it propped up against the wall of the garage and had been on the point of putting it back when Mma Makutsi had called her inside to take a telephone call. So the spare wheel remained in Tlokweng Road

Speedy Motors, and she was here, on the side of the road, where it was needed.

She felt a momentary irritation with herself. There was really no excuse for driving without a spare wheel; tyres were always going flat with all those sharp stones on the road and dropped nails and the like. If it had happened to somebody else, she would have had no hesitation in saying: *Well, it's not very clever, is it, to drive a car without a spare wheel*; and here it had happened to her, and she richly deserved such self-reproach.

She drew over to the left, to keep the car away from the traffic, not that there was much of that along this quiet residential road. She looked about her. She was not far from Zebra Drive— about half an hour's walk, at the most—and she could easily walk home and wait for Mr. J.L.B. Matekoni to come round for dinner. Then they could rescue the tiny white van together. Or, and this made more sense in terms of avoiding extra journeys, she could telephone him at Tlokweng Road Speedy Motors, where he was working late, and ask him to bring the spare wheel with him on his way to Zebra Drive.

She looked about her. There was a public telephone in the shopping centre at the end of the road, or, and this was the obvious answer, there was Dr. Moffat's house, close to which the tiny white van was now parked. Dr. Moffat, who had helped Mr. J.L.B. Matekoni recover from his depressive illness, lived with his wife in a rambling old house, surrounded by a generous-sized garden, the gate of which Mma Ramotswe now opened tentatively, bearing in mind how careful one had to be about dogs in yards like that. But there was no dog barking defiance, only the surprised voice of Mrs. Moffat, who emerged from behind a shrub which she had been tending.

"Mma Ramotswe! You are always creeping up on people!"

Mma Ramotswe smiled. "I am not here on business," she said.

"I am here because my van out there has a flat tyre and I need to phone Mr. J.L.B. Matekoni for help. Would you mind, Mma?"

Mrs. Moffat slipped her garden secateurs into her pocket. "We can telephone straightaway," she said. "And then we can have a cup of tea while we are waiting for Mr. J.L.B. Matekoni."

They went into the house, where Mma Ramotswe telephoned Mr. J.L.B. Matekoni, told him of her misfortune, and explained where she was. Then, invited by the doctor's wife to join her on the verandah, they sat around a small table and talked.

There was much to talk about. Mrs. Moffat had lived in Mochudi when her husband had run the small hospital there, and she had known Obed Ramotswe and many of the families who were friendly with the Ramotswes. Mma Ramotswe liked nothing more than to talk about those days, long past now, but so important to her sense of who she was.

"Do you remember my father's hat?" she asked, stirring sugar into her tea. "He wore the same hat for many years. It was very old."

"I remember it," said Mrs. Moffat. "The doctor used to describe it as a very wise hat."

Mma Ramotswe laughed. "I suppose a hat sees many things," she said. "It must learn something." She paused. The memory was coming back to her of the day that her father lost his hat. He had taken it off for some reason and had forgotten where he had left it. For the best part of a day they had gone round Mochudi, trying to remember where he might have left it, asking people whether they had seen it. And at last it had been found on a wall near the kgotla, placed there by somebody who must have picked it up from the road. Would somebody in Gaborone put a hat in a safe place if it were found in the road? She thought not. We do not care about other people's hats in the same way these days, do we? We do not.

"I miss Mochudi," said Mrs. Moffat. "I miss those mornings when we listened to the cattle bells. I miss hearing the singing of the children from the school when the wind was in the right direction."

"It is a good place," said Mma Ramotswe. "I miss listening to people talking about very small things."

"Like hats," ventured Mrs. Moffat.

"Yes, like hats. And special cattle. And which babies have arrived and what they are called. All those things."

Mrs. Moffat refilled the teacups, and for a few minutes they sat in easy silence, each with her own thoughts. Mma Ramotswe thought of her father, and of Mochudi, and her childhood, and of how happy it had been even without a mother. And Mrs. Moffat thought of her parents, and of her father, an artist who had become blind, and of how hard it must have been to move into a world of darkness.

"I have some photographs which may interest you," Mrs. Moffat said after a while. "There are some photographs of Mochudi in those days. You will know the people in them."

She went off into the living room and returned with a large cardboard box.

"I have been meaning to put these into albums," she said, "but I have never got round to it. I shall do it one day, maybe."

"I am the same," said Mma Ramotswe. "I will do these things one day."

The photographs were taken out and examined, one by one. There were many people Mma Ramotswe remembered; here was Mrs. de Kok, the wife of the missionary, standing in front of a rosebush; here was the schoolteacher from the primary school giving a prize to a small child; here was the doctor himself playing tennis. And there, in a group of men in front of the kgotla, was

Obed Ramotswe himself, wearing his hat, and the sight made her catch her breath.

"There," said Mrs. Moffat. "That's your father, isn't it?"

Mma Ramotswe nodded.

"You take that," said Mrs. Moffat, handing her the photograph.

She accepted the gift gratefully and they looked at more photographs.

"Who is this?" asked Mma Ramotswe, pointing to a photograph of an elderly woman sitting at a table in a shady part of a garden, playing cards with the Moffat children.

"That is the doctor's mother," said Mrs. Moffat.

"And this person standing behind them? This man who is looking at the camera?"

"That is somebody who comes to stay with us from time to time," said Mrs. Moffat. "He writes books."

Mma Ramotswe examined the photograph more closely. "It seems that he is looking at me," she said. "He is smiling at me."

"Yes," said Mrs. Moffat. "Maybe he is."

Mma Ramotswe looked again at the photograph of her father which Mrs. Moffat had given to her. Yes, that was his smile; hesitant at first, and then broader and broader; and his hat, of course. . . . She wondered what the occasion had been, why these people were standing outside the gate of the kgotla, the meeting place; the doctor would know, perhaps, as he must have taken the photograph. Perhaps it was something to do with the hospital; people raised money for it and had meetings about it. That might have been it.

Everybody in the photograph was smartly dressed, even under the sun, and everybody was looking at the camera with *courtesy*, with an attitude of moral attention. That was the old Botswana way—to deal with others in this way—and that was passing, was it not, just as the world and the people captured in this photograph were passing. She touched the photograph with her finger, briefly, as if to communicate with, to touch, those in it, and as she did so, she felt her eyes fill with tears.

"Please excuse me, Mma," she said to Mrs. Moffat. "I am thinking of how this old Botswana is going away."

"I understand," said Mrs. Moffat, reaching out for her friend's arm. "But we remember it, don't we?" And she thought, yes, this woman, this daughter of Obed Ramotswe, whom everybody agreed was a good man, would remember things about the old Botswana, about that country that had been—and still was—a beacon of light in Africa, a country of integrity and generosity in both the simple and the big things.

THAT EVENING the typing class went particularly well. Mma Makutsi had planned a test for her students, to determine their speed, and had been pleasantly surprised by the results. One or two of the men were not very good—indeed, one of them was talking about giving up but had been persuaded by the other members of the class to persist. Most, however, had worked hard and were beginning to feel the benefits of practice and the expert tuition provided by Mma Makutsi. Mr. Bernard Selelipeng was doing particularly well and, entirely on the basis of merit, had attained the highest words-per-minute score in the class.

"Very good, Mr. Selelipeng," said Mma Makutsi as she looked at his score. She was determined to keep their professional relationship formal, although as she spoke to him, she felt a warm flush of feeling for this man who treated her with such respect and admiration. And he, in turn, treated her as his teacher, not as his girlfriend; there was no familiarity, no assumption that he would be given special treatment.

After the class ended and she had locked the hall, Mma

Makutsi went outside and found him, as they had agreed, sitting in his car, waiting for her. He suggested that they go to the cinema that evening, and afterwards to a café for something to eat. This idea appealed to Mma Makutsi, who relished the thought that rather than going to the cinema by herself, as was often her lot, she would this time be sitting with a man, like most of the other women.

The film was full of silly, rich people living in conditions of unimaginable luxury, but Mma Makutsi was barely interested in it and scarcely followed what was happening on screen. Her thoughts were with Mr. Bernard Selelipeng, who, halfway through the performance, slipped his hand into hers and whispered something heady into her ear. She felt excited and happy. Romance had arrived in her life at last, after all these years and all that waiting; a man had come to her and given her life a new meaning. That impression—or delusion—so common to lovers, of personal transformation, was strong upon her, and she closed her eyes at the sheer pleasure and happiness of it all. She would make him happy, this man who was so kind to her.

They went to a café after the cinema and ordered a meal. Then, sitting at a table near the door, they talked about one another, as lovers do, their hands joined under the table. That is where they were when Mma Ramotswe came in, with Mr. J.L.B. Matekoni. Mma Makutsi introduced her friend to Mma Ramotswe, who smiled and greeted him politely.

Mma Ramotswe and Mr. J.L.B. Matekoni did not stay long in the café.

"You are upset about something," said Mr. J.L.B. Matekoni to Mma Ramotswe as they made their way back to the van.

"I am very sad," said Mma Ramotswe. "I have found something out. But I am too upset to talk about it. Please drive me back to my house, Mr. J.L.B. Matekoni. I am very sad."

CHAPTER SEVENTEEN

FINDING TEBOGO

YES, THOUGHT Mma Ramotswe, the world can be very discouraging. But we cannot sit and think about all the things that have gone wrong, or could go wrong. There was no point in doing that because it only made things worse. There was much for which we could be grateful, whatever the sorrows of this world. Besides, dwelling on the trials and tribulations of life was time-consuming, and ordinary duties still have to be performed; livings have to be earned, and in the case of Mma Ramotswe, this meant that she had to do something about Mr. Molefelo and his conscience. It was over a week since she had found Mma Tsolamosese, which had been the easy part; now she had to find Tebogo, the girl who had been so badly treated by Mr. Molefelo.

The information she had was slender, but if Tebogo had become a nurse, then she would have been registered, and might be registered still. That would be a starting point, and then, if Mma Ramotswe found nothing there, she still had various other lines of enquiry. Tebogo had come from Molepolole, Mma Ramotswe had been told. She could go there and find somebody who knew the family.

It did not take her long to exhaust the nursing route. Once she had found the civil servant in charge of nurse training, it had been easy to ascertain whether anybody of that name had been registered as a nurse in Botswana. There had not, which meant that Tebogo had either not trained or, having been trained, had not completed her registration. Mma Ramotswe was thoughtful; it might be that the consequences of Tebogo's involvement with Mr. Molefelo had had much greater repercussions for her life than she had imagined. People's lives are delicate; you cannot interfere with them without running the risk of changing them profoundly. A chance remark, a careless involvement, may make the difference between a life of happiness and one of sorrow.

A trip out to Molepolole would not be unwelcome and would give Mma Ramotswe the chance to speak to several old friends whom she knew out there. One, in particular, a retired bankteller, knew everybody in the town and would be able to tell her about Tebogo's family. Perhaps Tebogo herself would be living there now, and Mma Ramotswe would be able to visit her. That would require tact, particularly if she was married. She might not have told her husband about the baby, and men can be possessive and unreasonable about these things. They, of course, did not have to bear the children; they did not have to carry the babies around on their backs for the first few years; they did not have to attend to the daily, hourly, minute-by-minute needs of the baby, and yet they could have very strong views on the subject of babies.

She chose a fine morning for the trip out to Molepolole, a

morning when the air was crisp and clean and the sun not too hot. As she drove, she thought of the events of the last few days, and in particular of the disturbing discovery she had made of Mma Makutsi's involvement with Mr. Bernard Selelipeng. She had been shocked by what she had found out, and the following morning her dismay had been compounded when Mma Makutsi had talked at some length about Mr. Selelipeng and about how well suited they were.

"I would have told you about this earlier," she said to her employer. "But I wanted to be sure first that this was going to last. I did not want to come to you and say that I had found the right man for me, and then to have to tell you, one week later, that it was all off. I did not want that."

As Mma Makutsi spoke, Mma Ramotswe's sense of foreboding grew. There was much to be said in favour of honesty; she could tell Mma Makutsi right now what the truth of the matter was, and indeed not to do so would be to shelter her from information which she had the right to know. Would she not feel more betrayed, wondered Mma Ramotswe, if she were to find out that she, Mma Ramotswe, had known all along and not warned her that Mr. Selelipeng was married? If one could not get this information from a friend and colleague, then from whom might one expect it? And yet, to tell her now would be so brutal, and it would also preclude the possibility of doing something in the background to ease the pain of discovery—whatever that something might be.

She would just have to think about it further, although she knew that at the end of the day there was inevitably going to be disappointment for Mma Makutsi, who could not be protected forever from the truth about Mr. Bernard Selelipeng. But then, she thought, did she know? She had assumed all along that he would have misled her into thinking that he was single, or divorced, but it might be that Mma Makutsi knew full well that there was a wife and family in the background. Was this likely? If a person was desperate enough, she might well be prepared to take any man who came along, even one who was married. Now that she came to think of it, she knew of many cases where women had been quite prepared to consort with married men in the full knowledge of their matrimonial status, hoping, perhaps, to prise the man away from his wife or even calculating that this would never happen but at least they would have some fun along the way. Men would do the same thing, too, although they seemed less willing to share a woman with another man. But Mma Ramotswe certainly knew of cases where men had conducted affairs with married women, fully aware of the fact that the woman would never leave her husband.

Would Mma Makutsi do this, she wondered. She remembered the awkward conversation she had had with her not all that long ago, when Mma Makutsi had remarked despairingly on the fact that it was no use trying to meet men in bars because they were all married. This suggested that she considered such men to be out of bounds. And yet, faced with such a man, particularly with a charming one with a centre parting and a winning smile; might she not, in such circumstances, decide that even if he was married, this was nonetheless her chance? Time was ticking by for Mma Makutsi; soon younger men would no longer consider her, and then she would be left with only the possibility of an old man. Perhaps she did feel desperate; perhaps she was fully aware of the situation in which Mr. Bernard Selelipeng found himself. But no. No, thought Mma Ramotswe, she was not. She would not have spoken to me with that enthusiasm had she known this was a relationship that could not go any further. She would have been guarded, or resigned, or even sad; she would not have been enthusiastic.

Mma Ramotswe was pleased that she had to put such troubling thoughts to one side, as she had now arrived in Molepolole and had driven the tiny white van over the rutted track that led to the house of her old friend Mma Ntombi Boko, formerly deputy chief teller of the Standard Bank in Gaborone, a position from which she had retired at the age of fifty-four to take up residence in Molepolole and to run there the local branch of the Botswana Rural Women's Association.

She found Mma Boko at the side of her house, under a canvas awning which she had erected to create an informal shady porch. A small brick oven had been built there, and on the top of this was a large blackened saucepan.

Mma Boko's greeting was warm. "Precious Ramotswe! Yes, it is you! I can see you, Mma!"

"It is me," said Mma Ramotswe. "I have come to see you."

"I am very glad," said Mma Boko. "I was sitting here stirring this jam and thinking: Where is everybody today? Why has nobody come to talk to me?"

"And then I arrived," said Mma Ramotswe. "Just in time." She knew that her friend was gregarious, and that a day without a chance to have a good gossip was a trial for her. Not that the gossip was at all malicious; Mma Boko spoke ill of nobody but was nevertheless extremely interested in what others were doing. Impressed by the orations that she gave at funerals, where people were entitled to stand up and speak of the doings of the deceased, friends had tried to persuade her to stand for the legislature, but she had declined, saying that she liked to talk about interesting things, and that there was never any talk of interesting things in Parliament.

"All they do is talk about money and roads and things like that," she had said. "Those are important things, and somebody has to talk about them, but let the men do that. We women have more important things to talk about."

"No, no, Mma!" they said. "That is precisely the wrong attitude. That is what men want us to think. They want us to think that these important things they discuss are not really important to women. But they are! They are very important. And if we let the men talk about them and decide them, then suddenly we wake up and find out that the men have made all the decisions, and these decisions all suit men."

Mma Boko had considered this carefully. "There is some truth in that," she had said. "In the bank the decisions were made by men. They did not ask me first."

"You see!" they said. "You see how it works. They are always doing this, the men. We women must stand up on our legs and talk."

Mma Ramotswe examined the jam which Mma Boko was making, and took the small spoonful which her friend offered her.

"It is good," she said. "This is the best jam in Botswana, I think."

Mma Boko shook her head. "There are ladies here in Molepolole who make much better jam than this. I will bring you some of their jam one day, and you will see."

"I cannot believe it will be better," said Mma Ramotswe, licking the spoon clean.

They sat down and talked. Mma Boko told Mma Ramotswe of her grandchildren, of whom she had sixteen. They were all clever, she said, although one of her daughters had married a rather unintelligent man. "He is kind, though," she said. "Even if he says very stupid things, he is kind."

Mma Ramotswe told her about Mr. J.L.B. Matekoni's illness, and how he had been nursed back to health by Mma Potokwane. She told her about the move to Tlokweng Road Speedy Motors and the sharing of the offices, and of how well he had been handled by Mma Makutsi. She told her about the children; how Motholeli had been bullied and how Puso had been through a difficult patch.

"Boys do go through times like that," said Mma Boko. "It can last for fifty years."

Then they talked about Molepolole and about the Botswana Rural Women's Association and about its plans. Eventually, after these multitudinous subjects had been exhausted, Mma Ramotswe asked Mma Boko the question which had brought her out on the visit.

"There is a girl," she began, "or was a girl—she is a woman now—called Tebogo Bathopi. About twenty years ago she came to Gaborone from Molepolole to train to be a nurse. I am not sure if she ever managed to finish—I do not think that she did. Something happened to her in Gaborone which somebody now wants to set right. I cannot tell you what that thing was, but I can tell you that the person involved is very serious about righting what he now sees was a wrong. He means it. But he does not know where this girl is. He has no idea. That is why I have come to you. You know everybody. You see everything. I thought you could help me to find out where this woman is, if she is still alive."

Mma Boko laid down the spoon with which she had been stirring her jam.

"Of course she is still alive," she said, laughing. "Of course she is still alive. She is now called Mma Tshenyego."

Mma Ramotswe's surprise showed itself in a broad smile. She had not imagined that it would be this easy, but her instinct to ask Mma Boko had proved correct. It was always the best way of finding out information; just go and ask a woman who keeps her eyes and ears open and who likes to talk. It always worked. It was no use asking men; they simply were not interested enough in other people and the ordinary doings of people. That is why the real historians of Africa had always been the grandmothers, who remembered the lineage and the stories that went with it.

"I am very glad to hear that, Mma," she said. "Can you tell me where she is?"

"Over there," answered Mma Boko. "She is right there. At that house over there. Do you see it? And look, there she is herself, coming out of the house with one of the children, that girl, who is sixteen now. That is her firstborn, her first daughter."

Mma Ramotswe looked in the direction in which Mma Boko was pointing. She saw a woman coming out of the house, together with a girl in a yellow dress. The woman threw some grain to the chickens in the yard, and then they stood and watched the chickens peck away at the food.

"She has many hens," said Mma Boko, "and she is also one of those ladies who makes good jam. She is always in that house, cleaning and cooking and making things. She is a good person."

"So she did not become a nurse?" asked Mma Ramotswe.

"No, she is not a nurse," said Mma Boko. "But she is a clever lady and she could have been a nurse. Maybe one of her daughters will become a nurse."

Mma Ramotswe rose to take her leave.

"I must go and see that lady," she said to Mma Boko. "But first I must give you a present which I have brought for you. It is in my van."

She walked over to the van and took out a parcel wrapped in brown paper. This she gave to Mma Boko, who unwrapped it and saw that it contained a length of printed cotton, enough for a dress. Mma Boko held the material up against her.

"You are a very kind lady, Mma Ramotswe," she said. "This will be a very fine dress."

"And you are a useful friend," said Mma Ramotswe.

CHAPTER EIGHTEEN

A RADIO IS A SMALL THING

MR. MOLEFELO arrived at the No. 1 Ladies' Detective Agency the following morning. Mma Ramotswe had telephoned him the previous evening and had suggested an appointment in a few days' time, but such had been his eagerness to hear what she had found out that he begged her to see him sooner.

"Please, Mma," he had pleaded. "I cannot wait. After all this time, I must know soon. Please do not make me wait. I shall be sitting here thinking, thinking, all the time."

There were other things that Mma Ramotswe had to do, but these were not urgent and she understood his anxiety. So she agreed to see him at her office the next day when, she said, she would be able to give him the information he wanted. This required arrangements to be made, of course, and there was the older apprentice to dispatch on an errand. But that could be done.

Mr. Molefelo was punctual, waiting outside in his car until exactly eleven o'clock, the time at which Mma Ramotswe had agreed to see him. Mma Makutsi showed him into the office and then returned to her desk. Mr. Molefelo greeted Mma Ramotswe and then looked at Mma Makutsi.

"I wonder, Mma . . ." he began.

Mma Ramotswe caught Mma Makutsi's eye, and that was enough. They both understood that there were things that could be said to one but not to two. And there were other reasons.

"I have to go to the post, Mma," said Mma Makutsi. "Should I go now?"

"A very good idea," said Mma Ramotswe.

Mma Makutsi left the office, throwing an injured look in Mr. Molefelo's direction, but he did not notice. As soon as she had left, Mr. Molefelo spoke.

"I must know, Mma," he said, wringing his hands as he spoke. "I must know. Are they late? Are they late?"

"No, they are not late, Rra," said Mma Ramotswe. "Mr. Tsolamosese has died, but his widow is still alive. You came to me in time."

Mr. Molefelo's relief was palpable. "In that case, I can do what I need to do."

"Yes," said Mma Ramotswe. "You can do what needs to be done." She paused. "I shall tell you first about Tebogo. I found her, you know."

Mr. Molefelo nodded eagerly. "Good. And . . . and what had happened to her? Was she well?"

"She was fine," said Mma Ramotswe. "I found her in Molepolole, very easily. I drank tea with her and we talked. She told me about her life."

"I am . . ." Mr. Molefelo tried to speak but found that he had nothing to say.

"She said that she did not train as a nurse after all. She was very upset when you made her deal with the baby in that way. She said that she cried and cried, and for many months she had bad dreams about what she had done."

"That was my fault," said Mr. Molefelo. "My fault."

"Yes it was," said Mma Ramotswe. "But you were a young man then, weren't you? Young men do these things. It is only later that they regret them."

"It was wrong of me to say that she should end that baby. I know that."

Mma Ramotswe looked at him. "It is not that simple, Rra. There are times when you cannot expect a woman to have a baby. It is not always right. Many women would tell you that."

"I am not questioning that," said Mr. Molefelo meekly. "I am just telling you what I feel."

"She was upset about you, too, you know," went on Mma Ramotswe. "She said that she loved you and that you had told her that, too. Then you changed your mind, and she was very upset. She said that you had a hard heart."

Mr. Molefelo looked down at the floor. "It is true. I had a hard heart. . . ."

"But then she said that she met another boy and he asked her to marry him. He joined the police, and then later on he found a job as a bus driver. They live out at Molepolole, and they have been happy. They have five children. I met the oldest girl."

Mr. Molefelo listened attentively. "Is that all?" he said. "Is that all that happened? Did you tell her how sorry I was?"

"I did," said Mma Ramotswe.

"And what did she say?"

"She said that you must not worry. She said that her life had turned out very well and she bore you no ill will. She said that she hoped that you had been happy, too." She paused. "I think that you wanted to help her in some way, didn't you, Rra?"

Mr. Molefelo was smiling. "I said that, Mma, and I meant it. I want to give her some money."

"That might not be the best way to do it," said Mma Ramotswe. "What do you think the husband of this woman would think if she received money from an old boyfriend? He might not like it at all."

"Then what can I do?"

"I met her daughter," said Mma Ramotswe. "I told you that. She is a clever girl. She is the one who would like to be a nurse now. She is very keen. I spoke to her about it. But there are not many places for nurse training, and it is the girls who get the best results who will get the places."

"Is she clever?" asked Mr. Molefelo. "Her mother was clever."

"She is clever enough, I think," said Mma Ramotswe. "But she would stand an even better chance if she went for a year or two to one of those schools where they charge high fees. They teach the children very carefully there. It would be a very good chance for her."

Mr. Molefelo was silent. "The fees are high," he said. "That costs a lot of money."

Mma Ramotswe looked at him, meeting his gaze. "I do not think that you can make up for things cheaply, Rra. Do you?"

Mr. Molefelo looked at her, hesitated, and then he smiled. "You are a very astute lady, Mma, and I think you are right. I will pay for that girl to go to one of those schools here in Gaborone. I will pay that."

Half the medicine, thought Mma Ramotswe. *Now for the other half.* She looked out of the window. The apprentice had left shortly before nine o'clock, and allowing for delays at the roundabouts and for one or two wrong turnings, he should be back very soon. She could start, though, by telling him of how she had found Mma Tsolamosese.

"The father died," she said. "He retired from prison service and then he died. But Mma Tsolamosese herself is well, and she is living on her widow's pension from the department. I think that she has enough. Her house seemed comfortable, and she is with her people. I think she is happy."

"That is very good," said Mr. Molefelo. "But was she also cross with me when you told her what had happened?"

"She was very surprised," said Mma Ramotswe. "At first she did not believe that you could have done it. I had to persuade her that it was true. Then she said that she thought that you were very brave to confess what had happened. That's what she said."

Mr. Molefelo, who had looked cheerful before, now looked miserable again. "She must think I am very bad. She must think that I abused her hospitality. That is a very bad thing to do."

"She understands," said Mma Ramotswe. "She is a woman who has lived quite a long time. She understands that young men can behave like that. Do not think that she is filled with anger, or anything like that."

"She is not?"

"No. And she is also happy that you should apologise in person. She is prepared for that."

"Then I must go out there," said Mr. Molefelo.

Mma Ramotswe glanced out of her window. The tiny white van was being driven up to the back of the garage.

"No need to go out there, Rra," she said. "Mma Tsolamosese has just arrived. She will be here in a moment." She paused. "Are you all right, Rra?"

Mr. Molefelo gulped. "I am very embarrassed, Mma. I feel very bad. But I think I am ready."

MMA TSOLAMOSESE looked at the man standing before her.

"You are looking very well," she said. "You were thinner in those days. You were a boy."

"You were my mother, Mma. You looked after me well."

She smiled at him. "I was your mother in Gaborone. You were my son while you were here. Now I am proud of you. Mma Ramotswe has told me how well you have done."

"But I did a very bad thing to you," said Mr. Molefelo. "Your radio—"

Mma Tsolamosese interrupted him. "A radio is a small thing. A man is a big thing."

"I am sorry, Mma," said Mr. Molefelo. "I am sorry for what I did. I have never stolen anything else. That was the only time."

"Do not worry, Rra," she said. "I have told you already. A radio is a small thing."

They sat down together while Mma Ramotswe prepared the tea. Then, over the strong, sweet liquid, they talked about what had happened in their lives. At the end of the conversation, Mma Ramotswe drew Mr. Molefelo to one side and spoke to him quietly.

"There is something you can do for this woman," she said. "It will not cost you too much money, but it is something that you can do."

He glanced over his shoulder at Mma Tsolamosese. "She is such a kind woman," he whispered. "She was like that then, and she still is. I will do whatever I can."

"There is a grandchild," said Mma Ramotswe quietly. "There is a little girl. She may not live very long because of this cruel illness. But in the meantime, you could make a difference to that life. You could give Mma Tsolamosese money to use for that child.

The right food. Meat. Pretty clothes. Even if the life of that child is short, it would be made a happy one, and if you did that, Rra, then you would have more than made up for what you did all those years ago."

Mr. Molefelo looked at her. "You are right, Mma. I can do that. It is not a big thing to do."

"Then you tell Mma Tsolamosese," said Mma Ramotswe, gesturing towards the older woman. "You go ahead and tell her."

Mma Tsolamosese listened quietly as Mr. Molefelo spoke. Then, her head bowed, she spoke.

"I always thought that you were a good person, Rra," she said. "All those years ago, I thought that. Nothing that I have heard, nothing, has made me change my mind about you."

She looked up and reached for his hand, while Mma Ramotswe turned away. Mr. Molefelo had earned this moment for himself, she thought, and there should be no spectator.

NO. 42 LIMPOPO COURT

MR. MOLEFELO had written two cheques that day: one to Mma Ramotswe, for her professional services (three thousand pula, a steep fee, but one which he was well able to afford), and another for two thousand pula, to be deposited in a post office savings account in the name of Mma Tsolamosese, for the benefit of her grandchild. More cheques would need to be made out for school fees, but again, Mr. Molefelo had made a considerable amount of money, and these sums would not be noticed. In return, after all, as Mma Ramotswe was at pains to explain to him, he had corrected the moral balance of his past and earned the right to an easy conscience.

But Mma Ramotswe's sense of achievement was marred by the question brought to her attention by Mma Selelipeng, the physiotherapist from Mochudi. Mma Ramotswe would dearly have loved this issue to have gone away, but it remained stubbornly present and would have to be dealt with. At least she had now decided what to do; she had Mr. Bernard Selelipeng's address right there in her hand, and she would go and see him early that evening, shortly after he arrived home from work.

She knew Limpopo Court, a newish block of flats near Tlok-weng Road. She had been in one of the flats there before, visiting a distant cousin, and its shape and its stuffiness had discouraged her. Mma Ramotswe liked the old round shapes of traditional architecture; hard edges and sharp roofs struck her as being unfriendly and uncomfortable. And a traditional house *smelled* better, because there was no concrete, which has such a bad odour, dank and acrid. A traditional house smelled of wood smoke, the earth, and of thatch; all good smells, the smell of life itself.

No. 42 was on the first floor, reached by an ugly concrete walkway that ran the length of the building. She glanced at the door, with its shiny blue paint, and at the name, Selelipeng, which had been stencilled on it in pride of ownership. She felt unhappy and concerned, even anxious; what she had to do was not easy, but she could see no way out of it. She had agreed to act on behalf of Mma Selelipeng, and she could not go back on her word. At the same time, she was aware of the fact that she was interfering in Mma Makutsi's affairs in a way to which her employee might object. Would she, were she in the shoes of Mma Makutsi, want her employer meddling in a romance which clearly meant so much to her? She thought not. But then were she in Mma Makutsi's position, she would not have to worry about the obligation she owed to Mma Selelipeng. So it was not as simple as Mma Makutsi might imagine.

Unaware of the moral quandary which he had created for Mma Ramotswe, Mr. Bernard Selelipeng, his tie loosened after a demanding day in the diamond office, opened the door to Mma

Ramotswe's knock. He saw before him a large, well-built lady, vaguely familiar to him in some context. Who was she? A relative? Cousins of cousins were always appearing on his doorstep wanting something. At least this woman did not look hungry.

"Mr. Selelipeng?"

"My name is on the door, Mma."

Mma Ramotswe smiled at him. She saw the centre parting and the expensive blue shirt. She noticed the shoes, which were shinier than the shoes that most men wore.

"I have to speak to you, Rra, about an important matter. Please, will you invite me in?"

Mr. Selelipeng drew back from the door, gesturing for Mma Ramotswe to enter. Pointing to a chair, he invited her to sit down.

"I am not sure who you are, Mma," he began. "I think I have met you, but I am sorry, I am not sure."

"I am Precious Ramotswe," she said. "I am the owner of the No. 1 Ladies' Detective Agency. You may have heard of us."

Mr. Selelipeng looked surprised. "I have heard of your agency," he said. "There was an interview in the newspaper the other day."

Mma Ramotswe bit her lip. "That was not us, Rra. That was another business. Nothing to do with us." She made an effort to keep the irritation out of her voice, but she was afraid that it showed, as Mr. Selelipeng seemed to become tense as she spoke.

"The No. 1 Ladies' Detective Agency," went on Mma Ramotswe, "is run by two women. There is me—I am the manager—and there is a lady who works for me as assistant detective. She is a person who came from the Botswana Secretarial College and is now working for me. I think you know her."

Mr. Selelipeng said nothing.

"She is called Mma Makutsi," said Mma Ramotswe. "That is the name of this lady."

Mr. Selelipeng did not lower his eyes, but Mma Ramotswe noticed that he was no longer smiling. She noticed how he was drumming the fingers of his right hand on the arm of his chair. His other hand lay on his lap but was slightly clenched, she saw.

Mma Ramotswe took a deep breath. "I know that you are seeing this lady, Rra. She has spoken of you."

Still Mr. Selelipeng said nothing.

"She was very happy when you invited her out," she continued. "I could tell from the way that she was behaving that something good was happening in her life. And then she mentioned your name. She said—"

Suddenly Mr. Selelipeng interrupted. "So," he said, his voice raised. "So what has this got to do with you, Mma? I don't like to be rude, but is this any of your business? You are her boss, but you do not own her life, do you?"

Mma Ramotswe sighed. "I can understand how you feel, Rra. I can imagine that you think I am a busybody woman who is trying to put her nose into matters that do not concern her."

"Well?" said Mr. Selelipeng. "There, you have said it yourself. You yourself have said that it is only a busybody who talks about these things, like some old woman in a village, watching, watching."

"I am only doing what I have to do, Rra," said Mma Ramotswe defensively.

"Hah! Why do you have to do this? Why do you have to come and talk to me about this private matter? You tell me that."

"Because your wife asked me to," said Mma Ramotswe quietly. "That is why."

Her words had the effect that she had thought they would. Mr. Selelipeng opened his mouth, and then he closed it. He swallowed. Then he opened his mouth again, and Mma Ramotswe saw that he had a gold cap on a tooth slightly to the right side. His mouth closed.

"You are worried, Rra? Did you not tell Mma Makutsi that you were a married man?"

Mr. Selelipeng now seemed crumpled. He had moved back slightly in his chair, and his shoulders had slumped.

"I was going to tell her," he said lamely. "I was going to tell her, but I had not got round to it yet. I am very sorry."

Mma Ramotswe looked into his eyes and saw the lie. This did not surprise her; indeed, Mr. Selelipeng had behaved true to form and had not caused her to rethink her strategy in any way. It would have been different, of course, if he had laughed when she mentioned his wife, but he had not done that. This was not a man who was going to leave his wife; that was very apparent.

She now had the advantage. "So, Mr. Selelipeng, what do you think we should do about this? Your wife has instructed me to report on your activities. I have a professional duty to her. I also have to think about the interests of my employee, Mma Makutsi. I do not want her to be hurt . . . by a man who has no intention of staying with her."

At this, Mr. Selelipeng made an attempt to glower at her, but she met his gaze and held it, and he wilted.

"Please do not tell my wife about this, Mma," he said, his voice thin and pleading. "I am sorry that I have inconvenienced Mma Makutsi. I do not want to hurt her."

"Perhaps you should have thought about that earlier, Rra. Perhaps you should have . . ." She stopped herself. She was a kind woman, and the sight of this man, so wretched and fearful, made it difficult for her to say anything to exacerbate his discomfort. *I could never be a judge,* she thought; *I could not sit there and punish people after they have begun to feel sorry for what they have done.*

"We could try to sort this out," she said. "We could try to make sure that Mma Makutsi is not too badly upset. In particular, Rra, I do not want her to think that she has been thrown over . . . thrown over by somebody who no longer loves her. And I do not want her to find out that she has been seeing a married man. That would make her feel bad about herself, which is what I definitely do not want to happen. Do you understand me?"

Mr. Selelipeng nodded eagerly. "I will do what you tell me to do, Mma."

"I thought, Rra, that it might be better if you were to move back to Mochudi for a while. You could tell Mma Makutsi that you have to go away and that you are not giving her up because you do not love her. Then you must tell her that you do not think that you are worthy of her, even if you are still in love with her. Then you will buy her a very fine present and some flowers. You will know what to do. But you must make sure that she is not being thrown away. That would be very bad, and I would find it difficult then not to talk to your wife about all this. Do you understand me?"

"I understand you very well," said Mr. Selelipeng. "You can be sure that I will try to make it easy for her."

"That is what you must do, Rra."

She rose to her feet, preparing to leave.

"And another thing, Rra," she said. "I would like you to remember that in the future these things may not work out quite so easily for you. Bear that in mind."

"There is not going to be a next time," said Mr. Bernard Selelipeng.

BUT AS she made her way back to the tiny white van, he was watching from his window, and he thought: *I have no happiness now. I am just a man who provides for that woman and her children. She does not love me, but she will not let me find somebody who does love me. And I am too much of a coward to walk away and tell her that I have my own life, which will soon be gone anyway, because I am getting older. And now I no longer have that lady, who was so good to me. One day I will put a stop to all this. One day.*

And Mma Ramotswe, glancing up, saw him at his window before he retreated, and she thought: *Poor man! It could have been different for him, if he had not lied to Mma Makutsi. Why is it that there are always these problems and misunderstandings between men and women? Surely it would have been better if God had made only one sort of person, and the children had come by some other means, with the rain, perhaps.*

She thought about this as she started the van and began to drive away. But if there were only one sort of person, would this person be more like a man than a woman? The answer was obvious, thought Mma Ramotswe. One hardly even had to think about it.

CHAPTER TWENTY

TWO AWKWARD MEN
SATISFACTORILY DISPOSED OF

I T SEEMED to Mma Ramotswe that the run of misfortune that had begun with the illness of Mr. J.L.B. Matekoni, and which had continued through events such as the foreshortened affair of Mma Makutsi with Mr. Bernard Selelipeng and the establishing of the rival agency, was now coming to an end. She had still been concerned about the Selelipeng matter, but she need not have been. Shortly after Mma Ramotswe's visit to No. 42 Limpopo Court, Mma Makutsi explained to her, quite spontaneously, that Mr. Selelipeng had unfortunately been called back to look after aged relatives in Mochudi. As a result of this, he was, most regrettably of course, not in a position to see her as regularly as he might have wished.

"A bit of a relief," she said. "I liked him to begin with, but then, you know how it is, Mma, I rather went off him."

For a moment Mma Ramotswe's composure deserted her.

"You went off . . . you . . ."

"I was bored with him," said Mma Makutsi airily. "He was a very nice man in many ways, but he was a bit too concerned about his appearance. He also just sat there and smiled at me all the time. He was definitely in love with me, which is nice, but you can get a bit bored with that sort of thing, can't you?"

"Of course," said Mma Ramotswe hurriedly.

"He would just sit there and look into my eyes," went on Mma Makutsi. "After a while, it made me go cross-eyed."

Mma Ramotswe laughed. "Some girls would like a man like that."

"Perhaps," said Mma Makutsi. "But then, I'm looking for somebody with a bit more . . ."

"Intelligence?"

"Yes."

"You are very wise," said Mma Ramotswe.

Mma Makutsi threw a hand in the air, as might one who could have her pick of men. "When he said that he was going off to Mochudi, I was very pleased. I said immediately that it would not be easy for us to see one another anymore and that perhaps it was best to say good-bye. He seemed surprised, but I tried to make it easy for him. So we agreed on that. He gave me a very nice present, too. A necklace with a very small diamond in it. He said that he could get them at a special price from the company."

She took a silver chain out of a small packet and showed it to Mma Ramotswe. Suspended on the chain was a small chip of diamond, almost invisible. He could have been more generous, thought Mma Ramotswe, but at least he did it, which was the important thing.

Mma Ramotswe looked at Mma Makutsi. She wondered whether she was putting a brave face on it, or whether she really had been intending to get rid of Mr. Bernard Selelipeng. No, there was only one possibility. Mma Makutsi was a scrupulously truthful person, and she would not—she could not—sit there and tell Mma Ramotswe a skein of lies. So she had made the first move after all. It was astonishing how life had a way of working out, even when everything looked so complicated and unpromising.

EVEN MORE astonishing, though, was the arrival later that day of Mr. Buthelezi, who knocked on the door, entered uninvited, and cheerfully extended a greeting to both Mma Ramotswe and Mma Makutsi.

"So this is your place," he said, looking about the office with a rather condescending air. "I wondered what sort of office you ladies would have. I thought there might be more feminine things. Curtains, you know, things like that."

Mma Ramotswe looked at Mma Makutsi. If there was a limit to this man's nerve, then they had yet to plumb it.

"You people are very busy, I hear," he said. "Lots of cases. This and that."

"Yes," said Mma Ramotswe, adding: "Some clients even came from—"

"Oh, I know about that," said Mr. Buthelezi. "That woman! I told her the truth, I told—"

Mma Ramotswe coughed loudly. She had inadvertently mentioned Mma Selelipeng, forgetting for a moment the careful steps she had taken to prevent Mma Makutsi from hearing anything about it. "Yes, yes, Rra. Let's forget all about that. It was nothing. Now, what can we do for you today? Do you need a detective?"

At this Mma Makutsi burst out laughing but was silenced by a look from Mr. Buthelezi.

"Very funny, Mma," he said. "The truth of the matter is that you can keep the detective business. I have had enough of it. I do not think it is the right business for me."

For a moment Mma Ramotswe was speechless. It was true: the natural order was indeed restoring itself after all these setbacks.

"It's a very boring business, I've decided," said Mr. Buthelezi. "This is a small town. People in this place lead very boring lives. They have no problems to sort out. It is not like Johannesburg."

"Or New York?" interjected Mma Makutsi.

"Yes," said Mr. Buthelezi. "It is not like New York, either."

"So what are you going to do, Rra?" asked Mma Ramotswe. "Are you going to find another business?"

"I'll try to think of something," said Mr. Buthelezi. "Something will turn up."

"What about a driving school?" asked Mma Makutsi. "You would be good at that."

Mr. Buthelezi spun round to face Mma Makutsi's desk. "That is a very good idea, Mma. It is a very good idea. My, my! You are a clever lady. Not just beautiful but clever, too."

"You could call it *Learn to Drive with Jesus*," Mma Makutsi suggested. "You would get many safe, religious people coming to you."

"Hah!" said Mr. Buthelezi, his voice raised. And then, "Hah!" again.

They have such loud voices, these people, thought Mma Ramotswe; *they are all like that. They just are.*

THE FOLLOWING week, because life now seemed to be more ordered and satisfactory, Mma Ramotswe, Mma Makutsi, and Mr. J.L.B. Matekoni organised a gathering by the side of the dam. Not only did they invite the two apprentices, but they also asked Mma Potokwane and her husband, Mma Boko, who was fetched from Molepolole by one of the apprentices, and Mr. Molefelo and his family. Mma Ramotswe and Mma Makutsi worked hard at preparing fried chicken and sausages, together with ample quantities of rice and maize pap. At the picnic itself, the apprentices made a small fire on which thick slices of beef were grilled.

There were other groups picnicking there at the same time, including several families with teenage girls. The apprentices soon started talking to these girls and sat on a rock away from the others, exchanging jokes and conversation of a sort which Mr. J.L.B. Matekoni could only imagine.

"What do these young people talk about?" he said to Mma Ramotswe. "Just look at them. Even the religious one is talking to those girls and trying to touch them on the arm."

"He has gone back to girls," said Mma Makutsi, picking up a tempting bit of chicken and popping it into her mouth. "I have noticed that. He will not be religious for long."

"I thought that might happen," said Mma Ramotswe. "People do not change all that much."

She looked at Mr. J.L.B. Matekoni, who was poking at a piece of meat on the fire. It was good that people did not change, except, she supposed, where there was room for improvement. Mr. J.L.B. Matekoni was perfect as he was, she thought; a good man, with a profound feeling for machinery and possessed of a nature made up of utter kindness. There were so few men like that around; how satisfactory it was, then, that she had one of them.

Mma Potokwane filled a plate with chicken and rice and passed it to her husband.

"How fortunate we are," she said. "How fortunate that we have been given these kind friends, and that we are living in this place, which is so good to us. We are lucky people."

"We are," echoed her husband, who agreed with everything his wife said, without exception.

"Mma Potokwane," said Mr. J.L.B. Matekoni, "is that new pump of yours working well?"

"Very well," said Mma Potokwane. "But one of the house-mothers says that the hot-water system in her house is making a gurgling noise. I was wondering—"

"I will come and fix it," said Mr. J.L.B. Matekoni. "I will come tomorrow."

Mma Ramotswe smiled, but only to herself.

africa
africa africa
africa africa africa
africa africa
africa

MORALITY FOR BEAUTIFUL GIRLS

While trying to resolve some financial problems for her business, Mma Ramotswe finds herself investigating the alleged poisoning of a government official as well as the moral character of the four finalists of the Miss Beauty and Integrity contest. Other difficulties arise at her fiancé's Tlokweng Road Speedy Motors, as Mma Ramotswe discovers he is more complicated than he seems.

Volume 3
1-4000-3136-2 (pbk)

The mysteries are "smart and sassy . . . [with] the power to amuse or shock or touch the heart, sometimes all at once."
—*Los Angeles Times*

THE KALAHARI TYPING SCHOOL FOR MEN

Mma Precious Ramotswe is content. But, as always, there are troubles. Mr J.L.B. Matekoni has not set the date for their wedding, her assistant Mma Makutsi wants a husband, and worst of all, a rival detective agency has opened up in town. Of course, Precious will manage these things, as she always does, with her uncanny insight and good heart.

Volume 4
1-4000-3180-X (pbk)
0-375-42217-X (hc)

THE FULL CUPBOARD OF LIFE

Mma Ramotswe has weighty matters on her mind. She has been approached by a wealthy lady to check up on several suitors. Are these men interested in her or just her money? This may be difficult to find out, but it's just the kind of case Mma Ramotswe likes.

Volume 5
1-4000-3181-8 (pbk)
0-375-42218-8 (hc)

IN THE COMPANY OF CHEERFUL LADIES

Precious Ramotswe is busier than usual at the No. 1 Ladies' Detective Agency when the appearance of a strange intruder in her house and a mysterious pumpkin in her yard add to her concerns. But what finally rattles Mma Ramotswe's normally unshakable composure is the visitor who forces her to confront a painful secret from her past.

Volume 6
0-375-42271-4 (hc)
Paperback available Spring 2006

A New Series Begins

THE SUNDAY PHILOSOPHY CLUB

**THE SUNDAY
PHILOSOPHY CLUB**
Isabel Dalhousie is fond of problems,
and sometimes she becomes
interested in problems that are,
quite frankly, none of her business—
including some that are best left to
the police. Filled with endearingly
thorny characters and a Scottish
atmosphere as thick as a highland
mist, *The Sunday Philosophy Club* is
an irresistible pleasure.

**Volume 1
1-4000-7709-5 (pbk)
0-375-42298-6 (hc)**

**FRIENDS, LOVERS,
CHOCOLATE**
While taking care of her niece Cat's
delicatessen, Isabel meets a heart
transplant patient who has had some
strange experiences in the wake of
surgery. Against the advice of her
housekeeper, Isabel is intent on
investigating. Matters are further
complicated when Cat returns from
vacation with a new boyfriend, and
Isabel's fondness for him lands her in
another muddle.

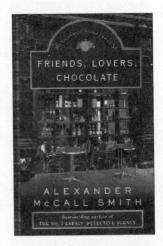

**Volume 2
0-375-42299-4 (hc)
Paperback available Fall 2006**

ANCHOR BOOKS
ORIGINAL TRADE PAPERBACKS

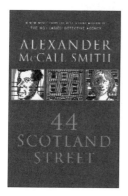

44 SCOTLAND STREET
All of Alexander McCall Smith's trademark warmth and wit come into play in this novel chronicling the lives of the residents of an Edinburgh boardinghouse. Complete with colorful characters, love triangles, and even a mysterious art caper, this is an unforgettable portrait of Edinburgh society.
1-4000-7944-6

THREE NEW NOVELLAS
INTRODUCING THE ECCENTRIC AND EVER-LIKABLE
PROFESSOR DR VON IGELFELD

Welcome to the insane and rarified world of Professor Dr Moritz-Maria von Igelfeld of the Institute of Romance Philology. Von Igelfeld is engaged in a never-ending quest to win the respect he feels certain is due him—a quest which has a way of going hilariously astray.

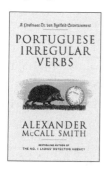

1-4000-7708-7

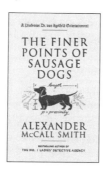

1-4000-9508-5

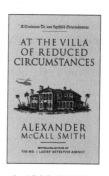

1-4000-9509-3

"Witty, elegant, compassionate and exotic. . . . [McCall Smith is] a treasure of a writer whose books deserve immediate devouring."
—*The Guardian* (London)

"Today, when most books about Africa describe hardship, Alexander McCall Smith brings us further glimpses of Mma Precious Ramotswe and her friends that refresh our souls. . . . We become caught up in the lives of these gentle Botswanans. We share a mug of bush tea with them, and sit together under the shade of a jacaranda."
—*The Christian Science Monitor*

"Delightful. . . . Up to the high standard established with the first book and each succeeding one. . . . The relentless warmth, generosity, cheerfulness, and simple wisdom of the heroine are guaranteed to charm you."
—*The New York Sun*

"*The Full Cupboard of Life* delivers . . . the perfect journey to a faraway place. . . . Mma Ramotswe, her able assistant Mma Makutsi and her fiancé, Mr J.L.B. Matekoni, are brilliant creations. . . . McCall Smith's unique voice, with its African rhythms, elegant, formal turns of phrase and subtle humor . . . is remarkable."
—*The Globe and Mail* (Toronto)

"What makes the stories so charming is their vivid sense of place."
—*W* magazine

"An act of divine ventriloquism. . . . [McCall Smith] give[s] voice to the life and work, sorrows and joys, of the only lady detective in Gaborone, Botswana. . . . There is deep wisdom [here]."
—*The Times-Picayune* (New Orleans)

"A reassuring book, calm, good-humored . . . strong on winsome charm. . . . McCall Smith's writing . . . harks back to a more tranquil age, where gentle ironies and strict proprieties prevail. . . . The pleasure of the novel lies in its simplicity."
—*The Independent* (London)

Alexander McCall Smith

THE FULL CUPBOARD OF LIFE

In addition to the huge international phenomenon The No. 1 Ladies' Detective Agency series, Alexander McCall Smith is the author of The Sunday Philosophy Club series, the Portuguese Irregular Verbs series, *The Girl Who Married a Lion*, and *44 Scotland Street*. He was born in what is now Zimbabwe and taught law at the University of Botswana and Edinburgh University. He lives in Scotland and returns regularly to Botswana.

THE FULL CUPBOARD OF LIFE

Alexander McCall Smith

Anchor Books
A Division of Random House, Inc.
New York

FIRST ANCHOR BOOKS EDITION, JANUARY 2005

Copyright © 2003 by Alexander McCall Smith

The Library of Congress has cataloged the Pantheon edition as follows:
McCall Smith, Alexander, 1948–
The full cupboard of life / Alexander McCall Smith.
p. cm.
1. Ramotswe, Precious (Fictitious character)—Fiction.
2. Women private investigators—Botswana—Fiction. 3. Botswana—Fiction. I. Title.
PR6063.C326F85 2004   823'.914—dc22
2003062379

Anchor ISBN-10: 1-4000-3181-8
Anchor ISBN-13: 978-14000-3181-8

www.anchorbooks.com

Printed in the United States of America
10

This book is for
Soula Ross
and
Vicky Taylor

THE FULL CUPBOARD OF LIFE

CHAPTER ONE

A GREAT SADNESS AMONG
THE CARS OF BOTSWANA

PRECIOUS RAMOTSWE was sitting at her desk at the No. 1
Ladies' Detective Agency in Gaborone. From where she sat she
could gaze out of the window, out beyond the acacia trees, over
the grass and the scrub bush, to the hills in their blue haze of
heat. It was such a noble country, and so wide, stretching for mile
upon mile to brown horizons at the very edge of Africa. It was late
summer, and there had been good rains that year. This was
important, as good rains meant productive fields, and productive
fields meant large, ripened pumpkins of the sort that traditionally
built ladies like Mma Ramotswe so enjoyed eating. The yellow
flesh of a pumpkin or a squash, boiled and then softened with a
lump of butter (if one's budget stretched to that), was one of
God's greatest gifts to Botswana. And it tasted so good, too, with a
slice of fine Botswana beef, dripping in gravy.

Oh yes, God had given a great deal to Botswana, as she had
been told all those years ago at Sunday school in Mochudi.
"Write a list of Botswana's heavenly blessings," the teacher had
said. And the young Mma Ramotswe, chewing on the end of her
indelible pencil, and feeling the sun bearing down on the tin roof
of the Sunday school, heat so insistent that the tin creaked in

protest against its restraining bolts, had written: *(1) the land;* *(2) the people who live on the land; (3) the animals, and specially the fat cattle.* She had stopped at that, but, after a pause, had added: *(4) the railway line from Lobatse to Francistown.* This list, once submitted for approval, had come back with a large blue tick after each item, and the comment written in: *Well done, Precious! You are a sensible girl. You have correctly shown why Botswana is a fortunate country.*

And this was quite true. Mma Ramotswe was indeed a sensible person and Botswana was a fortunate country. When Botswana had become independent all those years ago, on that heart-stilling night when the fireworks failed to be lit on time, and when the dusty wind had seemed to augur only ill, there had been so little. There were only three secondary schools for the whole country, a few clinics, and a measly eight miles of tarred road. That was all. But was it? Surely there was a great deal more than that. There was a country so large that the land seemed to have no limits; there was a sky so wide and so free that the spirit could rise and soar and not feel in the least constrained; and there were the people, the quiet, patient people, who had survived in this land, and who loved it. Their tenacity was rewarded, because underneath the land there were the diamonds, and the cattle prospered, and brick by brick the people built a country of which anybody could be proud. That was what Botswana had, and that is why it was a fortunate country.

Mma Ramotswe had founded the No. 1 Ladies' Detective Agency by selling the cattle left her by her father, Obed Ramotswe, a good man whom everybody respected. And for this reason she made sure that his picture was on the office wall, alongside, but slightly lower than, the picture of the late President of Botswana, Sir Seretse Khama, paramount chief of the Bangwato, founding president of Botswana, and gentleman. The last of these attributes was perhaps the most important in Mma Ramotswe's eyes. A man could be a hereditary ruler, or an elected president, but not be a gentleman, and that would show in his every deed. But if you had a leader who was a gentleman, with all that this meant, then you were lucky indeed. And Botswana had been very lucky in that respect, because all three of her presidents had been good men, gentlemen, who were modest in their bearing, as a gentleman should be. One day, perhaps, a woman might become president, and Mma Ramotswe thought that this would be even better, provided, of course, that the lady in question had the right qualities of modesty and caution. Not all ladies had those qualities, Mma Ramotswe reflected; some of them being quite conspicuously lacking in that respect.

Take that woman who was always on the radio—a political woman who was always telling people what to do. She had an irritating voice, like that of a jackal, and a habit of flirting with men in a shameless way, provided that the men in question could do something to advance her career. If they could not, then they were ignored. Mma Ramotswe had seen this happening; she had seen her ignoring the Bishop at a public function, in order to talk to an important government minister who might put in a good word for her in the right place. It had been transparent. Bishop Theophilus had opened his mouth to say something about the rain and she had said, "Yes, Bishop, yes. Rain is very important." But even as she spoke, she was looking in the direction of the minister, and smiling at him. After a few minutes, she had slipped away, leaving the Bishop behind, and sidled up to the minister to whisper something to him. Mma Ramotswe, who had watched the whole thing, was in no doubt about what that something had been, for she knew women of this sort and there were many of them. So they would have to be careful before choosing a woman as president. It would have to be the right sort of woman; a woman who knew what hard work was and what it was like to bear half the world upon your shoulders.

On that day, sitting at her desk, Mma Ramotswe allowed her thoughts to wander. There was nothing in particular to do. There were no outstanding matters to investigate, as she had just completed a major enquiry on behalf of a large store that suspected, but could not prove, that one of its senior staff was embezzling money. Its accountants had looked at the books and had found discrepancies, but had been unable to find how and where the money had disappeared. In his frustration at the continuing losses, the managing director had called in Mma Ramotswe, who had compiled a list of all the senior staff and had decided to look into their circumstances. If money was disappearing, then there was every likelihood that somebody at the other end would be spending it. And this elementary conclusion—so obvious really— had led her straight to the culprit. It was not that he had advertised his ill-gotten wealth; Mma Ramotswe had been obliged to elicit this information by placing temptation before each suspect. At length, one had succumbed to the prospect of an expensive bargain and had been able to offer payment in cash—a sum beyond the means of a person in such a position. It was not the sort of investigation which she enjoyed, because it involved recrimination and shame, and Mma Ramotswe preferred to forgive, if at all possible. "I am a forgiving lady," she said, which was true. She did forgive, even to the extent of bearing no grudge against Note Mokoti, her cruel former husband, who had caused her such suffering during their brief, ill-starred marriage. She had forgiven Note, even though she did not see him any more, and she would tell him that he was forgiven if he came to her now. Why, she asked herself, why keep a wound open when forgiveness can close it?

Her unhappiness with Note had convinced her that she

would never marry again. But then, on that extraordinary evening some time ago, when Mr J.L.B. Matekoni had proposed to her after he had spent all afternoon fixing the dispirited engine of her tiny white van, she had accepted him. And that was the right decision, for Mr J.L.B. Matekoni was not only the best mechanic in Botswana, but he was one of the kindest and most gracious of men. Mr J.L.B. Matekoni would do anything for one who needed help, and, in a world of increasing dishonesty, he still practised the old Botswana morality. He was a good man, which, when all is said and done, is the finest thing that you can say about any man. He was a good man.

It was strange at first to be an engaged lady; a status somewhere between spinsterhood and marriage; committed to another, but not yet another's spouse. Mma Ramotswe had imagined that they would marry within six months of the engagement, but that time had passed, and more, and still Mr J.L.B. Matekoni had said nothing about a wedding. Certainly he had bought her a ring and had spoken freely, and proudly, of her as his fiancée, but nothing had been said about the date of the wedding. She still kept her house in Zebra Drive, and he lived in his house in the Village, near the old Botswana Defence Force Club and the clinic, and not far from the old graveyard. Some people, of course, did not like to live too close to a graveyard, but modern people, like Mma Ramotswe, said that this was nonsense. Indeed, there were many differences of opinion here. The people who lived around Tlokweng, the Batlokwa, had a custom of burying their ancestors in a small, mud-walled round house, a rondavel, in the yard. This meant that those members of the family who died were always there with you, which was a good practice, thought Mma Ramotswe. If a mother died, then she might be buried under the hut of the children, so that her spirit could watch over them. That must have been comforting for children, thought Mma

Ramotswe, to have the mother under the stamped cattle-dung floor.

There were many good things about the old ways, and it made Mma Ramotswe sad to think that some of these ways were dying out. Botswana had been a special country, and still was, but it had been more special in the days when everybody—or almost everybody—observed the old Botswana ways. The modern world was selfish, and full of cold and rude people. Botswana had never been like that, and Mma Ramotswe was determined that her small corner of Botswana, which was the house on Zebra Drive, and the office that the No. 1 Ladies' Detective Agency and Tlokweng Road Speedy Motors shared, would always remain part of the old Botswana, where people greeted one another politely and listened to what others had to say, and did not shout or think just of themselves. That would never happen in that little part of Botswana, ever.

That morning, sitting at her desk, a steaming mug of bush tea before her, Mma Ramotswe was alone with her thoughts. It was nine o'clock, which was well into the working morning (which started at seven-thirty), but Mma Makutsi, her assistant, had been instructed to go to the post office on her way to work and would not arrive for a little while yet. Mma Makutsi had been hired as a secretary, but had quickly proved her value and had been promoted to assistant detective. In addition to this, she was Assistant Manager of Tlokweng Road Speedy Motors, a role which she had taken on with conspicuous success when Mr J.L.B. Matekoni had been ill. Mma Ramotswe was lucky to have such an assistant; there were many lazy secretaries in Gaborone, who sat in the security of their jobs tapping at a keyboard from time to time or occasionally picking up the telephone. Most of these lazy secretaries answered the telephone in the same tone of voice, as if the cares of being a secretary were overwhelming and there was nothing that they could possibly do for the caller. Mma Makutsi was quite unlike these; indeed she answered the telephone rather too enthusiastically, and had sometimes scared callers away altogether. But this was a minor fault in one who brought with her the distinction of being the most accomplished graduate of her year from the Botswana Secretarial College, where she had scored ninety-seven per cent in the final examinations.

As Mma Ramotswe sat at her desk, she heard sounds of activity from the garage on the other side of the building. Mr J.L.B. Matekoni was at work with his two apprentices, young men who seemed entirely obsessed with girls and who were always leaving grease marks about the building. Around each light switch, in spite of many exhortations and warnings, there was an area of black discolouration, where the apprentices had placed their dirty fingers. And Mma Ramotswe had even found greasy fingerprints on her telephone receiver and, more irritatingly still, on the door of the stationery cupboard.

"Mr J.L.B. Matekoni provides towels and all that lint for wiping off grease," she had said to the older apprentice. "They are always there in the washroom. When you have finished working on a car, wash your hands before you touch other things. What is so hard about that?"

"I always do that," said the apprentice. "It is not fair to talk to me like that, Mma. I am a very clean mechanic."

"Then is it you?" asked Mma Ramotswe, turning to the younger apprentice.

"I am very clean too, Mma," he said. "I am always washing my hands. Always. Always."

"Then it must be me," said Mma Ramotswe. "I must be the one with greasy hands. It must be me or Mma Makutsi. Maybe we get greasy from opening letters."

The older apprentice appeared to think about this for a moment. "Maybe," he said.

"There's very little point in trying to talk to them," Mr J.L.B. Matekoni had observed when Mma Ramotswe subsequently told him of this conversation. "There is something missing in their brains. Sometimes I think it is a large part, as big as a carburettor maybe."

Now Mma Ramotswe heard the sound of voices coming from the garage. Mr J.L.B. Matekoni was saying something to the apprentices, and then there came a mumbling sound as one of the young men answered. Another voice; this time raised; it was Mr J.L.B. Matekoni.

Mma Ramotswe listened. They had done something again, and he was reprimanding them, which was unusual. Mr J.L.B. Matekoni was a mild man, who did not like conflict, and always spoke politely. If he felt it necessary to raise his voice, then it must have been something very annoying indeed.

"Diesel fuel in an ordinary engine," he said, as he entered her office, wiping his hands on a large piece of lint. "Would you believe it, Mma Ramotswe? That . . . that silly boy, the younger one, put diesel fuel into the tank of a non-diesel vehicle. Now we have to drain everything out and try to clean the thing up."

"I'm sorry," said Mma Ramotswe. "But I am not surprised." She paused for a moment. "What will happen to them? What will happen when they are working somewhere else—somewhere where there is no longer a kind person like you to watch over them?"

Mr J.L.B. Matekoni shrugged. "They will ruin cars left, right, and centre," he said. "That is what will happen to them. There will be great sadness among the cars of Botswana."

Mma Ramotswe shook her head. Then, on a sudden impulse,

and without thinking at all why she should say this, she asked, "And what will happen to us, Mr J.L.B. Matekoni?"

The words were out, and Mma Ramotswe looked down at her hands on the desk, and at the diamond ring, which looked back up at her. She had said it, and Mr J.L.B. Matekoni had heard what she had said.

Mr J.L.B. Matekoni looked surprised. "Why do you ask, Mma? What do you mean when you ask what will happen to us?"

Mma Ramotswe raised her eyes. She thought that she might as well continue, now that she had begun. "I was wondering what would happen to us. I was wondering whether we would ever get married, or whether we would continue to be engaged people for the rest of our lives. I was just wondering, that was all."

Mr J.L.B. Matekoni stood quite still. "But we are engaged to be married," he said. "That means that we will get married. Everybody knows that."

Mma Ramotswe sighed. "Yes, but now they are saying: when will those two get married? That is what they are all saying. And maybe I should say that too."

For a few moments Mr J.L.B. Matekoni said nothing. He continued to wipe his hands on the lint, as if concentrating on a delicate task, and then he spoke. "We will get married next year. That is the best thing to do. By then we will have made all the arrangements and saved enough money for a big wedding. Weddings cost a lot, you know. Maybe it will be next year, or the year after that, but we shall certainly get married. There is no doubt about that."

"But I have got money in the Standard Chartered Bank," said Mma Ramotswe. "I could use that or I could sell some cattle. I still have some cattle that my father left me. They have multiplied. I have almost two hundred now."

"You must not sell cattle," said Mr J.L.B. Matekoni. "It is good to keep cattle. We must wait."

He stared at her, almost reproachfully, and Mma Ramotswe looked away. The subject was too awkward, too raw, to be discussed openly, and so she did not pursue the matter. It seemed as if he was frightened of marriage, which must be the reason why he was proving so slow to commit himself. Well, there were men like that; nice men who were fond enough of women but who were wary of getting married. If that was the case, then she would be realistic about it and continue to be an engaged lady. It was not a bad situation to be in, after all; indeed, there were some arguments for preferring an engagement to a marriage. You often heard of difficult husbands, but how often did you hear of difficult fiancés? The answer to that, thought Mma Ramotswe, was never.

Mr J.L.B. Matekoni left the room, and Mma Ramotswe picked up her mug of bush tea. If she was going to remain an engaged lady, then she would make the most of it, and one of the ways to do this would be to enjoy her free time. She would read a bit more and spend more time on her shopping. And she might also join a club of some sort, if she could find one, or perhaps even form one herself, perhaps something like a Cheerful Ladies' Club, a club for ladies in whose lives there was some sort of gap—in her case a gap of waiting—but who were determined to make the most of their time. It was a sentiment of which her father, the late Obed Ramotswe, would have approved; her father, that good man who had always used his time to good effect and who was always in her thoughts, as constantly and supportively as if he were buried under the floor directly beneath her.

———————————

HOW TO RUN AN ORPHAN FARM

MMA SILVIA POTOKWANE, the matron of the orphan farm, was sorting out bits of carpeting for a jumble sale. The pieces of carpet were scattered about the ground under a large syringa tree, and she and several of the housemothers were busy placing them in order of desirability. The carpets were not old at all, but were off-cuts which had been donated by a flooring firm in Gaborone. At the end of every job, no matter how careful the carpet layers were, there would always be odd pieces which simply did not fit. Sometimes these were quite large, if the end of a roll had been used, or the room had been a particularly awkward shape. But none of them was square or rectangular, and this meant that their usefulness was limited.

"Nobody has a room this shape," said one of the housemothers, drawing Mma Potokwane's attention to a triangular piece of flecked red carpet. "I do not know what we can do with this."

Mma Potokwane bent down to examine the carpet. It was not easy for her to bend, as she was an unusually traditional shape. She enjoyed her food, certainly, but she was also very active, and one might have thought that all that walking about the orphan farm, peering into every corner just to keep everybody on their toes, would have shed the pounds, but it had not. All the women in her family had been that build, and it had brought them good fortune and success; there was no point, she felt, being a thin and unhappy person when the attractions of being a comfortable person were so evident. And men liked women like that too. It was a terrible thing that the outside world had done to Africa, bringing in the idea that slender ladies, some as thin as a sebokoldi, a millipede, should be considered desirable. That was not what men really wanted. Men wanted women whose shape reminded them of good things on the table.

"It is a very strange shape," agreed Mma Potokwane. "But if you put together two triangles, then do you not get a square, or something quite close to a square? Do you not think that is true, Mma?"

The housemother looked blank for a moment, but then the wisdom of Mma Potokwane's suggestion dawned upon her and she smiled broadly. There were other triangular pieces, and she now reached for one of these, and held it in position alongside the awkward red piece. The result was an almost perfect square, even if the two pieces of carpet were a different colour.

Mma Potokwane was pleased with the result. Once they had sorted out the carpets, they would put up a notice in the Tlokweng Community Centre and invite people to a carpet sale. They would have no difficulty in selling everything, she thought, and the money would go into the fund that they were building up for book prizes for the children. At the end of each term, those who had done well would receive a prize for their efforts; an atlas, perhaps, or a Setswana Bible, or some other book which would be useful at school. Although she was not a great reader, Mma Potokwane was a firm believer in the power of the book. The more books that Botswana had, in her view, the better. It would be on books that the future would be based; books and the people who knew how to use them.

It would be wonderful, she thought, to write a book which would help other people. In her case, she would never have the time to do it, and even if she had the time, then she very much doubted whether she would have the necessary ability. But if she were to write a book, then the title would undoubtedly be *How to Run an Orphan Farm*. That would be a useful book for whomever took over from her when she retired, or indeed for the many other ladies who ran orphan farms elsewhere. Mma Potokwane had spent some time thinking about the contents of such a work. There would be a great deal about the ordinary day-to-day business of an orphan farm: the arranging of meals, the sorting out of duties and so on. But there would also be a chapter on the psychology which went into running an orphan farm. Mma Potokwane knew a great deal about that. She could tell you, for example, of the importance of keeping brothers and sisters together, if at all possible, and of how to deal with behavioural problems. These were almost always due to insecurity and had one cure and one cure alone: love. That, at least, had been her experience, and even if the message was a simple one, it was, in her view, utterly true.

Another chapter—a very important one—would be on fund raising. Every orphan farm needed to raise money, and this was a task which was always there in the background. Even when you had successfully performed every other task, the problem of money always remained, a persistent, nagging worry at the back of one's mind. Mma Potokwane prided herself on her competence in this. If something was needed—a new set of pots for one of the houses, or a pair of shoes for a child whose shoes were wearing thin—she would find a donor who could be persuaded to come up with the money. Few people could resist Mma Potokwane, and there had been an occasion when the Vice-President of Botswana himself, a generous man who prided himself on his open door policy, had thought ruefully of those countries where it was inconceivable that any citizen could claim the right to see the second most important person in the country. Mma Potokwane had made him promise to find somebody to sell her building materials, and he had agreed before he had thought much about it. The building materials had been purchased from a firm which was prepared to sell them cheaply, but it had taken up a great deal of time.

At the very head of Mma Potokwane's list of supporters was Mr J.L.B. Matekoni. She had relied on him for years to take care of various bits of machinery on the orphan farm, including the water pump, which he had now insisted on being replaced, and the minivan in which the orphans were driven into town. This was an old vehicle, exhausted by years of bumping along on the dusty road to the orphanage, and had it not been for Mr J.L.B. Matekoni's expert hand, it would have long since come to the end of its life. But it was a van which he understood, and it was blessed with a Bedford engine that had been built to last and last, like a strong old mule that pulls a cart. The orphan farm could probably afford a new van, but Mma Potokwane saw no reason to spend money on something new when you had something old which was still working.

That Saturday morning, as they sorted out the carpet pieces for the sale, Mma Potokwane suddenly looked at her watch and saw that it was almost time for Mr J.L.B. Matekoni to arrive. She had asked him whether he could come out to look at a ladder which was broken and needed welding. A new ladder would not have cost a great deal, and would probably have been safer, but why buy a new ladder, Mma Potokwane had asked herself. A new ladder might be shiny, but would hardly have the strength of their old metal ladder, which had belonged to the railways and had been given to them almost ten years ago.

She left the housemothers discussing a round piece of green carpet and returned to her office. She had baked a cake for Mr J.L.B. Matekoni, as she usually did, but this time she had taken particular care to make it sweet and rich. She knew that Mr J.L.B. Matekoni liked fruit cake, and particularly liked raisins, and she had thrown several extra handfuls of these into the mixture, just for him. The broken ladder might have been the ostensible reason for his invitation, but she had other business in mind and there was nothing better than a cake to facilitate agreement.

When Mr J.L.B. Matekoni eventually did arrive, she was ready for him, sitting directly in front of the fan in her office, feeling the benefit of the blast of air from the revolving blades, looking out of the window at the lushness of the trees outside. Although Botswana was a dry country, at the end of the rainy season it was always green, and there were pockets of shade at every turn. It was only at the beginning of the summer, before the rains arrived, that everything was desiccated and brown. That was when the cattle became thin, sometimes painfully so, and it broke the heart of a cattle-owning people to see the herds nibbling at the few dry shreds of grass that remained, their heads lowered in lassitude and in weakness. And it would be like that until the purple clouds stacked up to the east and the wind brought the smell of rain—rain which would fall in silver sheets over the land.

That, of course, was if the rain came. Sometimes there were droughts, and a whole season would go by with very little rainfall, and the dryness would become an ache, always there, like dust in the throat. Botswana was lucky of course; she could import grain, but there were countries which could not, for they had no money, and in those places there was nothing to stand between the people and starvation. That was Africa's burden, and by and large it was borne with dignity; but it still caused pain to Mma Potokwane to know that her fellow Africans faced such suffering.

Now, though, the trees were covered with green leaves, and it was easy for Mr J.L.B. Matekoni to find a shady place for his car outside the orphan farm offices. As he emerged from the car, a small boy came up to him and took his hand. The child looked up at him with grave eyes, and Mr J.L.B. Matekoni smiled down on him. Reaching into his pocket, he withdrew a handful of wrapped peppermints, and slipped these into the palm of the child's hand.

"I saw you there, Mr J.L.B. Matekoni," said Mma Potokwane, as her visitor entered her room. "I saw you give sweets to that child. That child is cunning. He knows you are a kind man."

"I am not a kind man," said Mr J.L.B. Matekoni. "I am an ordinary mechanic."

Mma Potokwane laughed. "You are not an ordinary mechanic. You are the best mechanic in Botswana! Everybody knows that."

"No," said Mr J.L.B. Matekoni. "Only you think that."

Mma Potokwane shook her head vigorously. "Then why does the British High Commissioner take his car to you? There are many big garages in Botswana who would like to service a car like that. But he still goes to you. Always."

"I cannot say why," said Mr J.L.B. Matekoni. "But I think that he is a good man and likes to go to a small garage." He was too modest to accept her praise, and yet he was aware of his reputation. Of course, if people knew about his apprentices, and how bad they were, they might think differently of Tlokweng Road Speedy Motors, but the apprentices were not going to be there forever. In fact, they were due to complete their training in a couple of months and that would be the end of them. How peaceful it would be once they had moved on! How comfortable it would be not to have to think of the damage that they were doing to the cars entrusted to him. It would be a new freedom for him; a release from a worry which hung about his shoulders each day. He had done his best to train them properly, and they had picked up something over the years, but they were impatient, and that was a fatal flaw in the personality of any mechanic. Donkeys and cars required patience.

One of the older girls had made tea, and now she brought this in, together with the rich fruit cake on a plate. Mr J.L.B. Matekoni saw the cake, and for a moment he frowned. He knew Mma Potokwane, and the presence of a large cake, specially made for the occasion, was an unambiguous signal that she had a request to make of him. A cake of this size, and emitting such a strong smell of raisins, would mean a major mechanical problem. The minivan? He had replaced the brake pads recently, but he was concerned about the engine seals. At that age, engine seals could go and the block could heat up and . . .

"I've made you a cake," said Mma Potokwane brightly.

"You are a very generous person, Mma," said Mr J.L.B. Matekoni flatly. "You always remember that I like raisins."

"I have many more packets of raisins," said Mma Potokwane, making a generous gesture, as might one with an unlimited supply of raisins. She reached over to the plate and cut a large portion of cake for her guest. Mr J.L.B. Matekoni watched her, and he thought: once I eat this cake I will have to say yes. But then he went on to think: I always say yes anyway, cake or no cake. What difference is there?

"I should think that Mma Ramotswe makes you many cakes these days," said Mma Potokwane as she slid a generous portion of cake onto her own plate. "She is a good cook, I think."

Mr J.L.B. Matekoni nodded. "She is best at cooking pumpkin and things like that," he said. "But she can also make cakes. You ladies are very clever."

"Yes," agreed Mma Potokwane, pouring the tea. "We are much cleverer than you men, but unfortunately you do not know that."

Mr J.L.B. Matekoni looked at his shoes. It was probably true, he thought. It was difficult being a man sometimes, particularly when women reminded one of the fact that one was a man. But there were clever men about, he thought, and these men would give ladies like Mma Potokwane a good run for their money. The problem was that he was not one of these clever men.

Mr J.L.B. Matekoni looked out of the window. He thought that perhaps he should say something, but nothing came into his mind. Outside the window, the branch of the flamboyant tree, on which a few red flowers still grew, moved almost imperceptibly. New seed pods were growing, while last year's pods, long blackened strips, clung to branches here and there. They were good trees, flamboyants, he thought, with their shade and their red flowers, and their delicate fronds of tiny leaves, like feathers, swaying gently in the wind . . . He stopped. The thin green branch just outside the open window seemed to be unwinding itself and extending tentatively, as if some exaggerated process of growth were occurring.

He rose to his feet, putting down his half-finished piece of cake.

"You've seen something?" asked Mma Potokwane. "Are the children up to something out there?"

Mr J.L.B. Matekoni took a step closer to the window and then stopped. "There is a snake on that branch out there, Mma. A green snake."

Mma Potokwane gasped and stood up to peer out of her window. She narrowed her eyes briefly, peering into the foliage, and then reached suddenly for Mr J.L.B. Matekoni's arm.

"You are right, Rra! There is a snake! Ow! Look at it!"

"Yes," said Mr J.L.B. Matekoni. "It's a long snake too. Look, its tail goes all the way down there."

"You must kill it, Rra," said Mma Potokwane. "I will fetch you a stick."

Mr J.L.B. Matekoni nodded. He knew that people were always telling you not to kill snakes on sight, but you could not allow snakes to come so close to all the orphans. It might be different in the bush, where there was a place for snakes, and they had their own roads and paths, going this way and that, but here it was different. This was the orphan farm front yard, and at any moment the snake could drop down on an orphan as he or she walked under that tree. Mma Potokwane was right; he would have to kill the snake.

Armed with the broomstick which Mma Potokwane had fetched from a cupboard, Mr J.L.B. Matekoni, followed at a discreet distance by the matron, walked round the corner of the office building. The syringa tree seemed higher when viewed from outside, and he wondered whether he would be able to reach the branch on which the snake had been sitting. If he could not, then there was nothing that he could do. They would simply have to warn the orphans to stay away from that tree for the time being.

"Just climb up there and hit it," whispered Mma Potokwane. "Look! There it is. It is not moving now."

"I cannot go up there," protested Mr J.L.B. Matekoni. "If I get too close, it could bite me." He shuddered as he spoke. These green tree snakes, boomslangs they called them, were amongst the most poisonous snakes, worse even than the mambas, some people said, because they had no serum in Botswana to deal with their bite. They had to telephone through to South Africa to get supplies of it if somebody was bitten.

"But you must climb up," urged Mma Potokwane. "Otherwise, it will get away."

Mr J.L.B. Matekoni looked at her, as if to confirm the order. He looked for some sign that she did not really mean this, but there was none. He could not climb up the tree, into the snake's domain; he simply could not.

"I cannot," he said. "I cannot climb up there. I shall try to reach him with my stick from here. I shall poke at the branch."

Mma Potokwane looked doubtful, standing back as he took a tentative step forward. She raised a hand to watch as the broom handle moved up into the foliage of the tree. For his part Mr J.L.B. Matekoni held his breath; he was not a cowardly man, and indeed was braver than most. He never shirked his duty and knew that he had to deal with this snake, but the way to deal with snakes was to keep an advantage over them, and while it was in the tree this snake was in its element.

What happened next was the subject of much discussion amongst the staff of the orphan farm and amongst the small knot of orphans which was by now watching from the security of the office verandah. Mr J.L.B. Matekoni might have touched the snake with the broom handle or he might not. It is possible that the snake saw the stick approaching and decided on evasive action, for these are shy snakes, in spite of their powerful venom, and do not seek confrontation. It moved, and moved quickly, slipping through the leaves and branches with a fluid, undulating motion. Within a few seconds it was sliding down the trunk of the tree, impossibly attached, and then was upon the ground and darting, arrow-like, across the baked earth. Mma Potokwane let out a shriek, as the snake seemed to be heading for her, but then it swerved and shot away towards a large hibiscus bush that grew on a patch of grass behind the office. Mr J.L.B. Matekoni gave a shout, and pursued it with his broom, thumping the end of the stick upon the earth. The snake moved faster, and reached the grass, which seemed to help it in its flight. Mr J.L.B. Matekoni stopped; he did not wish to kill this long green stripe of life, which would surely not linger here any longer and was no danger to anyone. He turned to Mma Potokwane, who had raised her hand to her mouth and had uttered a brief ululation, as was traditional, and quite proper, at moments of celebration.

"You brave man!" she shouted. "You chased that snake away!"

"Not really," said Mr J.L.B. Matekoni. "I think it had decided to go anyway."

Mma Potokwane would have none of this. Turning to the group of orphans, who were chattering excitedly amongst themselves, she said, "You see this uncle? You see how he has saved us all from this snake?"

"Ow!" called out one of the orphans. "You are very brave, uncle."

Mr J.L.B. Matekoni looked away in embarrassment. Handing back the broom to Mma Potokwane, he turned to go back into the office, where the rest of his cake was awaiting him. He noticed that his hands were shaking.

"NOW," SAID Mma Potokwane as she placed another, particularly generous, slice of cake on Mr J.L.B. Matekoni's plate. "Now we can talk. Now I know you are a brave man, which I always suspected anyway."

"You must stop calling me that," he said. "I am no braver than any other man."

Mma Potokwane seemed not to hear. "A brave man," she went on. "And I have been looking for a brave man now for over a week. At last I have found him."

Mr J.L.B. Matekoni frowned. "You have had snakes for that long? What about the men around here? What about the husbands of all those housemothers? Where are they?"

"Oh, not snakes," said Mma Potokwane. "We have seen no other snakes. This is about something else. I have a plan which needs a brave man. And you are the obvious person. We need a brave man who is also well-known."

"I am not well-known," said Mr J.L.B. Matekoni quickly.

"But you are! Everybody knows your garage. Everybody has seen you standing outside it, wiping your hands on a cloth. Everybody who drives past says, 'There's Mr J.L.B. Matekoni in front of his garage. That is him.'"

Mr J.L.B. Matekoni looked down at his plate. He felt a strong sense of foreboding, but he would eat the cake nonetheless while Mma Potokwane revealed whatever it was that she had in store for him. He would be strong this time, he thought. He had stood up to her not all that long ago on the question of the pump, and the need to replace it; now he would stand up to her again. He picked up the piece of cake and bit off a large piece. The raisins tasted even better now, in the presence of danger.

"I want you to help me raise money," said Mma Potokwane,"We have a boy who can sing very well. He is sixteen now, one of the older boys, and Mr Slater at the Maitisong Festival wants to send him to Cape Town to take part in a competition. But this costs money, and this boy has none, because he is just an orphan. He can only go if we raise the money for him. It will be a big thing for Botswana if he goes, and a big thing for that boy too."

Mr J.L.B. Matekoni put down the rest of the cake. He need not have worried, he thought: this sounded like a completely reasonable request. He would sell raffle tickets at the garage if she wanted, or donate a free car service as a prize. Why that should require courage, he could not understand.

And then it became clear. Mma Potokwane picked up her tea cup, took a sip of tea, and then announced her plan.

"I'd like you to do a sponsored parachute jump, Mr J.L.B. Matekoni," she said.

CHAPTER THREE

MMA RAMOTSWE VISITS HER COUSIN
IN MOCHUDI, AND THINKS

MMA RAMOTSWE did not see Mr J.L.B. Matekoni that Saturday, as she had driven up to Mochudi in her tiny white van. She planned to stay there until Sunday, leaving the children to be looked after by Mr J.L.B. Matekoni. These were the foster children from the orphan farm, whom Mr J.L.B. Matekoni had agreed to take into his home, without consulting Mma Ramotswe. But she had been unable to hold this against him, even if many women would have felt that they should have been consulted about the introduction of children into their lives; it was typical of his generosity that he should do something like this. After a few days, the children had come to stay with her, which was better than their living in his house, with its engine parts that littered the floor and with its empty store cupboards (Mr J.L.B. Matekoni did not bother to buy much food). And so they had moved to the house in Zebra Drive, the girl and her brother; the girl in a wheelchair, for illness had left her unable to walk, and the brother, much younger than she, and still needing special attention after all that had happened to him.

Mma Ramotswe had no particular reason to go up to Mochudi, but it was the village in which she had grown up and one never really needed an excuse to visit the place in which one had spent one's childhood. That was the marvellous thing about going back to one's roots; there was no need for explanation. In Mochudi everybody knew who she was: the daughter of Obed Ramotswe, who had gone off to Gaborone, where she had made a bad marriage to a trumpet player she had met on a bus. That was all common knowledge, part of the web of memories which made up the village life of Botswana. In that world, nobody needed to be a stranger; everybody could be linked in some way with others, even a visitor; for visitors came for a reason, did they not? They would be associated, then, with the people whom they were visiting. There was a place for everybody.

Mma Ramotswe had been thinking a great deal recently about how people might be fitted in. The world was a large place, and one might have thought that there was enough room for everybody. But it seemed that this was not so. There were many people who were unhappy, and wanted to move. Often they wished to come to the more fortunate countries—such as Botswana—in order to make more of their lives. That was understandable, and yet there were those who did not want them. This is our place, they said; you are not welcome.

It was so easy to think like that. People wanted to protect themselves from those they did not know. Others were different; they talked different languages and wore different clothes. Many people did not want them living close to them, just because of these differences. And yet, they were people, were they not? They thought the same way, and had the same hopes as anybody else did. They were our brothers and sisters, whichever way you looked at it, and you could not turn a brother or sister away.

Mochudi was busy. There was to be a wedding at the Dutch Reformed Church that afternoon, and the relatives of the bride were arriving from Serowe and Mahalapye. There was also some-

thing happening at one of the schools—a sports day, it seemed—
and as she passed the field (or patch of dust, she noted ruefully) a
teacher in a green floppy hat was shouting at a group of children
in running shorts. Ahead of her on the road a couple of donkeys
ambled aimlessly, flicking at the flies with their moth-eaten tails.
It was, in short, a typical Mochudi Saturday.

Mma Ramotswe went to her cousin's house and sat on a stool
in the lelapa, the small, carefully swept yard which forms the
immediate curtilage of the traditional Botswana house. Mma
Ramotswe was always pleased to see her cousin, as these visits
gave her the opportunity to catch up on village news. This was
information one would never see in any newspaper, yet it was every
bit as interesting—more so, in many respects—than the great
events of the world which the newspapers reported. So she sat on a
traditional stool, the seat of which was woven from thin strips of
rough-cured leather, and listened to her cousin tell her what had
taken place. Much had happened since Mma Ramotswe's last
visit. A minor headman, known for his tendency to drink too
much beer, had fallen into a well, but had been saved because a
young boy passing by had happened to mention that he had seen
somebody jump into the well.

"They almost didn't believe that boy," said the cousin. "He
was a boy who was always telling lies. But happily somebody
decided to check."

"That boy will grow up to be a politician," said Mma
Ramotswe. "That will be the best job for him."

The cousin had shrieked with laughter. "Yes, they are very
good at lying. They are always promising us water for every house,
but they never bring it. They say that there are not enough pipes.
Maybe next year."

Mma Ramotswe shook her head. Water was the source of

many problems in a dry country and the politicians did not make it any easier by promising water when they had none to deliver.

"If the opposition would only stop arguing amongst themselves," the cousin went on, "they would win the election and get rid of the government. That would be a good thing, do you not think?"

"No," said Mma Ramotswe.

The cousin stared at her. "But it would be very different if we had a new government," she said.

"Would it?" asked Mma Ramotswe. She was not a cynical woman, but she wondered whether one set of people who looked remarkably like another set of people would run things any differently. But she did not wish to provoke a political argument with her cousin, and so she changed the subject by asking after the doings of a local woman who had killed a neighbour's goat because she thought that the neighbour was flirting with her husband. It was a long-running saga and was providing a great deal of amusement for everyone.

"She crept out at night and cut the goat's throat," said the cousin. "The goat must have thought she was a tokolosh, or something like that. She is a very wicked woman."

"There are many like that," said Mma Ramotswe. "Men think that women can't be wicked, but we are quite capable of being wicked too."

"Even more wicked than men," said the cousin. "Women are much more wicked, don't you agree?"

"No," said Mma Ramotswe. She thought that the levels of male and female wickedness were about the same; it just took slightly different forms.

The cousin looked peevishly at Mma Ramotswe. "Women have not had much of a chance to be wicked in a big way," she muttered. "Men have taken all the best jobs, where you can be truly wicked. If women here were allowed to be generals and presidents and the like, then they would be very wicked, same as all those wicked men. Just give them the chance. Look at how those lady generals have behaved."

Mma Ramotswe picked up a piece of straw and examined it closely. "Name one," she said.

The cousin thought, but no names came to her, at least no names of generals. "There was an Indian lady called Mrs Gandhi."

"And did she shoot people?" asked Mma Ramotswe.

"No," said the cousin. "Somebody shot her. But . . ."

"There you are," said Mma Ramotswe. "I assume that it was a man who shot her, or was it some lady, do you think?"

The cousin said nothing. A small boy was peering over the wall of the lelapa, staring at the two women. His eyes were large and round, and his arms, which protruded from a scruffy red shirt, were thin. The cousin pointed at him.

"He cannot speak, that little boy," she said. "His tongue does not work properly. So he just watches the other children play."

Mma Ramotswe smiled at him, and called out to him gently in Setswana. But the little boy might not have heard, for he turned away without replying and walked slowly away on his skinny legs. Mma Ramotswe was silent for a moment, imagining what it would be like to be a little boy like that, thin and voiceless. I am fortunate, she thought, and turned to say to her cousin, "We are lucky, aren't we? Here we are, traditionally built ladies, and there's that poor little boy with his thin arms and legs. And we can talk and he can make no sound at all."

The cousin nodded. "We are very lucky to be who we are," she said. "We are fortunate ladies, sitting here in the sun with so much to talk about."

So much to talk about—and so little to do. Here in Mochudi, away from the bustle of Gaborone, Mma Ramotswe could feel herself lapsing again into the rhythms of country life, a life much slower and more reflective than life in town. There was still time and space to think in Gaborone, but it was so much easier here, where one might look out up to the hill and watch the thin wisps of cloud, no more than that, float slowly across the sky; or listen to the cattle bells and the chorus of the cicadas. This was what it meant to live in Botswana; when the rest of the world might work itself into a frenzy of activity, one might still sit, in the space before a house with ochre walls, a mug of bush tea in one's hand, and talk about very small things: headmen in wells, goats and jealousy.

CHAPTER FOUR

_____

A WOMAN WHO KNOWS ABOUT HAIR

THAT MONDAY, Mma Ramotswe had an appointment. Most of her clients did not bother to arrange a time to see her, preferring to drop in unannounced and—in some cases—without disclosing their identity. Mma Ramotswe understood why people should wish to do this. It was not easy to consult a detective agency, especially if one had a problem of a particularly private nature, and many people had to pluck up considerable courage before they knocked on her door. She understood that doctors sometimes encountered similar behaviour; that patients would talk about everything except the real problem and then, at the last moment, mention what was really troubling them. She had read somewhere—in one of the old magazines that Mma Makutsi liked to page through—of a doctor who had been consulted by a man wearing a paper bag over his head. Poor man, thought Mma Ramotswe. It must be terrible to feel so embarrassed about something that one would have to wear a paper bag over one's head! What was wrong with that man? she wondered. Things did go wrong with men sometimes that they were ashamed to talk about, but there was really no need to feel that way.

Mma Ramotswe had never encountered embarrassment of

such a degree, but she had certainly had to draw stories out of people. This happened most commonly with women who had been let down by their husbands, or who suspected that their husbands were having an affair. Such women could feel anger and a sense of betrayal, both of which were entirely understandable, but they could also feel shame that such a thing had happened to them. It was as if it was their fault that their husband had taken up with another woman. This could be so, of course; there were women who drove their husbands away, but in most cases it was because the husband had become bored with his marriage and wanted to see a younger woman. They were always younger, Mma Ramotswe reflected; only rich ladies were able to take up with younger men.

The thought of rich ladies reminded her: the woman who was coming to see her that day was undoubtedly a rich lady. Mma Holonga was well-known in Gaborone as the founder of a chain of hairdressing salons. The salons were successful, but what had proved even more profitable was her invention, and marketing, of Special Girl Hair Braiding Preparation. This was one of those mixtures which women put on their hair before they braided it; its efficacy was doubtful, but the hair products market was not one which required a great deal of scientific evidence. What mattered was that there was a sufficient number of people who believed that their favourite preparation worked.

Mma Ramotswe had never met Mma Holonga. She had seen her picture in *Mmegi* and the *Botswana Guardian* from time to time, and in the photographs she had noticed a pleasant, rather round face. She knew, too, that Mma Holonga lived in a house in the Village, not far from Mr J.L.B. Matekoni. She was intrigued to meet her, because from what she had seen in the newspapers she had formed the impression that Mma Holonga was an unusual rich lady. Many such women were spoilt and demanding, and frequently had an exaggerated idea of their own importance. Mma Holonga did not seem like that.

And when she arrived for her appointment, at exactly the right time (which was another point in her favour), Mma Holonga confirmed Mma Ramotswe's advance impressions.

"You are very kind to see me," she said as she sat down on the chair in front of Mma Ramotswe's desk. "I can imagine how busy you must be."

"Sometimes I am busy," said Mma Ramotswe. "And then sometimes I am not. I am not busy today. I am just sitting here."

"That is very good," said Mma Holonga. "It is good just to sit sometimes. I like to do that, if I get the chance. I just sit."

"There is a lot to be said for that," agreed Mma Ramotswe. "Although we would not want people to do it all the time, would we?"

"Oh no," said Mma Holonga hurriedly. "I would never recommend that."

For a few moments there was silence. Mma Ramotswe looked at the woman in front of her. As the newspaper photographs had suggested, she was traditionally built about the face, but also everywhere else, and her dress was straining at the sides. She should move up a size or two, thought Mma Ramotswe, and then those panels on the side would not look as if they were about to rip. There really was no point in fighting these things: it is far better to admit one's size and indeed there is even a case for buying a slightly larger size. That gives room for manoeuvre.

Mma Holonga was also taking the opportunity to sum up Mma Ramotswe. Comfortable, she thought; not one of these undernourished modern ladies. That is good. But her dress is a bit tight, and she should think of getting a slightly larger size. But she has a friendly face—a good, old-fashioned Botswana face that one can trust, unlike these modern faces which one saw so much of these days.

"I am glad that I came to see you," said Mma Holonga. "I had heard that you were a good person for this sort of thing. That's what people tell me."

Mma Ramotswe smiled. She was a modest person, but a compliment was never unwelcome. And she knew, of course, how important it was to compliment others; not in any insincere way, but to encourage people in their work or to make them feel that their efforts had been worthwhile. She had even complimented the apprentices on one occasion, when they had gone out of their way to help a customer, and for a short time it seemed as if this had inspired them to take a pride in their work. But after a few days she assumed that her words had been forgotten, as they forgot everything else, since they returned to their usual, sloppy habits.

"Oh yes," Mma Holonga continued. "You may not know it, Mma, but your reputation in this town is very high. People say that you are one of the cleverest women in Botswana."

"Oh that cannot be true," said Mma Ramotswe, laughing. "There are many much cleverer ladies in Botswana, ladies with BAs and BScs. There are even lady doctors at the hospital. They must be much cleverer than I am. I have just got my Cambridge Certificate, that is all."

"And I haven't even got that," said Mma Holonga. "But I don't think that I am any less intelligent than those apprentices out there in the garage. I assume they have their Cambridge Certificate too."

"They are a special case," said Mma Ramotswe. "They have passed their Cambridge Certificate, but they are not a very good advertisement for education. Their heads are quite empty. They have nothing in them except thoughts of girls."

Mma Holonga glanced through the doorway to where one of the apprentices could be seen sitting on an upturned oil-drum. She appeared to study him for a moment before she turned back to Mma Ramotswe. Mma Ramotswe noticed; it was only a momentary stare, she thought, but it told her something: Mma Holonga was interested in men. And why should she not be? The days when women had to pretend not to be interested in men were surely over, and now they could talk about it. Mma Ramotswe was not sure whether it was a good idea to talk too openly about men—she had heard some quite shocking things being said by some women, and she would never condone such shamelessness—but it was, on the whole, better for women to be able to express themselves.

"I have come to see you about men," said Mma Holonga suddenly. "That is why I am here."

Mma Ramotswe was taken aback. She had wondered why Mma Holonga had come and had assumed that it was something to do with one of her businesses. But now it seemed it was going to be something rather more personal than that.

"There are many women who come to see me about men," she said quietly. "Men are a major problem for many women."

Mma Holonga smiled at this. "That is no exaggeration, Mma. But many women have problems just with one man. I have problems with four men."

Mma Ramotswe gave a start. This was unexpected: four men! It was conceivable that somebody might have two boyfriends, and hope that neither found out about the other, but to have four! That was an invitation for trouble.

"It's not what you may think," said Mma Holonga hurriedly. "I do not have four boyfriends. At the moment I have no boyfriend, except for these four . . ."

Mma Ramotswe raised her hand. "You should start at the

beginning," she said. "I am getting confused already." She paused. "And to help you talk, I shall make some bush tea. Would you like that?"

Mma Holonga nodded. "I will talk while you are making the tea. Then you will hear all my troubles while the water is boiling."

"I AM a very ordinary lady," Mma Holonga began. "I did not do very well at school, as I have told you. When other girls were looking at their books, I was always looking at magazines. I liked the fashion magazines with all their pictures of bright clothes and smart models. And I specially liked looking at pictures of people's hair and of how hair could be braided and made beautiful with all those beads and henna and things like that.

"I thought it very unfair that God had given African ladies short hair and all the long hair had been taken by everybody else. But then I realised that there was no reason why African hair should not be very beautiful too, although it is not easy to do things with it. I used to braid my friends' hair, and soon I had quite a reputation amongst the other girls at school. They came to see me on Friday afternoons to have their hair braided for the week-end, and I would do it outside our kitchen. The friends would sit on a chair and I would stand behind them, talking and braiding hair in the afternoon sun. I was very happy doing that.

"You'll know all about hair braiding, Mma. You'll know that it can sometimes take a long time. Most of the time I would only spend an hour or two on somebody's hair, but there were times when I spent over two days on a design. I was very proud of all the circles and lines, Mma. I was very proud.

"By the time I was ready to leave school, there was no doubt in my mind what I wanted to do for a living. I had been promised a job in a hair salon that a lady had opened in the African Mall.

She had seen my work and knew that I would bring a lot of business because I was so well-known as a hair braider. She was right. All my friends came to this salon although now they had to pay for me to do their hair.

"After a while I started my own business. I found a small tuck shop that was closing down and I started off in there. It was very cramped, and I had to bring the water I needed in a bucket, but all my customers moved with me and said that they did not mind if the new place was very small. They said that the important thing was to have somebody who really knew about hair, and they said I was such a person. One of them said that a person who knew as much about hair only comes along once or twice in a century. I was very pleased to hear this and asked that person to write out what they had said. I then had a sign-writer paint it on a board and passers-by would stop and read that remark and look at me with respect as I stood there with my scissors ready to cut their hair. I was very happy, Mma. I was very happy.

"I built up my business and eventually I bought a proper salon. Then I bought another one and another after that up in Francistown. Everything went very well and all this time the money was piling up in the bank. I had so much money that I could not really spend it all myself, and so I gave some to my brother and asked him to use it to buy some other businesses for me. He bought me a shop and a place where they make dresses. So I had a factory now, and this made me even richer. I was very happy with all that money, and I went into the bank every Thursday to check how much I had. They were very polite to me now, as I had all that money and banks like people with lots of money.

"But you know what I didn't have, Mma? I didn't have a husband. I had been so busy cutting hair and making money that I had forgotten to get married. Three months ago, when I had my fortieth birthday, I suddenly thought: where is your husband?

THE FULL CUPBOARD OF LIFE

Where are all your children? And the answer was that there were none of these. So I decided that I would find a husband. It may be too late to have children now, but at least I would find a husband.

"And do you think that was easy, Mma? What do you think?"

Mma Ramotswe had by now made the bush tea and was pouring it into her client's cup. "I think it would be easy for a lady like you," she said. "I would not think you would find it hard."

"Oh?" said Mma Holonga. "And why would I not find it hard?"

Mma Ramotswe hesitated. She had answered without thinking very much about it, and now she wondered how she would explain herself. She had probably thought that it would be easy for Mma Holonga to find a husband because she was rich. It was easy for rich people to do anything, even to find a husband. But could she say that? Would it not seem insulting to Mma Holonga that the only reason why Mma Ramotswe should think she could find a husband was because she was rich, and not because she was beautiful or desirable.

"There are many men . . ." began Mma Ramotswe, and then stopped. "There are many men looking for wives."

"But many women say that it is not all that easy," said Mma Holonga. "Why should they find it hard while I should find it easy? Can you explain that?"

Mma Ramotswe sighed. It was best to be honest, she thought, and so she said, quite simply, "Money, Mma. That is the reason. You are a lady with a large chain of hair salons. You are a rich lady. There are many men who like rich ladies."

Mma Holonga sat back in her chair and smiled. "Exactly, Mma. I was waiting to see if you would say that. Now I know that you really do understand things."

"But they would also like you because you are an attractive

lady," added Mma Ramotswe hurriedly. "Traditional Botswana men like ladies who are more traditionally shaped. You and I, Mma. We remind men of how things used to be in Botswana before these modern-shaped ladies started to get men all confused."

Mma Holonga nodded, but in a rather distracted fashion. "Yes, Mma. That may be quite true, but I think that my problem remains. I must tell you what happened when I let it be known that I was looking for a suitable husband. A very interesting thing happened." She paused. "But would you pour me more of that tea, Mma? It is very fine tea and I am thirsty again."

"It is bush tea," said Mma Ramotswe as she reached for the tea-pot. "Mma Makutsi—my assistant—and I drink bush tea because it helps us to think."

Mma Holonga raised her refilled cup to her lips and drained it noisily.

"I shall buy bush tea instead of ordinary tea," she said. "I shall put honey in it and drink it every day."

"That would be a very good thing to do," said Mma Ramotswe. "But what about this husband business? What happened?"

Mma Holonga frowned. "It is very difficult for me," she said. "When word got round, then I received many telephone calls. Ten, twenty calls. And they were all from men."

Mma Ramotswe raised an eyebrow. "That is a large number of men," she said.

Mma Holonga nodded. "Of course, I realised that some of them were no good right there and then. One even telephoned from the prison and the telephone was snatched away from him. And one was only a boy, about thirteen or fourteen, I think. But I agreed to see the others, and from these I ended up with a list of four."

"That is a good number to choose from," said Mma Ramotswe. "Not too large a list of men, but not too small."

Mma Holonga seemed pleased by this. She looked at Mma Ramotswe uncertainly. "You do not think it strange to have a list, Mma? Some of my friends . . ."

Mma Ramotswe raised a hand to interrupt her. Many of her clients referred to advice from friends, and in her experience this advice was often wrong. Friends tried to be helpful, but tended to misadvise, largely because they had unrealistic ideas of what the friend whom they were advising was really like. Mma Ramotswe believed that it was usually better to seek the advice of a stranger—not just any stranger, of course, as one could hardly go out onto the street and confide in the first person one encountered, but a stranger whom you knew to be wise. We do not talk about wise men or wise ladies any more, she reflected; their place had been taken, it seemed, by all sorts of shallow people—actors and the like—who were only too ready to pronounce on all sorts of subjects. It was worse, she thought, in other countries, but it was beginning to happen in Botswana and she did not like it. She, for one, would never pay any attention to the views of such people; she would far rather listen to a person who had done something real in life; these people knew what they were talking about.

"I'm not sure if you should worry too much about what your friends think, Mma," she said. "I think that it is a good idea to have a list. What is the difference between a list of things to buy at a shop, or a list of things to do, and a list of men? I do not see the difference."

"I am glad that you think that," said Mma Holonga. "In fact, I have been glad to hear everything that you have said."

Mma Ramotswe was always embarrassed by compliments, and rapidly went on.

"You must tell me about this list," she said. "And you must tell me about what you want me to do."

"I want you to find out about these men," said Mma Holonga. "I want you to see which men are interested in my money and which are interested in me."

Mma Ramotswe clapped her hands in delight. "Oh, this is the sort of work I like," she said. "Judging men! Men are always looking at women and judging them. Now we have the chance to do some judging back. Oh, this is a very good case to take on."

"I can pay you very well," said Mma Holonga, reaching for the large black handbag she had placed by the side of her chair. "If you tell me how much it will cost, I shall pay it."

"I shall send you a bill," said Mma Ramotswe. "That is what we do. Then you can pay me for my time." She paused. "But first, you must tell me about these men, Mma. I shall need some information on them. Then I shall set to work."

Mma Holonga sat back in her seat. "I am happy to talk about men, Mma. And now I shall begin with the first of these men."

Mma Ramotswe looked into her tea cup. It was still half-full of bush tea. That would be enough to see her through one man, perhaps, but not four. So she reached forward, picked up the teapot, and offered to fill Mma Holonga's cup before attending to her own. That was the old Botswana way of doing things, and that is how Mma Ramotswe behaved. Modern people could say what they liked, but nobody had ever come up with a better way of doing things and in Mma Ramotswe's view nobody ever would.

MR J.L.B. MATEKONI HAS CAUSE
TO REFLECT

T WAS some time before it dawned on Mr J.L.B. Matekoni that Mma Potokwane may have thought that he was agreeing to her proposition. His own recollection of what had happened was very clear. He had said, "I shall think about it, Mma," which is very different—as anybody could see—from saying that one would definitely do something. It might have been better had he refused her there and then, but Mr J.L.B. Matekoni was a kind man and like all kind men he did not enjoy saying no. There were many who had no such compunction, of course; they would refuse things outright, even if it meant hurting another's feelings.

Mr J.L.B. Matekoni thought very carefully. After the initial bombshell, when Mma Potokwane had revealed what she had in mind, he had remained silent for a moment. At first, he thought that he had misheard her, and that she had said that she wanted him to *fix* a parachute, just as she was always asking him to fix some piece of equipment. But of course she had not asked him that, as there would have been plenty of people around the orphan farm who would be much better placed to fix a parachute than he. Fixing a parachute was a sewing job, he assumed, and most of the housemothers were adept at that; they were always sewing the orphans' clothes, repairing rents in the seats of boys' trousers or undoing the hems of skirts that were now a little bit too short. These ladies could easily have stitched up a torn parachute, even if the parachute would end up with a patch made out of a boy's trousers. No, that was not what Mma Potokwane could have had in mind.

Her next remark made this clear. "It's a very good way of raising money," she had said. "The hardship project did it last year. That man from the radio—the well-known one with the funny voice—he agreed to jump. And then that girl who almost became Miss Botswana said she would jump too. They raised a lot of money. A lot."

"But I cannot jump," Mr J.L.B. Matekoni had protested. "I have never even been in an aeroplane. I would not like to jump from one."

It was as if Mma Potokwane had not heard him. "It is a very easy thing to do. I have spoken to somebody in the Flying Club and they say that they can teach you how to do it. They have a book, too, which shows you how to put your feet when you land. It is very simple. Even I could do it."

"Then why don't you?" he had said, but not loudly enough to be heard, for Mma Potokwane had continued as if he had not spoken.

"There is no reason to be afraid," she said. "I think that it will be very comfortable riding down in the air like that. They might drop you over one of our fields and I will get one of the housemothers to have a cake ready for you when you land. And we have a stretcher too. We can have that close by, just in case."

"I do not want to do it," Mr J.L.B. Matekoni had intended to say, but for some reason the words came out as, "I'll think about it."

And that, he realised, was where he had made his mistake. Of course it would be easy enough to undo. All that he would have to do would be to telephone Mma Potokwane and tell her, as unambiguously and as finally as he could, that he had now thought about it and he had decided that he would not do it. He would be happy to give some money to whomsoever she managed to persuade to do it for her, but that person, he was sorry to say, would not be him. This was the only way with Mma Potokwane. One had to be firm with her, just as he had been firm with her on the issue of the pump. One had to stand up to a woman like that.

The difficulty, of course, with standing up to women was that it appeared to make little difference. At the end of the day, a man was no match for a woman, especially if that woman was somebody like Mma Potokwane. The only thing to do was to try to avoid situations where women might corner you. And that was difficult, because women had a way of ensuring that you were neatly boxed in, which was exactly what had happened to him. He should have been more careful. He should have been on his guard when she offered him cake. That was her technique, he now understood; just as Eve had used an apple to trap Adam, so Mma Potokwane used fruit cake. Fruit cake, apples; it made no difference really. Oh foolish, weak men!

Mr J.L.B. Matekoni looked at his watch. It was nine o'clock in the morning, and he should have been at the garage by eight, at the latest. The apprentices had plenty to do—simple servicing tasks that morning—and he could probably leave them to get on with it, but he did not like to leave the business in their hands for too long. He looked out of the window. It was a comfortable sort of day, not too hot for the time of year, and it would be good to drive out into the lands somewhere and just walk along a path. But he could not do that, as he had his clients to think of. The best thing to do was to stop thinking about it, and to get on with the ordinary business of the day. There were exhaust pipes to be looked at, tyres to be changed, brake linings to be renewed; these were the things that really mattered, not some ridiculous parachute drop which Mma Potokwane had dreamed up and which he was not proposing to do anyway. That could be disposed of—with a little resolve. All he had to do was to lift up the telephone and say no to Mma Potokwane. He imagined the conversation.

"No, Mma. That's all: no."

"No what?"

"No. I'm not doing it."

"What do you mean no?"

"By no, I mean no. That's what I mean. No."

"No? Oh."

That, at least, was the theory. When it came actually to speaking, it might be considerably more difficult than that. But at least he had an idea of what he might say and the tone he would adopt.

MR J.L.B. MATEKONI, trying—and largely succeeding—not to think of parachutes or aeroplanes, or even the sky, started the short journey from his house to Tlokweng Road Speedy Motors. It was a journey that he had made so often that he knew every bump in the road, every gateway past which he drove, and, extraordinarily, the people whom he would often see standing at much the same place as they always stood. People like their places, Mr J.L.B. Matekoni reflected. There was that rather ragged man who used to walk about the end of Maratadiba Road, looking as if he had lost something. He was the father, he believed, of the maid who worked in one of the houses there and she had given him the spare room in her quarters. That was the right thing for a daughter to do, of course, but if Mr J.L.B. Matekoni were that man, or the daughter for that matter, he would think that the best place for a father who was slightly confused would be back in the village, or even out at the lands or at a cattle post. In the village he would be able to stand in one spot and watch everything happen without his moving about. He could watch cattle, which was very important for older people, and a good hobby for older men. There was a great deal to be learned just by watching cattle and noting their different colours. That would have kept that man busy.

And then, just round the corner, on Boteli Road, on Fridays and Saturdays one might see a very interesting car parked under the shade of a thorn tree. The car belonged to the brother of a man who lived in one of the houses on Boteli Road. He was a butcher from Lobatse, who came up to Gaborone for the weekends, which started, for him, on Friday morning. Mr J.L.B. Matekoni had seen his butchery store down in Lobatse. It was large and modern, with a picture of a cow painted on the side. In addition, this man owned a plastering business, and so Mr J.L.B. Matekoni imagined that he was a fairly wealthy man, at least by the standards of Lobatse, if not the standards of Gaborone. But it was not his prosperity which singled him out in the eyes of Mr J.L.B. Matekoni; it was the fact that he had such a fine car and had clearly taken such good care of it.

This car was a Rover 90, made in 1955, and therefore very old. It was painted blue, and on the front there was a silver badge showing a boat with a high prow. The first time he had driven past it, Mr J.L.B. Matekoni had stopped to examine it and had noted the fine red leather seats and the gleaming silver of the gear lever. These external matters had not impressed him; it was the knowledge of what lay within: the knowledge of the 2.6-litre engine with its manual transmission *and its famous free wheel option*. That was something one would not see these days, and indeed Mr J.L.B. Matekoni had once brought his apprentices to look at the car, from the outside, so that they could get some sense of fine engineering. He knew of course that there was very little chance of that, but he tried anyway. The apprentices had whistled, and the older one, Charlie, had said, "That is a very fine car, Rra! Ow!" But no sooner had Mr J.L.B. Matekoni turned his back for a moment than that very same apprentice had leant forward to admire himself in the car's wing mirror.

Mr J.L.B. Matekoni had realised then that it was hopeless. Between these young men and himself there was a gulf that simply could not be crossed. The apprentice had recognised that it was a fine car, but had he really understood what it was that made it fine? He doubted that. They were impressed with the spoilers and flashy aluminium wheels that car manufacturers added these days; things which meant nothing, just nothing, to a real mechanic like Mr J.L.B. Matekoni. These were the externals, the outside trim designed, as often as not, to impress those who had no knowledge of cars. For the real mechanic, mechanical beauty lay in the accuracy and intricacy of the thousand moving pieces within the breast of the car: the rods, the cogs, the pistons. These were the things that mattered, not the inanimate parts that did nothing but reflect the sun.

Mr J.L.B. Matekoni slowed down and gazed at the fine car under the thorn tree. As he did so, he noticed, to his alarm, that there was something under the car—something that a casual observer might not notice but which he would never miss. Drawing up at the side of the road, he switched off the engine of his truck and got out of the cab. Then, walking over to the blue Rover, he went down on his hands and knees and peered at the dark underbelly of the car. Yes, it was as he thought; and now he went down on his stomach and crawled under the car to get a better view. It took him only a moment to realise what was wrong, of course, but the sight made him draw in his breath sharply. A pool of oil had leaked out onto the ground below the car and had stained the sand black.

"What are you doing, Rra?"

The sound surprised Mr J.L.B. Matekoni, but he knew better than to lift his head up sharply; that was the sort of thing that the apprentices kept doing. They often bumped their heads on the bottom of cars when the telephone rang or when something else disturbed them. It was a normal human reaction to look up when disturbed, but a mechanic learned quickly to control it. Or a mechanic should learn that quickly; the apprentices had not done so, and he suspected that they never would. Mma Makutsi knew this, of course, and she had once rather mischievously called out Charlie's name when he was underneath a car. "Charlie," she had cried, and there had followed a dull thump as the unfortunate young man had sat up and hit his head on the sump of the car. Mr J.L.B. Matekoni had not really approved of this little joke, but he had found it difficult not to smile when he caught her eye. "I was just checking up that you were all right," shouted Mma Makutsi. "Be careful of your head down there. That brain needs to be looked after, you know."

Mr J.L.B. Matekoni wriggled his way out from under the car and stood up, dusting his trousers as he did so. As he had thought, it was the butcher himself, a corpulent man with a thick neck, like the neck of a bull. It was obvious to anyone, from the very first glance, that this was a wealthy man, even if they did not know about the butchery and the plastering business, nor indeed about this wonderful car with its silver badge.

"I was looking at your car, Rra," he said. "I was underneath it."

"So I see," said the butcher. "I saw your legs sticking out. When I saw that, I knew that there was somebody under my car."

Mr J.L.B. Matekoni smiled. "You must be wondering what I was doing, Rra."

The butcher nodded. "You are right. That is what I was wondering."

"You see, I am a mechanic," said Mr J.L.B. Matekoni. "I have always thought very highly of this car. It is a very good car."

The butcher seemed to relax. "Oh, I see, Rra. You are one who understands old cars like this. I am happy for you to go back under and look."

Mr J.L.B. Matekoni acknowledged the generosity of the offer. He would go back under the car, but it would be more than out of mere curiosity. If he went back, it would be on a mission of repair. He would have to tell the butcher of what he had seen.

"There is oil, Rra," he began. "Your car is leaking oil."

The butcher lifted up a hand in a gesture of tiredness. There was always oil. It was a risk with old cars. Oil; the smell of burning rubber; mysterious rattles: old cars were like the bush at night—there were always strange sounds and smells. He kept taking the car back to the garage and getting them to fix this problem and that problem, and yet these problems always recurred. And now here was another mechanic—one he did not even know—who was talking about oil leaks.

"I have had trouble with oil," he said. "There are always oil leaks and I always have to put more oil in the front. Every time I make the journey up from Lobatse, I have to put in more oil."

Mr J.L.B. Matekoni grimaced. "That is bad, Rra. But you should not have to do it. If the person who serviced this car made sure that the rubber seal on the rod that holds the oil cylinder was in its proper place, then this sort of thing would not happen." He paused. "I could fix this for you. I could do it in ten minutes."

The butcher looked at him. "I cannot bring the car in to your garage now," he said. "I have to talk to my brother about our sister's boy. He is a difficult boy, that one, and we have to work something out. And anyway, I cannot be paying all sorts of mechanics to look at this car. I have already paid a lot of money to the garage."

Mr J.L.B. Matekoni looked down at his shoes. "I would not have charged you, Rra. That is not why I offered."

For a few moments there was silence. The butcher looked at Mr J.L.B. Matekoni and knew, immediately, what sort of man he was dealing with. And he knew, too, that his assumption that Mr J.L.B. Matekoni would want payment was a gross misreading of the situation; for there were people in Botswana who still believed in the old Botswana ways and who were prepared to do things for others just to help them and not in prospect of some reward. This man, whom he had found lying underneath his car, was such a man. And yet he had paid such a great deal of money to those mechanics and they had assured him that all was in order. And the car, after all, worked reasonably well, even if there was a small problem with oil.

The butcher frowned, slipping a hand inside his collar and tugging at it, as if to loosen the material. "I do not think there can be anything wrong with my car," he said. "I think that you must be wrong, Rra."

Mr J.L.B. Matekoni shook his head. Without saying anything, he pointed to the edge of the dark oil stain, just discernible beneath the body of the car. The butcher's gaze followed his hand, and he shook his head vigorously. "It is impossible," he said. "I take this car to a good garage. I pay a great deal of money to have it looked after. They are always tinkering with the engine."

Mr J.L.B. Matekoni raised an eyebrow. "Always tinkering? Who are these people?" he asked.

The butcher gave the name of the garage, and Mr J.L.B. Matekoni knew immediately. He had spent years trying to improve the image of the motor trade, but whatever he, and others like him, did they would always be thwarted by the activities of people like the butcher's mechanics; if indeed they were mechanics at all—Mr J.L.B. Matekoni had strong doubts about the qualifications of some of them.

Mr J.L.B. Matekoni took his handkerchief out of his pocket and wiped his brow.

'If you would let me look at the engine, Rra," he said. "I could very quickly check your oil level. Then we would know whether it was safe for you to drive off to have more oil put in."

The butcher hesitated for a moment. There was something humiliating about being called to account in this way, and yet it would be churlish to reject an offer of help. This man was obviously sincere, and seemed to know what he was talking about; so he reached into his pocket for the car keys, opened the driver's door, and set about pulling the silver-topped lever that would release the catch on the engine cover.

Mr J.L.B. Matekoni stood back respectfully. The revealing of an engine of this nature—an engine which was older than the Republic of Botswana itself—was a special moment, and he did not want to show unseemly curiosity as the beautiful piece of engineering was exposed to view. So he stood where he was and only leaned forward slightly once he could see the engine; and quickly drew in his breath, and was silent—not in admiration, as he had expected, but in shock. For this was not the engine of a 1955 Rover 90, lovingly preserved; he saw, instead, an engine which had been cobbled together with all manner of parts. A flimsy carburettor, of recent vintage and crude construction; a modern oil filter, adapted and tacked onto the only original part that he could make out—the great, solid engine block that had been put into the car at its birth all those years ago. That at least was intact, but what mechanical company it had been obliged to keep!

The butcher looked at him expectantly. "Well, Rra?"

Mr J.L.B. Matekoni found it hard to reply. There were times

when, as a mechanic, one had to give bad news. It was never easy, and one often wished that there were some way round the brute truth. But there were occasions when just nothing could be done, and he feared that this was one of them. "I'm sorry, Rra," he began. "This is very sad. A terrible thing has been done to this car. The engine parts . . ." He could not go on. What had been done was an act of such mechanical vandalism that Mr J.L.B. Matekoni could not find the words to express the feelings within him. So he turned away and shook his head, as might one who had seen some great work of art destroyed before his eyes, cast low by the basest Philistines.

CHAPTER SIX

MR MOPEDI BOBOLOGO

MMA HOLONGA sat back in her chair and closed her eyes. From the other side of the desk, Mma Ramotswe watched her client. She had observed that some people found it easier to tell a story if they shut their eyes, or if they looked down, or focused on something in the distance—something that was there but not there. It did not matter to her; the important thing was that clients should feel comfortable and that they should be able to talk without embarrassment. It might not be easy for Mma Holonga to talk about this, as these were intimate matters of the heart, and if closing her eyes would help, then Mma Ramotswe thought that a good idea. One of her clients, ashamed of what he had to say, had talked from behind cupped hands; that had been difficult, as what he had said had been far from clear. At least Mma Holonga, addressing her from her private darkness, could be understood perfectly well.

"I'll start with the man I like best," she said. "Or at least I think he is the one I like the best."

Then why not marry him? thought Mma Ramotswe. If you liked a man, then surely you could trust your judgment? But no, there were men who were likeable—charming in fact—but who were dangerous to women: Note Makoti, thought Mma Ramotswe. Her own first husband, Note Makoti, was immensely attractive to women, and only later would they discover what sort of man he really was. So Mma Holonga was right: the man you liked might not be the right man.

"Tell me about this man," said Mma Ramotswe. "What does he do?"

Mma Holonga smiled. "He is a teacher."

Mma Ramotswe noted this information on a piece of paper. *First man,* she wrote. *Teacher.* It was important information, because everybody in Botswana had their place, and one simple word could describe a world. Teachers were respected in Botswana, even if so many attitudes were changing. In the past, of course, it had been an even more important thing to be a schoolteacher, and the moral authority of the teacher was recognised by all. Today, more people had studied for diplomas and certificates and these people considered themselves to be every bit as good as teachers. But often they were not, because teachers had wisdom, while many of these people with paper qualifications had not. The wisest man Mma Ramotswe had ever known—her own father, Obed Ramotswe, had no Cambridge Certificate, not even his Standard Six, but that had made no difference. He had wisdom, and that counted for very much more.

She looked out of the window while Mma Holonga began to explain who the teacher was. She tried to concentrate, but the thought of her father had taken her back to Mochudi, and to the memories that the village had for her; of afternoons in the hot season when nothing happened but the heat and when it seemed that nothing could ever have happened; when there was time to sit in front of one's house in the evening and watch the birds flying back to the trees and the sky to the West fill with swathes of red as the sun went down over the Kalahari; when it seemed that

you would be fifteen years old for ever and would always be here
in Mochudi. And you were not to know then what the world
would bring; that the life you imagined for yourself elsewhere
might not be as good as the life you already had. Not that this was
the case with Mma Ramotswe's life, which had on the whole
been a happy one; but for many it was true—those quiet days in
their village would prove to be the best time for them.

Mma Ramotswe's thoughts were interrupted by Mma
Holonga. "A teacher, Mma," the other woman said. "I said that he
was a teacher."

"I'm sorry," said Mma Ramotswe. "I was dreaming there for a
moment. A teacher. Yes, Mma, that is a good job to have, in spite
of the cheekiness of young people these days. It is still a good
thing to be a teacher."

Mma Holonga nodded, acknowledging the truth of this
observation. "His name is Bobologo," she went on. "Mopedi
Bobologo. He is a teacher at the school over there near the University gate. You know that one."

"I have driven past it many times," said Mma Ramotswe.
"And Mr J.L.B. Matekoni, who is the man who runs this garage
behind us; he has a house nearby and he says that he can hear the
children singing sometimes if the wind is coming from that
school."

Mma Holonga listened to this, but was not interested. She
did not know Mr J.L.B. Matekoni, and could not picture him, as
Mma Ramotswe now did, standing on his verandah, listening to
the singing of the children.

"This man is called Mr Mopedi Bobologo, although he is not
like the famous Bobologo. This one is tall and thin, because he
comes from the North, and they are often tall up there. Like the
trees. They are just like the trees up in the North.

"He is a very clever man, this Bobologo. He knows everything about everything. He has read many books, and can tell you what is in all of them. This books says that. This book says this. He knows the contents of many books."

"Oh," said Mma Ramotswe. "There are many, many books. And all the time, more books are coming. It is difficult to read them all."

"It is impossible to read them all," said Mma Holonga. "Even those very clever people at the University of Botswana—people like Professor Tlou—they have not read everything."

"It must be sad for them," observed Mma Ramotswe reflectively. "If it is your job to read books and you can never get to the end of them. You think that you have read all the books and suddenly you see that there are some new ones that have arrived. Then what do you do? You have to start over again."

Mma Holonga shrugged. "I don't know what you do. It is the same with every job, I suppose. Look at hairdressing. You braid one head of hair and then another head of unbraided hair comes along. And so it goes on. You cannot finish your work." She paused. "Even you, Mma. Look at you. You deal with one case and then somebody knocks at the door and there is another case. Your work is never finished."

They were both silent for a moment, thinking of the endless nature of work. It was true, thought Mma Ramotswe, but it was not something to worry too much about. If it were not true, one might have real cause to be concerned.

"Tell me more about this Mr Bobologo," said Mma Ramotswe. "Is he a kind man?"

Mma Holonga thought for a moment. "He is kind, I think. I have seen him smiling at the schoolchildren and he has never spoken roughly to me. I think he is kind."

"Then why has he not been married?" asked Mma Ramotswe. "Or is his wife late?"

"There was a wife," said Mma Holonga. "But she died. He did not have time to get married again, as he was so busy reading. Now he thinks that it is time."

Mma Ramotswe looked out of the window. There was something wrong with this Mr Bobologo; she could sense it. So she wrote on her piece of paper: *No wife. Reads books. Tall and thin.* She looked up. It would not take long to deal with Mr Bobologo, she thought; then they could move on to the second, third, and fourth man. There would be something to worry about with each of them, she thought pessimistically, but then she corrected herself, reminding herself that it was no use giving up on a case before one even started. Clovis Andersen, author of *The Principles of Private Detection*, would never have countenanced that. *Be confident,* he wrote—and Mma Ramotswe remembered the very passage—*Everything can be found out in time. There are very few circumstances in which the true facts are waiting to be tripped over. And never, ever reach a decision before you start.*

That was very wise advice, and Mma Ramotswe was determined to follow it. So while Mma Holonga continued to talk about Mr Bobologo, she deliberately thought of the positive aspects of this man who was being described to her. And there were many. He was very neat, she heard, and he did not drink too much. On one occasion, when they had a meal together, he had made sure that she had the bigger piece of meat and he had taken the smaller. That was a very good sign, was it not? A man who did that must have very fine qualities. And of course he was educated, which would mean that he could teach Mma Holonga things, and improve her outlook on life. All of this was positive, and yet there was still something wrong, and she could not drive the suspicion from her mind. Mr Bobologo would have an ulterior motive. Money? That was the obvious one, but was there something more to it than that?

*   *   *

MMA HOLONGA had just finished talking that morning when Mr
J.L.B. Matekoni arrived at the garage. He was preoccupied with
his encounter with the butcher and he was eager to tell Mma
Ramotswe about it. He had heard a great deal about that other
garage, and from time to time he had seen the results of their
fumbling when one of their disgruntled clients had switched to
Tlokweng Road Speedy Motors. But those cases were but as
nothing compared with the deliberate fraud—and there really
was no other word for it—which his glance at the engine of the
Rover 90 had revealed. This was dishonesty of a calculated and
prolonged variety, all perpetrated against a man who had trusted
them, and, what was perhaps even more shocking, against an
important car that had been placed in their hands. That was a
particular and aggravated wrong: a mechanic had a duty towards
machinery, and these ones had demonstrably failed to discharge
that duty. If you were a conscientious mechanic you would never
deliberately subject an engine to stress. Engines had their dignity—yes, that was the word—and Mr J.L.B. Matekoni, as one of
Botswana's finest mechanics, was not ashamed to use such
terms. It was a question of morality. That was what it was.

As he parked his truck in its accustomed place—under the
acacia tree at the side of the garage—Mr J.L.B. Matekoni
reflected on the sheer effrontery of those people. He imagined
the butcher going into the garage and describing some problem,
and being reassured, when he collected the car, that it had been
attended to. Perhaps they even lied about the difficulties of
obtaining parts; he was sure that they would have charged him
for the genuine spare parts, which they would have had to order
from a special dealer in South Africa, or even England, all that
way away. He thought of the factory in England where they made

Rover cars; under a grey sky, with rain, which they had in such abundance and of which Botswana had so little; and he thought too of those Englishmen, his brother mechanics, standing over the metal lathes and drills that would produce those beautiful pieces of machinery. What would they have felt, he wondered, if they were to know that far away in Botswana there were unscrupulous mechanics prepared to put all sorts of unsuitable parts into the engine which they had so lovingly created? What would they think of Botswana if they knew that? It made him burn with indignation just to contemplate. And he was sure that Mma Ramotswe would share his outrage when he told her. He had noticed her reaction to wrongdoing when she heard about it. She would go quiet, and shake her head, and then she would utter some remark which always expressed exactly what he was feeling, but in a way which he could never achieve. He was a man of machinery, of nuts and bolts and engine blocks, not a man of words. But he appreciated the right words when he heard them, and particularly when they came from Mma Ramotswe, who, in his mind, spoke for Botswana.

Rather than enter the garage through the workshop, Mr J.L.B. Matekoni went round to the side, to the door of the No. 1 Ladies' Detective Agency. Normally this was kept open, which meant that chickens sometimes wandered in and annoyed Mma Makutsi by pecking at the floor around her toes, but today it was closed, which suggested that Mma Ramotswe and Mma Makutsi were out, or that there was a client inside. Mr J.L.B. Matekoni leaned forward to listen at the keyhole, to see if he could hear voices within, and at that moment, as he bent forward, the door was suddenly opened from inside.

Mma Holonga stared in astonishment at the sight of Mr J.L.B. Matekoni, bent almost double. She half turned to Mma

Ramotswe. "There is a man here," she said. "There is a man here listening."

Mma Ramotswe shot Mr J.L.B. Matekoni a warning glance. "He has hurt his back, I think, Mma. That is why he is standing like that. And anyway, it's only Mr J.L.B. Matekoni, who owns the garage. He is entitled to be standing there. He is quite harmless."

Mma Holonga looked again at Mr J.L.B. Matekoni, who, feeling that he had to authenticate Mma Ramotswe's explanation, put a hand to his back and tried to look uncomfortable.

"I thought that he was trying to listen to us," said Mma Holonga. "That's what I thought, Mma."

"No, he would not do that," said Mma Ramotswe. "Sometimes men just stand around. I think that is what he was doing."

"I see," said Mma Holonga, making her way past Mr J.L.B. Matekoni with a sideways glance. "I shall go now, Mma. But I shall wait to hear from you."

"Well, well!" said Mma Ramotswe as they watched Mma Holonga get into her car. "That was very awkward. What were you doing listening in at the keyhole?"

Mr J.L.B. Matekoni laughed. "I was not listening. Or I was not listening, but just trying to hear . . ." He trailed off. He was not explaining it well.

"You wanted to see if I was busy," prompted Mma Ramotswe. "Is that it?"

Mr J.L.B. Matekoni nodded. "That was all I was doing."

Mma Ramotswe smiled. "You could always knock and say Ko, Ko. That is how we normally do things, is it not?"

Mr J.L.B. Matekoni took the reproach in silence. He did not wish to argue with Mma Ramotswe over this; he was keen to tell her about the butcher's car and he looked eagerly at the tea-pot. They could sit over a cup of bush tea and he would tell her about the awful thing that he had discovered quite by chance and she would tell him what to do. So he made a remark about being thirsty, as it was such a hot day, and Mma Ramotswe immediately suggested a cup of tea. She could sense that there was something on his mind and it was surely the function of a wife to listen to her husband when there was something troubling him. Not that I'm actually a wife, she told herself; I'm only a fiancée. But even then, fiancées should listen too, and could give exactly the same sort of advice as wives gave. So she put on the kettle and they had bush tea together, sitting in the shade of the acacia tree, beside Mr J.L.B. Matekoni's parked truck. And in the tree above them, an African grey dove watched them from its branch, silently, before it flew off in search of the mate which it had lost.

MMA RAMOTSWE'S reaction to Mr J.L.B. Matekoni's story was exactly as he had thought it would be. She was angry; not angry in the loud way in which some people were angry, but quietly, with only pursed lips and a particular look in her eye to show what she was feeling. She had never been able to tolerate dishonesty, which she thought threatened the very heart of relationships between people. If you could not count on other people to mean what they said, or to do what they said they would do, then life could become utterly unpredictable. The fact that we could trust one another made it possible to undertake the simple tasks of life. Everything was based on trust, even day-to-day things like crossing the road—which required trust that the drivers of cars would be paying attention—to buying the food from a roadside vendor, whom you trusted not to poison you. It was a lesson that we learned as children, when our parents threw us up into the sky and thrilled us by letting us drop into their waiting arms. We trusted those arms to be there, and they were.

Mma Ramotswe was silent for a while after Mr J.L.B. Matekoni finished speaking. "I know that garage," she said. "A long time ago, when I first had my white van, I used to go there. That was before I started coming to Tlokweng Road Speedy Motors of course."

Mr J.L.B. Matekoni listened intently. This explained the state of the tiny white van when he had first seen it. He had assumed that the worn brake pads and the loose clutch were the results of neglect by Mma Ramotswe herself, rather than a consequence of the van having been looked after—if one could call it that—by First Class Motors, as it had the temerity to call itself. The thought made his heart skip a beat; it would have been so very easy for Mma Ramotswe to have had an accident as a result of her faulty brakes, and if that had happened he might never have met her and he would never have been what he was today— the fiancé of one of the finest women in Botswana. But he recognised that there was no point in entertaining such thoughts. History was littered with events that had changed everything and might easily not have done so. Imagine if the British had given in to South African pressure and had agreed to make what was then the Bechuanaland Protectorate into part of the Cape Province. They might easily have done that, and then there would be no Botswana today, and that would have been a loss for everybody. And his people would have suffered so much too if that had happened; all those years of suffering which others had borne but which they had been spared; and all that had stood between them and that was the decision of some politician somewhere who may never even have visited the Protectorate, or cared very much. And then, of course, there was Mr Churchill, whom Mr J.L.B. Matekoni admired greatly, although he had been no more than a small boy when Mr Churchill had died. Mr J.L.B. Matekoni had read in one of Mma Makutsi's magazines that Mr

Churchill had almost been run over by a car when he was visiting America as a young man. If he had been standing six inches further into the road when the car hit him he would not have survived, and that would have made history very different, or so the article suggested. And then there was President Kennedy, who might have leaned forward just at the moment when that trigger was pulled, and might have lived to change history even more than he had already done. But Mr Churchill had survived, as had Mma Ramotswe, and that was the important thing. Now the tiny white van was scrupulously maintained, with its tight clutch and its responsive brakes. And Mr J.L.B. Matekoni had fitted a new, extra-large seat belt in the front, so that Mma Ramotswe could strap herself in without feeling uncomfortable. She was safe, which was what he wanted above all else; it would be unthinkable for anything to happen to Mma Ramotswe.

"You will have to do something about this," said Mma Ramotswe suddenly. "You cannot leave it be."

"Of course not," said Mr J.L.B. Matekoni. "I have told the butcher to bring the car round here next week, and I shall start to fix it for him. I shall have to order special parts, but I think I know where I can find them. There is a man in Mafikeng who knows all about these old cars and the parts they need. I shall ask him."

Mma Ramotswe nodded. "That will be a kind thing to do," she said. "But I was really thinking that you would have to do something about First Class Motors. They are the ones who have been cheating him. And they will be cheating others."

Mr J.L.B. Matekoni looked thoughtful. "But I don't know what I can do about them," he said. "You can't make good mechanics out of bad ones. You cannot teach a hyena to dance."

"Hyenas have nothing to do with it," said Mma Ramotswe firmly. "But jackals do. Those men in that garage are jackals. You will have to stop them."

Mr J.L.B. Matekoni felt alarmed. Mma Ramotswe was right about those mechanics, but he really did not see what he could do to stop them. There was no Chamber of Mechanics to which he could complain (Mr J.L.B. Matekoni had often thought that a Chamber of Mechanics would have been a good idea), and he had no proof that they had committed a crime. He would never be able to convince the police that fraud had been perpetrated because there would be no proof of what they had said to the butcher. They could argue that they had told him all along that they would have to put in substitute parts, and there would be many other mechanics who could go into court and testify that this was a reasonable thing for any mechanic to do in the circumstances. And if there were no help from the police, then Mr J.L.B. Matekoni would have to speak to the manager of First Class Motors, and he did not relish the prospect of that. This man had an unpleasant look on his face and was known to be something of a bully. He would not stand for allegations being made by somebody like Mr J.L.B. Matekoni, and the situation could rapidly turn threatening. It was all very well, then, for Mma Ramotswe to tell him to go and deal with the dishonest garage, but she did not understand that one could not police the motor trade single-handed.

Mr J.L.B. Matekoni said nothing. He felt that the whole day had taken an unsatisfactory turn—right from the beginning. He had encountered a shocking case of dishonesty, he had been suspected of listening in at doors (when all he had been doing was listening in), and now there was this uncomfortable expectation on the part of Mma Ramotswe that he would confront the unpleasant mechanics at First Class Motors. This was all very unsettling to a man who in general only wanted a quiet life; who liked nothing more than to be bent over the engine of a car, coaxing machinery back into working order. Everything, it seemed to him, was becoming more complicated than it need be, and—here he shuddered as the thought occurred to him—there was also hanging over him the awful threat of an involuntary parachute descent. This was far worse than anything else; a summons to a seat of judgment, an undischarged debt that sooner or later he would have to pay.

He turned to Mma Ramotswe. He should tell her now, as it would be so much easier if there was somebody to share his anxiety. She might accompany him to see Mma Potokwane to make it clear to her that there would be no parachute jump, at least not one made by him. She could handle Mma Potokwane, as women were always much better at dealing with other dominant women than were men. But when he opened his mouth to tell her, he found that the words were not there.

"Yes?" said Mma Ramotswe. "What is it, Mr J.L.B. Matekoni?'

He looked at her appealingly, willing her to help him in his torment, but Mma Ramotswe, seeing only a man staring at her with a vague longing, smiled at him and touched him gently on the cheek.

"You are a good man," she said. "And I am a very lucky woman to have such a fiancé."

Mr J.L.B. Matekoni sighed. There were cars to fix. This hill of problems could wait for its resolution until that evening when he went to Mma Ramotswe's house for dinner. That would be the time to talk, as they sat in quiet companionship on the verandah, listening to the sounds of the evening—the screeching of insects, the occasional snatch of music drifting across the waste ground behind her house, the barking of a dog somewhere in the darkness. That was when he would say, "Look, Mma Ramotswe, I am not very happy." And she would understand, because she always understood, and he had never once seen her make light of another's troubles.

But that evening, as they sat on the verandah, the children were with them, Motholeli and Puso, the two orphans whom Mr J.L.B. Matekoni had so precipitately fostered, and the moment did not seem to right to discuss these matters. So nothing was said then, nor at the kitchen table, where, as they ate the meal which Mma Ramotswe had prepared for them, the talk was all about a new dress which Motholeli had been promised and about which it seemed there was great deal to say.

CHAPTER SEVEN

EARLY MORNING AT TLOKWENG
ROAD SPEEDY MOTORS

MMA MAKUTSI woke early that day, in spite of having been to bed late and having slept very little. She had arisen at five, just before the first signs of dawn in the sky, and had gone outside to wash at the tap which she shared with two other houses. It was not ideal this sharing, and she looked forward to the day when she would have her own tap—and perhaps even a shower. This day was coming, which was one of the reasons why she had found it difficult to sleep. The previous afternoon she had found a couple of rooms to rent in another, rather better, part of town, which made up almost half—and the best half, too—of a low-cost house, and which had rudimentary plumbing all of their own. She had been told that it would not be expensive to install a simple shower, and was assured that this could be arranged within a week or two of her moving in. The information had prompted her into paying a deposit straightaway, which meant that she could make the move in little more than a week.

The rent of the new rooms was almost three times the rent which she was currently paying, but, rather to her surprise, she found that she could easily afford it. Her financial position had improved out of all recognition since she had started her part-time typing school, the Kalahari Typing School for Men. This school met several evenings a week in a church hall and offered supportive and discreet typing instruction for men. There had been many takers—she had been obliged to keep a waiting list— and the money which she had made had been carefully husbanded. Now there was enough for the deposit and more: if she chose to empty her account, she would be able to pay at least eight months' rent and still send a substantial sum back to her family in Bobonong. She had already doubled the amount that she sent to them, and had received an appreciative letter from an aunt. "We are eating well now," her aunt had written. "You are a kind girl, and we think of you every time we eat the good food which you make it possible for us to buy. Not all girls are like you. Many are interested only in themselves (and I have a long list of such girls), but you are interested in aunties and cousins. That is a very good sign."

Mma Makutsi had smiled as she had read this letter. This aunt was a favourite of hers and one day she would pay for her to come on a visit to Gaborone. The aunt had never been out of Bobonong and it would be a great treat for her to come all the way down to Gaborone. But would it be an altogether good idea, she wondered? If you had never been anywhere in your life it could be disturbing suddenly to discover a new place. The aunt was content in Bobonong, but if she were to see how much bigger and more exciting was Gaborone, then she might find it hard to return to Bobonong, to all those rocks, and baked land, and hot sun. So perhaps the aunt would stay where she was, but Mma Makutsi could perhaps send her a picture of Gaborone, so that she would have some idea of what it was like to be in a city.

Mma Makutsi made her way out of her room and walked towards the tap at the side of the neighbouring house. She and the other people who used this tap paid the neighbour twenty pula a month for the privilege, and even then they were discouraged from using too much water. If the tap was left running while one doused one's face under it, then the owner was apt to appear and make a comment about the shortage of water in Botswana.

"We are a dry country," she had once said while Mma Makutsi was trying to wash her hair in the running water.

"Yes," said Mma Makutsi from under the stream of deliciously cool water. "That is why we have taps."

The owner had stormed off. "It is people like you," she had remarked over her shoulder, "it is people like you who are causing droughts and making all the dams empty. You be careful or the whole country will dry up and we shall have to go somewhere else. You just be careful."

This had irritated Mma Makutsi, as she was a careful user of water. But one had to turn the tap on sometimes; there was no point just standing there and looking at it, even if that is what the tap's owner would really have wanted.

This morning there was no sign of the owner, and Mma Makutsi got down on her hands and knees and allowed the water to run over her head and shoulders. After a while, she changed her position and put her feet under the water, in this way experiencing a satisfactory tingling sensation that went all the way up her calves to her knees. Then, washed and refreshed, she returned to her room. She would make breakfast now, and give her brother Richard a bowl of freshly boiled porridge . . . She stopped. For a few moments she had forgotten that Richard was no longer there, and that the corner of her room which she had curtained off for his sickbed was now empty.

Mma Makutsi stood in her doorway, looking down at the place where his bed had been. Only four months ago he had been there, struggling with the illness which was causing his life to ebb away. She had nursed him, doing her best to make him comfortable in the morning before she went off for work, and bringing him whatever small delicacies she could afford from her meagre salary. They had told her to make sure that he ate, even if his appetite was tiny. And she had done so, bringing him sticks of biltong, ruinously expensive though they were, and watermelons, which cooled his mouth and gave him the sugar that he needed.

But none of this—none of the special food, the nursing, or the love which she so generously provided—could alter the dreadful truth that the disease which was making his life so hard could never be beaten. It could be slowed down, or held in check, but it would always assert itself in the long run.

She had known, on that awful day, that he might not be there when she came back from work, because he had looked so tired, and his voice had been so reedy, like the voice of a thin bird. She had toyed with the idea of staying at home, but Mma Ramotswe was away from the office during the morning and there had to be somebody there. So she had said goodbye to him in a fairly matter-of-fact way, although she knew that this might be the last time she spoke to him, and indeed her intuition had been right. Shortly after lunchtime she had been summoned by a neighbour who looked in on him several times a morning, and she had been told to come home. Mma Ramotswe had offered to drive her back in the tiny white van, and she had accepted. As they made their way past the Botswana Technical College, she had suddenly felt that it was too late, and she had sat back in her seat, her head sunk in her hands, knowing what she would find when she arrived at her room.

Sister Banjule was there. She was the nurse from the Anglican Hospice and the neighbour had known to call her too. She was sitting by his bedside, and when Mma Makutsi came in she rose to her feet and put her arm around her, as did Mma Ramotswe.

"He said your name," she whispered to Mma Makutsi. "That is what he said before the Lord took him. I am telling you the truth. That is what he said."

They stood together for several minutes, the three women; Sister Banjule in the white uniform of her calling, Mma Ramotswe in her red dress, that she would now change for black, and Mma Makutsi in the new blue dress that she had treated herself to with some of the proceeds of the typing school classes. And then the neighbour, who had been standing near the door, led Mma Makutsi away so that Sister Banjule could ensure in private the last dignities for a man whose life had not amounted to much, but who now received, as of right, the unconditional love of one who knew how to give just that. *Receive the soul of our brother, Richard,* said Sister Banjule as she gently took from the body its stained and threadbare shirt and replaced it with a garment of white, that a poor man might leave this world in cleanliness and light.

SHE WISHED that he could have seen her new place, as he would have appreciated the space and the privacy. He would have loved the tap too, and she would have probably ended up being as bad as the woman who watched the water, telling him off for using too much. But that was not to be, and she accepted that, because she knew now that his suffering was at an end.

The new place, when she moved into it, would be much closer to work. It was not far from the African Mall, in an area which everybody called Extension Two. The streets there were nothing like Zebra Drive, which was leafy and quiet, but at least they were recognisably streets, with names of their own, rather than being the rutted tracks which dodged this way and that round Naledi. And the houses there were neatly set in the middle of small plots of land, with paw-paw trees or flowering bushes dotted about the yards. These houses, although small, were suitable for clerks, or the managers of small stores, or even teachers. It was not at all inappropriate that somebody of her status—a graduate of the Botswana Secretarial College and an assistant detective—should live in a place like that, and she felt proud when she thought of her impending move. There would be less smell, too, which would be good, as there were proper drains and not so much litter. Not that Botswana smelled; anything but, though there were small corners of it—one of these near Mma Makutsi's room—where one was reminded of humanity and heat.

The fact that Mma Makutsi had two rooms in a house of four rooms meant, in her mind, that she could say that she would now be living in a house. *My house*—she tried the words out, and at first they seemed strange, almost meretricious. But it was true; she would shortly be responsible for half a roof and half a yard, and that justified the expression *my house*. It was a comforting thought—anther milestone on the road that had led her from that constrained life in Bobonong, with its non-existent possibilities and its utter isolation, via the Botswana Secretarial College, with its crowning moment of the award of ninety-seven per cent in the final examinations, to the anticipated elevation to the status of householder, with a yard, and paw-paw trees of her own, and a place where the washing could be hung out to dry in the wind.

The furnishing and decoration of the new house was a matter of the utmost importance, and had been the subject of lengthy discussion with Mma Ramotswe. There were long hours at the office when nothing very much happened, and these might be spent in conversation, or crocheting perhaps, or in simply looking up at the ceiling, with its little fly tracks, like miniature paths through the bush. Mma Ramotswe had strong views on the subject of decoration, and had put these into effect in the house on Zebra Drive, where the living room was unquestionably the most comfortable room Mma Makutsi had ever seen. When she had first visited Mma Ramotswe at home, Mma Makutsi had stood for a moment in the living room doorway, marvelling at the matching suite of sofa and chairs, with their thick cushions, so inviting for a tired or discouraged person, and at the treasures on the shelves—the commemorative plate of Sir Seretse Khama and the Queen Elizabeth II tea cup, with the Queen smiling out in such a reassuring way; and the framed picture of Nelson Mandela with the late King Moshoeshoe II of Lesotho; and the illuminated motto which called for peace and understanding in the house. She had stood there and realised that there had been little beauty in her life; that she had never had a room which in any way expressed her striving for something better, but that perhaps one day she would. And now it was happening.

Mma Ramotswe had been generous. When she first heard of the move, she had taken Mma Makutsi to the house on Zebra Drive and she had gone through the whole place, room by room, identifying household effects which she could pass on to her assistant. There was a chair which nobody used any more, but which had a bright red seat. She could have that. And then there were the yellow curtains, which had been replaced by a new set; Mma Makutsi had scarcely dared to ask for those, but they had been offered, and she had accepted with alacrity.

Now, sitting at her desk in the morning, it seemed to her that her life could hardly get any better. There was her new home to look forward to, furnished in part with Mma Ramotswe's generous gifts; there was the prospect of having a little spare money in her pocket, rather than having to count every thebe; and there was the knowledge that she had a good job, with good people, and that her work made things better, at least for some. Since she had started at the No. 1 Ladies' Detective Agency, she had managed to help quite a number of clients. They had gone away feeling the better for what she had done for them, and that, more than any fee, made her work worthwhile. So those glamorous girls who had gone to work in those companies with new offices; those girls who had never achieved much more than fifty per cent in the examinations at the Botswana Secretarial College; those girls may have highly paid jobs, *but did they enjoy their work?* Mma Makutsi was sure that they did not. They sat at their desks, pretending to type, watching the hands of the clock approach five. And then, exactly on the hour, they disappeared, eager to get as far away as possible from their offices. Well, it was not like that for Mma Makutsi. Sometimes she would be there in the office well after six, or even seven. Occasionally she found that she was so absorbed in what she was doing that she would not even notice that it had become dark, and when she walked home it would be through the night, with all its sounds and the smells of woodsmoke from cooking fires, and with the sky up above like a great black blanket.

Mma Makutsi rose from her chair and went to look out of the window. Charlie, the older apprentice, was getting out of a minibus which had drawn off the main road. He waved to somebody who remained inside, and then began to walk towards the garage, his hands stuck in his pockets, his lips moving as he whistled one of those irritating tunes which he picked up. Just as he reached the garage, he began a few steps of a dance, and Mma Makutsi grimaced. He was thinking of girls, of course, as he always did. That explained the dance.

She drew back from the window, shaking her head. She knew that the apprentices were popular with girls, but she could not imagine what anybody saw in them. It was not that they had much to talk about—cars and girls seemed to be their only interest—and yet there were plenty of girls who were prepared to giggle and flirt with them. Perhaps those girls were in their own way as bad as the apprentices themselves, being interested only in boys and make-up. There were plenty of girls like that, Mma Makutsi thought, and maybe they would make very good wives for these apprentices when they were ready to marry.

The door, which was ajar, was now opened and the apprentice stuck his head round.

"Dumela, Mma," he said. "You have slept well?"

"Dumela, Rra," Mma Makutsi replied. "Yes, I have. Thank you. I was here very early and I have been thinking."

The apprentice smiled. "You must not think too much, Mma," he said. "It is not good for women to think too much."

Mma Makutsi decided to ignore this remark, but after a moment she had to reply. She could not let this sort of thing go unanswered; he would never have said something like that if Mma Ramotswe had been present, and if he thought that he could get away with it then she would have to disabuse him of that idea.

"It is not good for men if women think too much," she retorted. "Oh yes, you are right there. If women start thinking about how useless some men are, then it is bad for men in general. Oh yes, that is true."

"That is not what I meant," said the apprentice.

"Hah!" said Mma Makutsi. "So now you are changing your mind. You did not know what you were saying because your tongue is out of control. It is always walking away on its own and leaving your head behind. Perhaps there is some medicine for that. Maybe there is an operation that can fix it for you!"

The apprentice looked cross. He knew that there was no point in trying to better Mma Makutsi in an argument, but anyway he had not come into the office to argue; he had come in to impart some very important news.

"I have read something in the paper," he said. "I have read something very interesting."

Mma Makutsi glanced at the paper which he had extracted from his pocket. Already it had been smudged with greasy fingerprints, and she wrinkled her nose in distaste.

"There is something about Mr J.L.B. Matekoni in here," said the apprentice. "It is on the front page."

Mma Makutsi drew in her breath. Had something happened to Mr J.L.B. Matekoni? Newspapers were full of bad news about people, and she wondered whether something unpleasant had happened to Mr J.L.B. Matekoni. Or perhaps Mr J.L.B. Matekoni had been arrested for something or other; no, that was impossible. Nobody would ever arrest Mr J.L.B. Matekoni. He was the last person who would ever do anything that would send him to jail. They would have to arrest the whole population of Botswana before they got to Mr J.L.B. Matekoni.

The apprentice, relishing the interest which his comment had aroused, unfolded the newspaper and handed it to Mma Makutsi. "There," he said. "The Boss is going to do something really brave. Ow! I'm glad that it's him and not me!"

Mma Makutsi took the newspaper and began to read. "Mr J.L.B. Matekoni, proprietor of Tlokweng Road Speedy Motors, and a well-known figure in the Gaborone motor trade," began the report, "has agreed to perform a parachute jump to raise money for the Tlokweng orphan farm. Mma Silvia Potokwane, the matron of the orphan farm, said that Mr J.L.B. Matekoni made the surprise offer only a few days ago. She expects him to be able to raise at least five thousand pula in sponsorship. Sponsorship forms have already been distributed and many sponsors are coming forward."

She read the report aloud, the apprentice standing before her and smiling.

"You see," said the apprentice. "None of us would have imagined that the Boss would be so brave, and there he is planning to jump out of an aeroplane. And all to help the orphan farm! Isn't that good of him?"

"Yes," said Mma Makutsi. It was very kind, but she had immediately wondered what Mma Ramotswe would think of her fiancé making a parachute jump. If she had a fiancé herself, then she was not sure whether she would approve of that; indeed the more she thought about it the more she realised that she would not approve. Parachute jumps went wrong; everybody knew that.

"They go wrong, these parachute jumps," said the apprentice, as if he had picked up the direction of her thoughts. "There was a man in the Botswana Defence Force whose parachute didn't open. That man is late now."

"That is very sad," said Mma Makutsi. "I am sorry for that man."

"The other men were watching from the ground," the apprentice continued. "They looked up and shouted to him to open his emergency parachute—they always carry two, you see—but he did not hear them."

Mma Makutsi looked at the apprentice. What did he mean: *he didn't hear them?* Of course he wouldn't hear them. This was typical of the curious, ill-informed way in which the apprentices, and so many young men like them, viewed the world. It was astonishing to think that they had been to school, and yet there they were, with a good Cambridge Certificate. As Mma Ramotswe pointed out, it must be very difficult being the Minister of Education and having to deal with raw material like this.

"But he would never be able to hear them," said Mma Makutsi. "They were wasting their breath."

"Yes," said the apprentice. "It is possible that he had fallen asleep."

Mma Makutsi sighed. "You would not fall asleep while you were jumping from an aeroplane. That doesn't happen."

"Oh yes?" challenged the apprentice. "And what about falling asleep at the wheel—while you're driving? I saw a car go off the Francistown Road once, just because of that. The driver had gone to sleep and the next thing he knew he had hit a tree and the car rolled over. You can go to sleep anywhere."

"Driving is different," said Mma Makutsi. "You do that for a long time. You become hot and drowsy. But when you jump out of an aeroplane, you are not likely to feel hot and drowsy. You will not go to sleep."

"How do you know?" said the apprentice. "Have you jumped out of an aeroplane, Mma? Hah! You would have to watch your skirt! All the boys would be standing down below and whistling because your skirt would be over your head. Hah!"

Mma Makutsi shook her head. "It is no good talking to somebody like you," she said. "And anyway, here's Mr J.L.B. Matekoni's truck. We can ask him about this parachute business. We can find out if what the paper says is true."

MR J.L.B. Matekoni parked his truck in the shade under the acacia tree beside the garage, making sure to leave enough room for Mma Ramotswe to park her tiny white van when she arrived. She would not arrive until nine o'clock, she had told him, because she was taking Motholeli to the doctor. Dr Moffat had telephoned to say that a specialist was visiting the hospital and that he had agreed to see Motholeli. "I do not think that he will be able to say much more than we have said," Dr Moffat had warned. "But there's no harm in his seeing her." And Dr Moffat had been right; nothing new could be said.

Mr J.L.B. Matekoni was pleased that he was getting to know

the children better. He had always been slightly puzzled by children, and felt that he did not really understand them. There were children all round Botswana, of course, and nobody could be unaware of them, but he had been surprised at how these orphans thought about things. The boy, Puso, was a case in point. He was behaving very much better than he had in the past—and Mr J.L.B. Matekoni was thankful for that—but he was still inclined to be on the moody side. Sometimes, when he was driving with Mr J.L.B. Matekoni in his truck, he would sit there, staring out of the window, and saying nothing at all.

"What are you thinking of?" Mr J.L.B. Matekoni would ask, and Puso would shake his head and reply, "Nothing."

That could not be true. Nobody thought of nothing, but it was difficult to imagine what thoughts a boy of that age would have. What did boys do? Mr J.L.B. Matekoni tried to remember what he had done as a boy, but there was a curious gap, as if he had done nothing at all. This was strange, he thought. Mma Ramotswe remembered everything about her childhood and was always describing the details of events which had happened all those years ago. But when he tried to do that, Mr J.L.B. Matekoni could not even remember the names of the other boys in his class, apart from one or two very close friends with whom he had kept in touch. And it was the same with the initiation school, when all the boys were sent off to be inducted into the traditions of men. That was a great moment in your life, and you were meant to remember it, but he had only the vaguest memories.

Engines were different, of course. Although his memory for people's names and for people themselves was not terribly good, Mr J.L.B. Matekoni remembered virtually every engine that he had ever handled, from the large and loyal diesels which he had learned to deal with during his apprenticeship to the clinically efficient, and characterless, motors of modern cars. And not only did he remember the distinguished engines—such as that which powered the British High Commissioner's car—but he also remembered their more modest brothers, such as that which drove the only NSU Prinz which he had ever seen on the roads of Botswana; a humble car, indeed, which looked the same from the front or the back and which had an engine very like the motor on Mma Ramotswe's sewing machine. All of these engines were like old friends to Mr J.L.B. Matekoni—old friends with all the individual quirks which old friends inevitably had, but which were so comfortable and reassuring.

Mr J.L.B. Matekoni got out of his truck and stretched his limbs. He had a busy day ahead of him, with four cars booked in for a routine service, and another which would require the replacement of the servo system on its brakes. This was a tricky procedure, because it was difficult to get at in the first place, and then, when one got there, it was very easy to replace incorrectly. The problem, as Mr J.L.B. Matekoni had explained to the apprentices on numerous occasions, was that the ends of the brake pipes were flared and one had to put a small nut into these flared ends. This nut allowed you to connect the servo mechanism to the pipes, but, and this was the real danger, if you cross-threaded the nuts you would get a leak. And if you avoided this danger, but if you were too rough, then you could twist a brake pipe. That was a terrible thing to do, as it meant that you had to replace the entire brake pipe, and these pipes, as everybody knew, ran through the body of the car like arteries. The apprentices had caused both of these disasters in the past, and he had been obliged to spend almost a whole day sorting things out. Now he no longer trusted them to do it. They could watch if they wished, but they would not be allowed to touch. This was the main problem with the apprentices; they had the necessary theoretical knowledge, or some of it, but so often they were slipshod in the way they finished a job—as if they had become bored with it—and Mr J.L.B. Matekoni knew that you could never be slipshod when it came to brake pipes.

He went into the garage and, hearing voices from the detective agency, he knocked on the door and looked in to see Mma Makutsi handing Charlie a folded-up newspaper. They turned and stared at him.

"Here's the Boss," said the apprentice. "Here's the brave man himself."

"The hero," echoed Mma Makutsi, smiling.

Mr J.L.B. Matekoni frowned. "What is this?" he asked. "Why are you calling me a brave man?"

"Not just us," said the apprentice, handing him the newspaper. "The whole town will be calling you brave now."

Mr J.L.B. Matekoni took the newspaper. It can only be one thing, he thought, and as his eye fell upon the article his fears were confirmed. He stood there, his hands shaking slightly as he held the offending newspaper, the dismay mounting within him. This was Mma Potokwane's doing. Nobody else could have told the newspaper about the parachute jump, as he had spoken to nobody about it. She had no right to do this, he thought. She had no right at all.

"Is it true?" asked Mma Makutsi. "Did you really say that you would jump out of an aeroplane?"

"Of course he did," exclaimed the apprentice. "The Boss is a brave man."

"Well," began Mr J.L.B. Matekoni, "Mma Potokwane said to me that I should and then . . ."

"Oh!" said Mma Makutsi, clapping her hands with delight. "So it is true then! This is very exciting. I will sponsor you, Rra. Yes, I will sponsor you up to thirty pula!"

"Why do you say 'up to'?" asked the apprentice.

"Because that's what these sponsorship forms normally say," said Mma Makutsi. "You put down a maximum amount."

"But that's only because when a person is doing something like a sponsored walk they may not reach the end," said the apprentice. "In the case of a parachute jump, the person you have sponsored usually reaches the end—one way or the other." He laughed at his observation, but Mr J.L.B. Matekoni merely stared at him.

Mma Makutsi was annoyed with the apprentice. It was not right to make remarks like that in the presence of one who would be taking such a great personal risk for a good cause. "You must not talk like that," she said severely. "This is not a joke for you to laugh at. This is a brave thing that Mr J.L.B. Matekoni is doing."

"Oh it's brave all right," said the apprentice. "It is surely a brave thing, Mma. Look what happened to that poor Botswana Defence Force man . . ."

"What happened to him?" asked Mr J.L.B. Matekoni.

Mma Makutsi glowered at the apprentice. "Oh that has nothing to do with you, Mr J.L.B. Matekoni," she said quickly. "That is another thing. We do not need to talk about that thing."

Mr J.L.B. Matekoni looked doubtful. "But he said that something happened to a Botswana Defence Force man. What is that thing?"

"It is not an important thing," said Mma Makutsi. "Sometimes the Botswana Defence Force makes silly mistakes. It is only human after all."

"How do you know it was the Defence Force's mistake?" interjected the apprentice. "How do you know that it wasn't that man's fault?"

"What man?" asked Mr. J.L.B. Matekoni.

"I do not know his name," said Mma Makutsi. "And anyway, I

am tired of talking about these things. I want to get some work done before Mma Ramotswe comes in. There is a letter here which we shall have to reply to. There is a lot to do."

The apprentice smiled. "All right," he said. "I am also busy, Mma. You are not the only one." He gave a small jump, which could have been the beginnings of one of his dances, but which also could have been just a small jump. Then he left the office.

Mma Makutsi returned to her desk in a businesslike fashion. "I have drawn up the accounts for last month," she said. "It was a much better month."

"Good," said Mr J.L.B. Matekoni. "Now about this Defence Force man . . ."

He did not finish, as Mma Makutsi interrupted him with a screech. "Oh," she cried, "I have forgotten something. Oh, I am very stupid. Sorry, Mr J.L.B. Matekoni, I have forgotten to enter those receipts over there. I am going to have to check everything."

Mr J.L.B. Matekoni shrugged. There was something which she did not want him to be told, but he thought that he knew exactly what it was. It was about a parachute that had not opened.

CHAPTER EIGHT

TEA IS ALWAYS THE SOLUTION

MMA RAMOTSWE swept up to the premises of Tlokweng Road Speedy Motors, bringing her tiny white van to a halt under the acacia tree. She had been thinking as she drove in, not of work, but of the children, who were proving such surprising people to live with. Children were never simple—she knew that—but she had always assumed that brothers and sisters had at least something in common in their tastes and behaviour. Yet here were these two orphans, who were children of the same mother and same father (or so Mma Potokwane had told her) and yet who were so thoroughly different. Motholeli was interested in cars and trucks, and liked nothing better than to watch Mr J.L.B. Matekoni with his spanners and wrenches and all the other mysterious tools of his calling. She was adamant that she would be a mechanic, in spite of her wheelchair and in spite of the fact that her arms were not as strong as the arms of other girls of her age. The illness which had deprived her of the use of her legs had touched at other parts of her body too, weakening the muscles and sometimes constricting her chest and lungs. She never complained, of course, as it was not in her nature to do so, but Mma Ramotswe could tell when a momentary shadow of discomfort passed over her face, and her heart went out to the brave, uncomplaining girl whom Mr J.L.B. Matekoni, almost by accident, had brought into her life. Puso, the boy, whom Motholeli had rescued from burial with their mother, scraping the hot sand from his face and breathing air into his struggling lungs, shared none of his sister's interest in machinery. He was indifferent to cars, except as a means of getting around, and he was happiest in his own company, playing in the patch of scrub bush behind Mma Ramotswe's house in Zebra Drive, throwing stones at lizards or tricking those minute creatures known as ant lions into showing themselves. These insects, small as ticks but quicker and more energetic, created little conical wells in the sand, snares for any ants that might wander that way. Once on the edge of the trap, the ant would inevitably trigger a miniature landslide, tumbling down the sides of it. The ant lion, hidden under grains of sand at the bottom, would burrow out and seize its prey, dragging it back underground to provide a tasty meal. If you were a boy, and so minded, you could tickle the edge of the trap with a blade of grass and create a false alarm to bring the ant lion out of its lair. Then you could flip it out with a twig and witness its confusion. That was an entertaining pastime for a boy, and Puso liked to do this for hours on end.

Mma Ramotswe had imagined that he would play with other boys, but he seemed to be quite happy on his own. She had invited a friend to send her sons over, and these boys had arrived, but Puso had simply stared at them and said nothing.

"You should talk to these boys," Mma Ramotswe admonished him. "They are your guests, and you should talk to them."

He had mumbled something, and they had gone off into the garden together, but when she had looked out of the window a few minutes later, Mma Ramotswe had seen the two visiting boys entertaining themselves by climbing a tree while Puso busied himself with a nest of white ants which he had found underneath a mopipi tree.

"Leave him to do what he wants to do," Mr J.LB. Matekoni had advised her. "Remember where he comes from. Remember his people."

Mma Ramotswe knew exactly what he meant. These children, although not pure-bred Masarwa, had at least some of that blood in their veins. It was easy to forget that, because they did not look like bushmen, and yet here was the boy taking this strange, almost brooding interest in the bush and in creatures that most other people would not ever notice. That, she imagined, was because he had been given the eyes to see these things; as we are given the eyes of those who have gone before us, and can see the world in the way in which they saw it. In her case, she knew that she had her father's eye for cattle, and could tell their quality in an instant, at first glance. That was something she just knew—she just knew it. Perhaps Mr J.L.B. Matekoni could do the same with cars; one glance, and he would know.

She got out of the tiny white van and walked round the side of the building to the door that led directly into the No. 1 Ladies' Detective Agency. She could tell that they were busy in the garage, and she did not want to disturb them. In an hour or so it would be time for tea-break, and she could chat to Mr J.L.B. Matekoni then. In the meantime there was a letter to sign— Mma Makutsi had started to type it yesterday—and there might be new mail to go through. And sooner or later she would have to begin the investigation of Mma Holonga's list of suitors. She had no idea how she was going to tackle that, but Mma Makutsi might be able to come up with a suggestion. Mma Makutsi had a good mind—as her ninety-seven per cent at the Botswana Secretarial College had demonstrated to the world—but she was inclined to unrealistic schemes. Sometimes these worked, but on other occasions Mma Ramotswe had been obliged to pour cold water on over-ambitious ideas.

She entered the office to find Mma Makutsi polishing her large spectacles, staring up at the ceiling as she did so. This was always a sign that she was thinking, and Mma Ramotswe wondered what she was thinking about. Perhaps the morning post, which Mma Makutsi now picked up from the post office on her way into work, had contained an interesting letter, possibly from a new client. Or perhaps it had brought one of those anonymous letters which people inexplicably sent them; letters of denunciation which the senders thought that they would be interested to receive, but which were no business of theirs. Such letters were usually mundane, revealing nothing but human pettiness and jealousy. But sometimes they contained a snippet of information which was genuinely interesting, or gave an insight into the strange corners of people's lives. Mma Makutsi could be thinking about one of these, thought Mma Ramotswe, or she could just be staring at the ceiling because there was nothing else to do. Sometimes, when people stared, there was nothing else in their minds, and all they were doing was thinking of the ceiling, or of the trees, or of the sky, or of any of the things that it was so satisfying just to stare at.

"You're thinking of something, Mma," said Mma Ramotswe. "Whenever I see you polishing your glasses like that, I know that you are thinking of something."

Mma Makutsi looked round sharply, disturbed by the sudden sound of her employer's voice. "You surprised me, Mma," she said. "I was sitting here and I suddenly heard your voice. It made me jump."

Mma Ramotswe smiled. "Mr J.L.B. Matekoni says that I creep up on him too. But I do not mean to do that." She paused. "So what were you thinking about, Mma?"

Mma Makutsi replaced her glasses and adjusted their position on the bridge of her nose. She had been thinking about Mr J.L.B. Matekoni and his parachute drop and about how Mma Ramotswe would react to the news, that is assuming that she had not heard it already.

"Have you seen the paper today?" she asked.

Mma Ramotswe shook her head as she walked over to her desk. "I have not seen it," she said. "I have been busy taking the children here and there. I have had no time to sit down." She threw Mma Makutsi a quizzical glance. "Is there something special in it?"

So she does not know, thought Mma Makutsi. Well, she would have to tell her, and it would probably be a shock for her.

"Mr J.L.B. Matekoni is going to jump," she said. "It is in the paper this morning."

Mma Ramotswe stared at Mma Makutsi. What was she talking about? What was this nonsense about Mr J.L.B. Matekoni jumping?

"Out of a plane," went on Mma Makutsi quickly. "Mr J.L.B. Matekoni is going to do a parachute jump."

Mma Ramotswe laughed. "What nonsense!" she said. "Mr J.L.B. Matekoni would never do something like that. Who has put such nonsense in the newspapers?"

"It's true," said Mma Makutsi. "It's one of these charity jumps. Mma Potokwane . . ."

She had to say no more. At the mention of Mma Potokwane's name, Mma Ramotswe's expression changed. "Mma Potokwane?" she said sharply. "She has been forcing Mr J.L.B. Matekoni to do things again? A parachute jump?"

Mma Makutsi nodded. "It is in the paper," she said. "And I have spoken to Mr J.L.B. Matekoni myself. He has confirmed that it is true."

Mma Ramotswe sat quite still. For a moment she said nothing, as the implications of Mma Makutsi's revelations sank in. Then she thought, I shall be a widow. I shall be a widow before I am even married.

Mma Makutsi could see the effect the news was having on Mma Ramotswe and she searched for words that might help.

"I don't think he wants to do it," she said quietly. "But now he is trapped. Mma Potokwane has told the newspapers."

Mma Ramotswe said nothing, while Mma Makutsi continued. "You must go into the garage right now," she said. "You must put a stop to it. You must forbid him. It is too dangerous."

Mma Ramotswe nodded. "I do not think that it is a good idea. But I'm not sure that I can forbid him. He is not a child."

"But you are his wife," said Mma Makutsi. "Or you are almost his wife. You have the right to stop him doing something dangerous."

Mma Ramotswe frowned. "No, I do not have that right. I can talk to him about it, but if you try to stop people from doing things they can resent it. I do not want Mr J.L.B. Matekoni to think that I am telling him what to do all the time. That is not a good start for a marriage."

"But it hasn't started yet," protested Mma Makutsi. "You are just an engaged lady. And you've been an engaged lady for a long time now. There is no sign of a wedding." She stopped, realising that perhaps she had gone too far. What she said was quite true, but it did not help to draw attention to their long engagement and to the conspicuous absence of any wedding plans.

Mma Ramotswe was not offended. "You are right," she said. "I am a very engaged lady. I have been waiting for a long time. But you cannot push men around. They do not like it. They like to feel that they are making their own decisions."

"Even when they are not?" interjected Mma Makutsi.

"Yes," said Mma Ramotswe. "We all know that it is women who take the decisions, but we have to let men think that the decisions are theirs. It is an act of kindness on the part of women."

Mma Makutsi took off her glasses and polished them on her lace handkerchief, now threadbare but so loved. This was the handkerchief that she had bought when she was at the Botswana Secretarial College, at a time when she had virtually nothing else, and it meant a great deal to her.

"So we should say nothing at the moment?" she said. "And then . . ."

"And then we find a chance to say something very small," said Mma Ramotswe. "We shall find some way to get Mr J.L.B. Matekoni out of this. But it will be done carefully, and he will think that he has changed his mind."

Mma Makutsi smiled. "You are very clever with men, Mma. You know how their minds work."

Mma Ramotswe shrugged. "When I was a girl I used to watch little boys playing and I saw what they did. Now that I am a lady, I know that there is not much difference. Boys and men are the same people, in different clothes. Boys wear short trousers and men wear long trousers. But they are just the same if you take their trousers off."

Mma Makutsi stared at Mma Ramotswe, who, suddenly flustered, added quickly, "That is not what I meant to say. What I meant to say is that trousers mean nothing. Men think like boys, and if you understand boys, then you understand men. That is what I meant to say."

"I thought so," said Mma Makutsi. "I did not think that you meant anything else."

"Good," said Mma Ramotswe briskly. "Then let us have a cup of tea and think about how we are going to deal with this problem which Mma Holonga brought us the other day. We cannot sit here all day talking about men. We must get down to work. There is much to do."

Mma Makutsi made the bush tea and they sipped on the dark red liquid as they discussed the best approach to the issue of Mma Holonga's suitors. Tea, of course, made the problem seem smaller, as it always does, and by the time they reached the bottom of their cups, and Mma Makutsi had reached for the slightly chipped tea-pot to pour a refill, it had become clear what they would have to do.

CHAPTER NINE

HOW TO HANDLE YOUNG MEN THROUGH THE APPLICATION OF PSYCHOLOGY

AT THE end of that day's work Mma Ramotswe so engineered matters that she was standing at the door of her tiny white van at precisely the time—one minute to five—that the two apprentices came out of the garage entrance, wiping their greasy hands on a handful of the loose white lint provided by Mr J.L.B. Matekoni. Mr J.L.B. Matekoni knew all about oil-dermatitis, the condition which stalked mechanics and which had struck several of his brother mechanics over the years, and he made every effort to drum the lesson into the heads of his apprentices. Not that this worked, of course; they were still inclined to limit themselves to a quick plunge of the hands into a bucket of lukewarm water, but at least on occasion they resorted to lint and made some effort to do it properly. There was an old barrel for the used lint, and for other detritus of their calling, but they tended to ignore this and now Mma Ramotswe saw the lint tossed casually to the ground. As they did so, the older apprentice looked up and saw her watching them. He muttered something to his friend, and they dutifully picked up the lint and walked off to deposit it in the barrel.

"You are very tidy," called out Mma Ramotswe when they re-emerged. "Mr J.L.B. Matekoni will be pleased."

"We were going to put it there anyway," said the younger apprentice reproachfully. "You don't have to tell us to do it, Mma."

"Yes," said Mma Ramotswe. "I knew that. I thought perhaps you had just dropped it by mistake. That sometimes happens, doesn't it? I have often seen you drop things by mistake. Sweet papers. Chip bags. Newspapers."

The apprentices, who had now drawn level with the tiny white van, looked at their shoes sheepishly. They were no match for Mma Ramotswe, and they knew it.

"But I don't want to talk about litter," said Mma Ramotswe kindly. "I can see that you have been working very hard today, and I thought I would drive you both home. It will save you waiting for a minibus."

"You are very kind, Mma," said the older apprentice.

Mma Ramotswe gestured to the passenger seat. "You sit in there, Charlie. You are the older one. And you," she looked at the younger apprentice and pointed to the back of the van, "you can go there. Next time you can ride in front."

She had a rough idea where the two young men lived. The younger one stayed with his uncle in a house beyond the Francistown Road brewery and the older one lodged with an aunt and uncle near the orphan farm at Tlokweng. It would take over half an hour to deliver them both, and the children would be waiting for her at home, but this was important and she would do it cheerfully.

She would deliver the younger one first, skirting the edge of the town, driving past the university and the Sun Hotel and the road to Maru-a-Pula. Then Nyerere Drive bore left, past the end of Elephant Road, and ran down to Nelson Mandela Drive, which she still thought of as the old Francistown Road. They crossed the dry course of the Segoditshane River and then the older apprentice directed her to a side road lined by a row of small, well-kept houses.

"That is his uncle's place over there," he said, pointing to one of the houses. "He lives in that shack on the side. That is where he sleeps, but he eats inside with the family."

They stopped outside the gate and the younger apprentice jumped out of the van and clapped his hands in gratitude. Mma Ramotswe smiled and said through the open window, "I am glad that I saved you a walk." Then she waved and they drove off.

"He is a good boy," said Mma Ramotswe. "He will make a good husband for some girl one day."

"Hah!" said the older apprentice. "That girl will have to catch him first. He is a quick runner, that boy. It will not be easy for the girls!"

Mma Ramotswe pretended to look interested. "But what if a very beautiful girl with lots of money saw him? What then? Surely he would like to marry a girl like that and have a large car? Perhaps even one of those German cars that you think are so smart. What then?"

The apprentice laughed. "Oh, I would marry a girl like that double-quick. But girls like that won't look at boys like us. We are just apprentice mechanics. Girls like that want boys from rich families or with very good jobs. Accountants. People like that. We just get ordinary girls."

Mma Ramotswe clucked her tongue. "Oh! That is very sad. It is a pity that you don't know how to attract more glamorous girls. It is a great pity." She paused before saying, almost as an aside, "I could tell you, of course."

The apprentice looked at her incredulously. "You, Mma? You could tell me how to attract that sort of girl?"

"Of course I could," said Mma Ramotswe. "I am a woman,

remember? I used to be a girl. I know how girls think. Just because I am a bit older now and I do not run round looking at boys doesn't mean that I have forgotten how girls think."

The apprentice raised an eyebrow. "You tell me then," he said. "You tell me this secret."

Mma Ramotswe was silent. This, she thought, was the difficult part. She had to make sure that the apprentice would take what she had to say seriously, and that meant that she should not be too quick to impart the information.

"I don't know whether I should tell you," she said. "I cannot just tell anybody. I would only want to tell a man who would be kind to these glamorous girls. Just because they are glamorous doesn't mean that they do not have their feelings. Maybe I should wait a few years before I tell you."

The apprentice, who had been smiling, now frowned. "I would treat such a girl very well, Mma. You can count on me."

Mma Ramotswe concentrated on her driving. There was an elderly man on a bicycle ahead of them, a battered hat perched on his head, and a red hen tied to the carrier on the back of his cycle. She slowed down, giving him a wide berth.

"That hen is making its last journey," she said. "He will be taking it to somebody who will eat it."

The apprentice glanced behind him. "That is what happens to all hens. That is what they are for."

"They may not think that," said Mma Ramotswe.

The apprentice laughed. "They cannot think. They have very small heads. There are no brains in a chicken."

"What is in their heads, then?" asked Mma Ramotswe.

"There is just blood and some bits of meat," said the apprentice. "I have seen it. There is no brain."

Mma Ramotswe nodded. "Oh," she said. There was no point

in arguing with these boys about matters of this sort; they were usually quite adamant that they were right, even if there was no basis for what they said.

"But what is this thing about girls?" the apprentice persisted. "You can tell me, Mma. I may talk about girls a lot, but I am very kind to them. You ask Mr J.L.B. Matekoni. He has seen how well I treat girls."

They were now nearing the Tlokweng Road, and Mma Ramotswe thought that the time was ripe. She had aroused the apprentice's attention and now he was listening to her.

"Well then," she began, "I will tell you a very certain way to attract the attention of one of these glamorous girls. You must become well-known. If you are well-known—if your name is in the papers—then these girls cannot resist you. You look about you and see what sort of man has that sort of lady. It is always the ones who are in the papers. They get those girls every time."

The apprentice looked immediately defeated. "That is not good news for me," he said. "I shall never be well-known. I shall never get into the papers."

"Why not?" asked Mma Ramotswe. "Why give up before you have started?"

"Because nobody is ever going to write about me," said the apprentice. "I am just an unknown person. I am not going to be famous."

"But look at Mr J.L.B. Matekoni," said Mma Ramotswe. "Look at him. He was in the papers today. Now he is well-known."

"That is different," the apprentice retorted. "He is in the papers because he is going to do a parachute jump."

"But you could do that," said Mma Ramotswe, as if the idea had just occurred. "If you were to jump out of an aeroplane you would be all over the papers and the glamorous girls would notice all right. They would be all over you. I know how these girls think."

"But . . ." began the apprentice.

He did not finish. "Oh yes they would," Mma Ramotswe went on. "There is nothing—nothing—that they like more than bravery. If you jumped out of the plane—maybe instead of Mr J.L.B. Matekoni, who is possibly too old to do that these days—then you would be the one who would get all the attention. I guarantee it. Those girls would be waiting for you. You could take your pick. You could choose the one with the biggest car."

"If she had the biggest car then she would also have the biggest bottom," said the apprentice, smiling. "She would need a big car to fit her bottom in. Such a girl would be very nice."

Mma Ramotswe would normally not have let such a remark pass without a sharp retort, but this was not the occasion, and she simply smiled. "It seems simple to me," she said. "You do the jump. You get the girl. It's perfectly safe."

The apprentice thought for a moment. "But what about that Botswana Defence Force man? The one whose parachute didn't open. What about him?"

Mma Ramotswe shook her head. "You are wrong there, Charlie. His parachute would have opened *if he had pulled the cord*. You yourself said to Mma Makutsi that that man had probably gone to sleep. There was nothing wrong with his parachute, you see. You are much cleverer than that man. You will not forget to pull the cord."

The apprentice thought for a moment. "And you think that the papers will write about me?"

"Of course they will," said Mma Ramotswe. "I shall get Mma Potokwane to talk to them again. She is always giving them stories about the orphan farm. She will tell them to put a big photograph of you on the front page. That will certainly be read by the sort of girl we are talking about."

Mma Ramotswe slowed down. A small herd of donkeys had wandered onto the road ahead of them and had stopped in the middle, looking at the tiny white van as if they had never before encountered a vehicle. She brought the van to a halt, glancing quickly at the apprentice as she did so. Psychology, she thought; that is what they called it these days, but in her view it was something much older than that. It was woman's knowledge, that was what it was; knowledge of how men behaved and how they could be persuaded to do something if one approached the matter in the right way. She had told the apprentice no lies; there were girls who would be impressed by a young man who did a parachute jump and who had his photograph in the papers. If men were prepared to use psychology, which they usually were not, then they too could get women to do what they wanted them to do. Perhaps it was fortunate, then, that men were so bad at psychology. Men got women to do what they wanted through making them feel sorry for them, or making them feel guilty. Men did not do this deliberately, of course, but that was the effect.

The apprentice leaned out of his window and shouted at the donkeys, who looked at him balefully before they began to move slowly out of the way. Then, sitting back in his seat, he turned to Mma Ramotswe. "I think I will do it, Mma. I think that maybe it is a good idea to help the orphan farm. We should all do that we can."

WHEN MMA RAMOTSWE returned to Zebra Drive it was already beginning to get dark. Mr J.L.B. Matekoni's truck was parked at the side of the house, in the special spot that she had set aside for him, and she tucked the tiny white van into its own place near the kitchen door. Lights were on in the house, and she heard the sound of voices. They would be wondering, she thought, where she was, and they would be hungry.

She went into the kitchen, kicking off her shoes as she entered. Motholeli was in her wheelchair, behind the kitchen table, chopping carrots, and Puso was stirring something on the stove. Mr J.L.B. Matekoni, standing just behind the boy, was dropping a pinch of salt into the mixture in the pot.

"We are cooking your dinner tonight," said Mr J.L.B. Matekoni. "You can go and sit down, with your feet on a stool. We will call you when everything is ready."

Mma Ramotswe gave a cry of delight. "That is a very big treat for me," she said. "I am very tired for some reason."

She went through to the sitting room and dropped into her favourite chair. Although the children helped in the kitchen, it was unusual for them to cook a full meal. It must have been Mr J.L.B. Matekoni's idea, she reflected, and the thought filled her with gratitude that she had such a man who would think to cook a meal. Most husbands would never do that—would regard it as beneath their dignity to work in the house—but Mr J.L.B. Matekoni was different. It was as if he knew what it was like to be a woman, to have all that cooking to do, for the rest of one's life, a whole procession of pots and pans stretching out into the distance, seemingly endless. Women knew all about that, and dreamed about cooking and pots and the like, but here was a man who seemed to understand.

When they sat down to table half an hour later, Mma Ramotswe watched proudly as Mr J.L.B. Matekoni and Puso brought in the plates of good rich food and set them at each place. Then she said grace, as she always did, her eyes lowered to the tablecloth, as was proper.

"May the Lord look down kindly on Botswana," said Mma

Ramotswe. "And now we thank Him for the food on our plates which has been cooked so well." She paused. There was more to be said about that, but for the time being she felt that what she had said was enough and since everybody was very hungry they should all begin.

"This is very good," she said after the first mouthful. "I am very happy that I have such good cooks right here in my own house."

"It was Mr J.L.B. Matekoni's idea," said Motholeli. "Maybe he could start a Tlokweng Road Speedy Restaurant."

Mr J.L.B. Matekoni laughed. "I could not do that. I am only good at fixing cars. That is all I can do."

"But you can jump by parachute," said Motholeli. "You can do that too. They were talking about it at school."

There was a sudden silence, and it seemed as if a cloud had passed over the gathering. Mr J.L.B. Matekoni's fork paused where it was, half way to his mouth, and Mma Ramotswe's knife stopped cutting into a large piece of pumpkin. She looked up at Mr J.L.B. Matekoni, who held her glance only for a moment before he looked away.

"Oh that," said Mma Ramotswe. "That is all a mistake. Mr J.L.B. Matekoni was going to do a parachute jump, but now Charlie, the apprentice at the garage, has offered to do it instead. I have already spoken to Mma Potokwane about it and she is very pleased with the new arrangements. She said that she was sure that Mr J.L.B. Matekoni would want to give that young man a chance, and I said I would ask him what he thought."

They all looked at Mr J.L.B. Matekoni, whose eyes had opened wide as Mma Ramotswe spoke.

"Well?" said Mma Ramotswe, returning to her task of cutting the pumpkin. "What would you like to do, Mr J.L.B. Matekoni? Would you like to give that boy a chance?"

Mr J.L.B. Matekoni looked up at the ceiling. "I could do, I suppose," he said.

"Good," said Mma Ramotswe. "You are a very generous man. Charlie will be very pleased."

Mr J.L.B. Matekoni smiled. "It is nothing," he said. "Nothing."

They continued with the meal. Mma Ramotswe noticed that Mr J.L.B. Matekoni appeared to be in a very good mood and made several amusing remarks about the day's events, including a joke about a gearbox, which they all laughed at but which none of them understood. Then, when the plates were cleared away and the children were out of the room, Mr J.L.B. Matekoni left his chair and, standing over Mma Ramotswe's chair, he took her hand and said, "You are a kind woman, Mma Ramotswe, and I am very lucky to have found a lady like you. My life is a very happy one now."

"And I am happy too," said Mma Ramotswe. She was not going to be a widow after all, and she had managed to make it seem as if it had been his decision. That was what men liked— she was sure of it—and why should men not be allowed to think that they were getting what they liked, occasionally at least? She saw no reason why not.

MR J.L.B. MATEKONI'S DREAM

MR J.L.B. Matekoni was, of course, immensely relieved that Mma Ramotswe had presented him with the opportunity to withdraw from the parachute jump. She had done it so graciously, and so cleverly, that he had been saved all embarrassment. Throughout that day he had been plagued by anxiety as he reflected on the position in which Mma Potokwane had placed him. He was not a cowardly man, but he had felt nothing but fear, sheer naked fear, when he thought about the parachute jump. Eventually, by mid-afternoon, he had reached the conclusion that this was going to be the way in which he would die, and he had spent almost an hour thinking about the terms of a will which he would draw up the following day. Mma Ramotswe would get the garage, naturally, and she could run it with Mma Makutsi, who could become Manager again. His house would be sold—it would get a very good price—and the money could then be distributed amongst his cousins, who were not well-off and who would be able to use it to buy cattle. Mma Ramotswe should keep some of it, perhaps as much as half, as this would help to keep the children, who were his responsibility after all. And then there was his truck, which could go to the orphan farm, where a good use would be found for it.

At this point he stopped. Leaving the truck to the orphan farm was tantamount to leaving it to Mma Potokwane, and he was not at all sure whether this was what he wanted. It was Mma Potokwane, after all, who had caused this crisis in the first place and he saw no reason why she should profit from it. In one view of the matter, Mma Potokwane would be responsible for his death, and perhaps she should even be put on trial. That would teach her to push people around as she did. That would be a lesson to all powerful matrons, and he suspected that there were many such women. Men would simply have to fight back, and this could be done, on their behalf, by the Attorney-General of Botswana himself, who could start a show trial of Mma Poto-kwane—for homicide—for the sake of all men. That would at least be a start.

Such unworthy thoughts were now no longer necessary, and after that glorious release pronounced by Mma Ramotswe at the dinner table, Mr J.L.B. Matekoni felt no need to plan his will. That night, after he had returned to his house near the old Botswana Defence Force Club, he contemplated his familiar possessions, not with the eye of one who was planning their testamentary disposal, but with the relief of one who knew that he was not soon to be separated from them. He looked at his sofa, with its stained arms and cushions, and thought about the long Saturday afternoons that he had spent just sitting there, listening to the radio and thinking about nothing in particular. Then he looked at the velvet picture of a mountain that hung on the wall opposite the sofa. That was a fine picture which must have taken the artist a great deal of time to make. Mr J.L.B. Matekoni knew every detail of it. All of this would go over to Mma Ramotswe's house one of these days, but for the time being it was reassuring to see things so firmly and predictably in their proper place.

It was almost midnight by the time Mr J.L.B. Matekoni went to bed. He read the paper for a few minutes before he put out the light, drowsily dropping the paper by his bedside, and then, enveloped in darkness, he drifted into the sleep that had always come so easily to him after a day of hard work. Sleep was welcome; the nightmare that he had experienced had been a diurnal one, and now it was resolved. There was to be no drop, no plummet to the ground, no humiliation as his fear made itself manifest to all . . .

That was in the waking world; the sleeping world of Mr J.L.B. Matekoni had not caught up with the events of that evening, with the release from his torment, and at some point that night, he found himself standing on the edge of the tarmac at the airport, with a small white plane of the sort used by the Kalahari Flying Club taxi-ing towards him. A door of the plane was opened, and he was beckoned within by the pilot, who, as it happened, was Mma Potokwane herself.

"Get in, Mr J.L.B. Matekoni," shouted Mma Potokwane above the noise of the engine. She seemed vaguely annoyed that he was holding things up in some way, and Mr J.L.B. Matekoni obeyed, as he always did.

Mma Potokwane seemed quite confident, leaning forward to flick switches and adjust instruments. Mr J.L.B. Matekoni reached to touch a switch that appeared to need attention, as an orange light was flashing behind it, but his hand was brushed away by Mma Potokwane.

"Don't touch!" she shouted, as if addressing an orphan. "Dangerous!"

He sat back, and the little plane shot forward down the runway. The trees were so close, he thought, the grass so soft that he could jump out now, roll over, and escape; but there was no getting away from Mma Potokwane, who looked at him crossly and shook a finger in admonition. And then they were airborne, and he looked out of the window of the plane at the land below him, which was growing smaller and smaller, a miniaturised Botswana of cattle like ants and roads like thin strips of twisting brown thread. Oh, it was so beautiful to look down on his land and see the clouds and the blue and all the air. One might so easily step out onto such clouds and drift away, off to the West, over the great brown, and alight somewhere where the lions walked and where there were springs of water and tall trees and little sign of man.

Mma Potokwane pulled on the controls of the plane and they circled, hugging the edge of the town so far below. He looked down and he saw Zebra Drive; it was so easy to spot it, and was that not Mma Ramotswe waving to him from her yard, and Mma Makutsi, in her new green shoes? They were waving, smiling up at him, pointing to a place on the ground where he might land. He turned to Mma Potokwane, who smiled at him now and pointed to the handle of the door.

He reached out and no more than touched the door before it flew open. He felt the wind on his face, and the panic rose in him, and he tried to stop himself falling, holding onto one of the levers in the plane, a little thing that gave him no purchase. Mma Potokwane was shouting at him, taking her hands off the controls of the plane to shove him out, and now kicked him firmly in the back with those flat brown shoes which she wore to walk about the orphan farm. "Out!" she cried, and Mr J.L.B. Matekoni, mute with fear, slipped out into the empty air and tumbled, head over heels, now looking at the sky, now at the ground, down to the earth that was still so far away beneath him.

There was no parachute, of course, just pyjamas, and they were billowing about him, hardly slowing him up at all. *This is how it ends*, thought Mr J.L.B. Matekoni, and he began to think of how good life had been, and how precious; but he could not think of these things for long, for his fall was over in seconds and he landed on his feet, perfectly, as if he might have hopped off an old orange box at the garage; and there he was, out in the bush, beside a termite mound. He looked about him; it was an unfamiliar landscape, perhaps Tlokweng, perhaps not, and he was studying it when he heard his father's voice behind him. He turned round, but there was no sign of his father, who was there but not quite there, in the way in which the dead can come to us in our dreams. There was much that he wanted to ask his father, there was much that he wanted to tell him about the garage, but his father spoke first, in a voice which was strange and reedy—for a dead man has no breath to make a voice—and asked a question which woke up Mr J.L.B. Matekoni, wrenching him from his dream with its satisfactory soft landing by the termite mound.

"When are you going to marry Mma Ramotswe?" asked his father. "Isn't it about time?"

CHAPTER ELEVEN

MEETING MR BOBOLOGO

MMA RAMOTSWE had not been ignoring Mma Holonga's case. It was true that she had as yet done nothing, but that did not mean that she had not been thinking about how she would approach this delicate issue. It would not do for any of the men to discover that they were being investigated, as this would give offence and could easily drive away any genuine suitor. This meant that she would have to make enquiries with discretion, talking to people who knew these men and, if at all possible, engineering a meeting with them herself. That would require a pretext, but she was confident that one could be found.

The first thing she would have to do, she thought, was to talk to somebody who worked at Mr Bobologo's school. This was not difficult, as Mma Ramotswe's maid, Rose, had a cousin who had for many years been in charge of the school kitchen. She had stopped working now, and was living in Old Naledi, where she looked after the children of one of her sons. Mma Ramotswe had never met her, but Rose had mentioned her from time to time and assured her employer that a visit would be welcome.

"She is one of these people who is always talking," said Rose.

"She talks all day, even if nobody listens to her. She will be very happy to talk to you."

"Such people are very helpful in our work," said Mma Ramotswe. "They tell us things we need to know."

"This is such a lady," said Rose. "She will tell you everything she knows. It makes her very happy to do that. You will need a long, long time."

There were many people like that in Botswana, Mma Ramotswe reflected, and she was glad that this was so. It would be strange to live in a country where people were silent, passing one another in the street wordlessly, as if frightened of what the other might think or say. This was not the African way, where people would call out and converse with one another from opposite sides of a road, or across a wide expanse of bush, careless of who heard. Such conversations could be carried on by people walking in different directions, until voices grew too faint and too distant to be properly heard and words were swallowed by the sky. That was a good way of parting from a friend, so less abrupt than words of farewell followed by silence. Mma Ramotswe herself often shouted out to the children after they had left the house for school, reminding Puso to be careful of how he crossed the road or telling him to make sure that his shoelaces were tied properly, not that boys ever bothered about that sort of thing. Nor did boys ensure that their shirts were tucked into their trousers properly, but that was another issue which she could think about later, when the demands of clients were less pressing.

Rose's cousin, Mma Seeonyana, was at home when Mma Ramotswe called on her. Her house was not a large one—no more than two small rooms, Mma Ramotswe saw—but her yard was scrupulously clean, with circles traced in the sand by her wide-headed broom. This was a good sign; an untidy yard was a sign of a woman who no longer bothered with the traditional Botswana virtues, and such people, Mma Ramotswe found, were almost always unreliable or rude. They had no idea of *botho,* which meant respect or good manners. *Botho* set Botswana apart from other places; it was what made it a special place. There were people who mocked it, of course, but what precisely did they want instead? Did they want people to be selfish? Did they want them to treat others unkindly? Because if you forgot about *botho,* then that was surely what would happen; Mma Ramotswe was sure of that.

She saw Mma Seeonyana standing outside her front door, a brown paper bag in her hand. As she parked the tiny white van at the edge of the road, she noticed the older woman watching her. This was another good sign. It was a traditional Botswana pursuit to watch other people and wonder what they were up to; this modern habit of indifference to others was very hard to understand. If you watched people, then it was a sign that you cared about them, that you were not treating them as complete strangers. Again, it was all a question of manners.

Mma Ramotswe stood at the gate and called out to Mma Seeonyana. The other woman responded immediately, and warmly, inviting Mma Ramotswe to come in and sit with her at the back of the house, where it was shadier. She did not ask her visitor what she wanted, but welcomed her, as if she were a friend or neighbour who had called in for a chat.

"You are the woman who lives over that way, on Zebra Drive," said Mma Seeonyana. "You are the woman who employs Rose. She has told me about you."

Mma Ramotswe was surprised that she had been recognised, but further explanation was quickly provided. "Your van is very well-known," said Mma Seeonyana. "Rose told me about it, and I have seen you driving through town. I have often thought: I would like to get to know that lady, but I never thought I would have the chance. I am very happy to see you here, Mma."

"I have heard of you too," said Mma Ramotswe. "Rose has spoken very well of you. She was very proud that you were in charge of those school kitchens."

Mma Seeonyana laughed. "When I was in that place I was feeding four hundred children every day," she said. "Now I am feeding two little boys. It is much easier."

"That is what we women must do all the time," said Mma Ramotswe. "I am feeding three people now. I have a fiancé and I have two children who are adopted and who come from the orphan farm. I have to make many meals. It seems that women have been put in the world to cook and keep the yard tidy. Sometimes I think that is very unfair and must be changed."

Mma Seeonyana agreed with this view of the world, but frowned when she thought of the implications. "The trouble is that men would never be able to do what we do," she said. "Most men will just not cook. They are too lazy. They would rather go hungry than cook. That is a big problem for us women. If we started to do other things, then the men would fade away and die of hunger. That is the problem."

"We could train them," said Mma Ramotswe. "There is much to be said for training men."

"But you have to find a man to train," said Mma Seeonyana. "And they just run away if you try to tell them what to do. I have had three men run away from me. They said that I talked too much and that they had no peace. But that is not true."

Mma Ramotswe clicked her tongue in sympathy. "No, Mma, it cannot be true. But sometimes men seem not to like us to talk to them. They think they have already heard what we have to say."

Mma Seeonyana sighed. "They are very foolish."

"Yes," said Mma Ramotswe. Some men were foolish, she

thought, but by no means all. And there were some very foolish women too, if one thought about it.

"Even teachers," said Mma Seeonyana. "Even teachers can be foolish sometimes."

Mma Ramotswe looked up sharply. "You must have known many teachers, Mma," she said. "When you were working in that place you must have known all the teachers."

"Oh I did," said Mma Seeonyana. "I knew many teachers. I saw them come as junior teachers and I saw them get promotion and become senior teachers. I saw all that happening. And I saw some very bad teachers too."

Mma Ramotswe affected surprise. "Bad teachers, Mma? Surely not."

"Oh yes," said Mma Seeonyana. "I was astonished over what I found out. But I suppose teachers are the same as anybody else and they can be bad sometimes."

Mma Ramotswe looked down at the ground. "Who were these bad teachers?" she asked. "And why were they bad?"

Mma Seeonyana shook her head. "They came and went," she said. "I do not remember all their names. But I do remember a man who came to the school for six months and then the police took him away. They said he had done a very bad thing, but they never told us what it was."

Mma Ramotswe shook her head. "That must have been very bad." She paused, and then, "The good teachers must have been ashamed. Teachers like Mr Bobologo, for example. He's a good teacher, isn't he?"

She had not expected the reply, which was a peal of laughter. "Oh that one! Yes, Mma. He's very good all right."

Mma Ramotswe waited for something more to be said, but Mma Seeonyana merely smiled, as if she were recalling some private, amusing memory. She would have to winkle this out without giving the impression of being too interested. "Oh," she said. "So he's a ladies' man, is he? I might have suspected it. There are so many ladies' men these days. I am surprised that there are any ordinary husbands left at all."

This brought forth another burst of laughter from Mma Seeonyana, who wiped at her eyes with the cuff of her blouse. "A ladies' man, Mma? Yes, I suppose you could say that! A ladies' man! Yes. Mr Bobologo would be very pleased to hear that, Mma."

Mma Ramotswe felt a momentary irritation with Mma Seeonyana. It was discourteous, in her view, to make vague allusions in one's conversation with another—allusions which the other could not understand. There was nothing more frustrating than trying to work out what another person was saying in the face of coyness or even deliberate obfuscation. If there was something which Mma Seeonyana wanted to say about Mr Bobologo, then she should say it directly rather than hinting at some private knowledge.

"Well, Mma," said Mma Ramotswe in a firm tone. "Is Mr Bobologo a ladies' man, or is he not?"

Mma Seeonyana stared at her. She was still smiling, but she had picked up the note of irritation in her visitor's voice and the smile was fading. "I'm sorry, Mma," she said. "I didn't mean to laugh like that. It's just that . . . well, it's just that you touched upon a very funny thing with that man. He is a ladies' man, but only in a very special sense. That was what was so funny."

Mma Ramotswe nodded encouragingly. "In what sense is he a ladies' man then?"

Mma Seeonyana chuckled. "He is one of those men who is worried about street ladies. These bad girls who hang about in bars. That sort of woman. He disapproves of them very strongly and he and some friends of his have been trying for years to save these girls from their bad ways. It is his hobby. He goes to the bus station and hands leaflets to young girls coming in from the villages. He warns them about what can happen in Gaborone."

Mma Ramotswe narrowed her eyes. This was very interesting information, but it was difficult to see what exactly it told her. Everybody was aware of the problem of bar girls, who were the scourge of Africa. It was sad to see them, dressed in their shoddy finery, flirting with older men who should know better, but who almost inevitably did not. Nobody liked this, but most people did nothing about it. At least Mr Bobologo and his friends were trying.

"It's a hopeless task," Mma Seeonyana continued. "They have set up some sort of place where these girls can go and live while they try to get honest jobs. It is over there by the African Mall." She stopped and looked at Mma Ramotswe. "But I'm sure that you didn't come here to talk about Mr Bobologo, Mma. There are better things to talk about."

Mma Ramotswe smiled. "I have been very happy to talk about him," she replied. "But if there are other things you would like to talk about, I am happy with that."

Mma Seeonyana sighed. "There are so many things to talk about, Mma. I don't really know where to start."

This, thought Mma Ramotswe, was a good cue, and she took it. She remembered Rose's warning, and she could see the afternoon, her precious Sunday afternoon, disappearing before her. "Well, I could always come back to visit you, Mma . . ."

"No," said Mma Seeonyana quickly. "You must stay, Mma. I will make you some tea and then I can tell you about something that has been happening around here that is very strange."

"You are very kind, Mma."

Mma Ramotswe sat down on the battered chair which Mma Seeonyana had pulled out of the doorway. This was duty, she supposed, and there were more uncomfortable ways of earning a living than listening to ladies like Mma Seeonyana gossiping about neighbourhood affairs. And one never knew what one might learn from such conversations. It was her duty to keep herself informed, as one could not tell when some snippet of information gathered in such a way would prove useful; just as the information about Mr Bobologo and the bar girls might prove useful, or might not. It was difficult to tell.

MMA MAKUTSI was also busy that Sunday, not on the affairs of the No. 1 Ladies' Detective Agency, but on the move to her new house. The simplest way of doing this would have been to ask Mma Ramotswe to bring her tiny white van to carry over her possessions, but she was unwilling to impose in this way. Mma Ramotswe was generous with her time, and would have readily agreed to help her, but Mma Makutsi was independent and decided to hire a truck and a driver for the hour or so it would take to move her effects to their new home. There was not much to move, after all: her bed, with its thin coir mattress which she would soon replace, her single chair, her black tin trunk with her clothes folded within it, and a box containing her shoes, her pot, pan, and small primus stove. These were the worldly goods of Mma Makutsi which were quickly piled up in the back of the truck by the muscular young man who drove up the bumpy track that morning.

"You have packed this well," he said, making conversation as they drove the short distance to her new house. "I move things for people all the time. But they often have many boxes and plastic bags full of things. Sometimes they also have a grandmother to be moved, and I have to put the old lady in the back of the truck with all the other things."

"That is no way to treat a grandmother," said Mma Makutsi. "The grandmother should ride in the front."

"I agree, Mma," said the young man. "Those people who put their grandmother in the back of the truck, they will feel sorry when the grandmother is late. They will remember that they put her in the back of the truck, and it will be too late to do anything about it."

Mma Makutsi replied to this observation civilly, and the rest of the journey was completed in silence. She had the key of the house in the pocket of her blouse and she felt for it from time to time just to reassure herself that it was really there. She was thinking, too, of how she would arrange the furniture—such as it was—and how she might see about a rug for her new bedroom. That was a previously undreamed-of luxury; she had woken every day of her life to a packed earth floor or to plain concrete. Now she might afford a rug which would feel so soft underfoot, like a covering of new grass. She closed her eyes and thought of what lay ahead—the luxury of having her own shower—with hot water!—and the pleasure, the sheer pleasure, of having an extra room in which she could entertain people if she wished. She could invite friends to have a meal with her, and nobody would have to sit on a bed or look at her tin trunk. She could buy a radio and they could listen to music together, Mma Makutsi and her friends, and they would talk about important things, and all the humiliations of the shared stand-pipe would be a thing of the past.

She kept her eyes closed until they were almost there and then opened them and saw the house, which seemed smaller now than she had remembered it, but which was still so beautiful in her eyes, with its sloping roof and its paw-paw trees.

"This is your place, Mma?" asked the driver.

"It's my house," said Mma Makutsi, savouring the words.

"You're lucky," said the young man. "This is a good place to live. How many pula is the rent? What do you pay?"

Mma Makutsi told him and he whistled. "That is a lot! I

could not afford a place like this. I have to live in half a room over that way, half way to Molepolole."

"That cannot be easy," said Mma Makutsi.

They drew up in front of the gate, and Mma Makutsi walked down the short path that led to the front door. She had that door, and the part of the house which was lived in by the other tenants was reached by the door at the back. She felt proud that the front door was hers, even if it looked as if it was in need of a coat of paint. That could be dealt with later; what counted now was that she had the key to this door in her hand, paid for by the first month's rent, and hers by right.

It took the young man very little time to move her possessions into the front room. She thanked him, and gave him a ten-pula tip—overly generous, perhaps, but she was a proper householder now and these things would be expected of her. As she handed over the money, which he took from her with a wide smile, she reflected on the fact that she had never done this before. She had never before been in a position where she had given largesse, and the thought struck her forcibly. It was an unfamiliar, slightly uncomfortable feeling; I am just Mma Makutsi, from Bobonong, and I am giving this young man a ten-pula note. I have more money than he has. I have a better house. I am where he would like to be, but isn't.

By herself now, in the house, Mma Makutsi moved about her two rooms. She touched the walls; they were solid. She loosened a window latch, letting in a warm breeze for a moment, and then closed the window again. She switched on a light, and a bulb glowed above her; she turned on a tap, and water, fresh, cold water came out and splashed into a stainless steel sink, so polished and shiny that she could see her face reflected at her, the face of a person who was looking at the world with the cautious wonder of ownership, or at least of something close to it, of tenancy.

There was a side door to the house, and she opened this and peered out onto the yard. The paw-paw trees had incipient fruit upon them, which would be ready in a month or so. There were one or two other plants, shrubs that had wilted in the heat but which had the dogged determination of indigenous Botswana vegetation. These would survive even if never watered; they would cling on in the dry ground, making the most of what little moisture they could draw from the soil, tenacious because they lived here in this dry country, and had always lived here. Mma Ramotswe had once described the traditional plants of Botswana as loyal and yes, that was right, thought Mma Makutsi, that is what they are—our old friends, our fellow survivors in this brown land that I love and love so much. Not that she thought about that love very often, but it was there, as it was in the hearts of all Batswana. And that was surely what most people wanted, at the end of the day; to live on the land that they love, and nowhere else; to be where their people had been before them, as long as anybody could remember.

She drew back from the door, and looked about her house again. She did not see the grubby finger marks on the wall, nor the place where the floor had buckled. What she saw was a room with bright curtains and with friends about a table, and herself at the head; what she heard was a pot of water boiling on a stove, to the soft hissing of a flame.

MR BOBOLOGO TALKS ON THE SUBJECT
OF LOOSE WOMEN

THE FACT that the schools were on holiday was convenient. Had Mr Bobologo been teaching, then Mma Ramotswe would have been obliged to wait until half past three, when she could have accosted him on his way to the house that he occupied in the neat row of teachers' houses at the back of the school. As it was, that Monday she was able to arrive at his house at ten o'clock and find him, as Mma Seeonyana said she would, sitting on a chair in the sun outside his back door, a Bible on his lap. She approached him carefully, as one always should when coming across somebody reading the Bible, and greeted him in the approved, traditional fashion. Had he slept well? Was he well? Would he mind if she talked to him?

Mr Bobologo looked up at her, squinting against the sunlight, and Mma Ramotswe saw a tall man of slim build, carefully dressed in khaki trousers and an open-necked white shirt, and wearing a pair of round, pebble-lensed glasses. Everything about him, from the carefully polished brown shoes to the powerful glasses, said *teacher*, and she had to make an effort to prevent herself from smiling. People were so predictable, she thought, so true to type. Bank managers dressed exactly as bank managers were expected to dress—and behaved accordingly; you could always tell a lawyer from that careful, rather watchful way they listened to what you had to say, as if they were ready to pounce on the slightest slip; and, since she had come to know Mr J.L.B. Matekoni, there was no mistaking mechanics, who looked at things as if they were ready to take them apart and make them work better. Not that this applied to all mechanics, of course; the apprentices would be mechanics before too long and yet they looked at things as if they were about to break them. So perhaps it took years before a calling began to tell on a person.

Did she look like a detective, she wondered? This was an intriguing question. If somebody saw her in the street, they would probably not look twice at her. She was just an ordinary Motswana lady, in the traditional mould, going about her daily business as so many other women did. Surely nobody would suspect her of *watching*, which is what she had to do in her job. Perhaps it was different with Mma Makutsi, with those large glasses of hers. People noticed those glasses and clearly thought about them. They might wonder, might they not, why somebody would need such large glasses and they might conclude that this was because she was interested in looking closely at things, at magnifying them. That, of course, was an absurd vision of what she and Mma Makutsi did; they very rarely had to examine any physical objects—human behaviour was what interested them, and all that this required was observation and understanding.

Her observation of Mr Bobologo lasted only a few seconds. Now he stood up, closing the Bible with some regret, as one might close a riveting novel in which one had become immersed. Of course Mr Bobologo would know the end of the story—which was not a happy ending, if one thought about it carefully—but one might still be absorbed even in the completely familiar.

"I am sorry to disturb you," said Mma Ramotswe. "The school

holidays must be a good time for you teachers to catch up on your reading. You will not like people coming along and disturbing you."

Mr Bobologo responded well to this courteous beginning. "I am happy to see you, Mma. There will be plenty of time for reading later on. You may sit on this chair and I will fetch another."

Mma Ramotswe sat on the teacher's chair and waited for him to return. It was a good spot that he had chosen to sit, hidden from passers-by on the road, but with a view of the children's playground where even now in the holidays the children of the school staff were engaged in some complicated game with a ball. It would be good to sit here, she thought, knowing that the Government was still paying one's salary every month, and that reading, and becoming wiser and wiser, was exactly what one was expected to do.

Mr Bobologo returned with another chair and seated himself opposite Mma Ramotswe. He looked at her through the thick lenses of his spectacles, and then dabbed gently at the side of his mouth with a white handkerchief, which he then folded neatly and placed in the pocket of his shirt.

Mma Ramotswe looked back at him and smiled. Her initial impression of Mr Bobologo had been favourable, but she found herself wondering why it was that a successful, rather elegant person such as Mma Holonga should take up with this teacher, who, whatever his merits might be, was hardly a romantic figure. But such speculation was inevitably fruitless. The choices that people made in such circumstances were often inexplicable, and perhaps it was no more than sheer chance. If you were in the mood for falling in love, or marrying, then perhaps it did not matter very much whom you would see when you turned the corner. You were looking for somebody, and there was somebody, and you would convince yourself that this random person was what you were really looking for in the first place. *We find what we are looking for in life*, her father had once said to her; which was true—if you look for happiness, you will see it; if you look for distrust and envy and hatred—all those things—you will find those too.

"So, Mma," said Mr Bobologo. "Here I am. You have come to see me about your child, I assume. I hope I can say that this boy or this girl is doing well at school. I am sure I can. But first you must tell me what your name is, so I know which child it is that I am talking about. That is important."

For a few moments Mma Ramotswe was taken aback, but then she laughed. "Oh no, Rra. Do not worry. I am not some troublesome mother who has come to talk about her difficult child. I have come because I have heard of your other work."

Mr Bobologo took out his handkerchief and dabbed again at the side of his mouth.

"I see," he said. "You have heard of this work that I do." There was a note of suspicion in his voice, Mma Ramotswe noticed, and she wondered why this should be. Perhaps he was laughed at by others, or labelled a prude, and the thought irritated her. There was nothing to be ashamed of in the work that he did, even if it seemed strange for a man to have such strong views on such a matter. At least he was trying to help address a social problem, which was more than most people did.

"I have heard of it," said Mma Ramotswe. "And I thought that I would like to hear more about it. It is a good thing that you are doing, Rra."

Mr Bobologo's expression remained impassive. Mma Ramotswe thought that he was still unconvinced by what she had said, and so she continued, "The problem of these street girls is a very big one, Rra. Every time I see them going into bars, I think: *That girl is somebody's daughter*, and that makes me sad. That is what I think, Rra."

These words had a marked effect on Mr Bobologo. While she

was still speaking, he sat up in his chair, sharply, and stared intensely at Mma Ramotswe.

"You are right, Mma," he said. "They are all the daughters of some poor person. They are all children who have been loved by their parents, and by God himself, and now where are they? In bars! That is where. Or in the arms of some man. That is also where." He paused, looking down at the ground. "I am sorry to use such strong language, Mma. I am not a man who uses strong language, but when it comes to this matter, then I am like a dog who has been kicked in the ribs."

Mma Ramotswe nodded. "It is something that should make us all angry."

"Yes," said Mr Bobologo. "It should. It should. But what does the Government do about this? Do you see the Government going down to these bars and chasing these bad girls back to their villages? Do you see that, Mma?"

Mma Ramotswe mused for a moment. There were many things, she thought, that one could reasonably expect the Government to do, but it had never occurred to her that chasing bar girls back to their villages was one of them. For a moment she imagined the Minister of Roads, for example, a portly man who inevitably wore a wide-brimmed hat to shade him from the sun, chasing bar girls down the road to Lobatse, followed, perhaps, by his Under-Secretary and several clerks from the Ministry. It was an intriguing picture, and one which would normally have made her smile, but there was no question of smiling now, in front of the righteous indignation of Mr Bobologo.

"So I decided—together with some friends," continued Mr Bobologo, "that we should do something ourselves. And that is how we started the House of Hope."

Mma Ramotswe listened politely as Mr Bobologo listed the

difficulties he had encountered in finding a suitable building for
the House of Hope and how eventually they had obtained a
ruinously expensive lease on a house near the African Mall. It
had three bedrooms and a living room which was not enough, he
explained, for the fourteen girls who lived there. "Sometimes we
have even had as many as twenty bad girls in that place," he said.
"Twenty girls, Mma! All under one roof. When it is that full, then
there is not enough room for anybody to do anything. They must
sleep on the floor and doubled-up in bunks. That is not a good
thing, because when things get that crowded they run away and
we have to look for them again and persuade them to come back.
It is very trying."

Mma Ramotswe was intrigued. If the girls ran away, then it
implied that they were kept there against their will, which surely
could not be the case. You could keep children in one place
against their will, but you could not do that to bar girls, if they
were over eighteen. There were obviously details of the House of
Hope which would require further investigation.

"Would you show me this place, Rra?" she asked. "I can drive
you down there in my van if you would show me. Then I will be
able to understand the work that you are doing."

Mr Bobologo seemed to weigh this request for a moment, but
then he rose to his feet, taking his glasses off and stowing them in
his top pocket. "I am happy to do that, Mma. I am happy for
people to see what we are doing so that they may tell other people
about it. Perhaps they will even tell the Government and persuade them to give us money so that we can run the House of
Hope on a proper basis. There is never ever enough money, and
we have to rely on what we can get from churches and some
generous people. The Government should pay for this, but do
they help us? The answer to that, Mma, is no. The Government
is not concerned about the welfare of ladies in this country. They

think only of new roads and new buildings. That is what they think of."

"It is very unfair," agreed Mma Ramotswe. "I also have a list of things that I think the Government should do."

"Oh yes?" said Mr Bobologo. "And what is on your list, Mma?"

This question caught Mma Ramotswe by surprise. She had spoken of her list idly, as a conversational ploy; there was no list, really.

"So?" pressed Mr Bobologo. "So what is on this list of yours, Mma?"

Mma Ramotswe thought wildly. "I would like to see boys taught how to sew at school," she said. "That is on my list."

Mr Bobologo stared at her. "But that is not possible, Mma," he said dismissively. "That is not something that boys wish to learn. I am not surprised that the Government is not trying to teach boys this thing. You cannot teach boys to be girls. That is not good for boys."

"But boys wear clothes, do they not, Rra?" countered Mma Ramotswe. "And if these clothes are torn, then who is there to sew them up?"

"There are girls to do that," said Mr Bobologo. "There are girls and ladies. There are plenty of people in Botswana to do all the necessary sewing. That is a fact. I am a very experienced teacher and I know about these matters. Do you have anything else on your list, Mma?"

There would have been a time when Mma Ramotswe would not have allowed this to pass, but she was on duty now, and there was no need to antagonise Mr Bobologo. She owed it to her client to find out more about him, and that was a more immediate duty than her duty to the women of Botswana. So she merely looked up at the sky, as if looking for inspiration.

"I would like the Government to do many things," she said. "But I do not want to make them too tired. So I shall have to think about my list and make it a bit smaller."

Mr Bobologo looked at her approvingly. "I think that is very wise, Mma. If one asks for too many things at the same time, then one does not usually get them. If you ask for one thing, then you may get that one thing. That is what I have found in life."

"Ow!" exclaimed Mma Ramotswe. "You are a clever man, Rra!"

Mr Bobologo acknowledged the compliment with a brief nod of the head, and then indicated that he was now ready to follow Mma Ramotswe to the van. She stood aside and invited him to precede her, as was proper when dealing with a teacher. Whatever Mr Bobologo might prove to be like, he was first and foremost a teacher, and Mma Ramotswe believed very strongly that teachers should be treated with respect, as they always had been before the old Botswana morality had started to unravel. Now people treated teachers like anybody else, which was a grave mistake; no wonder children were so cheeky and ill-behaved. A society that undermined its teachers and their authority only dug away at its own sure foundations. Mma Ramotswe thought this was obvious; the astonishing thing was that many people simply did not understand that this was the case. But there was a great deal that people did not understand and would only learn through bitter experience. In her view, one of these things was the truth of the old African saying that it takes an entire village to raise a child. Of course it does; of course it does. Everybody in a village had a role to play in bringing up a child—and cherishing it—and in return that child would in due course feel responsible for everybody in that village. That is what makes life in society possible. We must love one another and help one another in our daily lives. That was the traditional African way and there was no substitute for it. None.

IT WAS only a few minutes' drive from the teachers' quarters to the House of Hope, a drive during which Mr Bobologo held on firmly to the side of the passenger seat, as if fearing that any moment Mma Ramotswe would steer the tiny white van off the road. Mma Ramotswe noticed this, but said nothing; there were some men who would never be happy with women drivers, even although the statistics were plain for them to see. Women had fewer accidents because they drove more sedately and were not trying to prove anything to anybody. It was men who were the reckless drivers—particularly young men (such as the apprentices) who felt that girls would be more impressed by speed than by safety. And it was young men in red cars who were the most dangerous of all. Such people were best given a wide berth, both in and out of the car.

"That is the House of Hope," said Mr Bobologo. "You can park under the tree here. Carefully, Mma. You do not wish to hit the tree. Careful!"

"I have never hit a tree in my life," retorted Mma Ramotswe. "But I have known many men who have hit trees, Rra. Some of those men are late now."

"It may not have been their fault," muttered Mr Bobologo.

"Yes," said Mma Ramotswe evenly. "It could have been the fault of the trees. That is always possible."

She was incensed by his remark and struggled to contain her anger. Unfortunately, her battle with her righteous indignation overcame her judgment, and she hit the tree; not hard, but with enough of a jolt to make Mr Bobologo grab onto his seat once again.

"There," he said, turning to her in triumph. "You have hit the tree, Mma."

Mma Ramotswe turned off the engine and closed her eyes. Clovis Andersen, author of her professional vade mecum, *The Principles of Private Detection,* had advice which was appropriate to this occasion, and Mma Ramotswe now called it to mind. *Never allow your personal feelings to cloud the issue*, he had written. *You may be seething with anger over something, but do not— and I repeat not—do not allow it to overcome your professional judgment. Keep your calm. That is the most important thing. And if you find it difficult, close your eyes and count to ten.*

By the time she reached ten, Mr Bobologo had opened his door and was waiting for her outside. So Mma Ramotswe swallowed hard and joined him, following him up the short garden path that led to the doorway of an unexceptional white-washed house, of much the same sort as could be seen on any nearby street, and which from the road would never have been identified—without special knowledge—as a house of hope, or indeed of despair, or of anything else for that matter. It was just a house, and yet here it was, filled to the brim with bad girls.

"Here we are, Mma," said Mr Bobologo as he approached the front door. "Take up hope all you who enter here. That is what we say, and one day we shall have it written above the door."

Mma Ramotswe looked at the unprepossessing door. Her reservations about Mr Bobologo were growing, but she was not quite sure why this should be so. He was irritating, of course, but so were many people, and being irritating was not enough for him to be written off. No, there was something more than that. Was it smugness, or singularity of purpose? Perhaps that was it. It was always disconcerting to meet those who had become so obsessed with a single topic that they could not see their concerns in context. Such people were uncomfortable company purely because they lacked normal human balance, and this, she thought, might be the case with Mr Bobologo. And yet she had not been asked to find out whether Mr Bobologo was an interesting man, or even a nice man. She had been asked to find out whether he was after Mma Holonga's money. That was a very specific question, and her feelings for Mr Bobologo had nothing to do with the answer to that question. So she would give him the benefit of the doubt, and keep her personal opinions to herself. She herself would never marry Mr Bobologo—or any man like him—but it would be wrong of her to interfere until she had very concrete proof of the exact issue at stake. And that had not yet appeared, and might never appear. So for the time being, the only thing to do was to concentrate on inspecting the House of Hope and wait until Mr Bobologo put a foot wrong and gave himself away. And she had a feeling now—a fairly strong feeling—that he might never do that.

MR J.L.B. MATEKONI RECEIVES THE BUTCHER'S CAR; THE APPRENTICES RECEIVE AN ANONYMOUS LETTER

WHILE MMA RAMOTSWE was visiting Mr Bobologo and his House of Hope, Mr J.L.B. Matekoni was completing a tricky repair at Tlokweng Road Speedy Motors. He was relieved, of course, about the cancellation of the parachute jump, but at the same time he was concerned about the fact that one of the apprentices was going to do it in his stead. He knew that these boys were feckless, and he knew that they would do anything to impress girls, but he was their apprentice-master, after all, and he considered that he had a moral responsibility for them until they had served out their apprenticeship. Many people would say that this did not extend to cover what they did in their own time, but Mr J.L.B. Matekoni was not one to take a narrow view of these matters and he could not avoid feeling at least slightly paternal towards these young men, irritating though they undoubtedly were. He was not sure, though, how he could deal with this issue. If he persuaded the young man not to jump, then Mma Potokwane might insist that he do the jump after all. If she did so, then that would lead to a row between her and Mma Ramotswe, and that could become complicated. There might be no more fruit cake, for example, and he would miss his trips out to see the orphans, even if he was inevitably given some task to perform the moment he arrived at the orphan farm.

The repair took less time than he had anticipated, and well before it was time for the morning break Mr J.L.B. Matekoni found himself wiping the steering wheel and the driver's seat to make the car ready for collection by its owner. He was always very careful to ensure that cars were returned to the customer in a clean state—something he had attempted to drill into the apprentices, but without success.

"How would you feel if your car came back to you with greasy fingerprints all over it?" he said to them. "Would you like it?"

"I would not see them," said one of the young men. "I am not worried about fingerprints. As long as a car goes fast, that is the only thing."

Mr J.L.B. Matekoni could barely credit what he had heard. "Do you mean to say that the only thing that advantages is speed? Is that what you really think?"

The apprentice had looked at him blankly before he gave his reply. "Of course. If a car goes fast, then it is a good car. It has a strong engine. Everybody knows that, Boss."

Mr J.L.B. Matekoni shook his head in despair. How many times had he explained about solid engineering and the merits of a reliable gearbox? How many times had he spelled out to these young men the merits of an economical engine, particularly a good diesel engine that would give years and years of service with very little trouble? Diesel-powered cars did not usually go very fast, but that was not the point; they were good cars anyway. None of these lessons, it appeared, had sunk in. He sighed. "I have been wasting my time," he muttered. "Wasting my time."

The apprentice smiled. "Wasting your time, Boss? What have you been doing? Dancing? You and Mma Ramotswe going dancing at one of those clubs? Hah!"

Mr J.L.B. Matekoni wanted to say, "Trying to teach a hyena to dance," but did not. Where had he heard that expression before? It seemed familiar, and then he remembered he had said it himself only a few days ago when he had been discussing First Class Motors with Mma Ramotswe. The memory made him start, and put the apprentices quite out of his mind. There was something hanging over him; he had forgotten what it was, but now it came back: he still had to deal with the issue of the butcher's car, which was due to be brought into the garage that morning. The thought appalled him: he would be able to effect a temporary repair, until such time as he tracked down the right parts, but there was more to it than that. He had agreed that he would confront the Manager of First Class Motors and tell him that his wrongdoing had been discovered. He did not relish this, in view of the other man's reputation. Indeed, it might have been moderately more attractive to do a parachute jump, perhaps, rather than meet the Manager of First Class Motors.

"You look worried," said the apprentice. "Is there something troubling you, Boss?"

Mr J.L.B. Matekoni sighed. "I have an unpleasant duty to do," he said. "I have to go and speak to some bad mechanics about their work. That is what is troubling me."

"Who are these bad mechanics?" asked the apprentice.

"Those people at First Class Motors," said Mr J.L.B. Matekoni. "The man who owns it and the men who work for him. They are all bad, every one of them."

The apprentice whistled. "Yes, they are bad all right. I have seen those people. They know nothing about cars. They are not like you, Mr J.L.B. Matekoni, who knows everything about all sorts of cars."

The compliment from the apprentice was unexpected, and

Mr J.L.B. Matekoni, in spite of his modesty, was touched by the young man's tribute.

"I am not a great mechanic," he said softly. "I am just careful, that is all, and that is what I have always wanted you to be. I would want you to be careful mechanics. It would make me very happy if you would be that."

"We will be," said the apprentice. "We will try to be like you. We hope that people will always look at our work and think: they learned that from Mr J.L.B. Matekoni."

Mr J.L.B. Matekoni smiled. "*Some* of your work, maybe . . ." he began, but the apprentice interrupted him.

"You see," he said, "my father is late. He became late when I was a small boy—just that high—very small. And I did not have uncles who were any good, and so I think of you as my father, Rra. That is what I think. You are my father."

Mr J.L.B. Matekoni was silent. He had always had difficulty in expressing his emotions—as mechanics often do, he thought—and it was hard for him now. He wanted to say to this young man: What you have said makes me very proud, and very sad, all at the same time—but he could not find these words. He could, however, place a hand on the young man's shoulder and leave it there for a moment, to show that he understood what had been said.

"I have never said thank you, Rra," went on the apprentice. "And I would not want you to die without being thanked by me."

Mr J.L.B. Matekoni gave a start. "Am I going to die?" he asked. "I am not all that old surely. I am still here."

The apprentice smiled. "I did not mean that you were going to die soon, Rra. But you will die one of these days, like everybody else. And I wanted to say thank you before that day came."

"Well," said Mr J.L.B. Matekoni, "what you say is probably true, but we have spent too much time standing here talking about these things. There is work to be done in the garage. We have to get rid of that dirty oil over there. You can take it over to the special dump for burning. You can take the spare truck."

"I will do that now," said the apprentice.

"And don't pick up any girls in the truck," warned Mr J.L.B. Matekoni. "You remember what I told you about the insurance."

The apprentice, who had been already walking away, suddenly stopped in his tracks, guiltily, and Mr J.L.B. Matekoni knew immediately that this was precisely what he had been planning to do. The young man had made a moving statement, and Mr J.L.B. Matekoni had been touched by what he had said, but some things obviously never changed.

A FEW HOURS later, as the sun climbed up the sky and made shadows short and even the birds were lethargic, when the screeching of the cicadas from the bush behind Tlokweng Road Speedy Motors had reached a high insistent pitch, the butcher drew up in his handsome old Rover. He had had the time to reflect on what Mr J.L.B. Matekoni had told him, and he now spoke angrily of First Class Motors, with whom he intended to have no further dealings. Only shame, the shame of being a victim, prevented him from returning there to ask for his money back.

"I shall do that for you, Rra," said Mr J.L.B. Matekoni. "I feel responsible for what my brother mechanics have done to you."

The butcher took Mr J.L.B. Matekoni's hand and shook it firmly. "You have been very good to me, Rra. I am glad that there are still some honest men left in Botswana."

"There are many honest men in Botswana," said Mr J.L.B. Matekoni. "I am no better than anybody else."

"Oh yes you are," said the butcher. "I see many men in my work and I can tell . . ."

Mr J.L.B. Matekoni cut him short. This was clearly a day for excessive compliments, and he was beginning to feel embarrassed. "You are very kind, Rra, but I must get on with my work. The flies will be settling on the cars if I don't look out."

He had spoken the words without thinking that a butcher might take such a remark as a slight, as a suggestion that his own meat was much beset by flies. But the butcher did not appear to mind, and he smiled at the metaphor. "There are flies everywhere," he said. "We butchers know all about that. I would like to find a country without flies. Is there such a place, do you think, Rra?"

"I have not heard of such a country," said Mr J.L.B. Matekoni. "I think that in very cold places there are no flies. Or in some very big towns, where there are no cattle to bring the flies. Perhaps in such places. Places like New York."

"Are there no cattle in New York?" asked the butcher.

"I do not think so," said Mr J.L.B. Matekoni.

The butcher thought for a moment. "But there is a big green part of the town. I have seen a photograph. This part, this bit of bush, is in the middle. Perhaps they keep the cattle there. Do you think that is the place for cattle, Rra?"

"Perhaps," said Mr J.L.B. Matekoni, glancing at his watch. It was time for him to go home for his lunch, which he always ate at noon. Then, after lunch, fortified by a plate of meat and beans, he would drive round to First Class Motors and speak to the Manager.

MMA MAKUTSI ate her own lunch in the office. Now that she had a bit more money from the Kalahari Typing School for Men, she was able to treat herself to a doughnut at lunchtime, and this she ate with relish, a magazine open on the desk before her, a cup of bush tea at her side. It was best, of course, if Mma Ramotswe was there too, as they could exchange news and opinions, but it was still enjoyable to be by oneself, turning the pages of the magazine with one hand and licking the sugar off the fingers of the other.

The magazine was a glossy one, published in Johannesburg, and sold in great numbers at the Botswana Book Centre. It contained articles about musicians and actors and the like, and about the parties which these people liked to attend in places like Cape Town and Durban. Mma Ramotswe had once said that she would not care to go to that sort of party, even if she were to be invited to one—which she never had been, as Mma Makutsi helpfully pointed out—but she was still sufficiently interested to peer over Mma Makutsi's shoulder and comment on the people in the pictures.

"That woman in the red dress," Mma Ramotswe had said. "Look at her. She is a lady who is only good for going to parties. That is very clear."

"She is a very famous lady, that one," Mma Makutsi had replied. "I have seen her picture many times. She knows where there are cameras and she stands in front of them, like a pig trying to get to the food. She is a very fashionable lady over in Johannesburg."

"And what is she famous for?"

"The magazine has never explained that," Mma Makutsi had said. "Maybe they do not know either."

This had made Mma Ramotswe laugh. "And then that woman there, that one in the middle, standing next to . . ." She had stopped, suddenly, as she recognised the face in the photograph. Mma Makutsi, engrossed in the contemplation of another photograph, had not noticed anything untoward. So she did not see the expression on Mma Ramotswe's face as she recognised, in the middle of the group of smiling friends, the face of Note Mokoti, trumpet player, and, for a brief and unhappy time, husband of Precious Ramotswe and father—not that it had meant anything to him—of her tiny child, the one who had left her after only those few, cherished hours.

Now, though, Mma Makutsi paged through the magazine on her own, while from within the garage there came the sound of a car's wheels being taken off. The sounds of wheel-nuts being thrown into an upturned hub-cap was one she recognised well, and was reassuring, in a strange way, just as the sound of the cicadas in the bush was a comforting one. The sounds that were alarming were those that came from nowhere, strange sounds that occurred at night, which might be anything.

She abandoned her magazine and reached for her tea cup, and it was at that point that she saw the envelope at the end of her desk. She had not noticed it when she came in that day, and it was not there last night, which meant that it must have been put there first thing in the morning. Mr J.L.B. Matekoni had opened the garage and the office, and he must have found it slipped under a door. Sometimes customers left notes that way, when they passed by and the garage was closed. Bills were even settled like this, with the money tucked into an envelope and pushed into the office through a crack in the door. That worried Mma Makutsi, who imagined that it would be very easy for money to go missing, but Mr J.L.B. Matekoni seemed unconcerned about it, and said that his customers had always paid in all sorts of ways and money had never been lost.

"One man used to pay his bills with bags of coins," he said. "Sometimes he would drive past, throw out one of those old white Standard Bank bags, wave, and drive off. That is how he settled his bills."

"That's all very well," Mma Makutsi had said. "But that would never have been recommended to us at the Botswana Secretarial College. They taught us there that the best way to pay bills was by cheque, and to ask for a receipt."

That was undoubtedly true, and Mr J.L.B. Matekoni had not cared to argue with one who had achieved the since then unequalled score of ninety-seven per cent in her final examinations at the Botswana Secretarial College. This letter, though, was plainly not a bill. As Mma Makutsi stretched across her desk to pick it up, she saw, written across the front of the envelope: *To Mr Handsome, Tlokweng Road Speedy Motors.*

She smiled. There was no means of telling who this Mr Handsome was—there were, after all, three men who worked at the garage and it could be addressed to any one of them—and this meant that she would be quite within her rights to open it.

There was a single sheet of paper inside the envelope, and Mma Makutsi unfolded this and began to read. *Dear Mr Handsome*, the letter began. *You do not know who I am, but I have been watching out for you! You are very handsome. You have a handsome face and handsome legs. Even your neck is handsome. I hope that you will talk to me one day. I am waiting for you. There is a lot we could talk about. Your admirer.*

Mma Makutsi finished reading and then folded the letter up and put it back in the envelope. People did send such notes to one another, she knew, but the senders usually made sure that the letters were picked up by those for whom they were intended. It was strange that this person, this admirer, whoever she was, should have put the letter under the door without giving any further clue as to which Mr Handsome she had in mind. Now it was up to her to decide who should get this letter. Mr J.L.B. Matekoni? No. He was not a handsome man; he was pleasant-looking in a comfortable sort of way, but he was not handsome, in that sense. And anyway, whoever it was who had left the letter had no business in sending a letter like that to an engaged man and she, Mma Makutsi, would most certainly never pass on a letter of this nature to Mr J.L.B. Matekoni, even if it had been intended for him.

It was much more likely, then, that the letter was intended for the apprentices. But which one? Charlie, the older apprentice, was certainly good-looking, in a cheap sort of way she thought, but the same could probably be said of the younger one, perhaps even more so, when one considered the amount of hair gel that he seemed to rub on his head. If one were a young woman, somebody aged perhaps seventeen or eighteen, it is easy to see how one would be taken in by the looks of these young men and how one might even write a letter of this sort. So there was really no way of telling which of the young men was the intended recipient. It might be simpler, then, to throw the letter in the bin, and Mma Makutsi had almost decided to do this when the older apprentice walked into the room. He saw the envelope on the desk before her and, with a typical lack of respect for what is right, peered at the writing on the envelope.

"To Mr Handsome," he exclaimed. "That letter must be for me!"

Mma Makutsi snorted. "You are not the only man around here. There are two others, you know. Mr J.L.B. Matekoni and that friend of yours, that one with the oil on his hair. It could be for either of them."

The apprentice stared at her uncomprehendingly. "But Mr J.L.B. Matekoni is at least forty," he said. "How can a man of forty be called Mr Handsome?"

"Forty is not the end," said Mma Makutsi. "People who are forty can look very good."

"To other people who are forty maybe," said the apprentice, "but not to the general public."

Mma Makutsi drew in her breath, and held it. If only Mma

Ramotswe had been here to listen to this; what would she have done? She certainly would not have let any of this pass. The effrontery of this young man! The sheer effrontery! Well, she would teach him a lesson, she would tell him what she thought of his vanity; she would spell it out . . . She stopped. A better idea had materialised; a wonderful trick that would amuse Mma Ramotswe when she told her about it.

"Call the young one in," she said. "Tell him I want to tell him about this letter you have received. He will be impressed, I think."

Charlie left and soon returned with the younger apprentice.

"Charlie here has received a letter," said Mma Makutsi. "It was addressed to Mr Handsome and I shall read it out to you."

The younger apprentice glanced at Charlie, and then looked back at Mma Makutsi. "But that could be for me," he said petulantly. "Why should he think that such a letter is addressed to him? What about me?"

"Or Mr J.L.B. Matekoni?" asked Mma Makutsi, smiling. "What about him?"

The younger apprentice shook his head. "He is an old man," he said. "Nobody would call him Mr Handsome. It is too late."

"I see," said Mma Makutsi. "Well, at least you are agreed on that. Well, let me read out the letter, and then we can decide."

She opened the envelope again, extracted the piece of paper, and read out the contents. Then, putting the letter down on the table, she smiled at the two young men. "Now who is being described in that letter? You tell me."

"Me," they both said together, and then looked at one another.

"It could be either," said Mma Makutsi. "Of course, I now remember who must have put that letter there. I have remembered something."

"You must tell me," said the older apprentice. "Then I can look out for this girl and talk to her."

"I see," said Mma Makutsi. She hesitated; this was a delicious moment. Oh, silly young men! "Yes," she continued, "I saw a man outside the garage this morning, first thing. Yes, there was a man."

There was complete silence. "A man?" said the younger apprentice eventually. "Not a girl?"

"It was for him, I think," said the older apprentice, gesturing at the younger one. And the younger one, his mouth open, was for a few moments unable to talk.

"It was not for me," he said at last. "I do not think so."

"Then I think that we should throw the letter into the bin, where it belongs," said Mma Makutsi. "Anonymous letters should always be ignored. The best place for them is the bin."

Nothing more was said. The apprentices returned to their work and Mma Makutsi sat at her desk and smiled. It was a wicked thing to have done, but she could not resist it. After all, one could not be good all the time, and occasional fun at the expense of another was harmless. She had told no lies, strictly speaking; she had seen a man walking away from the garage, but she had recognised him as one who did occasionally take a short-cut that way. The real sender of the letter was obviously some young girl who had been dared to write it by her friends. It was a piece of adolescent nonsense which everybody would soon forget about. And perhaps the boys had been taught some sort of lesson, about vanity certainly, but also, in an indirect way, about tolerance of the feelings of others, who might be a bit different from oneself. She doubted if they had learned the latter lesson, but it was there, she thought, visible if one bothered to think hard enough about it.

CHAPTER FOURTEEN

INSIDE THE HOUSE OF HOPE

MMA RAMOTSWE surveyed the House of Hope. It was a rather grand name for a modest bungalow which had been built in the early seventies, at a time when Gaborone was a small town, inching out from the cluster of buildings around Government Headquarters and the small square of shops nearby. These houses had been built for government employees or for expatriates who came to the country on short-term contracts. They were comfortable, and were large by the standards of most people's houses, but it seemed ambitious to use them for institutions, such as the House of Hope. But there was no choice, she imagined: larger buildings simply were not available, least of all to charities, which would have to scrimp and save to meet their costs.

There was a large garden, though, and this had been well-tended. In addition to a stand of healthy-looking paw-paw trees at the back, there were several clusters of bougainvillea and a mopipi tree. A vegetable garden, rather like the vegetable garden which Mr J.L.B. Matekoni had established in Mma Ramotswe's own yard, appeared to be growing beans and carrots with some success, although Mma Ramotswe reflected that in the case of carrots one could never really tell until one pulled them out of the ground. There were all sorts of insects which competed with us for carrots, and often what appeared from above to be a healthy plant would reveal itself as riddled with holes once pulled out of the soil.

There was a verandah to the side of the house, and somebody had thoughtfully placed shade netting over the side of this. That would be a good place to sit, thought Mma Ramotswe, and one might even drink tea there, on a hot afternoon, and feel the sun on one's face, but filtered by the shade netting. And then the thought occurred to her that all of Gaborone, the whole town, might be covered with shade netting, held aloft on great poles, and that this would keep the town cool and hold in the water which people put on their plants. It would be comfortable under this shade netting in summer, and then when winter came, and the air was cooler, they could roll back the shade netting to let in the winter sun, which would warm them, like the smile of an old friend. It was such a good idea, and it would surely not be too expensive for a country that had all those diamonds, but she knew that nobody would ever take it seriously. So they would continue to complain about the hot weather when it was hot and about the cold weather when it was cold.

The front door of the House of Hope opened immediately into the living room. This was a large room for that style of house, but the immediate and overwhelming impression it gave Mma Ramotswe was one of clutter. There were three or four chairs in the centre of the room—tightly arranged in a circle—and around them there were tables, storage boxes, and, here and there, a suitcase. On the wall, fixed with drawing pins, were pictures ripped from magazines; pictures of families and of mothers and children; of Mother Teresa with her characteristic headscarf; of Nelson Mandela waving to a crowd; and of a line of African nuns, all clad in white, walking down a path through thick undergrowth, their hands joined in prayer. Mma Ramotswe's eye dwelt on the picture of the nuns. Where was the photograph taken, and where were these ladies going? They looked so peaceful, she thought, that perhaps it did not matter whether they were going anywhere, or nowhere in particular. People sometimes walked simply because walking was an enjoyable thing to do, and better than standing still, perhaps, if that was all you otherwise had to do. Sometimes she herself walked around her garden for no reason, and found it very relaxing, as perhaps it was for those nuns.

"You are interested in the pictures," said Mr Bobologo, behind her. "We think that it is important that these bar girls should be reminded of a better life. They can sit here and look at the pictures."

Mma Ramotswe nodded. She was not convinced that it would be much fun for a bar girl, or for anybody else for that matter, to be sitting on one of those chairs in that crowded room, looking at these pictures from the magazines. But then it would be better than listening to Mr Bobologo, she thought.

Mr Bobologo now came to Mma Ramotswe's side and pointed in the direction of the corridor that led off the living room. "I will be happy to show you the dormitories," he said. "We may find some of the bad girls in their rooms."

Mma Ramotswe raised an eyebrow. It was not very tactful of him to call them bad girls, even if they were. People rose to the descriptions of themselves, and it might have been better, she thought, to call them young ladies, in the hope that they might behave as young ladies behaved. But then, to be realistic, they probably would not behave that way, as it took a great deal to change somebody's ways.

The corridor was tidy enough, with only a small bookcase along one wall and the floor well-polished with that fresh-smelling polish that Mma Ramotswe's maid, Rose, so liked to use. They stopped outside a half-open bedroom door and Mr Bobologo knocked upon this before he pushed it open.

Mma Ramotswe looked inside. There were two bunk-beds in the room, both of them triple-deckers. The top bed was just below the ceiling, barely allowing enough space for anybody to fit in. Mma Ramotswe reflected that she herself would never fit in that space, but then these girls were younger, and some of them might be quite small.

There were three girls in the room, two lying fully clothed on the lower bunks and one wearing a dressing gown, and sitting on a middle bunk, her legs hanging down over the edge. As Mr Bobologo and Mma Ramotswe entered the room, they stared at them, not with any great interest, but with a rather vacant look.

"This lady is a visitor," Mr Bobologo announced, somewhat obviously, thought Mma Ramotswe.

One of the girls muttered something, which may have been a greeting but which was difficult to make out. The other one on the lower bunk nodded her head, while the girl sitting on the middle bunk managed a weak smile.

"You have a nice house here," said Mma Ramotswe. "Are you happy?"

The girls exchanged glances.

"Yes," said Mr Bobologo. "They are very happy."

Mma Ramotswe watched the girls, who did not appear inclined to contradict Mr Bobologo.

"And do you get good food here, ladies?" she asked.

"Very good food," said Mr Bobologo. "These good-time bar girls do not eat properly. They just drink dangerous liquor. When they are here they are given good, Botswana cooking. The food is very healthy."

"It is good to hear you telling me all this," Mma Ramotswe said, pointedly addressing her remark to the girls.

"That is all right," said Mr Bobologo. "We are happy to talk to visitors." He touched Mma Ramotswe's elbow and pointed out into the corridor. "I must show you the kitchen," he said. "And we must allow these girls to get on with their work."

It was not very apparent to Mma Ramotswe what this work was, and she had to suppress a smile as they walked back down the corridor towards the kitchen. He really was a most irritating man, this Mr Bobologo, with his tendency to speak for others and his one-track mind. Mma Holonga had struck Mma Ramotswe as being a reasonable woman, and yet she was seriously entertaining Mr Bobologo as a suitor, which seemed very strange. Surely Mma Holonga, with her wealth and position, could find somebody better than this curious teacher with his ponderous, didactic style.

They now stood at the door of the kitchen, in which two young women, barefoot and wearing light pink housecoats, were chopping vegetables on a large wooden chopping board. A pot of stew was boiling on the stove—boiling too vigorously, thought Mma Ramotswe—and a large cup of tea was cooling on the table. It would be good to be offered tea, she thought longingly, and that very cup looked just right.

"These girls are chopping vegetables," said Mr Bobologo solemnly. "And there is stew for our meal tonight."

"So I see," said Mma Ramotswe. "And I see, too, that they have just made tea."

"It is better for them to drink tea than strong liquor," intoned Mr Bobologo, looking disapprovingly at one of the girls, who cast her eyes downwards, in shame.

"Those are my views too," said Mma Ramotswe. "Tea refreshes. It clears the mind. Tea is good at any time of the day, but especially at mid-day, when it is so hot." She paused, and then added, "As it is today."

"You are right, Mma," said Mr Bobologo. "I am a great drinker of tea. I cannot understand why anybody would want to drink anything else when there is tea to be had. I have never been able to understand that."

Mma Ramotswe now used an expression which is common in Setswana and which indicates understanding, and firm endorsement of what another has said. "Eee, Rra," she said, with great depth of feeling, drawing out the vowels. If anything could convey to this man that she needed a cup of tea, this would. But it did not.

"This habit of drinking coffee is a very bad thing," went on Mr Bobologo. "Tea is better for the heart than coffee is. People who drink coffee strain their hearts. Tea has a calming effect on the heart. It makes the heart go more slowly. Thump, thump. That is what the heart should sound like. I have always said that."

"Yes," agreed Mma Ramotswe, weakly. "That is very true."

"That is why I am in favour of tea," pronounced Mr Bobologo with an air of finality, as might a speaker at a kgotla meeting make his concluding statement.

They stood there in silence. Mr Bobologo looked at the girls, who were still chopping vegetables with an air of studied concentration. Mma Ramotswe looked at the cup of tea. And the girls looked at the vegetables.

AFTER THEY had finished inspecting the kitchen—which was very clean, Mma Ramotswe noticed—they went out and sat on the verandah. There was still no tea, and when Mma Ramotswe, in a last desperate bid, mentioned that she was thirsty, a glass of water was called for. She sipped on this in a resigned way, imagining that it was bush tea, which helped slightly, but not a great deal.

"Now that you have seen the House of Hope," said Mr Bobologo, "you can ask me anything you like about it. Or you can tell me what you think. I don't mind. We have nothing to hide in the House of Hope."

Mma Ramotswe lifted her glass to her lips, noticing the greasy fingerprints around its rim, the fingerprints of those girls in the kitchen, she imagined. But this did not concern her. We all have fingerprints, after all.

"I think that this is a very good place," she began. "You are doing very good work."

"Yes, I am," said Mr Bobologo.

Mma Ramotswe looked out at the garden, at the rows of beans. A large black dung beetle was optimistically rolling a tiny trophy, a fragment of manure from the vegetable beds, back towards its home somewhere—a small bit of nature struggling with another small bit of nature, but as important as anything else in the world.

She turned to Mr Bobologo. "I was wondering, Rra," she began. "I was wondering why the girls come here. And why do they stay, if they want to be bar girls in the first place?"

Mr Bobologo nodded. This was clearly the obvious question to ask. "Some of them are very young and are sent here by the social work department or the police when they see them going into bars. Those girls have to stay, or the police will take them back to their village.

"Then there are the other bad girls, the ones our people meet down at the bus station or outside the bars. They may have nowhere to stay. They may be hungry. They may have been beaten up by some man. They are ready to come here then."

Mma Ramotswe listened carefully. The House of Hope

might be a rather dispiriting place, but it was better than the alternative.

"This is very interesting. Most of us are doing nothing about these things. You are doing something. That is very good." She paused. "But how did you come to do this work, Rra? Why do you give up all your time to this thing? You are a busy teacher, and you have much to do at the school. Instead, you very kindly come and give up all your time to this House of Hope."

Mr Bobologo thought for a moment. Mma Ramotswe noticed that his hands were clasped together; her question had unsettled him.

"I will tell you something, Mma," he said after a few moments. "I would not like you to speak about it, please. Will you give me your word that you will not speak about it?"

Instinctively Mma Ramotswe nodded, immediately realising that this would put her in difficulty if he said something that she needed to report to her client. But she had agreed to keep his secret, and she would honour that.

Mr Bobologo spoke quietly. "Something happened to me, Mma. Something happened some years ago, and I have not forgotten this thing. I had a daughter, you see, by my wife who is late. She was our first born, and our only child. I was very proud of her, as only a father can be proud. She was clever and did well at Gaborone Secondary School.

"Then one day she came back from school, and she was a different girl. Just like that. She paid no attention to me and she started to go out at night. I tried to keep her in and she would scream at me and stamp her feet. I did not know what to do. I could not raise a hand to her, as there was no mother, and a father does not strike a motherless child. I tried to reason with her, and she just said that I was an old man and I did not understand the things that she now understood.

"And then she left. She was just sixteen when this happened. She left, and I looked everywhere and asked everybody about her. Until one day I heard that she had been seen over the border, down in Mafikeng, and that this place where she had been seen, this place . . ." He faltered, and Mma Ramotswe reached out to him, in a gesture of sympathy and reassurance.

"You can carry on when you are ready, Rra," she said. But she already knew what he was going to say and he need not have continued.

"This place was a bar down there. I went there and my heart was hammering within me. I could not believe that my daughter would be in such a place. But she was, and she did not want to talk to me. I cried out to her and a man with a broken nose, a young man in a smart suit, a tsotsi type, came and threatened me. He said, *Go home, uncle. Your daughter is not your property. Go home, or pay for one of these girls, like everybody else.* Those were his words, Mma."

Mma Ramotswe was silent. Her hand was on his shoulder, and it remained there.

Mr Bobologo raised his head and looked up into the sky, high above the shade netting. "And so I said to myself that I would work to help these girls, because there are other fathers, just like me, who have this awful thing happen to them. These men are my brothers, Mma. I hope that you understand that."

Mma Ramotswe swallowed. "I understand very well," she said. "I understand. Your heart is broken, Rra. I understand that."

"It is broken inside me," echoed Mr Bobologo. "You are right about that, Mma."

There was not much else to be said, and they made their way down the path to Mma Ramotswe's tiny white van, parked under a tree. But as they walked, Mma Ramotswe decided to ask another question, more by way of making conversation than to elicit information.

"What are your plans for the House of Hope, Rra?"

Mr Bobologo turned and looked back at the house. "We are going to build an extension there at the side," he said. "We shall have new showers and a room where the girls can learn sewing. That is what we are going to do."

"That will be expensive," said Mma Ramotswe. "Extensions always seem to cost more than the house itself. These builders are greedy men."

Mr Bobologo laughed. "But I will shortly be in a position to pay," he said. "I think that I may be a rich man before too long."

Had Mma Ramotswe been less experienced than she was, had she not been the founder of the No. 1 Ladies' Detective Agency, this remark would have caused her to falter, to miss her step. But she was an experienced woman, whose job had shown her all of human life, and so she appeared quite unperturbed by what he had said. But these last few words that Mr Bobologo uttered—every one of them—fell into the pond of memory with a resounding splash.

CHAPTER FIFTEEN

BAD MEN ARE JUST
LITTLE BOYS, UNDERNEATH

T HE FOLLOWING morning at Tlokweng Road Speedy
Motors, when the morning rush had abated, Mma Ramotswe
decided to stretch her legs. She had been sitting at her desk, dic-
tating a letter to a client, while Mma Makutsi's pencil moved over
the page of her notepad with a satisfactory squeak. Shorthand
had been one of her strongest subjects at the Botswana Secretarial College, and she enjoyed taking dictation.

"Many secretaries these days don't have shorthand," Mma
Makutsi had remarked to Mma Ramotswe. "Can you believe it,
Mma? They call themselves secretaries, and they don't have
shorthand. What would Mr Pitman think?"

"Who is this Mr Pitman?" asked Mma Ramotswe. "What is
he thinking about?"

"He is a very famous man," said Mma Makutsi. "He invented
shorthand. He wrote books about it. He is one of the great heroes
of the secretarial movement."

"I see," said Mma Ramotswe. "Perhaps they should put up a
statue to him at the Botswana Secretarial College. In that way he
would be remembered."

"That is a very good idea," said Mma Makutsi. "But I do not

think they will do it. They would have to raise the money from the graduates, and I do not think that some of those girls—the ones who do not know anything about shorthand, and who only managed to get something like fifty per cent in the exams—I do not think they would pay."

Mma Ramotswe nodded vaguely. She was not particularly interested in the affairs of the Botswana Secretarial College, although she always listened politely when Mma Makutsi sounded off about such matters. Most people had something in their lives that was particularly important to them, and she supposed that the Botswana Secretarial College was as good a cause as any. What was it in her own case, she wondered? Tea? Surely she had something more important than that; but what? She looked at Mma Makutsi, as if for inspiration, but none came, and she decided to return to the subject later, in an idle moment, when one had time for this sort of unsettling philosophical speculation.

Now, the morning's dictation finished and the letters duly signed, Mma Ramotswe arose from her desk, leaving Mma Makutsi to address the envelopes and find the right postage stamps in the mail drawer. Mma Ramotswe glanced out of the window; it was precisely the sort of morning she appreciated—not too hot, and yet with an empty, open sky, flooded with sunlight. This was the sort of morning that birds liked, she thought; when they could stretch their wings and sing out; the sort of morning when you could fill your lungs with air and inhale nothing but the fragrance of acacia and the grass and the sweet, sweet smell of cattle.

She left the office by the back door and stood outside, her eyes closed, the sun on her face. It would be good to be back in Mochudi, she thought, to be sitting in front of somebody's house peeling vegetables, or crocheting something perhaps. That's what she had done when she was a girl, and had sat with her cousin, who was adept at crocheting and made place mat after place mat in fine white thread; so many place mats that every table in Botswana could have been covered twice over, but which somebody, somewhere, bought and sold on. These days she had no time for crocheting, and she wondered whether she would even remember how to do it. Of course, crocheting was like riding a bicycle, which people said that you never forgot how to do once you had learned it. But was that true? Surely there were things that one might forget how to do, if enough time elapsed between the occasions on which one had to do whatever it was that one had forgotten. Mma Ramotswe had once come across somebody who had forgotten his Setswana, and she had been astonished, and shocked. This person had gone to live in Mozambique as a young man and had spoken Tsonga there, and had learned Portuguese too. When he came back to Botswana, thirty years later, it seemed as if he were a foreigner, and she had seen him look puzzled when people used quite simple, everyday Setswana words. To lose your own language was like forgetting your mother, and as sad, in a way. We must not lose Setswana, she thought, even if we speak a great deal of English these days, because that would be like losing part of one's soul.

Mma Makutsi, of course, had another language tucked away in her background. Her mother had been a speaker of Ikalanga, because she had come from Marapong, where they spoke a dialect of Ikalanga called Lilima. That made life very complicated, thought Mma Ramotswe, because that meant that she spoke a minor version of a minor language. Mma Makutsi had been brought up speaking both Setswana, her father's language, and this strange version of Ikalanga, and then had learned English at school, because that was how one got on in life. You could never even get to the Botswana Secretarial College if you spoke no English, and you would certainly never get anywhere near ninety-seven per cent unless your English was almost faultless, like the English that schoolteachers *used* to speak.

Mma Ramotswe had more or less forgotten that Mma Makutsi spoke Ikalanga until one day she had used an Ikalanga word in the middle of a sentence, and it had stuck out.

"I have hurt my gumbo," Mma Makutsi had said.

Mma Ramotswe had looked at her in surprise. "Your gumbo?"

"Yes," said Mma Makutsi. "When I was walking to work today, I stepped into a pothole and hurt my gumbo." She paused, noticing the look of puzzlement on Mma Ramotswe's face. Then she realised. "I'm sorry," she said. "*Gumbo* is foot in Ikalanga. If you speak Ikalanga, your foot is your gumbo."

"I see," said Mma Ramotswe. "That is a very strange word. Gumbo."

"It is not strange," said Mma Makutsi, slightly defensively. "There are many different words for foot. It is *foot* in English. In Setswana it is *lonao,* and in Ikalanga it is *gumbo,* which is what it really is."

Mma Ramotswe laughed. "There is no *real* word for foot. You cannot say it is really gumbo, because that is true only for Ikalanga-speaking feet. Each foot has its own name, depending on the language which the foot's mother spoke. That is the way it works, Mma Makutsi."

That had ended the conversation, and no more was said of gumbos.

These, and other, thoughts went through Mma Ramotswe's head as she stood outside the office that morning, stretching, and allowing her mind to wander this way and that. After a few minutes, though, she decided that it was time to get back into the office. Mma Makutsi would have finished addressing the letters by now, and she wanted to tell her about yesterday's visit to the House of Hope. There was a lot to be said about that, and she thought it would be useful to discuss it with her assistant. Mma Makutsi often came up with very shrewd observations, although in the case of Mr Bobologo no particular shrewdness was required to work out what his motives were. And yet, and yet . . . One could not say that he was an insincere man. He was patently sincere when it came to bar girls, but marriage, perhaps, was another matter. Mma Makutsi might have valuable insights into this, and this would help clarify the situation in Mma Ramotswe's mind.

Mma Ramotswe opened her eyes and started to make her way back into the office. She was intercepted in the doorway, though, by Mma Makutsi, who looked anxious.

"There is something wrong," Mma Makutsi whispered to her. "There is something wrong with Mr J.L.B. Matekoni. Back there." She gestured towards the garage. "There is something wrong with him."

"Has he hurt himself?" Mma Ramotswe always dreaded the possibility of an accident, particularly with those careless apprentices being allowed to raise cars on ramps and do other dangerous things. Mechanics hurt themselves, it was well-known, just as butchers often had parts of fingers missing, a sight which always made Mma Ramotswe's blood run cold, although the enthusiasm of the butchers for their great chopping knives—the guilty blades, no doubt—seemed undiminished.

Mma Makutsi set her mind at rest. "No, there has not been an accident. But I saw him sitting in the garage with his head in his hands. He looked very miserable, and he hardly greeted me when I walked past him. I think something has happened."

This was not good news. Even if there had been no accident, Mr J.L.B. Matekoni's recovery from his depressive illness was recent enough to make any apparent drop in mood a cause for concern. Dr Moffat, who had treated Mr J.L.B. Matekoni during his illness—with the assistance of Mma Potokwane, it must be recalled, who had taken Mr J.L.B. Matekoni in hand and made him take his pills—had warned that these illnesses could recur. Mma Ramotswe remembered his very words: "You must be watchful, Mma Ramotswe," the doctor had said, in that kind voice he used when he spoke to everybody, even to his rather ill-tempered brown spaniel. "You must be watchful because this illness is like a dark cloud in the sky. It is often there, just over the horizon, but it can blow up very quickly. Watch, and tell me if anything happens."

So far, the recovery had seemed complete, and Mr J.L.B. Matekoni had been as equable and as constant as he always had been. There had been no sign of the lassitude that had come with the illness; no sign of the dark, introspective brooding which had so reduced him. But perhaps this was it coming back. Perhaps the cloud had blown over and had covered his sky.

Mma Ramotswe thanked Mma Makutsi and made her way into the garage. The two apprentices were bent over the engine of a car, spanners in hand, and Mr J.L.B. Matekoni was sitting on his old canvas chair near the compressor, his head sunk in his hands, just as Mma Makutsi had seen him.

"Now then, Mr J.L.B. Matekoni," said Mma Ramotswe breezily. "You seem to be thinking very hard about something. Can I make you a cup of tea to help you think?"

Mr J.L.B. Matekoni looked up, and as he did so Mma Ramotswe realised, with relief, that the illness had not returned. He looked worried, certainly, but it was a very different look from the haunted look he had developed during the illness. This was a real worry, she thought; not a worry about shadows and imaginary wrongs and dying; all those things which had so tormented him when he was ill.

"Yes, I am thinking," he said. "I am thinking that I have dug myself into a mess. I am like a potato in . . ." He stopped, unable to complete the metaphor.

"Like a potato?" asked Mma Ramotswe.

"Like a potato in a . . ." He stopped again. "I don't know. But I have done a very foolish thing in involving myself in this business."

Mma Ramotswe was perplexed, and asked him what business he meant.

"This whole business with that butcher's car," he said. "I went round to First Class Motors yesterday afternoon."

"Ah!" said Mma Ramotswe, and thought: this is my fault. I urged him to go and now this has happened. So, rather than say Ah! again, she said, "Oh!"

"Yes," went on Mr J.L.B. Matekoni miserably. "I went up there yesterday afternoon. The man who runs the place was at a funeral in Molepolole, and so I spoke to one of his assistants. And this man said that he had seen the butcher's car round at my garage and he had mentioned it to his boss, who was very cross. He said that I was taking his clients, and that he was going to come round and see me about it this morning, when he arrived back from Molepolole. He said that his boss was going to 'sort me out.' That's what he said, Mma Ramotswe. Those were his words. I didn't even have the chance to complain, as I had intended to. I didn't even have the chance."

Mma Ramotswe folded her arms. "Who is this man?" she snapped angrily. "What is his name, and who does he think he is? Where is he from?"

Mr J.L.B. Matekoni sighed. "He is called Molefi. He is a horrible man from Tlokweng. People are scared of him. He gives mechanics a bad name."

Mma Ramotswe said nothing for a moment. She felt sorry for

Mr J.L.B. Matekoni, who was a very peaceful man and who did not like conflict. He was not one to start an argument, and yet she rather wished that he would stand up to this Molefi man a bit more. Such people were bullies and the only thing to do was to stand up to them. If only Mr J.L.B. Matekoni were a bit braver . . . Did she really want him to fight, though? It was quite out of character, and that was just as well. She could not abide men who threw their weight around, and that was one of the reasons why she so admired Mr J.L.B. Matekoni. Although he was physically strong from all that lifting of engines, he was gentle. And she loved him for that, as did so many others.

She unfolded her arms and walked over to stand beside Mr J.L.B. Matekoni. "When is this man coming?" she asked.

"Any time now. They said this morning. That is all they said."

"I see." She turned away, intending to go over to the apprentices and have a word with them. They would have to rally round to deal with this Molefi person. They were young men . . . She stopped. Tlokweng. Mr J.L.B. Matekoni had said that Molefi was from Tlokweng, and Tlokweng was where the orphan farm was, and the orphan farm made her think of Mma Potokwane.

She turned back again, ignoring the apprentices, and walked briskly back into her office. Mma Makutsi looked up at her expectantly as she came in.

"Is he all right? I was worried."

"He is fine," she said. "He is worried about something. That man at First Class Motors has been threatening him. That's what's going on."

Mma Makutsi whistled softly, as she sometimes did in moments of crisis. "That is very bad, Mma. That is very bad."

Mma Ramotswe nodded. "Mma Makutsi," she said. "I am going out to Tlokweng right now. This very minute. Please telephone Mma Potokwane and tell her that I am coming to fetch her in my van and that we need her help. Please do that right now. I am going."

WHEN MMA RAMOTSWE arrived at the orphan farm, Mma Potokwane was not in her office. The door was open, but the large, rather shabby chair in which Mma Potokwane was often to be found—when she was not bustling round the kitchens or the houses—was empty. Mma Ramotswe rushed outside again and looked about anxiously. It had not occurred to her that Mma Potokwane might not be found; she was always on duty, it seemed. And yet she could be in town, doing some shopping, or she could even be far away, down in Lobatse, perhaps, picking up some new orphan.

"Mma Ramotswe?"

She gave a start, looking about her. It was Mma Potokwane's voice, but where was she?

"Here!" came the voice. "Under this tree! Here I am, Mma Ramotswe."

The matron of the orphan farm was in the shade of a large mango tree, merging with the shadows. Mma Ramotswe had looked right past her, but now Mma Potokwane stepped out from under the drooping branches of the tree.

"I have been watching a special mango," she said. "It is almost ready and I have told the children that they are not to pick it. I am keeping it for my husband, who likes to eat a good mango." She dusted her hands on her skirts as she walked towards Mma Ramotswe. "Would you like to see this mango, Mma Ramotswe?" she asked. "It is very fine. Very yellow now."

"You are very kind, Mma," called out Mma Ramotswe. "I will

come and see it some other time, I think. Right now there is something urgent to talk to you about. Something very urgent."

Mma Potokwane joined her friend outside the office, and Mma Ramotswe quickly explained that she needed her to come to the garage, "to help with Mr J.L.B. Matekoni." Mma Potokwane listened gravely and nodded her agreement. They could go straight away, she said. No, she would not need to fetch anything from her office. "All I need is my voice," she said, pointing to her chest. "And it is all there. Ready to be used."

They travelled back to the garage in the tiny white van, now heavily laden and riding low on its shock absorbers. Mma Ramotswe drove more quickly than she normally did, sounding the horn impatiently at indolent donkeys and children on wobbling cycles. There was only one hold-up—a small herd of rickety cattle, badly looked after by all appearances, which blocked the road until Mma Potokwane opened her window and shouted at them in a stentorian voice. The cattle looked surprised, and indignant, but they moved, and the tiny white van continued its journey.

They drew up at Tlokweng Road Speedy Motors a few minutes after the arrival of Molefi. A large red truck was parked outside the garage, blocking the entrance, and on this was written FIRST CLASS MOTORS in ostentatious lettering. Mma Potokwane, to whom the situation had been explained by Mma Ramotswe on the way back, saw this and snorted.

"Big letters," she murmured. "Big nothing."

Mma Ramotswe smiled. She was sure that the summoning of Mma Potokwane was the right thing to do and this remark made her even more certain. Now, as they negotiated their way round the aggressively parked truck and she saw Molefi standing in front of Mr J.L.B. Matekoni, who was looking down at the

ground as his visitor remonstrated with him, she realised that
they had not arrived a minute too early.

Mma Potokwane bustled forward. "So," she said. "Who do we
find here in Mr J.L.B. Matekoni's garage? Molefi? It's you, isn't it?
You've come to discuss some difficult mechanical problem with
Mr J.L.B. Matekoni, have you? Come for his advice?"

Molefi looked round and glowered. "I am here on business,
Mma. It's business between me and Mr J.L.B. Matekoni." His
tone was rude and he compounded the offence by turning his
back on Mma Potokwane and facing Mr J.L.B. Matekoni again.
Mma Potokwane glanced at Mma Ramotswe, who shook her
head in disapproval of Molefi's rudeness.

"Excuse me, Rra," said Mma Potokwane, stepping forward. "I
think that perhaps you might have forgotten who I am, but I certainly know exactly who you are."

Molefi turned around in irritation. "Listen, Mma . . ."

"No, you listen to me, Rra," Mma Potokwane said, her voice
rising sharply. "I know you, Herbert Molefi. I know your mother.
She is my friend. And I have often felt sorry for her, with a son
like you."

Molefi opened his mouth to speak, but no sound came.

"Oh yes," went on Mma Potokwane, shaking a finger at him.
"You were a bad little boy, and now you are a bad man. You are just
a bully, that's what you are. And I have heard this thing about the
butcher's car. Oh, yes, I have heard it. And I wonder whether your
mother knows it, or your uncles? Do they know it?"

Molefi's collapse was sudden and complete. Mma Ramotswe
watched the effect of these words and saw the burly figure shrink
visibly in the face of Mma Potokwane's tongue-lashing.

"No? They have not heard about it?" she pressed on. "Well, I
think I might just let them know. And you, you, Herbert Molefi,
who thinks that he can go round bullying people like Mr J.L.B.

Matekoni here, had better think again. Your mother can still tell you a thing or two, can't she? And your uncles. They will not be pleased and they might just give their cattle to somebody else when they die, might they not? I think so, Rra. I think so."

"Now, Mma," said Molefi. "I am just talking to Mr J.L.B. Matekoni, that is all I am doing."

"Pah!" retorted Mma Potokwane. "Don't you try to tell me your lies. You just shut that useless mouth of yours for a little while and let Mr J.L.B. Matekoni tell you what to do about that poor man you've cheated. And I'll just stand here and listen, just in case. Then we'll think about whether your people out at Tlokweng need to be told about this."

Molefi was silent, and he remained silent while Mr J.L.B. Matekoni quietly and reasonably told him that he would have to make a refund to the butcher and that he should be careful in the future, as other garages in the town would be watching what he did. "You let us all down, you see," said Mr J.L.B. Matekoni. "If one mechanic cheats, then all mechanics are blamed. That is what happens, and that is why you should change your ways."

"Yes," said Mma Ramotswe, making her first contribution. "You just be careful in future, or Mma Potokwane will hear of it. Do you understand?"

Molefi nodded silently.

"Has a goat eaten your tongue?" asked Mma Ramotswe.

"No," said Molefi quietly. "I understand what you have said, Mma."

"Good," said Mma Potokwane. "Now the best thing you can do is to move that truck of yours and get back to your garage. I think that you will have an envelope in your office. That will do for the letter you are going to write to that man in Lobatse." She paused before adding, "And send me a copy, if you don't mind."

There was not much more to be said after that. Molefi reversed

his truck and drove angrily away. Mr J.L.B. Matekoni thanked
Mma Potokwane, rather sheepishly, thought Mma Ramotswe, and
the two women went into the office of the No. 1 Ladies' Detective
Agency, where Mma Makutsi had boiled the kettle for tea. Mma
Makutsi had listened to the encounter from the doorway. She
was somewhat in awe of Mma Potokwane, but now she asked her
a question.

"Is his mother that fierce?"

"I have no idea," said Mma Potokwane. "I've only seen his
mother; I've never met her, and I took a bit of a risk with that. But
usually bullies have severe mothers and bad fathers, and they are
usually frightened of them. That is why they are bullies, I think.
There is something wrong at home. I have found that with children in general and this applies to men as well. I think that I shall
have to write about that if I ever write a book about how to run an
orphan farm."

"You must write that book, Mma," urged Mma Ramotswe. "I
would read it, even if I was not planning to run an orphan farm."

"Thank you," said Mma Potokwane. "Maybe I shall do that
one day. But at the moment I am so busy looking after all those
orphans and making tea and baking fruit cake and all those
things. There seems very little time for writing books."

"That is a pity," said Mma Makutsi. It had just occurred to
her that she might write a book herself, if Mma Potokwane, of all
people, was considering doing so. *The Principles of Typing*, perhaps, although that was not perhaps the most exciting title one
might imagine. *How to Get Ninety-Seven Per Cent*. Now that was
much, much better, and would be bought by all those people,
those many, many people who would love to get ninety-seven per
cent in whatever it was that they were doing and who knew that
perhaps they never would. At least they could hope, which was
an important thing. We must be able to hope. We simply must.

CHAPTER SIXTEEN

MMA POTOKWANE AND MMA
RAMOTSWE DISCUSS MARRIAGE

THESE MATTERS were distractions, of course, but at least the matter of the butcher's car was now sorted out and Mr J.L.B. Matekoni, only so recently worried on two fronts—the parachute jump and First Class Motors—could now look forward to the immediate future with greater equanimity. Mma Potokwane had been magnificent, as she always was, and had dispatched the bullying Herbert Molefi with the same ease as she dealt with ten-year-old bullies. She had been happy to do this, as she owed Mr J.L.B. Matekoni a great deal, with his constant and unquestioning availability to fix bits and pieces of machinery on the orphan farm. And Mma Potokwane, like everybody else who came into contact with him, recognised in Mr J.L.B. Matekoni those qualities which endeared him to so many and which meant that most people would do anything for him: his courtesy, his reliability, his sheer decency. If only all men, or even more men, were like that, thought Mma Potokwane, indeed thought all the women of Botswana. If only you could trust men in the same way in which you could trust a close woman friend; instead of which, men tended to let women down, not always deliberately, but just because they were selfish or they became bored, or their heads were turned in some way. It was very easy to turn a man's head; a glamorous woman could do it just by looking at a man and lowering her eyelids once or twice. That could make an apparently steadfast man quite unpredictable, particularly if that man were of an age where he was starting to feel unsure of himself as a man.

Mma Ramotswe was lucky to be engaged to Mr J.L.B. Matekoni, thought Mma Potokwane. He was exactly the right choice for her, as she was a fine woman and she deserved a good man like Mr J.L.B. Matekoni with whom to share her life. It was hard being a woman by oneself, particularly when one was in a job such as Mma Ramotswe's, and it was important to have a man on whom one could call for assistance and support. So Mma Ramotswe had made a wise choice, even if all those years ago she had shown a distinct lack of judgment in marrying Note Mokoti, the trumpet player. Mokoti, Matekoni: similar names, reflected Mma Potokwane, but how different the men who bore the names.

Of course there was the question of the length of the engagement and the slowness with which preparations were being made for the wedding, indeed if any preparations were being made at all. This was a puzzle to Mma Potokwane, and while Mma Makutsi made tea that day, after the disposal of Herbert Molefi, Mma Potokwane decided to raise the matter with Mma Ramotswe. She was direct rather than allusive; rather too direct, thought Mma Makutsi, who listened but did not say anything. She tended to feel inhibited in the presence of Mma Potokwane, largely because she felt the other woman was so much more confident and experienced than she was. There was also an element of disapproval in Mma Makutsi's attitude—not that she would ever have expressed it. She thought that Mma Potokwane was too ready to take advantage of Mr J.L.B. Matekoni's good nature. The kindness of men like that could be exploited by forceful women, and there was no doubt but that Mma Potokwane was in the vanguard

THE FULL CUPBOARD OF LIFE   167

of the forceful women of Botswana, their very standard bearer, their champion.

So Mma Makutsi said nothing, but listened very carefully as Mma Potokwane raised the subject of marriage and weddings, virtually under the nose of Mr J.L.B. Matekoni, who had resumed work on a car next door. And what if he had walked in the door and heard her speaking in these terms; what then? Mma Makutsi was astonished at the matron's tactlessness.

"Such a very good man," came the opening gambit. "He has been very helpful to us at the orphan farm. All the children love him and call him their special uncle. So there he is an uncle, but not yet a husband!"

Mma Ramotswe smiled. "Yes, he is a fine man. And he will make a good husband one day. That is why I agreed to his proposal."

Mma Potokwane looked at her fingernails, as if absorbed by some cuticular matter. "One day?" she said. "Which day? When is this day you are talking about? Next week, do you think? Or next year?"

"Not next week," said Mma Ramotswe evenly. "Maybe next year. Who knows?"

Mma Potokwane was quick to press home on this question. "But does he know? That's the important thing. Does Mr J.L.B. Matekoni know?"

Mma Ramotswe made a gesture which indicated that she did not know the answer and that indeed the matter was not important as far as she was concerned. "Mr J.L.B. Matekoni is not a man who makes hasty decisions. He likes to think about things for a long time."

Mma Potokwane shook her head. "That is a weakness, Mma Ramotswe," she said. "I'm sorry to have to say this, but there are some men who need to be organised by women. Every woman

knows this. It is only now, in these modern days, with men getting ideas about running their lives without any help from
women—those dangerous, bad ideas—it is only now that we see
how much these poor men need our assistance. It is a very sad
thing."

"I don't know about that," countered Mma Ramotswe. "I
know that ladies have to help men in many things. Sometimes it
is necessary to push men a little bit. But one should not take it
too far."

"Well it's not going too far to push men to the altar," retorted
Mma Potokwane. "Women have always done that, and that is how
marriages take place. If you left it up to men, they would never
get there. Nobody would be married. You have to remind men to
get married."

Mma Ramotswe looked at her guest thoughtfully. Should she
allow Mma Potokwane to help her to get Mr J.L.B. Matekoni a little bit further along the road to matrimony? It was awkward for
her; she did not want him to form the impression that she was
interfering too much in his life; men did not like that, and many
men would simply leave if they felt this was happening. At the
same time, if Mr J.L.B. Matekoni did need slight prompting, it
would be easier for this to come from Mma Potokwane, who had a
long history of pushing Mr J.L.B. Matekoni about, most of it with
considerable success. One only had to remember the matter of
that old pump at the orphan farm which she had cajoled him into
maintaining well beyond the point where he had formed the professional opinion that it should be scrapped. And one only had to
recall the recent instance of the parachute jump, which was
another example of Mr J.L.B. Matekoni being made to agree to
something to which he did not wish to agree. Perhaps there was a
case for assistance in this matter too . . .

No, no, no! thought Mma Makutsi, willing her employer not

to yield to the imprecations of the manipulative Mma Potokwane. She could see that Mma Ramotswe was tempted, and if only Mma Potokwane had not been there she would have urged Mma Ramotswe in the most vocal terms not to do anything which could have serious consequences for the engagement or, even more importantly, for Mr J.L.B. Matekoni's state of health. Dr Moffat had told them all that Mr J.L.B. Matekoni was not to be put under any stress, and what could be more stressful than to be the object of a determined campaign by Mma Potokwane? Look at that Herbert Molefi man, crushed by her tongue and unable to do anything to defend himself. If only the Botswana Defence Force could have seen it, thought Mma Makutsi, they would have signed her up immediately and made her a sergeant-major or a general or whatever they called those soldiers who ordered all the other soldiers about. Or even better, Mma Potokwane could have been used as a weapon to intimidate the enemy, whoever they were. They would see Mma Potokwane coming towards them and they would be incapable of doing anything, reduced by the sight to mute and helpless boys.

None of these thoughts reached Mma Ramotswe, although she did briefly glance across the room to where Mma Makutsi was busying herself with the tea. But Mma Makutsi was turned away at the time and Mma Ramotswe did not see her expression, so she had no idea of the other woman's feelings.

"Well," began Mma Ramotswe cautiously, "how would we help Mr J.L.B. Matekoni to make a decision? How would we do it?"

"We don't have to help him make any decision," replied Mma Potokwane firmly. "He has already made the decision to marry you, has he not? What is an engagement? It is an agreement to marry. That decision is made, Mma. No, all we have to do is to arrange for him to carry it out. We need to get a date, and then we need to make sure that he gets to the right place on the date. And in my view that means that we should make all the plans and then pick him up on the day and take him there. That's right, we'll *take* him there."

At this, Mma Makutsi spun round and stared at Mma Ramotswe open-mouthed. Surely Mma Ramotswe would see the danger in this? If you took a man to the church, he would simply run away. No man would be forced in this way, and certainly not a mature and intelligent man like Mr J.L.B. Matekoni. This was the stuff of disaster, and Mma Ramotswe should put a stop to these ridiculous fantasies at once. But instead—and here Mma Makutsi drew in her breath in astonishment—instead she was nodding her head in agreement!

"Good," said Mma Potokwane enthusiastically. "I can see that you agree with me. So now all we have to do is to plan the wedding and get everything ready—in secret of course—and then on the day get him into a suit somehow . . ."

"And how would you do that?" interrupted Mma Ramotswe. "You know the sort of clothes that Mr J.L.B. Matekoni normally wears. Those overalls. That old hat with grease round the rim. Those suede veldschoens. How will we get him out of those and into suitable clothes for church?"

"Leave that side of it to me," said Mma Potokwane confidently. "In fact, simply leave the whole thing to me. We can have the wedding out at the orphan farm. I will get my housemothers to cook all the food. I will make all the arrangements and all you will have to do is to get there at the time I will tell you. Then you will be married. I promise you."

Mma Ramotswe looked doubtful and was about to open her mouth to say something when Mma Potokwane continued. "You needn't worry, Mma Ramotswe. I am a very tactful person. I know how to do these things. You know that."

Mma Makutsi's eyes widened, but she knew that there was

no stopping Mma Potokwane now, and that events would run their course whatever she tried to do. And what was there for her to do? She could attempt to persuade Mma Ramotswe to forbid Mma Potokwane from proceeding with her plan, but that would be unlikely to happen once Mma Ramotswe had agreed to it. She could warn Mr J.L.B. Matekoni that he was in danger of being pushed into his own wedding, but then that would seem appallingly disloyal to Mma Ramotswe, and if she did that she might be responsible for his doing something really foolish, such as calling off the engagement altogether. No, there was only one thing for Mma Makutsi to do, and that was to keep out of the whole affair, although she would allow herself one remark, perhaps, just as an aside, to register her disapproval of the whole scheme.

Mma Potokwane did not stay long, but every minute of the visit seemed to drag terribly. An icy atmosphere had developed, with Mma Makutsi sitting in almost complete silence, responding to Mma Potokwane's remarks only in the briefest and most unhelpful of terms.

"You must be very busy," the matron said to her, pointing to the papers on her desk. "I have heard that you are a very efficient secretary. Perhaps you will come out to the orphan farm one day and sort out my office! That would be a good thing to do. You could have a big bonfire of all the spare papers. The children would like that."

"I am too busy," said Mma Makutsi. "Perhaps you should employ a secretary. There is a very fine secretarial college, you know, the Botswana Secretarial College. They will provide you with a name. They will also tell you what the right salary will be."

Mma Potokwane took a sip of her tea and looked at Mma Makutsi over the rim of the cup.

"Thank you, Mma," she said. "That is a good suggestion. But

of course we are an orphan farm and we do not have very much money for secretaries and the like. That is why kind people—people like Mr J.L.B. Matekoni—offer their services free."

"He is a kind man," agreed Mma Makutsi. "That is why people take advantage of him."

Mma Potokwane put down her cup and turned to Mma Ramotswe. "You are very lucky to have an assistant who can give you good advice," she said politely. "That must make your life easier."

Mma Ramotswe, who had been quite aware of the developing tension, did her best to smooth over the situation.

"Most tasks in this life are better done by two people," she said. "I am sure that you get a lot of support from the housemothers. I am sure that they have good advice to give too."

Mma Potokwane rose to her feet to leave. "Yes, Mma," she said, glancing at Mma Makutsi. "We must all help one another. That is very true."

One of the apprentices was detailed to drive Mma Potokwane back to the orphan farm, leaving Mma Ramotswe and Mma Makutsi alone in the office once again. Mma Makutsi, sitting at her desk, looked down at her shoes, as she often did in moments of crisis; her shoes, always her allies, but now so unhelpfully mute, as if to convey: *don't look at us, we said nothing. You were the one, Boss.* (In her mind, her shoes always addressed her as Boss, as the apprentices addressed Mr J.L.B. Matekoni. This was right for shoes, which should know their place.)

"I'm sorry, Mma," Mma Makutsi suddenly burst out. "I had to stand there making tea while that woman gave you that terrible, terrible advice. And I couldn't say anything because I always feel too small to say anything when she's around. She makes me feel as if I'm still six years old."

Mma Ramotswe looked at her assistant with concern. "She is

just trying to help. She's bossy, of course, but that is because she is a matron. Every matron is bossy; if they weren't then nothing would get done. Mma Potokwane's job is to be bossy. But she is just trying to help."

"But it won't help," wailed Mma Makutsi. "It won't help at all. You can't force Mr J.L.B. Matekoni to get married."

"Nobody's forcing him," said Mma Ramotswe. "He asked me to marry him. I said yes. He has never once, not once, said that he does not want to get married. Have you ever heard him say that? No, well there you are."

"But he will agree to a wedding one day," said Mma Makutsi. "You can wait."

"Can I, Mma?" said Mma Ramotswe quickly. "Can I wait forever? And why should I wait all this time and put up with all this uncertainty? My life is going past. Tick, tick. Like a clock that is running too fast. And all the time I remain an engaged lady. People are talking, believe me. They say: there's that lady who's engaged forever to Mr J.L.B. Matekoni. That's what they are saying."

Mma Makutsi was silent, and Mma Ramotswe continued, "I don't want to force Mr J.L.B. Matekoni to do anything he doesn't want to do. But in this case I think that there is some sort of block—there is some sort of reason why he cannot make up his mind. I think it is in his nature. Dr Moffat said that when people had that illness—that depression thing—then they might not be able to make decisions. Even when they seem quite well. Maybe there is a little corner of that in Mr J.L.B. Matekoni. So all we are trying to do is help him."

Mma Makutsi shook her head. "I don't know, Mma. You may be right, but I am very worried. I do not think that you should let Mma Potokwane stick her nose into this business."

"I understand what you are saying to me," said Mma Ramotswe. "But I have reached the end of waiting. I have waited,

waited, waited. No date has been mentioned. Nothing has been said. No cattle have been bought for the feast. No chairs have been fixed up. No aunties have been written to. Nothing has been done. Nothing. No lady can accept that, Mma."

Mma Makutsi again looked down at her shoes. This time the shoes were vocal: *you just be quiet now*, they said rather rudely.

CHAPTER SEVENTEEN

MR SPOKES SPOKESI, THE AIRWAVE RIDER

F MMA Ramotswe was still on the shelf, then the following day she was on the wall. She was sitting on the wall in question, the waist-high wall that surrounded the car park of Radio Gabs, enjoying the effervescent company of two seventeen-year-old girls. They were attractive girls, dressed in jeans and bright-coloured blouses that must have cost them a great deal, thought Mma Ramotswe; too much, in fact, because the most expensive parts of their outfit, the labels, were prominently displayed. Mma Ramotswe had never been able to understand why people wanted to have their labels on the outside. In her day, labels had been tucked in, which is where they belonged in her view. One did not walk around the town with one's birth certificate stuck on one's back; why then should clothes have their labels on the outside? It was a very vulgar display, she felt, but it did not really matter with these nice girls, who were talking so quickly and in such an amusing way about all the things which interested them, which was not very much, at the end of the day; in fact which was only one subject when one came to think of it, or two, possibly, if one included fashion.

"Some people say that there are no good-looking men in

Gaborone," said Constance, the girl sitting to Mma Ramotswe's right. "But I think that is nonsense. There are many good-looking men in Gaborone. I have seen hundreds, just in one day. Hundreds."

Her friend, Kokotso, looked dubious. "Oh?" she said. "Where can I go to see all these good-looking men? Is there a club for good-looking men maybe? Can I go and stand outside the door and watch?"

"There is no such club," laughed Constance. "And if there were, then the men would not be able to get near it, for all the girls standing at the door. It would not work."

Mma Ramotswe decided to join in. It was many years since she had participated in such a conversation, and she was beginning to enjoy it. "It all depends on what you mean by good-looking," she said. "Some men are good-looking in one department and not so good-looking in another. Some men have nice wide shoulders, but very thin legs. Very thin legs are not so good. I know one girl who left a good boyfriend because his legs were too thin."

"Ow!" exclaimed Kokotso. "That girl made a very bad move. If he was a good boyfriend in other ways, then why leave him because of his thin legs?"

"Perhaps she felt that she wanted to laugh whenever she saw his legs," suggested Constance. "That would not have made him happy. Men do not like to be laughed at. Men do not think they are funny."

This made Mma Ramotswe smile. "That is very amusing! Men do not think they are funny! That is very true, Mma. Very true. You must not laugh at a man, or he will go and hide away like a village dog."

"But there is a serious point," said Kokotso. "Can you call a man good-looking if he has a handsome face but very short legs? I have known men like that. They are good-looking when they are sitting down, but when they stand up and you see how short their legs are you think Oh my God, these are short, short legs!"

"And sometimes, have you noticed," Constance interjected, "have you noticed how men's legs go out at the knees and make a circle? Have you seen that? That is very funny. I always want to laugh when I see men like that."

Kokotso now lowered herself off the wall and began to walk in a circle, her arms hanging loose, her chin stuck out. "This is how men walk," she said. "Have you seen it? They walk like this, almost like monkeys."

It was difficult not to laugh, and if she had thought that these girls seriously entertained this low opinion of men she would have frowned instead, but she knew that these were girls who liked men, a great deal, and so joined Constance in shrieking with laughter at Kokotso's imitation of . . . of the apprentices! How accurate she was, and she did not even know them. To imitate one young man of that sort, then, was to imitate them all.

Kokotso resumed her seat on the wall and for a moment there was silence. Mma Ramotswe was rather surprised at herself, sitting there on a wall with two young women less than half her age, talking about good-looking men. She had seen them when she had driven past the Radio Gabs station at lunch-time, not intending to call in until later that afternoon, but realising that this was exactly the opportunity she was looking for. So she had parked the tiny white van round the corner and had walked back, casually, as one who was spending the lunch hour in a quiet ramble. She had stopped at the entrance to the car park and had gone up to the girls to ask them if they knew the correct time. From there it had been easy. The question about the time had been followed by a remark on how tiring it was to have to walk all the way into town and would they mind if she sat on the wall with them for a few minutes while she summoned up her energy?

Of course she had suspected that these girls were not sitting
on the wall just because it was any wall. This was the Radio Gabs
wall, and these young ladies were watching the entrance to the
radio station. And if one were to ask oneself why girls like this
would be watching the entrance to the radio station, it was surely
not to see who went in, but who came out. And amongst those
who were likely to come out, in terms of good looks and general
interest to fashion-conscious girls of seventeen or so, who could
it be but Mr Spokes Spokesi, the well-known disc-jockey and
radio personality? Spokes Spokesi's show, which stretched from
nine in the morning until one-thirty in the afternoon, *Cool Time
with Spokes*, was a favourite of younger people in Gaborone. The
apprentices listened to it while they were working—although Mr
J.L.B. Matekoni, when he could bear it no longer, would switch
off their radio in a gesture of defiance. He at least had good taste
and a limited tolerance for the inane patter which such radio sta-
tions pumped out with great enthusiasm. Mma Ramotswe would
have had a similar lack of interest in Spokes except for one thing:
he was the second name on the list of Mma Holonga's suitors,
unlikely though that was, and this meant that she would have to
speak to him at some stage.

"Do you listen to this station?" she asked casually.

Constance clapped her hands. "All the time! All the time! It's
the best station there is. The latest music, the latest everything,
and . . ."

"And Spokes, of course," supplied Kokotso. "Spokes!"

Mma Ramotswe pretended to look blank. "Spokes? Who is
this Spokes? Is he a band?"

Kokotso laughed. "Oh, Mma, you're out of touch. Spokes
does a show—the best show you can listen to. Can he talk! Oh
my! You hear him talking about music and you can just see him
sitting there in front of the mike. Oh!"

"And is he good-looking too?" asked Mma Ramotswe.

"He's fabulous," said Constance. "The best-looking man in Gaborone."

"In all Botswana," suggested Kokotso.

"My!" said Mma Ramotswe. "And will we see him if we sit here long enough? Will we see him coming out?"

"Yes," said Constance. "We come here once a week usually just to see Spokes. He talks to us sometimes; sometimes he just waves. He thinks that we work in that building over there and are just sitting here to pass the lunch hour. He doesn't know that we come to see him."

Mma Ramotswe tried to look intrigued. "How old is this Spokes?" she asked.

"Just the right age," said Constance. "He's twenty-eight. And his birthday is . . ."

"The twenty-fourth of July," said Kokotso. "We shall come here on that day with a present for him. He will like that."

"You are very kind," said Mma Ramotswe. She studied the girls for a moment, trying to imagine what it must be like to worship somebody who was, after all, almost a stranger to them. Why did people behave this way with entertainers? What was so special about them? And then she stopped, for she had remembered Note Mokoti and her own feelings for him all those years ago when she was hardly older than these girls. And the memory made her humble; for we should not forget what it is to be young and to have ideas and attitudes that may later seem so fanciful.

"Will he be out soon?" she asked. "Will we have to wait long?"

"It depends," said Constance. "Sometimes he sits inside and talks to the station manager for hours. But on other days he comes out the moment his show goes off the air and he gets into his car. That is his car over there, that red one with the yellow curtains in the back. It is a very smart car."

Mma Ramotswe glanced at the car. First Class Motors, she thought dismissively, but then Kokotso grabbed her arm and Constance whispered in her ear: Spokes!

He came out of the front door, dressed in his hip-hugging jeans, his shirt open to the third button down, a gold chain round his neck; Spokes Spokesi himself, Gaborone icon, silver-tongued rider of the airwaves, good-looking, confident, ice-cool, flashing white teeth.

"Spokes!" murmured Kokotso, and as if he had heard her barely articulated prayer, he turned in their direction, waved, and began to make his way over the car park to where they sat.

"Hiya, girls! Dumela and all the rest of it, etcetera, etcetera, etcetera!"

Kokotso dug Mma Ramotswe in the ribs. "He's coming to speak to us," she whispered. "He's seen us!"

"Hallo there, Spokes," called out Constance. "Your show today was great. Fantastic. That band you played at ten o'clock. To die for!"

"Yes," said Spokes, who was now standing before them, smiling his devastating smile. "Good sound. A good sound."

"This lady hasn't listened to you yet, Spokes," said Kokotso, gesturing towards Mma Ramotswe. "Now she knows. She'll be listening tomorrow morning, won't you, Mma."

Mma Ramotswe smiled. She did not like to lie and would not lie now. "No," she said. "I won't be listening."

Spokes looked at her quizzically. "Why not, Mma? My music's wrong for you? Is that it? Maybe I can play some more oldies."

"That would be nice," said Mma Ramotswe politely. "But please don't worry about me. You play what your listeners want to hear. I'll be all right."

"I like to please everybody," said Spokes agreeably. "Radio Gabs is for everyone."

"And everyone listens, Spokes," said Kokotso. "You know we listen."

"What are you doing today, Spokes?" asked Constance.

Spokes winked at her. "You know I'd like to take you to the movies, but I have to go and look after the cattle. Sorry about that."

They all laughed at this witticism, Mma Ramotswe included. Then Mma Ramotswe spoke.

"Haven't I seen you before, Rra?" she said, looking at him closely, as if inspecting him. "I'm sure that I've seen you."

Spokes drew back slightly, but seemed bemused. "You see me here and there. Gaborone is not a big place. You might have seen my picture in the papers."

Mma Ramotswe looked doubtful. "No, it wasn't in the papers. No . . ." She paused, as if trying to drag something out of her memory, and then continued, "Yes! That's it. I remember now. I've seen you with that lady who owns the hair-braiding salons. You know the one. I've seen you with her somewhere or other. A party maybe. You were with her. Is she your girlfriend, Rra?"

Her remark made, she watched its effect on him. The easy smile disappeared, and in its place there was a look of anxiety. He glanced at the young girls, who were looking at him eagerly. "Oh that lady! She is my aunty! She is not my girlfriend!"

The girls giggled, and Spokes leaned forward to touch Kokotso lightly on the shoulder. "Meet you later?" he asked. "Metro Club?"

Kokotso squirmed with pleasure. "We'll be there."

"Good," said Spokes, and then, to Mma Ramotswe, "Nice meeting you, aunty. Go carefully."

*   *   *

MMA MAKUTSI listened intently to what Mma Ramotswe had to say when she returned that afternoon from her meeting with Constance, Kokotso, and Spokes.

"I have spent two days on this matter so far," said Mma Ramotswe. "I have met and interviewed two of the suitors on Mma Holonga's list, and neither of them is in the slightest bit suitable. Both can only be interested in her money. One by his own admission—he said it himself, Mma—and the other by the way he behaved."

"Poor Mma Holonga," said Mma Makutsi. "I have read that it is not easy being rich. I have read that you can never tell who is really interested in you or who is interested only in your money."

Mma Ramotswe agreed. "I am going to have to speak to her soon and tell her what progress I have made. I am going to have to say that the first two are definitely unsuitable."

"That is very sad," said Mma Makutsi, thinking how sad it was, too, that there was Mma Holonga with four suitors and there was she with none.

CHAPTER EIGHTEEN

THE PARACHUTE JUMP, AND A UNIVERSAL TRUTH ABOUT THE GIVING AND TAKING OF ADVICE

MMA RAMOTSWE was hoping that Mma Potokwane would forget all about the parachute jump which Charlie, the older apprentice, had agreed to take over from Mr J.L.B. Matekoni. Unfortunately, neither Mma Potokwane nor Charlie himself forgot, and indeed Charlie had actively been seeking sponsorship. People were generous; a parachute jump was a considerably more exciting project than a sponsored walk or run—anybody could do those. A parachute jump required courage and there was always the possibility that it could go badly wrong. This made it difficult to refuse a donation.

The jump was planned for a Saturday. The plane would take off from the airport, out near the ostrich abattoir, would circle the town and would then fly out towards Tlokweng and the orphan farm. At the appropriate moment the apprentice would be given the signal to jump and would land, it was hoped, in a large field at the edge of the orphan farm. All the children would be there, waiting to see the parachute come down, and the ranks of the children would be swelled by several press photographers, an official from the Mayor's office—the Mayor himself would be away at the time—a colonel from the Botswana Defence Force (invited by Mr J.L.B. Matekoni) and the Principal of the Botswana Secretarial College (invited by Mma Makutsi). Mma Ramotswe had invited Dr Moffat, and had asked him whether he could possibly bring his medical bag with him—just in case anything went wrong, which she was certain it would not. She had also invited Mma Holonga, not only because she was something of a public figure who might be expected to attend a charity event as a matter of course, but also because she wanted to speak to her. Apart from these people, the public at large could attend, if it wished. The event had been given wide publicity in the papers, and even Spokes Spokesi had mentioned it on his show on Radio Gabs. He claimed to have done a parachute jump himself, and that it was nothing, "as long as you were brave enough." But things could go wrong, he warned, although he did not propose to say anything more on that subject just then.

Charlie himself seemed very calm. On the day before the jump, Mma Ramotswe had a private word with him at the garage, telling him that there would be no dishonour in his withdrawing, even at this late stage.

"Nobody will think the less of you if you phone Mma Poto-kwane right now and tell her that you have changed your mind. Nobody will think that you are a coward."

"Yes, they will," said Charlie. "And anyway, I want to do it. I have been practising and I know everything there is to know about parachutes now. You count ten—or is it fifty?—and then you pull the cord. So. Like that. Then you keep your feet together and you roll over on the ground once you land. That is all there is to it."

Mma Ramotswe wanted to say that it was not so simple, but she kept her own counsel.

"You could come with me, Mma Ramotswe," said Charlie, jokingly. "They could make an extra big parachute for you."

Mma Ramotswe ignored this. He could be right, of course; perhaps you needed an especially large parachute if you were of traditional build, or perhaps you just came down faster. But then parachutists of traditional build would land more softly and comfortably, being better padded, and those of particularly traditional build might just roll over when they landed, as barrels do when you drop them.

"Well," she said, after a while, "in your case you must be hoping to land on your bottom, which is much bigger than normal. That will be the best place for you to land. Put your feet up when you get close to the ground and sit down."

The apprentice looked annoyed, but he did not say anything. Instead, he looked in a small mirror which he had hung on a pin near the door that led from the garage into the office. He could often be found standing before this mirror, preening himself, or doing a small, shuffling dance while he looked at his reflection.

ON THE day in question, they all met at Tlokweng Road Speedy Motors: Mma Ramotswe; the two children, Motholeli and Puso; Mr J.L.B. Matekoni; Mma Makutsi; and the younger apprentice. Charlie himself had been collected from his home several hours earlier and driven to the airfield by the pilot of the light aircraft from which he was to jump.

They drove out to the orphan farm in Mma Ramotswe's tiny white van and in Mr J.L.B. Matekoni's truck, Mma Makutsi travelling in the van with Mma Ramotswe and the children sitting in the back. Motholeli's wheelchair was secured in the back of the van by a system of ropes which Mr J.L.B. Matekoni had devised, and this gave her a very good view of the passing countryside. People waved to her, and she waved back, "like the Queen," she said. Mma Ramotswe had told her all about the Queen Elizabeth and about how she had been a friend of Sir Seretse Khama himself. She loved Botswana, explained Mma Ramotswe, and she did her duty all the time, all the time, visiting people and shaking their hands and being given flowers by children. She had been on duty for fifty years, Mma Ramotswe said, just like Mr Mandela, who had given his whole life for justice and had never once thought of himself. How unlike these people were modern politicians, who thought only of power and tricks.

By the time they drew up at the orphan farm, the trees outside the office already had cars under them, and they were obliged to leave the tiny white van out on the road. People had obviously already begun to arrive, and some of the children were on duty at the gate, standing smartly and greeting the guests, telling them where they should go for tea and cake before the jump took place. Some of the younger children were wearing cardboard aeroplane badges which they had cut out and coloured themselves, and some of these were on sale for two pula at a small table under a tree.

Mma Potokwane saw them from her office, and she rushed out to meet them just as Mr J.L.B. Matekoni and the younger apprentice arrived in the truck. Then Dr Moffat arrived, with his wife, in his pick-up truck, and Mma Potokwane immediately seized him and led him off to look at one of the children who had developed a high fever and was being watched over by her housemother. Mrs Moffat stayed with Mma Ramotswe and Mma Makutsi and together they made their way to the spot under a wide jacaranda tree where two of the housemothers were dispensing heavily-sugared tea from a very large brown tea-pot. There was cake too, but it was not free. Mma Ramotswe bought a slice for all of them and they sat down on stools and drank the tea and ate the cake while further spectators arrived. Then, after half an hour or so, they heard the distant drone of an aircraft engine and the children began to squeal with excitement, pointing at the sky to the west. Mma Ramotswe looked up, straining her eyes; the sound was clear enough now, and yes, there it was, a small plane, white against the great empty sky, much higher than she had imagined it would be. How small we must all look from up there, she thought; and poor Charlie, for all his faults, now just a tiny dot in the sky, a tiny dot that would come tumbling down to the hard earth below.

"I shouldn't have asked him to do this," she said to Mma Makutsi. "What if he's killed?"

Mma Makutsi put a reassuring hand on Mma Ramotswe's forearm. "He won't be," she said. "These things are very safe these days. They check everything two or three times."

"But it still might not open. And what if he freezes with shock and doesn't pull the cord? What then?"

"His instructor will be jumping with him," soothed Mma Makutsi. "He would dive down and pull the cord for him. I saw a picture in the *National Geographic* of that being done. It is very easy for these people."

They became silent as the plane passed overhead. Now they could see the markings underneath the wings and the undercarriage, and then the opening door and a figure and a blur of shapes. Suddenly there were two little packages, but packages with arms and legs flailing about in the rushing wind, and some of the children shrieked and pointed upwards. Mr J.L.B. Matekoni looked up too, and gulped, imagining that it could have been him up there, and remembering that disturbing dream. Mma Ramotswe closed her eyes, and then opened them again, and still the figures were falling against the empty sky, and she thought: his parachute is not going to open, and she clutched at Mma Makutsi who had muttered something under her breath, a prayer perhaps.

But the parachutes did open, and Mma Ramotswe let out her

breath and felt weak at the knees. Mrs Moffat smiled at her and said, "I was worried then. It seemed such a time," and Mma Ramotswe was too overcome to say anything in response, but vowed to herself that she would make it up to this boy in the future; she would be kind to him and not be so impatient at the irritating things he said and did.

As they drifted down, floating beneath the great white canopies, the two figures separated. One of them waved to the other, and seemed to be gesturing, but the other did nothing and continued to float away. The gesturing one was now getting fairly close to the ground, and within seconds he had landed in the field, scarcely a few hundred yards from the spectators. There was a cheer, and the children ran forward, in spite of the calls from the housemothers to stay where they were until the second parachutist had landed safely.

They need not have worried. The other parachutist, now revealed to be Charlie, had so drifted off course that he did not land in the field at all, but disappeared behind the tree tops of the scrub bush on the other side. The spectators watched silently as this happened, and then people turned to one another in uncertainty.

"He will be dead," cried out one of the smaller children. "We must fetch a box."

IT WAS Mr J.L.B. Matekoni, Mma Potokwane's husband, and the instructor (not freed of his equipment) who discovered Charlie. He was hanging a few feet above the ground, his parachute covering the upper branches of a large acacia tree, snagged and snared by the thorny limbs of the tree. He shouted out to them as they approached, and the instructor soon had him out of the harness and down on the ground.

"That was a soft landing," said the instructor. "Well done. You were just a bit off target, that's all. I think you were pulling on the wrong side of the canopy. That's why you sailed off here."

The apprentice nodded. He had a curious expression on his face, half way between sheer relief and pain.

"I think that I am injured," he said.

"You can't be," said the instructor, dusting down the green parachute suit. "The tree completely broke your fall."

The apprentice shook his head. "There is something hurting me. It is very sore. It is there. Please see what it is."

Mr J.L.B. Matekoni looked at the seat of Charlie's trousers. There was a large rip in the fabric and a very nasty-looking acacia thorn, several inches long, embedded in the flesh. Deftly he took this between his fingers and extracted it with one swift movement. The apprentice gave a yelp.

"That was all," said Mr J.L.B. Matekoni. "A big thorn . . ."

"Please do not tell them," said the apprentice. "Please do not tell them where it was."

"Of course I will not," said Mr J.L.B. Matekoni. "You are a brave, brave young man."

The apprentice smiled. He was recovering from his shock now. "Are the newspaper people there?" he asked. "Did they come?"

"They are there," said Mma Potokwane's husband. "And many girls too."

Back under the trees he received a hero's welcome. The children ran round him, tugging at his sleeves, the housemothers fussed over him with mugs of tea and large slices of cake, and the girls looked on admiringly. Charlie basked in the glory of it all, smiling at the photographers when they approached with their cameras, and patting children on the head, just as an experienced hero might do. Mma Ramotswe watched with amusement, and considerable relief, and then went off to talk to Mma Holonga, whom she had spotted arriving rather late, when the jump had already taken place. She took her client a mug of tea and led her to a private place under a tree, where they could both sit in privacy and talk.

"I have started making enquiries for you," she began. "I have spoken to two of the men on your list and I can give you a report on what I have found out so far."

Mma Holonga nodded. "Well, yes. I must say that there have been developments since I saw you. But tell me anyway. Then I shall tell you what I have decided to do."

Mma Ramotswe could not conceal her surprise. What was the point of consulting her if Mma Holonga was going to make a decision before receiving even a preliminary report?

"You've decided something?" she asked.

"Yes," said Mma Holonga, in a matter-of-fact voice. "But you go ahead and tell me what you found out. I'm very interested."

Mma Ramotswe began her account. "A few days ago I met your Mr Spokesi," she said. "I had a conversation with him and in the course of this conversation I realised that he was not being honest with you. He is a man who likes younger ladies and I do not think that he is serious about marrying you. I think that he would like to have a good time using your money, and then he would go back to the other ladies. I'm sorry about that, Mma, but there it is."

"Of course," said Mma Holonga, tossing back her head. "That man is very vain and is interested only in himself. I think I knew that all along. You have confirmed my views, Mma."

Mma Ramotswe was slightly taken aback by this. She had expected a measure of disappointment on Mma Holonga's part, an expression of regret, instead of which Mr Spokes Spokesi, who must have been a lively suitor, was being consigned to oblivion quite insouciantly.

"Then there is the teacher," Mma Ramotswe went on. "Mr Bobologo. He is a much more serious man than that Spokesi person. He is a clever man, I think; very well-read."

Mma Holonga smiled. "Yes," she said. "He is a good man."

"But a very dull one too," said Mma Ramotswe. "And he is interested only in getting hold of your money to use for his House of Hope. That is all that interests him. I think that . . ."

Mma Ramotswe tailed off. Her words were having a strange effect on Mma Holonga, she thought. Her client was now sitting bolt upright, her lips pursed in disapproval of what Mma Ramotswe was telling her.

"That is not true!" Mma Holonga expostulated. "He would never do a thing like that."

Mma Ramotswe sighed. "I am sorry, Mma. In my job I often have to tell people things that they do not want to hear. I think that you might not want to hear what I have to say, but I must say it nonetheless. That is my duty. That man is after your money."

Mma Holonga stared at Mma Ramotswe. She rose to her feet, dusting at her skirts as she did so. "You have been very good, Mma," she said coldly. "I am very grateful to you for finding out about Spokesi. Oh yes, you have done well there. But when it comes to my fiancé, Mr Bobologo, you must stop talking about him in this way. I have decided to marry him, and that is it."

Mma Ramotswe did not know what to say and for a few moments she struggled with herself. Clovis Andersen, as far as she could remember, had never written about what to do in this precise situation and she was thrown back on first principles. There was her duty to her client, which was to carry out the enquiries which she had been asked to conduct. But then there was her duty to warn—a simple human duty which involved warning somebody of danger which they were courting. That duty existed, of course, but at the same time one should not be paternalistic and interfere in matters in which another person wished to choose for themselves. It was not for Mma Ramotswe to make Mma Holonga's decisions for her.

She decided to be cautious. "Are you sure about this, Mma?" she asked. "I hope that you do not think I am being rude in asking, but are you sure that you wish to marry this man? It is a very major decision."

Mma Holonga seemed to be pacified by Mma Ramotswe's tone, and she smiled as she replied. "Well, Mma, you are right about its being a very major decision. I am well aware of that. But I have decided that my destiny lies with that man."

"And you know all about his . . . his interests?"

"You mean his good works? His work for others?"

"The House of Hope. The bar girls . . ."

Mma Holonga looked out over the orphan farm field, as if searching for bar girls. "I know all about that. In fact, I am very much involved in that good work. Since I came to see you, he has shown me the House of Hope and I have been doing work there. I have started hair-braiding classes for those bad girls and then they can come and work in my salons."

"That is a very good idea," said Mma Ramotswe. "And then there is the possible extension . . ."

"That too," interrupted Mma Holonga. "I shall be paying for that. I have already talked to a builder I know. Then, after that is done, I am going to build a House of Hope out at Molepolole, for bad girls from that region. That was all my idea, not Bobologo's."

Mma Ramotswe listened to all this and realised that she was in the presence of a woman who had found her vocation. So there was nothing more for her to say, other than to congratulate her on her forthcoming marriage and to reflect on the truth that when people ask for advice they very rarely want your advice and will go ahead and do what they want to do anyway, no matter what you say. That applied in every sort of case; it was a human truth of universal application, but one which most people knew little or nothing about.

CHAPTER NINETEEN

A VERY RICH CAKE IS SERVED

AFTER SHE had finished her surprising discussion with
Mma Holonga, Mma Ramotswe moved over to join Mr J.L.B.
Matekoni and Mma Makutsi, who were sitting at a table under a
tree near the children's dining room. More tea had been produced and was being served by the housemothers, and Mma
Ramotswe noticed that there were many people in the crowd
whom she knew. Indeed, some of them were relatives of hers;
her cousin and husband, for example, and some of Mr J.L.B.
Matekoni's people. Mma Potokwane had obviously been very
active in gathering people for the parachute drop.

She walked over to join her cousin, who said that she would
not be prepared to do a parachute drop, even if asked by the President himself. "I would have to say, I'm sorry Rra, but there are
some things one cannot do, even for Botswana. I cannot jump
from an aeroplane. I would die straightaway."

The cousin's husband agreed. He would be prepared to give
all his money, and all his cattle, to charity rather than jump.

"You should not let Mma Potokwane hear that," said Mma
Ramotswe. "It might give her ideas."

Then there was a conversation with the Reverend Trevor

Mwamba from the Anglican Cathedral. He, too, confessed that he would not like to do a parachute jump, and he felt that the same could be said for the Bishop. For a moment Mma Ramotswe entertained a mental picture of the Bishop jumping from an aeroplane, dressed in his episcopal robes and clutching his mitre as he fell.

"It is nothing, you know," said Charlie, who had come up to join them, a glass of beer in his hand, and clearly enjoying his fame. "I wasn't at all frightened. I just jumped and then bump! the chute opened above me and I came down. That's all there is to it. I will do it again tomorrow if Mma Potokwane asks me. In fact, I think I might offer to join the Botswana Defence Force. I could look after their aeroplane engines and then do some jumping in my spare time."

Mma Ramotswe saw that this made Mr J.L.B. Matekoni look anxious, but the conversation moved on to another topic and no more was said of the looking-after of aeroplane engines.

The event had now turned into something of a party. Some of the older children, who had been helping with the tea cups and with arranging chairs under the trees, now formed up as a choir and sang several songs while one of them, a talented marimba player, provided an accompaniment. Then, after the singing, Mma Potokwane came over to Mma Ramotswe's side and invited her to join her for a moment in the office. The same invitation was extended to Mr J.L.B. Matekoni, and it was explained that a very special cake had been prepared for him but that it could not be produced in public as there was not enough for everybody.

They went into the office. The Reverend Trevor Mwamba was already there, a plate of cake before him. He stood up and smiled at Mr J.L.B. Matekoni.

"Now," said Mma Potokwane, putting a large slice of the special cake on Mr J.L.B. Matekoni's plate. "Here is the special cake I have made."

"You are very kind to us, Mma," said Mr J.L.B. Matekoni. "This looks like a very rich cake. Very rich." He paused, the cake half way to his mouth. He looked at Mma Potokwane. Then he looked at the Reverend Trevor Mwamba. Finally he looked at Mma Ramotswe. Nobody spoke.

Mma Potokwane broke the silence. "Mr J.L.B. Matekoni," she said. "We all know how proud you are of Mma Ramotswe. We all know how proud you are to be her fiancé and how you wish to be her husband. I am right, am I not, in saying that you wish to be her husband?"

Mr J.L.B. Matekoni nodded. "I do. Of course I do."

"Well, do you not think that the moment has come?" she went on. "Do you not think that this would be the right time to marry Mma Ramotswe? Right now. Not next month or next year or whenever, but right now. Because if you do not do something about this, you may never do it. Life is perilous. At any time it could be too late. When you love another person, you must tell her, but you must also show her. You must do that thing that says to the world that you love that person. And this must never be put off, never."

She paused, watching the effect of her words on Mr J.L.B. Matekoni. He was staring at her, his eyes slightly moist, as if he was about to burst into tears.

"You do wish to marry Mma Ramotswe, do you not?" Mma Potokwane urged.

Now there was a further silence. The Reverend Trevor Mwamba slipped a small piece of cake into his mouth and chewed on it. Mma Ramotswe herself looked down at the ground, at the edge of Mma Potokwane's carpet. And then Mr J.L.B. Matekoni spoke.

"I will marry Mma Ramotswe right now," he said. "If that is what Mma Ramotswe wishes, then I shall do that. I shall be proud to do that. There is no other lady I would ever wish to marry. Just Mma Ramotswe. That is all."

It was a long speech for Mr J.L.B. Matekoni, but every word was filled with passion and a new determination.

"In that case," said the Reverend Trevor Mwamba, wiping the crumbs from the edge of his lips. "In that case I have the prayer books in my car and I have the Bishop's authority to perform the ceremony right here."

"We can do it under the big tree," said Mma Potokwane. "I will tell the children's choir to get ready. And I will also tell the guests to prepare themselves. They will be surprised."

THEY ASSEMBLED under the boughs of the great jacaranda tree. A table had been covered with a clean white sheet and served as an altar, and before this altar stood Mr J.L.B. Matekoni, waiting for Mma Ramotswe to be led up to him by Mma Potokwane's husband, who had offered to give the bride away on behalf of her late father, Obed Ramotswe. Mma Potokwane had produced a suitable dress for Mma Ramotswe, in just the right size as it happened, and Mr J.L.B. Matekoni had been put into a suit by Mma Potokwane's husband. The Reverend Trevor Mwamba had fetched his robes from his car.

When Mma Ramotswe came out of the office and walked with Mma Potokwane's husband up to the group of people and the waiting groom, there were enthusiastic ululations from the crowd. This was how people showed their delight and pleasure and the sound was strong that day.

"Dearly beloved," began the Reverend Trevor Mwamba, "we are gathered here together in the sight of God and in the presence of this congregation to join this man and this woman in holy matrimony, which is an honourable estate . . ."

The words which Mma Ramotswe had heard so many times for others, those echoing words, she now heard for herself, and she made the responses clearly, as did Mr J.L.B. Matekoni. Then, taking their hands and placing them together, in accordance with the authority vested in him, the Reverend Trevor Mwamba pronounced them man and wife, and the ladies present, led by Mma Potokwane, ululated with pleasure.

The choir had been waiting, and now they sang, while Mma Ramotswe and Mr J.L.B. Matekoni sat down on chairs which had been placed before the altar, and signed the register which the Reverend Trevor Mwamba had also happened to have in the back of his car. The choir sang, the sweet voices of the children rising through the branches of the tree above them, and filling the still, clear air with sound. There was an old Botswana hymn, one which everybody knew, and then, because it was a favourite of Mma Ramotswe's father, they sang that song which distils all the suffering and the hope of Africa; that song which had inspired and comforted so many, "Nkosi Sikeleli Afrika," God Bless Africa, give her life, watch over her children.

Mma Ramotswe turned to face her friends, and smiled, and they smiled back. Then she and Mr J.L.B. Matekoni stood up and walked down through the crowd to the place where the children had taken more tables and where, quite miraculously, as at Cana of Galilee, the housemothers had set out large plates of food, ready for the wedding feast.

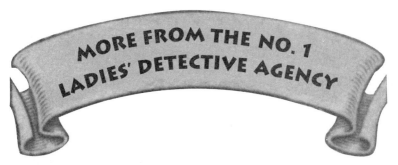

MORE FROM THE NO. 1 LADIES' DETECTIVE AGENCY

Alexander McCall Smith
**THE NO.1
LADIES' DETECTIVE
AGENCY**
"The Miss Marple of Botswana."
—*The New York Times Book Review*

THE NO. 1 LADIES' DETECTIVE AGENCY

Millions of readers have fallen in love with the witty, wise Mma Ramotswe and her Botswana adventures. Share the magic of Alexander McCall Smith's No. 1 Ladies' Detective Agency series in two alternate editions:

1-4000-3477-9 (pbk)
0-375-42387-7 (hc)

TEARS OF THE GIRAFFE

The No. 1 Ladies' Detective Agency is growing, and in the midst of solving her usual cases—from an unscrupulous maid to a missing American—eminently sensible and cunning detective Mma Ramotswe ponders her impending marriage, promotes her talented secretary, and finds her family suddenly and unexpectedly increased by two.

**Volume 2
1-4000-3135-4 (pbk)**

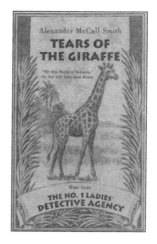

Alexander McCall Smith
**TEARS OF
THE GIRAFFE**
"The Miss Marple of Botswana."
—*The New York Times Book Review*

More from
**THE NO. 1 LADIES'
DETECTIVE AGENCY**

MORALITY FOR BEAUTIFUL GIRLS

While trying to resolve some financial problems for her business, Mma Ramotswe finds herself investigating the alleged poisoning of a government official as well as the moral character of the four finalists of the Miss Beauty and Integrity contest. Other difficulties arise at her fiancé's Tlokweng Road Speedy Motors, as Mma Ramotswe discovers he is more complicated than he seems.

Volume 3
1-4000-3136-2 (pbk)

The mysteries are "smart and sassy . . . [with] the power to amuse or shock or touch the heart, sometimes all at once."
—*Los Angeles Times*

THE KALAHARI TYPING SCHOOL FOR MEN

Mma Precious Ramotswe is content. But, as always, there are troubles. Mr J.L.B. Matekoni has not set the date for their wedding, her assistant Mma Makutsi wants a husband, and worst of all, a rival detective agency has opened up in town. Of course, Precious will manage these things, as she always does, with her uncanny insight and good heart.

Volume 4
1-4000-3180-X (pbk)
0-375-42217-X (hc)

THE FULL CUPBOARD OF LIFE

Mma Ramotswe has weighty matters on her mind. She has been approached by a wealthy lady to check up on several suitors. Are these men interested in her or just her money? This may be difficult to find out, but it's just the kind of case Mma Ramotswe likes.

Volume 5
1-4000-3181-8 (pbk)
0-375-42218-8 (hc)

IN THE COMPANY OF CHEERFUL LADIES

Precious Ramotswe is busier than usual at the No. 1 Ladies' Detective Agency when the appearance of a strange intruder in her house and a mysterious pumpkin in her yard add to her concerns. But what finally rattles Mma Ramotswe's normally unshakable composure is the visitor who forces her to confront a painful secret from her past.

Volume 6
0-375-42271-4 (hc)
Paperback available Spring 2006

A New Series Begins

THE SUNDAY PHILOSOPHY CLUB

**THE SUNDAY
PHILOSOPHY CLUB**
Isabel Dalhousie is fond of problems,
and sometimes she becomes
interested in problems that are,
quite frankly, none of her business—
including some that are best left to
the police. Filled with endearingly
thorny characters and a Scottish
atmosphere as thick as a highland
mist, *The Sunday Philosophy Club* is
an irresistible pleasure.

Volume 1
1-4000-7709-5 (pbk)
0-375-42298-6 (hc)

"The literary equivalent of herbal tea and a cozy fire. . . .
McCall Smith's Scotland [is] well worth future visits."
—*The New York Times*

THE SUNDAY PHILOSOPHY CLUB

FRIENDS, LOVERS, CHOCOLATE

While taking care of her niece Cat's delicatessen, Isabel meets a heart transplant patient who has had some strange experiences in the wake of surgery. Against the advice of her housekeeper, Isabel is intent on investigating. Matters are further complicated when Cat returns from vacation with a new boyfriend, and Isabel's fondness for him lands her in another muddle.

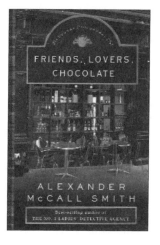

Volume 2
0-375-42299-4 (hc)
Paperback available Fall 2006

ANCHOR BOOKS
ORIGINAL TRADE PAPERBACKS

44 SCOTLAND STREET
All of Alexander McCall Smith's trademark warmth and wit come into play in this novel chronicling the lives of the residents of an Edinburgh boardinghouse. Complete with colorful characters, love triangles, and even a mysterious art caper, this is an unforgettable portrait of Edinburgh society.

1-4000-7944-6

THREE NEW NOVELLAS
INTRODUCING THE ECCENTRIC AND EVER-LIKABLE PROFESSOR DR VON IGELFELD

Welcome to the insane and rarified world of Professor Dr Moritz-Maria von Igelfeld of the Institute of Romance Philology. Von Igelfeld is engaged in a never-ending quest to win the respect he feels certain is due him—a quest which has a way of going hilariously astray.

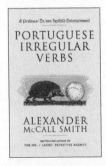

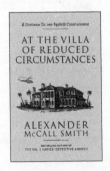

1-4000-7708-7   **1-4000-9508-5**   **1-4000-9509-3**

The Official Home of Alexander McCall Smith on the Web

WWW.ALEXANDERMCCALLSMITH.COM

A comprehensive Web site for new readers and
longtime fans alike, with five exclusive content areas:

• THE NO. 1 LADIES' DETECTIVE AGENCY

The original site for McCall Smith's bestselling series. Explore
Precious Ramotswe's Botswana through book descriptions, a
photo gallery, advice from Mma Ramotswe, and more.

• THE SUNDAY PHILOSOPHY CLUB

Enter a Scottish atmosphere as thick as a highland mist,
complete with a photo tour of Isabel Dalhousie's Edinburgh.

• PROFESSOR DR VON IGELFELD ENTERTAINMENTS

Three original paperback novellas introducing the eccentric and
ever-likable Professor Dr von Igelfeld, his colleagues, and their
comic adventures.

• ABOUT THE AUTHOR

Read about Alexander McCall Smith and get updates on
tour events and other author activities.

• JOIN THE COMMUNITY

Share the world of Alexander McCall Smith with friends,
family, and fellow book club members. Print our free Reading
Group Guides and sign up for the Alexander McCall Smith
Fan Club and e-Newsletter.

ALEXANDER McCALL SMITH

JOIN THE FAN CLUB TODAY!

Photo © Chris Watt

WWW.ALEXANDERMCCALLSMITH.COM

Membership to the Alexander McCall Smith Fan Club is absolutely FREE! You can register online at **www.alexandermccallsmith.com** or simply complete the form below and mail it to: **Alexander McCall Smith Fan Club, c/o Anchor Books, 1745 Broadway, New York, NY 10019**. As a member, you will receive a quarterly newsletter covering all of Alexander McCall Smith's beloved series, his latest work and travels, and details about where you can see him on tour. Additionally, members will have exclusive opportunities to hear from the author, participate in contests, and receive excerpts of McCall Smith's titles before the books are available in stores. Don't miss this chance to have a greater connection to one of your favorite authors!

NAME: _____

ADDRESS: _____

CITY: _____ STATE: _____ ZIP: _____

E-MAIL: _____

WHERE DO YOU BUY BOOKS? _____

CHAPTER ONE FROM

BLUE SHOES
AND
HAPPINESS

by Alexander McCall Smith

The new novel in
The No. 1 Ladies' Detective Agency series

DEAR AUNTY EMANG

HEN YOU ARE JUST THE RIGHT AGE, as Mma Ramotswe was, and when you have seen a bit of life, as Mma Ramotswe certainly had, then there are some things that you just know. And one of the things that was well known to Mma Ramotswe, only begetter of the No 1 Ladies' Detective Agency (Botswana's only detective agency) was that there were two sorts of problem in this life. Firstly, there were those problems—and they were major ones—about which one could do very little, other than to hope, of course. These were the problems of the land, of fields that were too rocky, of soil which blew away in the wind, or of places where crops would just not thrive for some sickness that lurked in the very earth. But looming greater than anything else there was the problem of drought. It was a familiar feeling in Botswana, this waiting for rain, which often simply did not come, or came too late to save the crops. And then the land, scarred and exhausted, would dry and crack under the relentless sun, and it would seem that nothing short of a miracle would ever bring it to life. But that miracle would eventually arrive, as it always had, and the landscape would turn from brown to green within hours under the kiss of the rain. And there were other colors that would follow the green; yellows, blues, reds would appear in patches across the veld as if great cakes of dye had been crumbled and scattered by an unseen hand. These were the colors of the wild flowers that had been lurking there, throughout the dry season, waiting for the first drops of moisture to awaken them. So at least that sort of problem had its solution, although one often had to wait long, dry months for that solution to arrive.

The other sort of problems were those which people made for themselves. These were very common, and Mma Ramotswe had seen many of them in the course of her work. Ever since she has set up this agency, armed only with a copy of Clovis Andersen's *Principles of Private Detection*—and a great deal of common sense—scarcely a day had gone by without her encountering some problem which people had brought upon themselves. Unlike the first sort of problem—drought and the like—these were problems that could have been avoided. If people were only more careful, or behaved themselves as they should, then they would not find themselves faced with problems of this sort. But of course people never behaved themselves as they should. "We are all human beings," Mma Ramotswe had once observed to Mma Makutsi, "and human beings can't really help themselves. Have you noticed that, Mma? We can't really help ourselves from doing things that land us in all sorts of trouble."

Mma Makutsi pondered this for a few moments. In general, she thought that Mma Ramotswe was right when she expressed her views on matters of this sort, but she felt that this particular proposition needed a little bit more thought. She knew that there were some people who were unable to make of their lives what they wanted them to be, but then there were many others who were quite capable of keeping themselves under control. In her own case, she thought that she was able to resist temptation quite effectively. She did not consider herself to be particularly strong, but at the same time she did not seem to be markedly weak. She did not drink, nor did she over-indulge in food, or chocolate or anything of that sort. No, Mma Ramotswe's observation was just a little bit too sweeping and she would have to disagree. But then the thought struck her: could she resist a fine new pair of shoes, even if she knew that she had plenty of shoes already (which was not the case).

"I think you're right, Mma," she said. "Everybody has a weakness and most of us are not strong enough to resist it."

Mma Ramotswe looked at her assistant. She had an idea what Mma Makutsi's weakness might be, and indeed there might even be more than one.

"Take Mr J.L.B. Matekoni, for example," said Mma Ramotswe.

"All men are weak," said Mma Makutsi. "That is well-known." She paused. Now that Mma Ramotswe and Mr J.L.B. Matekoni were married it was possible that Mma Ramotswe had discovered new weaknesses in him, and it would be interesting to hear about these. The mechanic was a quiet man, but it was often the mildest-looking people who did the most colourful things, in secret of course. What could Mr J.L.B. Matekoni get up to? It would be very interesting to hear.

"Cake," said Mma Ramotswe quickly. "That is Mr J.L.B. Matekoni's great weakness. He cannot help himself when it comes to cake. He can be manipulated very easily if you have a plate of cake in your hand."

Mma Makutsi laughed. "Mma Potokwane knows that, doesn't she?" she said. "I have seen her getting Mr J.L.B. Matekoni to do all sorts of things for her just by offering him pieces of that fruit cake of hers."

Mma Ramotswe rolled her eyes up towards the ceiling. Mma Potokwane, the matron of the Orphan Farm, was her friend, and when all was said and done she was good woman, but she was quite ruthless when it came to getting things done for the children in her care. She it was who had

cajoled Mr J.L.B. Matekoni into fostering the two children
who now lived in their house; that had been a good thing,
of course, and the children were dearly loved, but Mr J.L.B.
Matekoni had not thought the thing through and had failed
even to consult Mma Ramotswe about the whole matter.
And then there were the numerous occasions on which she
had prevailed upon him to spend hours of his time fixing
that unreliable old water pump at the Orphan Farm—a
pump which dated back to the days of the Protectorate and
which should have been retired and put into a museum
long ago. And Mma Potokwane achieved all of this because
she had a profound understanding of how men worked and
what their weakness were; that was the secret of so many
successful women—they knew about the weaknesses
of men.

That conversation with Mma Makutsi had taken place
some days before. Now Mma Ramotswe was sitting on the
veranda of her house on Zebra Drive, late on a Saturday
afternoon, reading the paper. She was the only person in
the house at the time, which was unusual for a Saturday.
The children were both out: Motheleli had gone to spend
the weekend with a friend whose family lived out at
Mogiditishane. This friend's mother had picked her up in
her small truck and had stored the wheelchair in the back
with some bales of string that had aroused Mma
Ramotswe's interest but which she had not felt it her place
to ask about. What could anybody want with such large
balls of string, she wondered? Most people needed very

little string, if any, in their lives, but this woman, who was a beautician, seemed to need a great deal. Did beauticians have a special use for string that the rest of us knew nothing about, Mma Ramotswe asked herself. People spoke about face-lifts; did string come into face-lifts?

Puso, the boy, who had caused them such concern over his unpredictable behavior but who had recently become much more settled, had gone off with Mr J.L.B. Matekoni to see an important football match at the stadium. Mma Ramotswe did not consider it important in the least—she had no interest in football and she could not see how it could possibly matter in the slightest who succeeded in kicking the ball into the goal the most times—but Mr J.L.B. Matekoni clearly thought differently. He was a close follower and supporter of the Zebras, a local football team, and he tried to get to the stadium whenever the national team was playing. Fortunately the Zebras were doing well at the moment, and this, thought Mma Ramotswe, was a good thing: it was quite possible, she felt, that Mr J.L.B. Matekoni's depression, from which he had made a good recovery, could recur if he, or the Zebras, were to suffer any serious setback.

So now she was alone in the house, and it seemed very quiet to her. She had made a cup of bush tea and had drunk that thoughtfully, gazing out over the rim of her cup onto the garden to the front of the house. The sausage fruit tree, the *moporoto*, which she had never paid much attention to, had taken upon itself to produce abundant fruit this year, and four heavy sausage-shaped pods had appeared at the end of a branch, bending that limb of the tree under their weight. She would have to do something about that, she thought. People knew that it was dangerous to sit under such trees, as the heavy fruit could crack open a skull if it chose to fall when a person was below. That had happened to a friend of her father's many years ago, and the blow that he had received had cracked his skull and damaged his brain, making it difficult for him to speak. She remembered him as a child, struggling to make himself understood, and her father had explained that he had sat under a sausage tree and had gone to sleep and this was the result.

She made a mental note to warn the children and to get Mr J.L.B. Matekoni to knock the fruit down with a pole before anybody was hurt. And then she turned back to her cup of tea and to her perusal of the copy of *The Daily News* which she had unfolded on her lap. She had read the first four pages of the paper, and gone through the small advertisements with her usual care. There was much to be learned from the small advertisements, with their offers of irrigation pipes for farmers, used vans, jobs of various sorts, plots of land with house construction permission, and bargain furniture. Not only could one keep up to date with what things cost, but there was also a great deal of social detail to be garnered from this source. That day, for instance, there was a statement by a Mr Herbert Motimedi that he would not be responsible for any debts incurred by Mrs Boipelo Motimedi, which effectively informed the public that Herbert and Boipelo were no longer on close terms—which did not surprise Mma Ramotswe, as it happened, because she had always felt that that particular marriage was not a good idea, in view of the fact that Boipelo Motimedi had gone through three husbands before she found Herbert, and two of these previous husbands had both been declared bankrupt. She smiled at that and skimmed over the remaining advertisements before turning the page and getting to the column that interested her more than anything else in the newspaper.

Some months earlier, the newspaper had announced to its readers that they would be starting a new feature. "If you have any problems," the paper said, "then you should write to our new exclusive columnist, Aunty Emang, who will give you advice on what to do. Not only is Aunty Emang a B.A. from the University of Botswana, but she also has the wisdom of one who has lived fifty-eight years and knows all about life." This advance notice brought in a flood of letters, and the paper had expanded the amount of space available for Aunty Emang's sound advice. Soon she had become so popular that she was viewed as something of a national institution and was even named in Parliament when an opposition member brought the house down when he suggested that the policy proposed by some hapless Minister would never have been approved of by Aunty Emang.

Mma Ramotswe had chuckled over that, as she now chuckled over the plight of a young student who had written a passionate love letter to a girl and had delivered it, by mistake, to her sister. "I am not sure what to do," he had written to Aunty Emang. "I think that the sister is very pleased with what I wrote to her as she is smiling at me all the time. Her sister, the girl I really like, does not know that I like her and maybe her own sister has told her about the letter which she has received from me. So she thinks now that I am in love with her sister, and does not know that I am in love with her. How can I get out of this difficult situation?" And Aunty Emang, with her typical robustness, had written: "Dear Anxious in Molepolole: the simple answer to your question is that you cannot get out of this. If you tell one of the girls that she has received a letter intended for her sister, then she will become very sad. Her sister (the one you really wanted to write to in the first place) will then think that you have been unkind to her sister and made her upset. She will not like you for this. The answer is that you must give up seeing both of these girls and you should spend your time working harder on your examinations. When you have a good job and are earning some money, then you can find another girl to fall in love with. But make sure that you address any letter to that girl very carefully."

There were two other letters. One was from a boy of fourteen who had been moved to write to Aunty Emang about being picked upon by his teacher. "I am a hard-working boy," he wrote. "I do all my school-work very carefully and neatly. I never shout in the class or push people about (like most other boys). When my teacher talks, I always pay attention and smile at him. I do not trouble the girls (like most other boys). I am a very good boy in every sense. Yet my teacher always blames me for anything that goes wrong and gives me low marks in my work. I am very unhappy. The more I try to please this teacher, the more he dislikes me. What am I doing wrong?"

Everything, thought Mma Ramotswe. That's what you are doing wrong: everything. But how could one explain to a fourteen-year-old boy that one should not try too hard; which was what he was doing and which irritated teachers. It was better, she thought, to be a little bit bad in this life, and not too perfect. If you were too perfect, then you invited exactly this sort of reaction, even if teachers should be above that sort of thing. But what, she wondered, would Aunty Emang say?

"Dear Boy," wrote Aunty Emang. "Teachers do not like boys like you. You should not say you are not like other boys, or people will think that you are like a girl." And that is all that Aunty Emang seemed prepared to say on the subject—which was a bit dismissive, thought Mma Ramotswe, and now that poor, over-anxious boy would think that not only did his teacher not like him, but neither did Aunty Emang. But perhaps there was not enough space in the newspaper to go into the matter in any great depth and, anyway, there was the final letter to be printed, which was not a short one.

"Dear Aunty Emang," the letter ran, "Four years ago my wife gave birth to our first born. We had been trying for this baby for a long time and we were very happy when the baby arrived. When it came to choosing a name for this child, my wife suggested that we should call him after my brother, who lives in Mahalapye but who comes to see us every month. She said that this would be a good thing, as my brother does not have a wife himself and it will be good to have a name from a member of the family. I was happy with this and agreed.

"As my son has been growing up, my brother has been very kind to him. He has given him many presents and packets of sweets when he comes to see him. The boy likes his uncle very much and always listens very carefully to the stories that he tells him. My wife thinks that this is a good thing—that a boy should love his kind uncle like this.

"Then somebody said to me: *Your son looks very like his uncle. It is almost as if he is his own son.* And that made me think for the first time: is my brother the father of my son? I looked at the two of them when they were sitting together and I thought that too. They are very alike.

"I am very fond of my brother. He is my twin, and we have done everything together all our lives. But I do not like the thought that he is the father of my son. I would like to talk to him about this, but I do not want to say anything that may cause trouble in the family. You are a wise lady, Aunty: what do you think I should do?"

Mma Ramotswe finished reading the letter and thought: surely a twin should know how funny this sounds—after all, *they are twins.* If Aunty Emang had laughed on reading this letter, then it was not apparent in her answer.

"I am very sorry that you are worrying about this," she wrote. "Look at yourself in the mirror. Do you look like your brother?" And once again that was all she had to say on the subject.

Mma Ramotswe reflected on what she had read. It seemed to her that she and Aunty Emang had at least something in common. Both of them dealt with the problems of others and both were expected by others to provide some solution to their difficulties. But there the similarity ended. Aunty Emang had the easier role: she merely had to give a pithy response to the facts presented to her. In Mma Ramotswe's case, the facts were often unknown and required to be coaxed out of obscurity. And once she had done that, then she had to do rather more than make a clever or dismissive suggestion.She had to see matters through to their conclusion, and these conclusions were not always as simple as somebody like Aunty Emang might imagine.

It would be tempting, she thought, to write to Aunty Emang when next she had a particularly intractable problem to deal with. She would write and ask her what she would do in the circumstances. *Here, Aunty Emang, just you solve this one!* Yes, it would be interesting to do that, she thought, but completely unprofessional. If you were a private detective, as Mma Ramotswe was, you could not reveal your client's problem to the world; indeed, Clovis Andersen had something to say on this subject. "Keep your mouth shut," he had written in *The Principles of Private Detection.* "Keep your mouth shut at all times, but at the same time encourage others to do precisely the opposite."

Mma Ramotswe had remembered this advice, and had to agree that even if it sounded like hypocrisy (if it was indeed hypocrisy to do one thing and encourage others to do the opposite), it was at the heart of good detection to get other people to talk. People loved to talk, especially in Botswana, and if you only gave them the chance they would tell you everything that you needed to know. Mma Ramotswe had found this to be true in so many of her cases. If you want the answer to something, then ask somebody. It always worked.

She put the paper aside and marshalled her thoughts. It was all very well sitting there on her verandah thinking about the problems of others, but it was getting late in the afternoon and there were things to do. In the kitchen at the back of the house there was a packet of green beans that needed to be washed and chopped. There was a pumpkin that was not going to cook itself. There were onions to be put in a pan of boiling water and cooked until soft. That was part of being a woman, she thought; one never reached the end. Even if one could sit down and drink a cup of bush tea, or even two cups, one always knew that at the end of the tea somebody was waiting for something. Children or men were waiting to be fed; a dirty floor cried out to be washed; a crumpled skirt called for the iron. And so it would continue. Tea was just a temporary solution to the cares of the world, although it was certainly helped. Perhaps she should write and tell Aunty Emang that. Most problems could be diminished by the drinking of tea and the thinking through things that could be done while tea was being drunk. And even if that did not solve problems, at least it could put them off for a little while, which we sometimes needed to do, we really did.

NOW AVAILABLE IN PAPERBACK
THE FULL CUPBOARD OF LIFE

COMING IN APRIL 2006 IN HARDCOVER
BLUE SHOES AND HAPPINESS